3 BY GRAHAM GREENE

Also by Graham Greene

3

This Gun for Hire

The Confidential Agent

The Ministry of Fear

BY **GRAHAM GREENE**

NEW YORK · THE VIKING PRESS

PZ

3

.G8319

Thi

(1)

Contents

This Gun for Hire

One

Murder didn't mean much to Raven. It was just a new job. You had to be careful. You had to use your brains. It was not a question of hatred. He had seen the minister only once: he had been pointed out to Raven as he walked down the new housing estate between the little lit Christmas trees—an old, rather grubby man without any friends, who was said to love humanity.

The cold wind cut his face in the wide Continental street. It was a good excuse for turning the collar of his coat well up above his mouth. A harelip was a serious handicap in his profession. It had been badly sewn in infancy, so that now the upper lip was twisted and scarred. When you carried about you so easy an identification you couldn't help becoming ruthless in your methods. It had always, from the first, been necessary for Raven to eliminate the evidence.

He carried an attaché case. He looked like any other youngish man going home after his work; his dark overcoat had a clerical air. He moved steadily up the street like hundreds of his kind. A tram went by, lit up in the early dusk; he didn't take it. An economical young man, you might have thought, saving money for his home. Perhaps even now he was on his way to meet his girl.

But Raven had never had a girl. The harelip prevented that. He had learned when he was very young how repulsive it was. He turned into one of the tall grey houses and climbed the stairs, a sour, bitter, screwed-up figure.

Outside the top flat he put down his attaché case and put on gloves. He took a pair of clippers out of his pocket and cut through the telephone wire where it ran out from above the door to the lift shaft. Then he rang the bell.

He hoped to find the minister alone. This little top-floor flat was the Socialist's home. He lived in a poor, bare solitary way, and Raven had been told that his secretary always left him at half-past six—he was very considerate with his employees. But Raven was a minute too early and the minister half an hour too late. A woman opened the door, an elderly woman with pince-nez and several gold teeth. She had her hat on, and her coat was over her arm. She had been on the point of leaving, and she was furious at being caught. She didn't allow him to speak, but snapped at him in German, "The minister is engaged."

He wanted to spare her, not because he minded a killing but because his employers might prefer him not to exceed his instructions. He held the letter of introduction out to her silently; as long as she didn't hear his foreign voice or see his harelip she was safe. She took the letter bitterly and held it up close to her pince-nez. Good, he thought, she's shortsighted. "Stay where you are," she said and walked primly back up the passage. He could hear her disapproving governess's voice, then she was back in the passage, saying, "The minister will see you. Follow me, please." He couldn't understand the foreign speech, but he knew what she meant from her behaviour.

His eyes, like little concealed cameras, photographed the room instantaneously: the desk, the easy chair, the map on the wall, the door to the bedroom behind, the wide window above the bright cold Christmas street. A little oilstove was all the heating, and the minister was using it now to boil a saucepan. A kitchen alarm clock on the desk marked seven o'clock. A voice said, "Emma, put another egg in the saucepan." The minister came out from the bedroom. He had tried to tidy himself, but he had forgotten the cigarette ash on his trousers. He was old and small and rather dirty. The secretary took an egg out of one of the drawers in the desk. "And the salt. Don't forget the salt," the minister said. He explained in slow English, "It prevents the shell cracking. Sit down, my friend. Make yourself at home. Emma, you can go."

Raven sat down and fixed his eyes on the minister's chest. He thought, I'll give her three minutes by the alarm clock to get well away. He kept his eyes on the minister's chest. Just there I'll shoot. He let his coat collar fall and saw with bitter rage how the old man turned away from the sight of his harelip.

The minister said, "It's years since I heard from him. But I've never forgotten him, never. I can show you his photograph in the other room. It's good of him to think of an old friend. So rich and powerful too. You must ask him when you go back if he remembers the time—" A bell began to ring furiously.

Raven thought, The telephone. I cut the wire. It shook his nerve. But it was only the alarm clock drumming on the desk. The minister turned it off. "One egg's boiled," he said and stooped for the saucepan. Raven opened his attaché case; in the lid he had fixed his automatic fitted with a silencer. The minister said, "I'm sorry the bell made you jump. You see, I like my egg just four minutes."

Feet ran along the passage. The door opened. Raven turned furiously in his seat, his harelip flushed and raw. It was the secretary. He thought, My God, what a household. They won't let a man do things tidily. He forgot his lip, he was angry; he had a grievance. She came in, flashing her gold teeth, prim and ingratiating. She said, "I was just going out when I heard the telephone." Then she winced slightly, looked the other way, showed a clumsy delicacy before his deformity which he couldn't help noticing. It condemned her. He snatched the automatic out of the case and shot the minister twice in the back.

The minister fell across the oilstove; the saucepan upset, and the two eggs broke on the floor. Raven shot the minister once more in the head, leaning across the desk to make quite certain, driving the bullet hard into the base of the skull, smashing it open like a china doll's. Then he turned on the secretary. She moaned at him; she hadn't any words; the old mouth couldn't hold its saliva. He supposed she was begging him for mercy. He pressed the trigger again; she staggered as if she had been kicked in the side by an animal. But he had miscalculated. Her unfashionable dress, the swathes of useless material in which she hid her body, perhaps confused him. And she was tough, so tough he couldn't believe his eyes: she was through the door before he could fire again, slamming it behind her.

But she couldn't lock it; the key was on his side. He twisted the handle and pushed. The elderly woman had amazing strength; it only gave two inches. She began to scream some word at the top of her voice.

There was no time to waste. He stood away from the door and shot twice through the woodwork. He could hear the pince-nez fall on the floor and break. The voice screamed again and stopped; there was a sound outside as if she were sobbing. It was her breath going out through her wounds. Raven was satisfied. He turned back to the minister.

There was a clue he had been ordered to leave; a clue he had to remove. The letter of introduction was on the desk. He put it in his pocket, and between the minister's stiffened fingers he inserted a scrap of paper. Raven had little curiosity; he had only glanced at the introduction, and the nickname at its foot conveyed nothing to him; he was a man who could be depended on. Now he looked round the small bare room to see whether there was any clue he had overlooked. The suitcase and the automatic he was to leave behind. It was all very simple.

He opened the bedroom door. His eyes again photographed the scene: the single bed, the wooden chair, the dusty chest of drawers, a photograph of a young Jew with a small scar on his chin as if he had been struck there with a club, a pair of brown wooden hairbrushes initialled *J. K.*, everywhere cigarette ash—the home of a lonely untidy old man, the home of the minister for war.

A low voice whispered an appeal quite distinctly through the door. Raven picked up the automatic again. Who would have imagined an old woman could be so tough? It touched his nerve a little just in the same way as the bell had done, as if a ghost were interfering with a man's job. He opened the study door—he had to push it against the weight of her body. She looked dead enough, but he made quite sure with his automatic almost touching her eyes.

It was time to be gone. He took the automatic with him.

2

They sat and shivered side by side as the dusk came down. They were borne in their bright small smoky cage above the streets. The bus rocked down to Hammersmith. The shop windows sparkled like ice and—"Look," she said, "it's snowing." A few large flakes went drifting by as they crossed the bridge, falling like paper scraps into the dark Thames.

He said, "I'm happy as long as this ride goes on."

"We're seeing each other tomorrow—Jimmy." She always hesitated before his name. It was a silly name for anyone of such bulk and gravity.

He said, "It's the nights that bother me, Anne."

She laughed. "It's going to be wearing." But immediately she became serious. "I'm happy too." About happiness she was always serious; she preferred to laugh when she was miserable. She couldn't avoid being serious about things she cared for, and happiness made her grave at the thought of all the things which might destroy it. She said, "It would be dreadful now if there was a war."

"There won't be a war."

"The last one started with a murder."

"That was an archduke. This is just an old politician."

She said, "Be careful. You'll break the record—Jimmy."

"Damn the record."

She began to hum the tune she'd bought it for, "It's Only Kew to You," and the large flakes fell past the window, melted on the pavement—"a snowflower a man brought from Greenland."

He said, "It's a silly song."

She said, "It's a lovely song—Jimmy. I simply can't call you Jimmy. You aren't Jimmy. You're outsize. Detective Sergeant Mather. You're the reason why people make jokes about policemen's boots."

"What's wrong with dear, anyway?"

"Dear, dear." She tried it out on the tip of her tongue, between lips as vividly stained as a winter berry. "Oh no," she decided, "it's cold. I'll call you that when we've been married ten years."

"Well—darling?"

"Darling, darling. I don't like it. It sounds as if I'd known you a long, long time." The bus went up the hill past the fish-and-chip shops. A brazier glowed, and they could smell the roasting chestnuts. The ride was nearly over; there were only two more streets and a turn to the left by the church, which was already visible, the spire lifted like a long icicle above the houses. The nearer they got to home the more miserable she became; the nearer they got to home the more lightly she talked. She was keeping things off and out of mind: the peeling wallpaper, the long flights to her room, cold supper with Mrs. Brewer, and next day the walk to the agent's, perhaps a job again in the provinces away from him.

Mather said heavily, "You don't care for me like I care for you. It's nearly twenty-four hours before I see you again."

"It'll be more than that if I get a job."

"You don't care. You simply don't care."

She clutched his arm. "Look. Look at that poster." But it was gone before he could see it through the steamy pane. "Europe Mobilizing" lay like a weight on her heart.

"What was it?"

"Oh, just the same old murder again."

"You've got that murder on your mind. It's a week old now. It's got nothing to do with us."

"No, it hasn't, has it?"

"If it had happened here, we'd have caught him by now."

"I wonder why he did it."

"Politics. Patriotism."

"Well. Here we are. It might be a good thing to get off. Don't look so miserable. I thought you said you were happy?"

"That was five minutes ago."

"Oh," she said out of her light and heavy heart, "one lives quickly these days." They kissed under the lamp; she had to stretch to reach him. He was comforting like a large dog, even when he was sullen and stupid, but one didn't have to send away a dog alone in the cold dark night.

"Anne," he said, "we'll be married, won't we, after Christmas?"

"We haven't a penny," she said, "you know. Not a penny—Jimmy."

"I'll get a rise."

"You'll be late for duty."

"Damn it, you don't care."

She jeered at him, "Not a scrap—dear," and walked away from him up the street to Number 54, praying, Let me get some money quick; let *this* go on *this* time. She hadn't any faith in herself. A man passed her, going up the road. He looked cold and strung-up as he passed in his black overcoat. He had a harelip. Poor devil, she thought, and forgot him, opening the door of 54, climbing the long flights to the top floor (the carpet stopped on the first), putting on the new record, hugging to her heart the silly, senseless words, the slow, sleepy tune:

> *It's only Kew*
> *To you,*
> *But to me*
> *It's Paradise.*
> *They are only blue*
> *Petunias to you,*
> *But to me*
> *They are your eyes.*

The man with the harelip came back down the street. Fast walking hadn't made him warm; like Kay in "The Snow Queen," he bore the cold within him as he walked. The flakes went on falling, melting into slush on the pavement; the words of a song dropped from the lit room on the third floor, the scrape of a used needle.

They say that's a snowflower
A man brought from Greenland.
I say it's the lightness, the coolness, the whiteness
Of your hand.

The man hardly paused. He went on down the street, walking fast. He felt no pain from the chip of ice in his breast.

3

Raven sat at an empty table in the Corner House, near a marble pillar. He stared with distaste at the long list of sweet iced drinks, of parfaits and sundaes and coupes and splits. Somebody at the next little table was eating brown bread and butter and drinking Horlick's. He wilted under Raven's gaze and put up his newspaper. One word, "Ultimatum," ran across the top line.

Mr. Cholmondeley picked his way between the tables.

He was fat and wore an emerald ring. His wide square face fell in folds over his collar. He looked like a real-estate man or perhaps a man more than usually successful in selling women's belts. He sat down at Raven's table and said, "Good evening."

Raven said, "I thought you were never coming, Mr. Chol-mondeley," pronouncing every syllable.

"Chumley, my dear man, Chumley," Mr. Cholmondeley corrected him.

"It doesn't matter how it's pronounced. I don't suppose it's your own name."

"After all, I chose it," Mr. Cholmondeley said. His ring flashed under the great inverted bowls of light as he turned the pages of the menu. "Have a parfait."

"It's odd wanting to eat ice in this weather. You've only got to stay outside if you're hot. I don't want to waste any time, Mr. Cholmon-deley. Have you brought the money? I'm broke."

Mr. Cholmondeley said, "They do a very good Maiden's Dream. Not to speak of Alpine Glow. Or the Knickerbocker Glory."

"I haven't had a thing since Calais."

"Give me the letter," Mr. Cholmondeley said. "Thank you." He told the waitress, "I'll have an Alpine Glow with a glass of kümmel over it."

"The money," Raven said.

"Here in this case."

"They are all fivers."

"You can't expect to be paid two hundred in small change. And it's nothing to do with me," Mr. Cholmondeley said; "I'm merely the agent." His eyes softened as they rested on a Raspberry Split at the next table. He confessed wistfully to Raven, "I've got a sweet tooth."

"Don't you want to hear about it?" Raven said. "The old woman—"

"Please, please," Mr. Cholmondeley said, "I want to hear nothing. I'm just an agent. I take no responsibility. My clients—"

Raven twisted his harelip at him with sour contempt. "That's a fine name for them."

"How long the waitress is with my parfait," Mr. Cholmondeley complained. "My clients are really quite the best people. These acts of violence—they regard them as war."

"And I and the old man—" Raven said.

"Are in the front trench." He began to laugh softly at his own humour. His great white open face was like a curtain on which you can throw grotesque images: a rabbit, a man with horns. His small eyes twinkled with pleasure at the mass of ice cream which was borne towards him in a tall glass. He said, "You did your work very well, very neatly. They are quite satisfied with you. You'll be able to take a long holiday now." He was fat, he was vulgar, he was false, but he gave an impression of great power as he sat there with the cream dripping from his mouth. He was prosperity, he was one of those who possessed things; but Raven possessed nothing but the contents of the wallet, the clothes he stood up in, the harelip, the automatic he should have left behind.

He said, "I'll be moving."

"Good-bye, my man, good-bye," Mr. Cholmondeley said, sucking through a straw.

Raven rose and went. Dark and thin and made for destruction, he wasn't at ease among the little tables, among the bright fruit drinks. He went out into the Circus and up Shaftesbury Avenue. The shop windows were full of tinsel and hard red Christmas berries. It maddened him, the sentiment of it. His hands clenched in his pockets. He leaned his face against a modiste's window and jeered silently through the glass. A Jewish girl with a neat curved figure bent over a dummy. He fed his eyes contemptuously on her legs and hips; so much flesh, he thought, on sale in the Christmas window.

A kind of subdued cruelty drove him into the shop. He let his harelip loose on the girl when she came towards him with the same pleasure that he might have turned a machine gun on a picture gallery. He said, "That dress in the window. How much?"

She said, "Five guineas." She wouldn't "sir" him. His lip was like a badge of class. It revealed the poverty of parents who couldn't afford a clever surgeon.

He said, "It's pretty, isn't it?"

She lisped at him genteelly, "It's been vewwy much admired."

"Soft. Thin. You'd have to take care of a dress like that, eh? Do for someone pretty and well off?"

She lied without interest, "It's a model." She was a woman; she knew all about it; she knew how cheap and vulgar the little shop really was.

"It's got class, eh?"

"Oh yes," she said, catching the eye of a dago in a purple suit through the pane, "it's got class."

"All right," he said. "I'll give you five pounds for it." He took a note from Mr. Cholmondeley's wallet.

"Shall I pack it up?"

"No," he said. "The girl'll fetch it." He grinned at her with his raw lip. "You see, she's class. This the best dress you have?" And when she nodded and took the note away he said, "It'll just suit Alice then."

And so out into the avenue with a little of his scorn expressed, out into Frith Street and round the corner into the German café where he kept a room. A shock awaited him there, a little fir tree in a tub hung with coloured glass, a crib. He said to the old man who owned the café, "You believe in this? This junk?"

"Is there going to be war again?" the old man said. "It's terrible what you read."

"All this business of no room in the inn. They used to give us plum pudding. A decree from Caesar Augustus. You see I know the stuff, I'm educated. We used to have it read us once a year."

"I have seen one war."

"I hate the sentiment."

"Well," the old man said, "it's good for business."

Raven picked up the bambino. The cradle came with it, all of a piece—cheap painted plaster. "They put him on the spot, eh? You see I know the whole story. I'm educated."

He went upstairs to his room. It hadn't been seen to: there was still dirty water in the basin, and the ewer was empty. He remembered the fat man saying, "Chumley, my man, Chumley. It's pronounced Chumley," flashing his emerald ring. He called furiously, "Alice," over the banisters.

She came out of the next room, a slattern, one shoulder too high, with wisps of fair bleached hair over her face. She said, "You needn't shout."

He said, "It's a pigsty in there. You can't treat me like that. Go in and clean it." He hit her on the side of the head, and she cringed away from him, not daring to say anything but, "Who do you think you are?"

"Get on," he said, "you humpbacked bitch." He began to laugh at her when she crouched over the bed. "I've bought you a Christmas dress, Alice. Here's the receipt. Go and fetch it. It's a lovely dress. It'll suit you."

"You think you're funny," she said.

"I've paid a fiver for this joke. Hurry, Alice, or the shop'll be shut." But she got her own back, calling up the stairs, "I won't look worse than what you do with that split lip." Everyone in the house could hear her: the old man in the café, his wife in the parlour, the customers at the counter. He imagined their smiles. "Go it, Alice, what an ugly pair you are." He didn't really suffer; he had been fed the poison from boyhood drop by drop; he hardly noticed its bitterness now.

He went to the window and opened it and scratched on the sill. The kitten came to him, making little rushes along the drainpipe, feinting at his hand. "You little bitch," he said, "you little bitch." He took a small twopenny carton of cream out of his overcoat pocket and spilled it in his soap dish. She stopped playing and rushed at him with a tiny cry. He picked her up by the scruff and put her on top of his chest of drawers with the cream. She wriggled from his hand; she was no larger than the rat he'd trained in the home, but softer. He scratched her behind the ear, and she struck back at him in a preoccupied way. Her tongue quivered on the surface of the milk.

Dinnertime, he told himself. With all that money he could go anywhere. He could have a slap-up meal at Simpson's with the businessmen—cut off the joint and any number of vegs.

When he got by the public call box in the dark corner below the stairs he caught his name, "Raven." The old man said, "He always has a room here. He's been away."

"You," a strange voice said, "what's your name—Alice—show me his room. Keep an eye on the door, Saunders."

Raven went on his knees inside the telephone box. He left the door ajar because he never liked to be shut in. He couldn't see out, but he had no need to see the owner of the voice to recognize police, plain clothes, the Yard accent. The man was so near that the floor of the box vibrated to his tread. Then he came down again. "There's no one there. He's taken his hat and coat. He must have gone out."

"He might have," the old man said. "He's a soft-walking sort of fellow."

The stranger began to question them. "What's he like?"

The old man and the girl both said in a breath, "A harelip."

"That's useful," the detective said. "Don't touch his room. I'll be sending a man round to take his fingerprints. What sort of a fellow is he?"

Raven could hear every word. He couldn't imagine what they were after. He knew he'd left no clues; he wasn't a man who imagined things, he knew. He carried the picture of that room and flat in his brain as clearly as if he had the photographs. They had nothing against him. It had been against his orders to keep the automatic, but he could feel it now safe under his armpit. Besides, if they had picked up any clue they'd have stopped him at Dover. He listened to the voices with a dull anger. He wanted his dinner; he hadn't had a square meal for twenty-four hours, and now with two hundred pounds in his pocket he could buy anything, anything.

"I can believe it," the old man said. "Why, tonight he even made fun of my poor wife's crib."

"A bloody bully," the girl said. "*I* shan't be sorry when you've locked him up."

He told himself with surprise, They hate me.

She said, "He's ugly through and through. That lip of his. It gives you the creeps."

"An ugly customer all right."

"I wouldn't have him in the house," the old man said. "But he pays. You can't turn away someone who pays. Not in these days."

"Has he friends?"

"You make me laugh," Alice said. "Him friends. What would he do with friends?"

He began to laugh quietly to himself on the floor of the little dark box. That's me they're talking about, me. He stared up at the pane of glass with his hand on his automatic.

"You seem kind of bitter. What's he been doing to you? He was going to give you a dress, wasn't he?"

"Just his dirty joke."

"You were going to take it, though."

"You bet I wasn't. Do you think I'd take a present from him? I was going to sell it back to them and show him the money, and wasn't I going to laugh!"

He thought again with bitter interest, They hate me. If they open this door I'll shoot the lot.

"I'd like to take a swipe at that lip of his. I'd laugh. I'd say I'd laugh."

"I'll put a man," the strange voice said, "across the road. Tip him the wink if our man comes in." The café door closed.

"Oh," the old man said. "I wish my wife was here. She would not miss this for ten shillings."

"I'll give her a ring," Alice said. "She'll be chatting at Mason's. She can come right over and bring Mrs. Mason too. Let 'em all join in the fun. It was only a week ago Mrs. Mason said she didn't want to see his ugly face in her shop again."

"Yes, be a good girl, Alice. Give her a ring."

Raven reached up his hand and took the bulb out of the fitment; he stood up and flattened himself against the wall of the box. Alice opened the door and shut herself in with him. He put his hand over her mouth before she had time to cry. He said, "Don't you put the pennies in the box. I'll shoot if you do. I'll shoot if you call out. Do what I say." He whispered in her ear. They were as close together as if they were in a single bed. He could feel her crooked shoulder pressed against his chest. He said, "Lift the receiver. Pretend you're talking to the old woman. Go on. I don't care a damn if I shoot you. Say, Hello, Frau Groener."

"Hello, Frau Groener."

"Spill the whole story."

"They are after Raven."

"Why?"

"That five-pound note. They were waiting at the shop."

"What do you mean?"

"They'd got its number. It was stolen."

He'd been double-crossed. His mind worked with mechanical accuracy like a ready-reckoner. You only had to supply it with the figures and it gave you the answer. He was possessed by a deep sullen rage. If Mr. Cholmondeley had been in the box with him he would have shot him; he wouldn't have cared a damn.

"Stolen from where?"

"You ought to know that."

"Don't give me any lip. Where from?"

He didn't even know who Cholmondeley's employers were. It was obvious what had happened: they hadn't trusted him. They had arranged this so that he might be put away. A newsboy went by outside, calling, "Ultimatum. Ultimatum." His mind registered the fact, but no more; it seemed to have nothing to do with him. He repeated, "Where from?"

"I don't know. I don't remember."

With the automatic stuck against her back he tried to plead with her. "Remember, can't you? It's important. I didn't do it."

"I bet you didn't," she said bitterly into the unconnected phone.

"Give me a break. All I want you to do is remember."

She said, "On your life I won't."

"I gave you that dress, didn't I?"

"You didn't. You tried to plant your money, that's all. You didn't know they'd circulated the numbers to every shop in town. We've even got them in the café."

"If I'd done it, why should I want to know where they came from?"

"It'll be a bigger laugh than ever if you get jugged for something you didn't do."

"Alice," the old man called from the café, "is she coming?"

"I'll give you ten pounds."

"Phony notes. No thank you, Mr. Generosity."

"Alice," the old man called again; they could hear him coming along the passage.

"Justice," he said bitterly, jabbing her between the ribs with the automatic.

"You don't need to talk about justice," she said. "Driving me like I was in prison. Hitting me when you feel like it. Spilling ash all over the floor. I've got enough to do with your slops. Milk in the soap dish. Don't talk about justice."

Pressed against him in the tiny dark box she suddenly came alive to him. He was so astonished that he forgot the old man till he had the door of the box open. He whispered passionately, out of the dark, "Don't say a word or I'll plug you." He had them both out of the box in front of him. He said, "Understand this. They aren't going to get me. I'm not going to prison. I don't care a damn if I plug one of you. I don't care if I hang. My father hanged. What's good enough for him— Get along in front of me up to my room. There's hell coming to somebody for this."

When he had them there he locked the door. A customer was ringing the café bell over and over again. He turned on them. "I've got a good mind to plug you. Telling them about my harelip. Why can't you play fair?" He went to the window; he knew there was an easy way down: that was why he had chosen the room. The kitten caught his eye, prowling like a toy tiger in a cage up and down the edge of the chest of drawers, afraid to jump. He lifted her up and threw her on his bed; she tried to bite his finger as she went. Then he got through onto the leads. The clouds were massing up across the moon, and the earth seemed to move with them, an icy barren globe, through the vast darkness.

4

Anne Crowder walked up and down the small room in her heavy tweed coat; she didn't want to waste a shilling on the gas meter, because she wouldn't get her shilling's worth before morning. She told herself, I'm lucky to have got that job. I'm glad to be going off to work again. But she wasn't convinced. It was eight now; they would have four hours together till midnight. She would have to deceive him and tell him she was catching the nine-o'clock, not the five-o'clock train, or he would be sending her back to bed early. He was like that. No romance. She smiled with tenderness and blew on her fingers.

The telephone at the bottom of the house was ringing. She thought it was the doorbell and ran to the mirror in the wardrobe. There wasn't enough light from the dull globe to tell her if her makeup would stand the brilliance of the Astoria Dance Hall. She began making up all over again; if she was pale he would take her home early.

The landlady stuck her head in at the door and said, "It's your gentleman. On the phone."

"On the phone?"

"Yes," the landlady said, sidling in for a good chat, "he sounded all of a jump. Impatient, I should say. Half barked my head off when I wished him good evening."

"Oh," she said despairingly, "it's only his way. You mustn't mind him."

"He's going to call off the evening, I suppose," the landlady said. "It's always the same. You girls who go travelling round never get a square deal. You said *Dick Whittington,* didn't you?"

"No, no; *Aladdin.*"

She pelted down the stairs. She didn't care a damn who saw her hurry. She said, "Is that you, darling?" There was always something wrong with their telephone. She could hear his voice so hoarsely vibrating against her ear she could hardly realize it was his. He said, "You've been ages. This is a public call box. I've put in my last pennies. Listen, Anne, I can't be with you. I'm sorry. It's work. We're onto the man in that safe robbery I told you about. I shall be out all night on it. We've traced one of the notes." His voice beat excitedly against her ear.

She said, "Oh, that's fine, darling. I know you wanted—" But she couldn't keep it up. "Jimmy," she said, "I shan't be seeing you again. For weeks."

He said, "It's tough, I know. I'd been dreaming of— Listen. You'd better not catch that early train; what's the point? There isn't a nine-o'clock. I've been looking them up."

"I know. I just said—"

"You'd better go tonight. Then you can get a rest before rehearsals. Midnight from Euston."

"But I haven't packed."

He took no notice. It was his favourite occupation, planning things, making decisions. He said, "If I'm near the station, I'll try—"

"Your two minutes up."

He said, "Oh hell, I've no coppers. Darling, I love you."

She struggled to bring it out herself, but his name stood in the way, impeded her tongue. She could never bring it out without hesitation. "Ji—" The line went dead on her. She thought bitterly, He oughtn't to go out without coppers. She thought, It's not right, cutting off a detective like that. Then she went back up the stairs. She wasn't crying; it was just as if somebody had died and left her alone and scared, scared of the new faces and the new job, the harsh provincial jokes, the fellows who were fresh; scared of her-

self, scared of not being able to remember clearly how good it was
to be loved.

The landlady said, "I just thought so. Why not come down and
have a cup of tea and a good chat? It does you good to talk. Really
good. A doctor said to me once it clears the lungs. Stands to reason,
don't it? You can't help getting dust up, and a good talk blows it
out. I wouldn't bother to pack yet. There's hours and hours. My old
man would never of died if he'd talked more. Stands to reason. It
was something poisonous in his throat cut him off in his prime. If
he'd talked more he'd have blown it out. It's better than spitting."

5

The crime reporter couldn't make himself heard. He kept on
trying to say to the chief reporter, "I've got some stuff on that safe
robbery."

The chief reporter had had too much to drink. They'd all had
too much to drink. He said, "You can go home and read *The
Decline and Fall*—"

The crime reporter was a young earnest man who didn't drink
and didn't smoke; it shocked him when someone was sick in one of
the telephone boxes. He shouted at the top of his voice, "They've
traced one of the notes."

"Write it down, write it down, old boy," the chief reporter said,
"and then smoke it."

"The man escaped—held up a girl. It's a terribly good story,"
the earnest young man said. He had an Oxford accent; that was
why they had made him crime reporter: it was the news editor's
joke.

"Go home and read Gibbon."

The earnest young man caught hold of someone's sleeve. "What's
the matter? Are you all crazy? Isn't there going to be any paper or
what?"

"War in forty-eight hours," somebody bellowed at him.

"But this is a wonderful story I've got. He held up a girl and an
old man, climbed out of a window—"

"Go home. There won't be any room for it."

"They've killed the annual report of the Kensington Kitten
Club."

"No 'Round the Shops.' "

"They've made the Limehouse Fire a News in Brief."

"Go home and read Gibbon."

"He got clean away with a policeman watching the front door. The Flying Squad's out. He's armed. The police are taking revolvers. It's a lovely story."

The chief reporter said, "Armed. Go away and put your head in a glass of milk. We'll all be armed in a day or two. They've published their evidence. It's clear as daylight a Serb shot him. Italy's supporting the ultimatum. They've got forty-eight hours to climb down. If you want to buy armament shares hurry and make your fortune."

"You'll be in the army this day week," somebody said.

"Oh no," the young man said; "no, I won't be that. You see, I'm a pacifist."

The man who was sick in the telephone box said, "I'm going home. There isn't any more room in the paper if the Bank of England's blown up."

A little thin piping voice said, "My copy's going in."

"I tell you there isn't any room."

"There'll be room for mine. Gas Masks for All. Special Air Raid Practices for Civilians in every town of more than fifty thousand inhabitants." He giggled.

"The funny thing is—it's—it's—" But nobody ever heard what it was. A boy opened the door and flung them in a pull of the middle page: damp letters on a damp grey sheet; the headlines came off on your hands. "Yugoslavia Asks for Time. Adriatic Fleet at War Stations. Paris Rioters Break into Italian Embassy." Everyone was suddenly quite quiet as an airplane went by, driving low overhead through the dark, heading south, a scarlet tail-lamp, pale transparent wings in the moonlight. They watched it through the great glass ceiling, and suddenly nobody wanted to have another drink.

The chief reporter said, "I'm tired. I'm going to bed."

"Shall I follow up this story?" the crime reporter said.

"If it'll make you happy, but *that's* the only news from now on."

They stared up at the glass ceiling, the moon, the empty sky.

6

The station clock marked three minutes to midnight. The ticket collector at the barrier said, "There's room in the front."

"A friend's seeing me off," Anne Crowder said. "Can't I get in at this end and go up front when we start?"

"They've locked the doors."

She looked desperately past him. They were turning out the lights in the buffet; no more trains from that platform.

"You'll have to hurry, miss."

The poster of an evening paper caught her eye, and as she ran down the train, looking back as often as she was able, she couldn't help remembering that war might be declared before they met again. He would go to it. He always did what other people did, she told herself with irritation, but she knew that that was the reliability she loved. She wouldn't have loved him if he'd been queer, had his own opinions about things; she lived too closely to thwarted genius, to second-touring-company actresses who thought they ought to be Cochran stars, to admire difference. She wanted her man to be ordinary; she wanted to be able to know what he'd say next.

A line of lamp-struck faces went by her. The train was full, so full that in the first-class carriages you saw strange shy awkward people who were not at ease in the deep seats, who feared the ticket collector would turn them out. She gave up the search for a third-class carriage, opened a door, dropped her *Woman and Beauty* on the only seat, and struggled back to the window over legs and protruding suitcases. The engine was getting up steam, the smoke blew back up the platform; it was difficult to see as far as the barrier.

A hand pulled at her sleeve. "Excuse me," a fat man said, "if you've quite finished with that window. I want to buy some chocolate."

She said, "Just one moment, please. Somebody's seeing me off."

"He's not here. It's too late. You can't monopolize the window like that. I must have some chocolate." He swept her to one side and waved an emerald ring under the light. She tried to look over his shoulder to the barrier; he almost filled the window. He called, "Boy, boy," waving the emerald ring. He said, "What chocolate have you got? No, not Motorist's, not Mexican. Something sweet."

Suddenly through a crack she saw Mather. He was past the barrier, he was coming down the train, looking for her, looking in all the third-class carriages, running past the first-class. She implored the fat man, "Please, please do let me come. I can see my friend."

"In a moment. In a moment. Have you Nestlé's? Give me a shilling packet."

"Please let me."

"Haven't you anything smaller," the boy said, "than a ten-shilling note?"

Mather went by, running past the first-class. She hammered on the window, but he didn't hear her among the whistles and the beat of trolley wheels, the last packing cases rolling into the van. Doors slammed, a whistle blew, the train began to move.

"Please. Please."

"I must get my change," the fat man said, and the boy ran beside the carriage, counting the shillings into his palm. When she got to the window and leaned out they were past the platform; she could only see on a wedge of asphalt a small figure who couldn't see her. An elderly woman said, "You oughtn't to lean out like that. It's dangerous."

She trod on their toes getting back to her seat; she felt unpopularity well up all around her; everyone was thinking, She oughtn't to be in the carriage. What's the good of our paying first-class fares when— But she wouldn't cry; she was fortified by all the conventional remarks which came automatically to her mind about spilled milk and it will all be the same in fifty years. Nevertheless she noted with deep dislike, on the label dangling from the fat man's suitcase his destination, which was the same as hers, Nottwich. He sat opposite her with the *Spectator* and the *Evening News* and the *Financial Times* on his lap, eating sweet milk chocolate.

Two

1

Raven walked with his handkerchief over his lip across Soho Square, Oxford Street, up Charlotte Street. It was dangerous, but not so dangerous as showing his harelip. He turned to the left and then to the right into a narrow street, where big-breasted women in aprons called across to each other and a few solemn children scooted up the gutter. He stopped by a door with a brass plate: Dr. Alfred Yogel on the second floor, on the first floor the North American Dental Company. He went upstairs and rang the bell. There was a smell of greens from below, and somebody had drawn a naked torso in pencil on the wall.

A woman in nurse's uniform opened the door, a woman with a mean lined face and untidy grey hair. Her uniform needed washing; it was spotted with grease marks and what might have been blood or iodine. She brought with her a harsh smell of chemicals and disinfectants. When she saw Raven holding his handkerchief over his mouth she said, "The dentist's on the floor below."

"I want to see Doctor Yogel."

She looked him over closely, suspiciously, running her eyes down his dark coat. "He's busy."

"I can wait."

One naked globe swung behind her head in the dingy passage. "He doesn't generally see people as late as this."

"I'll pay for the trouble," Raven said. She judged him with just the same appraising stare as the doorkeeper at a shady night club. She said, "You can come in." He followed her into a waiting room: the same bare globe, a chair, a round oak table splashed with dark paint. She shut him in, and he heard her voice start in the next room. It went on and on. He picked up the only magazine, *Good Housekeeping* of eighteen months back, and began mechanically to read. "Bare walls are very popular today, perhaps one picture to give the necessary point of colour . . ."

The nurse opened the door and jerked her hand. "He'll see you." Dr. Yogel was washing his hands in a fixed basin behind his long yellow desk and swivel chair. There was no other furniture in the room except a kitchen chair, a cabinet, and a long couch. His hair was jet black. It looked as if it had been dyed, and there was not much of it. It was plastered in thin strands across the scalp. When he turned he showed a plump, hard, bonhomous face, a thick sensual mouth. He said, "And what can we do for you?" You felt he was more accustomed to deal with women than with men. The nurse stood harshly behind, waiting.

Raven lowered his handkerchief. He said, "Can you do anything about this lip quickly?"

Dr. Yogel came up and prodded it with a little fat forefinger. "I'm not a surgeon."

Raven said, "I can pay."

Dr. Yogel said, "It's a job for a surgeon. It's not in my line at all."

"I know that," Raven said and caught the quick flicker of glances between the nurse and Dr. Yogel. Dr. Yogel lifted up the lip on each side; his fingernails were not quite clean. He watched Raven carefully and said, "If you come back tomorrow at ten . . ." His breath smelled faintly of brandy.

"No," Raven said. "I want it done now, at once."

"Ten pounds," Dr. Yogel said quickly.

"All right."

"In cash."

"I've got it with me."

Dr. Yogel sat down at his desk. "And now if you'll give me your name . . ."

"You don't need to know my name."

Dr. Yogel said gently, "Any name."

"Chumley, then."

"C-h-o-l-m-o —"

"No. Spell it C-h-u-m-l-e-y."

Dr. Yogel filled up a slip of paper and handed it to the nurse. She went outside and closed the door behind her. Dr. Yogel went to the cabinet and brought out a tray of knives. Raven said, "The light's bad."

"I'm used to it," Dr. Yogel said. "I've a good eye." But as he held up a knife to the light his hand very slightly trembled. He said softly, "Lie down on the couch, old man."

Raven lay down. He said, "I knew a girl who came to you. Name of Page. She said you did her trick fine."

Dr. Yogel said, "She oughtn't to talk about it."

"Oh," Raven said, "you are safe with me. I don't go back on a fellow who treats me right." Dr. Yogel took a case like a portable gramophone out of his cabinet and carried it over to the couch. He produced a long tube and a mask. He smiled gently and said, "We don't run to anesthetists here, old man."

"Stop," Raven said; "you're not going to give me gas."

"It would hurt without it, old man," Dr. Yogel said, approaching with the mask; "it would hurt like hell."

Raven sat up and pushed the mask aside. "I won't have it," he said, "not gas. I've never had gas. I've never passed out yet. I like to see what's going on."

Dr. Yogel laughed gently and pulled at Raven's lip in a playful way. "Better get used to it, old man. We'll all be gassed in a day or two."

"What do you mean?"

"Well, it looks like war, doesn't it?" Dr. Yogel said, talking rapidly and unwinding more tube, turning screws in a soft, shaking, inexorable way. "The Serbs can't shoot a minister of war like that and get away with it. Italy's ready to come in. And the French are warming up. We'll be in it ourselves inside a week."

Raven said, "All that because an old man—" He explained, "I haven't read the papers."

"I wish I'd known beforehand," Dr. Yogel said, making conversation, fixing his cylinder. "I'd have made a fortune in munitions shares. They've gone up to the sky, old man. Now lean back. It won't take a moment." He again approached the mask. He said, "You've only got to breathe deep, old man."

Raven said, "I told you I wouldn't have gas. Get that straight. You can cut me about as much as you like, but I won't have gas."

"It's very silly of you, old man," Dr. Yogel said. "It's going to hurt." He went back to the cabinet and again picked up a knife, but his hand shook more than ever. He was frightened of something. And then Raven heard from outside the tiny tinkle a telephone makes when the receiver is lifted. He jumped up from the couch. It was bitterly cold, but Dr. Yogel was sweating. He stood by the cabinet holding his surgical knife, unable to say a word. Raven said, "Keep quiet. Don't speak." He flung the door suddenly open, and there was the nurse in the little dim hall with the telephone at her ear. Raven stood sideways so that he could keep his eye on both of them. "Put back that receiver," he said. She put it back, watching him with her little mean conscienceless eyes. He said furiously, "You double-crossing — !" He said, "I've got a mind to shoot you both."

"Old man," Dr. Yogel said, "old man, you've got it all wrong"; but the nurse said nothing. She had all the guts in their partnership; she was toughened by a long career of illegalities, by not a few deaths.

Raven said, "Get away from that phone." He took the knife out of Dr. Yogel's hand and hacked and sawed at the telephone wire. He was touched by something he had never felt before; a sense of injustice stammered on his tongue. These people were of his own kind; they didn't belong inside the legal borders; for the second time in one day he had been betrayed by the lawless. He had always been alone, but never as alone as this. The telephone wire gave. He wouldn't speak another word for fear his temper might master him and he might shoot. This wasn't the time for shooting. He went downstairs in a dark loneliness of spirit, his handkerchief over his face, and from the little wireless shop at the street corner heard, "We have received the following notice . . ." The same voice followed him down the street from the open windows of the little impoverished homes, the suave, expressionless voice from every house,

"New Scotland Yard. Wanted. James Raven. Aged about twenty-eight. Easily recognizable by his harelip. A little above the middle height. Last seen wearing a dark overcoat and a black felt hat. Any information leading to the arrest . . ." Raven walked away from the voice, out into the traffic of Oxford Street, bearing south.

There were too many things he didn't understand—this war they were talking of, why he had been double-crossed. He wanted to find Cholmondeley. Cholmondeley was of no account: he was acting under orders; but if he found Cholmondeley he could squeeze out of him— He was harassed, hunted, lonely; he bore with him a sense of great injustice and a curious pride. Going down the Charing Cross Road, past the music shops and the rubber-goods shops, he swelled with it; after all it needed a man to start a war as he was doing.

He had no idea where Cholmondeley lived; the only clue he had was an accommodation address. It occurred to him that there was a faint chance that if he watched the small shop to which Cholmondeley's letters were sent he might see him—a very faint chance, but it was strengthened by the fact of his escape. Already the news was on the air; it would be in the evening papers. Cholmondeley might want to clear out of the way for a while, and there was just a possibility that before he went he would call for letters. But that depended on whether he used that address for other letters besides Raven's. Raven wouldn't have believed there was one chance in a thousand if it were not that Cholmondeley was a fool. You didn't have to eat many ices with him to learn that.

The shop was in a side street opposite a theatre. It was a tiny one-roomed place in which was sold nothing above the level of *Film Fun* and *Breezy Stories*. There were postcards from Paris in sealed envelopes, American and French magazines, and books on flagellation in paper jackets for which the pimply youth or his sister, whoever was in the shop, charged twenty shillings—fifteen shillings back if you returned the book.

It wasn't an easy shop to watch. A woman policeman kept an eye on the tarts at the corner, and opposite there was just the long blank theatre wall, the gallery door. Against the wall you were as exposed as a fly against wallpaper, unless, he thought, waiting for the lights to flash green and let him pass, unless the play was popular.

And it was popular. Although the doors wouldn't open for another hour, there was quite a long queue for the gallery. Raven hired a camp stool with almost his last small change and sat down. The shop was only just across the way. The youth wasn't in charge, but his sister. She sat there just inside the door in an old green dress that might have been stripped from one of the billiard tables in the pub next door. She had a square face that could never have looked young, a squint that her heavy steel spectacles did nothing to disguise. She might have been any age from twenty to forty; a parody of a woman, dirty and depraved, crouched under the most lovely figures, the most beautiful vacant faces, the smut photographers could hire.

Raven watched; with a handkerchief over his mouth, one of sixty in the gallery queue, he watched. He saw a young man stop and eye *Plaisirs de Paris* furtively and hurry on; he saw an old man go into the shop and come out again with a brown paper parcel. Somebody from the queue went across and bought cigarettes.

An elderly woman in pince-nez sat beside him. She said over her shoulder, "That's why I always liked Galsworthy. He was a gentleman. You knew where you were, if you know what I mean."

"It always seems to be the Balkans."

"I liked *Loyalties*."

"He was such a humane man."

A man stood between Raven and the shop, holding up a little square of paper. He put it in his mouth and held up another square. A tart ambled by on the other side of the road and said something to the girl in the shop. The man put the second piece of paper in his mouth.

"They say the fleet—"

"He makes you *think*. That's what I like."

Raven thought, If he doesn't come before the queue begins to move I'll have to go.

"Anything in the papers?"

"Nothing new."

The man in the road took the papers out of his mouth and began to tear them and fold them and tear them. Then he opened them out, and it was a paper St. George's Cross, blowing flimsily in the cold wind.

"He used to subscribe heavily to the Antivivisection Society. Mrs. Milbanke told me. She showed me one of his cheques with his signature."

"He was really humane."

"And a *really* great writer."

A girl and a boy who looked happy applauded the man with the paper flag, and he took off his cap and began to come down the queue, collecting coppers. A taxi drew up at the end of the street, and a man got out. It was Cholmondeley. He went into the bookshop, and the girl got up and followed him. Raven counted his money. He had two and sixpence and a hundred and ninety-five pounds in stolen notes he could do nothing with. He sank his face deeper in his handkerchief and got up hurriedly like a man taken ill. The paper tearer reached him, held out his cap, and Raven saw with envy the odd dozen pennies, a sixpence, a threepenny bit. He would have given a hundred pounds for the contents of that cap. He pushed the man roughly and walked away.

At the other end of the road there was a taxi rank. He stood there bowed against the wall, a sick man, until Cholmondeley came out.

He said, "Follow that taxi," and sank back with a sense of relief, moving back up Charing Cross Road, Tottenham Court Road, the Euston Road, where all the bicycles had been taken in for the night and the secondhand-car dealers from that end of Great Portland Street were having a quick one before they bore their old school ties and their tired, tarnished bonhomie back to their lodgings. He wasn't used to being hunted; this was better, to hunt.

Nor did the metre fail him. He had a shilling to spare when Mr. Cholmondeley led the way in by the Euston war memorial to the great smoky entrance, and rashly he gave it to the driver; rashly because there was a long wait ahead of him with nothing but his hundred and ninety-five pounds to buy a sandwich with. For Mr. Cholmondeley led the way with two porters behind him to the left-luggage counter, depositing there three suitcases, a portable typewriter, a bag of golf clubs, a small attaché case, and a hatbox. Raven heard him ask from which platform the midnight train went.

Raven sat down in the great hall beside a model of Stephenson's Rocket. He had to think. There was only one midnight train. If Cholmondeley was going to report, his employers were somewhere in the smoky industrial north, for there wasn't a stop before Nottwich. But again he was faced with his wealthy poverty; the numbers of the notes had been circulated everywhere; the booking clerks would almost certainly have them. The trail for a moment seemed to stop at the barrier to number 3 platform.

But slowly a plan did form in Raven's mind as he sat under the Rocket among the bundles and crumbs of sandwich eaters. He *had* a chance, for it was possible that the ticket collectors on the trains had not been given the numbers. It was the kind of loophole the authorities might forget. There remained, of course, this objection: that the note would eventually give away his presence on the north-bound train. He would have to take a ticket to the limit of the journey, and it would be easy enough to trace him to the town where he alighted. The hunt would follow him, but there might be a time lag of half a day in which his own hunt could get nearer to *his* prey. Raven could never realize other people; they didn't seem to him to live in the same way as he lived; and though he bore a grudge against Mr. Cholmondeley, hated him enough to kill him, he couldn't imagine Mr. Cholmondeley's own fears and motives. He was the greyhound and Mr. Cholmondeley only the mechanical hare; only in this case the greyhound was chased in its turn by another mechanical hare.

He was hungry, but he couldn't risk changing a note. He hadn't even a copper to pass him into the lavatory. After a while he got up and walked the station to keep warm among the frozen smuts, the icy turbulence. At eleven-thirty he saw from behind a chocolate machine Mr. Cholmondeley fetch his luggage, followed him at a distance until he passed through the barrier and down the length of the lit train. The Christmas crowds had begun. They were different from the ordinary crowd: you had a sense of people going home. Raven stood back in the shadow of an indicator and heard their laughter and calls, saw smiling faces raised under the great lamps. The pillars of the station had been decorated to look like enormous crackers. The suitcases were full of presents; a girl had a sprig of holly in her coat; high up under the roof dangled a bough of mistletoe lit by floodlamps. When Raven moved he could feel the automatic rubbing beneath his arm.

At two minutes to twelve Raven ran forward. The engine smoke was blowing back along the platform, the doors were slammed. He said to the collector at the barrier, "I haven't time to get a ticket. I'll pay on the train."

He tried the first carriages. They were full and locked. A porter shouted to him to go up front, and he ran on. He was only just in time. He couldn't find a seat but stood in the corridor with his face pressed against the pane to hide his harelip, watching London recede from him: a signal box lit up so that you could see the saucepan of cocoa heating on the stove, a signal going green, a long line of blackened houses standing rigid against the cold-starred sky;

watching because there was nothing else to do to keep his lip hidden, but like a man watching something he loves slide back from him out of his reach.

2

Mather walked back up the platform. He was sorry to have missed Anne, but it wasn't important. He would be seeing her again in a few weeks. It was not that his love was any less than hers but that his mind was more firmly anchored. He was on a job. If he pulled it off, he might be promoted: they could marry. Without any difficulty at all he wiped his mind clear of her.

Saunders was waiting on the other side of the barrier. Mather said, "We'll be off."

"Where next?"

"Charlie's."

They sat in the back seat of a car and dived back into the narrow dirty streets behind the station. A prostitute put her tongue out at them. Saunders said, "What about J-J-J-Joe's?"

"I don't think so, but we'll try it."

The car drew up two doors away from a fried fish shop. A man sitting beside the driver got down and waited for orders. "Round to the back, Frost," Mather said. He gave him two minutes and then hammered on the door of the fish shop. A light went on inside, and Mather could see through the window the long counter, the stock of old newspapers, the dead grill. The door opened a crack. He put his foot in and pushed it wide. He said, "Evening, Charlie," looking round.

"Mr. Mather," Charlie said. He was as fat as an eastern eunuch, and he swayed his great hips coyly when he walked, like a street woman.

"I want to talk to you," Mather said.

"Oh, I'm delighted," Charlie said. "Step this way, Mr. Mather. I was just off to bed."

"I bet you were," Mather said. "Got a full house down there tonight?"

"Oh, Mr. Mather. What a wag you are. Just one or two Oxford boys."

"Listen. I'm looking for a fellow with a harelip. About twenty-eight years old."

"He's not here."

"Dark coat, black hat."

"I don't know him, Mr. Mather."

"I'd like to take a look over your basement."   ⟍

"Of course, Mr. Mather. There are just one or two Oxford boys. Do you mind if I go down first? Just to introduce you, Mr. Mather." He led the way down the stone stairs. "It's safer."

"I can look after myself," Mather said. "Saunders, stay in the shop."

Charlie opened a door. "Now, boys, don't be scared. Mr. Mather's a friend of mine." They faced him in an ominous line at the end of the room, the Oxford boys, with their broken noses and their cauliflower ears, the dregs of pugilism.

"Evening," Mather said. The tables had been swept clear of drink and cards. He plodded down the last steps into the stone-floored room.

Charlie said, "Now, boys, you don't need to get scared."

"Why don't you get a few Cambridge boys into this club?" Mather said.

"Oh, what a wag you are, Mr. Mather."

They followed him with their eyes as he crossed the floor. They wouldn't speak to him; he was the Enemy. They didn't have to be diplomats like Charlie, they could show their hatred. They watched every move he made. Mather said, "What are you keeping in that cupboard?" Their eyes followed him as he went towards the cupboard door.

Charlie said, "Give the boys a chance, Mr. Mather. They don't mean any harm. This is one of the best-run clubs—" Mather pulled open the door of the cupboard. Four women fell into the room. They were like toys turned from the same mould with their bright, brittle hair.

Mather laughed. He said, "The joke's on me. That's a thing I never expected in one of your clubs, Charlie. Good night all." The girls got up and dusted themselves. None of the men spoke.

"Really, Mr. Mather," Charlie said, blushing all the way up-stairs, "I do wish this hadn't happened in my club. I don't know what you'll think. But the boys didn't mean any harm. Only you know how it is. They don't like to leave their sisters alone."

"What's that?" Saunders said at the top of the stairs.

"So I said they could bring their sisters, and the dear girls just sit around . . ."

"What's that?" Saunders said. "G-g-g-girls?"

"Don't forget, Charlie," Mather said. "Fellow with a harelip. You'd better let me know if he turns up here. You don't want your club closed up."

"Is there a reward?"

"There'd be a reward for you all right."

They got back into the car. "Pick up Frost," Mather said. "Then Joe's." He took his notebook out and crossed off another name. "And after Joe's six more—"

"We shan't be f-f-finished till three," Saunders said.

"Routine. He's out of town by now. But sooner or later he'll cash another note."

"Fingerprints?"

"Plenty. There was enough on his soap dish to stock an album. Must be a clean sort of fellow. Oh, he doesn't stand a chance. It's just a question of time."

The lights of Tottenham Court Road flashed across their faces. The windows of the big shops were still lit up. "That's a nice bedroom suite," Mather said.

"It's a lot of f-fuss, isn't it?" Saunders said. "About a few notes, I mean. When there may be a w-w-w-w—"

Mather said, "If those fellows over there had our efficiency there mightn't be a war. We'd have caught the murderer by now. Then all the world could see whether the Serbs— Oh," he said softly, as Heal's went by, a glow of soft colour, a gleam of steel, allowing himself about the furthest limits of his fancy, "I'd like to be tackling a job like that. A murderer with all the world watching."

"Just a few n-notes," Saunders complained.

"No, you are wrong," Mather said. "It's the routine which counts. Five-pound notes today. It may be something better next time. But it's the routine which matters. That's how I see it," he said, letting his anchored mind stretch the cable as far as it could go as they drove round St. Giles's Circus and on towards Seven Dials, stopping every hole the thief might take, one by one. "It doesn't matter to me if there is a war. When it's over I'll still want to be going on with this job. It's the organization I like. I always want to be on the side that organizes. On the other you get your geniuses, of course, but you get all your shabby tricksters, you get all the cruelty and the selfishness and the pride."

You got it all, except the pride, in Joe's, where they looked up from their bare tables and let him run the place through, the extra aces back in the sleeve, the watered spirit out of sight, facing him

each with his individual mark of cruelty and egotism. Even pride
was perhaps there in a corner, bent over a sheet of paper, playing
an endless game of double noughts and crosses against himself because there was no one else in that club he deigned to play with.

Mather again crossed off a name and drove southwest towards
Kensington. All over London there were other cars doing the
same: he was part of an organization. He did not want to be a
leader, he did not even wish to give himself up to some God-sent
fanatic of a leader. He liked to feel that he was one of thousands,
more or less equal, working for a concrete end: not equality of opportunity, not government by the people or by the richest or by the
best, but simply to do away with crime, which meant uncertainty.
He liked to be certain, to feel that one day quite inevitably he
would marry Anne Crowder.

The loud speaker in the car said, "Police cars proceed back to
the King's Cross area for intensified search. Raven driven to Euston
Station about seven P.M. May not have left by train." Mather leaned
across to the driver. "Right about and back to Euston." They were
by Vauxhall. Another police car came past them through the Vauxhall tunnel. Mather raised his hand. They followed it back over the
river. The floodlit clock on the Shell-Mex building showed half-
past one. The light was on in the clock tower at Westminster: Parliament was having an all-night sitting as the opposition fought their
losing fight against mobilization.

It was six o'clock in the morning when they drove back towards
the Embankment. Saunders was asleep. He said, "That's fine." He
was dreaming: he had no impediment in his speech; he had an independent income; he was drinking champagne with a girl; everything
was fine. Mather totted things up in his notebook. He said to Saunders, "He got on a train for sure, I'd bet you——" Then he saw that
Saunders was asleep and slipped a rug across his knees and began
to consider again. They turned in at the gates of New Scotland
Yard.

Mather saw a light in the chief inspector's room and went up.

"Anything to report?" Kusack asked.

"Nothing. He must have caught a train, sir."

"We've got a little to go on at this end. Raven followed somebody to Euston. We are trying to find the driver of the first car. And
another thing, he went to a doctor called Yogel to try and get his
lip altered. Offered some more of those notes. Still handy, too, with
that automatic. We've got him taped. As a kid he was sent to an

industrial school. He's been smart enough to keep out of our way since. I can't think why he's broken out like this. A smart fellow like that. He's blazing a trail."

"Has he much money besides the notes?"

"We don't think so. Got an idea, Mather?"

Colour was coming into the sky above the city. Kusack switched off his table lamp and left the room grey. "I think I'll go to bed."

"I suppose," Mather said, "that all the booking offices have the numbers of those notes."

"Every one."

"It looks to me," Mather said, "that if you had nothing but phony notes and wanted to catch an express—"

"How do we know it was an express?"

"Yes, I don't know why I said that, sir. Or perhaps—if it was a slow train with plenty of stops near London, surely someone would have reported by this time."

"You may be right."

"Well, if I wanted to catch an express, I'd wait till the last minute and pay on the train. I don't suppose the ticket collectors carry the numbers."

"I think you're right. Are you tired, Mather?"

"No."

"Well, I am. Would you stay here and ring up Euston and King's Cross and St. Pancras, all of them. Make a list of all the outgoing expresses after seven. Ask them to telephone up the line to all stations to check up on any man travelling without a ticket who paid on the train. We'll soon find out where he stepped off. Good night, Mather."

"Good morning, sir." He liked to be accurate.

3

There was no dawn that day in Nottwich. Fog lay over the city like a night sky with no stars. The air in the streets was clear. You had only to imagine that it was night. The first tram crawled out of its shed and took the steel track down towards the market. An old piece of newspaper blew up against the door of the Royal Theatre and flattened out. In the streets on the outskirts of Nottwich nearest the pits an old man plodded by with a pole, tapping at the windows. The stationer's window in the High Street was full of prayer books and Bibles. A printed card remained among them, a relic of Armistice Day, like the old drab wreath of Haig poppies by the War Memorial: "Look up, and swear by the slain of the war that you'll never forget." Along the line a signal lamp winked green in the dark day, and the lit carriages drew slowly in past the cemetery, the glue factory, over the wide, tidy, cement-lined river. A bell began to ring from the Roman Catholic cathedral. A whistle blew.

The packed train moved slowly into another morning; smuts were thick on all the faces; everyone had slept in his clothes. Mr. Cholmondeley had eaten too many sweets: his teeth needed cleaning; his breath was sweet and stuffy. He put his head into the corridor, and Raven at once turned his back and stared out at the sidings, the trucks heaped with local coal. A smell of bad fish came in from the glue factory. Mr. Cholmondeley dived back across the carriage to the other side, trying to make out at which platform the train was drawing in. He said, "Excuse me," trampling on the feet. Anne smiled softly to herself and hacked his ankle. Mr. Cholmondeley glared at her. She said, "I'm sorry," and began to mend her face with her Pond's tissues and her powder, to bring it up to standard so that she could bear the thought of the Royal Theatre, the little dressing rooms and the oil heating, the rivalry and the scandals.

"If you'll let me by," Mr. Cholmondeley said fiercely, "I'm getting down here."

Raven saw his ghost in the windowpane getting down. But he didn't dare follow him closely. It was almost as if a voice blown over many foggy miles, over the long swelling fields of the hunting counties, the villaed suburbs creeping up to town, had spoken to him. "Any man travelling without a ticket," he thought, with the slip of white paper the collector had given him in his hand. He opened the door and watched the passengers flow by him to the barrier. He needed time, and the paper in his hand would so quickly identify him. He needed time, and he realized now that he wouldn't have even so much as a twelve-hour start. They would visit every boarding house, every lodging in Nottwich; there was nowhere for him to stay.

Then it was that the idea struck him—by the slot machine on number 2 arrival platform—which thrust him finally into other people's lives, broke the world in which he walked alone.

Most of the passengers had gone now, but one girl waited for a returning porter by the buffet door. He went up to her and said, "Can I help and carry your bags?"

"Oh, if you would," she said. He stood with his head a little bent, so that she mightn't see his lip.

"What about a sandwich?" he said. "It's been a hard journey."

"Is it open," she said, "this early?"

He tried the door. "Yes, it's open."

"Is it an invitation?" she said. "You're standing treat?"

He gazed at her with faint astonishment: her smile, the small neat face with the eyes rather too wide apart. He was more used to the absent-minded routine endearments of prostitutes than to this natural friendliness, this sense of rather lost and desperate amusement. He said, "Oh yes. It's on me." He carried the bags inside and hammered on the counter. "What'll you have?" he said. In the pale light of the electric globe he kept his back to her: he didn't want to scare her yet.

"There's a rich choice," she said. "Bath buns, penny buns, last year's biscuits, ham sandwiches. I'd like a ham sandwich and a cup of coffee. Or will that leave you broke? If so, leave out the coffee."

He waited till the girl behind the counter had gone again, till the other's mouth was full of sandwich so that she couldn't have screamed if she'd tried. Then he turned his face on her. He was disconcerted when she showed no repulsion but smiled as well as she could with her mouth full. He said, "I want your ticket. The police are after me. I'll do anything to get your ticket."

She swallowed the bread in her mouth and began to cough. She said, "For God's sake, hit me on the back." He nearly obeyed her; she'd got him rattled: he wasn't used to normal life, and it upset his nerve. He said, "I've got a gun," and added lamely, "I'll give you this in return." He laid the paper on the counter, and she read it with interest between the coughs. "First class. All the way to . . . Why, I'll be able to get a refund on this. I call that a fine exchange; but why the gun?"

He said, "The ticket."

"Here."

"Now," he said, "you are going out of the station with me. I'm not taking any chances."

"Why not eat your ham sandwich first?"

"Be quiet," he said. "I haven't the time to listen to your jokes."

She said, "I like he-men. My name's Anne. What's yours?" The train outside whistled; the carriage began to move, a long line of light going back into the fog; the steam blew along the platform. Raven's eyes left her for a moment. She raised her cup and dashed

the hot coffee at his face. The pain drove him backwards with his
hands to his eyes; he moaned like an animal; this was pain. This
was what the old war minister had felt, the woman secretary, his
father when the trap sprang and the neck took the weight. His right
hand felt for the automatic, his back was against the door. People
were driving him to do things, to lose his head. He checked himself;
with an effort he conquered the agony of the burns, the agony
which drove him to kill. He said, "I've got you covered. Pick up
those cases. Go out in front of me with that paper."

She obeyed him, staggering under the weight. The ticket collector
said, "Changed your mind? This would have taken you to Edin-
burgh. Do you want to break the journey?"

"Yes," she said, "yes. That's it." He took out a pencil and began
to write on the paper. An idea came to Anne: she wanted him to
remember her and the ticket. There might be enquiries. "No," she
said, "I'll give it up. I don't think I'll be going on. I'll stay here,"
and she went out through the barrier, thinking, He won't forget that
in a hurry.

The long street ran down between the small dusty houses. A milk
float clattered round a corner out of sight. She said, "Well, can I
go now?"

"You think me a fool," he said bitterly. "Keep on walking."

"You might take one of these bags." She dropped one in the
road and went on; he had to pick it up. It was heavy. He carried it
in his left hand; he needed his right for the automatic.

She said, "This isn't taking us into Nottwich. We ought to have
turned right at that corner."

"I know where I'm going."

"I wish I did."

The little houses went endlessly on under the fog. It was very
early. A woman came to a door and took in the milk. Through a
window Anne saw a man shaving. She wanted to scream to him,
but he might have been in another world. She could imagine his
stupid stare, the slow working of the brain before he realized anything was wrong. On they went, Raven a step behind. She wondered
if he were bluffing her; he must be wanted for something very
serious if he was really ready to shoot.

She spoke her thoughts aloud, "Is it murder?" and the lapse of
her flippancy, the whispered fear, came to Raven like something
familiar, friendly: he was used to fear. It had lived inside him for

twenty years. It was normality he couldn't cope with. He answered
her without strain, "No. I'm not wanted for that."

She challenged him. "Then you wouldn't dare to shoot," but he
had the answer pat, the answer which never failed to convince because it was the truth. "I'm not going to prison. I'd rather hang. My
father hanged."

She said again, "Where are we going?" watching all the time for
her chance. He didn't answer.

"Do you know this place?" But he had said his say. And suddenly the chance was there: outside a little stationer's, where the
morning posters leaned, looking in the window filled with cheap
notepaper, pens, and ink bottles—a policeman. She felt Raven come
up behind her. It was all too quick: she hadn't time to make up her
mind; they were past the policeman and on down the mean road.
It was too late to scream now: he was twenty yards away; there'd
be no rescue. She said in a low voice, "It *must* be murder."

The repetition stung him into speech. "That's justice for you.
Always thinking the worst. They've pinned a robbery onto me, and
I don't even know where the notes were stolen." A man came out
of a public house and began to wipe the steps with a wet cloth; they
could smell frying bacon; the suitcases weighed on their arms.
Raven couldn't change his hands for fear of leaving hold of the
automatic. He said, "If a man's born ugly, he doesn't stand a
chance. It begins at school. It begins before that."

"What's wrong with your face?" she said with bitter amusement.
There seemed hope while he talked. It must be harder to murder
anyone with whom you'd had any kind of relationship.

"My lip, of course."

"What's up with your lip?"

He said with astonishment, "Do you mean you haven't noticed—"

"Oh," Anne said, "I suppose you mean your harelip. I've seen
worse things than that." They had left the little dirty houses behind
them. She read the name of the new street: Shakespeare Avenue.
Bright red bricks and Tudor gables and half-timbering, doors with
stained glass, names like Restholme. These houses represented
something worse than the meanness of poverty, the meanness of
the spirit. They were on the very edge of Nottwich now, where the
speculative builders were running up their hire-purchase houses. It
occurred to Anne that he had brought her here to kill her in the

scarred fields behind the housing estate, where the grass had been trampled into the clay and the stumps of trees showed where an old wood had been. Plodding on, they passed a house with an open door, which at any hour of the day visitors could enter and inspect, from the small square parlour to the small square bedroom and the bathroom and water closet off the landing. A big placard said:

COME IN AND INSPECT A COZYHOLME
TEN POUNDS DOWN AND A HOUSE IS YOURS

"Are you going to buy a house?" she said with desperate humour.

He said, "I've got a hundred and ninety pounds in my pocket, and I couldn't buy a box of matches with them. I tell you, I was double-crossed. I never stole these notes. A fellow gave them to me."

"That was generous."

He hesitated outside Sleepy Nuik. It was so new that the builder's paint had hardly been removed from the panes. He said, "It was for a piece of work I did. I did the work well. He ought to have paid me properly. I followed him here. A fellow called Chol-mon-deley."

He pushed her through the gate of Sleepy Nuik, up the unmade path and round to the back door. They were at the edge of the fog here: it was as if they were at the boundary between night and day; it faded out in long streamers into the grey winter sky. He put his shoulder against the back door, and the little doll's house lock snapped at once out of the cheap rotten wood. They stood in the kitchen, a place of wires waiting for bulbs, of tubes waiting for the gas cooker. "Get over to the wall," he said, "where I can watch you."

He sat down on the floor with the pistol in his hand. He said, "I'm tired. All night standing in that train. I can't think properly. I don't know what to do with you."

Anne said, "I've got a job here. I haven't a penny if I lose it. I'll give you my word I'll say nothing if you'll let me go." She added hopelessly, "But you wouldn't believe me."

"People don't trouble to keep their word to me," Raven said. He brooded darkly in his dusty corner by the sink. He said, "I'm safe here for a while as long as you are here too." He put his hand to his face and winced at the soreness of the burns. Anne made a movement. He said, "Don't move. I'll shoot if you move."

"Can't I sit down?" she said. "I'm tired too. I've got to be on my

feet all the afternoon." But while she spoke she saw herself bundled
into a cupboard with the blood still wet. She said, "Dressed up as a
Chink. Singing." But he wasn't listening to her; he was making his
own plans in his own darkness. She tried to keep her courage up
with the first song that came into her head, humming it because it
reminded her of Mather, the long bus ride home, the "see you tomorrow."

> It's only Kew
> To you,
> But to me
> It's Paradise.

He said, "I've heard that tune." He couldn't remember where.
He remembered a dark night and a cold wind and hunger and the
scratch of a needle. It was as if something sharp and cold were
breaking in his heart with great pain. He sat there under the sink
with the automatic in his hand and began to cry. He made no
sound: the tears seemed to run like flies of their own will from the
corners of his eyes. Anne didn't notice for a while, humming the
song, "They say that's a snowflower a man brought from Greenland." Then she saw. She said, "What's the matter?"

Raven said, "Keep back against that wall, or I'll shoot."

"You're all in."

"That doesn't matter to you."

"Well, I suppose I'm human," Anne said. "You haven't done me
any harm yet."

He said, "This doesn't mean anything. I'm just tired." He looked
along the bare, dusty boards of the unfinished kitchen. He tried to
swagger. "I'm tired of living in hotels. I'd like to fix up this kitchen.
I learned to be an electrician once. I'm educated." He said, "Sleepy
Nuik. It's a good name when you are tired. But they've gone and
spelled Nook wrong."

"Let me go," Anne said. "You can trust me. I'll not say a thing.
I don't even know who you are."

He laughed miserably. "Trust you! I'd say I can. When you get
into the town you'll see my name in the papers and my description,
what I'm wearing, how old I am. I never stole the notes, but *I* can't
put a description in of the man I want: name Chol-mon-deley, profession double-crosser, fat, wears an emerald ring—"

"Why," she said, "I believe I travelled down with a man like
that. I wouldn't have thought he'd have the nerve—"

"Oh, he's only the agent," Raven said, "but if I could find him I'd squeeze the names—"

"Why don't you give yourself up? Tell the police what happened?"

"That's a great idea, that is. Tell them it was Cholmondeley's friends got the old Czech killed. You're a bright girl."

"The old Czech?" she exclaimed. A little more light came into the kitchen as the fog lifted over the housing estate, the wounded fields. She said, "You don't mean what the papers are so full of?"

"That's it," he said with gloomy pride.

"You know the man who shot him?"

"As well as myself."

"And Cholmondeley's mixed up in it. . . . Doesn't that mean —that everyone's all wrong?"

"They don't know a thing about it, these papers. They can't give credit where credit's due."

"And you know and Cholmondeley. Then there won't be a war at all if you find Cholmondeley."

"I don't care a damn whether there's a war or not. I only want to know who it is who double-crossed me. I want to get even," he explained, looking up at her across the floor, with his hand over his mouth, hiding his lip, noticing that she was young and flushed and lovely, with no more personal interest than a mangy wolf will show from the cage in the groomed, well-fed bitch beyond the bars. "A war won't do people any harm," he said. "It'll show them what's what, it'll give them a taste of their own medicine. I know. There's always been a war for me." He touched the automatic. "All that worries me is what to do with you to keep you quiet for twenty-four hours."

She said under her breath, "You wouldn't kill me, would you?"

"It is the only way," he said. "Let me think a bit."

"But I'd be on your side," she implored him, looking this way and that for anything to throw, for a chance of safety.

"Nobody's on my side," Raven said. "I've learned that. Even a crook doctor . . . You see—I'm ugly. I don't pretend to be one of your handsome fellows. But I'm educated. I've thought things out." He said quickly, "I'm wasting time. I ought to get started."

"What are you going to do?" she said, scrambling to her feet.

"Oh," he said in a tone of disappointment, "you are scared again. You were fine when you weren't scared." He faced her across the kitchen with the automatic pointed at her breast. He

pleaded with her. "There's no need to be scared. This lip—"
"I don't mind your lip," she said desperately. "You aren't bad-
looking. You ought to have a girl. She'd stop you worrying about
that lip."

He shook his head. "You're talking that way because you are
scared. You can't get round me that way. But it's hard luck on you,
my picking on you. You shouldn't be so afraid of death. We've all
got to die. If there's a war, you'll die anyway. It's sudden and
quick; it doesn't hurt," he said, remembering the smashed skull of
the old man. Death was like that: no more difficult than breaking
an egg.

She whispered, "Are you going to shoot me?"

"Oh no, no," he said, trying to calm her; "turn your back and go
over to that door. We'll find a room where I can lock you up for a
few hours." He fixed his eyes on her back; he wanted to shoot her
clean: he didn't want to hurt her.

She said, "You aren't so bad. We might have been friends if we
hadn't met like this. If this was the stage door. Do you meet girls at
stage doors?"

"Me?" he said. "No. They wouldn't look at me."

"You aren't ugly," she said. "I'd rather you had that lip than a
cauliflower ear like all those fellows have who think they are tough.
The girls go crazy on them when they are in shorts. But they look
silly in a dinner jacket." Raven thought, If I shoot her here anyone may see her through a window; I'll shoot her upstairs in the
bathroom. He said, "Go on. Walk."

She said, "Let me go this afternoon. Please. I'll lose my job if I'm
not at the theatre."

They came out into the little glossy hall, which smelled of paint.
She said, "I'll give you a seat for the show."

"Go on," he said, "up the stairs."

"It's worth seeing. Alfred Bleek as the Widow Twankey." There
were only three doors on the little landing; one had ground-glass
panes. "Open the door," he said, "and go in there." He decided that
he would shoot her in the back as soon as she was over the threshold. Then he would only have to close the door, and she would be
out of sight. A small aged voice whispered agonizingly in his memory through a closed door. Memories had never troubled him. He
didn't mind death: it was foolish to be scared of death in this bare,
wintry world. He said hoarsely, "Are you happy? I mean, you like
your job?"

"Oh, not the job," she said. "But the job won't go on forever. Don't you think someone might marry me? I'm hoping."

He whispered, "Go in. Look through that window," his finger touching the trigger. She went obediently forward. He brought the automatic up; his hand didn't tremble; he told himself that she would feel nothing. Death wasn't a thing she need be scared about. She had taken her handbag from under her arm. He noticed the odd, sophisticated shape; a circle of twisted glass on the side and within it chromium initials, A. C. She was going to make her face up.

A door closed, and a voice said, "You'll excuse me bringing you here this early, but I have to be at the office till late—"

"That's all right, that's all right, Mr. Graves. Now don't you call this a snug little house?"

He lowered the pistol as Anne turned. She whispered breathlessly, "Come in here quick." He obeyed her. He didn't understand; he was still ready to shoot her if she screamed. She saw the automatic and said, "Put it away. You'll only get into trouble with that."

Raven said, "Your bags are in the kitchen."

"I know. They've come in by the front door."

"Gas and electric," a voice said, "laid on. Ten pounds down, and you sign along the dotted line and move in the furniture."

A precise voice which went with pince-nez and a high collar and thin flaxen hair said, "Of course I shall have to think it over."

"Come and look upstairs, Mr. Graves."

They could hear them cross the hall and climb the stairs, the agent talking all the time. Raven said, "I'll shoot if you—"

"Be quiet," Anne said. "Don't talk. Listen, have you those notes? Give me two of them." When he hesitated she whispered urgently, "We've got to take a risk." The agent and Mr. Graves were in the best bedroom now.

"Just think of it, Mr. Graves," the agent was saying, "with flowered chintz."

"Are the walls soundproof?"

"By a special process. Shut the door—" The door closed, and the agent's voice went thinly, distinctly on—"and in the passage you couldn't hear a thing. These houses were specially made for family men."

"And now," Mr. Graves said, "I should like to see the bathroom."

"Don't move," Raven threatened her.

"Oh, put it away," Anne said, "and be yourself." She closed the bathroom door behind her and walked to the door of the bedroom. It opened, and the agent said with the immediate gallantry of a man known in all the Nottwich bars, "Well, well, what have we here?"

"I was passing," Anne said, "and saw the door open. I'd been meaning to come and see you, but I didn't think you'd be up this early."

"Always on the spot for a young lady," the agent said.

"I want to buy this house."

"Now look here," Mr. Graves said, a young-old man in a black suit who carried about with him in his pale face and irascible air the idea of babies in small, sour rooms, of insufficient sleep, "you can't do that. I'm looking over this house."

"My husband sent me here to buy it."

"I'm here first."

"Have you bought it?"

"I've got to look it over first, haven't I?"

"Here," Anne said, showing two five-pound notes. "Now all I have to do—"

"Is sign along the dotted line," the agent said.

"Give me time," Mr. Graves said. "I like this house." He went to the window. "I like the view." His pale face stared out at the damaged fields stretching under the fading fog to where the slag heaps rose along the horizon. "It's quite country," Mr. Graves said. "It'll be good for the children and the wife."

"I'm sorry," Anne said, "but you see I'm ready to pay and sign."

"References?" the agent said.

"I'll bring them this afternoon."

"Let me show you another house, Mr. Graves." The agent belched slightly and apologized, "I'm not used to business before breakfast."

"No," Mr. Graves said, "if I can't have this I won't have any." Pallid and aggrieved, he planted himself in the best bedroom of Sleepy Nuik and presented his challenge to fate, a challenge which he knew from long and bitter experience was always accepted.

"Well," the agent said, "you can't have this. First come, first served."

Mr. Graves said, "Good morning"; carried his pitiful, narrow-chested pride downstairs. At least he could claim that, if he had been always too late for what he really wanted, he had never accepted substitutes.

"I'll come with you to the office," Anne said, "straight-away," taking the agent's arm, turning her back on the bathroom where the dark, pinched man stood waiting with his pistol, going downstairs into the cold overcast day, which smelled to her as sweet as summer because she was safe again.

4

"What did Aladdin say
When he came to Pekin?"

Obediently the long, shuffling row of them repeated with tired vivacity, bending forward, clapping their knees, "Chin chin." They had been rehearsing for five hours.

"It won't do. It hasn't got any sparkle. Start again, please."

"What did Aladdin say . . ."

"How many of you have they killed so far?" Anne said under her breath. "Chin chin."

"Oh, half a dozen."

"I'm glad I got in at the last minute. A fortnight of this! No thank you."

"Can't you put some Art into it?" the producer implored them. "Have some pride. This isn't just any panto."

"What did Aladdin say . . ."

"You look washed out," Anne said.

"You don't look too good yourself."

"Things happen quick in this place."

"Once more, girls, and then we'll go on to Miss Maydew's scene."

"What did Aladdin say
When he came to Pekin?"

"You won't think that when you've been here a week."

Miss Maydew sat sideways in the front row with her feet up on the next stall. She was in tweeds and had a golf and grouse-moor air about her. Her real name was Binns, and her father was Lord Fordhaven. She said in a voice of penetrating gentility to Alfred Bleek, "I said I won't be presented."

"Who's the fellow at the back of the stalls?" Anne whispered. He was only a shadow to her.

"I don't know. Hasn't been here before. One of the men who put up the money, I expect, waiting to get an eyeful." She began to mimic an imaginary man. "Won't you introduce me to the girls, Mr. Collier? I want to thank them for working so hard to make this panto a success. What about a little dinner, missy?"

"Stop talking, Ruby, and make it snappy," said Mr. Collier.

*"What did Aladdin say
When he came to Pekin?"*

"All right. That'll do."

"Please, Mr. Collier," Ruby said, "may I ask you a question?"

"Now, Miss Maydew, your scene with Mr. Bleek. Well, what is it you want to know?"

"What *did* Aladdin say?"

"I want discipline," Mr. Collier said, "and I'm going to have discipline." He was rather undersized, with a fierce eye and straw-coloured hair and a receding chin. He was continually glancing over his shoulder in fear that somebody was getting at him from behind. He wasn't a good producer: his appointment was due to more wheels within wheels than you could count. Somebody owed money to somebody else who had a nephew . . . but Mr. Collier was not the nephew: the chain of causes went much further before you reached Mr. Collier. Somewhere it included Miss Maydew, but the chain was so long you couldn't follow it. You got a confused idea that Mr. Collier must owe his position to merit. Miss Maydew didn't claim that for herself. She was always writing little articles in the cheap women's paper on "Hard Work the only Key to Success on the Stage." She lit a new cigarette and said, "Are you talking to *me?*" She said to Alfred Bleek, who was in a dinner jacket with a red knitted shawl round his shoulders, "It was to get away from all that: royal garden parties . . ."

Mr. Collier said, "Nobody's going to leave this theatre." He looked nervously over his shoulder at the stout gentleman emerging into the light from the back of the stalls, one of the innumerable wheels within wheels that had spun Mr. Collier into Nottwich, into this exposed position at the front of the stage, into this fear that nobody would obey him.

"Won't you introduce me to the girls, Mr. Collier?" the stout gentleman said. "If you are finishing. I don't want to interrupt."

"Of course," Mr. Collier said. He said, "Girls, this is Mr. Davenant, one of our chief backers."

"Davis, not Davenant," the fat man said. "I bought out Davenant." He waved his hand: the emerald ring on his little finger flashed and caught Anne's eye. He said, "I want to have the pleasure of taking every one of you girls out to dinner while this show lasts. Just to tell you how I appreciate the way you are working to make the panto a success. Who shall I begin with?" He had an air of desperate jollity. He was like a man who suddenly finds he has nothing to think about and somehow must fill the vacuum.

"Miss Maydew," he said half-heartedly, as if to show to the chorus the honesty of his intentions by inviting the principal boy.

"Sorry," Miss Maydew said, "I'm dining with Bleek."

Anne walked out on them. She didn't want to high hat Davis, but his presence there shocked her. She believed in Fate and God and Vice and Virtue, Christ in the stable, all the Christmas stuff; she believed in unseen powers that arranged meetings, drove people along ways they didn't mean to go; but she, she was quite determined, wouldn't help. She wouldn't play God's or the Devil's game. She had evaded Raven, leaving him there in the bathroom of the little empty house, and Raven's affairs no longer concerned her. She wouldn't give him away—she was not yet on the side of the big organized battalions—but she wouldn't help him either. It was a strictly neutral course she steered out of the changing room, out of the theatre door into Nottwich High Street.

But what she saw there made her pause. The street was full of people; they stretched along the southern pavement, past the theatre entrance, as far as the market. They were watching the electric bulbs above Wallace's, the big drapers, spelling out the night's news. She had seen nothing like it since the last election, but this was different, because there were no cheers. They were reading of the troop movements over Europe, of the precautions against gas raids. Anne was not old enough to remember how the last war began; but she had read of the crowds outside the palace, the enthusiasm, the queues at the recruiting offices, and that was how she had pictured every war beginning. She had feared it only for herself and Mather. She had thought of it as a personal tragedy played out against a background of cheers and flags. But this was different: this silent crowd wasn't jubilant, it was afraid. The white faces were turned towards the sky with a kind of secular entreaty; they weren't praying to any God, they were just willing that the electric bulbs would tell a different story. They were caught there, on the way back from work with tools and attaché cases, by the rows of bulbs spelling out complications they simply didn't understand.

Anne thought, Can it be true that that fat fool—that the boy with the harelip *knows*— Well, she told herself, I believe in fate; I suppose I can't just walk out and leave them. I'm in it up to the neck. If only Jimmy were here. But Jimmy, she remembered with pain, was on the other side; he was among those hunting Raven down. And Raven must be given his chance to finish *his* hunt first. She went back into the theatre.

Mr. Davenant—Davis—Cholmondeley, whatever his name was, was telling a story. Miss Maydew and Alfred Bleek had gone. Most of the girls had gone too, to change. Mr. Collier watched and listened nervously: he was trying to remember who Mr. Davis was. Mr. Davenant had been silk stockings and had known Callitrope, who was the nephew of the man Dreid owed money to. Mr. Collier had been quite safe with Mr. Davenant, but he wasn't certain about Davis. This panto wouldn't last forever, and it was as fatal to get *in* with the wrong people as to get *out* with the right. It was possible that Davis was the man Cohen had quarrelled with, or he might be the uncle of the man Cohen had quarrelled with. The echoes of that quarrel were still faintly reverberating through the narrow backstage passages of provincial theatres in the second-class touring towns. Soon they would reach the third companies, and everyone would either move up one or move down one, except those who couldn't move down any lower. Mr. Collier laughed nervously and glared in a miserable attempt to be in and out simultaneously.

"I thought somebody breathed the word dinner," Anne said. "I'm hungry."

"First come, first served," Mr. Davis-Cholmondeley said cheerily. "Tell the girls I'll be seeing them. Where shall it be, miss?"

"Anne."

"That's fine," Mr. Davis-Cholmondeley said. "I'm Willie."

"I bet you know this town well," Anne said. "I'm new." She came close to the footlights and deliberately showed herself to him —she wanted to see whether he recognized her—but Mr. Davis never looked at a face. He looked past you. His large square face didn't need to show its force by any eye-to-eye business. Its power lay in its existence at all. You couldn't help wondering, as you wondered with an outsize mastiff, how much sheer weight of food had daily to be consumed to keep him fit.

Mr. Davis winked at Mr. Collier, who decided to glare back at

him, and said, "Oh yes, I know this town. In a manner of speaking
I made this town." He said, "There isn't much choice. There's the
Grand or the Metropole. The Metropole's more intimate."

"Let's go to the Metropole."

"They have the best sundaes, too, in Nottwich."

The street was no longer crowded; just the usual number of
people looking in the windows, strolling home, going into the Im-
perial Cinema. Anne thought, Where is Raven now? How can I find
Raven?

"It's not worth taking a taxi," Mr. Davis said, "the Metropole's
only just round the corner. You'll like the Metropole," he repeated.
"It's more intimate than the Grand." But it wasn't the kind of hotel
you associated with intimacy. It came in sight at once all along one
side of the market place; as big as a railway station, of red and
yellow stone, with a big clock face in a pointed tower.

"Kind of Hotel-de-Ville, eh?" Mr. Davis said. You could tell
how proud he was of Nottwich.

There were sculptured figures in between every pair of windows;
all the historic worthies of Nottwich stood in stiff neo-Gothic attitudes, from Robin Hood up to the Mayor of Nottwich in 1864.
"People come a long way to see this," Mr. Davis said.

"And the Grand? What's the Grand like?"

"Oh, the Grand," Mr. Davis said. "The Grand's gaudy."

He pushed her in ahead of him through the swing doors, and
Anne saw how the porter recognized him. It wasn't going to be
hard, she thought, to trace Mr. Davis in Nottwich. But how to find
Raven?

The restaurant had room for the passengers of a liner; the roof
was supported on pillars painted in stripes of sage green and gold.
The curved ceiling was blue, scattered with gold stars arranged in
their proper constellations. "It's one of the sights of Nottwich," Mr.
Davis said. "I always keep a table under Venus." He laughed nervously, settling in his seat, and Anne noticed that they weren't under
Venus at all, but under Jupiter.

"You ought to be under the Great Bear," she said.

"Ha ha, that's good," Mr. Davis said. "I must remember that."
He bent over the wine list. "I know you ladies always like a sweet
wine." He confessed, "I've a sweet tooth myself." He sat there
studying the card, lost to everything. He wasn't interested in her.
He seemed interested at that moment in nothing but a series of
tastes, beginning with the lobster he had ordered. This was his

chosen home, the huge stuffy palace of food; this was his idea of intimacy, one table set among two hundred tables.

Anne thought he had brought her there for a flirtation. She had imagined that it would be easy to get on terms with Mr. Davis, even though the ritual a little scared her. Five years of provincial theatres had not made her adept at knowing how far she could go without arousing in the other more excitement than she could easily cope with. Her retreats were always sudden and dangerous. Over the lobster she thought of Mather, of security, of loving one man. Then she put out her knee and touched Mr. Davis's. Mr. Davis took no notice, cracking his way through a claw. He might just as well have been alone. It made her uneasy, to be so neglected. It didn't seem natural. She touched his knee again and said, "Anything on your mind, Willie?"

The eyes he raised were like the lenses of a large, powerful microscope focused on an empty slide. He said, "What's that? This lobster all right, eh?" He stared past her over the wide, rather empty restaurant, all the tables decorated with holly and mistletoe. He called, "Waiter, I want an evening paper," and set to again at his claw. When the paper was brought he turned first of all to the financial page. He seemed satisfied: what he read there was as good as a lollipop.

Anne said, "Would you excuse me a moment, Willie?" She took three coppers out of her bag and went to the ladies' lavatory. She stared at herself in the glass over the wash basin: there didn't seem to be anything wrong. She said to the old woman there, "Do I look all right to you?"

The woman grinned. "Perhaps he doesn't like so much lipstick."

"Oh no," Anne said, "he's the lipstick type. A change from home. Hubbie on the razzle." She said, "Who is he? He calls himself Davis. He says he made this town."

"Excuse me, dear, but your stocking's laddered."

"It's not his doing anyway. Who is he?"

"I've never heard of him, dear. Ask the porter."

"I think I will."

She went to the front door. "The restaurant's so hot," she said. "I had to get a bit of air." It was a peaceful moment for the porter of the Metropole. Nobody came in, nobody went out. He said, "It's cold enough outside." A man with one leg stood on the curb and sold matches. The trams went by, little lighted homes full of smoke and talk and friendliness. A clock struck half-past eight, and you could hear from one of the streets outside the square the shrill voices of children singing a tuneless carol. Anne said, "Well, I must be getting back to Mr. Davis." She said; "Who *is* Mr. Davis?"

"He's got plenty," the porter said.

"He says he made this town."

"That's boasting," the porter said. "It's Midland Steel made this town. You'll see their offices in the Tanneries. But they're ruining the town now. They *did* employ fifty thousand. Now they don't have ten thousand. I was a doorkeeper there once myself. But they even cut down the doorkeepers."

"It must have been cruel," Anne said.

"It was worse for him," the porter said, nodding through the door at the one-legged man. "He had twenty years with them. Then he lost his leg, and the court brought it in wilful negligence, so they didn't give him a tanner. They economized there too, you see. It was negligence, all right: he fell asleep. If you tried watching a machine do the same thing once every second for eight hours, you'd feel sleepy yourself."

"But Mr. Davis?"

"Oh, I don't know anything about Mr. Davis. He may have something to do with the boot factory. Or he may be one of the directors of Wallace's. They've got money to burn."

A woman came through the door carrying a Pekingese. She wore a heavy fur coat. She said, "Has Mr. Alfred Piker been in here?"

"No, ma'am."

"There. It's just what his uncle was always doing. Disappearing," she said. "Keep hold of the dog," and she rolled away across the square.

"That's the mayoress," the porter said.

Anne went back. But something had happened. The bottle of wine was almost empty, and the paper lay on the floor at Mr. Davis's feet. Two sundaes had been laid, but Mr. Davis hadn't touched his. It wasn't politeness; something had put him out. He growled at her, "Where have you been?" She tried to see what he had been reading. It wasn't the financial page any more, but she could make out only the main headlines. "Decree Nisi for Lady——" the name was too complicated to read upside down; "Manslaughter Verdict on Motorist." Mr. Davis said, "I don't know what's wrong with this place. They've put salt or something in the sundaes." He turned his furious, dewlapped face at the passing waiter. "Call this a Knickerbocker Glory?"

"I'll bring you another, sir."

"You won't. My bill."

"So we call it a day," Anne said.

Mr. Davis looked up from the bill with something very like fear. "No, no," he said, "I didn't mean that. You won't go and leave me flat now?"

"Well, what do you want to do, the flickers?"

"I thought," Mr. Davis said, "you might come back with me to my place and have a tune on the radio and a glass of something good. We might foot it together a bit, eh?" He wasn't looking at her; he was hardly thinking of what he was saying. He didn't look dangerous. Anne thought she knew his type: you could pass them off with a kiss or two, and when they were drunk tell them a senti-mental story until they began to think you were their sister. This would be the last: soon she would be Mather's; she would be safe. But first she was going to learn where Mr. Davis lived.

As they came out into the square the carol singers broke on them —six small boys without an idea of a tune among them. They wore wool gloves and mufflers, and they stood across Mr. Davis's path, chanting, "Mark my footsteps well, my page."

"Taxi, sir?" the porter asked.

"No." Mr. Davis explained to Anne, "It saves threepence to take one from the rank in the Tanneries." But the boys got in his way, holding out their caps for money. "Get out of the way," Mr. Davis said. With the intuition of children they recognized his uneasiness and baited him, pursuing him along the curb, singing, "Follow in them boldly." The loungers outside the Crown turned to look. Somebody clapped. Mr. Davis suddenly turned and seized the hair of the boy nearest him. He pulled it till the boy screamed; pulled it till a tuft came out between his fingers. He said, "That will teach you," and sinking back a moment later in the taxi from the rank in the Tanneries, he said with pleasure, "They can't play with me." His mouth was open, and his lip was wet with saliva; he brooded over his victory in the very same way as he had brooded over the lobster; he didn't look to Anne as safe as he had done. She re-minded herself that he was only an agent. He *knew* the murderer, Raven said; he hadn't committed it himself.

"What's that building?" she asked, seeing a great black glass front stand out from the Victorian street of sober offices where once the leather-workers had tanned their skins.

"Midland Steel," Mr. Davis said.

"Do you work there?"

Mr. Davis for the first time returned look for look. "What made you think that?"

"I don't know," Anne said and recognized with uneasiness that Mr. Davis was only simple when the wind stood one way.

"Do you think you could like me?" Mr. Davis said, fingering her knee.

"I daresay I might."

The taxi had left the Tanneries. It heaved over a net of tram-lines and came out into the station approach. "Do you live out of town?"

"Just at the edge," Mr. Davis said.

"They ought to spend more on lighting in this place."

"You're a cute little girl," Mr. Davis said. "I bet you know what's what."

"It's no good looking for eggshell, if that's what you mean," Anne said, as they drove under the great steel bridge that carried the line on to York. There were only two lamps on the whole of the long, steep gradient to the station. Over a wooden fence you could see the shunted trucks on the side line, the stacked coal ready for entrainment. An old taxi and a bus waited for passengers outside the small dingy station entrance. Built in 1860, it hadn't kept pace with Nottwich.

"You've got a long way to go to work," Anne said.

"We are nearly there."

The taxi turned to the left. Anne read the name of the road: Khyber Avenue, a long row of mean villas showing apartment cards. The taxi stopped at the end of the road. Anne said, "You don't mean you live *here?*" Mr. Davis was paying off the driver. "Number sixty-one," he said (Anne noticed there was no card in this window between the pane and the thick lace curtains). He smiled in a soft, ingratiating way and said, "It's really nice inside, dear." He put a key in the lock and thrust her firmly forward into a little dimly lit hall with a hatstand. He hung up his hat and walked softly towards the stairs on his toes. There was a smell of gas and greens. A blue fan of flame lit up a dusty plant.

"We'll turn on the wireless," Mr. Davis said, "and have a tune."

A door opened in the passage, and a woman's voice said, "Who's that?"

"Just Mr. Cholmondeley."

"Don't forget to pay before you go up."

"The first floor," Mr. Davis said. "The room straight ahead of you. I won't be a moment," and he waited on the stairs till she passed him. The coins chinked in his pocket as his hand groped for them.

There *was* a wireless in the room, standing on a marble washstand, but there was certainly no space to dance in, for the big double bed filled the room. There was nothing to show the place was ever lived in; there was dust on the wardrobe mirror, and the ewer beside the loudspeaker was dry. Anne looked out of the window behind the bedposts on a little dark yard. Her hand trembled against the sash; this was more than she had bargained for. Mr. Davis opened the door.

She was badly frightened. It made her take the offensive. She said at once, "So you call yourself Mr. Cholmondeley?"

He blinked at her, closing the door softly behind him. "What if I do?"

"And you said you were taking me home. This isn't your home."

Mr. Davis sat down on the bed and took off his shoes. He said, "We mustn't make a noise, dear. The old woman doesn't like it." He opened the door of the washstand and took out a cardboard box; it spilled soft icing sugar out of its cracks all over the bed and the floor as he came towards her. "Have a piece of Turkish Delight."

"This isn't your home," she persisted.

Mr. Davis, with his fingers halfway to his mouth, said, "Of course it isn't. You don't think I'd take you to my home, do you? You aren't as green as that. I'm not going to lose my reputation." He said "We'll have a tune, shall we, first?" And turning the dials, he set the instrument squealing and moaning. "Lot of atmospherics about," Mr. Davis said, twisting and turning the dials until very far away you could hear a dance band playing, a dreamy rhythm underneath the shrieking in the air. You could just discern the tune: "Night light, Love light." "It's our own Nottwich programme," Mr. Davis said. "There isn't a better band on the Midland Regional. From the Grand. Let's do a step or two," and, grasping her round the waist, he began to shake up and down between the bed and the wall.

"I've known better floors," Anne said, trying to keep up her spirits with her own hopeless form of humour, "but I've never known a worse crush." And Mr. Davis said, "That's good. I'll remember that." Quite suddenly, blowing off the relics of icing sugar which clung round his mouth, he grew passionate. He fastened his lips on her neck. She pushed him away and laughed at him at the same time. She had to keep her head. "Now I know what a rock feels like," she said, "when the sea amen—anem— Damn, I can never say that word."

"That's good," Mr. Davis said mechanically, driving her back.

She began to talk rapidly about anything which came into her head. She said, "I wonder what this gas practice will be like. Wasn't it terrible the way they shot the old woman through her eyes?"

He loosed her at that, though she hadn't really meant anything by it. He said, "Why do you bring that up?"

"I was just reading about it," Anne said. "The man must have made a proper mess in that flat."

Mr. Davis implored her, "Stop. Please stop." He explained weakly, leaning back for support against the bedpost, "I've got a weak stomach. I don't like horrors."

"I like thrillers," Anne said. "There was one I read the other day—"

"I've got a very vivid imagination," Mr. Davis said.

"I remember once when I cut my finger—"

"Don't. Please don't."

Success made her reckless. She said, "I've got a vivid imagination too. I thought someone was watching this house."

"What do you mean?" Mr. Davis said. He was scared all right. But she went too far. She said, "There was a dark fellow watching the door. He had a harelip."

Mr. Davis went to the door and locked it. He turned the wireless low. He said, "There's no lamp within twenty yards. You couldn't have seen his lip."

"I just thought—"

"I wonder how much he told you," Mr. Davis said. He sat down on the bed and looked at his hands. "You wanted to know where I lived, whether I worked—" He cut his sentence short and looked up at her with horror. But she could tell from his manner that he was no longer afraid of her: it was something else that scared him. He said, "They'd never believe you."

"Who wouldn't?"

"The police. It's a wild story." To her amazement he began to sniffle, sitting on the bed, nursing his great hairy hands. "There must be some way out. I don't want to hurt you. I don't want to hurt anyone. I've got a weak stomach."

Anne said, "I don't know a thing. Please open the door."

Mr. Davis said in a low, furious voice, "Be quiet. You've brought it on yourself."

She said again, "I don't know anything."

"I'm only an agent," Mr. Davis said. "I'm not responsible." He explained gently, sitting there in his stockinged feet with tears in his deep, selfish eyes. "It's always been our policy to take no risks. It's not my fault that fellow got away. I did my best. I've always done my best. But he won't forgive me again."

"I'll scream if you don't open the door."

"Scream away. You'll only make the old woman cross."

"What are you going to do?"

"There's more than half a million at stake," Mr. Davis said. "I've got to make sure this time." He got up and came towards her with his hands out. She screamed and shook the door, then fled from it because there was no reply and ran around the bed. He just let her run: there was no escape in the tiny cramped room. He stood there muttering to himself, "Horrible. Horrible." You could tell he was on the verge of sickness, but the fear of somebody else drove him on.

Anne implored him, "I'll promise anything."

He shook his head. "He'd never forgive me." He sprawled across the bed and caught her wrist. He said thickly, "Don't struggle. I won't hurt you if you don't struggle," pulling her to him across the bed, feeling with his other hand for the pillow. She told herself even then, It isn't me. It's other people who are murdered. Not me. The urge to life which made her disbelieve that this could possibly be the end of everything for her, for the loving, enjoying I, comforted her even when the pillow was across her mouth, never allowed her to realize the full horror as she fought against his hands, strong and soft and sticky with icing sugar.

5

The rain blew up along the River Weevil from the east. It turned to ice in the bitter night and stung the asphalt walks, pitted the paint on the wooden seats. A constable came quietly by in his heavy raincoat gleaming like wet macadam, moving his lantern here and there in the dark spaces between the lamps. He said "Good night" to Raven without another glance. It was couples he expected to find, even in December under the hail, the signs of poor, cooped provincial passion.

Raven, buttoned to the neck, went on, looking for any shelter. He wanted to keep his mind on Cholmondeley, on how to find the man in Nottwich. But continually he found himself thinking instead of the girl he had threatened that morning. He remembered the kitten he had left behind in the Soho café. He had loved that kitten.

It had been sublimely unconscious of his ugliness. "My name's Anne." "You aren't ugly." She never knew, he thought, that he had meant to kill her; she had been as innocent of his intention as a cat he had once been forced to drown. And he remembered with astonishment that she had not betrayed him, although he had told her that the police were after him. It was even possible that she had believed him.

These thoughts were colder and more uncomfortable than the hail. He wasn't used to any taste that wasn't bitter on the tongue. He had been made by hatred; it had constructed him into this thin, smoky, murderous figure in the rain, hunted and ugly. His mother had borne him when his father was in jail, and six years later, when his father was hanged for another crime, she had cut her own throat with a kitchen knife. Afterwards there had been the home. He had never felt the least tenderness for anyone; he was made in this image, and he had his own odd pride in the result; he didn't want to be unmade. He had a sudden terrified conviction that he must be himself now as never before if he was to escape. It was not tenderness that made you quick on the draw.

Somebody in one of the larger houses on the river front had left his garage gate ajar. It was obviously not used for a car, but only to house a pram, a child's playground, and a few dusty dolls and bricks. Raven took shelter there: he was cold through and through except in the one spot that had lain frozen all his life. That dagger of ice was melting with great pain. He pushed the garage gate a little farther open: he had no wish to appear furtively hiding if anyone passed along the river beat. Anyone might be excused for sheltering in a stranger's garage from *this* storm, except, of course, a man with a harelip wanted by the police.

These houses were only semidetached. They were joined by their garages. Raven was closely hemmed in by the red brick walls. He could hear the wireless playing in both houses. In the one house it switched and changed as a restless finger turned the screw and beat up the wave lengths, bringing a snatch of rhetoric from Berlin, of opera from Stockholm. On the National Programme from the other house an elderly critic was reading verse. Raven couldn't help but hear, standing in the cold garage by the baby's pram, staring out at the black hail.

> *"A shadow flits before me,*
> *Not thou, but like to thee;*
> *Ah Christ, that it were possible*
> *For one short hour to see*
> *The souls we loved, that they might tell us*
> *What and where they be."*

He dug his nails into his hands, remembering his father who had been hanged and his mother who had killed herself in the basement kitchen, and all the long parade of those who had done him down. The elderly cultured Civil Service voice read on:

> *"And I loathe the squares and streets,*
> *And the faces that one meets,*
> *Hearts with no love for me . . ."*

He thought, Give her time, and she too will go to the police. That's what always happens in the end with a skirt—

> *"My whole soul out to thee . . ."*

—trying to freeze again as hard and safe as ever the icy fragment.

"That was Mr. Druce Winton, reading a selection from *Maud* by Lord Tennyson. This ends the National Programme. Good night, everybody."

Three

1

Mather's train got in at eleven that night, and with Saunders he drove straight through the almost empty streets to the police station. Nottwich went to bed early; the cinemas closed at ten-thirty, and a quarter of an hour later everyone had left the middle of Nottwich by tram or bus. Nottwich's only tart hung round the market place, cold and blue under her umbrella, and one or two businessmen were having a last cigar in the hall of the Metropole. The car slid on the icy road. Just before the police station Mather noticed the posters of *Aladdin* outside the Royal Theatre. He said to Saunders, "My girl's in that show." He felt proud and happy.

The chief constable had come down to the police station to meet Mather. The fact that Raven was known to be arméd and desperate gave the chase a more serious air than it would otherwise have had. The chief constable was fat and excited. He had made a lot of money as a tradesman and during the war had been given a commission and the job of presiding over the local military tribunal. He prided himself on having been a terror to pacifists. It atoned a little for his own home life and a wife who despised him. That was why he had come down to the station to meet Mather: it would be something to boast about at home.

Mather said, "Of course, sir, we don't *know* he's here. But he was on the train all right, and his ticket was given up. By a woman."

"Got an accomplice, eh?" the chief constable said.

"Perhaps. Find the woman, and we may have Raven."

The chief constable belched behind his hand. He had been drinking bottled beer before he came out, and it always repeated itself. The superintendent said, "Directly we heard from the Yard we circulated the number of the notes to all shops, hotels, and boarding houses."

"That a map, sir," Mather asked, "with your beats marked?"

They walked over to the wall, and the superintendent pointed out the main points in Nottwich with a pencil: the railway station, the river, the police station.

"And the Royal Theatre," Mather said, "will be about there?"

"That's right."

"What's brought 'im to Nottwich?" the chief constable asked.

"I wish we knew, sir. Now these streets round the station, are they hotels?"

"A few boarding houses. But the worst of it is," the superintendent said, absent-mindedly turning his back on the chief constable, "a lot of these houses take occasional boarders."

"Better circulate them all."

"Some of them wouldn't take much notice of a police request. Houses of call, you know. Quick ten minutes and the door always open."

"Nonsense," the chief constable said, "we don't 'ave that kind of place in Nottwich."

"If you wouldn't mind my suggesting it, sir, it wouldn't be a bad thing to double the constables on any beats of that kind. Send the sharpest men you've got. I suppose you've had his description in the evening paper. He seems to be a pretty smart safe-breaker."

"There doesn't seem to be much more we can do tonight," the superintendent said. "I'm sorry for the poor devil if he's found nowhere to sleep."

"Keep a bottle of whisky here, Super?" the chief constable asked. "Do us all good to 'ave a drink. Had too much beer. It returns. Whisky's better, but the wife doesn't like the smell." He leaned back in his chair with his fat thighs crossed and watched the inspector with a kind of childlike happiness; he seemed to be saying, What a spree this is, drinking again with the boys. Only the superintendent knew what an old devil he was with anyone weaker than himself. "Just a splash, Super." He said over his glass, "You caught that old swine Baines out nicely," and explained to Mather, "Street betting. He's been a worry for months."

"He was straight enough. I don't believe in harrying people. Just because he was taking money out of Macpherson's pocket."

"Ah," the chief constable said, "but that's legal. Macpherson's got an office and a telephone. He's got expenses to carry. Cheerio, boys. To the ladies." He drained his glass. "Just another two fingers, Super." He blew out his chest. "What about some more coal on the fire? Let's be snug. There's no work we can do tonight."

Mather was uneasy. It was quite true there wasn't much one could do, but he hated inaction. He stayed by the map. It wasn't such a large place, Nottwich. They ought not to take long to find Raven, but here he was a stranger. He didn't know what dives to raid, what clubs and dance halls. He said, "We think he's followed someone here. I'd suggest, sir, that first thing in the morning we interview the ticket collector again. See how many local people he can remember leaving the train. We might be lucky."

"Do you know that story about the Archbishop of York?" the chief constable asked. "Yes, yes. We'll do that. But there's no hurry. Make yourself at 'ome, man, and take some scotch. You're in the Midlands now. The slow Midlands—eh, Super? We don't 'ustle, but we get there just the same."

Of course, he was right. There *was* no hurry, and there wasn't anything anyone could do at this hour, but as Mather stood beside the map it was just as if someone were calling to him, "Hurry. Hurry. Hurry. Or you may be too late." He traced the main streets with his finger; he wanted to be as familiar with them as he was with central London. Here was the G.P.O., the market, the Metropole, the High Street. What was this? The Tanneries. "What's this big block in the Tanneries, sir?" he asked.

"That'll be Midland Steel," the superintendent said and, turning to the chief constable, he went on patiently, "No, sir. I hadn't heard that one. That's a good one, sir."

"The mayor told me that," the chief constable said. "He's a sport, old Piker. You'd think he wasn't a day under forty. Do you know what he said when we had that committee on the gas practice? He said, 'This'll give us a chance to get into a strange bed.' He meant the women couldn't tell who was who in a gas mask. You see?"

"Very witty man, Mr. Piker, sir."

"Yes, Super, but I was too smart for him there. I was on the spot that day. Do you know what I said?"

"No, sir."

"I said, '*You* won't be able to find a strange bed, Piker.' Catch me meaning? He's a dog, old Piker."

"What are your arrangements for the gas practice, sir?" Mather asked with his finger jabbed on the Town Hall.

"You can't expect people to buy gas masks at twenty-five bob a time, but we're having a raid the day after tomorrow with smoke bombs from Hanlow aerodrome, and anyone found in the street without a mask will be carted off by ambulance to the General Hospital. So anyone who's too busy to stop indoors will have to buy a mask. Midland Steel are supplying all their people with masks, so it'll be business as usual there."

"Kind of blackmail," the inspector said. "Stay in or buy a mask. The transport companies have spent a pretty penny on masks."

"What hours, sir?"

"We don't tell them that. Sirens hoot. You know the idea. Boy Scouts on bicycles. They've been lent masks. But of course we know it'll be all over before noon."

Mather looked back at the map. "These coal yards," he said, "round the station. You've got them well covered?"

"We are keeping an eye on those," the superintendent said. "I saw to that as soon as the Yard rang through."

"Smart work, boys, smart work," the chief constable said, swallowing the last of his whisky. "I'll be off home. Busy day before us all tomorrow. You'd like a conference with me in the morning, I daresay, Super?"

"Oh, I don't think we'll trouble you that early, sir."

"Well, if you do need any advice, I'm always at the end of the phone. Good night, boys."

"Good night, sir. Good night."

"The old boy's right about one thing." The superintendent put the whisky away in his cupboard. "We can't do anything more tonight."

"I won't keep you up, sir," Mather said. "You mustn't think I'm fussy. Saunders will tell you I'm as ready to knock off as any man, but there's something about this case . . . I can't leave it alone. It's a queer case. I was looking at this map, sir, and trying to think where I'd hide. What about these dotted lines out here on the east?"

"It's a new housing estate."

"Half-built houses?"

"I've put two men on special beat out there."

"You've got everything taped pretty well, sir. You don't really need us."

"You mustn't judge us by *him*."

"I'm not quite easy in my mind. He's followed someone here. He's a smart lad. We've never had anything on him before, and yet for the last twenty-four hours he's done nothing but make mistakes. The chief said he's blazing a trail, and it's true. It strikes me that he's desperate to get someone."

The superintendent glanced at the clock.

"I'm off, sir," Mather said. "See you in the morning. Good night, Saunders. I'm just going to take a stroll around a bit before I come to the hotel. I want to get this place clear."

He walked out into the High Street. The rain had stopped and was freezing in the gutters. He slipped on the pavement and had to put his hand on the lamp standard. They turned the lights very low in Nottwich after eleven. Over the way, fifty yards down towards the market, he could see the portico of the Royal Theatre. No lights at all to be seen there. He found himself humming, "But to me it's Paradise," and thought, It's good to love, to have a centre, a certainty, not just to be *in* love floating around. He liked organization. He wanted that too to be organized as soon as possible; he wanted love stamped and sealed and signed and the license paid for. He was filled with a dumb tenderness he would never be able to express outside marriage. He wasn't a lover; he was already like a married man, but a married man with years of happiness and confidence to be grateful for.

He did the maddest thing he'd done since he had known her: he went and took a look at her lodgings. He had the address. She'd given it to him over the phone, and it fitted in with his work to find his way to All Saints Road. He learned quite a lot of things on the way, keeping his eyes open; it wasn't really a waste of time. He learned, for instance, the name and address of the local papers, the Nottwich *Journal* and the Nottwich *Guardian,* two rival papers facing each other across Chatton Street, one of them next a great gaudy cinema. From their posters he could even judge their publics: the *Journal* was popular; the *Guardian* was "class." He learned too where the best fish-and-chip shops were and the public houses where the pitmen went. He discovered the park, a place of dull wilted trees and palings and gravel paths for perambulators. Any of these facts might be of use, and they humanized the map of Nottwich so that he could think of it in terms of people, just as he thought of London, when he was on a job, in terms of Charlie's and Joe's.

All Saints Road was two rows of stone-tiled neo-Gothic houses lined up as carefully as a company on parade. He stopped outside Number 14 and wondered if she were awake. She'd get a surprise in the morning: he had posted a card at Euston, telling her he was putting up at the Crown, the commercial house. There was a light on in the basement: the landlady was still awake. He wished that he could send a quicker message than that card: he knew the dreariness of new lodgings, of waking to the black tea and the unfriendly face. It seemed to him that life couldn't treat her well enough.

The wind froze him, but he lingered there on the opposite pavement, wondering whether she had enough blankets on her bed, whether she had any shillings for the gas metre. Encouraged by the light in the basement, he nearly rang the bell to ask the landlady whether Anne had all she needed. But he made his way instead towards the Crown. He wasn't going to look silly; he wasn't even going to tell her that he'd been and had a look at where she slept.

2

A knock on the door woke him. It was barely seven. A woman's voice said, "You're wanted on the phone," and he could hear her trailing away downstairs, knocking a broom handle against the banisters. It was going to be a fine day.

Mather went downstairs to the telephone, which was behind the bar in the empty saloon. He said, "Mather. Who's that?" and heard the station sergeant's voice: "We've got some news for you. He slept last night in St. Mark's, the Roman Catholic cathedral. And someone reports he was down by the river earlier."

But by the time he was dressed and at the station more evidence had come in. The agent of a housing estate had read in the local paper about the stolen notes and brought to the station two notes he had received from a girl who said she wanted to buy a house. He'd thought it odd because she had never turned up to sign the papers.

"That'll be the girl who gave up his ticket," the superintendent said. "They are working together on this."

"And the cathedral?" Mather asked.

"A woman saw him come out early this morning. Then when she got home (she was on the way to chapel) and read the paper, she told a constable on point duty. We'll have to have the churches locked."

"No, watched," Mather said. He warmed his hand over the iron stove. "Let me talk to this house agent."

The man came breezily in in plus fours from the outer room. "Name of Green," he said.

"Could you tell me, Mr. Green, what this girl looked like?"

"A nice little thing," Mr. Green said.

"Short? Below five-feet four?"

"No, I wouldn't say that."

"You said little?"

"Oh," Mr. Green said, "term of affection, you know. Easy to get on with."

"Fair? Dark?"

"Oh, I couldn't say that. Don't look at their hair. Good legs."

"Anything strange in her manner?"

"No, I wouldn't say that. Nicely spoken. She could take a joke."

"Then you wouldn't have noticed the colour of her eyes?"

"Well, as a matter of fact, I did. I always look at a girl's eyes. They like it. 'Drink to me only,' you know. A bit of poetry. That's my gambit. Kind of spiritual, you know."

"And what colour were they?"

"Green with a spot of gold."

"What was she wearing? Did you notice that?"

"Of course I did," Mr. Green said. He moved his hands in the air. "It was something dark and soft. You know what I mean."

"And the hat? Straw?"

"No. It wasn't straw."

"Felt?"

"It might have been a kind of felt. That was dark too. I noticed that."

"Would you know her again if you saw her?"

"Of course I would," Mr. Green said. "Never forget a face."

"Right," Mather said. "You can go. We may want you later to identify the girl. We'll keep these notes."

"But I say," Mr. Green said, "those are good notes. They belong to the company."

"You can consider the house is still for sale."

"I've had the ticket collector here," the superintendent said. "Of course he doesn't remember a thing that helps. In these stories you read people always remember *something,* but in real life they just say she was wearing something dark or something light."

"You've sent someone up to look at the house? Is this the man's story? It's odd. She must have gone there straight from the station. Why? And why pretend to buy the house and pay him with a stolen note?"

"It looks as if she was desperate to keep the other man from buying. As if she'd got something hidden there."

"Your man had better go through that house with a comb, sir. But of course they won't find anything. If there was still anything to find she'd have turned up to sign the papers."

"No, she'd have been afraid," the superintendent said, "in case he'd found out they were stolen notes."

"You know," Mather said, "I wasn't much interested in this case. It seemed sort of petty—chasing down a small thief when the whole world will soon be fighting because of a murderer those fools in Europe couldn't catch. But now it's getting me. There's something odd about it. I told you what my chief said about Raven? He said he was blazing a trail. But he's managed so far to keep just ahead of us. Could I see the ticket collector's statement?"

"There's nothing in it."

"I don't agree with you, sir," Mather said, while the superintendent turned it up from the file of papers on his desk. "The books are right. People generally do remember something. If they remembered nothing at all it would look very queer. It's only spooks that don't leave any impression. Even that agent remembered the colour of her eyes."

"Probably wrong," the superintendent said. "Here you are. All he remembers is that she carried two suitcases. It's something, of course, but it's not worth much."

"Oh, one could make guesses from that," Mather said. "Don't you think so?" He didn't believe in making himself too clever in front of the provincial police: he needed their cooperation. "She was coming for a long stay (a woman can get a lot in one suitcase), or else, if she was carrying his case too, he was the dominant one. Believes in treating her rough and making her do all the physical labour. That fits in with Raven's character. As for the girl—"

"In these gangster stories," the superintendent said, "they call her a moll."

"Well, this moll," Mather said, "is one of those girls who like being treated rough. Sort of clinging and avaricious, I picture her. If she had more spirit he'd carry one of the suitcases or else she'd split on him."

"I thought this Raven was about as ugly as they are made."

"That fits too," Mather said. "Perhaps she likes 'em ugly. Perhaps it gives her a thrill."

The superintendent laughed. "You've got a lot out of those suitcases. Read the report and you'll be giving me her photograph. Here you are. But he doesn't remember a thing about her, not even what she was wearing."

Mather read it. He read it slowly. He said nothing, but something in his manner of shock and incredulity was conveyed to the superintendent. He said, "Is anything wrong? There's nothing *there,* surely?"

"You said I'd be giving you her photograph," Mather said. He took a slip of newspaper from the back of his watch. "There it is, sir. You'd better circulate that to all stations in the city and to the press."

"But there's nothing in the report," the superintendent said.

"Everybody remembers something. It wasn't anything you could have spotted. I seem to have private information about this crime, but I didn't know it till now."

The superintendent said, "He doesn't remember a thing. Except the suitcases."

"Thank God for those," Mather said. "It may mean— You see he says here that one of the reasons he remembers her—he calls it remembering her—is that she was the only woman who got out of the train at Nottwich. And this girl I happen to know was travelling by it. She'd got an engagement at the theatre here."

The superintendent said bluntly—he didn't realize the full extent of the shock, "And is she of the type you said? Likes 'em ugly?"

"I thought she liked them plain," Mather said, staring out through the window at a world going to work through the cold early day. "Sort of clinging and avaricious?"

"No, damn it."

"But if she'd had more spirit—" the superintendent mocked. He thought Mather was disturbed because his guesses were wrong.

"She had all the spirit there was," Mather said. He turned back from the window. He forgot the superintendent was his superior officer; he forgot you had to be tactful to these provincial police officers; he said, "Goddam it, don't you see? He didn't carry his suitcase because he had to keep her covered. He *made* her walk out to that housing estate." He said, "I've got to go there. He meant to murder her."

"No, no," the superintendent said. "You are forgetting: she paid the money to Green and walked out of the house with him alone. He saw her off the estate."

"But I'd swear," Mather said, "she isn't in this. It's absurd. It doesn't make sense." He said, "We're engaged to be married."

"That's tough," the superintendent said. He hesitated, picked up a dead match and cleaned a nail, then he pushed the photograph back. "Put it away," he said. "We'll go about this differently."

"No," Mather said. "I'm on this case. Have it printed. It's a bad smudged photo." He wouldn't look at it. "It doesn't do her justice. But I'll wire home for a better likeness. I've got a whole strip of Photomatons at home. Her face from every angle. You couldn't have a better lot of photos for newspaper purposes."

"I'm sorry, Mather," the superintendent said. "Hadn't I better speak to the Yard? Get another man sent?"

"You couldn't have a better on the case," Mather said. "I know her. If she's to be found, I'll find her. I'm going out to the house now. You see, your man may miss something. I *know* her."

"There may be an explanation," the superintendent said.

"Don't you see," Mather said, "that if there's an explanation it means—why, that she's in danger. She may even be—"

"We'd have found her body."

"We haven't even found a living man," Mather said. "Would you ask Saunders to follow me out? What's the address?" He wrote it carefully down: he always noted facts; he didn't trust his brain for more than theories, guesses.

It was a long drive out to the housing estate. He had time to think of many possibilities. She might have fallen asleep and been carried on to York. She might not have taken the train . . . and there was nothing in the hideous little house to contradict him. He found a plain-clothes man in what would one day be the best front room. In its flashy fireplace, its dark-brown picture rail and the cheap oak of its wainscotting, it bore already the suggestion of heavy unused furniture, dark curtains, and Gosse china. "There's nothing," the detective said, "nothing at all. You can see, of course, that someone's been here. The dust has been disturbed. But there wasn't enough dust to take a footprint. There's nothing to be got here."

"There's always something," Mather said. "Where did you find traces? All the rooms?"

"No, not all of them. But that's not evidence. There was no sign in this room, but the dust isn't as thick here. Maybe the builders swept up better. You can't say no one was in here."

"How did she get in?"

"The lock of the back door's busted."

"Could a girl do that?"

"A cat could do it. A determined cat."

"Green says he came in at the front. Just opened the door of this room and then took the other fellow straight upstairs, into the best bedroom. The girl joined them there just as he was going to show the rest of the house. Then they all went straight down and out of the house, except the girl went into the kitchen and picked up her suitcases. He'd left the front door open and thought she'd followed them in."

"She was in the kitchen all right. And in the bathroom."

"Where's that?"

"Up the stairs and round to the left."

The two men—they were both large—nearly filled the cramped bathroom. "Looks as if she heard them coming," the detective said, "and hid in here."

"What brought her up? If she was in the kitchen she had only to slip out at the back." Mather stood in the tiny room between the bath and the lavatory seat and thought, *She* was here yesterday. It was incredible. It didn't fit in at any point with what he knew of her. They had been engaged for six months: she couldn't have disguised herself so completely. On the bus ride from Kew that evening, humming the song—what was it?—something about a snowflower; the night they sat two programmes round at the cinema because he'd

spent his week's pay and hadn't been able to give her dinner. She
never complained as the hard, mechanized voices began all over
again: "A wise guy, huh?" "Baby, you're swell," "Siddown, won't
you?" "Thenks" at the edge of their consciousness. She was straight,
she was loyal, he could swear that, but the alternative was a danger
he hardly dared contemplate. Raven was desperate. He heard himself saying with harsh conviction, "Raven was here. He drove her
up at the point of his pistol. He was going to shut her in here—or
maybe shoot her. Then he heard voices. He gave her the notes and
told her to get rid of the other fellows. If she'd tried anything on,
he'd have shot her. Damn it, isn't it plain?" But the detective only
repeated the substance of the superintendent's criticism: "She
walked right out of the place alone with Green. There was nothing
to prevent her going to the police station."

"He may have followed at a distance."

"It looks to me," the detective said, "as if you are taking the
most *unlikely* theory," and Mather could tell from his manner how
puzzled he was at the Yard man's attitude: these Londoners were
a little too ingenious; he believed in good sound Midland common
sense. It angered Mather in his professional pride; he even felt a
small chill of hatred against Anne for putting him in a position
where his affection warped his judgment. He said, "We've no proof
that she didn't try to tell the police," and wondered, Do I want her
dead and innocent or alive and guilty? He began to examine the
bathroom with meticulous care. He even pushed his finger up the
taps in case . . . He had a wild idea that if it were really Anne
who had stood here she would have wanted to leave a message. He
straightened himself impatiently. "There's nothing here." He remembered there was a test; she might have missed her train. "I
want a telephone," he said.

"There'll be one down the road at the agent's."

Mather rang up the theatre. There was no one there except a
caretaker, but as it happened she could tell him that no one had
been absent from rehearsal. The producer, Mr. Collier, always
posted absentees on the board inside the stage door. He was great
on discipline, Mr. Collier. Yes, and she remembered that there *was*
a new girl. She happened to see her going out with a man at dinnertime after the rehearsal just as she came back to the theatre to tidy
up a bit, and thought, That's a new face. She didn't know who the
man was. He must be one of the backers. "Wait a moment, wait a
moment," Mather said. He had to think what to do next. She *was*

the girl who had given the agent the stolen notes; he had to forget that she was Anne, who had so wildly wished that they could marry before Christmas, who had hated the promiscuity of her job, who had promised him that night on the bus from Kew that she would keep out of the way of all rich business backers and stage-door loungers. He said, "Mr. Collier? Where can I find him?"

"He'll be at the theatre tonight. There's a rehearsal at eight."

"I want to see him at once."

"You can't. He's gone up to York with Mr. Bleek."

"Where can I find any of the girls who were at the rehearsal?"

"I dunno. I don't have the address book. They'll be all over the town."

"There must be *someone* who was there last night."

"You could find Miss Maydew, of course."

"Where?"

"I don't know where she's staying. But you've only got to look at the posters of the jumble."

"The jumble? What do you mean?"

"She's opening the jumble up at St. Luke's at two."

Through the window of the agent's office Mather saw Saunders coming up the frozen mud of the track between the Cozyholmes. He rang off and intercepted him. "Any news come in?"

"Yes," Saunders said. The superintendent had told him everything. He was deeply distressed. He loved Mather. He owed everything to Mather; it was Mather who had brought him up every stage of promotion in the police force, who had persuaded the authorities that a man who stammered could be as good a policeman as the champion reciter at police concerts. But he would have loved him anyway for a quality of idealism, for believing so implicitly in what he did.

"Well? Let's have it."

"It's about your g-girl. She's disappeared." He took the news at a run, getting it out in one breath. "Her landlady rang up the station, said she was out all night and never came back."

"Run away," Mather said.

Saunders said, "D-Don't you believe it. You t-t-t-told her to take that train. She wasn't going till the m-m-m-m-morning."

"You're right," Mather said. "I'd forgotten that. Meeting him must have been an accident. But it's a miserable choice, Saunders. She may be dead now."

"Why should he do that? We've only got a theft on him. What are you going to do next?"

"Back to the station. And then at two—" he smiled miserably— "a jumble sale."

3

The vicar was worried. He wouldn't listen to what Mather had to say; he had too much to think about himself. It was the curate, the new, bright, broad-minded curate from a London East End parish, who had suggested inviting Miss Maydew to open the jumble sale. He thought it would be a draw, but as the vicar explained to Mather, holding him pinned there in the pitch-pine anteroom of St. Luke's Hall, a jumble was always a draw. There was a queue fifty yards long of women with baskets waiting for the door to open. They hadn't come to see Miss Maydew; they had come for bargains. St. Luke's jumble sales were famous all over Nottwich.

A dry, perky woman with a cameo brooch put her head in at the door. "Henry," she said, "the committee are rifling the stalls again. Can't you *do* something about it? There'll be nothing left when the sale starts."

"Where's Mander? It's *his* business," the vicar said.

"Mr. Mander, of course, is off fetching Miss Maydew." The perky woman blew her nose and disappeared into the hall, crying, "Constance, Constance."

"You can't really do anything about it," the vicar said. "It happens every year. These good women give their time voluntarily. The Altar Society would be in a very bad way without them. They *expect* to have first choice of everything that's sent in. Of course the trouble is, *they* fix the prices."

"Henry," the perky woman said, appearing again in the doorway, "you *must* interfere. Mrs. Penny has priced that very good hat Lady Cundifer sent at eighteenpence and bought it herself."

"My dear, how can I say anything? They'd never volunteer again. You must remember they've given time and trouble—" but he was addressing a closed door. "What worries me," he said to Mather, "is that this young lady will expect an ovation. She won't understand that nobody's interested in *who* opens a jumble sale. Things are so different in London."

"She's late," Mather said.

"They are quite capable of storming the doors," the vicar said with a nervous glance through the window at the lengthening queue. "I must confess to a little stratagem. After all she is our guest. She is giving time and trouble." Time and trouble were the gifts of which the vicar was always most conscious. They were given more readily than coppers in the collection. He went on, "Did you see any young boys outside?"

"Only women," Mather said.

"Oh dear, oh dear. I *told* Troop Leader Lance. You see, I thought if one or two Scouts, in plain clothes of course, brought up autograph books, it would please Miss Maydew, seem to show we appreciated—the time and trouble." He said miserably, "The St. Luke's Troop is always the least trustworthy."

A grey-haired man with a carpet bag put his head in at the door. He said, "Mrs. 'Arris said as there was something wrong with the 'eating."

"Ah, Mr. Bacon," the vicar said, "so kind of you. Step into the hall. You'll find Mrs. Harris there. A little stoppage, so I understand."

Mather looked at his watch. He said, "I must speak to Miss Maydew directly—"

A young man entered at a rush. He said to the vicar, "Excuse me, Mr. Harris, but will Miss Maydew be speaking?"

"I hope not. I profoundly hope not," the vicar said. "It's hard enough as it is to keep the women from the stalls till after I've said a prayer. Where's my prayer book? Who's seen my prayer book?"

"Because I'm covering it for the *Journal,* and if she's not, you see, I can get away . . ."

Mather wanted to say, Listen to me. Your damned jumble is of no importance. My girl's in danger. She may be dead. He wanted to do things to people, but he stood there heavy, immobile, patient, even his private passion and fear subdued by his training: one didn't give way to anger, one plodded on calmly, adding fact to fact. If one's girl was killed, one had the satisfaction of knowing one had done one's best according to the standards of the best police force in the world. He wondered bitterly, as he watched the vicar search for his prayer book, whether that would be any comfort.

Mr. Bacon came back and said, "She'll 'eat now," and disappeared with a clank of metal. A boisterous voice said, "Upstage a little, upstage, Miss Maydew," and the curate entered. He wore suede shoes, he had a shiny face and plastered hair, and he carried an umbrella under his arm like a cricket bat; he might have been returning to the pavilion after scoring a duck in a friendly, taking his failure noisily, as a good sportsman should. "Here is my C.O., Miss Maydew, on the O.P. side." He said to the vicar, "I've been telling Miss Maydew about our dramatics."

Mather said, "May I speak to you a moment privately, Miss Maydew?"

But the vicar swept her away. "A moment, a moment; first our little ceremony. Constance. Constance," and almost immediately the anteroom was empty, except for Mather and the journalist, who sat on the table swinging his legs, biting his nails. An extraordinary noise came from the next room; it was like the trampling of a herd of animals, a trampling suddenly brought to a standstill at a fence. In the sudden silence one could hear the vicar hastily finishing off the Lord's Prayer, and then Miss Maydew's clear, immature, principal boy's voice saying, "I declare this jumble well and truly . . ." and then the trampling again. She had got her words wrong: it had always been foundation stones her mother laid, but no one noticed. Everyone was relieved because she hadn't made a speech. Mather went to the door. Half a dozen boys were queued up in front of Miss Maydew with autograph albums; the St. Luke's Troop hadn't failed after all. A hard, astute woman in a toque said to Mather, "This stall will interest *you*. It's a Man's Stall," and Mather looked down at a dingy array of penwipers and pipe cleaners and hand-embroidered tobacco pouches. Somebody had even presented a lot of old pipes. He lied quickly, "I don't smoke."

The astute woman said, "You've come here to spend money, haven't you, as a duty? You may as well take *some*thing that will be of use. You won't find anything on any of the other stalls," and between the women's shoulders, as he craned to follow the movements of Miss Maydew and the St. Luke's Troop, he caught a few grim glimpses of discarded vases, chipped fruit stands, yellowing piles of babies' napkins. "I've got several pairs of braces. You may just as well take a pair of braces."

Mather, to his own astonishment and distress, said, "She may be dead."

The woman said, "Who dead?" and bristled over a pair of mauve suspenders.

"I'm sorry," Mather said. "I wasn't thinking." He was horrified at himself for losing grip. He thought, I ought to have let them exchange me. It's going to be too much. He said, "Excuse me," seeing the last Scout shut his album.

He led Miss Maydew into the anteroom. The journalist had gone. He said, "I'm trying to trace a girl in your company called Anne Crowder."

"Don't know her," Miss Maydew said.

"She only joined the cast yesterday."

"They all look alike," Miss Maydew said; "like Chinamen. I never can learn their names."

"This one's fair. Green eyes. She has a good voice."

"Not in *this* company," Miss Maydew said, "not in *this* company. I can't listen to them. It sets my teeth on edge."

"You don't remember her going out last night with a man at the end of rehearsal?"

"Why should I? Don't be so sordid."

"He invited you out too."

"The fat fool," Miss Maydew said.

"Who was he?"

"I don't know. Davenant, I think Collier said, or did he say Davis? Never saw him before. I suppose he's the man Cohen quarrelled with. Though somebody said something about Callitrope."

"This is important, Miss Maydew. The girl's disappeared."

"It's always happening on these tours. If you go into their dressing room it's always *men* they are talking about. How can they ever hope to act? So sordid."

"You can't help me at all? You've no idea where I can find this man Davenant?"

"Collier will know. He'll be back tonight. Or perhaps he won't. I don't think he knew him from Adam. It's coming back to me now. Collier called him Davis, and he said No, he was Davenant. He'd bought out Davis."

Mather went sadly away. Some instinct that always made him go where people were, because clues were more likely to be found among a crowd of strangers than in empty rooms or deserted streets, drove him through the hall. You wouldn't have known among these avid women that England was on the edge of war. "I said to Mrs. 'Opkinson, if you are addressing me, I said." "That'll look tasty on Dora." A very old woman said across a pile of artificial silk knickers, " 'E lay for five hours with 'is knees drawn up." A girl giggled and said in a hoarse whisper, "Artful. I'd say so. 'E put 'is fingers right down." Why should these people worry about war?

They moved from stall to stall in an air thick with their own deaths and sicknesses and loves. A woman with a hard, driven face touched Mather's arm. She must have been about sixty years old. She had a way of ducking her head when she spoke, as if she expected a blow, but up her head would come again with a sour unconquerable malice. He had watched her without really knowing it as he walked down the stalls. Now she plucked at him; he could smell fish on her fingers. "Reach me that bit of stuff, dear," she said. "You've got long arms. No, not that. The pink," and began to fumble for money —in Anne's bag.

4

Mather's brother had committed suicide. More than Mather he had needed to be part of an organization, to be trained and disciplined and given orders, but unlike Mather he hadn't found his organization. When things went wrong he had killed himself, and Mather was called to the mortuary to identify the body. He had hoped it was a stranger until they exposed the pale, drowned, lost face. All day he had been trying to find his brother, hurrying from address to address, and the first feeling he had when he saw him there was not grief. He thought, I needn't hurry, I can sit down. He went out to an A.B.C. and ordered a pot of tea. He began to feel his grief only after the second cup.

It was the same now. He thought, I needn't have hurried; I needn't have made a fool of myself before that woman with the braces. She must be dead. I needn't have felt so rushed.

The old woman said, "Thank you, dear," and thrust the little piece of pink material away. He couldn't feel any doubt whatever about the bag. He had given it her himself. It was an expensive bag, not of a kind you would expect to find in Nottwich, and to make it quite conclusive you could still see, within a little circle of twisted glass, the place where two initials had been removed. It was all over forever; he hadn't got to hurry any more. A pain was on its way worse than he had felt in the A.B.C. (a man at the next table had been eating fried plaice, and now, he didn't know why, he associated a certain kind of pain with the smell of fish). But first it was a perfectly cold, calculating satisfaction he felt, that he had the devils in his hands already. Someone was going to die for this. The old woman had picked up a small brassière and was testing the elastic with a malicious grin because it was meant for someone young and pretty with breasts worth preserving. "The silly things they wear," she said.

He could have arrested her at once, but already he had decided that wouldn't do; there were more in it than the old woman. He'd get them all, and the longer the chase lasted the better: he wouldn't have to begin thinking of the future till it was over. He was thankful now that Raven was armed, because he himself was forced to carry a gun, and who could say whether chance might not allow him to use it?

He looked up, and there on the other side of the stall, with his eyes fixed on Anne's bag, was the dark, bitter figure he had been seeking, the harelip imperfectly hidden by a few days' growth of moustache.

Four

1

Raven had been on his feet all the morning. He had to keep moving; he couldn't use the little change he had on food, because he did not dare to stay still, to give anyone the chance to study his face. He bought a paper outside the post office and saw his own description there, printed in black type inside a frame. He was angry because it was on a back page; the situation in Europe filled the front page. By midday, moving here and moving there with his eyes always open for Cholmondeley, he was dog-tired. He stood for a moment and stared at his own face in a barber's window. Ever since his flight from the café he had remained unshaven. A moustache might hide his deformity, but he knew from experience how his hair grew in patches, strong on the chin, weak on the lip, and not at all on either side the red deformity. Now the scrubby growth on his chin was making him conspicuous, and he didn't dare go into the barber's for a shave. He passed a chocolate machine, but it would take only sixpenny or shilling pieces, and his pocket held nothing but half-crowns, florins, halfpennies. If it had not been for his bitter hatred he would have given himself up—they couldn't give him more than five years—but the death of the old minister lay, now that he was so tired and harried, like an albatross round his neck. It was hard to realize that he was wanted only for theft.

He was afraid to haunt alleys, to linger in culs-de-sac, because

if a policeman passed and he was the only man in sight he felt conspicuous—the man might give him a second glance—and so he
walked all the time in the most crowded streets and took the risk
of innumerable recognitions. It was a dull, cold day, but at least it
wasn't raining. The shops were full of Christmas gifts; all the absurd useless junk which had lain on back shelves all the year was
brought out to fill the windows: foxhead brooches, book rests in
the shape of the Cenotaph, woollen cosies for boiled eggs, innumerable games with counters and dice, and absurd patent variations on
darts or bagatelle, "Cats on a Wall," the old shooting game, and
"Fishing for Gold Fish." In a religious shop by the Catholic cathedral he found himself facing again the images that had angered
him in the Soho café: the plaster mother and child, the wise men,
and the shepherds. They were arranged in a cavern of brown paper
among the books of devotion, the little pious scraps of St. Theresa.
"The Holy Family"—he pressed his face against the glass with a
kind of horrified anger that that tale still went on. "Because there
was no room for them in the inn . . ." He remembered how they
had sat in rows on the benches, waiting for Christmas dinner, while
the thin precise voice read on about Caesar Augustus and how
everyone went up to his own city to be taxed. Nobody was beaten
on Christmas Day; all punishments were saved for Boxing Day.
Love, Charity, Patience, Humility: he was educated, he knew all
about those virtues; he'd seen what they were worth. They twisted
everything, even that story in there. It was historical, it had happened, but they twisted it to their own purposes. They made him a
god because they could feel fine about it all; they didn't have to
consider themselves responsible for the raw deal they'd given him.
He'd consented, hadn't he? That was the argument, because he
could have called down "a legion of angels" if he'd wanted to escape hanging there. On your life he could, he thought, with bitter
lack of faith; just as easily as his own father, taking the drop at
Wandsworth, could have saved himself when the trap opened. He
stood there, with his face against the glass, waiting for somebody
to deny *that* reasoning, staring at the swaddled child with a horrified
tenderness—"the little bastard"—because he was educated and
knew what the child was in for: the damned Jews and the double-
crossing Judas, with no one even to draw a knife on his side when
the soldiers came for him in the garden.

A policeman came up the street as Raven stared into the window,
and passed without a glance. It occurred to him to wonder how

much they knew. Had the girl told them her story? He supposed she had by this time. It would be in the paper, and he looked. There was not a word about her there. It shook him. He'd nearly killed her, and she hadn't gone to them; that meant she had believed what he'd told her. He was momentarily back in the garage again beside the Weevil in the rain and dark with the dreadful sense of desolation, of having missed something valuable, of having made an irretrievable mistake, but he could no longer comfort himself with any conviction with his old phrase, "Give her time—it always happens with a skirt." He wanted to find her, but he thought, What a chance. I can't even find Cholmondeley. He said bitterly to the tiny scrap of plaster in the plaster cradle, "If you were a god you'd know I wouldn't harm her. You'd give me a break—you'd let me turn and see her on the pavement," and he turned with a half a hope, but of course there was nothing there.

As he moved away he saw a sixpence in the gutter. He picked it up and went back the way he had come, to the last chocolate slot machine he had passed. It was outside a sweet shop and next a church hall, where a queue of women waited along the pavement for some kind of sale to open. They were getting noisy and impatient; it was after the hour when the doors should have opened; and he thought what fine game they would be for a really expert bag picker. They were pressed against each other and would never notice a little pressure on the clasp. There was nothing personal in the thought; he had never fallen quite so low, he believed, as picking women's bags. But it made him idly pay attention to them as he walked along the line. One stood out from the others. Carried by an old, rather dirty woman, the bag was new, expensive, sophisticated, of a kind he had seen before. He remembered at once the occasion: the little bathroom, the raised pistol, the compact she had taken from the bag.

The door was opened, and the women pushed in. Almost at once he was alone on the pavement beside the slot machine and the jumble-sale poster: "Entrance 6d." It couldn't be her bag, he told himself, there must be hundreds like it; but nevertheless he pursued it through the pitch-pine door. "And lead us not into temptation," the vicar was saying from a dais at one end of the hall above the old hats and the chipped vases and the stacks of women's underwear. When the prayer was finished Raven was flung by the pressure of the crowd against a stall of fancy goods: little framed amateur water colours of lakeland scenery, gaudy cigarette boxes from Italian holidays, brass ash trays, and a row of discarded novels. Then the crowd lifted him and pushed him on towards the favourite stall. There was nothing he could do about it. He couldn't seek for any individual in the crowd, but that didn't matter, for he found himself pressed against a stall on the other side of which the old woman stood. He leaned across and stared at the bag. He remembered how the girl had said, "My name's Anne," and there, impressed on the leather, was a faint initial *A*, where a chromium letter had been removed. He looked up. He didn't notice that there was another man beside the stall; his eyes were filled with the image of a dusty, wicked face.

He was shocked by it just as he had been shocked by Mr. Cholmondeley's duplicity. He felt no guilt about the old war minister. He was one of the great ones of the world, one of those who "sat." He knew all the right words, he was educated, "in the chief seats at the synagogues," and if he was sometimes a little worried by the memory of the secretary's whisper through the imperfectly shut door, he could always tell himself that he had shot her in self-defence. But this was evil, that people of the same class should prey on each other. He thrust himself along the edge of the stall until he was by her side. He bent down. He whispered, "How did you get that bag?" but an arrowhead of predatory women forced themselves between; she couldn't even have seen who had whispered to her. As far as she knew it might have been a woman mistaking it for a bargain on one of the stalls, but nevertheless the question had scared her. He saw her elbowing her way to the door, and he fought to follow her.

When he got out of the hall she was just in sight, trailing her long old-fashioned skirt round a corner. He walked fast. He didn't notice in his hurry that he in his turn was followed by a man whose clothes he would immediately have recognized, the soft hat and overcoat worn like a uniform. Very soon he began to remember the road they took; he had been this way with the girl. It was like retracing in mind an old experience. A newspaper shop would come in sight next moment. A policeman had stood just there. He had intended to kill her, to take her out somewhere beyond the houses and shoot her quite painlessly in the back. The wrinkled, deep malice in the face he had seen across the stall seemed to nod at him, "You needn't worry; we have seen to all that for you."

It was incredible how quickly the old woman scuttled.

She held the bag in one hand, lifted the absurd long skirt with the other; she was like a female Rip van Winkle who had emerged from her sleep in the clothes of fifty years ago. He thought, They've done something to her, but who are "they"? She hadn't been to the police; she'd believed his story; it was only to Cholmondeley's benefit that she should disappear. For the first time since his mother died he was afraid for someone else, because he knew only too well that Cholmondeley had no scruples.

Past the station she turned to the left up Khyber Avenue, a line of dingy apartment houses. Coarse grey lace quite hid the interior of little rooms save when a plant in a jardinière pressed glossy green palms against the glass between the lace. There were no bright geraniums lapping up the air behind closed panes; those scarlet flowers belonged to a poorer class than the occupants of Khyber Avenue—to the exploited. In Khyber Avenue they had progressed to the aspidistra of the small exploiters. They were all Cholmondeleys on a tiny scale. Outside Number 61 the old woman had to wait and fumble for her key; it gave Raven time to catch her up. He put his foot against the closing door and said, "I want to ask you some questions."

"Get out," the old woman said. "We don't 'ave anything to do with your sort."

He pressed the door steadily open. "You'd better listen," he said. "It'd be good for you." She stumbled backwards among the crowded litter of the little dark hall. He noted it all with hatred: the glass case with a stuffed pheasant, the moth-eaten head of a stag picked up at a country auction to act as a hatstand, the black metal umbrella holder painted with gold stars, the little pink glass shade over the gas jet. He said, "Where did you get that bag? Oh," he said, "it wouldn't take much to make me squeeze your old neck."

"Acky," the old woman screamed. "Acky."

"What do you do here, eh?" He opened one of the two doors at random off the hall and saw a long cheap couch with the ticking coming through the cover, a large gilt mirror, a picture of a naked girl knee-deep in the sea. The place reeked of scent and stale gas.

"Acky," the old woman screamed again. "Acky."

He said, "So that's it, eh? You old bawd," and turned back into the hall. But she was supported now. She had Acky with her; he had come through to her side from the back of the house on rubber-soled shoes, making no sound. Tall and bald, with a shifty pious look, he faced Raven.

"What d'you want, my man?" He belonged to a different class

altogether: a good school and a theological college had formed his accent; something else had broken his nose.

"What names," the old woman said, turning on Raven from under Acky's protecting arm.

Raven said, "I'm in a hurry. I don't want to break up this place. Tell me where you got that bag."

"If you refer to my wife's reticule," the bald man said, "it was given her—was it not, Tiny?—by a lodger."

"When?"

"A few nights ago."

"Where is she now?"

"She only stayed one night."

"Why did she give her bag to you?"

"We only pass this way once," Acky said, "and therefore—you know the quotation."

"Was she alone?"

"Of course she wasn't alone," the old woman said. Acky coughed, put his hand over her face, and pushed her gently behind him. "Her betrothed," he said, "was with her." He advanced towards Raven. "That face," he said, "is somehow familiar. Tiny, my dear, fetch me a copy of the *Journal.*"

"No need," Raven said. "It's me all right." He said, "You've lied about that bag. If the girl was here, it was last night. I'm going to search this bawdy house of yours."

"Tiny," her husband said, "go out at the back and call the police." Raven's hand was on his gun, but he didn't move, he didn't draw it. His eyes were on the old woman as she trailed indeterminately through the kitchen door. "Hurry, Tiny, my dear."

Raven said, "If I thought she was going, I'd shoot you straight, but she's not going to any police. You're more afraid of them than I am. She's in the kitchen now, hiding in a corner."

Acky said, "Oh no, I assure you she's gone; I heard the door. You can see for yourself," and as Raven passed him he raised his hand and struck with a knuckle-duster at a spot behind Raven's ear.

But Raven had expected that. He ducked his head and was safely through in the kitchen doorway with his gun out. "Stay put," he said. "This gun doesn't make any noise. I'll plug you where you'll feel it if you move." The old woman was where he had expected her to be, between the dresser and the door, squeezed in a corner. She moaned, "Oh, Acky, you ought to 'ave 'it 'im."

Acky began to swear. The obscenity trickled out of his mouth effortlessly like dribble, but the tone, the accent never changed; it was still the good school, the theological college. There were a lot of Latin words Raven didn't understand. He said impatiently, "Now where's the girl?" But Acky simply didn't hear. He stood there in a kind of nervous seizure with his pupils rolled up almost under the lids. He might have been praying; for all Raven knew some of the Latin words might be prayers: "saccus stercoris," "fauces." He said again, "Where's the girl?"

"Leave 'im alone," the old woman said. " 'E can't 'ear you. Acky," she moaned from her corner by the dresser, "it's all right, love, you're at 'ome." She said fiercely to Raven, "The things they did to 'im."

Suddenly the obscenity stopped. He moved and blocked the kitchen door. The hand with the knuckle-duster grasped the lapel of Raven's coat. Acky said softly, "After all, my lord Bishop, you too, I am sure—in your day—among the haycocks . . ." and tittered.

Raven said, "Tell him to move. I'm going to search this house." He kept his eye on both of them. The little stuffy house wore on his nerves; madness and wickedness moved in the kitchen. The old woman watched him with hatred from her corner. Raven said, "My God, if you've killed her . . ." He said, "Do you know what it feels like to have a bullet in your belly? You'll just lie there and bleed." It seemed to him that it would be like shooting a spider. He suddenly shouted at her husband, "Get out of my way."

Acky said, "Even St. Paul . . ." watching him with glazed eyes, barring the door. Raven struck him in the face, then backed out of reach of the flailing arm. He raised the pistol, and the woman screamed at him.

"Stop. I'll get 'im out." She said, "Don't you dare to touch Acky. They've treated 'im bad enough in 'is day." She took her husband's arm; she only came halfway to his shoulder, grey and soiled and miserably tender. "Acky dear," she said, "come into the parlour." She rubbed her old wicked wrinkled face against his sleeve. "Acky, there's a letter from the bishop."

His pupils moved down again like those of a doll. He was almost himself again. He said, "Tut tut, I gave way, I think, to a little temper." He looked at Raven with half-recognition. "That fellow's still here, Tiny."

"Come into the parlour, Acky dear. I've got to talk to you." He

let her pull him away into the hall, and Raven followed them and
mounted the stairs. All the way up he heard them talking: they
were planning something between them. As like as not, when he
was out of sight and round the corner, they'd slip out and call the
police. If the girl was really not here or if they had disposed of her,
they had nothing to fear from the police. On the first-floor landing
there was a tall cracked mirror; he came up the stairs into its reflection—unshaven chin, harelip, and ugliness. His heart beat against
his ribs; if he had been called on to fire now, quickly, in self-
defence, his hand and eye would have failed him. He thought hopelessly, This is ruin . . . I'm losing grip . . . a skirt's got me
down. He opened the first door to hand and came into what was
obviously the best bedroom: a wide double bed with a flowery
eiderdown, veneered walnut furniture, a little embroidered bag for
hair combings, a tumbler of Lysol on the washstand for someone's
false teeth. He opened the big wardrobe door, and a musty smell
of old clothes and camphor balls came out at him. He went to the
closed window and looked out at Khyber Avenue, and all the while
he looked he could hear the whispers from the parlour: Acky and
Tiny plotting together. His eye for a moment noted a large, rather
clumsy-looking man in a soft hat chatting to a woman at the house
opposite; another man came up the road and joined him, and they
strolled together out of sight. He recognized at once: the police.
They mightn't, of course, have seen him there; they might be engaged on a purely routine inquiry. He went quickly out onto the
landing and listened; Acky and Tiny were quite silent now. He
thought at first they might have left the house, but when he listened
carefully he could hear the faint whistling of the old woman's breath
somewhere near the foot of the stairs.

There was another door on the landing. He tried the handle. It
was locked. He wasn't going to waste any more time with the old
people downstairs. He shot through the lock and crashed the door
open. But there was no one there. The room was empty. It was a
tiny room almost filled by its double bed, its dead fireplace hidden
by a smoked brass trap. He looked out of the window and saw
nothing but a small stone yard, a dustbin, a high sooty wall keeping
out neighbours, the grey, waning afternoon light. On the washstand
was a wireless set, and the wardrobe was empty. He had no doubt
what this room was used for.

But something made him stay—some sense uneasily remaining
in the room, of someone's terror. He couldn't leave it, and there

was the locked door to be accounted for. Why should they have locked up an empty room unless it held some clue, some danger to themselves? He turned over the pillows of the bed and wondered, his hand loose on the pistol, his brain stirring with another's agony. Oh, to know, to know. He felt the painful weakness of a man who had depended always on his gun. I'm educated, aren't I?—the phrase came mockingly into his mind, but he knew that one of the police out there could discover in this room more than he. He knelt down and looked under the bed. Nothing there. The very tidiness of the room seemed unnatural, as if it had been tidied after a crime. Even the mats looked as if they had been shaken.

He asked himself whether he had been imagining things. Perhaps the girl had really given the old woman her bag. But he couldn't forget that they had lied about the night she'd stayed with them, had picked the initial off the bag. And they had locked this door. But people did lock doors—against burglars, against sneak thieves. Oh, there was an explanation, he was only too aware of that, for everything; why should you leave another person's initials on a bag? When you had many lodgers, naturally you forgot which night . . . There were explanations, but he couldn't get over the impression that something had happened here, that something had been tidied away; and it came over him with a sense of great desolation that only he could not call in the police to find his girl. Because he was an outlaw she had to be an outlaw too. "Ah, Christ, if it were possible . . ." The rain beating on the Weevil, the plaster child, the afternoon light draining from the little stone yard, the image of his own ugliness fading in the mirror, and from belowstairs Tiny's whistling breath. "For one short hour to see . . ."

He went back onto the landing, but something all the time pulled him back, as if he were leaving a place which had been dear to him. It dragged on him as he went upstairs to the second floor and into every room in turn. There was nothing in any of them but beds and wardrobes and the stale smell of scent and toilet things, and in one cupboard a broken cane. They were all of them more dusty, less tidy, more used than the room he'd left. He stood up there among the empty rooms, listening. There wasn't a sound to be heard now: Tiny and her Acky were quite silent below him, waiting for him to come down. He wondered again if he had made a fool of himself and risked everything. But if they had nothing to hide, why hadn't they tried to call the police? He had left them alone, they had nothing to fear while he was upstairs, but something kept them to the house just as something kept him tied to the room on the first floor.

It took him back to it. He was happier when he had closed the door behind him and stood again in the small cramped space between the big bed and the wall. The drag at his heart ceased. He was able to think again. He began to examine the room thoroughly, inch by inch. He even moved the radio on the washstand. Then he heard the stairs creak and, leaning his head against the door, he listened to someone he supposed was Acky mounting the stairs step by step with clumsy caution. Then he was crossing the landing, and there he must be, just outside the door, waiting and listening. It was impossible to believe that those old people had nothing to fear. Raven went along the walls, squeezing by the bed, touching the glossy, flowery paper with his fingers; he had heard of people before now papering over a cavity. He reached the fireplace and unhooked the brass trap.

Propped up inside the fireplace was a woman's body, the feet in the grate, the head out of sight in the chimney. The first thought he had was of revenge: if it's the girl, if she's dead, I'll shoot them both. I'll shoot them where it hurts most so that they die slow. Then he went down on his knees to ease the body out.

The hands and feet were roped; an old cotton vest had been tied between the teeth as a gag; the eyes were closed. He cut the gag away first. He couldn't tell whether she was alive or dead. He cursed her. "Wake up, you bitch, wake up." He leaned over her, imploring her. "Wake up." He was afraid to leave her; there was no water in the ewer; he couldn't do a thing. When he had cut away the ropes he just sat on the floor beside her with his eyes on the door and one hand on his pistol and the other on her breast. When he could feel her breathing under his hand it was like beginning life over again.

She didn't know where she was. She said, "Please. The sun. It's too strong." There was no sun in the room—it would soon be too dark to read. He thought, What ages have they had her buried there? and held his hand over her eyes to shield them from the dim winter light of early evening. She said in a tired voice, "I could go to sleep now. There's air."

"No, no," Raven said, "we've got to get out of here," but he wasn't prepared for her simple acquiescence. "Yes, where to?"

He said, "You don't remember who I am. I haven't anywhere. But I'll leave you some place where it's safe."

She said, "I've been finding out things." He thought she meant things like fear and death, but as her voice strengthened she explained quite clearly. "It was the man you said. Cholmondeley."

"So you know me," Raven said. But she took no notice. It was as if all the time in the dark she had been rehearsing what she had to say when she was discovered, at once, because there was no time to waste.

"I made a guess at somewhere where he worked. Some company. It scared him. He must work there. I don't remember the name. I've got to remember."

"Don't worry," Raven said. "You're fine. It'll come back. But how it is you aren't crazy—Christ, you've got nerve."

She said, "I remembered till just now. I heard you looking for me in the room, and then you went away and I forgot everything."

"Do you think you could walk now?"

"Of course I could walk. We've got to hurry."

"Where to?"

"I had it all planned. It'll come back. I had plenty of time to think things out."

"You sound as if you weren't scared at all."

"I knew I'd be found all right. I was in a hurry. We haven't got much time. I thought about the war all the time."

He said again admiringly, "You've got nerve."

She began to move her hands and feet up and down quite methodically as if she was following a programme she had drawn up for herself. "I thought a lot about that war. I read somewhere, but I'd forgotten, about how babies can't wear gas masks because there's not enough air for them." She knelt up with her hand on his shoulder. "There wasn't much air there. It made things sort of vivid. I thought, We've got to stop it. It seems silly, doesn't it?—us two, but there's nobody else." She said, "My feet have got pins and needles bad. That means they are coming alive again." She tried to stand up, but it wasn't any good.

Raven watched her. He said, "What else did you think?"

She said, "I thought about you. I wished I hadn't had to go away like that and leave you."

"I thought you'd gone to the police."

"I wouldn't do that." She managed to stand up this time with her hands on his shoulders. "I'm on your side."

Raven said, "We've got to get out of here. Can you walk?"

"Yes."

"Then leave go of me. There's someone outside." He stood by the door with his gun in his hand, listening. They'd had plenty of time, those two, to think up a plan, longer than he. He pulled the door open. It was very nearly dark. He could see no one on the landing. He thought, The old devil's at the side, waiting to get a hit at me with the poker. I'll take a run for it. And immediately he tripped across the string they had tied across the doorway. He was on his knees with the gun on the floor. He couldn't get up in time, and Acky's blow got him on the left shoulder. It staggered him; he couldn't move; he had just time to think, It'll be the head next time; I've gone soft; I ought to have thought of a string—when he heard Anne speak. "Drop the poker."

He got painfully to his feet. The girl had snatched the gun as it fell and had Acky covered.

He said with astonishment, "You're fine."

At the bottom of the stairs the old woman cried out, "Acky, where are you?"

"Give me the gun," Raven said. "Get down the stairs; you needn't be afraid of the old bitch." He backed after her, keeping Acky covered, but the old couple had shot their bolt. He said regretfully, "If he'd only rush I'd put a bullet in him."

"It wouldn't upset *me*," Anne said. "I'd have done it myself."

He said again, "You're fine." He nearly forgot the detectives he had seen in the street, but with his hand on the door he remembered. He said, "I may have to make a bolt for it if the police are outside." He hardly hesitated before he trusted her. "I've found a hideout for the night. In the goods yard. A shed they don't use any longer. I'll be waiting by the wall tonight fifty yards down from the station." He opened the door. Nobody moved in the street. They walked out together and down the middle of the road into a vacant dusk.

Anne said, "Did you see a man in the doorway opposite?"

"Yes," Raven said. "I saw him."

"I thought it was like—but how could it—?"

"There was another at the end of the street. They were police all right, but they didn't know who I was. They'd have tried to get me if they'd known."

"And you'd have shot?"

"I'd have shot all right. But they didn't know it was me." He laughed with the night damp in his throat. "I've fooled them properly." The lights went on in the city beyond the railway bridge, but where they were it was just a grey dusk with the sound of an engine shunting in the yard.

"I can't walk far," Anne said. "I'm sorry. I suppose I'm a bit sick after all."

"It's not far now," Raven said. "There's a loose plank. I got it all fixed up for myself early this morning. Why, there's even sacks —lots of sacks. It's going to be like home," he said.

"Like home?"

He didn't answer, feeling along the tarred wall of the goods yard, remembering the kitchen in the basement and the first thing very nearly he could remember, his mother bleeding across the table. She hadn't even troubled to lock the door—that was all she had cared about him. He'd done some ugly things in his time, he told himself, but he'd never been able to equal that ugliness. Someday he would. It would be like beginning life over again, to have something else to look back to when somebody spoke of death or blood or wounds or home.

"A bit bare for a home," Anne said.

"You needn't be scared of me," Raven said. "I won't keep you. You can sit down a bit and tell me what he did to you, what Chol-mon-deley did, and then you can be getting along anywhere you want."

"I couldn't go any farther if you paid me." He had to put his hands under her shoulders and hold her up against the tarred wood, while he put more will into her from his own inexhaustible reserve. He said, "Hold on. We're nearly there." He shivered in the cold, holding her with all his strength, trying in the dusk to see her face. He said, "You can rest in the shed. There are plenty of sacks there." He was like somebody describing with pride some place he lived in, that he'd bought with his own money or built with his own labour, stone by stone.

2

Mather stood back in the shadow of the doorway. It was worse in a way than anything he'd feared. He put his hand on his revolver. He had only to go forward and arrest Raven—or stop a bullet in the attempt. He was a policeman; he couldn't shoot first. At the end of the street Saunders was waiting for him to move. Behind, a uniformed constable waited on them both. But he made no move.

He let them go off down the road in the belief that they were alone. Then he followed as far as the corner and picked up Saunders. Saunders said, "The d-d-devil."

"Oh no," Mather said, "it's only Raven—and Anne." He struck a match and held it to the cigarette which he had been holding between his lips for the last twenty minutes. They could hardly see the man and woman going off down the dark road by the goods yard, but beyond them another match was struck. "We've got them covered," Mather said. "They won't be able to get out of our sight now."

"W-will you take them b-b-both?"

"We can't have shooting with a woman there," Mather said. "Can't you see what they'd make of it in the papers if a woman got hurt? It's not as if he was wanted for murder."

"We've got to be careful of your girl," Saunders brought out in a breath.

"Get moving again," Mather said. "We don't want to lose touch. I'm not thinking about *her* any more. I promise you that's over. She's led me up the garden properly. I'm just thinking of what's best with Raven—and any accomplice he's got in Nottwich. If we've got to shoot, we'll shoot."

Saunders said, "They've stopped." He had sharper eyes than Mather. Mather said, "Could you pick him off from here if I rushed him?"

"No," Saunders said. He began to move forward quickly. "He's loosened a plank. They are getting through."

"Don't worry," Mather said. "I'll follow. Bring up three more men and post one of them at the gap where I can find him. We've got all the gates into the yard picketed already. Bring the rest inside. But keep it quiet." He could hear the slight shuffle of cinders where the two were walking. It wasn't so easy to follow them because of the sound his own feet made. They disappeared round a stationary truck, and the light failed more and more. He caught a glimpse of their moving shadows, and then an engine hooted and belched a grey plume of steam round him; for a moment it was like walking in a mountain fog. A warm, dirty spray settled on his face. When he was clear he had lost them. He began to realize the difficulty of finding anyone in the yard at night. There were trucks everywhere; they could slip into one and lie down. He barked his shin and swore softly. Then quite distinctly he heard Anne whisper, "I can't make it."

There were only a few trucks between them. Then the movements began again, heavier movements, as if someone was carrying a weight. Mather climbed onto the truck and stared across a dark, desolate waste of cinders and points, a tangle of lines and sheds and piles of coal and coke. It was like a no man's land full of torn iron across which one soldier picked his way with a wounded companion in his arms. Mather watched them with an odd sense of shame, as if he were a spy. The thin limping shadow became a human being who knew the girl he loved. There was a kind of relationship between them. He thought, How many years will he get for that robbery? He no longer wanted to shoot. He thought, Poor devil, he must be pretty driven by now. He's probably looking for a place to sit down in, and there the place was—a small wooden workman's shed between the lines.

Mather struck a match again, and presently Saunders was below him, waiting for orders. "They are in that shed," Mather said. "Get the men posted. If they try to get out, nab them quick. Otherwise wait for daylight. We don't want any accidents."

"You aren't s-staying?"

"You'll be easier without me," Mather said. "I'll be at the station tonight." He said gently, "Don't think about me. Just go ahead. And look after yourself. Got your gun?"

"Of course."

"I'll send the men along to you. It's going to be a cold watch, I'm afraid, but it's no good trying to rush that shed. He might shoot his way clear out."

"It's t-t-t-tough on you," Saunders said. The dark had quite come, healing the desolation of the yard. Inside the shed there was no sign of life, no glimmer of light. Soon Saunders couldn't have told that it existed, sitting there with his back to a truck, out of the wind's way, hearing the breathing of the policeman nearest him, and saying over to himself to pass the time (his mind's words free from any impediment) the line of a poem he had learned at school about a dark tower: "He must be wicked to deserve such pain." It was a comforting line, he thought. Those who followed his profession couldn't be taught a better; that's why he had remembered it.

3

"Who's coming to dinner, dear?" the chief constable asked, putting his head in at the bedroom door.

"Never you mind," Mrs. Calkin said, "you'll change."

The chief constable said, "I was thinking, dear, as·'ow—"

"As how," Mrs. Calkin said firmly.

"The new maid. You might teach her that I'm *Major* Calkin."

Mrs. Calkin said, "You'd better hurry."

"It's not the mayoress again, is it?" He trailed drearily out towards the bathroom, but on second thought nipped quietly downstairs to the dining room. Must see about the drinks. But if it was the mayoress there wouldn't be any. Piker never turned up; he didn't blame him. While there he might just as well take a nip. He took it neat for speed and cleaned the glass afterwards with a splash of soda and his handkerchief. He put the glass, as an afterthought, where the mayoress would sit. Then he rang up the police station.

"Any news?" he asked hopelessly. He knew there was no real hope that they'd ask him down for a consultation.

The inspector's voice said, "We know where he is. We've got him surrounded. We are just waiting till daylight."

"Can I be of any use? Like me to come down, eh, and talk things over?"

"It's quite unnecessary, sir."

He put the receiver down miserably, sniffed the mayoress's glass (she'd never notice that), and went upstairs. Major Calkin, he thought wistfully, Major Calkin. The trouble is, I'm a man's man. Looking out of the window of his dressing room at the spread gleam of Nottwich, he remembered for some reason the war, the tribunal, the fun it had all been giving hell to the conchies. His uniform still hung there, next the tails he wore once a year at the Rotarian dinner, when he was able to get among the boys. A faint smell of mothballs came out at him. His spirits suddenly lifted. He thought, My God, in a week's time we may be at it again. Show the devils what we are made of. I wonder if the uniform will fit? He couldn't resist trying on the jacket over his evening trousers. It was a bit tight, he couldn't deny that, but the general effect in the glass was not too bad—a bit pinched; it would have to be let out. With his influence in the county he'd be back in uniform in a fortnight. With any luck he'd be busier than ever in this war.

"Joseph," his wife said, "whatever are you doing?" He saw her in the mirror, posed statuesquely in the doorway in her new black-and-sequined evening dress like a shop-window model of an outsize matron. She said, "Take it off at once. You'll smell of mothballs now all dinnertime. The mayoress is taking off her things, and any moment Sir Marcus—"

"You might have told me," the chief constable said. "If I'd known Sir Marcus was coming— How did you snare the old boy?"

"He invited himself," Mrs. Calkin said proudly. "So I rang up the mayoress."

"Isn't old Piker coming?"

"He hasn't been home all day."

The chief constable slipped off his uniform jacket and put it away carefully. If the war had gone on another year they'd have made him a colonel; he had been getting on the very best terms with the regimental headquarters, supplying the mess with groceries at very little more than the cost price. In the next war he'd make the grade. The sound of Sir Marcus's car on the gravel brought him downstairs. The mayoress was looking under the sofa for her Pekingese, which had gone to ground defensively to escape strangers; she was on her knees with her head under the fringe, saying, "Chinky, Chinky," ingratiatingly. Chinky growled invisibly.

"Well, well," the chief constable said, trying to put a little warmth into his tones, "and how's Alfred?"

"Alfred," the mayoress said, coming out from under the sofa. "It's not Alfred, it's Chinky. Oh," she said, talking very fast, for it was her habit to work towards another person's meaning while she talked, "you mean how is he? Alfred? He's gone again."

"Chinky?"

"No, Alfred." One never got much further with the mayoress.

Mrs. Calkin came in. She said, "Have you got him, dear?"

"No, he's gone again," the chief constable said, "if you mean Alfred."

"He's under the sofa," the mayoress said. "He won't come out."

Mrs. Calkin said, "I ought to have warned you, dear. I thought of course you knew the story of how Sir Marcus hates the very sight of dogs. Of course, if he stays there quietly—"

"The poor dear," Mrs. Piker said; "so sensitive, he could tell at once he wasn't wanted."

The chief constable suddenly could bear it no longer. He said, "Alfred Piker's my best friend. I won't have you say he wasn't wanted," but no one took any notice of him. The maid had announced Sir Marcus.

Sir Marcus entered on the tips of his toes. He was a very old and very sick man with a little wisp of white beard on his chin like chicken fluff. He gave the effect of having withered inside his clothes like a kernel in a nut. He spoke with the faintest foreign accent, and it was difficult to determine whether he was Levantine or of an old English family. He gave the impression that very many cities had rubbed him smooth. If there was a touch of Alexandria, there was also a touch of St. James's; if of Vienna or some Central European slum, there were also marks of the most exclusive clubs in Cannes.

"So good of you, Mrs. Calkin," he said, "to give me this opportunity." It was difficult to hear what he said; he spoke in a whisper. His old scaly eyes took them all in. "I have always been hoping to make the acquaintance—"

"May I introduce the Lady Mayoress, Sir Marcus?"

He bowed with the very slightly servile grace of a man who might have been pawnbroker to the Pompadour. "So famous a figure in the city of Nottwich." There was no sarcasm or patronage in his manner. He was just old. Everyone was alike to him. He didn't trouble to differentiate.

"I thought you were on the Riviera, Sir Marcus," the chief constable said breezily. "Have a sherry. It's no good asking the ladies."

"I don't drink, I'm afraid," Sir Marcus whispered. The chief constable's face fell. "I came back two days ago."

"Rumours of war, eh? Dogs delight to bark—"

"Joseph," Mrs. Calkin said sharply, and glanced with meaning at the sofa.

The old scaly eyes cleared a little. "Yes. Yes," Sir Marcus repeated. "Rumours."

"I see you've been taking on more men at Midland Steel, Sir Marcus."

"So they tell me," Sir Marcus whispered.

The maid announced dinner. The sound startled Chinky, who growled under the sofa, and there was an agonizing moment while they all watched Sir Marcus. But he had heard nothing, or else the noise had just faintly stirred his subconscious mind, for as he took Mrs. Calkin into the dining room he whispered venomously, "The dogs drove me away."

"Some lemonade for Mrs. Piker, Joseph," Mrs. Calkin said. The chief constable watched her drink with some nervousness. She seemed a little puzzled by the taste. She sipped and tried again.

"Really," she said, "what delicious lemonade. It has quite an aroma."

Sir Marcus passed the soup. He passed the fish. When the entree was served he leaned across the large silver-plated flower bowl inscribed "To Joseph Calkin from the assistants in Calkin and Calkin's on the occasion . . ." (the inscription ran round the corner out of sight) and whispered, "Might I have a dry biscuit and a little hot water?" He explained, "My doctor won't allow me anything else at night,"

"Well, that's hard luck," the chief constable said. "Food and drink as a man gets older . . ." He glared at his empty glass. What a life! Oh, for a chance to get away for a bit among the boys, throw his weight about and know that he was a man.

The Lady Mayoress said suddenly, "How Chinky would love those bones," and choked.

"Who is Chinky?" Sir Marcus whispered.

Mrs. Calkin said quickly, "Mrs. Piker has the most lovely cat."

"I'm glad it isn't a dog," Sir Marcus whispered. "There is something about a dog—" the old hand gestured hopelessly with a piece of cheese biscuit—"and of all dogs the Pekingese." He said with extraordinary venom, "Yap, yap, yap," and sucked up some hot water. He was a man almost without pleasures. His most vivid emotion was venom, his main object defence—defence of his fortune, of the pale flicker of vitality he gained each year in the Cannes sun, of his life. He was quite content to eat cheese biscuits to the end of them if eating biscuits would extend his days.

The old boy couldn't have many left, the chief constable thought, watching Sir Marcus wash down the last dry crumb and then take a white tablet out of a little flat gold box in his waistcoat pocket. He had a heart; you could tell it in the way he spoke, from the special coaches he travelled in when he went by rail, the bath chairs which propelled him softly down the long passages in Midland Steel. The chief constable had met him several times at civic receptions; after the general strike Sir Marcus had given a fully equipped gymnasium to the police force in recognition of their services; but never before had Sir Marcus visited him at home.

Everyone knew a lot about Sir Marcus. The trouble was, what they knew was contradictory. There were people who, because of his Christian name, believed that he was a Greek; others were quite as certain that he had been born in a ghetto. His business associates said that he was of an old English family. His face was no evidence either way—you found plenty of faces like that in Cornwall and the west country. His name did not appear at all in Who's Who, and an enterprising journalist who had once tried to write his life found extraordinary gaps in registers; it wasn't possible to follow any rumour to its source. There was even a gap in the legal records of Marseilles, where one rumour said that Sir Marcus as a youth had been charged with theft from a visitor to a bawdy house. Now he sat there in the heavy Edwardian dining room, brushing biscuit crumbs from his waistcoat, one of the richest men in Europe.

No one even knew his age, unless perhaps his dentist; the chief constable had an idea that you could tell the age of a man by his teeth. But then they probably were *not* his teeth at his age—another gap in the records.

"Well, we shan't be leaving them to their drinks, shall we?" Mrs. Calkin said in a sprightly way, rising from the table and fixing her husband with a warning glare. "But I expect they have a lot to talk about together."

When the door closed Sir Marcus said, "I've seen that woman somewhere with a dog. I'm sure of it."

"Would you mind if I gave myself a spot of port?" the chief constable said. "I don't believe in lonely drinking, but if you really won't— Have a cigar?"

"No," Sir Marcus whispered, "I don't smoke." He said, "I wanted to see you—in confidence—about this fellow Raven. Davis is worried. The trouble is he caught a glimpse of the man. Quite by chance. At the time of the robbery at a friend's office in Victoria Street. This man called on some pretext. He has an idea that the wild fellow wants to put him out of the way. As a witness."

"Tell him," the chief constable said proudly, pouring himself out another glass of port, "that he needn't worry. The man's as good as caught. We know where he is at this very moment. He's surrounded. We are only waiting till daylight, till he shows himself."

"Why wait at all? Wouldn't it be better," Sir Marcus whispered, "if the silly, desperate fellow were taken at once?"

"He's armed, you see. In the dark anything might happen. He might shoot his way clear. And there's another thing. He has a girl friend with him. It wouldn't do if he escaped and the girl got shot."

Sir Marcus bowed his old head above the two hands that lay idly, with no dry biscuit or glass of warm water or white tablet to occupy them, on the table. He said gently, "I want you to understand. In a way it is our responsibility. Because of Davis. If there were any trouble, if the girl were killed, all our money would be behind the police force. If there had to be an inquiry the best counsel—I have friends too, as you may suppose."

"It would be better to wait till daylight, Sir Marcus. Trust me. I know how things stand. I've been a soldier, you know."

"Yes, I understood that," Sir Marcus said.

"Looks as if the old bulldog will have to bite again, eh? Thank God for a government with guts."

"Yes, yes," Sir Marcus said. "I should say it was almost certain now." The old scaly eyes shifted to the decanter. "Don't let me stop you having your glass of port, Major."

"Well, if you say so, Sir Marcus, I'll just have one more glass for a nightcap."

Sir Marcus said, "I'm very glad that you have such good news for me. It doesn't look well to have an armed ruffian loose in Nottwich. You mustn't risk any of your men's lives, Major. Better that this—waste product should be dead than one of your fine fellows." He suddenly leaned back in his chair and gasped like a landed fish. He said, "A tablet. Please. Quick."

The chief constable picked the gold box from his pocket, but Sir Marcus had already recovered. He took the tablet himself. The chief constable said, "Shall I order your car, Sir Marcus?"

"No, no," Sir Marcus whispered, "there's no danger. It's simply pain." He stared with dazed old eyes down at the crumbs on his trousers. "What were we saying? Fine fellows, yes; you mustn't risk *their* lives. The country will need them."

"That's very true."

Sir Marcus whispered with venom, "To me this—ruffian is a traitor. This is a time when every man is needed. I'd treat him like a traitor."

"It's one way of looking at it."

"Another glass of port, Major."

"Yes, I think I will."

"To think of the number of able-bodied men this fellow will take from their country's service even if he shoots no one. Warders. Police guards. Fed and lodged at his country's expense when other men—"

"Are dying. You're right, Sir Marcus." The pathos of it all went deeply home. He remembered his uniform jacket in the cupboard; the buttons needed shining, the king's buttons. The smell of mothballs lingered round him still. He said, "Somewhere there's a corner of a foreign field that is forever—Shakespeare knew. Old timehonoured Gaunt when he said that—"

"It would be so much better, Major Calkin, if your men take no risks. If they shoot on sight. One must take up weeds—by the roots."

"It would be better."

"You're the father of your men."

"That's what old Piker said to me once. God forgive him, he meant it differently. I wish you'd drink with me, Sir Marcus. You're an understanding man. You know how an officer feels. I was in the Army once."

"Perhaps in a week you will be in it again."

"You know how a man feels. I don't want anything to come between us, Sir Marcus. There's one thing I'd like to tell you. It's on my conscience. There *was* a dog under the sofa."

"A dog?"

"A Pekingese called Chinky. I didn't know as 'ow—"

"She said it was a cat."

"She didn't want you to know."

Sir Marcus said, "I don't like being deceived. I'll see to Piker at the elections." He gave a small tired sigh as if there were too many things to be seen to, to be arranged, revenges to be taken, stretching into an endless vista of time, and so much time already covered— since the ghetto, the Marseilles brothel, if there had ever been a ghetto or a brothel. He whispered abruptly, "So you'll telephone now to the station and tell them to shoot at sight? Say you'll take the responsibility. I'll look after you."

"I don't see as 'ow, as how—"

The old hands moved impatiently; so much to be arranged. "Listen to me. I never promise anything I can't answer for. There's a training depot ten miles from here. I can arrange for you to have nominal charge of it, with the rank of colonel, directly war's declared."

"Colonel Banks?"

"He'll be shifted."

"You mean if I telephone?"

"No. I mean if you are successful."

"And the man's dead?"

"He's not important. A young scoundrel. There's no reason to hesitate. Take another glass of port."

The chief constable stretched out his hand for the decanter. He thought with less relish than he would have expected, "Colonel Calkin," but he couldn't help remembering other things. He was a sentimental middle-aged man. He remembered his appointment; it had been "worked," of course, no less than his appointment to the training depot would be worked, but there came vividly back to him his sense of pride at being head of one of the best police forces in the country. "I'd better not have any more port," he said lamely. "It's bad for my sleep, and the wife—"

Sir Marcus said, "Well, Colonel," blinking his old eyes, "you'll be able to count on me for anything."

"I'd like to do it," the chief constable said imploringly. "I'd like to please you, Sir Marcus. But I don't see as how— The police couldn't do that."

"It would never be known."

"I don't suppose they'd take my orders. Not on a thing like that."

Sir Marcus whispered, "Do you mean in your position you haven't any *hold?*" He spoke with the astonishment of a man who had always been careful to secure his hold on the most junior of his subordinates.

"I'd like to please you."

"There's the telephone," Sir Marcus said. "At any rate, you can use your influence. I never ask a man for more than he can do."

The chief constable said, "They are a good lot of boys. I've been down often to the station of an evening and had a drink or two. They're keen. You couldn't have keener men. They'll get him. You needn't be afraid, Sir Marcus."

"You mean dead?"

"Alive or dead. They won't let him escape. They are good boys."

"But he has got to be dead," Sir Marcus said. He sneezed. The intake of breath seemed to have exhausted him. He lay back again, panting gently.

"I couldn't ask them, Sir Marcus, not like that. Why, it's like murder."

"Nonsense."

"Those evenings with the boys mean a lot to me. I wouldn't even be able to go down there again after doing that. I'd rather stay what I am. They'll give me a tribunal. As long as there's wars there'll be conchies."

"There'd be no commission of any kind for you," Sir Marcus said. "I could see to that." The smell of mothballs came up from Calkin's evening shirt to mock him. "I can arrange, too, that you shan't be chief constable much longer. You and Piker." He gave a queer little whistle through the nose. He was too old to laugh, to use his lungs wastefully. "Come. Have another glass."

"No. I don't think I'd better. Listen, Sir Marcus, I'll put detectives at your office. I'll have Davis guarded."

"I don't much mind about Davis," Sir Marcus said. "Will you get my chauffeur?"

"I'd like to do what you want, Sir Marcus. Won't you come back and see the ladies?"

"No, no," Sir Marcus whispered, "not with that dog there." He had to be helped to his feet, and his stick brought him. A few dry crumbs lay in his beard. He said, "If you change your mind tonight you can ring me up. I shall be awake." A man at his age, the chief constable thought charitably, would obviously think differently of death; it threatened him every moment on the slippery pavement, in a piece of soap at the bottom of a bath. It must seem quite a natural thing he was asking. Great age was an abnormal condition; you had to make allowances. But watching Sir Marcus helped down the drive and into his deep, wide car, he couldn't help saying over to himself, "Colonel Calkin. Colonel Calkin." After a moment he added, "C.B."

The dog was yapping in the drawing room. They must have lured it out. It was very highly bred and nervous, and if a stranger spoke to it too suddenly or sharply it would rush round in circles, foaming at the mouth and crying out in a horribly human way, its low fur sweeping the carpet like a vacuum cleaner. I might slip down, the chief constable thought, and have a drink with the boys. But the idea brought no lightening of his gloom and indecision. Was it possible that Sir Marcus could rob him of even that? But he had robbed him of it already. He couldn't face the superintendent or the inspector with this on his mind. He went into his study and sat down by the telephone. In five minutes Sir Marcus would be home. So much stolen from him already, surely there was little more he could lose by acquiescence. But he sat there doing nothing, a small, plump, bullying, henpecked profiteer.

His wife put her head in at the door. "Whatever are you doing, Joseph?" she said. "Come at once and talk to Mrs. Piker."

4

Sir Marcus lived with his valet, who was also a trained nurse, at the top of the big building in the Tanneries. It was his only home. In London he stayed at Claridge's, in Cannes at the Ritz. His valet met him at the door of the building with his bath chair and pushed him into the lift, then out along the passage to his study. The heat of the room had been turned up to the right degree, the tape machine was gently ticking beside his desk. The curtains were not drawn, and through the wide double panes the night sky spread out over Nottwich, striped by the searchlights from Hanlow aerodrome.

"You can go to bed, Mollison. I shan't be sleeping."

Sir Marcus slept very little these days. In the little time left him to live a few hours of sleep made a distinct impression. And he didn't really need the sleep. No physical exertion demanded it. Now, with the telephone within reach, he began to read first the memorandum on his desk, then the strips of tape. He read the arrangements for the gas drill in the morning. All the clerks on the ground floor who might happen to be needed for outside work were already supplied with gas masks. The sirens were expected to go almost immediately the rush hour was over and work in the offices had begun. Members of the transport staff, lorry drivers, and special messengers would wear their masks immediately they started work. It was the only way to ensure that they wouldn't leave them behind somewhere and be caught unprotected during the hours of the practice and so waste in hospital the valuable hours of Midland Steel.

More valuable than they had ever been since November 1918. Sir Marcus read the tape prices. Armament shares continued to rise, and with them steel. It made no difference at all that the British government had stopped all export licenses; the country itself was now absorbing more armaments than it had ever done since the peak year of Haig's assaults on the Hindenburg Line. Sir Marcus had many friends, in many countries; he wintered with them regularly at Cannes or in Soppelsa's yacht off Rhodes; he was the intimate friend of Mrs. Cranbeim. It was impossible now to export arms, but it was still possible to export nickel and most of the other metals which were necessary to the arming of nations. Even when war was declared, Mrs. Cranbeim was able to say quite definitely that evening, when the yacht pitched a little and Rosen was so distressingly sick over Mrs. Ziffo's black satin, that the British government would not forbid the export of nickel to Switzerland or other neutral countries so long as the British requirements were first met. So the future really was very rosy indeed, for you could trust Mrs. Cranbeim's word. She spoke directly from the horse's mouth, if you could so describe the elder statesman whose confidence she shared.

It seemed quite certain now; Sir Marcus read in the tape messages that the two governments chiefly concerned would not either amend or accept the terms of the ultimatum. Probably within five days at least four countries would be already at war and the consumption of munitions have risen to a million pounds a day.

And yet Sir Marcus was not quite happy. Davis had bungled things. When he had told Davis that a murderer ought not to be allowed to benefit from his crime, he had never expected all this silly business of the stolen notes. Now he must wait up all night for the telephone to ring. The old thin body made itself as comfortable as it could on the air-blown cushion—Sir Marcus was as painfully aware of his bones as a skeleton must be, wearing itself away against the leaden lining of its last suit. A clock struck midnight; he had lived one more whole day.

Five

1

Raven groped through the dark of the small shed till he had found the sacks. He piled them up, shaking them as one shakes a pillow. He whispered anxiously, "You'll be able to rest there a bit?" Anne let his hand guide her to the corner. She said, "It's freezing."

"Lie down, and I'll find more sacks." He struck a match, and the tiny flame went wandering through the close, cold darkness. He brought the sacks and spread them over her, dropping the match.

"Can't we have a little light?" Anne said.

"It's not safe. Anyway," he said, "it's a break for me. You can't see me in the dark. You can't see *this*." He touched his lip secretly. He was listening at the door; he heard feet stumble on the tangle of metal and cinders, and after a time a low voice speak. He said, "I've got to think. They know I'm here. Perhaps you'd better go. They've got nothing on you. If they come there's going to be shooting."

"Do you think they know I'm here?"

"They must have followed us all the way."

"Then I'll stay," Anne said. "There won't be any shooting while I'm here..They'll wait till morning, till you come out."

"That's friendly of you," he said with sour incredulity, all his suspicion of friendliness coming back.

"I've told you. I'm on your side."

"I've got to think of a way," he said.

"You may as well rest now. You've all the night to think in."

"It *is* sort of—good in here," Raven said, "out of the way of the whole damned world of them. In the dark." He wouldn't come near her, but sat down in the opposite corner with the automatic in his lap. He said suspiciously, "What are you thinking about?" He was astonished and shocked by the sound of a laugh. "Kind of homey," Anne said.

"I don't take any stock in homes," Raven said. "I've been in one."

"Tell me about it. What's your name?"

"You know my name. You've seen it in the papers."

"I mean your Christian name."

"Christian. That's a good joke, that one. Do you think anyone ever turns the other cheek these days?" He tapped the barrel of the automatic resentfully on the cinder floor. "Not a chance." He could hear her breathing there in the opposite corner, out of sight, out of reach, and he was afflicted by the odd sense that he had missed something. He said, "I'm not saying you aren't fine. I daresay you're Christian all right."

"Search me," Anne said.

"I took you out to that house to kill you."

"To kill me?"

"What did you think it was for? I'm not a lover, am I? Girl's dream? Handsome as the day?"

"Why didn't you?"

"Those men turned up. That's all. I didn't fall for you. I don't fall for girls. I'm saved that. You won't find me ever going soft on a skirt." He went desperately on, "Why didn't you tell the police about me? Why don't you shout to them now?"

"Well," she said, "you've got a gun, haven't you?"

"I wouldn't shoot."

"Why not?"

"I'm not all that crazy," he said. "If people go straight with me, I'll go straight with them. Go on. Shout. I won't do a thing."

"Well," Anne said, "I don't have to ask your leave to be grateful, do I? You saved me tonight."

"That lot wouldn't have killed you. They haven't the nerve to kill. It takes a man to kill."

"Well, your friend Cholmondeley came pretty near it. He nearly throttled me when he guessed I was in with you."

"In with me?"

"To find the man you're after."

"The double-crossing bastard." He brooded over his pistol, but his thoughts always disturbingly came back from hate to this dark safe corner; he wasn't used to that. He said, "You've got sense all right. I like you."

"Thanks for the compliment."

"It's no compliment. You don't have to tell me. I've got something I'd like to trust you with, but I can't."

"What's the dark secret?"

"It's not a secret. It's a cat I left back in my lodgings in London when they chased me out. You'd have looked after her."

"You disappoint me, Mr. Raven. I thought it was going to be a few murders at least." She exclaimed with sudden seriousness, "I've got it! The place where Davis works."

"Davis?"

"The man you call Cholmondeley. I'm sure of it. Midland Steel. In a street near the Metropole. A big palace of a place."

"I've got to get out of here," Raven said, beating the automatic on the freezing ground.

"Can't you go to the police?"

"Me?" Raven said. "Me go to the police?" He laughed. "That'd be fine, wouldn't it? Hold out my hands for the cuffs—"

"I'll think of a way," Anne said. When her voice ceased it was as if she had gone. He said sharply, "Are you there?"

"Of course I'm here," she said. "What's worrying you?"

"It feels odd to be alone." The sour incredulity surged back. He struck a couple of matches and held them to his face, close to his disfigured mouth. "Look," he said, "take a long look." The small flames burned steadily down. "You aren't going to help *me,* are you? Me?"

"You are all right," she said. "I like you." The flames touched his skin, but he held the two matches rigidly up and they burned out against his fingers; the pain was like joy. But he rejected it; it had come too late. He sat in the dark, feeling tears like heavy weights behind his eyes, but he couldn't weep. He had never known the particular trick that opened the right ducts at the right time. He crept a little way out of his corner towards her, feeling his way along the floor with the automatic. He said, "Are you cold?"

"I've been in warmer places," Anne said.

There were only his own sacks left. He pushed them over to her. "Wrap 'em round," he said.

"Have you got enough?"

"Of course I have. I can look after myself," he said sharply, as if he hated her. His hands were so cold that he would have found it hard to use the automatic. "I've got to get out of here."

"We'll think of a way. Better have a sleep."

"I can't sleep," he said; "I've been dreaming bad dreams lately."

"We might tell each other stories? It's about the children's hour."

"I don't know any stories."

"Well, I'll tell you one. What kind? A funny one?"

"They never seem funny to me."

"The three bears might be suitable."

"I don't want anything financial. I don't want to hear anything about money."

She could just see him now that he had come closer, a dark, hunched shape that couldn't understand a word she was saying. She mocked at him gently, secure in the knowledge that he would never realize she was mocking him. She said, "I'll tell you about the fox and the cat. Well, this cat met a fox in a forest, and she'd always heard the fox cracked up for being wise. So she passed him the time of day politely and asked how he was getting along. But the fox was proud. He said, 'How dare you ask me how I get along, you hungry mousehunter? What do you know about the world?' 'Well, I do know one thing,' the cat said. 'What's that?' said the fox. 'How to get away from the dogs,' the cat said. 'When they chase me, I just jump into a tree.' Then the fox went all high and mighty and said, 'You've only one trick, and I've a hundred. I've got a sackful of tricks. Come along with me, and I'll show you.' Just then a hunter ran quietly up with four hounds. The cat sprang into the tree and cried, 'Open your sack, Mr. Fox, open your sack.' But the dogs held him with their teeth. So the cat laughed at him, saying, 'Mr. Know-all, if you'd had just this one trick in your sack you'd be safe up the tree with me now.' " Anne stopped. She whispered to the dark shape beside her, "Are you asleep?"

"No," Raven said, "I'm not asleep."

"It's your turn now."

"I don't know any stories," Raven said sullenly, miserably.

"No stories like that? You haven't been brought up properly."

"I'm educated all right," he protested, "but I've got things on my mind. Plenty of them."

"Cheer up. There's someone who's got more."

"Who's that?"

"The fellow who began all this, who killed the old man—you know who I mean. Davis's friend."

"What do you say?" he said furiously. "Davis's friend?" He held his anger in. "It's not the killing I mind, it's the double-crossing."

"Well, of course," Anne said cheerily, making conversation under the pile of sacks, "I don't mind a little thing like killing myself."

He looked up and tried to see her through the dark, hunting a hope. "You don't mind that?"

"But there are killings and killings," Anne said. "If I had the man here who killed—what was the old man's name?"

"I don't remember."

"Nor do I. We couldn't pronounce it anyway."

"Go on. If he was here . . ."

"Why, I'd let you shoot him without raising a finger. And I'd say, 'Well done' to you, afterwards." She warmed to the subject. "You remember what I told you, that they can't invent gas masks for babies to wear? That's the kind of thing he'll have on his mind. The mothers alive in their masks, watching the babies cough up their insides."

He said stubbornly, "The poor ones'll be lucky. And what do I care about the rich? This isn't a world I'd bring children into." She could just see his tense, crouching figure. "It's just their selfishness," he said. "They have a good time, and what do they mind if someone's born ugly? Mother love—" He began to laugh, seeing quite clearly the kitchen table, the carving knife on the linoleum, the blood all over his mother's dress. He explained, "You see, I'm educated. In one of His Majesty's own homes. They call them that —homes. What do you think a home means?" But he didn't allow her time to speak. "You are wrong. You think it means a husband in work, a nice gas cooker and a double bed, carpet-slippers and cradles and the rest. That's not a home. A home's solitary confinement for a kid that's caught talking in the chapel, and the birch for almost anything you do. Bread and water. A sergeant knocking you around if you try to lark a bit. That's a home."

"Well, he was trying to alter all that, wasn't he? He was poor like we are."

"Who are you talking about?"

"Old What's-his-name. Didn't you read about him in the papers? How he cut down all the army expenses to help clear the slums?

There were photographs of him opening new flats, talking to the children. He wasn't one of the rich. He wouldn't have gone to war. That's why they shot him. You bet there are fellows making money now out of him being dead. And he'd done it all himself too, the obituaries said. His father was a thief and his mother committed—"

"Suicide?" Raven whispered. "Did you read how she—"

"She drowned herself."

"The things you read," Raven said. "It's enough to make a fellow think."

"Well, I'd say the fellow who killed old What's-his-name had something to think about."

"Maybe," Raven said, "he didn't know all the papers know. The men who paid him, they knew. Perhaps if we knew all there was to know—the kind of breaks the fellow had had—we'd see his point of view."

"It'd take a lot of talking to make me see that. Anyway, we'd better sleep now."

"I've got to think," Raven said.

"You'll think better after you've had a nap."

But it was far too cold for him to sleep; he had no sacks to cover himself with, and his black, tight overcoat was worn almost as thin as cotton. Under the door came a draught which might have travelled down the frosty rails from Scotland, a northeast wind bringing icy fogs from the sea. He thought to himself, I didn't mean the old man any harm; there was nothing personal . . . "I'd let you shoot him, and afterwards I'd say, 'Well done.' " He had a momentary crazy impulse to get up and go through the door with his automatic in his hand and let them shoot. "Mr. Know-all," she could say then, "if you'd only had this one trick in your sack, the dogs wouldn't . . ." But then it seemed to him that this knowledge he had gained of the old man was only one more count against Chol-mon-deley. Chol-mon-deley had known all this. There'd be one more bullet in his belly for this, and one more for Chol-mon-deley's master. But how was he to find the other man? He had only the memory of a photograph to guide him, a photograph which the old minister had somehow connected with the letter of introduction Raven had borne: a young, scarred boy's face which was probably an old man's now.

Anne said, "Are you asleep?"

"No," Raven said. "What's troubling you?"

"I thought I heard someone moving."

He listened. It was only the wind tapping a loose board outside. He said, "You go to sleep. You needn't be scared. They won't come till it's light enough to see." He thought, Where would those two have met when they were young? Surely not in the kind of home he'd known—the cold stone stairs, the cracked commanding bell, the tiny punishment cells. Quite suddenly he fell asleep, and the old minister was coming towards him, saying, "Shoot me. Shoot me in the eyes," and Raven was a child with a catapult in his hands. He wept and wouldn't shoot, and the old minister said, "Shoot, dear child. We'll go home together. Shoot."

Raven woke again as suddenly. In his sleep his hand had gripped the automatic tight. It was pointed at the corner where Anne slept. He gazed with horror into the dark, hearing a whisper like the one he had heard through the door when the secretary tried to call out. He said, "Are you asleep? What are you saying?"

Anne said, "I'm awake." She said defensively, "I was just praying."

"Do you believe in God?" Raven said.

"I don't know," Anne said. "Sometimes, maybe. It's a habit, praying. It doesn't do any harm. It's like crossing your fingers when you walk under a ladder. We all need any luck that's going."

Raven said, "We did a lot of praying in the home. Twice a day, and before meals too."

"It doesn't prove anything."

"No, it doesn't prove anything. Only you get sort of mad when everything reminds you of what's over and done with. Sometimes you want to begin fresh, and then someone praying or a smell or something you read in the paper, and it's all back again, the places and the people." He came a little nearer in the cold shed for company; it made you feel more than usually alone to know that they were waiting for you outside, waiting for daylight so that they could take you without any risk of your escaping or of your firing first. He had a good mind to send her out directly it was day and stick where he was and shoot it out with them. But that meant leaving Cholmon-deley and his employer free; it was just what would please them most. He said, "I was reading once—I like reading, I'm educated—something about psicko—psicko—"

"Leave it at that," Anne said. "I know what you mean."

"It seems as how your dreams mean things. I don't mean like tea leaves or cards."

"I knew someone once," Anne said. "She was so good with the

cards it gave you the creeps. She used to have those cards with queer pictures on them. The Hanged Man—"

"It wasn't like that," Raven said. "It was— Oh, I don't know properly. I couldn't understand it all. But it seems if you told your dreams— It was like you carrying a load around with you; you are born with some of it because of what your father and mother were and their fathers—seems as if it goes right back, like it says in the Bible about the sins being visited. Then when you're a kid the load gets bigger: all the things you need to do and can't, and then all the things you do. They get you either way." He leaned his sad, grim, killer's face on his hands. "It's like confessing to a priest. Only when you've confessed you go and do it all over again. I mean you tell these doctors everything, every dream you have, and afterwards you don't *want* to do it. But you have to tell them everything."

"Even the flying pigs?" Anne said.

"Everything. And when you've told everything it's gone."

"It sounds phony to me," Anne said.

"I don't suppose I've told it right. But it's what I read. I thought that maybe sometime it would be worth a trial."

"Life's full of funny things. Me and you being here. You thinking you wanted to kill me. Me thinking we can stop a war. Your psicko isn't any funnier than that."

"You see, it's the getting rid of it all that counts," Raven said. "It's not what the doctor does. That's how it seemed to me. Like when I told you about the home, about the bread and water and the prayers, they didn't seem so important afterwards." He swore softly and obscenely under his breath. "I'd always said I wouldn't go soft on a skirt. I always thought my lip'd save me. It's not safe to go soft. It makes you slow. I've seen it happen to other fellows. They've always landed in jail or got a razor in their guts. Now I've gone soft, as soft as all the rest."

"I like you," Anne said. "I'm your friend—"

"I'm not asking anything," Raven said. "I'm ugly, and I know it. Only one thing. Be different. Don't go to the police. Most skirts do. I've seen it happen. But maybe you aren't a skirt. You're a girl."

"I'm *someone's* girl."

"That's all right with me," he exclaimed with painful pride in the coldness and the dark. "I'm not asking anything but that, that you don't double-cross me."

"I'm not going to the police," Anne said. "I promise you I won't. I like you as well as any man—except my friend."

"I thought as how perhaps I could tell you a thing or two—dreams—just as well as any doctor. You see I know doctors. You can't trust them. I went to one before I came down here. I wanted him to alter this lip. He tried to put me to sleep with gas. He was going to call the police. You can't trust them. But I could trust you."

"You can trust me all right," Anne said. "I won't go to the police. But you'd better sleep first and tell me your dreams after, if you want to. It's a long night."

His teeth suddenly chattered uncontrollably with the cold, and Anne heard him. She put out a hand and touched his coat. "You're cold," she said. "You've given me all the sacks."

"I don't need 'em. I've got a coat."

"We're friends, aren't we?" Anne said. "We are in this together. You take two of these sacks."

He said, "There'll be some more about. I'll look," and he struck a match and felt his way round the wall. "Here are two," he said, sitting down farther away from her, empty-handed, out of reach. He said, "I can't sleep. Not properly. I had a dream just now. About the old man."

"What old man?"

"The old man that got murdered. I dreamed I was a kid with a catapult, and he was saying, 'Shoot me through the eyes,' and I was crying and he said, 'Shoot me through the eyes, dear child.' "

"Search *me* for a meaning," Anne said.

"I just wanted to tell it you."

"What did he look like?"

"Like he did look." Hastily he added, "Like I've seen in the photographs." He brooded over his memories with a low passionate urge towards confession. There had never in his life been anyone he could trust till now. He said, "You don't mind hearing these things?" and listened with a curious deep happiness to her reply—"We are friends." He said, "This is the best night I've ever had." But there were things he still couldn't tell her. His happiness was incomplete till she knew everything, till he had shown his trust completely. He didn't want to shock or pain her; he led slowly towards the central revelation. He said, "I've had other dreams of being a kid. I've dreamed I opened a door, a kitchen door, and there was my mother—she'd cut her throat—she looked ugly—her head nearly off—she'd sawn at it—with a breadknife."

Anne said, "That wasn't a dream."

"No," he said, "you're right, that wasn't a dream." He waited. He could feel her sympathy move silently towards him in the dark. He said, "That was ugly, wasn't it? You'd think you couldn't beat that for ugliness, wouldn't you? She hadn't even thought enough of me to lock the door so as I shouldn't see. And after that, there was a home. You know all about that. You'd say that was ugly too, but it wasn't as ugly as that other was. And they educated me, too, properly, so as I could understand the things I read in the papers. Like this psicko business. And write a good hand and speak the King's English. I got beaten a lot at the start, solitary confinement, bread and water, all the rest of the homey stuff. But that didn't go on when they'd educated me. I was too clever for them after that. They could never put a thing on me. They suspected all right, but they never had the proofs. Once the chaplain tried to frame me. They were right when they told us the day we left about it was like life. Jim and me and a bunch of soft kids." He said bitterly, "This is the first time they've had anything on me, and I'm innocent."

"You'll get away," Anne said. "We'll think up something together."

"It sounds good, your saying 'together' like that, but they've got me this time. I wouldn't mind if I could get that Chol-mon-deley and his boss first." He said with a kind of nervous pride, "Would you be surprised if I told you I'd killed a man?" It was like the first fence; if he cleared that he would have confidence. . . .

"Who?"

"Did you ever hear of Battling Kite?"

"No."

He laughed with a scared pleasure. "I'm trusting you with my life now. If you'd told me twenty-four hours ago that I'd trust my life to— But of course I haven't given you any *proof*. I was doing the races then. Kite had a rival gang. There wasn't anything else to do. He'd tried to bump my boss off on the course. Half of us took a fast car back to town. He thought we were on the train with him. But we were on the platform, see, when the train came in. We got round him directly he got outside the carriage. I cut his throat, and the others held him up till we were all through the barrier in a bunch. Then we dropped him by the bookstall and did a bolt." He said, "You see it was his lot or our lot. They'd had razors out on the course. It was war."

After a while Anne said, "Yes. I can see that. He had his chance."

"It sounds ugly," Raven said. "Funny thing is, it wasn't ugly. It was natural."

"Did you stick to that game?"

"No. It wasn't good enough. You couldn't trust the others. They either went soft or else they got reckless. They didn't use their brains." He said, "I wanted to tell you that about Kite. I'm not sorry. I haven't got religion. Only you said about being friendly, and I don't want you to get any wrong ideas. It was that mix-up with Kite brought me up against Chol-mon-deley. I can see now he was only in the racing game so as he could meet people. I thought he was a mug."

"We've got a long way from dreams."

"I was coming back to them," Raven said. "I suppose killing Kite like that made me nervous." His voice trembled very slightly from fear and hope, hope because she had accepted one killing so quietly and might, after all, take back what she had said ("Well done," "I wouldn't raise a finger"); fear because he didn't really believe that you could put such perfect trust in another and not be deceived. But it'd be fine, he thought, to be able to tell everything, to know that another person knew and didn't care; it would be like going to sleep for a long while. He said, "That spell of sleep I had just now was the first for two—three—I don't know how many nights. It looks as if I'm not tough enough after all."

"You seem tough enough to me," Anne said. "Don't let's hear any more about Kite."

"No one will hear any more about Kite. But if I was to tell you—" He ran away from the revelation. "I've been dreaming a lot lately it was an old woman I killed, not Kite. I heard her calling out through a door, and I tried to open the door, but she held the handle. I shot at her through the wood, but she held the handle tight. I had to kill her to open the door. Then I dreamed she was still alive and I shot her through the eyes. But even that—it wasn't *ugly*."

"You are tough enough in your dreams," Anne said.

"I killed an old man, too, in that dream. Behind his desk. I had a silencer. He fell behind it. I didn't want to hurt him. He didn't mean anything to me. I pumped him full. Then I put a bit of paper in his hand. I didn't have to take anything."

"What do you mean—you didn't have to take?"

Raven said, "They hadn't paid me to take anything. Chol-mon-deley and his boss."

"It wasn't a dream."

"No. It wasn't a dream." The silence frightened him. He began to talk rapidly to fill it. "I didn't know the old fellow was one of us. I wouldn't have touched him if I'd known he was like that. All this talk of war. It doesn't mean a thing to me. Why should I care if there's a war? There's always been a war for me. You talk a lot about the babies. Can't you have a bit of pity for the men? It was me or him. Two hundred pounds when I got back and fifty pounds down. It's a lot of money. It was only Kite over again. It was just as easy as it was with Kite." He said, "Are you going to leave me now?" and in the silence Anne could hear his rasping, anxious breath.

She said at last, "No. I'm not going to leave you."

He said, "That's good. Oh, that's good," putting out his hand, feeling hers cold as ice on the sacking. He put it for a moment against his unshaven cheek—he wouldn't touch it with his malformed lip. He said, "It feels good to trust someone with everything."

2

Anne waited for a long time before she spoke again. She wanted her voice to sound right, not to show her repulsion. Then she tried it on him, but all she could think of to say was again, "I'm not going to leave you." She remembered very clearly in the dark all she had read of the crime: the old woman secretary shot through the eyes, lying in the passage, the brutally smashed skull of the old Socialist. The papers had called it the worst political murder since the day when the king and queen of Serbia were thrown through the windows of their palace to ensure the succession of the wartime hero king.

Raven said again, "It's good to be able to trust someone like this," and suddenly his mouth, which had never before struck her as particularly ugly, came to mind, and she could have retched at the memory. Nevertheless, she thought, I must go on with this, I mustn't let him know. He must find Cholmondeley and Cholmondeley's boss, and then— She shrank from him into the dark.

He said, "They are out there waiting now. They've got cops down from London."

"From London?"

"It was all in the papers," he said with pride. "Detective Sergeant Mather from the Yard."

She could hardly restrain a cry of desolation and horror. "Here?"

"He may be outside now."

"Why doesn't he come in?"

"They'd never get me in the dark. And they'll know by now that *you* are here. They wouldn't be able to shoot."

"And you—you would?"

"There's no one *I* mind hurting," Raven said.

"How are you going to get out when it's daylight?"

"I shan't wait till then. I only want just light enough to see my way. And see to shoot. *They* won't be able to fire first; they won't be able to shoot to kill. That's what gives me a break. I only want a few clear hours. If I get away they'll never guess where to find me. Only you'll know I'm at Midland Steel."

She felt a desperate hatred. "You'll just shoot like that in cold blood?"

"You said you were on my side, didn't you?"

"Oh yes," she said warily, "yes," trying to think. It was getting too much to have to save the world—*and* Jimmy. If it came to a showdown the world would have to take second place. And what, she wondered, is Jimmy thinking? She knew his heavy, humourless rectitude; it would take more than Raven's head on a platter to make him understand why she had acted as she had with Raven and Cholmondeley. It sounded weak and fanciful even to herself to say that she wanted to stop a war.

"Let's sleep now," she said. "We've got a long, long day ahead."

"I think I could sleep now," Raven said. "You don't know how good it seems . . ." It was Anne now who could not sleep. She had too much to think about. It occurred to her that she might steal his pistol before he woke and call the police in. That would save Jimmy from danger, but what was the use? They'd never believe her story; they had no proof that he had killed the old man. And even then he might escape. She needed time, and there was no time. She could hear very faintly, droning up from the south, where the military aerodrome was, a troop of planes. They passed very high on special patrol, guarding the Nottwich mines and the key industry of Midland Steel, tiny specks of light the size of fireflies travelling fast in formation, over the railway, over the goods yard, over the shed where Anne and Raven lay, over Saunders beating his arms for warmth behind a truck out of the wind's way, over Acky dreaming that he was in the pulpit of St. Luke's, over Sir Marcus, sleepless beside the tape machine.

Raven slept heavily for the first time for nearly a week, holding the automatic in his lap. He dreamed that he was building a great bonfire on Guy Fawkes Day. He threw in everything he could find: a saw-edged knife, a lot of racing cards, the leg of a table. It burned warmly, deeply, beautifully. A lot of fireworks were going off all round him, and again the old war minister appeared on the other side of the fire. He said, "It's a good fire," stepping into it himself. Raven ran to the fire to pull him out, but the old man said, "Let me be. It's warm here," and then he sagged like a Guy Fawkes in the flames.

A clock struck. Anne counted the strokes, as she had counted them all through the night; it must be nearly day, and she had no plan. She coughed—her throat was stinging—and suddenly she realized with joy that there was fog outside—not one of the black upper fogs, but a cold, damp, yellow fog from the river, through which it would be easy, if it were thick enough, for a man to escape. She put out her hand unwillingly, because he was now so repulsive to her, and touched Raven. He woke at once. She said, "There's a fog coming up."

"What a break," he said, "what a break," laughing softly. "It makes you believe in Providence, doesn't it?" They could just see each other in the pale, earliest light. He was shivering now that he was awake. He said, "I dreamed of a big fire." She saw that he had no sacks to cover him, but she felt no pity at all. He was just a wild animal who had to be dealt with carefully and then destroyed. Let him freeze, she thought. He was examining the automatic; she saw him put down the safety catch. He said, "What about you? You've been straight with me. I don't want you to get into any trouble. I don't want them to think"—he hesitated and went on with questioning humility—"to know that we are in this together."

"I'll think up something," Anne said.

"I ought to knock you out. They wouldn't know then. But I've gone soft. I wouldn't hurt you, not if I was paid."

She couldn't resist saying, "Not for two hundred and fifty pounds?"

"He was a stranger," Raven said. "It's not the same. I thought he was one of the high and mighties. You're"—he hesitated again, glowering dumbly down at the automatic—"a friend."

"You needn't be afraid," Anne said. "I'll have a tale to tell."

He said with admiration, "You're clever." He watched the fog coming in under the badly fitting door, filling the small shed with its

freezing coils. "It'll be nearly thick enough now to take a chance."
He held the automatic in his left hand and flexed the fingers of the
right. He laughed to keep his courage up. "They'll never get me
now in this fog."

"You'll shoot?"

"Of course I'll shoot."

"I've got an idea," Anne said. "We don't want to take any risks.
Give me your overcoat and hat. I'll put them on and slip out first
and give them a run for their money. In this fog they'll never notice
till they've caught me. Directly you hear the whistles blow count
five slowly and make a bolt. I'll run to the right. You run to the
left."

"You've got nerve," Raven said. He shook his head. "No. They
might shoot."

"You said yourself they wouldn't shoot first."

"That's right. But you'll get a couple of years for this."

"Oh," Anne said, "I'll tell them a tale. I'll say you forced me."
She said with a trace of bitterness, "This'll give me a lift out of the
chorus. I'll have a speaking part."

Raven said shyly, "If you made out you were my girl, they
wouldn't pin it on you. I'll say that for them. They'd give a man's
girl a break."

"Got a knife?"

"Yes." He felt in all his pockets. It wasn't there; he must have
left it on the floor of Acky's best guest chamber.

Anne said, "I wanted to cut up my skirt. I'd be able to run
easier."

"I'll try and tear it," Raven said, kneeling in front of her, taking
a grip; but it wouldn't tear. Looking down, she was astonished at
the smallness of his wrists; his hands had no more strength or substance than a delicate boy's. The whole of his strength lay in the
mechanical instrument at his feet. She thought of Mather and felt
contempt now as well as repulsion for the thin, ugly body kneeling
at her feet.

"Never mind," she said. "I'll do the best I can. Give me the
coat."

He shivered, taking it off, and seemed to lose some of his sour
assurance without the tight black tube which had hidden a very
old, very flamboyant check suit in holes at both the elbows. It hung
on him uneasily. He looked undernourished. He wouldn't have impressed anyone as dangerous now. He pressed his arms to his sides

to hide the holes. "And your hat," Anne said. He picked it from the sacks and gave it her. He looked humiliated, and he had never accepted humiliation before without rage. "Now," Anne said, "remember. Wait for the whistles and then count."

"I don't like it," Raven said. He tried hopelessly to express the deep pain it gave him to see her go; it felt too much like the end of everything. He said, "I'll see you again—sometime," and when she mechanically reassured him, "Yes," he laughed with his aching despair. "Not likely, after I've killed—" But he didn't even know the man's name.

Six

1

Saunders had half fallen asleep. A voice at his side woke him. "The fog's getting thick, sir."

It was already dense, with the first light touching it with dusty yellow, and he would have sworn at the policeman for not waking him earlier if his stammer had not made him chary of wasting words. He said, "Pass the word round to move in."

"Are we going to rush the place, sir?"

"No. There's the girl there. We can't have any s-s-shooting. Wait till he comes out."

But the policeman hadn't left his side when he noticed, "The door's opening." Saunders put his whistle in his mouth and lowered his safety catch. The light was bad and the fog deceptive, but he recognized the dark coat as it slipped quickly to the right into the shelter of the coal trucks. He blew his whistle and was after it. The black coat had half a minute's start and was moving quickly into the fog. It was impossible to see at all more than twenty feet ahead. But Saunders kept doggedly just in sight, blowing his whistle continuously. As he hoped, a whistle blew in front. It confused the fugitive; he hesitated for a moment, and Saunders gained on him. They had him cornered, and this Saunders knew was the dangerous moment. He blew his whistle urgently three times into the fog to bring the police round in a complete circle, and the whistle was taken up in the yellow obscurity, passing in a wide invisible circle.

But he had lost pace; the fugitive spurted forward and was lost. Saunders blew two blasts: "Advance slowly and keep in touch." To the right and in front a single long whistle announced that the man had been seen, and the police converged on the sound. Each kept in touch with a policeman on either hand. It was impossible, as long as the circle was kept closed, for the man to escape. But the circle drew in, and there was no sign of him. The short, single, explanatory blasts sounded petulant and lost. At last Saunders, gazing ahead, saw the faint form of a policeman come out of the fog a dozen yards away. He halted them all with a whistled signal; the fugitive must be somewhere just ahead in the tangle of trucks in the center. Revolver in hand, Saunders advanced, and a policeman took his place and closed the circle.

Suddenly Saunders spied his man. He had taken up a strategic position where a pile of coal and an empty truck at his back made a wedge which guarded him from surprise. He was invisible to the police behind him, and he had turned sidewise, like a duellist, and presented only a shoulder to Saunders, while a pile of old sleepers hid him to the knees. It seemed to Saunders that it meant only one thing—that he was going to shoot it out. The man must be mad and desperate. The hat was pulled down over the face; the coat hung in an odd, loose way; the hands were in the pockets. Saunders called at him through the yellow coils of fog, "You'd better come quietly." He raised his pistol and advanced, his finger ready on the trigger. But the immobility of the figure scared him. It was in shadow, half hidden in the swirl of fog. It was he who was exposed, with the east, and the pale penetration of early light behind him. It was like waiting for execution, for he could not fire first. But all the same, knowing what Mather felt, knowing that this man was mixed up with Mather's girl, he did not want much excuse to fire. Mather would stand by him. A movement would be enough. He said sharply, without a stammer, "Put up your hands." The figure didn't move. He told himself again, with a kindling hatred for the man who had injured Mather, I'll plug him if he doesn't obey. They'll all stand by me. One more chance. "Put up your hands," and when the figure stayed as it was, with its hands hidden, a hardly discernible menace, he fired.

But as he pressed the trigger a whistle blew, a long urgent blast which panted and gave out like a rubber animal, from the direction of the wall and the road. There could be no doubt whatever what that meant, and suddenly he saw it all—he had shot at Mather's girl; she'd drawn them off. He screamed at the men behind him, "Back to the gate," and ran forward. He had seen her waver at his shot. He said, "Are you hurt?" and knocked the hat off her head to see her better.

"You're the third person who's tried to kill me," Anne said weakly, leaning hard against the truck. "Come to sunny Nottwich. Well, I've got six lives left."

Saunders' stammer came back. "W-w-w-w—"

"This is where you hit," Anne said, "if that's what you want to know," showing the long yellow sliver on the edge of the truck. "It was only an outer. You don't even get a box of chocolates."

Saunders said, "You'll have to c-c-come along with me."

"It'll be a pleasure. Do you mind if I take off this coat? I feel kind of silly."

At the gate four policemen stood round something on the ground. One of them said, "We've sent for an ambulance."

"Is he dead?"

"Not yet. He's shot in the stomach. He must have gone on whistling—"

Saunders had a moment of vicious rage. "Stand aside, boys," he said, "and let the lady see." They drew back in an embarrassed, unwilling way, as if they'd been hiding a dirty chalk picture on the wall, and showed the white, drained face, which looked as if it had never been alive, never known the warm circulation of blood. You couldn't call the expression peaceful; it was just nothing at all. The blood was all over the trousers the men had loosened, was caked on the charcoal of the path. Saunders said, "Two of you take this lady to the station. I'll stay here till the ambulance comes."

2

Mather said, "If you want to make a statement I must warn you that anything you say may be used in evidence."

"I haven't got a statement to make," Anne said. "I want to talk to you, Jimmy."

Mather said, "If the superintendent had been here, I should have asked him to take the case. I want you to understand that I'm not letting personal—that my not having charged you doesn't mean—"

"You might give a girl a cup of coffee," Anne said. "It's nearly breakfast time."

Mather struck the table furiously. "Where was he going?"

"Give me time," Anne said. "I've got plenty to tell. But you won't believe it."

"You saw the man he shot," Mather said. "He's got a wife and two children. They've rung up from the hospital. He's bleeding internally."

"What's the time?" Anne said.

"Eight o'clock. It won't make any difference, your keeping quiet. He can't escape us now. In an hour the air-raid signals go. There won't be a soul on the streets without a mask. He'll be spotted at once. What's he wearing?"

"If you'd give me something to eat. I haven't had a thing for twenty-four hours. I could think then."

Mather said, "There's only one chance you won't be charged with complicity. If you make a statement."

"Is this third degree?" Anne said.

"Why do you want to shelter him? Why keep your word to him when you don't—?"

"Go on," Anne said. "Be personal. No one can blame you. I don't. But I don't want you to think I'd keep my word to him. He killed the old man. He told me so."

"What old man?"

"The war minister."

"You've got to think up something better than that," Mather said.

"But it's true. He never stole those notes. They double-crossed him. It was what they'd paid him to do the job."

"He spun you a fancy yarn," Mather said. "But *I* know where those notes came from."

"So do I. I can guess. From somewhere in this town."

"He told you wrong. They came from United Rail Makers in Victoria Street."

Anne shook her head. "They didn't start from there. They came from Midland Steel."

"So that's where he's going, to Midland Steel—in the Tanneries?"

"Yes," Anne said. There was a sound of finality about the word which daunted her. She hated Raven now. The policeman she had seen bleeding on the ground called at her heart for Raven's death, but she couldn't help remembering the hut, the cold, the pile of sacks, his complete and hopeless trust. She sat with bowed head while Mather lifted the receiver and gave his orders.

"We'll wait for him there," he said. "Who is it he wants to see?"

"He doesn't know."

"There might be something in it," Mather said. "Some connection between the two. He's probably been double-crossed by some clerk."

"It wasn't a clerk who paid him all that money, who tried to kill me just because I knew—"

Mather said, "Your fairy tale can wait." He rang a bell and told the constable who came, "Hold this girl for further inquiries. You can give her a sandwich and a cup of coffee now."

"Where are you going?"

"To bring in your boy friend," Mather said.

"He'll shoot. He's quicker than you are. Why can't you let the others . . ." she implored him. "I'll make a full statement. How he killed Kite, too."

"Take it," Mather said to the constable. He put on his coat. "The fog's clearing."

She said, "Don't you see that if it's true—only give him time to find his man and there won't be—war."

"He was telling you a fairy story."

"He was telling me the truth—but, of course, you weren't there, you didn't hear him. It sounds different to you. I thought I was saving—everyone."

"All you did," Mather said brutally, "was get a man killed."

"The whole thing sounds so different in here. Kind of fantastic. But he believed. Maybe," she said hopelessly, "he was mad."

Mather opened the door. She suddenly cried to him, "Jimmy, he wasn't mad. They tried to kill *me*."

He said, "I'll read your statement when I get back," and closed the door.

Seven

1

They were all having the hell of a time at the hospital. It was the biggest rag they'd had since the day of the street collection when they kidnapped old Piker and ran him to the edge of the Weevil and threatened to duck him if he didn't pay a ransom. Good old Fergusson, good old Buddy, was organizing it all. They had three ambulances out in the courtyard, and one had a death's head banner on it for the dead ones. Somebody shrieked that Mike was taking out the petrol with a nasal syringe, so they began to pelt him with flour and soot—they had it ready in great buckets. It was the unofficial part of the programme; all the casualties were going to be rubbed with it, except the dead ones the death's-head ambulance picked up. *They* were going to be put in the cellar where the refrigerating plant kept the corpses for dissection fresh.

One of the senior surgeons passed rapidly and nervously across a corner of the courtyard. He was on the way to a Caesarian operation, but he had no confidence whatever that the students wouldn't pelt him or duck him. Only five years ago there had been a scandal and an inquiry because a woman had died on the day of a rag. The surgeon attending her had been kidnapped and carried all over town dressed as Guy Fawkes. Luckily she wasn't a paying patient, and, though her husband had been hysterical at the inquest, the coroner had decided that one must make allowance for youth. The coroner had been a student himself once and remembered with pleasure the day when they had pelted the vice-chancellor of the university with soot.

The senior surgeon had been present that day too. Once safely inside the glass corridor he could smile at the memory. The vice-chancellor had been unpopular; he had been a classic, which wasn't very suitable for a provincial university. He had translated Lucan's *Pharsalia* into some complicated metre of his own invention. The senior surgeon remembered something vaguely about stresses. He could still see the little wizened, frightened Liberal face trying to smile when his pince-nez broke, trying to be a good sportsman. But anyone could tell that he wasn't really a good sportsman. That's why they pelted him so hard.

The senior surgeon, quite safe now, smiled tenderly down at the rabble in the courtyard. Their white coats were already black with soot. Somebody had got hold of a stomach pump. Very soon they'd be raiding the shop in the High Street and seizing their mascot, the stuffed and rather moth-eaten tiger. Youth, youth, he thought, laughing gently when he saw Mander, the treasurer, scuttle from door to door with a scared expression. Perhaps they'll catch him— no, they've let him by. What a joke it all was, "trailing clouds of glory," "turn as swimmers into cleanness leaping."

Buddy was having the hell of a time. Everyone was scampering to obey his orders. He was the leader. They'd duck or pelt anyone he told them to. He had an enormous sense of power; it more than atoned for unsatisfactory examination results, for surgeons' sarcasms. Even a surgeon wasn't safe today if *he* gave an order. The soot and water and flour were his idea. The whole gas practice would have been a dull, sober, official piece of routine if he hadn't thought of making it a "rag." The very word "rag" was powerful; it conferred complete freedom from control. He'd called a meeting of the brighter students and explained, "If anyone's on the street without a gas mask he's a conchie. There are people who want to crab the practice. So when we get 'em back to the hospital we'll give 'em hell."

They boiled round him. "Good old Buddy." "Look out with that pump." "Who's the bastard who's pinched my stethoscope?" "What about Tiger Tim?" They surged round Buddy Fergusson, waiting for orders, and he stood superbly above them on the step of an ambulance, his white coat apart, his fingers in the pockets of his double-breasted waistcoat, his square, squat figure swelling with pride, while they shouted, "Tiger Tim. Tiger Tim. Tiger Tim."

"Friends, Romans, and Countrymen," he said, and they roared with laughter. Good old Buddy. Buddy always had the right word. He could make any party go. You never knew what Buddy would say next. "Lend me your—" They shrieked with laughter. He was a dirty dog, old Buddy. Good old Buddy.

Like a great beast which is in need of exercise, which has fed on too much hay, Buddy Fergusson was aware of his body. He felt his biceps; he strained for action. Too many exams, too many lectures. Buddy Fergusson wanted action. While they surged round him he imagined himself a leader of men. No Red Cross work for him when war broke: Buddy Fergusson, company commander; Buddy Fergusson, the daredevil of the trenches. The only exam he had ever successfully passed was Certificate A in the school O.T.C.

"Some of our friends seem to be missing," Buddy Fergusson said. "Simmons, Aitkin, Mallowes, Watt. They are bloody conchies, every one, grubbing up anatomy while we are serving our country. We'll pick 'em up in town. The Flying Squad will go to their lodgings."

"What about the women, Buddy?" someone screamed, and everyone laughed and began to hit at each other, wrestle and mill. For Buddy had a reputation with the women. He spoke airily to his friends of even the super-barmaid at the Metropole, calling her Juicy Juliet and suggesting to the minds of his hearers amazing scenes of abandonment over high tea at his digs.

Buddy Fergusson straddled across the ambulance step. "Deliver 'em to me. In wartime we need more mothers." He felt strong, coarse, vital, a town bull. He hardly remembered himself that he was virgin, guilty only of a shamefaced unsuccessful attempt on the old Nottwich tart. He was sustained by his reputation; it bore him magically in imagination into every bed. He knew women, he was a realist.

"Treat 'em rough," they shrieked at him, and, "You're telling me," he said magnificently, keeping well at bay any thought of the future: the small, provincial G.P.'s job, the panel patients in dingy consulting rooms, innumerable midwife cases, a lifetime of hard, underpaid fidelity to one dull wife. "Got your gas masks ready?" he called to them, the undisputed leader, daredevil Buddy. What the hell did examinations matter when you were a leader of men? He could see several of the younger nurses watching him through the panes. He could see the little brunette called Milly. She was coming to tea with him on Saturday. He felt his muscles taut with pride. What scenes, he told himself, there would be *this* time of disreputable revelry, forgetting the inevitable truth known only to himself and each girl in turn: the long silence over the muffins, the tentative references to League results, the peck at empty air on the doorstep.

The siren at the glue factory started its long mounting whistle rather like a lap dog with hysteria, and everyone stood still for a moment with a vague reminiscence of Armistice Day silences. Then they broke into three milling mobs, climbing onto the ambulance roofs, fixing their gas masks, and drove out into the cold, empty Nottwich streets. The ambulances shed a lot of them at each corner, and small groups formed and wandered down the streets with a predatory, disappointed air. The streets were almost empty. Only a few errand boys passed on bicycles, looking in their gas masks like bears doing a trick cycle act in a circus. They all shrieked at each other because they didn't know how their voices sounded outside. It was as if each of them were enclosed in a separate soundproof telephone cabinet. They stared hungrily through their big mica eyepieces into the doorways of shops, wanting a victim. A little group collected round Buddy Fergusson and proposed that they should seize a policeman who, being on point duty, was without a mask. But Buddy vetoed the proposal. He said this wasn't an ordinary rag. What they wanted were people who thought so little about their country that they wouldn't even take the trouble to put on a gas mask. "They are the people," he said, "who avoid boat drill. We had great fun with a fellow once in the Mediterranean who didn't turn up to boat drill."

That reminded them of all the fellows who weren't helping, who were probably getting ahead with their anatomy at that moment. "Watt lives near here," Buddy Fergusson said. "Let's get Watt and debag him." A feeling of physical well being came over him just as if he had drunk a couple of pints of bitter. "Down the Tanneries," Buddy said. "First left. First right. Second left. Number Twelve. First floor." He knew the way, he said, because he'd been to tea several times with Watt their first term before he'd learned what a hound Watt was. The knowledge of his early mistake made him unusually anxious to do something to Watt physically, to mark the severance of their relationship more completely than with sneers.

They ran down the empty Tanneries, half-a-dozen masked monstrosities in white coats smutted with soot. It was impossible to tell one from another. Through the great glass door of Midland Steel they saw three men standing by the lift, talking to the porter. There were a lot of uniformed police about, and in the square ahead they saw a rival group of fellow students, who had been luckier than they, carrying a little man (he kicked and squealed) towards an ambulance. The police watched and laughed, and a troop of planes zoomed overhead, diving low over the centre of the town to lend the practice verisimilitude. First left. First right. The centre of Nottwich, to a stranger, was full of sudden contrasts. Only on the edge of the town to the north, out by the park, were you certain of encountering street after street of well-to-do middle-class houses. Near the market you changed at a corner from modern chromium offices to little cats'-meat shops; from the luxury of the Metropole to seedy lodgings and the smell of cooking greens. There was no excuse in Nottwich for one half of the world being ignorant of how the other half lived.

Second left. The houses on one side gave way to bare rock, and the street dived steeply down below the Castle. It wasn't really a castle any longer; it was a yellow brick municipal museum full of flint arrowheads and pieces of broken brown pottery and a few stags' heads in the zoological section, suffering from moths, and one mummy brought back from Egypt by the Earl of Nottwich in 1843. The moths left that alone, but the custodian thought he had heard mice inside. Mike, with a nasal douche in his breast pocket, wanted to climb up the rock. He shouted to Buddy Fergusson that the custodian was outside without a mask, signalling to enemy aircraft. But Buddy and the others ran down the hill to Number Twelve.

The landlady opened the door to them. She smiled winningly and said Mr. Watt was in—she thought he was working. She button-holed Buddy Fergusson and said she was sure it would be good for Mr. Watt to be taken away from his books for half an hour. Buddy said, "We'll take him away."

"Why, that's Mr. Fergusson," the landlady said. "I'd know your voice anywhere, but I'd never 'ave known you without you spoke to me, not in them respiratorories. I was just going out when Mr. Watt reminded me as 'ow it was the gas practice."

"Oh, he remembers, does he?" Buddy said. He was blushing inside the mask at having been recognized by the landlady. It made him want to assert himself more than ever.

"He said I'd be taken to the 'ospital."

"Come on, men," Buddy said and led them up the stairs. But their number was an embarrassment. They couldn't all charge through Watt's door and seize him in a moment from the chair in which he was sitting. They had to go through one at a time after Buddy and then bunch themselves in a shy silence beside the table. This was the moment when an experienced man could have dealt with them, but Watt was aware of his unpopularity. He was afraid of losing dignity. He was a man who worked hard because he liked the work—he hadn't the excuse of poverty. He played no games because he didn't like games, without the excuse of physical weakness. He had a mental arrogance which would ensure his success. If he suffered agony from his unpopularity now, as a student, it was the price he paid for the baronetcy, the Harley Street consulting room, the fashionable practice of the future. There was no reason to pity him; it was the others who were pitiable, living in their vivid, vulgar way for five years before the long provincial interment of a lifetime.

Watt said, "Close the door, please. There's a draught," and his scared sarcasm gave them the chance they needed to resent him.

Buddy said, "We've come to ask why you weren't at the hospital this morning."

"That's Fergusson, isn't it?" Watt said. "I don't know why you want to know."

"Are you a conchie?"

"How old-world your slang is," Watt said. "No. I'm not a conchie. Now I'm just looking through some old medical books, and as I don't suppose they'd interest you, I'll ask you to show yourself out."

"Working? That's how fellows like you get ahead, working while others are doing a proper job."

"It's just a different idea of fun, that's all," Watt said. "It's my pleasure to look at these folios, it's yours to go screaming about the streets in that odd costume."

That let them loose on him. He was as good as insulting the king's uniform. "We're going to debag you," Buddy said.

"That's fine. It'll save time," Watt said, "if I take them off myself," and he began to undress. He said, "This action has an interesting psychological significance. A form of castration. My own theory is that sexual jealousy in some form is at the bottom of it."

"You dirty tyke," Buddy said. He took an inkpot and splashed it on the wallpaper. He didn't like the word "sex." He believed in barmaids and nurses and tarts, and he believed in love—something rather maternal with deep breasts. The word sex suggested that there was something in common between the two; it outraged him. "Wreck the room," he bawled, and all were immediately happy and at ease, exerting themselves physically like young bulls. Because they were happy again they didn't do any real damage, just pulled the books out of the shelves and threw them on the floor. They broke the glass of a picture frame in puritanical zeal because it contained the reproduction of a nude girl by Munke. Watt watched them. He was scared, and the more scared he was the more sarcastic he became. Buddy suddenly saw him as he was, standing there in his pants, marked from birth for distinction, for success, and hated him. He felt impotent; he hadn't "class" like Watt, he hadn't the brains. In a very few years nothing he could do or say would affect the fortunes or the happiness of the Harley Street specialist, the woman's physician, the baronet. What was the good of talking about free will? Only war and death could save Buddy from the confinements, the provincial practice, the one dull wife, and the bridge parties. It seemed to him that he could be happy if he had the strength to impress himself on Watt's memory. He took an inkpot and poured it over the open title page of the old folio on the table.

"Come on, men," he said. "This room stinks," and led his party out and down the stairs. He felt an immense exhilaration; it was as if he had proved his manhood.

Almost immediately they picked up an old woman. She didn't

in the least know what it was all about. She thought it was a street collection and offered them a penny. They told her she had to come along to the hospital. They were very courteous, and one offered to carry her basket; they reacted from violence to a more than usual gentility. She laughed at them. She said, "Well I never, what you boys will think up next." And when one took her arm and began to lead her gently up the street, she said, "Which of you's Father Christmas?" Buddy didn't like that; it hurt his dignity. He had suddenly been feeling rather noble: "women and children first," "although bombs were falling all round he brought the woman safely . . ." He stood still and let the others go on up the street with the old woman. She was having the time of her life; she cackled and dug them in the ribs—her voice carried a long distance in the cold air. She kept on telling them to "take off them things and play fair," and just before they turned a corner out of sight she was calling them Mormons. She meant Mohammedans, because she had an idea that Mohammedans went about with their faces covered up and had a lot of wives. An airplane zoomed overhead, and Buddy was alone in the street with the dead and dying until Mike appeared. Mike said he had a good idea. Why not pinch the mummy in the castle and take it to the hospital for not wearing a gas mask? The fellows with the death's-head ambulance had already got Tiger Tim and were driving round the town, crying out for old Piker.

"No," Buddy said, "this isn't an ordinary rag. This is serious." And suddenly, at the entrance to a side street, he saw a man without a mask double back at the sight of him. "Quick. Hunt him down," Buddy cried. "Tally-ho," and they pelted up the street in pursuit. Mike was the faster runner—Buddy was already a little inclined to fatness—and Mike was soon leading by ten yards. The man had a start, he was round one corner and out of sight. "Go on," Buddy shouted, "hold him till I come." Mike was out of sight too when a voice from a doorway spoke as he passed. "Hi," it said, "you. What's the hurry?"

Buddy stopped. The man stood there with his back pressed to a house door. He had simply stepped back, and Mike in his hurry had gone by. There was something serious and planned and venomous about his behaviour. The street of little Gothic villas was quite empty.

"You were looking for me, weren't you?" the man said.

Buddy demanded sharply, "Where's your gas mask?"

"Is this a game?" the man said angrily.

"Of course it's not a game," Buddy said. "You're a casualty. You'll have to come along to the hospital with me."

"I will, will I?" the man said, pressed back against the door, thin and undersized and out-at-elbows.

"You'd better," Buddy said. He inflated his chest and made his biceps swell. Discipline, he thought, discipline. The little brute didn't recognize an officer when he saw one. He felt the satisfaction of superior physical strength. He'd punch his nose for him if he didn't come quietly.

"All right," the man said, "I'll come." He emerged from the dark doorway, mean vicious face, harelip, a crude check suit, ominous and aggressive in his submission.

"Not that way," Buddy said, "to the left."

"Keep moving," the small man said, covering Buddy through his pocket, pressing the pistol against his side. "*Me* a casualty," he said, "that's a good one," laughing without mirth. "Get in through that gate or you'll be the casualty." (They were opposite a small garage. It was empty. The owner had driven to his office, and the little bare box stood open at the end of a few feet of drive.)

Buddy blustered, "What the hell," but he had recognized the face of which the description had appeared in both the local papers, and there was a control in the man's actions which horribly convinced Buddy that he wouldn't hesitate to shoot. It was a moment in his life that he never forgot; he was not allowed to forget it by friends who saw nothing wrong in what he did. All through his life the tale cropped up in print in the most unlikely places: serious histories, symposiums of famous crimes. It followed him from obscure practice to obscure practice. Nobody saw anything important in what he did. Nobody doubted that he would have done the same—walked into the garage, closed the gates at Raven's orders. But friends didn't realize the crushing nature of the blow; they hadn't just been standing in the street under a hail of bombs, they had not looked forward with pleasure and excitement to war, they hadn't been Buddy, the daredevil of the trenches, one minute before real war in the shape of an automatic in a thin, desperate hand broke on him.

"Strip," Raven said, and obediently Buddy stripped. But he was stripped of more than his gas mask, his white coat, his green tweed suit. When it was over he hadn't a hope left. It was no good hoping for a war to prove him a leader of men. He was just a stout, flushed, frightened young man shivering in his pants in the cold garage.

There was a hole in the seat of his pants, and his knees were pink and hairless. You could tell that he was strong, but you could tell too in the curve of his stomach, the thickness of his neck, that he was beginning to run to seed. Like a mastiff, he needed more exercise than the city could afford him, even though several times a week, undeterred by the frost, he would put on shorts and a singlet and run slowly and obstinately round the park, a little red in the face but undeterred by the grins of nursemaids and the shrill, veracious comments of unbearable children in prams. He was keeping fit, but it was a dreadful thought that he had been keeping fit for this, to stand shivering and silent in a pair of holey pants while the mean, thin, undernourished city rat, whose arm he could have snapped with a single twist, put on his clothes, his white coat and, last of all, his gas mask.

"Turn round," Raven said, and Buddy Fergusson obeyed. He was so miserable now that he would have missed a chance even if Raven had given him one—miserable and scared as well. He hadn't much imagination; he had never really visualized danger as it now gleamed at him under the garage globe in a long, grey, wicked-looking piece of metal charged with pain and death. "Put your hands behind you." Raven tied together the pink, strong, hamlike wrists with Buddy's tie—the striped chocolate-and-yellow old boys' tie of one of the obscurer public schools. "Lie down," and meekly Buddy Fergusson obeyed, and Raven tied his feet together with a handkerchief and gagged him with another. It wasn't very secure, but it would have to do. He'd got to work quickly. He left the garage and pulled the doors softly to behind him. He could *hope* for several hours' start now, but he couldn't count on as many minutes.

He came quietly and cautiously up under the castle rock, keeping his eye open for students. But the gangs had moved on; some were picketing the station for train arrivals, and the others were sweeping the streets which led out northwards towards the mines. The chief danger now was that at any moment the sirens might blow the all-clear. There were a lot of police about—he knew why —but he moved unhesitantly past them and on towards the Tanneries. His plan carried him no farther than the big glass doors of Midland Steel. He had a kind of blind faith in destiny, in a poetic justice; somehow when he was inside the building he would find the way to the man who had double-crossed him. He came safely round into the Tanneries and moved across the narrow roadway, where there was only room for a single stream of traffic, towards the great functional building of black glass and steel. He hugged the automatic to his hip with a sense of achievement and exhilaration. There was a kind of lightheartedness now about his malice and hatred that he had never known before; he had lost his sourness and bitterness, he was less personal in his revenge. It was almost as if he were acting for someone else.

Behind the door of Midland Steel a man peered out at the parked cars and the deserted street. He looked like a clerk. Raven crossed the pavement. He peered back through the panes of the mask at the man behind the door. Something made him hesitate—the memory of a face he had seen for a moment in the Soho café where he had lodged. He suddenly started away again from the door, walking in a rapid, scared way down the Tanneries. The police were there before him.

It meant nothing, Raven told himself, coming out into a silent High Street, empty except for a telegraph boy in a gas mask getting onto a bicycle by the post office. It merely meant that the police too had noted a connection between the office in Victoria Street and Midland Steel. It didn't mean that the girl was just another skirt who had betrayed him. Only the faintest shadow of the old sourness and isolation touched his spirits. She's straight, he swore with almost perfect conviction; *she* wouldn't double-cross. We are together in this—and he remembered with a sense of doubtful safety how she had said, "We are friends."

2

The producer had called a rehearsal early. He wasn't going to add to the expenses by buying everyone gas masks. They would be in the theatre by the time the practice started, and they wouldn't leave until the all-clear had sounded. Mr. Davis had said he wanted to see the new number, and so the producer had sent him notice of the rehearsal. He had it stuck under the edge of his shaving mirror next a card with the telephone numbers of all his girls.

It was bitterly cold in the modern central-heated bachelor's flat. Something, as usual, had gone wrong with the oil engines, and the constant hot water was barely warm. Mr. Davis cut himself shaving several times and stuck little tufts of cotton wool all over his chin. His eye caught Mayfair 632 and Museum 798. Those were Coral and Lucy. Dark and fair, nubile and thin. His fair and his dark angel. A little early fog still yellowed the panes, and the sound of a

car backfiring made him think of Raven safely isolated in the railway yard surrounded by armed police. He knew that Sir Marcus
was arranging everything, and he wondered how it felt to be waking
to your last day. "We know not the hour," Mr. Davis thought happily, plying his styptic pencil, sticking the cotton wool on the larger
wounds, but if one knew, as Raven must know, would one still feel
irritation at the failure of central heating, at a blunt blade? Mr.
Davis's mind was full of great dignified abstractions, and it seemed
to him a rather grotesque idea that a man condemned to death
should be aware of something so trivial as a shaving cut. But then,
of course, Raven would not be shaving in his shed.

Mr. Davis made a hasty breakfast: two pieces of toast, two cups
of coffee, four kidneys and a piece of bacon, sent up by lift from
the restaurant, some sweet silver-shred marmalade. It gave him a
good deal of pleasure to think that Raven would not be eating such
a breakfast; a condemned man in prison, possibly, but not Raven.
Mr. Davis did not believe in wasting anything. He had paid for the
breakfast, so on the second piece of toast he piled up all the remains
of the butter and the marmalade. A little of the marmalade fell off
onto his tie.

There was really only one worry left, apart from Sir Marcus's
displeasure, and that was the girl. He had lost his head badly, first
in trying to kill her and then in not killing her. It had all been Sir
Marcus's fault. He had been afraid of what Sir Marcus would do
to him if he learned of the girl's existence. But now everything
should be all right. The girl had come out into the open as an accomplice; no court would take a criminal's story against Sir Marcus's. He forgot about the gas practice, hurrying down to the theatre
for a little relaxation now that everything really seemed to have
been tidied up. On the way he got a sixpenny packet of toffee out
of a slot machine.

He found Mr. Collier worried. They'd already had one rehearsal
of the new number, and Miss Maydew, who was sitting at the front
of the stalls in a fur coat, had said it was vulgar. She said she didn't
mind sex, but this wasn't in the right class. It was music-hall, it
wasn't revue. Mr. Collier didn't care a damn what Miss Maydew
thought, but it might mean that Mr. Cohen . . . He said, "If you'd
tell me what's vulgar—I just don't see—"

Mr. Davis said, "I'll tell you if it's vulgar. Have it again," and
he sat back in the stalls just behind Miss Maydew with the warm
smell of her fur and her rather expensive scent in his nostrils, suck-

ing a toffee. It seemed to him that life could offer nothing better than this. And the show was his. At any rate forty per cent of it was his. He picked out his forty per cent as the girls came on again in diminutive blue shorts with a red stripe and postmen's caps, and brassières, carrying cornucopias: the dark girl with the oriental eyebrows on the right, the fair girl with the rather plump legs and the big mouth (a big mouth was a good sign in a girl). They danced between two pillar boxes, wriggling their little neat hips, and Mr. Davis sucked his toffee.

"It's called 'Christmas for Two,' " Mr. Collier said.

"Why?"

"Well, you see, those cornucops are meant to be Christmas presents made sort of classical. And 'for Two' just gives it a little sex. Any number with 'for Two' in it goes."

"We've already got 'An Apartment for Two,' " Miss Maydew said, "and 'Two Make a Dream.' "

"You can't have too much of 'for Two,' " Mr. Collier said. He appealed pitiably, "Can't you tell me what's vulgar?"

"Those cornucopias, for one thing."

"But they are classical," Mr. Collier said. "Greek."

"And the pillar boxes for another."

"The pillar boxes!" Mr. Collier exclaimed hysterically. "What's wrong with the pillar boxes?"

"My dear man," Miss Maydew said, "if you don't know what's wrong with the pillar boxes, I'm not going to tell you. If you'd like to get a committee of matrons I wouldn't mind telling *them*. But if you *must* have them, paint them blue and let them be air mail."

Mr. Collier said, "Is this a game or what is it?" He added bitterly, "What a time you must have when you write a letter." The girls went patiently on behind his back to the jingle of the piano, offering the cornucopias, offering their collar-stud tails. He turned on them fiercely. "Stop that, can't you, and let me think!"

Mr. Davis said, "It's fine. We'll have it in the show." It made him feel good to contradict Miss Maydew, whose perfume he was now luxuriously taking in. It gave him in a modified form the pleasure of beating her or sleeping with her—the pleasure of mastery over a woman of superior birth. It was the kind of dream he had indulged in in adolescence, while he carved his name on the desk and seat in a grim Midland board school.

"You really think that, Mr. Davenant?"

"My name's Davis."

"I'm sorry, Mr. Davis." Horror on horror, Mr. Collier thought; he was alienating the new backer now.

"I think it's lousy," Miss Maydew said.

Mr. Davis took another piece of toffee. "Go ahead, old man," he said. "Go ahead." They went ahead. The songs and dances floated agreeably through Mr. Davis's consciousness, sometimes wistful, sometimes sweet and sad, sometimes catchy. Mr. Davis liked the sweet ones best. When they sang, "You have my mother's way," he really did think of his mother; he was the ideal audience.

Somebody came out of the wings and bellowed at Mr. Collier. Mr. Collier screamed, "What do you say?" and a young man in a pale-blue jumper went on mechanically singing:

> *"Your photograph*
> *Is just the sweetest half . . ."*

"Did you say Christmas tree?" Mr. Collier yelled.

> *"In your December*
> *I shall remember . . ."*

Mr. Collier screamed, "Take it away."

The song came abruptly to an end with the words "Another mother." The young man said, "You took it too fast," and began to argue with the pianist.

"I can't take it away," the man in the wings said. "It was ordered." He wore an apron and a cloth cap. He said, "It took a van and two horses. You'd better come and have a look."

Mr. Collier disappeared and returned immediately. "My God!" he said, "it's fifteen feet high. Who can have played this fool trick?" Mr. Davis was in a happy dream; his slippers had been warmed by a log fire in a big baronial hall, a little exclusive perfume like Miss Maydew's was kind of hovering in the air, and he was just going to go to bed with a good but aristocratic girl to whom he had been properly married that morning by a bishop. She reminded him a little of his mother. "In your December . . ."

He was suddenly aware that Mr. Collier was saying, "And there's a crate of glass balls and candles."

"Why," Mr. Davis said, "has my little gift arrived?"

"Your—little—?"

"I thought we'd have a Christmas party on the stage," Mr. Davis said. "I like to get to know all you artists in a friendly, homey way.

A little dancing, a song or two"— there seemed to be a visible lack of enthusiasm—"plenty of pop."

A pale smile lit Mr. Collier's face. "Well," he said, "it's very kind of you, Mr. Davis. We shall certainly appreciate it."

"Is the tree all right?"

"Yes, Mr. Daven—Davis, it's a magnificent tree." The young man in the blue jumper looked as if he were going to laugh, and Mr. Collier scowled at him. "We all thank you very much, Mr. Davis, don't we, girls?" Everybody said in refined and perfect chorus as if the words had been rehearsed, *"Rather,* Mr. Collier," except Miss Maydew, and a dark girl with a roving eye who was two seconds late and said, "You bet."

That attracted Mr. Davis's notice. Independent, he thought approvingly, stands out from the crowd. He said, "I think I'll step behind and look at the tree. Don't let me be in the way, old man. Just you carry on," and made his way into the wings, where the tree stood blocking the way to the changing rooms. An electrician had hung some of the baubles on for fun, and among the litter of properties under the bare globes it sparkled with icy dignity. Mr. Davis rubbed his hands, a buried childish delight came alive. He said, "It looks lovely." A kind of Christmas peace lay over his spirit; the occasional memory of Raven was only like the darkness pressing round the little lighted crib.

"That's a tree, all right," a voice said. It was the dark girl. She had followed him into the wings; she wasn't wanted on the stage for the number they were rehearsing. She was short and plump and not very pretty. She sat on a case and watched Mr. Davis with gloomy friendliness.

"Gives a Christmas feeling," Mr. Davis said.

"So will a bottle of pop," the girl said.

"What's your name?"

"Ruby."

"What about meeting me for a spot of lunch after the rehearsal's over?"

"Your girls sort of disappear, don't they?" Ruby said. "I could do with a steak and onions, but I don't want any conjuring. I'm not a detective's girl."

"What's that?" Mr. Davis said sharply.

"She's the Yard man's girl. He was round here yesterday."

"That's all right," Mr. Davis said crossly, thinking hard, "you're safe with me."

"You see, I'm unlucky."

Mr. Davis, in spite of his new anxiety, felt alive, vital. This wasn't *his* last day; the kidneys and bacon he had had for breakfast returned a little in his breath. The music came softly through to them: "Your photograph is just the sweetest half . . ." He licked a little grain of toffee on a back tooth as he stood under the tall, dark, gleaming tree and said, "You're in luck now. You couldn't have a better mascot than me."

"You'll have to do," the girl said with her habitual gloomy stare.

"The Metropole? At one, sharp?"

"I'll be there. Unless I'm run over. I'm the kind of girl who *would* get run over before a free feed."

"It'll be fun."

"It depends what you call fun," the girl said and made room for him on the packing case. They sat side by side staring at the tree. *In your December, I shall remember* . . . Mr. Davis put his hand on her bare knee. He was a little awed by the tune, the Christmas atmosphere. His hand fell flatly, reverently, like a bishop's hand on a choirboy's head.

"Sinbad," the girl said.

"Sinbad?"

"I mean Bluebeard. These pantos get one all mixed up."

"You aren't frightened of *me?*" Mr. Davis protested, leaning his head against the postman's cap.

"If any girl's going to disappear, it'll be me for sure."

"She shouldn't have left me," Mr. Davis said softly, "so soon after dinner. Made me go home alone. She'd have been safe with me." He put his arm tentatively round Ruby's waist and squeezed her, then loosed her hastily as an electrician came along. "You're a clever girl," Mr. Davis said, "you ought to have a part. I bet you've got a good voice."

"Me a voice? I've got as much voice as a peahen."

"Give me a little kiss?"

"Of course I will." They kissed rather wetly. "What do I call you?" Ruby said. "It sounds silly to me to call a man who's standing me a free feed Mister."

Mr. Davis said, "You could call me—Willy?"

"Well," Ruby said, sighing gloomily, "I hope I'll be seeing you, Willy. At the Metropole. At one. I'll be there. I only hope *you'll* be there, or bang'll go a good steak and onions." She drifted back towards the stage. She was needed. *What did Aladdin say* . . .

She said to the girl next her, "He fed out of my hand." *When he came to Pekin* . . . "The trouble is," Ruby said, "I can't keep them. There's too much of this love and ride away business. But it looks as if I'll get a good lunch, anyway." She said, "There I go again. Saying that and forgetting to cross my fingers."

Mr. Davis had seen enough. He had got what he'd come for. All that had to be done now was to shed a little light and comradeship among the electricians and other employees. He made his way slowly out by way of the dressing rooms, exchanging a word here and there, offering his gold cigarette case. One never knew. He was fresh to this backstage theatre, and it occurred to him that even among the dressers he might find—well, youth and talent, something to be encouraged, and fed too, of course, at the Metropole. He soon learned better: all the dressers were old; they couldn't understand what he was after, and one followed him round everywhere to make sure that he didn't hide in any of the girls' rooms. Mr. Davis was offended, but he was always polite. He departed through the stage door into the cold, tainted street, waving his hand. It was about time, anyway, that he looked in at Midland Steel and saw Sir Marcus. There should be good news for all of them this Christmas morning.

The High Street was curiously empty, except that there were more police about than was usual; he had quite forgotten the gas practice. No one attempted to interfere with Mr. Davis: his face was well known to all the force, though none of them could have said what Mr. Davis's occupation was. They would have said, without a smile at the thin hair, the heavy paunch, the plump and wrinkled hands, that he was one of Sir Marcus's young men. With an employer so old you could hardly avoid being one of the young men by comparison. Mr. Davis waved gaily to a sergeant on the other pavement and took a toffee. It was not the job of the police to take casualties to hospital, and no one would willingly have obstructed Mr. Davis. There was something about his fat good nature which easily turned to malevolence. They watched him, with covert amusement and hope, sail down the pavement towards the Tanneries, rather as one watches a man of some dignity approach an icy slide. Up the street from the Tanneries a medical student in a gas mask was approaching.

It was some while before Mr. Davis noticed the student, and the sight of the gas mask for a moment quite shocked him. He thought, These pacifists are going too far; sensational nonsense; and when the man halted Mr. Davis and said something which he could not catch through the heavy mask, Mr. Davis drew himself up and said haughtily, "Nonsense. We're well prepared." Then he remembered and became quite friendly again; it wasn't pacifism after all, it was patriotism. "Well, well," he said, "I quite forgot. Of course, the practice." The anonymous stare through the thickened eyepieces, the muffled voice, made him uneasy. He said jocularly, "You won't be taking *me* to the hospital now, will you? I'm a busy man." The student seemed lost in thought, with his hand on Mr. Davis's arm. Mr. Davis saw a policeman go grinning down the opposite pavement, and he found it hard to restrain his irritation. There was a little fog still left in the upper air, and a troop of planes drove through it, flying low, filling the street with their deep murmur, out towards the south and the aerodrome. "You see," Mr. Davis said, keeping his temper, "the practice is over. The sirens will be going any moment now. It would be too absurd to waste a morning at the hospital. You know me. Davis is the name. Everyone in Nottwich knows me. Ask the police that. No one can accuse *me* of being a bad patriot."

"You think it's nearly over?" the man said.

"I'm glad to see you boys enthusiastic," Mr. Davis said. "I expect we've met sometime at the hospital. I'm up there for all the big functions, and I never forget a voice. Why," Mr. Davis said, "it was me who gave the biggest contribution to the new operating theatre." Mr. Davis would have liked to walk on, but the man blocked his way, and it seemed a bit undignified to step into the road and go round him. The man might think he was trying to escape. There might be a tussle, and the police were looking on from the corner. A sudden venom spurted up into Mr. Davis's mind like the ink a cuttlefish shoots, staining his thoughts with its dark poison. That grinning ape in uniform—I'll have him dismissed, I'll see Calkin about it. He talked on cheerily to the man in the gas mask, a thin figure, little more than a boy's figure, on whom the white medical coat hung loosely. "You boys," Mr. Davis said, "are doing a splendid work. There's no one appreciates that more than I do. If war comes—"

"You call yourself Davis," the muffled voice said.

Mr. Davis said with sudden irritation, "You're wasting my time. I'm a busy man. Of course I'm Davis." He checked his rising temper with an effort. "Look here. I'm a reasonable man. I'll pay anything you like to the hospital. Say, ten pounds' ransom."

"Yes," the man said, "where is it?"

"You can trust me," Mr. Davis said. "I don't carry that much on me," and was amazed to hear what sounded like a laugh. This was going too far. "All right," Mr. Davis said, "you can come with me to my office, and I'll pay you the money. But I shall expect a proper receipt from your treasurer."

"You'll get your receipt," the man said in his odd, toneless, mask-muffled voice and stood on one side to let Mr. Davis lead the way. Mr. Davis's good humour was quite restored. He prattled on. "No good offering you a toffee in that thing," he said. A messenger boy passed in a gas mask with his cap cocked absurdly on the top of it; he whistled derisively at Mr. Davis. Mr. Davis went a little pink. His fingers itched to tear the hair, to pull the ear, to twist the wrist. "The boys enjoy themselves," he said. He became confiding; a doctor's presence always made him feel safe and oddly important: one could tell the most grotesque things to a doctor about one's digestion, and it was as much material for them as an amusing anec-dote was for a professional humorist. He said, "I've been getting hiccups badly lately. After every meal. It's not as if I eat fast—but, of course, you're only a student still. Though you know more about these things than I do. Then too I get spots before my eyes. Perhaps I ought to cut down my diet a bit But it's difficult. A man in my position has a lot of entertaining to do. For instance"—he grasped his companion's unresponsive arm and squeezed it knowingly—"it would be no good, my promising you that I'd go without my lunch today. You medicos are men of the world, and I don't mind telling you I've got a little girl meeting me. At the Metropole. At one." Some association of ideas made him feel in his pocket to make sure his packet of toffee was safe.

They passed another policeman, and Mr. Davis waved his hand. His companion was very silent. The boy's shy, Mr. Davis thought, he's not used to walking about town with a man like me. It excused a certain roughness in his behaviour; even the suspicion Mr. Davis had resented was probably only a form of gawkiness. Mr. Davis, because the day was proving fine after all, a little sun sparkling through the cold, obscured air; because the kidneys and bacon had really been done to a turn; because he had asserted himself in the presence of Miss Maydew, who was the daughter of a peer; because he had a date at the Metropole with a little girl of talent; because, too, by this time Raven's body would be safely laid out on its icy slab in the mortuary—for all these reasons Mr. Davis felt kindness

and Christmas in his spirit. He exerted himself to put the boy at his
ease. He said, "I feel sure we've met somewhere. Perhaps the house
surgeon introduced us." But his companion remained glumly un-
forthcoming. "A fine singsong you all put on at the opening of the
new ward." He glanced again at the delicate wrists. "You weren't
by any chance the boy who dressed up as a girl and sang that
naughty song?" Mr. Davis laughed thickly at the memory, turning
into the Tanneries, laughed as he had laughed more times than he
could count over the port, at the club, among the good fellows, at
the smutty masculine jokes. "I was tickled to death." He put his
hand on his companion's arm and pushed through the glass door of
Midland Steel.

A stranger stepped out from round a corner, and the clerk behind the inquiries counter told him in a strained voice, "That's all
right. That's Mr. Davis."

"What's all this?" Mr. Davis asked in a harsh no-nonsense voice
now that he was back where he belonged.

The detective said, "We are just keeping an eye open."

"Raven?" Mr. Davis asked in a rather shrill voice. The man
nodded. Mr. Davis said, "You let him escape? What fools—"

The detective said, "You needn't be scared. He'll be spotted at
once if he comes out of hiding. He can't escape this time."

"But why," Mr. Davis said, "are you here? Why do you expect—"

"We've got our orders," the man said.

"Have you told Sir Marcus?"

"He knows."

Mr. Davis looked tired and old. He said sharply to his companion, "Come with me, and I'll give you the money. I haven't any
time to waste." He walked with lagging, hesitating feet down a passage paved with some black shining composition to the glass lift
shaft. The man in the gas mask followed him down the passage and
into the lift. They moved slowly and steadily upwards together, as
intimate as two birds caged. Floor by floor the great building sank
below them, a clerk in a black coat, hurrying on some mysterious
errand which required a pot of bulbs; a girl standing outside a
closed door with a file of papers, whispering to herself, rehearsing
some excuse; an errand boy walking erratically along a passage,
balancing a bundle of new pencils on his head. They stopped at an
empty floor.

There was something on Mr. Davis's mind. He walked slowly,

turned the handle of his door softly, almost as if he feared that someone might be waiting for him inside. But the room was quite empty. An inner door opened, and a young woman with fluffy gold hair and exaggerated horn spectacles said, "Willy," and then saw his companion. She said, "Sir Marcus wants to see you, Mr. Davis."

"That's all right, Miss Connett," Mr. Davis said. "You might go and find me an A.B.C."

"Are you going away—at once?"

Mr. Davis hesitated. "Look me up what trains there are for town —after lunch."

"Yes, Mr. Davis." She withdrew, and the two of them were alone. Mr. Davis shivered slightly and turned on his electric fire. The man in the gas mask spoke, and again the muffled, coarse voice pricked at Mr. Davis's memory.

"Are you scared of something?"

"There's a madman loose in this town," Mr. Davis said. His nerves were alert at every sound in the corridor outside—a footstep, the ring of a bell. It had needed more courage than he had been conscious of possessing to say "after lunch"; he wanted to be away at once, clear away from Nottwich. He started at the scrape of a little cleaner's platform, which was being lowered down the wall of the inner courtyard. He padded to the door and locked it; it gave him a better feeling of security to be locked into his familiar room, with his desk, his swivel chair, the cupboard where he kept two glasses and a bottle of sweet port, the bookcase which contained a few technical works on steel, a Whitaker's, a Who's Who, and a copy of *His Chinese Concubine,* than to remember the detective in the hall. He took everything in like something seen for the first time, and it was true enough that he had never so realized the peace and comfort of his small room. Again he started at the creak of the ropes from which the cleaner's platform hung. He shut down his double window. He said in a tone of nervous irritation, "Sir Marcus can wait."

"Who's Sir Marcus?"

"My boss." Something about the open door of his secretary's room disturbed him with the idea that anyone could enter that way. He was no longer in a hurry, he wasn't busy any more, he wanted companionship. He said, "You aren't in any hurry. Take that thing off, it must be stuffy, and have a glass of port." On his way to the cupboard he shut the inner door and turned the key. He sighed with relief, fetching out the port and the glasses. "Now we are *really* alone, I want to tell you about these hiccups." He poured two brimming glasses, but his hand shook and the port ran down the sides. He said, "Always just after a meal—"

The muffled voice said, "The money."

"Really," Mr. Davis said, "you are rather impudent. You can trust *me*. I'm Davis." He went to his desk and unlocked a drawer, took out two five-pound notes, and held them out. "Mind," he said, "I shall expect a proper receipt from your treasurer."

The man put them away. His hand stayed in his pocket. He said, "Are these phony notes too?" A whole scene came back to Mr. Davis's mind: a Lyons' Corner House, the taste of an Alpine Glow, the murderer sitting opposite him, trying to tell him of the old woman he had killed. Mr. Davis screamed—not a word, not a plea for help, just a meaningless cry such as a man gives under an anesthetic when the knife cuts the flesh. He ran, bolted, across the room to the inner door and tugged at the handle. He struggled uselessly as if he were caught on barbed wire between trenches.

"Come away from there," Raven said. "You've locked the door."

Mr. Davis came back to the desk. His legs gave way, and he sat on the floor beside the wastepaper basket. He said, "I'm sick. You wouldn't kill a sick man." The idea really gave him hope. He retched convincingly.

"I'm not going to kill you yet," Raven said. "Maybe I won't kill you if you keep quiet and do what I say. This Sir Marcus, he's your boss?"

"An old man," Mr. Davis protested, weeping beside the wastepaper basket.

"He wants to see you," Raven said. "We'll go along." He said, "I've been waiting days for this—to find the two of you. It almost seems too good to be true. Get up. Get up!" he repeated furiously to the weak, flabby figure on the floor. "Remember this: If you squeal I'll plug you so full of lead they'll be able to use you as a doorstop."

Mr. Davis led the way. Miss Connett came down the passage, carrying a slip of paper. She said, "I've got the trains down, Mr. Davis. The best is the three-five. The two-seven is really so slow that you wouldn't be up more than ten minutes earlier. Then there's only the five-ten before the night train."

"Put them on my desk," Mr. Davis said. He hung about there in front of her in the shining modern plutocratic passage as if he wanted to say good-bye to a thousand things if only he dared: to this wealth, this comfort, this authority. Lingering there ("Yes, put them on my desk, May"), he might even have been waiting to express at the last some tenderness that had never before entered his mind in connection with "little girls." Raven stood just behind him with his hand in his pocket. Her employer looked so sick that Miss Connett said, "Are you feeling well, Mr. Davis?"

"Quite well," Mr. Davis said. Like an explorer going into strange country, he felt the need of leaving some record behind at the edge of civilization, to say to the last chance comer, "I shall be going towards the north" or "the west." He said, "We are going to see Sir Marcus, May."

"He's in a hurry for you," Miss Connett said. A telephone bell rang. "I shouldn't be surprised if that's him now." She pattered down the corridor to her room on very high heels, and Mr. Davis felt again the remorseless pressure on his elbow to advance, to enter the lift. They rose another floor, and when Mr. Davis pulled the gates apart he retched again. He wanted to fling himself to the floor and take the bullets in his back. The long gleaming passage to Sir Marcus's study was like a mile-long stadium track to a winded and defeated runner.

Sir Marcus was sitting in his bath chair with a kind of bed table on his knees. He had his valet with him, and his back was to the door, but the valet could see with astonishment Mr. Davis's exhausted entrance in the company of a medical student in a gas mask. "Is that Davis?" Sir Marcus whispered. He broke a dry biscuit and sipped a little hot milk. He was fortifying himself for a day's work.

"Yes, sir." The valet watched with astonishment Mr. Davis's sick progress across the hygienic rubber floor; he looked as if he needed support, as if he was about to collapse at the knees.

"Get out then," Sir Marcus whispered.

"Yes, sir." But the man in the gas mask had turned the key of the door. A faint expression of joy, a rather hopeless expectation, crept into the valet's face, as if he were wondering whether something at last was going to happen, something different from pushing bath chairs along rubber floors, dressing and undressing an old man not strong enough to keep himself clean, bringing him the hot milk or the hot water or the dry biscuits.

"What are you waiting for?" Sir Marcus whispered.

"Get back against the wall," Raven suddenly commanded the valet.

Mr. Davis cried despairingly, "He's got a gun. Do what he says." But there was no need to tell the valet that. The gun was out now and had them all three covered, the valet against the wall, Mr. Davis dithering in the middle of the room, Sir Marcus, who had twisted the bath chair round to face them.

"What do you want?" Sir Marcus said.

"Are you the boss?"

Sir Marcus said, "The police are downstairs. You can't get away from here unless I—" The telephone began to ring. It rang on and on and on, and then ceased.

Raven said, "You've got a scar under that beard, haven't you? I don't want to make a mistake. He had your photograph. You were in the home together," and he glared angrily round the large, rich office room, comparing it in mind with his own memories of cracked bells and stone stairs and wooden benches, and of the small flat, too, with the egg boiling in the ring. This man had moved farther than the old minister.

"You're mad," Sir Marcus whispered. He was too old to be frightened; the revolver represented no greater danger to him than a false step in getting into his chair, a slip in his bath. He seemed to feel only a faint irritation, a faint craving for his interrupted meal. He bent his old lip forward over the bed table and sucked loudly at the rim of hot milk.

The valet spoke suddenly from the wall. "He's got a scar," he said. But Sir Marcus took no notice of any of them, sucking up his milk untidily over his thin beard.

Raven twisted his gun on Mr. Davis. "It was him," he said. "If you don't want a bullet in your guts tell me it was him."

"Yes, yes," Mr. Davis said in horrified subservient haste, "the thought of it. It was his idea. We were on our last legs here. We'd got to make money. It was worth more than half a million to him."

"Half a million," Raven said. "And he paid me two hundred phony pounds."

"I said to him we ought to be generous. He said, 'Stop your mouth.'"

"I wouldn't have done it," Raven said, "if I'd known the old man was like he was. I smashed his skull for him. And the old woman, a bullet in both eyes." He shouted at Sir Marcus, "That was your doing. How do you like that?" But the old man sat there apparently unmoved; old age had killed the imagination. The deaths he had ordered were no more real to him than the deaths he read about in the newspapers. A little greed (for his milk), a little vice (occasionally to put his old hand inside a girl's blouse), a little avarice and calculation (half a million against a death), a very small, persistent, almost mechanical, sense of self-preservation—these were his only passions. The last made him edge his chair imperceptibly towards the bell at the edge of his desk. He whispered gently, "I deny it all. You are mad."

Raven said, "I've got you now where I want you. Even if the police kill me"—he tapped the gun—"here's my evidence. This is the gun I used. They can pin the murder to this gun. You told me to leave it behind, but here it is. It would put you away a long, long time even if I didn't shoot you."

Sir Marcus whispered gently, imperceptibly twisting his silent, rubbered wheels, "A Colt number seven. The factories turn out thousands."

Raven said angrily, "There's nothing the police can't do now with a gun. There are experts." He wanted to frighten Sir Marcus before he shot him; it seemed unfair to him that Sir Marcus should suffer less than the old woman he hadn't wanted to kill. He said, "Don't you want to pray? Better people than you," he said, "believe in a God," remembering how the girl had prayed in the dark, cold shed. The wheel of Sir Marcus's chair touched the desk, touched the bell, and the dull ringing came up the well of the lift, going on and on. It conveyed nothing to Raven until the valet spoke. "The old bastard," he said, with the hatred of years, "he's ringing the bell." Before Raven could decide what to do someone was at the door, shaking the handle.

Raven said to Sir Marcus, "Tell them to keep back or I'll shoot."

"You fool," Sir Marcus whispered, "they'll only get you for theft. If you kill me, you'll hang." But Mr. Davis was ready to clutch at any straw. He screamed to the man outside, "Keep away. For God's sake keep away."

Sir Marcus said venomously, "You're a fool, Davis. If he's going to kill us anyway—" While Raven stood, pistol in hand, before the two men, an absurd quarrel broke out between them.

"He's got no cause to kill me," Mr. Davis screamed. "It's you who've got us into this. I only acted for you."

The valet began to laugh. "Two to one on the field," he said.

"Be quiet," Sir Marcus whispered venomously back at Mr. Davis. "I can put you out of the way at any time."

"I defy you," Mr. Davis screamed in a high peacock voice. Somebody flung himself against the door.

"I have the West Rand Goldfields filed," Sir Marcus said, "the East African Petroleum Company."

A wave of impatience struck Raven. They seemed to be disturbing some memory of peace and goodness which had been on the point of returning to him when he had told Sir Marcus to pray. He raised his pistol and shot Sir Marcus in the chest. It was the only way to silence them. Sir Marcus fell forward across the bed table, upsetting the glass of warm milk over the papers on his desk. Blood came out of his mouth.

Mr. Davis began to talk very rapidly. He said, "It was all him, the old devil. You heard him. What could I do? He had me. You've got nothing against me." He shrieked, "Go away from that door. He'll kill me if you don't go," and immediately began to talk again, while the milk dripped from the bed table to the desk, drop by drop. "I wouldn't have done a thing if it hadn't been for him. Do you know what he did? He went and told the chief constable to order the police to shoot you on sight." He tried not to look at the pistol which remained pointed at his chest. The valet was white and silent by the wall; he watched Sir Marcus's life bleeding away with curious fascination. So this was what it would have been like, he seemed to be thinking, if he himself had had courage—any time, during all these years.

A voice outside said, "You had better open this door at once, or we'll shoot through it."

"For God's sake," Mr. Davis screamed, "leave me alone. He'll shoot me," and the eyes watched him intently through the panes of the gas mask with satisfaction. "There's not a thing I've done to you," he began to protest. Over Raven's head he could see the clock; it hadn't moved more than three hours since his breakfast; the hot, stale taste of the kidneys and bacon was still on his palate. He couldn't believe that this was really the end. At one o'clock he had a date with a girl—you didn't die before a date. "Nothing," he murmured, "nothing at all."

"It was you," Raven said, "who tried to kill—"

"Nobody. Nothing." Mr. Davis moaned.

Raven hesitated. The word was still unfamiliar on his tongue "—my friend."

"I don't know. I don't understand."

"Keep back," Raven cried through the door. "I'll shoot him if you fire." He said, "The girl."

Mr. Davis shook all over. He was like a man with St. Vitus' dance. He said, "She wasn't a friend of yours. Why are the police here if she didn't—who else could have known—"

Raven said, "I'll shoot you for that and nothing else. She's straight."

"Why," Mr. Davis screamed at him, "she's a policeman's girl. She's the Yard man's girl. She's Mather's girl."

Raven shot him. With despair and deliberation he shot his last chance of escape, plugged two bullets in where one would do, as if he were shooting the whole world in the person of stout, moaning, bleeding Mr. Davis. And so he was. For a man's world is his life, and he was shooting that: his mother's suicide, the long years in the home, the race-course gangs, Kite's death, and the old man's and the woman's. There was no other way; he had tried the way of confession, and it had failed him for the usual reason. There was no one outside your own brain whom you could trust—not a doctor, not a priest, not a woman. A siren blew up over the town, its message that the sham raid was over, and immediately the church-bells broke into a noisy Christmas carol—the foxes have their holes, but the son of man . . . A bullet smashed the lock of the door. Raven, with his gun pointed stomach-high, said, "Is there a bastard called Mather out there? He'd better keep away."

While he waited for the door to open he couldn't help remembering many things. He did not remember them in detail; they fogged together and formed the climate of his mind as he waited there for the chance of a last revenge: a voice singing above a dark street as the sleet fell, "They say that's a snowflower a man brought from Greenland"; the cultivated, unlived voice of the elderly critic reading *Maud*: "Oh,, that 'twere possible after long grief . . ." While he stood in the garage and felt the ice melt at his heart with a sense of pain and strangeness as if he were passing the customs of a land he had never entered before and would never be able to leave; the girl in the café, saying, "He's bad and ugly . . ." the little plaster child lying in its mother's arms, waiting the double-cross, the whips, the nails. She had said to him, "I'm your friend. You can trust me." Another bullet burst in the lock.

The valet, white-faced by the wall, said, "For God's sake, give it up. They'll get you anyway. He was right. It *was* the girl. I heard them on the phone."

I've got to be quick, Raven thought, when the door gives. I must shoot first. But too many ideas besieged his brain at once. He couldn't see clearly enough through the mask, and he undid it clumsily with one hand and dropped it on the floor. The valet could see now the raw, inflamed lip, the dark and miserable eyes. He said, "There's the window. Get onto the roof." He was talking to a man whose understanding was dulled, who didn't know whether he wished to make an effort or not, who moved his face so slowly to see the window that it was the valet who noticed first the painter's platform swinging down the wide, tall pane. Mather was on the platform; it was a desperate attempt to catch Raven in the rear, but the detective had not allowed for his own inexperience. The little platform swung this way and that; he held a rope with one hand and reached for the window with the other; he had no hand free for his revolver as Raven turned. He dangled outside the window six floors above the narrow Tanneries, a defenceless mark for Raven's pistol.

Raven watched him with bemused eyes, trying to take aim. It wasn't a difficult shot, but it was almost as if he had lost interest in killing. He was only aware of a pain and despair which was more like a complete weariness than anything else. He couldn't work up any sourness, any bitterness, at his betrayal. The dark Weevil under the storm of frozen rain flowed between him and any human enemy. "Ah, Christ that it were possible," but he had been marked from his birth for this end, to be betrayed in turn by everyone until every avenue into life was safely closed: by his mother bleeding in the basement, by the chaplain at the home, by the soft kids who had left it with him, by the shady doctor off Charlotte Street. How could he have expected to escape the commonest betrayal of all, to go soft on a skirt? Even Kite would have been alive now if it hadn't been for a skirt. They all went soft at some time or another: Penrith and Carter, Jossy and Ballard, Barker and the Great Dane. He took aim slowly, absent-mindedly, with a curious humility, with almost a sense of companionship in his loneliness: the trooper and Mayhew. They had all thought at one time or another that their skirt was better than other men's skirts, that there was something exalted in *their* relation The only problem when you were once born was to get out of life more neatly and expeditiously than you had entered it For the first time the idea of his mother's suicide came to him without bitterness, as he fixed his aim at the long reluctant last and Saunders shot him in the back through the opening door Death came to him in the form of unbearable pain It was as if he had to deliver this pain as a woman delivers a child, and he sobbed and moaned in the effort. At last it came out of him, and he followed his only child into a vast desolation.

Eight

1

The smell of food came through into the lounge whenever somebody passed in or out of the restaurant. The local Rotarians were having a lunch in one of the private rooms upstairs, and when the door opened Ruby could hear a cork pop and the scrap of a limerick. It was five past one. Ruby went out and chatted to the porter. She said, "The worst of it is I'm one of the girls who turn up on the stroke. One o'clock, he said, and here I am, panting for a good meal. I know a girl ought to keep a man waiting, but what do you do if you're hungry? He might go in and start." She said, "The trouble is I'm unlucky. I'm the kind of girl who daren't have a bit of fun because she'd be dead sure to get a baby Well, I don't mean I've had a baby, but I did catch mumps once. Would you believe a grown man could give a girl mumps? But I'm that kind of girl." She said, "You look fine in all that gold braid with those medals. You might say something."

The market was more than usually full, for everyone had come out late to do their shopping now that the gas practice was over Only Mrs. Alfred Piker, as Lady Mayoress, had set an example by shopping in a mask. Now she was walking home, and Chinky trotted beside her, trailing his low fur and the feathers on his legs in the cold slush, carrying her mask between his teeth. He stopped by a lamp post and dropped it in a puddle "Oh, Chinky, you bad little thing," Mrs. Piker said. The porter in his uniform glared out over the market. He wore the Mons medal and the Military medal. He had been three times wounded. He swung the glass door as the businessmen came in for their lunch, the head traveller of Crosthwaite and Crosthwaite, the managing director of the big grocery business in the High Street. Once he darted out into the road and disentangled a fat man from a taxi. Then he came back and stood beside Ruby and listened to her with expressionless good humour

"Ten minutes late," Ruby said. "I thought he was a man a girl could trust. I ought to have touched wood or crossed my fingers It serves me right. I'd rather have lost my honour than that steak. Do you know him? He flings his weight about a lot. Called Davis."

"He's always in here with girls," the porter said.

A little man in pince-nez bustled by. "A merry Christmas, Hallows."

"A merry Christmas to you, sir." The porter said, "You wouldn't have got very far with him."

"I haven't got as far as the soup," Ruby said.

A newsboy went by, calling out a special midday edition of the *News,* the evening edition of the *Journal;* and a few minutes later another newsboy went past with a special edition of the *Post,* the evening edition of the more aristocratic *Guardian.* It was impossible to hear what they were shouting, and the northeast wind flapped their posters so that on one it was only possible to read the syllable "gedy" and on the other the syllable "der."

"There are limits," Ruby said. "A girl can't afford to make herself cheap. Ten minutes' wait is the outside limit."

"You've waited more than that now," the porter said.

Ruby said, "I'm like that. You'd say I flung myself at men, wouldn't you? That's what I think, but I never seem to hit them." She added with deep gloom, "The trouble is, I'm the kind that's born to make a man happy. It's written all over me. It keeps them away. I don't blame them. I shouldn't like it myself."

"There goes the chief constable," the porter said. "Off to get a drink at the police station. His wife won't let him have them at home. The best of the season to you, sir."

"He seems in a hurry." A newspaper poster flapped "Trag—" at them. "Is he the kind that would buy a girl a good rump steak with onions and fried potatoes?"

"I tell you what," the porter said. "You wait around another five minutes and then I shall be going off for lunch."

"That's a date," Ruby said. She crossed her fingers and touched wood. Then she went and sat inside and carried on a long conversation with an imaginary theatrical producer whom she imagined rather like Mr. Davis, but a Mr. Davis who kept his engagements. The producer called her a little woman with talent, asked her to dinner, took her back to a luxurious flat, and gave her several cocktails. He asked her what she would think of a West End engagement at fifteen pounds a week and said he wanted to show her his flat. Ruby's dark, plump, gloomy face lightened. She swung one leg excitedly and attracted the angry attention of a businessman who was making notes of the midday prices. He found another chair and muttered to himself. Ruby, too, muttered to herself. She was saying, "This is the dining room. And through here is the bathroom. And this—elegant, isn't it?—is the bedroom." Ruby said promptly that she'd like the fifteen pounds a week, but need she have the West End engagement? Then she looked at the clock and went outside. The porter was waiting for her.

"What?" Ruby said. "Have I got to go out with that uniform?"

"I only get twenty minutes," the porter said.

"No rump steak then," Ruby said. "Well, I suppose sausages would do."

They sat at a lunch counter on the other side of the market and had sausages and coffee. "That uniform," Ruby said, "makes me embarrassed. Everyone'll think you're a guardsman going with a girl for a change."

"Did you hear the shooting?" the man behind the counter said.

"What shooting?"

"Just round the corner from you at Midland Steel. Three dead. That old devil Sir Marcus, and two others." He laid the midday paper open on the counter, and the old wicked face of Sir Marcus, the plump anxious features of Mr. Davis, stared up at them beyond the sausages, the coffee cups, the pepper pot, beside the hot-water urn.

"So that's why he didn't come," Ruby said. She was silent for a while, reading.

"I wonder what this Raven was after," the porter said. "Look here," and he pointed to a small paragraph at the foot of the column, which announced that the head of the special political department of Scotland Yard had arrived by air and gone straight to the offices of Midland Steel.

"It doesn't mean a thing to me," Ruby said.

The porter turned the pages, looking for something. He said, "Funny thing, isn't it? Here we are just going to war again, and they fill up the front page with a murder. It's driven the war onto a back page."

"Perhaps there won't be a war."

They were silent over their sausages. It seemed odd to Ruby that Mr. Davis, who had sat on the box with her and looked at the Christmas tree, should be dead, so violently and painfully dead. Perhaps he had meant to keep the date. He wasn't a bad sort. She said, "I feel kind of sorry for him."

"Who? Raven?"

"Oh no, not him. Mr. Davis, I mean."

"I know how you feel. I almost feel sorry too—for the old man. I was in Midland Steel myself once. He had his moments. He used to send round turkeys at Christmas. He wasn't too bad. It's more than they do at the hotel."

"Well," Ruby said, draining her coffee, "life goes on."

"Have another cup."

"I don't want to sting you."

"That's all right." Ruby leaned against him on the high stool; their heads touched. They were a little quietened because each had known a man who was suddenly dead; but the knowledge they shared gave them a sense of companionship which was oddly sweet and reassuring. It was like feeling safe, like feeling in love without the passion, the uncertainty, the pain.

2

Saunders asked a clerk in Midland Steel the way to a lavatory. He washed his hands and thought, "That job's over." It hadn't been a satisfactory job; what had begun as a plain robbery had ended with two murders and the death of the murderer. There was a mystery about the whole affair—everything hadn't come out. Mather was up there on the top floor now with the head of the political department. They were going through Sir Marcus's private papers. It really seemed as if the girl's story might be true.

The girl worried Saunders more than anything. He couldn't help admiring her courage and impertinence at the same time as he hated her for making Mather suffer. He was ready to hate anyone who hurt Mather. "She'll have to be taken to the Yard," Mather had said. "There may be a charge against her. Put her in a locked carriage on the three-five. I don't want to see her until this thing's cleared up." The only cheerful thing about the whole business was that the constable whom Raven had shot in the coal yard was pulling through.

Saunders came out of Midland Steel into the Tanneries with an odd sensation of having nothing to do. He went into a public house at the corner of the market and had half a pint of bitter and two cold sausages. It was as if life had sunk again to the normal level, was flowing quietly by once more between its banks. A card hanging behind the bar next a few cinema posters caught his eye: "A

New Cure for Stammerers." Mr. Montague Phelps, M.A., was
holding a public meeting in the Masonic Hall to explain his new
treatment. Entrance was free, but there would be a silver collection.
Two o'clock sharp. At one cinema Eddie Cantor. At another
George Arliss. Saunders didn't want to go back to the police station
until it was time to take the girl to the train. He had tried a good
many cures for stammering; he might as well try one more.

It was a large hall. On the walls hung large photographs of Masonic dignitaries. They all wore ribbons and badges of strange significance. There was an air of oppressive well-being, of successful
groceries, about the photographs. They hung, the well fed, the successful, the assured, over the small gathering of misfits in old mackintoshes, in rather faded mauve felt hats, in school ties. Saunders
entered behind a fat, furtive woman, and a steward stammered at
him, "T-t-t—?" "One," Saunders said. He sat down near the front
and heard a stammered conversation going on behind him, like the
twitters of two Chinamen. Little bursts of impetuous talk and then
the fatal impediment. There were about fifty people in the hall.
They eyed each other rather as an ugly man eyes himself in shop
windows: from this angle, he thinks, I am really not too bad. They
gained a sense of companionship; their mutual lack of communication was in itself like a communication. They waited together for a
miracle.

Saunders waited with them; waited as he had waited on the wind-
less side of the coal truck, with the same patience. He wasn't unhappy. He knew that he probably exaggerated the value of what he
lacked. Even if he could speak freely, without care to avoid the
dentals which betrayed him, he would probably find it no easier to
express his admiration and his affection. The power to speak didn't
give you words.

Mr. Montague Phelps, M.A., came onto the platform. He wore a
frock coat, and his hair was dark and oiled. His blue chin was
lightly powdered, and he carried himself with a rather aggressive
sangfroid, as much as to say to the depressed, inhibited gathering,
"See what you too might become, with a little more self-confidence,
after a few lessons from me." He was a man of about forty-two who
had lived well, who obviously had a private life. One thought in his
presence of comfortable beds and heavy meals and Brighton hotels.
For a moment he reminded Saunders of Mr. Davis, who had
bustled so importantly into the offices of Midland Steel that morning and had died very painfully and suddenly half an hour later. It

almost seemed as if Raven's act had had no consequences; as if to kill was just as much an illusion as to dream. Here was Mr. Davis all over again; they were turned out of a mould, and you couldn't break the *mould*. And suddenly, over Mr. Montague Phelps's shoulder, Saunders saw the photograph of the Grand Master of the Lodge above the platform—an old face and a crooked nose and a tuft of beard: Sir Marcus.

3

Major Calkin was very white when he left Midland Steel. He had seen for the first time the effect of violent death. That was war. He made his way as quickly as he could to the police station and was glad to find the superintendent in. He asked quite humbly for a spot of whisky. He said, "It shakes you up. Only last night he had dinner at my house. Mrs. Piker was there with her dog. What a time we had, stopping him knowing the dog was there."

"That dog," the superintendent said, "gives us more trouble than any man in Nottwich. Did I ever tell you the time it got in the women's lavatory in Higham Street? That dog isn't much to look at, but every once in a while it goes crazy. If it wasn't Mrs. Piker's we'd have had it destroyed many a time."

Major Calkin said, "He wanted me to give orders to your men to shoot this fellow on sight. I told him I couldn't. Now I can't help thinking we might have saved two lives."

"Don't you worry, sir," the superintendent said, "we couldn't have taken orders like that. Not from the Home Secretary himself."

"He was an odd fellow," Major Calkin said. "He seemed to think I'd be certain to have a hold over some of you. He promised me all kinds of things. I suppose he was what you'd call a genius. We shan't see his like again. What a waste." He poured himself out some more whisky. "Just at a time too when we need men like him. War." Major Calkin paused with his hand on his glass. He stared into the whisky, seeing things: the remount depot, his uniform in the cupboard. He would never be a colonel now, but on the other hand Sir Marcus could not prevent— But curiously he felt no elation at the thought of once more presiding over the tribunal. He said, "The gas practice seems to have gone off well. But I don't know that it was wise to leave so much to the medical students. They don't know where to stop."

"There was a pack of them," the superintendent said, "went

howling past here looking for the mayor. I don't know how it is Mr. Piker seems to be like catmint to those students."

"Good old Piker," Major Calkin said mechanically.

"They go too far," the superintendent said. "I had a ring from Higginbotham, the cashier at the Westminster. He said his daughter went into the garage and found one of these students there without his trousers."

Life began to come back to Major Calkin. He said, "That'll be Rose Higginbotham, I suppose. Trust Rose. What did she do?"

"He said she gave him a dressing down."

"Dressing down's good," Major Calkin said. He twisted his glass and drained his whisky. "I must tell that to old Piker. What did you say?"

"I told him his daughter was lucky not to find a murdered man in the garage. You see, that's where Raven must have got his clothes and his mask."

"What was the boy doing at the Higginbothams' anyway?" Major Calkin asked. "I think I'll go and cash a cheque and ask old Higginbotham that." He began to laugh. The air was clear again; life was going on quite in the old way: a little scandal, a drink with the super, a story to tell old Piker. On his way to the Westminster he nearly ran into Mrs. Piker. He had to dive hastily into a shop to avoid her, and for a horrible moment he thought Chinky, who was some way ahead of her, was going to follow him inside. He made motions of throwing a ball down the street, but Chinky was not a sporting dog, and anyway he was trailing a gas mask in his teeth. Major Calkin had to turn his back abruptly and lean over a counter. He found it was a small haberdasher's. He had never been in the shop before.

"What can I get you, sir?"

"Suspenders," Major Calkin said desperately. "A pair of suspenders."

"What colour, sir?" Out of the corner of his eye Major Calkin saw Chinky trot on past the shop door, followed by Mrs. Piker.

"Mauve," he said with relief.

4

The old woman shut the front door softly and trod on tiptoe down the little dark hall. A stranger could not have seen his way, but she knew exactly the position of the hatrack, of the whatnot table, and the staircase. She was carrying an evening paper, and when she opened the kitchen door with the very minimum of noise so as not to disturb Acky, her face was alight with exhilaration and excitement. But she held it in, carrying her basket over to the draining board and unloading there her burden of potatoes, a tin of pineapple chunks, two eggs, and a slab of cod.

Acky was writing a long letter on the kitchen table. He had pushed his wife's mauve ink to one side and was using the best blue-black and a fountain pen which had long ceased to hold ink. He wrote slowly and painfully, sometimes making a rough copy of a sentence on another slip of paper. The old woman stood beside the sink, watching him, waiting for him to speak, holding her breath in, so that sometimes it escaped in little whistles. At last Acky laid down his pen. "Well, my dear?" he said.

"Oh, Acky," the old woman said with glee, "what do you think? That Mr. Cholmondeley is dead. Killed." She added, "It's in the paper. And that Raven too."

Acky looked at the paper. "Quite horrible," he said with satisfaction. "Another death as well. A holocaust." He read the account slowly.

"Fancy a thing like that 'appening 'ere in Nottwich."

"He was a bad man," Acky said, "though I wouldn't speak ill of him now that he's dead. He involved us in something of which I was ashamed. I think perhaps now it will be safe for us to stay in Nottwich." A look of great weariness passed over his face as he looked down at the three pages of small, neat, classical handwriting.

"Oh, Acky, you've been tiring yourself."

"I think," Acky said, "this will make it clear."

"Read it to me, love," the old woman said. Her little old vicious face was heavily creased with tenderness as she leaned back against the sink in an attitude of infinite patience. Acky began to read. He spoke at first in a low, hesitating way, but he gained confidence from the sound of his own voice; his hand went up to the lapel of his coat.

" 'My Lord Bishop—' " He said, "I thought it best to begin formally, not to trespass at all on my former acquaintanceship."

"That's right, Acky, you are worth the whole bunch."

" 'I am writing to you for the fourth time, after an interval of some eighteen months.' "

"Is it so long, love? It was after we took the trip to Clacton."

"Sixteen months. 'I am quite aware what your previous answers have been, that my case has been tried already in the proper church court, but I cannot believe, my Lord Bishop, that your sense of justice, if once I convince you of what a deeply injured man I am, will not lead you to do all that is in your power to have my case reheard. I have been condemned to suffer all my life for what in the case of other men is regarded as a peccadillo, a peccadillo of which I am not even guilty.' "

"It's written lovely, love."

"At this point, my dear, I come down to particulars. 'How, my Lord Bishop, could the hotel domestic swear to the identity of a man seen once, a year before the trial, in a darkened chamber, for in her evidence she agreed that he had not allowed her to draw up the blind? As for the evidence of the porter, my Lord Bishop, I asked in court whether it was not true that money had passed from Colonel and Mrs. Mark Egerton into his hands, and my question was disallowed. Is this justice, founded on scandal, misapprehension, and perjury?' "

The old woman smiled with tenderness and pride. "This is the best letter you've written, Acky, so far."

" 'My Lord Bishop, it was well known in the parish that Colonel Mark Egerton was my bitterest enemy on the church council, and it was at his instigation that the inquiry was held. As for Mrs. Mark Egerton, she was a bitch.' "

"Is that wise, Acky?"

"Sometimes, dear, one reaches an impasse when there is nothing to be done but to speak out. At this point I take the evidence in detail as I have done before, but I think I have sharpened my arguments more than a little. And at the end, my dear, I address the worldly man in the only way he can understand." He knew this passage by heart. He reeled it fierily off at her, raising his crazy, sunken, flawed saint's eyes. " 'But even assuming, my Lord Bishop, that this perjured and bribed evidence were accurate, what then? Have I committed the unforgivable sin that I must suffer all my life long, be deprived of my livelihood, depend on ignoble methods to raise enough money to keep myself and my wife alive? Man, my Lord Bishop—and no one knows it better than yourself; I have seen you among the fleshpots at the palace—is made up of body as well as soul. A little carnality may be forgiven even to a man of my cloth. Even you, my Lord Bishop, have in your time no doubt sported among the haycocks.' " He stopped; he was a little out of breath. They stared back at each other with awe and affection.

Acky said, "I want to write a little piece, dear, now, about you."
He took in with what could only have been the deepest and the
purest love the black, sagging skirt, the soiled blouse, the yellow
wrinkled face. "My dear," he said, "what I should have done without—" He began to make a rough draft of yet another paragraph,
speaking the phrases aloud as he wrote them. " 'What I should have
done during this long trial—no, martyrdom—I do not know—I
cannot conceive—if I had not been supported by the trust and the
unswerving fidelity—no, fidelity and unswerving trust of my dear
wife, a wife whom Mrs. Mark Egerton considered herself in a position to despise. As if Our Lord had chosen the rich and well-born
to serve Him. At least this trial—has taught me to distinguish between my friends and enemies. And yet at my trial *her* word, the
word of the woman who loved and believed in me, counted—for
nought beside the word—of that—that—trumpery and deceitful
scandalmonger.' "

The old woman leaned forward with tears of pride and importance in her eyes. She said, "That's lovely. Do you think the bishop's
wife will read it? Oh dear, I know I ought to go and tidy the
room upstairs (we might be getting some young people in), but
some'ow, Acky dear, I'd just like to stay right 'ere with you awhile.
What you write makes me feel kind of 'oly." She slumped down on
the kitchen chair beside the sink and watched his hand move on, as
if she were watching some unbelievably lovely vision passing
through the room, something which she had never hoped to see and
now was hers.

"And finally, my dear," Acky said, "I propose to write, 'In a
world of perjury and all manner of uncharitableness one woman
remains my sheet anchor, one woman I can trust until death and beyond.' "

"They ought to be ashamed of themselves. Oh, Acky, my dear"
—she wept—"to think they've treated you that way. But you've
said true. I won't ever leave you. I won't leave you, not even when
I'm dead. Never, never, never," and the two old vicious faces regarded each other with the complete belief, the awe and mutual
suffering of a great love, while they affirmed their eternal union.

5

Anne cautiously felt the door of the compartment in which she
had been left alone. It was locked, as she had thought it would be

in spite of Saunders' tact and his attempt to hide what he was doing. She stared out at the dingy Midland station with dismay. It seemed to her that everything which made her life worth the effort of living was lost—she hadn't even got a job—and she watched between an advertisement of Horlick's for night starvation and a bright blue-and-yellow picture of the Yorkshire coast the weary pilgrimage which lay before her from agent to agent. The train began to move past the waiting rooms, the lavatories, the sloping concrete, into a waste of rails.

What a fool, she thought, I have been, thinking I could save us from a war. Three men are dead, that's all. Now that she was herself responsible for so many deaths, she could no longer feel the same repulsion towards Raven. In this waste through which she travelled, between the stacks of coal, the tumbledown sheds, abandoned trucks in sidings where a little grass had poked up and died between the cinders, she thought of him again with pity and distress. They had been on the same side, he had trusted her, she had given her word to him, and then she had broken it without even the grace of hesitation. He must have known of her treachery before he died; in that dead mind she was preserved forever with the chaplain who had tried to frame him, with the doctor who had telephoned to the police.

Well, she had lost the only man she cared a damn about—it was always regarded as some kind of atonement, she thought, to suffer too—lost him for no reason at all. For *she* couldn't stop a war. Men were fighting beasts; they needed war. In the paper that Saunders had left for her on the opposite seat she could read how the mobilization in four countries was complete, how the ultimatum expired at midnight; it was no longer on the front page, but that was only because to Nottwich readers there was a war nearer at hand, fought out to a finish in the Tanneries. How they love it, she thought bitterly, as the dusk came up from the dark wounded ground and the glow of furnaces became visible beyond the long black ridge of slag heaps. This was war too—this chaos through which the train moved slowly, grinding over point after point like a dying creature dragging itself painfully away through no man's land from the scene of battle.

She pressed her face against the window to keep her tears away; the cold pressure of the frosting pane stiffened her resistance. The train gathered speed by a small neo-Gothic church, a row of villas, and then the country, the fields, a few cows making for an open gate, a hard, broken lane, and a cyclist lighting his lamp. She began to hum to keep her spirits up, but the only tunes she could remember were "Aladdin" and "It's Only Kew." She thought of the long bus ride home, the voice on the telephone, and how she couldn't get to the window to wave to him and he had stood there with his back to her while the train went by. It was Mr. Davis even then who had ruined everything.

And it occurred to her, staring out at the bleak, frozen country-side, that perhaps, even if she had been able to save the country from a war, it wouldn't have been worth the saving. She thought of Mr. Davis and Acky and his old wife, of the producer and Miss Maydew and the landlady at her lodging with the bead of liquid on her nose. What had made her play so absurd a part? If she had not offered to go out to dinner with Mr. Davis, Raven probably would be in jail and the others alive. She tried to remember the watching, anxious faces studying the sky signs in Nottwich High Street, but she couldn't remember them with any vividness.

The door into the corridor was unlocked, and, staring through the window into the grey, fading winter light, she thought, More questions. Will they never stop worrying me? She said aloud, "I've made my statement, haven't I?"

Mather's voice said, "There are still a few things to discuss."

She turned hopelessly towards him. "Need *you* have come?"

"I'm in charge of this case," Mather said, sitting down opposite her with his back to the engine, watching the country which she could see approach flow backward over her shoulder and disappear. He said, "We've been checking what you told us. It's a strange story."

"It's true," she repeated wearily.

He said, "We've had half the legations in London on the phone. Not to speak of Geneva. And the commissioner."

She said with a flicker of malice, "I'm sorry you've been troubled." But she couldn't keep it up. Her formal indifference was ruined by his presence—the large, clumsy, once friendly hands, the bulk of the man. "Oh, I'm sorry," she said. "I've said that before, haven't I? What else can I—? I'd say it if I'd spilled your coffee, and I've got to say it after all these people are killed. There are no other words, are there, which mean more? It all worked out wrong. I thought everything was clear. I've failed. I didn't mean to hurt you ever. I suppose the commissioner—" She began to cry without tears; it was as if those ducts were frozen.

He said, "I'm to have promotion. I don't know why. It seems to me as if I'd bungled it." He added gently and pleadingly, leaning forward across the compartment. "We could get married—at once —though I daresay if you don't want to now, you'll do all right. They'll give you a grant."

It was like going into the manager's office expecting dismissal and getting a rise instead—or a speaking part; but it never had happened that way. She stared silently back at him.

"Of course," he said gloomily, "you'll be the rage now. You'll have stopped a war. I know I didn't believe you. I've failed. I thought I'd always trust— We've found enough already to prove what you told me and I thought was lies. They'll have to withdraw their ultimatum now. They won't have any choice." He added with a deep hatred of publicity, "It'll be the sensation of a century," sitting back with his face heavy and sad.

"You mean," she said with incredulity, "that when we get in— we can go off straightaway and be married?"

"Will you?"

She said, "The taxi won't be fast enough."

"It won't be as quick as all that. It takes three weeks. We can't afford a special licence."

She said, "Didn't you tell me about a grant? I'll blow it on the licence," and suddenly, as they simultaneously laughed, it was as if the past three days left the carriage, were whirled backward down to the metals to Nottwich. It had all happened there, and they need never go back to the scene of it. Only a shade of disquiet remained, a fading spectre of Raven. If his immortality was to be on the lips of living men, he was fighting now his last losing fight against extinction.

"All the same," Anne said, as Raven covered her with his sack, as Raven touched her icy hand, "I failed."

"Failed?" Mather said. "You've been the biggest success," and it seemed to Anne for a few moments that this sense of failure would never die from her brain, that it would cloud a little every happiness. It was something she could never explain; her lover would never understand it. But already, as his face lost its gloom, she was failing again—failing to atone. The cloud was blown away by his voice; it evaporated under his large and clumsy and tender hand.

"Such a success." He was as inarticulate as Saunders, now that he was realizing what it meant. It was worth a little publicity. This darkening land, flowing backwards down the line, was safe for a few more years. He was a countryman, and he didn't ask for more than a few years' safety at a time for something he so dearly loved. The precariousness of its safety made it only the more precious. Somebody was burning winter weeds under a hedge, and down a dark lane a farmer rode home alone from the hunt in a queer old-fashioned bowler hat on a horse that would never take a ditch. A small lit village came up beside his window and sailed away like a little pleasure steamer hung with lanterns. He had just time to notice the grey English church squatted among the yews and graves, the thick deaths of centuries, like an old dog who will not leave his corner. On the little wooden platform as they whirled by a porter was reading the label on a tall Christmas tree.

"You haven't failed," he said.

London had its roots in her heart; she saw nothing in the dark countryside. She looked away from it to Mather's happy face. "You don't understand," she said, sheltering the ghost for a very short while longer. "I *did* fail." But she forgot it herself completely when the train drew into London over a great viaduct under which the small, bright, shabby streets ran off like the rays of a star with their sweet shops, their Methodist chapels, their messages chalked on the paving stones. Then it was she who thought, This is safe, and, wiping the glass free from steam, she pressed her face against the pane and happily and avidly and tenderly watched, as a child whose mother has died watches the family *she* must rear without being aware at all that the responsibility is too great. A mob of children went screaming down a street—she could tell they screamed because she was one of them; she couldn't hear their voices or see their mouths. A man was selling hot chestnuts at a corner, and it was on *her* face that his little fire glowed. The sweet shops were full of white gauze stockings crammed with cheap gifts. "Oh," she said, with a sigh of unshadowed happiness, "we're home."

The Confidential Agent

PART I

The Hunted

One

The gulls swept over Dover. They sailed out like flakes of the fog, and tacked back towards the hidden town, while the siren mourned with them; other ships replied, a whole wake lifted up their voices —for whose death? The ship moved at half-speed through the bitter autumn evening. It reminded D. of a hearse, rolling slowly and discreetly towards the "garden of peace," the driver careful not to shake the coffin, as if the body minded a jolt or two. Hysterical women shrieked among the shrouds.

The third-class bar was jammed: a rugger team was returning home and they scrummed boisterously for their glasses, wearing striped ties. D. couldn't always understand what they were shouting; perhaps it was slang—or dialect; it would take a little time for his memory of English completely to return; he had known it very well once, but now his memories were rather literary. He tried to stand apart, a middle-aged man with a heavy moustache and a scarred chin and worry like a habit on his forehead, but you couldn't go far in that bar—an elbow caught him in the ribs, and a mouth breathed bottled beer into his face. He was filled with a sense of amazement at these people: you could never have told from their smoky good-fellowship that there was a war on—not merely a war in the country from which he had come, but a war here, half a mile outside Dover breakwater. He carried the war with him. Wherever D. was, there was the war. He could never understand that people were not aware of it.

"Pass here, pass here," a player screamed at the barman, and somebody snatched his glass of beer and shouted "Offside!" "Scrum!" they all screamed together.

D. said, "With your permission. With your permission," edging out. He turned up the collar of his mackintosh and went up onto the cold and foggy deck where the gulls were mourning, blowing over his head towards Dover. He began to tramp—up and down beside the rail—to keep warm, his head down, the deck like a map marked with trenches, impossible positions, salients, deaths; bombing planes took flight from between his eyes, and in his brain the mountains shook with shell-bursts.

He had no sense of safety, walking up and down on this English ship sliding imperceptibly into Dover. Danger was part of him. It wasn't like an overcoat you sometimes left behind; it was your skin. You died with it; only corruption stripped it from you. The one person you trusted was yourself. One friend was found with a holy medal under the shirt, another belonged to an organization with the wrong initial letters. Up and down the cold, unsheltered third-class deck, into the stern and back, until his walk was interrupted by the little wooden gate with a placard: "First-Class Passengers Only." There had been a time when the class distinction would have read like an insult, but now the class divisions were too subdivided to mean anything at all. He stared up the first-class deck; there was only one man out in the cold like himself: collar turned up, he stood in the bow, looking out towards Dover.

D. turned and went back into the stern, and again as regular as his tread the bombing planes took off. You could trust nobody but yourself, and sometimes you were uncertain whether after all you could trust yourself. *They* didn't trust you, any more than they had trusted the friend with the holy medal; they were right then, and who was to say whether they were not right now? You—you were a prejudiced party; the ideology was a complex affair; heresies crept in. . . . He wasn't certain that he wasn't watched at this moment. He wasn't certain that it wasn't right for him to be watched. After all, there were aspects of economic materialism which, if he searched his heart, he did not accept. . . . And the watcher—was he watched? He was haunted for a moment by the vision of an endless distrust. In an inner pocket, a bulge over the breast, he carried what were called credentials, but credence no longer meant belief.

He walked slowly back—the length of his chain; through the fog a young female voice cried harshly and distinctly, "I want one more. I *will* have one more"; somewhere a lot of glass broke. Somebody was crying behind a lifeboat—it was a strange world wherever you were. He walked cautiously round the bow of the boat and saw a child, wedged in a corner. He stood and looked at it. It didn't mean a thing to him—it was like writing so illegible you didn't even try to decipher it. He wondered whether he would ever again share anybody's emotion. He said to it in a gentle, dutiful way, "What is the matter?"

"I bumped my head."

He said, "Are you alone?"

"Dad stood me here."

"Because you bumped your head?"

"He said it wasn't any cause to take on." The child had stopped crying; it began to cough, the fog in the throat; dark eyes stared out of their cave between boat and rail, defensively. D. turned and walked on; it occurred to him that he shouldn't have spoken; the child was probably watched—by a father or a mother. He came up to the barrier—"First-Class Passengers Only"—and looked through. The other man was approaching through the fog, walking the longer length of *his* chain. D. saw first the pressed trousers, then the fur collar, and last the face. They stared at each other across the low gate. Taken by surprise, they had nothing to say. Besides, they had never spoken to each other; they were separated by different initial letters, a great many deaths—they had seen each other in a passage years ago, once in a railway station, and once on a landing field. D. couldn't even remember his name.

The other man was the first to move away; thin as celery inside his thick coat, tall, he had an appearance of nerves and agility; he walked fast on legs like stilts, stiffly, but you felt they might fold up. He looked as if he had already decided on some action. D. thought, He will probably try to rob me, perhaps he will try to have me killed. He would certainly have more helpers and more money and more friends. He would bear letters of introduction to peers and ministers; he had once had some kind of title himself, years ago, before the republic—count, marquess—D. had forgotten exactly what. It was a misfortune that they were both travelling on the same boat and that they should have seen each other like that at the barrier between the two classes, two confidential agents wanting the same thing.

The siren shrieked again, and suddenly out of the fog, like faces looking through a window, came ships, lights, a wedge of break-water. They were one of a crowd. The engine went half-speed and then stopped altogether. D. could hear the water slap, slap the side. They drifted, apparently, sideways. Somebody shouted invis-ibly—as though from the sea itself. They sidled forward and were there; it was as simple as all that. A rush of people carrying suitcases was turned back by sailors who seemed to be taking the ship to pieces. A bit of rail came off, as it were, in their hands.

Then they all surged over with their suitcases, labelled with Swiss hotels and pensions in Biarritz. D. let the rush go by; he had nothing but a leather wallet containing a brush and comb, a toothbrush, a few oddments. He had got out of the way of wearing pajamas; it wasn't really worth while when you were likely to be disturbed twice in a night by bombs.

The stream of passengers divided into two for the passport examination: aliens and British subjects. There were not many aliens; a few feet away from D. the tall man from the first class shivered slightly inside his fur coat. Pale and delicate, he didn't seem to go with this exposed and windy shed upon the quay. But he was wafted quickly through—one glance at his papers had been enough Like an antique, he was very well authenticated, D. thought without enmity, a museum piece. They all on that side seemed to him museum pieces—their lives led in big cold houses like public galleries hung with rather dull old pictures and with buhl cabinets in the corridors.

D. found himself at a standstill. A very gentle man with a fair moustache said, "But do you mean that this photograph is—yours?"

D. said, "Of course." He looked down at it; it had never occurred to him to look at his own passport for—well, years. He saw a stranger's face, that of a man much younger and, apparently, much happier than himself; he was grinning at the camera. He said, "It's an old photograph." It must have been taken before he went to prison, before his wife was killed, and before the air raid of December 23, when he was buried for fifty-six hours in a cellar. But he could hardly explain all that to the passport officer.

"How old?"

"Two years perhaps."

"But your hair is quite grey now."

"Is it?"

The detective said, "Would you mind stepping to one side and letting the others pass?" He was polite and unhurried. That was because this was an island. At home soldiers would have been called in; they would immediately have assumed that he was a spy, the questioning would have been loud and feverish and long drawn out. The detective was at his elbow. He said, "I'm sorry to have kept you. Would you mind just coming in here a moment?" He opened the door of a room. D. went in. There were a table, two chairs, and a picture of King Edward VII naming an express train Alexandra; extraordinary period faces grinned over high white collars, an engine driver wore a bowler hat.

The detective said, "I'm sorry about this. Your passport seems to be quite correct, but this picture—well—you've only to look at yourself, sir."

He looked in the only glass there was—the funnel of the engine and King Edward's beard rather spoiled the view—but he had to confess that the detective was not unreasonable. He did look different now. He said, "It never occurred to me—that I had changed so much." The detective watched him closely.

There was the old D.—he remembered now; it was just three years ago. He was forty-two, but a young forty-two. His wife had come with him to the studio; he had been going to take six months' leave from the university and travel—with her, of course. The civil war broke out exactly three days later. He had been six months in a military prison; his wife had been shot—that was a mistake, not an atrocity—and then— He said, "You know war changes people. That was before the war." He had been laughing at a joke—something about pineapples; it was going to be the first holiday together for years. They had been married for fifteen. He could remember the antiquated machine and the photographer diving under a hood; he could remember his wife only indistinctly. She had been a passion, and it is difficult to recall an emotion when it is dead.

"Have you got any more papers?" the detective asked. "Or is there anyone in London who knows you? Your embassy?"

"Oh, no, I'm a private citizen—of no account at all."

"You are not travelling for pleasure?"

"No. I have a few business introductions." He smiled back at the detective. "But they might be forged."

He couldn't feel angry; the grey moustache, the heavy lines around the mouth—they were all new; and the scar on his chin. He touched it. "We have a war on, you know." He wondered what the other was doing now. He wouldn't be losing any time. Probably there was a car waiting. He would be in London well ahead of D.— there might be trouble. Presumably he had orders not to allow anyone from the other side to interfere with the purchase of coal. Coal used to be called black diamonds before people discovered electricity. Well, in his own country it was more valuable than diamonds, and soon it would be as rare.

The detective said, "Of course your passport's quite in order.

Perhaps if you'd let me know where you are staying in London—"

"I have no idea."

The detective suddenly winked at him. It happened so quickly D. could hardly believe it. "Some address," the detective said.

"Oh, well, there's a hotel, isn't there, called the Ritz?"

"There is, but I should choose something less expensive."

"Bristol. There's always a Bristol."

"Not in England."

"Well, where do you suppose somebody like myself would stay?"

"Strand Palace?"

"Right."

The detective handed back the passport with a smile. He said, "We've got to be careful. I'm sorry. You'll have to hurry for your train." Careful! D. thought. Was that what they considered careful in an island? How he envied them their assurance.

What with the delay, D. was almost last in the queue at the customs; the noisy young men were presumably on the platform where the train would be waiting, and as for his fellow-countryman —D. was convinced he hadn't waited for the train. A girl's voice said, "Oh, I've got plenty to declare." It was a harsh voice; he had heard it before, demanding one more in the bar. He looked at her without much interest; he had reached a time of life when you were either crazy or indifferent about women, and this one, very roughly speaking, was young enough to be his daughter.

She said, "I've got a bottle of brandy here, but it's been opened." He thought vaguely, waiting his turn, that she oughtn't to drink so much—her voice didn't do her justice: she wasn't that type. He wondered why she had been drinking in the third class; she was well dressed, like an exhibit. She said, "And then there's a bottle of Calvados—but that's been opened too." D. felt tired; he wished they'd finish with her and let him through. She was very young and blond and unnecessarily arrogant; she looked like a child who has got nothing she really wants and so is determined to obtain anything, whether she likes it or not.

"Oh, yes," she said, "that's more brandy. I was going to tell you if you'd given me time, but you can see—that's been opened, too."

"I'm afraid we shall have to charge," the customs officer said, "on some of these."

"You've no right to."

"You can read the regulations."

The wrangle went interminably on; somebody else looked

through D.'s wallet and passed it. "The London train?" D. asked.

"It's gone. You'll have to wait for the seven-ten." It was not yet a quarter to six.

"My father's a director of the line," the girl said furiously.

"I'm afraid this is nothing to do with the line."

"Lord Benditch."

"If you want to take these drinks with you, the duty will be twenty-seven and six."

So that was Benditch's daughter. He stood at the exit watching her. He wondered whether he would find Benditch as difficult as the customs man was finding his girl. A lot depended on Benditch: if he chose to sell his coal at a price they were able to pay, they could go on for years; if not, the war might be over before the spring.

She seemed to have got her own way, if that was any omen; she looked as if she were on top of the world as she came to the door which would let her out onto the bitter foggy platform. It was prematurely dark; a little light burned by a bookstall, and a cold iron trolley leaned against a tin advertisement for Horlick's. It was impossible to see as far as the next platform, so that this junction for the great naval port—that was how D. conceived it—might have been a little country station planked down between the dripping fields which the fast trains passed.

"God," the girl said, "it's gone!"

"There's another," D. said, "in an hour and a half." He could feel his English coming back to him every time he spoke; it seeped in like fog and the smell of smoke; any other language would have sounded out of place.

"So they tell you," she said. "It will be hours late in this fog."

"I've got to get to town tonight."

"Who hasn't?"

"It may be clearer inland."

But she'd left him and was pacing impatiently up the cold platform. She disappeared altogether beyond the bookstall, and then a moment later was back again, eating a bun. She held one out to him, as if he were something behind bars. "Like one?"

"Thank you." He took it with a solemn face and began to eat; this was English hospitality.

She said, "I'm going to get a car. Can't wait in this dull hole for an hour. It *may* be clearer inland" (so she had heard him). She threw the remains of her bun in the direction of the track; it was like a conjuring trick—a bun and then just no bun at all. "Care for a lift?" she said. When he hesitated, she went on, "I'm as sober as a judge."

"Thank you. I wasn't thinking that. Only what would be—most quick."

"Oh, I shall be quickest," she said.

"Then I'll come."

Suddenly a face loomed oddly up at the level of their feet—they must have been standing on the very edge of the platform—an aggrieved face. A voice said, "Lady, I'm not in a zoo."

She looked down without surprise. "Did I say you were?" she said.

"You can't go—hurtling buns like that."

"Oh," she said impatiently, "don't be silly."

"Assault," the voice said. "I could sue you, lady. It was a missile."

"It wasn't. It was a bun."

A hand and a knee came up at their feet; the face came a little nearer. "I'd have you know—" it said.

D. said, "It was not the lady who threw the bun. It was me. You can sue me—at the Strand Palace. My name is D." He took what-was-her-name? by the arm and moved her towards the exit. A voice wailed in disgust through the fog like a wounded sea animal. "A foreigner."

"You know," the girl said, "you don't really need to protect me —from that."

"You have my name now," he said.

"Oh, mine's Cullen, if you want to know. Rose Cullen. A hideous name, but then you see my father's crazy about roses. He invented—is that right?—the Marquise Pompadour. He likes tarts too, you see. Royal tarts. We have a house called Gwyn Cottage."

They were lucky over the car. The garage near the station was well lit up; it penetrated the fog for nearly fifty yards, and there was a car they could have—an old Packard. He said, "I have business to do with Lord Benditch. It is an odd coincidence."

"I don't see why. Everybody I ever meet has business with him."

She drove slowly in what she supposed was the direction of London, bumping over tram lines. "We can't go wrong if we follow the tram lines."

He said, "Do you always travel third class?"

"Well," she said, "I like to choose my company. I don't find my father's business friends there."

"I was there."

She said, "Oh, hell, the harbour!" and switched recklessly across the road and turned; the fog was full of grinding brakes and human annoyance. They moved uncertainly back the way they had come and began to climb a hill. "Of course," she said, "if we'd been Scouts we'd have known. You always go downhill to find water."

At the top of the hill the fog lifted a little; there were patches of cold grey afternoon sky, hedgerows like steel needles, and quiet everywhere. A lamb padded and jumped along the grass margin of the road, and two hundred yards away a light came suddenly out. This was peace. He said, "I suppose you are very happy here."

"Happy?" she said. "Why?"

He said, "All this—security." He remembered the detective winking at him in a friendly way and saying, "We've got to be careful."

"It's not so rich," she said in her immature, badly brought-up voice.

"Oh, no, no," he said. He explained laboriously, "You see, I come from two years of war. I should go along a road like this very slowly, ready to stop and get into a ditch if I heard a plane."

"Well, I suppose you're fighting for something," she said, "or aren't you?"

"I don't remember. One of the things which danger does to you after a time is—well, to kill emotion. I don't think I shall ever feel anything again except fear. None of us can hate any more—or love. You know it's a statistical fact that very few children are being born in our country."

"But your war goes on. There must be a reason."

"You have to feel something to stop a war. Sometimes I think we cling to it because there is still fear. If we were without that, we shouldn't have any feeling at all. None of us will enjoy the peace."

A small village appeared ahead of them like an island—an old church, a few graves, an inn. He said, "I shouldn't envy us if I were you—with this." He meant the casualness and quiet, the odd unreality of a road you could follow over any horizon.

"It doesn't need a war to flatten things. Money, parents, lots of things are just as good as war."

He said sadly, "After all, you are young—very pretty."

"Oh, hell," she said, "are you going to start on me?"

"No. Of course not. I've told you, I can't feel anything. Besides, I'm old."

There was a sharp report, the car swerved, and he flung his arms up over his face. The car came to a stop. She said, "They've given us a dud tire." He put his arms down. "I'm sorry," he said. "I do still feel that." His hands were trembling. "Fear."

"There's nothing to be afraid of here," she said.

"I'm not sure." He carried the war in his heart. Give me time, he thought, and I shall infect anything—even this. I ought to wear a bell like the old lepers.

"Don't be melodramatic," she said. "I can't stand melodrama." She pressed the starter, and they moved bumpingly forward. "We shall hit a roadhouse or a garage or something before long," she said; "it's too cold to change the wretched thing here." And a little later, "The fog again."

"Do you think you should go on driving? Without a tire?"

"Don't be afraid," she said.

He said apologetically, "You see, I have important work to do."

She turned her face to him—a thin, worried face, absurdly young; he was reminded of a child at a dull party. She couldn't be more than twenty. That was young enough to be his daughter. She said, "You lay on the mystery with a trowel. Do you want to impress me?"

"No."

"It's such a stale gag." The conjurer had not come off.

"Have so many people tried it with you?"

"I couldn't count them," she said. It seemed to him immeasurably sad that anyone so young should have known so much fraud. Perhaps because he was middle-aged it seemed to him that youth should be a season of—well, hope. He said gently, "I'm nothing mysterious. I am just a businessman."

"Do you stink of money, too?"

"Oh, no. I am the representative of a rather poor firm."

She smiled at him suddenly, and he thought without emotion, One could call her beautiful. "Married?"

"In a way."

"You mean separated?"

"Yes. That is to say, she's dead."

The fog turned primrose ahead of them; they slowed down and came bumpingly into a region of voices and tail lights. A high voice said, "I told Sally we'd get here." A long glass window came into view; there was soft music; a voice, very hollow and deep, sang, "I know I knew you only when you were lonely."

"Back in civilization," the girl said gloomily.

"Can we get the tire changed here?"

"I should think so." She opened the door, got out, and was submerged at once in fog and light and other people. He sat alone in the car; now the engine wasn't running, it was bitterly cold. He tried to think what his movements should be. First he had been directed to lodge at a number in a Bloomsbury street. Presumably the number had been chosen so that his own people could keep an eye on him. Then he had an appointment the day after next with Lord Benditch. They were not beggars; they could pay a fair price for the coal, and a profiteer's bonus when the war was over. Many of the Benditch collieries were closed down; it was a chance for both of them. He had been warned that it was inadvisable to bring in the Embassy—the Ambassador and the First Secretary were not trusted, although the Second Secretary was believed to be loyal. It was a hopelessly muddled situation—it was quite possible that really it was the Second Secretary who was working for the rebels. Anyway, the whole affair was to be managed quietly; nobody had expected the complication he had encountered on the Channel boat. It might mean anything—from a competitive price for the coal shipments to robbery or even murder. Well, he was somewhere in the fog ahead.

D. suddenly felt an inclination to turn off the lights of the car. Sitting in the dark, he transferred his credentials from his breast pocket; he hesitated with them in his hand and then stuffed them down into his sock. The door of the car was pulled open and the girl said, "Why on earth did you turn out the lights? I had an awful business finding you." She switched them on again and said, "There's nobody free at the moment—but they'll send a man."

"We've got to wait?"

"I'm hungry."

He came cautiously out of the car, wondering whether it was his duty to offer her dinner; he grudged every inessential penny he spent. He said, "Can we get dinner?"

"Of course we can. Have you got enough? I spent my last sou on the car."

"Yes. Yes. You will have dinner with me?"

"That was the idea."

He followed her into the house—hotel—whatever it was. This sort of thing was new since the days when he came to England as a youth to read at the British Museum. An old Tudor house—he could tell it was genuine Tudor—it was full of armchairs and sofas, and a cocktail bar where you expected a library. A man with a monocle took one of the girl's hands, the left one, and wrung it. "Rose. Surely it's Rose." He said, "Excuse me. I think I see Monty Crookham," and slid rapidly sideways.

"Do you know him?" D. said.

"He's the manager. I didn't know he was down this way. He used to have a place on Western Avenue." She said with contempt, "This is fine, isn't it? Why don't you go back to your war?"

But that wasn't necessary. He had indeed brought the war with him; the infection was working already; he saw beyond the lounge —sitting with his back turned at the first table inside the restaurant —the other agent. His hand began to shake just as it always shook before an air raid; you couldn't live six months in prison, expecting every day to be shot, and come out at the end of it anything else but a coward. He said, "Can't we have dinner somewhere else? Here—there are so many people." It was absurd, of course, to feel afraid, but, watching the narrow stooping back in the restaurant, he felt as exposed as if he were in a yard with a blank wall and a firing squad.

"There's nowhere else. What's wrong with it?" She looked at him with suspicion. "Why not a lot of people? Are you going to begin something after all?"

He said: "No. Of course not. It only seemed to me—"

"I'll get a wash and find you here."

"Yes."

"I won't be a minute."

As soon as she had gone he looked quickly round for a lavatory; he wanted cold water, time to think. His nerves were less steady than they had been on the boat—he was worried by little things like a tire bursting. He pursued the monocled manager across the lounge; the place was doing good business in spite of—or because of—the fog. Cars came yapping distractedly in from Dover and London. He found the manager talking to an old lady with white hair. He was saying, "Just so high. I've got a photograph of him here—if you'd like to see. I thought of your husband at once. . . ." All the time he kept his eye open for other faces; his words had no conviction; his lean brown face, carved into the right military lines by a few years' service in the Army, was unattached, like an animal's in a shop window. D. said, "Excuse me a moment."

"Of course I wouldn't sell him to anyone." He swivelled round and switched on a smile as he would a cigarette lighter. "Let me see. Where have we met?" He held a snapshot of a wire-haired terrier in his hand. He said, "Good lines. Stands square. Teeth—"

"I just wanted to know—"

"Excuse me, old man, I see Tony," and he was off and away. The old lady said suddenly and brusquely, "No use asking him anything. If you want the w.c., it's downstairs."

The lavatory was certainly not Tudor; it was all glass and black marble. He took off his coat and hung it on a peg—he was the only man in the place—and filled a basin with cold water. That was what his nerves needed; cold water worked with him on the base of the neck like an electric charge. He was so on edge that he looked quickly round when someone else came in—as if it could be anyone he knew; it was only a chauffeur from one of the cars. D. plunged his head down into the cold water and lifted it dripping. He felt for a towel and got the water out of his eyes. His nerves felt better now. His hand didn't shake at all when he turned and said, "What are you doing with my coat?"

"What do you mean?" the chauffeur said. "I was hanging up my coat. Are you trying to put something on me?"

"It seemed to me," D. said, "that you were trying to take something off me."

"Call a policeman then," the chauffeur said.

"Oh, there were no witnesses."

"Call a policeman or apologize." The chauffeur was a big man, over six feet. He came threateningly forward across the glassy floor. "I got a good mind to knock your block off. A bloody foreigner coming over here, taking our bread, thinking you can do what—"

"Perhaps," D. said gently, "I was mistaken." He was puzzled; the man after all might be only an ordinary sneak thief. No harm was done.

"*Per*haps you were mistaken. *Per*haps I'll knock your bloody block off. Call that an apology?"

"I apologize," D. said, "in any way you like." War doesn't leave you the sense of shame.

"Haven't even got the guts to fight," the chauffeur said.

"Why should I? You are the bigger man. And younger."

"I could take on any number of you bloody dagos—"

"I daresay you could."

"Are you saucing me?" the chauffeur said. One of his eyes was out of the straight; it gave him an effect of talking always with one eye on an audience—and perhaps, D. thought, there was an audience.

"If it seems so to you, I apologize again."

"Why, I could make you lick my boots."

"I shouldn't be at all surprised." Had the man been drinking—or had he perhaps been told by someone to pick a quarrel? D. stood with his back to the washbasin. He felt a little sick with apprehension. He hated personal violence; to kill a man with a bullet, or to be killed, was a mechanical process which conflicted only with the will to live or the fear of pain. But the fist was different; the fist humiliated; to be beaten up put you into an ignoble relationship with the assailant; he hated the idea as he hated the idea of promiscuous intercourse. He couldn't help it; this made him afraid.

"Saucing me again."

"I did not intend that." His pedantic English seemed to infuriate the other. He said, "Talk English or I'll smash your bloody lip."

"I am a foreigner."

"You won't be much of anything when I've finished." The man came nearer; his fists hung down ready at his side like lumps of dried meat; he seemed to be beating himself into an irrational rage. "Come on," he said, "put up your fists. You aren't a coward, are you?"

"Why not?" D. said. "I'm not going to fight you. I should be glad if you would allow me— There is a lady waiting for me upstairs."

"She can have what's left," the man said, "when I've finished with you. I'm going to show you you can't go about calling honest men thieves." He seemed to be left-handed, for he began to swing his left fist.

D. flattened himself against the basin. The worst was going to happen now; he was momentarily back in the prison yard as the warder came towards him, swinging a club. If he had had a gun he would have used it; he would have been prepared to answer any charge to escape the physical contact. He shut his eyes and leaned back against the mirror; he was defenceless. He didn't know the first thing about using his fists.

The manager's voice said, "I say, old chap. Not feeling well?" D. straightened himself. The chauffeur was hanging back with a look of self-conscious righteousness. D. said gently with his eyes on the man, "I get taken sometimes with—what is it you call it—giddiness?"

"Miss Cullen sent me to find you. Shall I see if there's a doctor about?"

"No. It's nothing at all."

D. checked the manager outside the lavatory. "Do you know that chauffeur?"

"Never seen him before, but one can't keep a check on the retainers, old man. Why?"

"I thought he went for my pockets."

The eye froze behind the monocle. "Most improbable, old man. Here, you know, we get—well, I don't mean to be snobbish—only the best people. Must have been mistaken. Miss Cullen will bear me out." He said with false indifference, "You an old friend of Miss Cullen's?"

"No. I would not say that. She was good enough to give me a lift from Dover."

"Oh, I see," the manager said icily. He detached himself briskly at the top of the stairs. "You'll find Miss Cullen in the restaurant."

He passed in; somebody in a high-necked jumper was playing a piano, and a woman was singing, very deep down in the throat and melancholy. He went stiffly by the table where the other sat.

"What's up?" the girl said. "I thought you'd walked out on me. You look as if you'd seen a ghost."

Where he sat he couldn't see L.—the name came back to him now. He said softly, "I was attacked—that is to say, I was going to be attacked—in the lavatory."

"Why do you tell stories like that?" she said. "Making yourself out mysterious. I'd rather have the Three Bears."

"Oh, well," he said, "I had to make some excuse, hadn't I?"

"You don't really believe it, do you?" she asked anxiously. "I mean, you haven't got shell-shock?"

"No. I don't think so. I am just not a good friend to know."

"If only you wouldn't be funny. You say these melodramatic things. I've told you—I don't like melodrama."

"Sometimes it just happens that way. There's a man sitting facing this way at the first table inside the door. Don't look yet. I will make a bet with you. He is looking at us. Now."

"He is, but what of it?"

"He is watching me."

"There's another explanation, you know. That he's just watching me."

"Why you?"

"People often do."

"Oh, yes, yes," he said hurriedly. "Of course. I can understand that." He sat back and watched her: the sullen mouth, transparent skin. He felt an unreasonable dislike for Lord Benditch; if he had been her father, he wouldn't have allowed her to go this way. The woman with the deep voice sang an absurd song about unrequited love:

> *It was just a way of talking—I hadn't learned.*
> *It was just daydreaming—but my heart burned.*
> *You said, "I love you"—and I thought you meant it.*
> *You said, "My heart is yours"—but you'd only lent it.*

People set down their wine and listened—as if it were poetry. Even the girl stopped eating for a while. The self-pity of it irritated him; it was a vice nobody in his country on either side the line had an opportunity of indulging.

> *I don't say you lie; it's just the modern way.*
> *I don't intend to die—in the old Victorian way.*

He supposed it represented the "spirit of the age," whatever that meant; he almost preferred the prison cell, the law of flight, the bombed house, his enemy by the door. He watched the girl moodily; there was a time in his life when he would have tried to write her a poem—it would have been better stuff than this.

> *It was just daydreaming—I begin to discern it.*
> *It was just a way of talking—and I've started to learn it.*

She said, "It's muck, isn't it? But it has a sort of appeal."

A waiter came over to their table. He said, "The gentleman by the door asked me to give you this, sir."

"For somebody who's just landed," she said, "you make friends quickly."

He read it; it was short and to the point, although it didn't specify exactly what was wanted. "I suppose," he said, "you wouldn't believe me if I told you I had just been offered two thousand pounds."

"Why should you tell me if you had?"

"That's true." He called the waiter. "Can you tell me if that gentleman has a chauffeur—a big man with something wrong about his eye?"

"I'll find out, sir."

"You play it fine," she said, "fine. The mystery man." It occurred to him that she'd been drinking too much again. He said, "We'll never get up to London if you do not go carefully."

The waiter came back and said, "That's his chauffeur, sir."

"A left-handed man?"

"Oh, stop it," she said, "stop it."

He said gently, "I'm not showing off. This has nothing to do with you. Things are going so fast—I had to be sure." He gave the waiter a tip. "Give the gentleman back his note."

"Any reply, sir?"

"No reply."

"Why not be a gentleman," she said, "and write 'Thank you for the offer'?"

"I wouldn't want to give him a specimen of my handwriting. He might forge it."

"I give up," she said. "You win."

"Better not drink any more." The singing woman had shut down —like a radio set, the last sound was a wail and a vibration; a few couples began to dance. He said, "We have a long drive in front."

"What's the hurry? We can always stay the night here."

"Of course," he said. "You can—but I must get to London somehow."

"Why?"

"My employers," he said, "wouldn't understand the delay." They would have timetabled his movements, he knew for certain, with exactly this kind of situation in mind—the meeting and the offer of money. No amount of service would ever convince them that he hadn't got, at some level, a price. After all, he recognized sadly, *they* had their price; the people had been sold out over and over again by their leaders. But if the only philosophy you had left was a sense of duty, that knowledge didn't prevent your going on.

The manager was swinging his monocle at Rose Cullen and inviting her to dance; this, he thought, gloomily, was going on all night—he would never get her away. They moved slowly round the room to the sad stiff tune; the manager held her firmly with one large hand splayed out on her spine; the other was thrust, with rather insulting insouciance, it seemed to D., in his pocket. He was talking earnestly, and looking every now and then in D.'s direction.

Once they came into earshot and D. caught the word "careful." The girl listened attentively, but her feet were awkward; she must be more drunk than he had imagined.

D. wondered whether anybody had changed that tire. If the car was ready, perhaps after this dance he could persuade her. He got up and left the restaurant. L. sat over a piece of veal; he didn't look up, he was cutting the meat up into tiny pieces—his digestion must be rotten. D. felt less nervous; it was as if the refusal of the money had put him into a stronger position than his opponent. As for the chauffeur, it was unlikely that he'd start anything now.

The fog was lifting a little; he could see the cars in the courtyard —half a dozen of them: a Daimler, a Mercedes, a couple of Morrises, their old Packard, and a little scarlet cad car. The tire had been fixed.

He thought, If only we could leave now, at once, while L. is at his dinner; and then heard a voice which could only be L.'s speaking to him in his own language. He was saying, "Excuse me. If we could have a few words together . . ."

D. felt a little envious of him as he stood there in the yard among the cars—he looked established. Five hundred years of inbreeding had produced him, set him against an exact background, made him at home, and at the same time haunted—by the vices of ancestors and the tastes of the past. D. said, "I don't think there's much to talk about." But he recognized the man's charm; it was like being picked out of a party by a great man to be talked to. "I can't help thinking," L. said, "that you don't understand the position." He smiled deprecatingly at his own statement, which might sound impertinent after two years of war. "I mean—you really belong to us."

"It didn't feel like that in prison."

The man had an integrity of a kind: he gave an impression of truth. He said, "You probably had a horrible time. I have seen some of our prisons. But, you know, they are improving; the beginning of a war is always the worst time; after all, it is no good at all our talking atrocities to each other. You have seen your own prisons. We are both guilty. And we shall go on being guilty, here and there, I suppose, until one of us has won."

"That is a very old argument. Unless we surrender, we are just prolonging the war. That's how it goes. It's not a good argument to use to a man who has lost his wife—"

"That was a horrible accident. You probably heard—we shot the commandant. What I want to say"—he had a long nose like the ones you see in picture galleries in old brown portraits; thin and worn, he ought to have carried a sword as supple as himself—"is this. If you win, what sort of a world will it be for people like you? They'll never trust you—you are a bourgeois—I don't suppose they even trust you now. And you don't trust them. Do you think you'll find among those people—the ones who destroyed the National Museum and Z.'s pictures—anyone interested in your work?" He said gently—it was like being recognized by a state academy—"I mean the Berne MS."

"I'm not fighting for myself," D. said. It occurred to him that if there had not been a war he might have been friends with this man; the aristocracy did occasionally fling up somebody like this thin tormented creature interested in scholarship or the arts, a patron.

"I didn't suppose you were," he said. "You are more of an idealist than I am. My motives, of course, are suspect. My property has been confiscated. I believe"—he gave a kind of painful smile which suggested that he knew he was in sympathetic company—"that my pictures have been burned—and my manuscript collection. I had nothing, of course, which was in your line; but there was an early manuscript of Augustine's *City of God*." It was like being tempted by a devil of admirable character and discrimination. He couldn't find an answer. L. went on, "I'm not really complaining. These horrible things are bound to happen in war—to the things one loves. My collection and your wife."

It was amazing that he hadn't seen his mistake. He waited there for D.'s assent—the long nose and the too sensitive mouth, the tall thin dilettante body. He hadn't the faintest conception of what it meant to love another human being; his house—which they had burned—was probably like a museum, old pieces of furniture, cords drawn on either side of the picture gallery on days when the public was admitted. He appreciated the Berne MS. very likely, but he had no idea that the Berne MS. meant nothing at all beside the woman you loved. He went fallaciously on, "We've both suffered." It was difficult to remember that he had for a moment sounded like a friend. It was worth killing a civilization to prevent the government of human beings from falling into the hands of—he supposed they were called the civilized. What sort of world would that be? A world full of preserved objects labelled "Not to be touched"; no religious faith, but a lot of Gregorian chants and picturesque ceremonies. Miraculous images which bled or waggled their heads on certain days would be preserved for their quaintness: superstition was interesting. There would be excellent libraries, but no new books. He preferred the distrust, the barbarity, the betrayals—even chaos. The Dark Ages, after all, had been his "period."

He said, "It isn't really any good our talking. We have nothing in common—not even a manuscript." Perhaps this was what he had been painfully saved from by death and war; appreciation and scholarship were dangerous things; they could kill the human heart.

L. said, "I wish you would listen."

"It would waste our time."

L. gave him a smile. "I'm so glad," he said, "at any rate that you finished your work on the Berne MS. before this—wretched—war."

"It doesn't seem to me very important."

"Ah," L. said, "now that is treachery." He smiled—wistfully. It wasn't that war in his case had killed emotion; it was that he had never possessed more than a thin veneer of it for cultural purposes. His place was among dead things. He said whimsically, "I give you up. You won't blame me, will you?"

"What for?"

"For what happens now." Tall and brittle, courteous and un-convincing, he disengaged himself—like a patron leaving an exhibition of pictures by somebody he has decided is, after all, not quite good enough; a little sad, the waspishness up the sleeve.

D. waited a moment and then went back into the lounge. Through the double-glass doors of the restaurant he could see the narrow shoulders bent again over the veal.

The girl wasn't at her table; she'd joined another party. A monocle flashed near her ear; the manager was imparting a confidence. He could hear their laughter—and the harsh childish voice he had heard from the bar in the third class. "I want one more. I *will* have another." She was set for hours. Her kindness was something which meant nothing at all: she gave you a bun on a cold platform, offered you a lift, and then left you abandoned halfway; she had the absurd mind of her class, which would give a pound note to a beggar and forget the misery of anybody out of sight. She belonged really, he thought, with L.'s lot, and he remembered his own, at this moment queueing up for bread or trying to keep warm in unheated rooms.

He turned abruptly on his heel; it was untrue that war left you no emotions except fear; he could still feel a certain amount of anger and disappointment. He came back into the yard, opened the door of the car; an attendant came round the hood and said, "Isn't the lady—?"

"Miss Cullen's staying the night," D. said. "You can tell her I'll leave the car—tomorrow—at Lord Benditch's." He drove away.

He drove carefully, not too fast; it would never do to be stopped by the police and arrested for driving without a licence. A finger-post said, "London 45 miles." With any luck he would be in well before midnight. He began to wonder what L.'s mission was. The note had given nothing away; it had simply said, "Are you willing to accept two thousand pounds?" On the other hand, the chauffeur had searched his coat. If they were after his credentials, they must know what it was he had come to England to get—without those papers he would have no standing at all with the English coal-owners. But there were only five people at home concerned in this affair—and every one of them was a cabinet minister. Yes, the people were certainly sold out by their leaders. Was it the old Liberal, he wondered, who had once protested at the executions? Or was it the young pushing Minister of the Interior who perhaps saw more scope for himself under a dictatorship? But it might be any of them. There was no trust anywhere. All over the world there were people like himself who didn't believe in being corrupted— simply because it made life impossible—as when a man or woman cannot tell the truth about anything. It wasn't so much a question of morality, but a question of simply existing.

A signpost said, "40 miles."

But was L. simply here to stop the purchase—or did the other side need the coal as badly? They had possession of the mines in the mountains, but suppose the rumour was true that the workmen had refused to go down the pits? He became aware of a headlight behind him; he put out his hand and waved the car on. It drew level—a Daimler; then he saw the driver. It was the chauffeur who had tried to rob him in the lavatory.

D. stepped on his accelerator; the other car refused to give way; they raced side by side recklessly through the thin fog. He didn't know what it was all about; were they trying to kill him? It seemed improbable in England, but for two years now he had been used to the improbable: you couldn't be buried in a bombed house for fifty-six hours and emerge incredulous of violence.

The race lasted only two minutes; his needle went up to sixty; he strained the engine on to sixty-two, sixty-three, for a moment he hit sixty-five, but the old Packard was no match for the Daimler.

The other car hesitated, for the fraction of a minute allowing him to edge ahead; then, as it were, it laid back its ears and raced on at eighty miles an hour. It was in front of him; it went ahead into the edge of the fog and slid across the road, blocking his way. He drew up; it wasn't probable, but it seemed to be true—they were going to kill him. He thought carefully, sitting in his seat, waiting for them, trying to find some way of fixing responsibility—the publicity would be appalling for the other side; his death might be far more valuable than his life had ever been. He had once brought out a scholarly edition of an old Romance poem—this would certainly be more worth while.

A voice said, "Here's the beggar." To his surprise it was neither L. nor his chauffeur who stood at the door; it was the manager. But L. was there—he saw his thin celery shape wavering at the edge of the fog. Could the manager be in league—? The situation was crazy. He said, "What do you want?"

"What do I want? This is Miss Cullen's car."

No; after all, this was England—no violence; he was safe. Just an unpleasant explanation. What did L. expect to get out of this? Or did they mean to take him to the police? Surely she wouldn't charge him. At the worst it meant a few hours' delay. He said gently, "I left a message for Miss Cullen—that I'd leave the car at her father's."

"You bloody dago!" the manager said. "Did you really think you could walk off with a girl's bags just like that? A fine girl like Miss Cullen. And her jewellery."

"I forgot about the bags."

"I bet you didn't forget about the jewellery. Come on. Get out of there."

There was nothing to be done. He got out. Two or three cars were hooting furiously somewhere behind. The manager shouted, "I say, old man, do you mind clearing the road now? I've got the beggar." He grasped D. by the lapel of his coat.

"That isn't necessary," D. said. "I'm quite ready to explain to Miss Cullen—or to the police."

The other cars went by. The chauffeur loomed up a few yards away. L. stood by the Daimler, talking to somebody through the window.

"You think you're damned smart," the manager said. "You know Miss Cullen's a fine girl—wouldn't charge you."

His monocle swung furiously; he thrust his face close to D.'s and said, "Don't think you can take advantage of her." One eye was a curious dead blue; it was like a fish's eye; it recorded none of the emotion. He said, "I know your sort. Worm your way in on board a boat. I spotted you from the first."

D. said, "I'm in a hurry. Will you take me to Miss Cullen—or to the police?"

"You foreigners," the manager said, "come over here, get hold of our girls—you are going to learn a lesson—"

"Surely your friend over there is a foreigner too?"

"He's a gentleman."

"I don't understand," D. said, "what you propose to do."

"If I had my way, you'd go to jail; but Rose—Miss Cullen—won't charge you." He had been drinking a lot of whisky; you could tell that from the smell. "We'll treat you better than you deserve—give you a thrashing, man to man."

"You mean—assault me?" he asked incredulously. "There are three of you."

"Oh, we'll let you fight. Take off your coat. You called this chap here a thief—you bloody thief. He wants a crack at you."

D. said with horror, "If you want to fight, can't we get—pistols—the two of us?"

"We don't go in for that sort of murder here."

"And you don't fight your own battles, either."

"You know very well," he said, "I've got a gammy hand." He drew it out of his pocket and waggled it—a gloved object with stiff formalized fingers like a sophisticated doll's.

"I won't fight," D. said.

"That's as you like." The chauffeur came edging up without a cap. He had taken off his overcoat but hadn't troubled about his jacket—tight, blue, and vulgar. D. said, "He's twenty years younger."

"This isn't the Sporting Club," the manager said. "This is a punishment." He let go of D.'s collar and said, "Go on. Take off your coat." The chauffeur waited with his fists hanging down. D. slowly took off his overcoat; all the horror of the physical contact was returning: the club swung, he could see the warder's face—this was degradation. Suddenly he became aware of a car coming up behind. He darted into the middle of the road and began to wave. He said, "For God's sake—these men—"

It was a small Morris. A thin nervous man sat at the wheel with a grey powerful woman at his side. She looked at the odd group in the road with complacent disapproval. "I say—I say," the man said. "What's all this about?"

"Drunks," his wife said.

"That's all right, old man," the manager said; he had his monocle back over the fishlike eye. "My name's Captain Currie. You know—the Tudor Club. This man stole a car."

"Do you want us to fetch the police for you?" the woman said.

"No. The owner—a fine girl, one of the best—doesn't want to charge. We're just going to teach him a lesson."

"Well, you don't want us," the man said. "I don't intend to be mixed up . . ."

"One of these foreigners," the manager explained. "Glib tongue, you know."

"Oh, a foreigner," the woman said with tight lips. "Drive on, dear." The car ground into gear and moved forward into the fog.

"And now," the manager said, "are you going to fight?" He said with contempt, "You needn't be afraid. You'll get fair play."

"We better go into the field," the chauffeur said. "Too many cars here."

"I won't move," D. said.

"All right, then." The chauffeur struck him lightly on the cheek, and D.'s hands automatically went up in defence. Immediately the chauffeur struck again on the mouth, all the time looking elsewhere with one eye; it gave him an effect of appalling casualness, as if he needed only half a mind in order to destroy. He followed up without science at all, smashing out—not seeking a quick victory so much as just pain and blood. D.'s hands were useless; he made no attempt to hit back (his mind remained a victim of the horror and indignity of the physical conflict), and he didn't know the right way to defend himself. The chauffeur battered him; D. thought with desperation, They'll have to stop soon; they don't want murder. He went down under a blow. The manager said, "Get up, you skunk; no shamming," and as he got to his feet he thought he saw his wallet in L.'s hands. Thank God, he thought, I hid the papers; they can't batter the socks off me. The chauffeur waited till he got up, and then knocked him against the hedge. He took a step back and waited, grinning. D. could see with difficulty, and his mouth was full of blood; his heart was jumping and he thought with reckless pleasure, The damned fools, they *will* kill me. That would be worth while, and with his last vitality he came back out of the hedge and struck out at the chauffeur's belly. "Oh, the swine," he

heard the manager cry, "hitting below the belt! Go on. Finish him."
He went down again before a fist which felt like a steel-capped boot.
He had an odd impression that someone was saying, "Seven, eight,
nine."

One of them had undone his coat; for a moment he believed he
was at home, buried in the cellar with the rubble and a dead cat.
Then he remembered—and his mind retained a stray impression
of fingers which lingered round his shirt, looking for something.
Sight returned, and he saw the chauffeur's face very big and very
close. He had a sense of triumph; it was he really who had won this
round. He smiled satirically up at the chauffeur.

The manager said, "Is he all right?"

"Oh, he's all right, sir," the chauffeur said.

"Well," the manager said, "I hope it's been a lesson to you." D.
got with some difficulty onto his feet; he realized with surprise that
the manager was embarrassed—he was like a prefect who has caned
a boy and finds the situation afterwards less clear-cut. He turned
his back on D. and said, "Come on. Let's get going. I'll take Miss
Cullen's car."

"Will you give me a lift?" D. said.

"A lift! I should damn well think not. You can hoof it."

"Then perhaps your friend will give me back my coat."

"Go and get it," the manager said.

D. walked up the ditch to where his coat lay—he couldn't remember leaving it there, near L.'s car—and his wallet too. He
stooped and as he painfully straightened again he saw the girl; she
had been sitting all the time in the back of L.'s Daimler. Again he
felt suspicion widen to include the whole world—was she an agent
too? But, of course, it was absurd; she was still drunk; she hadn't
an idea of what it all meant any more than the absurd Captain
Currie. The zip fastener of his wallet was undone; it always stuck
when pulled open, and whoever had been looking inside had not
had time to close it again. He held the wallet up to the window of
the car and said, "You see. These people are very thorough. But
they haven't got what they wanted." She looked back at him
through the glass with disgust; he realized that he was still bleeding
heavily.

The manager said, "Leave Miss Cullen alone."

He said gently, "It's only a few teeth gone. A man of my age
must expect to lose his teeth. Perhaps we shall meet at Gwyn Cottage." She looked hopelessly puzzled, staring back at him. He put

his hands to his hat—but he had no hat; it must have dropped somewhere in the road. He said, "You must excuse me now. I have a long walk ahead. But I do assure you—quite seriously—you ought to be careful of these people." He began to walk towards London; he could hear Captain Currie exclaiming indignantly in the darkness behind—the word "infernal." It seemed to him that it had been a long day, but on the whole a successful one.

It had not been an unexpected day. This was the atmosphere in which he had lived for two years; if he had found himself on a desert island, he would have expected to infect even the loneliness somehow with violence. You couldn't escape a war by changing your country; you only changed the technique—fists instead of bombs, the sneak thief instead of the artillery bombardment. Only in sleep did he evade violence; his dreams were almost invariably made up of peaceful images from the past. Compensation? Wish-fulfilment? He was no longer interested in his own psychology. He dreamed of lecture rooms, his wife, sometimes of food and wine, very often of flowers.

He walked in the ditch to escape cars; the world was blanketed in white silence; sometimes he passed a bungalow dark among chicken coops; the chalky cutting of the road took headlights like a screen. He wondered what L.'s next move would be; he hadn't much time left, and today had got L. nowhere at all. Except that by now he certainly knew about the appointment with Benditch; it had been indiscreet to mention it to Benditch's daughter, but he hadn't imagined then this meeting between the two. Practical things began to absorb him to the exclusion of weariness or pain. The hours went quite rapidly by; he moved automatically; only when he had thought long enough did he begin to consider his feet, the chance of a lift. Presently he heard a lorry grinding up a hill behind him and he stepped into the road and signalled—a battered middle-aged figure who carried himself with an odd limping sprightliness.

Two

The early morning trams swung round the public lavatory in Theobald's Road in the direction of Kingsway. The lorries came in from the eastern counties, aiming at Covent Garden. In a big leafless Bloomsbury square a cat walked homewards from some alien rooftop. The city to D. looked extraordinarily exposed and curiously undamaged; nobody stood in a queue; there was no sign of a war—except himself. He carried his infection past the closed shops, a tobacconist's, a twopenny library. He knew the number he wanted, but he put his hand in his pocket to check it; the notebook was gone. So they had got something for their trouble, though it had contained nothing but his address that was of any significance to them—the rest was a recipe he had noticed in a French paper for making the most of cabbage; a quotation he had found somewhere from an English poet of Italian origin which had expressed a mood connected with his own dead:

> . . . *the beat*
> *Following her daily of thy heart and feet,*
> *How passionately and irretrievably*
> *In what fond flight, how many ways and days.*

There was also a letter from a French quarterly on the subject of the *Song of Roland,* referring to an old article of his own. He wondered what L. or his chauffeur would make of the quotation. Perhaps they would look for a code; there was no limit to the credulity and also the mistrust inherent in human beings.

Well, he remembered the number—35. He was a little surprised to find that it was a hotel—not a good hotel. The open outer door was a sure mark of its nature in every city in Europe. He took stock of his surroundings; he remembered the district very slightly. It had attached to it a haze of sentiment from his British Museum days, days of scholarship and peace and courtship. The street opened at the end into a great square—trees blackened with frost, the fantastic cupolas of a great inexpensive hotel, an advertisement for Russian baths. He went in and rang at the glass inner door. Somewhere a clock struck six.

A peaky haggard face looked at him—a child, about fourteen. He said, "I think there is a room waiting for me. The name is D."

"Oh," the child said, "we were expecting you last night." She was struggling with the bow of an apron behind; sleep was still white at the corners of her eyes; he could imagine the cruel alarm clock dinning in her ears. He said gently, "Just give me the key and I'll go up." She was looking at his face with consternation. He said, "I had a little accident—with a car."

She said, "It's Number twenty-seven. Right at the top. I'll show you."

"Don't bother," he said.

"Oh, it's no bother. It's the short times that are the bother. In and out three times in a night." She had all the innocence of a life passed since birth with the guilty. For the first two flights there was a carpet; afterwards just wooden stairs. A door opened, and an Indian in a gaudy dressing gown gazed out with heavy and nostalgic eyes. His guide plodded up ahead; she had a hole in one heel, which slipped out of the trodden shoe. If she had been older she would have been a slattern, but at her age she was only sad. He asked, "Have there been any messages left for me?"

She said, "A man called last night. He left a note." She unlocked a door. "You'll find it on the washstand."

The room was small: an iron bedstead, a table covered with a fringed cloth, a basket chair, a blue, patterned cotton bedspread, clean and faded and spider-thin. "Do you want some hot water?" the child asked gloomily.

"No, no, don't bother."

"And what will you be wanting for breakfast? Most lodgers take kippers or boiled eggs."

"I won't want any this morning. I will sleep a little."

"Would you like me to call you later?"

"Oh, no," he said. "These are such long stairs. I am quite used to waking myself. You needn't bother."

She said passionately, "It's good working for a gentleman. Here they are all short time—you know what I mean—or else they're Indians." She watched him with the beginning of devotion; she was of an age when she could be won by a single word forever. "Haven't you any bags?"

"No."

"It's lucky as how you were introduced. We don't let rooms to people without luggage—not if they're by themselves."

There were two letters waiting for him, propped against the toothglass on the washstand. The first he opened contained letter paper headed "The Entrenationo Language Centre"—a typed message: "Our charge for a course of thirty lessons in Entrenationo is six guineas. A specimen lesson has been arranged for you at 8:45 o'clock tomorrow (the 16th inst.), and we very much hope that you will be encouraged to take a full course. If the time arranged is for any reason inconvenient, will you please give us a ring and have it altered to suit your requirements?" The other was from Lord Benditch's secretary, confirming the appointment.

He said, "I've got to be going out again very soon. I shall just take a nap."

"Would you like a hot bottle?"

"Oh, no, I shall do very well."

She hovered anxiously at the door. "There's a gas metre for pennies. Do you know how they work?" How little London altered! He remembered the ticking metre with its avidity for coins and its incomprehensible dial; on a long evening together they had emptied his pocket and her purse of coppers, until they had none left and the night grew cold and she left him till morning. He was suddenly aware that, outside, two years of painful memories still waited to pounce. "Oh, yes," he said quickly, "I know. Thank you." She absorbed his thanks passionately: he was a gentleman. Her soft closing of the door seemed to indicate that, in her eyes at any rate, one swallow made a whole summer.

D. took off his shoes and lay down on the bed, not waiting to wash the blood off his face. He told his subconscious mind, as if it were a reliable servant who needed only a word, that he must wake at eight-fifteen, and almost immediately was asleep. He dreamed that an elderly man with beautiful manners was walking beside him along a river bank; he was asking for D.'s views on the *Song of Roland,* sometimes arguing with great deference. On the other side of the river there was a group of tall cold beautiful buildings like pictures he had seen of Rockefeller Plaza in New York, and a band was playing. He woke exactly at eight-fifteen by his own watch.

He got up and washed the blood from his mouth. The two teeth he had lost had been at the back; it was lucky, he thought grimly, for life seemed determined to make him look less and less like his passport photograph. He was not so bruised and cut as he had expected. He went downstairs. In the hall there was a smell of fish from the dining room, and the little servant ran blindly into him, carrying two boiled eggs. "Oh," she said, "I'm sorry." Some instinct made him stop her. "What is your name?"

"Else."

"Listen, Else. I have locked the door of my room. I want you to see that nobody goes in while I am away."

"Oh, nobody would."

He put his hand gently on her arm. "Somebody might. You keep the key, Else. I trust you."

"I'll see to it. I won't let anybody," she swore softly while the eggs rolled on the plate.

The Entrenationo Language Centre was on the third floor of a
building on the south side of Oxford Street, over a bead shop, an
insurance company, and the offices of a magazine called *Mental
Health*. An old lift jerked him up; he was uncertain of what he
would find at the top. He pushed open a door marked "Inquiries"
and found a large draughty room with several armchairs, two filing
cabinets, and a counter at which a middle-aged woman sat knitting.
He said, "My name is D. I have come for a specimen lesson."·

"I'm so glad," she said and smiled at him brightly; she had a
wizened idealist's face and ragged hair, and she wore a blue woollen
jumper with scarlet bobbles. She said, "I hope you will soon be
quite an old friend," and rang a bell. What a country! he thought
with reluctant and ironic admiration. She said, "Dr. Bellows always
likes to have a word with new clients." Was it Dr. Bellows, he wondered, whom he had to see? A little door opened behind the counter
into a private office. "Would you just step through?" the woman
said, lifting the counter.

No, he couldn't believe that it was Dr. Bellows. Dr. Bellows
stood in the tiny inner room, all leather and walnut-stain, and the
smell of dry ink, and held out both hands. He had smooth white
hair and a look of timid hope. He said something which sounded
like *"Me tray joyass."* His gestures and his voice were more gran-
diloquent than his face, which seemed to shrink from innumerable
rebuffs. He said, "The first words of the Entrenationo Language
must always be ones of welcome."

"That is good of you," D. said. Dr. Bellows closed the door.
He said, "I have arranged that your lesson—I hope I shall be able
to say lessons—will be given by a compatriot. That is always, if
possible, our system. It induces sympathy and breaks the new
world order slowly. You will find Mr. K. is quite an able teacher."

"I'm sure of it."

"But first," Dr. Bellows said, "I always like to explain just a
little of our ideals." He still held D. by the hand, and he led him
gently on towards a leather chair. He said, "I always hope that a
new client has been brought here by love."

"Love?"

"Love of all the world. A desire to be able to exchange—ideas
—with—everybody. All this hate," Dr. Bellows said, "these wars
we read about in the newspapers, they are all due to misunderstanding. If we all spoke the same language—" He suddenly gave a little
wretched sigh which wasn't histrionic. He said, "It has always been

my dream to help." The rash unfortunate man had tried to bring his dream to life, and he knew that it wasn't good—the little leather chairs and the draughty waiting-room and the woman in a jumper, knitting. He had dreamed of universal peace—and he had two floors on the south side of Oxford Street. There was something of a saint about him, but saints are successful.

D. said, "I think it is a very noble work."

"I want everyone who comes here to realize that this isn't just a —commercial relationship. I want you all to feel my fellow workers."

"Of course."

"I know we haven't got very far yet, but we have done better than you may think. We have had Spaniards, Germans, a Siamese, one of your own countrymen—as well as English people. But of course it is the English who support us best. Alas, I cannot say the same of France."

"It is a question of time," D. said. He felt sorry for the old man.

"I have been at it now for thirty years. Of course the war was our great blow." He suddenly sat firmly up and said, "But the response this month has been admirable. We have given five sample lessons. You are the sixth. I mustn't keep you any longer away from Mr. K." A clock struck nine in the waiting-room *"La hora sonas,"* Dr. Bellows said with a frightened smile and held out his hand. "That is—the clock sounds." He held D 's hand again in his, as if he were aware of more sympathy than he was accustomed to. "I like to welcome an intelligent man—it is possible to do so much good." He said, "May I hope to have another interesting talk with you?"

"Yes. I am sure of it."

Dr. Bellows clung to him a little longer in the doorway. "I ought perhaps to have warned you. We teach by the direct method. We trust—to your honour, not to speak anything but Entrenationo." He shut himself back in his little room. The woman in the jumper said, "Such an interesting man, don't you think, Dr Bellows?"

"He has great hopes."

"One must—don't you think?" She came out from behind the counter and led him back to the lift "The tuition rooms are on the fourth floor. Just press the button. Mr. K. will be waiting." He rattled upwards. He wondered what Mr. K. would look like; surely he wouldn't fit in here if he belonged—well, to the ravaged world D. had himself emerged from.

But he did fit in—with the building if not with the idealism; a little shabby and ink-stained, he was any underpaid language master in a commercial school. He wore steel spectacles and economized on razor blades. He opened the lift door and said, *"Bona matina."*

"Bona matina," D. said, and Mr. K. led the way down a pitch-pine passage walnut-stained; one big room the size of the waiting-room below had been divided into four. D. couldn't help wondering whether he was not wasting his time—somebody might have made a mistake—but then who could have got his name and address? Or had L. arranged this to get him out of the hotel while he had his room searched? But that too was impossible. L. had had no means of knowing his address until he had the pocketbook.

Mr. K. ushered him into a tiny cubicle warmed by a tepid radiator. Double windows shut out the air and the noise of the traffic far below in Oxford Street. On one wall was hung a simple childlike picture on rollers—a family sat eating in front of what looked like a Swiss chalet; the father had a gun, and one lady an umbrella; there were mountains, a forest, a waterfall; the table was crammed with an odd mixture of food—apples, an uncooked cabbage, a chicken, pears, oranges and raw potatoes, a joint of meat. A child played with a hoop, and a baby sat up in a pram, drinking out of a bottle. On the other wall was a clock face with movable hands. Mr. K. said, *"Tablo,"* and rapped on the table. He sat down with emphasis on one of the two chairs and said, *"Essehgo."* D. followed suit. Mr. K. said, *"El timo es"*—he pointed at the clock—*"neuvo."* He began to take a lot of little boxes out of his pocket. He said, *"Attentio."*

D. said, "I'm sorry. There must be some mistake—"

Mr. K. piled the little boxes one on top of another, counting as he did so. *"Una, da, trea, kwara, vif."* He added in a low voice, "We are forbidden by the rules to talk anything but Entrenationo. I am fined one shilling if I am caught. So please speak low except in Entrenationo."

"Somebody arranged a lesson for me—"

"That is quite right. I have had instructions." He said, *"Que son la?"* pointing at the boxes, and replied to his own question, *"La son castes."* He lowered his voice again and said, "What were you doing last night?"

"Of course I want to see your authority."

Mr. K. took a card from his pocket and laid it in front of D. He said, "Your boat was only two hours late, and yet you were not in London last night."

"First I missed my train—delay.at the passport control—then a woman offered me a lift; the tire burst, and I was delayed—at a roadhouse. L. was there."

"Did he speak to you?"

"He sent me a note offering me two thousand pounds."

An odd expression came into the little man's eyes—it was like envy or hunger. He said, "What did you do?"

"Nothing, of course."

Mr. K. took off the old steel-rimmed spectacles and wiped the lenses. He said, "Was the girl connected with L.?"

"I think it's unlikely."

"What else happened?" He said suddenly, pointing at the picture, *"La es un famil. Un famil gentilbono."* The door opened, and Dr. Bellows looked in. *"Excellente, excellente,"* he said, smiling gently, and closed the door again. Mr. K. said, "Go on."

"I took her car. She was drunk and wouldn't go on. The manager of the roadhouse—a Captain Currie—followed me in his car. I was beaten up by L.'s chauffeur. I forgot to tell you he tried to rob me in the lavatory—the chauffeur, I mean. They searched my coat, but of course found nothing. I had to walk. It was a long time before I got a lift."

"Is Captain Currie—?"

"Oh, no. Just a fool, I think."

"It's an extraordinary story."

D. allowed himself to smile. "It seemed quite natural at the time. If you disbelieve me—there's my face. Yesterday I was not quite so battered."

The little man said, "To offer so much money— Did he say what —exactly—for?"

"No." It suddenly occurred to D. that the man didn't know what he had come to London to do—it would be just like the people at home to send him on a confidential mission and set other people whom they didn't trust with a knowledge of this object to watch him. Distrust in civil war went to fantastic lengths; it made wild complications. Who could wonder if it sometimes broke down more seriously than trust? It needs a strong man to bear distrust; weak men live up to the character they are allotted. It seemed to D. that Mr. K. was a weak man. He said, "Do they pay you much here?"

"Two shillings an hour."

"It isn't much."

Mr. K. said, "Luckily I do not have to live on it." But from his suit, his tired, evasive eyes, it wasn't probable that he had much more to live on from another source. Looking down at his fingers —the nails bitten close to the quick—he said, "I hope you have— everything—arranged?" One nail didn't meet with his approval; he began to bite it down to match the rest.

"Yes. Everything."

"Everyone you want is in town?"

"Yes."

He was fishing, of course, for information, but his attempts were pathetically inefficient they were probably right not to trust Mr. K. on the salary they paid him.

"I have to send in a report, Mr. K said. "I will say you have arrived safely, that your delay seems to have been accounted for." It was ignominious to have your movements checked up by a man of Mr. K.'s calibre. "When will you be through?"

"A few days at most."

"I understand that you should be leaving London at latest on Monday night."

"Yes."

"If anything delays you, you must let me know. If nothing does, you must leave not later than the eleven-thirty train."

"So I understand."

"Well," Mr. K. said wearily, "you can't leave this place before ten o'clock We had better go on with the lesson " He stood up beside the wall picture. a little weedy and undernourished figure. What had made them choose him? Did he conceal somewhere under his disguise a living passion for his party? He said, *"Un famil tray gentilbono* and, pointing to the joint, *"Vici el carnor."* Time went slowly by Once D thought he heard Dr Bellows pass down the passage on rubber-soled shoes. There wasn't much trust even in the centre of internationalism.

In the waiting-room he fixed another appointment—for Monday —and paid for a course of lessons. The elderly lady said, "I expect you found it a teeny bit hard?"

"Oh, I feel I made progress," D. said.

"I am so glad. For advanced students, you know, Dr. Bellows runs little soirées. Most interesting. On Saturday evenings, at eight. They give you an opportunity to meet people of all countries—

Spanish, German, Siamese—and exchange ideas. Dr. Bellows doesn't charge—you only have to pay for coffee and cake."

"I feel sure it is very good cake," D. said, bowing courteously.

He went out into Oxford Street; there was no hurry now, nothing to be done until he saw Lord Benditch. He walked, enjoying the sense of unreality—the shop windows full of goods, no ruined houses anywhere, women going into Buzzard's for coffee. It was like one of his own dreams of peace. He stopped in front of a bookshop and stared in—people had time to read books, new books. There was one called *A Lady in Waiting at the Court of King Edward,* with a photograph on the paper jacket of a stout woman in white silk with ostrich feathers. It was incredible. And there was *Safari Days,* with a man in a sun helmet standing on a dead lioness. What a country! he thought again with affection. He went on. He couldn't help noticing how well clothed everybody was. A pale winter sun shone, and the scarlet buses stood motionless all down Oxford Street; there was a traffic block. What a mark, he thought, for enemy planes! It was always about this time that they came over. But the sky was empty—or nearly empty. One winking, glittering little plane turned and dived on the pale clear sky, drawing in little puffy clouds a slogan: "Keep Warm with Ovo." He reached Bloomsbury. It occurred to him that he had spent a very quiet morning; it was almost as if his infection had met a match in this peaceful and preoccupied city. The great leafless square was empty, except for two Indians comparing lecture notes under the advertisement for Russian baths. He entered his hotel.

A woman he supposed was the manageress was in the hall—a dark bulky woman with spots round her mouth. She gave him an acute commercial look and called, "Else. Else. Where are you, Else?" harshly.

"It's all right," he said. "I will find her on my way up."

"The key ought to be here on its hook," the woman said.

"Never mind."

Else was sweeping the passage outside the room. She said, "Nobody's been in."

"Thank you. You are a good watcher."

But as soon as he was inside he knew that she hadn't told the truth. He had placed his wallet in an exact geometrical relationship to other points in the room, so that he could be sure. It had been moved. Perhaps Else had been dusting. He zipped the wallet open.

It contained no papers of importance, but their order had been altered. He called, "Else," gently. Watching her come in, small and bony, with that expression of fidelity she wore awkwardly like her apron, he wondered whether there was anybody in the world who couldn't be bribed. Perhaps he could be bribed himself—with what? He said, "Somebody *was* in here."

"Only me and—"

"And who?"

"The manageress, sir. I didn't think you'd mind *her*." He felt a surprising relief at finding that after all there was a chance of discovering honesty somewhere. He said, "Of course you couldn't keep *her* out, could you?"

"I did my best. She said as I didn't want her to see the untidiness. I said you'd told me—no one. She said, 'Give me that key.' I said, 'Mr. D. put this in my hands and said I wasn't to let anybody in.' Then she snatched it. I didn't mean her to come in. But afterwards I thought, well, no harm's done. I didn't see how you'd ever know." She said, "I'm sorry. I didn't ought to 'ave let her in." She had been crying.

"Was she angry with you?" he asked gently.

"She's given me the sack." She went hurriedly on, "It don't matter. It's slavery here—but you pick up things. There's ways of earning more—I'm not going to be a servant all my life."

He thought, The infection's still on me after all. I come into this place, breaking up God knows what lives. He said, "I'll speak to the manageress."

"Oh, I won't stay—not after this. She's"—the confession came out like a crime—"slapped my face."

"What will you do?"

Her innocence and her worldly knowledge filled him with horror "Oh, there's a girl who used to come here. She's got a flat of her own now. She always said as how I could go to her—to be her maid. I wouldn't have anything to do with the men, of course. Only open the door."

He exclaimed, "No! No!" It was as if he had been given a glimpse of the guilt which clings to all of us without our knowing it. None of us knows how much innocence we have betrayed. He would be responsible. He said, "Wait till I've talked to the manageress."

She said with a flash of bitterness, "It's not very different, what I do here, is it?" She went on, "It wouldn't be like being a servant at all. Me and Clara would go to cinemas every afternoon. She wants company, she says. She's got a Pekingese, that's all. You can't count men."

"Wait a little. I'm sure I can help you—somehow." He had no idea, unless perhaps Benditch's daughter—but that was unlikely after the episode of the car.

"Oh, I won't be leaving for a week." She was preposterously young to have such complete theoretical knowledge of vice. She said, "Clara's got a telephone which fits into a doll. All dressed up as a Spanish dancer. And she always gives her maid the chocolates, Clara says."

"Clara," he said, "can afford to wait." He seemed to be getting a very complete picture of that young woman; she probably had a kind heart, but so, he believed, had Benditch's daughter. She had given him a bun on a platform; it had seemed at the time a rather striking gesture of heedless generosity.

A voice outside said, "What are you doing here, Else?" It was the manageress.

"I called her in," D. said, "to ask who had been in here."

He hadn't yet had time to absorb the information the child had given him. Was the manageress another of his, as it were, collaborators, like K., anxious to see that he followed the narrow and virtuous path, or had she been bribed by L.? Why, in that case, should he have been sent to this hotel by the people at home? His room had been booked; everything had been arranged for him, so that they should never lose contact. But that, of course, might all have been arranged by whoever it was gave information to L.—if anybody had. There was no end to the circles in this hell.

"Nobody," the manageress said, "has been in here but myself—and Else."

"I told Else to let nobody in."

"You ought to have spoken to me." She had a square strong face ruined by ill health. "Besides, there's nobody would go into your room—except those with business there."

"Somebody seemed to take an interest in these papers of mine."

"Did you touch them, Else?"

"Of course I didn't."

She turned her big square spotty face to him like a challenge—an old keep-still capable of holding out. "You see, you *must* be wrong—if you believe the girl."

"I believe *her*."

"Then there's no more to be said—and no harm done."

He said nothing; it wasn't worth saying anything—she was either one of his own or one of L.'s party. It didn't matter which, for she had found nothing of interest, and he couldn't move from the hotel, he had his orders.

"And now perhaps you'll let me say what I came up here to say. There's a lady wants to speak to you on the telephone. In the hall."

He said with surprise, "A lady?"

"It's what I said."

"Did she give her name?"

"She did not." He saw Else watching him with anxiety; he thought, Good God, surely not another complication, calf love? He touched her sleeve as he went out of the door and said, "Trust me." Fourteen was a dreadfully early age at which to know so much and be so powerless. If this was civilization—the crowded prosperous streets, the women trooping in for coffee at Buzzard's, the lady in waiting at King Edward's court, and the sinking, drowning child —he preferred barbarity, the bombed streets, and the food queues; a child there had nothing worse to look forward to than death. Well, it was for *her* kind that he was fighting, to prevent the return of such a civilization to his own country.

He took up the receiver. "Hullo. Who's that, please?"

An impatient voice said, "This is Rose Cullen." What on earth, he thought, does that mean? Are they going to try to get at me, as in the story books, with a girl? "Yes?" he said. "Did you get home safely the other night—to Gwyn Cottage?" There was only one person who could have given her his address, and that was L.

"Of course I got home. Listen."

"I'm sorry I had to leave you in such questionable company."

"Oh," she said, "don't be a fool. Are you a thief?"

"I began stealing cars before you were born."

"But you *have* got an appointment with my father."

"Did he tell you so?"

An exclamation of impatience came up the wire. "Do you think Father and I are on speaking terms? It was written down in your diary. You dropped it."

"And this address too?"

"Yes."

"I'd like to have that back. The diary, I mean. It has sentimental associations—with my other robberies."

"Oh, for God's sake," the voice said, "if only you wouldn't . . ."

He stared gloomily away across the little hotel hall: an aspidistra on stilts, an umbrella rack in the form of a shell case. He thought, We could make an industry out of that, with all the shells we have at home. Empty shell cases for export. Give a tasteful umbrella stand this Christmas from one of the devastated cities. "Have you gone to sleep?" the voice said.

"No, I'm just waiting to hear what you want. It is—you see—a little embarrassing. Our last meeting was—odd."

"I want to talk to you."

"Well?" He wished he could make up his mind as to whether she was L.'s girl or not.

"I don't mean on the phone. Will you have dinner with me tonight?"

"I haven't, you know, got the right clothes."

It was strange—her voice sounded extraordinarily strained. If she was L.'s girl, of course, they might be getting anxious; time was very short. His appointment with Benditch was for tomorrow at noon.

"We'll go anywhere you like."

It didn't seem to him as if there would be any harm in their meeting as long as he didn't take his credentials with him, even in his socks. On the other hand, his room might be searched again. It was certainly a problem. He said, "Where should we meet?"

She said promptly, "Outside Russell Square Station, at seven." That sounded safe enough. He said, "Do you know anyone who wants a good maid? You or your father, for instance?"

"Are you crazy?"

"Never mind. We'll talk about that tonight. Good-bye."

He walked slowly upstairs; he wasn't going to take any chances. The credentials had to be hidden. He had only to get through twenty-four hours, and then he would be a free man—to return to his bombed and starving home. Surely they were not going to throw a mistress at his head; people didn't fall for that sort of thing except in melodrama. In melodrama a secret agent was never tired or uninterested or in love with a dead woman. But perhaps L. read melodramas; he represented, after all, the aristocracy—the marquises and generals and bishops—who lived in a curious formal world of their own, jingling with medals that they awarded to each other— like fishes in a tank, perpetually stared at through glass, and confined to a particular element by their physiological needs. They might take their ideas of the other world—of professional men and working people—partly from melodrama. It was wrong to underestimate the ignorance of the ruling class. Marie Antoinette had said of the poor, "Can't they eat cake?"

The manageress had gone; perhaps there was an extension and she had been listening to his conversation on another phone. The child was still cleaning the passage with furious absorption. He stood and watched her for a while. One had to take risks sometimes. He said, "Would you mind coming into my room for just a moment?" He closed the door behind them both. He said, "I want to speak low—because the manageress mustn't hear." Again he was startled by that look of devotion—what on earth had he done to earn it, a middle-aged foreigner with a face from which he had only recently cleaned the blood, scarred? He had given her half a dozen kind words; in her environment were they so rare that they evoked automatically—this? He said, "I want you to do something for me."

"Anything," she said. She was devoted too, he thought, to Clara. What a life when a child had to fix her love on an old foreigner and a prostitute for want of anything better.

He said, "Nobody at all must know. I have some papers people are looking for. I want you to keep them for me until tomorrow."

She asked, "Are you a spy?"

"No. No."

"I wouldn't mind," she said, "what you are." He sat down on the bed and took off his shoes; she watched him with fascination. She said, "That lady on the phone—"

He looked up with a sock in one hand and the papers in the other. "She mustn't know. You and me only." Her face glowed; he might have given her a jewel. He changed his mind quickly about offering her money. Later—perhaps—when he was leaving—some present she could turn into money if she chose, but not the brutal and degrading payment. "Where will you keep them?" he said.

"Where you did."

"And nobody must know."

"Cross my heart."

"Better do it now. At once." He turned his back and looked out of the window; the hotel sign in big gilt letters was strung just below; forty feet down the frosty pavement and a coal cart going slowly by. "And now," he said, "I'm going to sleep again." There were enormous arrears of sleep to make up.

"Won't you have some lunch?" she asked. "It's not so bad today

There's Irish stew and treacle pudding. It keeps you warm." She said, "I'll see you get big helpings—when her back's turned."

"I'm not used yet," he said, "to your big meals. Where I've come from, we've got out of the way of eating."

"But you have to eat."

"Oh," he said, "we've found a cheaper way. We look at pictures of food—in the magazines—instead."

"Go on," she said. "I don't believe you. You've got to eat. If it's the money—"

"No," he said, "it's not the money. I promise you I'll eat well tonight. But just now it's sleep I want."

"Nobody'll come in this time," she said. "Nobody." He could hear her moving in the passage outside like a sentry—a flap, flap, flap; she was probably pretending to dust.

He lay down again on his bed in his clothes. No need this time to tell his subconscious mind to wake him. He never slept for more than six hours at a time. That was the longest interval there ever was between raids. But this time he couldn't sleep at all; never before had he left those papers out of his possession. They had been with him all across Europe: on the express to Paris, to Calais, Dover; even when he was being beaten up, they were there, under his heel, a safeguard. He felt uneasy without them. They were his authority, and now he was nothing—just an undesirable alien, lying on a shabby bed in a disreputable hotel. Suppose the girl should boast of his confidence; but he trusted her more than he trusted anyone else. But she was simple. Suppose she should change her stockings and leave his papers lying about, forgotten. L., he thought grimly, would never have done a thing like that. In a way the whole future of what was left of his country lay in the stockings of an underpaid child. They were worth at least two thousand pounds on the nail—that had been proved. They would probably pay a great deal more if you gave them credit. He felt powerless, like Samson with his hair shorn. He nearly got up and called Else back. But if he did, what should he do with the papers? There was no-where in the little bare room to hide them. In a way, too, it was suitable that the future of the poor should depend upon the poor.

The hours passed slowly. He supposed that this was resting. There was silence in the passage after a while; she hadn't been able to spin out her dusting any longer. If only I had a gun, he thought, I shouldn't feel so powerless. But it had been impossible to bring one; it was to risk too much at the Customs. Presumably here there were ways of obtaining a revolver secretly, but he didn't know them. He discovered that he was a little frightened; time was so short—they were certain to spring something on him soon. If they began with a beating-up, their next attempt was likely to be drastic. It felt odd, lonely, terrifying to be the only one in danger; as a rule he had the company of a whole city. Again his mind returned to the prison and the warder coming across the asphalt; he had been alone then. Fighting was better in the old days. Roland had companions at Roncesvalles—Oliver and Turpin; the whole chivalry of Europe was riding up to help him. Men were united by a common belief. Even a heretic would be on the side of Christendom against the Moors; they might differ about the persons of the Trinity, but on the main issue they were like rock. Now there were so many varieties of economic materialism, so many initial letters.

A few street cries came up through the cold air: old clothes, and a man who wanted chairs to mend. He had said that war killed emotion; it was untrue. Those cries were an agony. He buried his head in the pillow as a young man might have done. They brought back with intensity the years before his marriage. They had listened to them together. He felt like a young man who has given all his trust and found himself mocked, cuckolded, betrayed. Or who has himself in a minute of lust spoiled a whole life together. To live was like perjury. How often they had declared that they would die within a week of each other—but he hadn't died; he had survived prison, the shattered house. The bomb that had wrecked four floors and killed a cat had left him alive. Did L. really imagine that he could trap him with a woman? And was this what London—a foreign peaceful city—had in store for him, the return of feeling, despair?

The dusk fell; lights came out like hoarfrost. He lay on his back again with his eyes open. Oh, to be home. Presently he got up and shaved. It was time to be gone. He buttoned his overcoat up round the chin as he stepped out into the bitter night. An east wind blew from the city; it had the stone cold of big business blocks and banks. You thought of long passages and glass doors and a spiritless routine. It was a wind to take the heart out of a man. He walked up Guilford Street; the after-office rush was over and the theatre traffic hadn't begun. In the small hotels dinners were being laid, and oriental faces peered out from bed-sitting rooms with gloomy nostalgia.

As he turned up a side street he heard a voice behind him, cultured, insinuating, weak. "Excuse me, sir. Excuse me." He stopped. A man dressed very oddly in a battered bowler and a long black overcoat from which a fur collar had been removed bowed with an air of excessive gentility; he had a white stubble on his chin, his eyes were bloodshot and pouchy, and he carried in front of him a thin worn hand as if it were to be kissed. He began at once to apologize in what remained of a university—or a stage—accent. "I felt sure you wouldn't mind my addressing you, sir. The fact of the matter is, I find myself in a predicament."

"A predicament?"

"A matter of a few shillings, sir." D. wasn't used to this; their beggars at home in the old days had been more spectacular, with lumps of rotting flesh uplifted at the doors of churches.

The man had an air of badly secreted anxiety. "I wouldn't have addressed you, sir, naturally, if I hadn't felt that you were, well, of one's own kind." Was there really a snobbery in begging—or was it just a method of approach which had proved workable? "Of course if it's inconvenient at the moment, say no more about it."

D. put his hand into his pocket.

"Not here, if you don't mind, sir, in the full light of day, as it were. If you would just step into this mews. I confess to a feeling of shame—asking a complete stranger for a loan like this." He sidled nervously sideways into the empty mews. "You can imagine my circumstances." One car stood there; big green closed gates; nobody about. "Well," D. said, "here's half a crown."

"Thank you, sir." He grabbed it. "Perhaps one day I shall be able to repay . . ." He was off with lanky strides, out of the mews, into the street, out of sight. D. began to follow. There was a small scraping sound behind him, and a piece of brick suddenly flew out of the wall and struck him sharply on the cheek. Memory warned him; he ran. In the street there were lights in windows, a policeman stood at a corner, he was safe. He knew that somebody had fired at him with a gun fitted with a silencer. Ignorance. You couldn't aim properly with a silencer.

The beggar, he thought, must have waited for me outside the hotel, acted as decoy into the mews; if they had hit him, the car was there ready to take his body. Or perhaps they meant only to maim him. Probably they hadn't made up their own minds which, and that was another reason why they had missed, just as in billiards if you have two shots in mind, you miss both. But how had they known the hour at which he would be leaving the hotel? He quickened his step and came up Bernard Street, with a tiny flame of anger at his heart. The girl, of course, would not be at the station.

But she was.

He said, "I didn't really expect to find you here. Not after your friends had tried to shoot me."

"Listen," she said, "there are things I won't and can't believe. I came here to apologize. About last night. I don't believe you meant to steal that car, but I was drunk, furious. I never thought they meant to smash you as they did. It was that fool Currie. But if you start being melodramatic again— Is it a new kind of confidence trick? Is it meant to appeal to the romantic female heart? Because you'd better know, it doesn't work."

He said, "Did L. know you were meeting me here at seven?"

She said, with a faint uneasiness, "Not L. Currie did." The confession surprised him; perhaps after all she *was* innocent. "He'd got your notebook, you see. He said it ought to be kept—in case you tried anything more on. I spoke to him on the telephone today—he was in town. I said I didn't believe you meant to steal that car and that I was going to meet you. I wanted to give it back to you."

"He let you have it?"

"Here it is."

"And perhaps you told him where, what time?"

"I may have done. We talked a lot. He argued. But it's no use you telling me Currie shot at you. I don't believe it."

"Oh, no. Nor do I. I suppose he happened to meet L. and told him."

She said, "He was having lunch with L." She exclaimed furiously, "But it's fantastic! How could they shoot at you in the street—here? What about the police, the noise, the neighbours? Why are you here at all? Why aren't you at the police station?"

He said gently, "One at a time. It was in a mews. There was a silencer. And as for the police station, I had an appointment here with you."

"I don't believe it. I won't believe it. Don't you see that if things like that happened life would be quite different? One would have to begin over again."

He said, "It doesn't seem odd to me. At home we live with bullets. Even here you'd get used to it. Life goes on much the same." He took her by the hand like a child and led her down Bernard Street, then into Grenville Street. He said, "It will be quite safe. He won't have stayed." They came to the mews. He picked up a scrap of brick at the entrance. He said, "You see, this was what he hit."

"Prove it. Prove it," she said fiercely.

"I don't suppose that's possible." He began to dig with his nail at the wall, looking for something; the bullet might have wedged. He said, "They are getting desperate. There was the business in the lavatory yesterday—and then what you saw. Today somebody searched my room—but that may be one of my own people. But this—tonight—is going pretty far. They can't do much more now than kill me. I don't think they'll manage that, though. I'm horribly hard to kill."

"Oh, God," she said suddenly, "it's true!" He turned. She held a bullet in her hand; it had ricocheted off the wall. She said, "It's true. So we've got to do something. The police—"

"I saw nobody. There's no evidence."

"You said last night that note offered you money."

"Yes."

"Why don't you take it?" she asked angrily. "You don't want to be killed."

It occurred to him that she was going to be hysterical. He took her arm and pushed her in front of him into a public house. "Two double brandies," he said. He began to talk cheerfully and quickly. "I want you to do me a favour. There's a girl at the hotel where I'm staying—she's done me a service and got the sack for it. She's a good little thing—only wild. God knows what mightn't happen to her. Couldn't you find her a job? You must have hundreds of smart friends."

"Oh, stop being so damned quixotic," she said. "I want to hear more about all this."

"There's not much I can tell you. Apparently they don't want me to see your father."

"Are you," she said with a kind of angry contempt, "what they call a patriot?"

"Oh, no, I don't think so. It's they, you know, who are always talking about something called our country."

"Then why don't you take their money?"

He said, "You've got to choose some line of action and live by it. Otherwise nothing matters at all. You probably end with a gas oven. I've chosen certain people who've had the lean portion for some centuries now."

"But your people are betrayed all the time."

"It doesn't matter. You might say it's the only job left for anyone —sticking to a job. It's no good taking a moral line; my people commit atrocities like the others. I suppose if I believed in a God it would be simpler."

"Do you believe," she said, "that *your* leaders are any better than L.'s?" She swallowed her brandy and began to tap the counter nervously with the little metal bullet.

"No. Of course not. But I still prefer the people they lead—even if they lead them all wrong."

"The poor, right or wrong," she scoffed.

"It's no worse, is it, than my country right or wrong? You choose your side once for all—of course it may be the wrong side. Only history can tell that." He took the bullet out of her hand and said, "I'm going to eat something. I haven't had anything since last night." He took a plate of sandwiches and carried them to a table. "Go on," he said, "eat a little. You are always drinking on an empty stomach when I meet you. It's bad for the nerves."

"I'm not hungry."

"I am." He took a large bite out of a ham sandwich. She began to squeak her finger up and down on the shiny china top. "Tell me," she said, "about what you were—before all this started."

"I was a lecturer," he said, "in medieval French. Not an exciting occupation." He smiled. "It had its moment. You've heard of the *Song of Roland?*"

"Yes."

"It was I who discovered the Berne MS."

"That doesn't mean a thing to me," she said. "I'm bone ignorant."

"The best MS. was the one your people had at Oxford; but it was too corrected—and there were gaps. Then there was the Venice MS. That filled in some of the gaps, not all; it was very inferior." He said proudly, "I found the Berne MS."

"You did, did you?" she said gloomily, with her eyes on the bullet in his hand. Then she looked up at the scarred chin and the bruised mouth. He said, "You remember the story—of that rearguard in the Pyrenees, and how Oliver, when he saw the Saracens coming, urged Roland to blow his horn and fetch back Charlemagne."

She seemed to be wondering about the scar. She began to ask, "How—?"

"And Roland wouldn't blow—swore that no enemy could ever make him blow. A big brave fool. In war one always chooses the wrong hero. Oliver should have been the hero of that song—instead of being given second place with the bloodthirsty bishop Turpin."

She said, "How did your wife die?" but he was determined to keep the conversation free from the infection of his war.

He said, "And then, of course, when all his men are dead or dying, and he himself is finished, he says he'll blow the horn. And the song-writer makes—what is your expression?—a great dance about it. The blood streams from his mouth, the bones of his temple are broken. But Oliver taunts him. He had had his chance to blow his horn at the beginning and save all those lives, but for his own glory he would not blow. Now because he is defeated and dying he will blow and bring disgrace on his race and name. Let him die quietly and be content with all the damage his heroism has done. Didn't I tell you Oliver was the real hero?"

"Did you?" she said. She was obviously not following what he said. He saw that she was nearly crying, and ashamed of it—self-pity, probably. It was a quality he didn't care for, even in an adolescent.

He said, "That's the importance of the Berne MS. It re-establishes Oliver. It makes the story tragedy, not just heroics. Because in the Oxford version Oliver is reconciled, he gives Roland his deathblow by accident, his eyes blinded by wounds. The story, you see, has been tidied up, to suit. But in the Berne version he strikes his friend down with full knowledge—because of what he has done to his men, all the wasted lives. He dies hating the man he loves—the big boasting courageous fool who was more concerned with his own glory than with the victory of his faith. But you can see how that version didn't appeal—in the castles, at the banquets, among the dogs and reeds and beakers; the jongleurs had to adapt it to meet the tastes of the medieval nobles, who were quite capable of being Rolands in a small way—it only needs conceit and a strong arm—but couldn't understand what Oliver was at."

"Give me Oliver," she said, "any day." He looked at her with some surprise. She said, "My father, of course, would be like one of your barons—all for Roland."

He said, "After I had published the Berne MS. the war came."

"And when it's over," she said, "what will you do then?"

It had never occurred to him to wonder that. He said, "Oh, I don't suppose I shall see the end."

"Like Oliver," she said, "you'd have stopped it if you could, but as it's happened—"

"Oh, I'm not an Oliver any more than the poor devils at home are Rolands. Or L. a Ganelon."

"Who was Ganelon?"

"He was the traitor."

She said, "You are sure about L.? He seemed to me pleasant enough."

"They know how to be pleasant. They've cultivated that art for centuries." He drank his brandy down. He said, "Well, I'm here. Why should we talk business? You asked me to come and I've come."

"I just wished I could help you. That's all."

"Why?"

She said, "After they'd beaten you up last night I was sick. Of course Currie thought it was the drink. But it was your face. Oh," she exclaimed, "you ought to know how it is! There's no trust anywhere. I'd never seen a face that looked medium honest. I mean about everything. My father's people—they're honest about —well, food and love perhaps—they have stuffy contented wives, anyway—but where coal is concerned—or the workmen—" She said, "If you hope for anything at all from them, for God's sake don't breathe melodrama—or sentiment. Show them a cheque book, a contract—let it be a cast-iron one."

In the public bar across the way they were throwing darts with enormous precision. He said, "I haven't come to beg."

"Does it really matter a lot to you?"

"Wars today are not what they were in Roland's time. Coal can be more important than tanks. We've got more tanks than we want. They aren't much good, anyway."

"But Ganelon can still upset everything?"

"It's not so easy for him."

She said, "I suppose they'll all be there when you see my father. There's honour among thieves. Goldstein and old Lord Fetting, Brigstock—and Forbes. You better know what you'll be up against."

He said, "Be careful. After all, they are *your* people."

"I haven't got a people. My grandfather was a workman, anyway."

"You're unlucky," he said. "You are in no-man's-land. Where

I am. We just have to choose our side—and neither side will trust us, of course."

"You can trust Forbes," she said, "about coal, I mean. Not of course all round the clock. He's dishonest about his name—his real name is Furtstein. And he's dishonest in love. He wants to marry me. That's how I know. He keeps a mistress in Shepherd's Market. A friend of his told me." She laughed. "We have fine friends."

For the second time that day D. was shocked. He remembered the child in the hotel. You learned too much in these days before you came of age. His own people knew death before they could walk; they got used to desire early—but this savage knowledge, that ought to come slowly, the gradual fruit of experience . . . In a happy life the final disillusionment with human nature coincided with death. Nowadays they seemed to have a whole lifetime to get through somehow after it.

"You are not going to marry him?" he asked anxiously.

"I may. He's better than most of them."

"Perhaps it's not true about the mistress."

"Oh, yes. I put detectives on to check up."

He gave it up; this wasn't peace. When he landed in England he had felt some envy—there had been a casualness, even a certain sense of trust at the passport control, but there was probably something behind that. He had imagined that the suspicion which was the atmosphere of his own life was due to civil war, but he began to believe that it existed everywhere; it was part of human life. People were united only by their vices; there was honour among adulterers and thieves. He had been too absorbed in the old days with his love and with the Berne MS. and the weekly lecture on romance languages to notice it. It was as if the whole world lay in the shadow of abandonment. Perhaps it was still propped up by ten just men—that was a pity; better scrap it and begin again with newts. "Well," she said, "let's go "

"Where?"

"Oh, anywhere One must do something. It's early yet. A cinema?"

They sat for nearly three hours in a kind of palace—gold winged figures, deep carpets, and an endless supply of refreshment carried round by girls got up to kill; these places were less luxurious when he was last in London. It was a musical play full of curious sacrifices and sufferings—a starving producer and a blond girl who had made good. She had her name up in neon lights on Piccadilly, but she flung up her part and came back to Broadway to save him. She put up the money—secretly—for a new production, and the glamour of her name gave it success. It was a revue all written in no time, and the cast was packed with starving talent. Everybody made a lot of money; everybody's name went up in neon lights— the producer's too; the girl's of course was there from the first. There was a lot of suffering—glycerine tears pouring down the big blond features—and a lot of happiness. It was curious and pathetic; everybody behaved nobly and made a lot of money. It was as if some code of faith and morality had been lost for centuries, and the world was trying to reconstruct it from the unreliable evidence of folk memories and subconscious desires—and perhaps some hieroglyphics upon stone.

He felt her hand rest on his knee; she wasn't romantic, she had said; this was an automatic reaction, he supposed, to the deep seats and the dim lights and the torch songs, as when Pavlov's dogs salivated. It was a reaction which went through all social levels like hunger. But he was short-circuited. He laid his hand on hers with a sense of pity—she deserved something better than a man called Furtstein who kept a girl in Shepherd's Market. She wasn't romantic, but he could feel her hand cold and acquiescent under his. He said gently, "I think we ve been followed "

She said, "It doesn't matter. If that's how the world is, I can take it. Is somebody going to shoot or a bomb go off? I don't like sudden noises. Perhaps you'll warn me."

"It's only a man who teaches Entrenationo I'm sure I saw his steel glasses in the lobby."

The blond heroine wept more tears; for people predestined for success by popular choice they were all extraordinarily sad and obtuse. If *we* lived in a world, he thought, which guaranteed a happy ending, should we be as long discovering it? Perhaps that's what the saints were at with their incomprehensible happiness— they had seen the end of the story when they came in and couldn't take the agonies seriously. Rose said, "I can't stand this any more. Let's go. You can see the ending half an hour away."

They got out with difficulty into the aisle; he discovered he was still holding her hand. He said, "I wish—sometimes—I could see *my* ending." He felt extraordinarily tired; two long days and the beating had weakened him.

"Oh," she said, "I can tell you that. You'll go on fighting for people who aren't worth fighting for. Someday you'll be killed. But you won't hit back at Roland—not intentionally. The Berne MS. is all wrong there."

They got into a taxi. She said to the driver, "The Carlton Hotel, Gabitas Street." He looked back through the little window; there was no sign of Mr. K. Perhaps it had been a coincidence—even Mr. K. must sometimes relax and watch the glycerine tears. He said more to himself than her, "I can't believe they'll really give up, so soon. After all, tomorrow—it's defeat. The coal is as good as a whole fleet of the latest bombers." They came slowly down Guilford Street. He said, "If only I had a gun . . ."

"They'd never dare, would they?" she said. She put her hand through his arm, as if she wanted him to stay with her in the taxi, safely anonymous. He remembered that he had momentarily thought she was one of L.'s agents; he regretted that. He said, "My dear, it's just like a sum in mathematics. It might cause diplomatic trouble—but then that might not be so bad for them as if we got the coal. It's a question of addition—which adds up to most."

"Are you afraid?"

"Yes."

"Why not stay somewhere else? Come back with me. I can give you a bed."

"I've left something here. I can't." The taxi stopped. He got out. She followed him and stood on the pavement at his side. She said, "Can't I come in with you—in case—?"

"Better not." He held her hand. It was an excuse to linger and make sure the street was empty. He wondered whether the manageress was his friend or not. Mr. K. . . . He said, "Before you go, I meant to ask again—could you find a job for this girl here? She's a good thing—trustworthy."

She said sharply, "I wouldn't lift a finger if she were dying." It was that voice he had heard ages ago in the bar of the Channel steamer, making her demands to the steward. "I want one more. I *will* have one more"—the disagreeable child at the dull party. She said, "Let go of my hand." He dropped it quickly. She said, "You damned quixote. Go on. Get shot, die—you're out of place."

He said, "You have it all wrong. The girl's young enough to be my—"

"Daughter," she said. "Go on. So am I. Laugh. This is what always happens. I know. I told you. I'm not romantic. This is what's called a father-fixation. You hate your own father—for a thousand reasons—and then you fall for a man the same age." She said, "It's grotesque. Nobody can pretend there's any poetry in it. You go telephoning, making appointments—"

He watched her uneasily, aware of that awful inability to feel anything but fear, a little pity. Seventeenth-century poets wrote as if you could give away your heart forever. That wasn't true according to modern psychologists, but you could feel such grief and such despair that you flinched away from the possibility of ever feeling again. He stood hopelessly in front of the open door of the shabby hotel to which short-timers came, inadequate.

He said, "If only this war was over . . ."

"It won't be over ever—you've said it—for you."

She was lovely; he had never, when he was young, known anyone so lovely—certainly not his wife; she had been quite a plain woman. That hadn't mattered. All the same it ought to be possible to feel desire with the help of a little beauty. He took her tentatively in his arms like an experiment. She said, "Can I come up?"

"Not here." He let her go; it hadn't worked.

"I knew there was something wrong with me when you came up to the car last night. Dithering. Polite. I felt sick when I heard them beating you—I thought I was drunk, and then when I woke up this morning it still went on. You know I've never been in love before. They have a name for it—haven't they?—calf love."

She used an expensive scent; he tried to feel more than pity. After all, it was a chance for a middle-aged ex-lecturer in the romance languages. "My dear," he said.

She said, "It doesn't last, does it? But then it won't have to last long. You'll be killed, won't you, as sure as eggs is eggs?"

He kissed her unconvincingly. He said, "My dear, I'll be seeing you—tomorrow. All this—business—will be over then. We'll meet —celebrate." He knew he was acting not very effectively; but this wasn't an occasion for honesty. She was too young to stand honesty.

She said, "Even Roland, I suppose, had a woman." But he remembered that *she*—her name was Alda—had fallen dead when they brought the news. Life didn't go on in a legend, after the loved one died, as his had done. It was taken for granted—the jongleur gave her only a few formal lines. He said, "Good night."

"Good night." She went back up the street towards the black trees. He thought to himself that after all L. might have had a worse agent. He discovered in himself a willingness to love which was like treachery—but what was the use? Tomorrow everything would be settled, and he would return. He wondered whether in the end she would marry Furtstein.

He pushed the glass inner door. It was ajar; he flashed his hand automatically to his pocket, but of course he had no gun. The light was out, but somebody was there; he could hear the breathing, not far from the aspidistra. He himself was exposed in front of the door, with the street lamp beyond. It was no good moving; they could always fire first. He took his hand out of his pocket again, with his cigarette case in it. He tried to stop his fingers from shaking, but he was afraid of pain. He put a cigarette in his mouth and felt for a wax match—they mightn't expect the sudden flash on the wall. He moved a little way forward and suddenly struck with the match sideways; it scraped against a picture frame and flared up. A white childish face sailed like a balloon out of the darkness. He said, "Oh, God, Else, you gave me a fright! What are you doing there?"

"Waiting for you," the thin immature voice whispered; the match went out.

"Why?"

"I thought you might be bringing her in here. It's my job," she said, "to see that clients get their rooms."

"That's nonsense."

"You kissed her, didn't you?"

"It wasn't a good kiss."

"But it's not that. You've got a right. It's what *she* said."

He wondered whether he had made a mistake in giving her his papers—suppose she destroyed them, out of jealousy? He asked, "What did she say?"

"She said they'd kill you sure as eggs is eggs."

He laughed with relief. "Well, we've got a war on at home. People do get killed. But she doesn't *know.*"

"And *here,*" she said, "they're after you too."

"They can't do much."

"I knew something awful was happening," she said. "They're upstairs now, talking."

"Who?" he asked sharply.

"The manageress—and a man."

"What sort of a man?"

"A little grey man, with steel spectacles." He must have slipped out of the cinema before them. She said, "They were asking *me* questions."

"What questions?"

"If you'd said anything to me. If I'd seen anything—papers. Of course I was mum. Nothing *they* could do would make me talk." He was moved with pity by her devotion—what a world to let such qualities go to waste! She said passionately, "I don't mind their killing me."

"There's no danger of that."

Her voice came shivering out from beside the aspidistra. *"She'd* do anything. She acts mad sometimes—if she's crossed. I don't mind. I won't let you down. You're a gentleman." It was a horribly inadequate reason. She went mournfully on, "I'd do anything that girl'll do."

"You are doing much more."

"Is she going back with you—there?"

"No, no."

"Can I?"

"My dear," he said, "you don't know what it's like there."

He could hear a long whistling sigh. "You don't know what it's like here."

"Where are they now?" he said. "The manageress and her friend."

"The first floor front," she said. "Are they your—deadly foes?" God knew out of what twopenny trash she drew her vocabulary.

"I think they're my friends. I don't know. Perhaps I'd better find out before they know I'm here."

"Oh, they'll know by now. *She* hears everything. What's said on the roof, she hears in the kitchen. She told me not to tell you." He was shaken by a doubt. Could this child be in danger? But he couldn't believe it. What could they do to her? He went cautiously up the unlighted stair; once a board creaked. The staircase made a half-turn and he came suddenly upon the landing; a door stood open; an electric globe, under a pink frilly silken shade, shone on the two figures waiting for him with immense patience.

D. said gently, *"Bona matina.* You didn't teach me the word for night."

The manageress said, "Come in—and shut the door." He obeyed her—there was nothing else to do; it occurred to him that never once yet had he been allowed the initiative. He had been like a lay figure other people moved about, used as an Aunt Sally. "Where have you been?" the manageress said. It was a bully's face; she should have been a man, with that ugly square jaw, the shady determination, the impetigo.

He said, "Mr. K. will tell you."

"What were you doing with the girl?"

"Enjoying myself." He looked curiously round at the den; that was the best word for it; it wasn't a woman's room at all, with its square unclothed table, its leather chairs, no flowers, no frippery, a cupboard for shoes; it seemed made and furnished for nothing but use. The cupboard door was open, full of heavy, low-heeled, sensible shoes.

"She knows L."

"So do I." Even the pictures were masculine—of a kind. Cheap coloured pictures of women, all silk stockings and lingerie. It seemed to him the room of an inhibited bachelor. It was dimly horrifying, like timid secret desires for unattainable intimacies. Mr. K. suddenly spoke. He was like a feminine element in the male room; there were traces of hysteria. He said, "When you were out—at the cinema—somebody rang up—to make you an offer."

"Why did they do that? They should have known I was out."

"They offered you your own terms not to keep your appointment tomorrow."

"I haven't made any terms."

"They left the message with me," the manageress said.

"They were quite prepared, then, that everybody should know? You and K."

Mr. K. squeezed his bony hands together. "We wanted to make sure," he said, "that you still have the papers."

"You were afraid I might have sold them already. On my way home."

"We have to be careful," he said, as if he were listening for Dr. Bellows' rubber soles. He was dreadfully under the domination, even here, of the shilling fine.

"Are you acting on instructions?"

"Our instructions are so vague. A lot is left to our discretion. Perhaps you would show us the papers." The woman didn't talk any more—she let the weak ones have their rope.

"No."

He looked from one to the other. It seemed to him that at last the initiative was passing into his hands; he wished he had more vitality to take it, but he was exhausted. England was full of tiresome memories which made him remember that this wasn't really his job; he should be at the Museum now reading romance. He said, "I accept the fact that we have the same employers. But I have no reason to trust you." The little grey man sat as if condemned, with his eyes on his own bitter fingertips; the woman faced him with that ugly, square, dominant face—which had nothing to dominate except a shady hotel. He had seen many people shot on both sides of the line for treachery; he knew you couldn't recognize them by their manners or faces; there was no Ganelon type. He said, "Are you just anxious to see that you get your cut out of the sale? But there won't be a cut—or a sale."

"Perhaps, then, you'll read this letter," the woman suddenly said; they had used up their rope.

He read it slowly; there was no doubt at all of its genuineness; he knew the signature and the notepaper of the ministry too well to be deceived. This, apparently, was the end of his mission—the woman was empowered to take over from him the necessary papers, for what purpose wasn't said.

"You see," the woman said, "they don't trust you."

"Why not have shown me this when I arrived?"

"It was left to my discretion. To trust you or not."

The position was fantastic. He had been entrusted with the papers as far as London; Mr. K. was told to check up on his movements before he reached the hotel but was not trusted with the secret of his mission; this woman seemed to have been trusted with both the secret and the papers—but only as a last resort, if his conduct was suspicious. He said suddenly, "Of course you know what these papers are."

She said stubbornly, "Naturally." But he was sure that after all she didn't; he could read that in her face—the obstinate poker features. There was no end to the complicated work of half-trust and half-deceit. Suppose the ministry had made a mistake. Suppose, if he handed the papers over, they should sell them to L. He knew he could trust himself. He knew nothing else. There was a horrid smell of cheap scent in the room—it was apparently her only female characteristic—and it was disturbing, like scent on a man.

"You see," she said, "you can go home now. Your job is finished."

It was all too easy and too dubious. The ministry didn't trust him or them or anybody. They didn't trust each other. Only each individual knew that one person was true or false. Mr. K. knew what Mr. K. meant to do with those papers. The manageress knew what she intended. You couldn't answer for anybody but yourself.

He said, "Those orders were not given to me. I shall keep the papers."

Mr. K.'s voice became shrill. He said, "If you go behind our backs—" His underpaid jumpy Entrenationo eyes gave away unguardedly secrets of greed and envy. What could you expect on that salary? How much treachery is always nourished in little overworked centres of somebody else's idealism. The manageress said, "You are a sentimental man. A bourgeois. A professor. Probably romantic. If you cheat us you'll find—oh, I can think up things." He couldn't face her; it was really like looking into the pit—she had imagination; the impetigo was like the relic of some shameful act from which she had never recovered. He remembered Else's saying, "She acts like mad."

He said, "Do you mean if I cheat you—or cheat our people at home?" He was genuinely uncertain of her meaning. He was lost and exhausted among potential enemies; the farther you got away from the open battle, the more alone you were. He felt envy of those who were now in the firing line. Then suddenly he was back there himself—a clang of bells, the roar down the street—fire engine, ambulance? The raid was over and the bodies were being uncovered; men picked over the stones carefully for fear they might miss a body; sometimes a pick wielded too carelessly caused agony. The world misted over—as in the dust which hung for an hour about a street. He felt sick and shaken; he remembered the dead tomcat close to his face; he couldn't move, he just lay there with the fur almost on his mouth.

The whole room began to shake. The manageress's head swelled up like a blister. He heard her say, "Quick. Lock the door," and tried to pull himself together. What were they going to do to him? Enemies . . . friends. . . . He was on his knees. Time slowed up. Mr. K. moved with appalling slowness towards the door. The manageress's black skirt was close to his mouth, dusty like the cat's fur. He wanted to scream, but the weight of human dignity lay like a gag over his tongue—one didn't scream, even when the truncheon struck. He heard her say, "Where are the papers?" leaning down to him. Her breath was all cheap scent and nicotine—half female and half male.

He said apologetically, "Fight yesterday. Shot at today." A thick decisive thumb came down towards his eyeballs; he was involved in a nightmare. He said, "I haven't got them."

"Where are they?" It hovered over his right eye; he could hear

Mr. K. fiddling at the door. Mr. K. said, "It doesn't lock." He felt horror as if her hand as well as her face carried infection.

"You turn it the other way." He tried to heave himself upwards, but a thumb pushed him back. A sensible·shoe trod firmly upon his hand. Mr. K. protested about something in low tones. A scared determined voice said, "Was it you who rang, ma'am?"

"Of course I didn't ring."

D. raised himself carefully. He said, "I rang, Else. I felt ill. Nothing much. Ambulance outside. I was buried once in a raid. If you'll give me your arm, I can get to bed." The little room swung clearly back—the boot cupboard and the epicene girls in black silk stockings and the masculine chairs. He said, "I'll lock my door tonight or I'll be walking in my sleep."

They climbed slowly up to the top floor. He said, "You came just in time. I might have done something silly. I think after tomorrow morning we'll go away from here."

"Me too?"

He promised rashly, as if in a violent world you could promise anything at all, beyond the moment of speaking. "Yes. You too."

Three

The cat's fur and the dusty skirt stayed with him all the night. The peace of his usual dreams was hopelessly broken—no flowers or quiet rivers or old gentlemen talking of lectures; he had always, after that worst raid, been afraid of suffocation. He was glad the other side shot their prisoners and didn't hang them—the rope round the neck would bring nightmare into life. Day came without daylight; a yellow fog outside shut visibility down to twenty yards. While he was shaving, Else came in with a tray, a boiled egg and a kipper, a pot of tea.

"You shouldn't have bothered," he said. "I would have come down."

"I thought," she said, "it would be a good excuse. You'll be wanting the papers back." She began to haul off a shoe and a stocking. She said, "Oh, Lord, what would they think if they came in now?" She sat on the bed and felt for the papers in the instep.

"What's that?" he said, listening hard. He found he dreaded the return of the papers; responsibility was like an unlucky ring you preferred to hand on to strangers. She sat upon the bed and listened too; then the footsteps creaked on the stairs going down.

"Oh," she said, "that's only Mr. Muckerji—a Hindu gentleman. He's not like the other Indian downstairs. Mr. Muckerji's very respectful."

He took the papers—well, he'd be free of them very soon now. She put on her stocking again. She said, "He's inquisitive. That's the only thing. Asks such questions."

"What sort of questions?"

"Oh, everything. Do I believe in horoscopes? Do I believe the newspapers? What do I think of Mr. Eden? And he writes down the answers too. I don't know why."

"Odd."

"Do you think it'll get me into trouble? When I'm in the mood I say such things—about Mr. Eden, anything. For fun, you know. But sometimes it gets me scared to think that every word is written down. And then I look up sometimes and there he is watching me like I was an animal. But always respectful."

He gave it up; Mr. Muckerji didn't concern him. He sat down to his breakfast. But the child didn't go; it was as if she had a reservoir of speech saved up for him—or Mr. Muckerji. She said, "You meant what you said last night about us going away?"

"Yes," he said. "Somehow I'll manage it."

"I don't want to be a burden to you." The novelette was on her tongue again. "There's always Clara."

"We'll do better for you than Clara." He would appeal to Rose again; last night she had been a little hysterical.

"Can't I go back with you?"

"It wouldn't be allowed."

"I've read," she said, "about girls who dressed up—"

"That's only in books."

"I'd be afraid to stay here any more—with *her*."

"You won't have to," he assured her.

A bell began to ring furiously down below. She said, "Oh, he's rightly called Row."

"Who is?"

"The Indian on the second floor." She moved reluctantly to the door. She said, "It's a promise, isn't it? I won't be here tonight?"

"I promise."

"Cross your heart." He obeyed her. "Last night," she said, "I couldn't sleep. I thought she'd do something—awful. You should 'ave seen her face when I came in. 'Was it you who rung?' I said. 'Of course it wasn't,' she said and looked—oh, daggers. I tell you I locked my door when I left you. What was it she was up to in there?"

"I don't know for certain. She couldn't do much. She's like the devil you know—more brimstone than bite. She can't do us any harm if we don't get scared."

"Oh," she said, "I tell you I'll be glad—to be off from here." She smiled at him from the door with joy; she was like a child on her birthday. "No more Mr. Row," she said, "or the short-timers— no Mr. Muckerji—no more of *her* forever. It's my lucky day, all right." It was as if she were paying an elaborate farewell to a whole way of life.

He stayed in his room with the door locked until the time came to start for Lord Benditch's. He was taking no chances at all now. He put the papers ready in the breast pocket of his jacket, and wore his overcoat fastened up to the neck. No pickpocket, he was certain, could get at them; as for violence, he had to risk that. They would all know now that he had the papers with him; he had to trust London to keep him safe. Lord Benditch's house was like home to a boy playing hide-and-seek in an elaborate and unfamiliar garden. In three-quarters of an hour, he thought, as a clock told eleven-fifteen, everything would be decided one way or another. They would probably try to take some advantage of the fog.

This was to be his route. Up Bernard Street to Russell Square Station—they could hardly attempt anything in the tube—then from Hyde Park Corner to Chatham Terrace—about ten minutes' walk in this fog. He could, of course, ring up a taxi and go the whole way by car, but it would be horribly slow; traffic blocks, noise, and fog gave opportunities to really driven men—and he was beginning to think that they were driven hard by now. Besides, it was not beyond their ingenuity to supply a taxi themselves. If he had to take a taxi to Hyde Park Corner, he would take one from a rank.

He came downstairs with his heart knocking; he told himself in vain that nothing could possibly happen in daylight, in London; he was safe. But he was glad, nevertheless, when the Indian looked out of his room on the second floor; he was still wearing his frayed and gaudy dressing gown. It was almost like having a friend at your back, to have any witness at all. He would have liked to leave visible footprints wherever he walked, to put it incontestably on record that he had been here.

The carpet began; he walked gently, he had no wish to advertise his departure to the manageress. But he couldn't escape without seeing her. She was there in her masculine room, sitting at the table with the door open, the same musty black dress of his nightmare. He paused at the door and said, "I'm off now."

She said, "You know best why you haven't obeyed instructions."

"I shall be back here in a few hours. I shan't be staying another night."

She looked at him with complete indifference; it startled him; it was as if she knew more of his plans than he knew himself, as if everything had been provided for, a long time ago, in her capricious brain. "I imagine," he said, "that you have been paid for my room."

"Yes."

"What isn't provided for—in my expenses—is a week's wages for the maid. I'll pay that myself."

"I don't understand."

"Else is leaving too. You've given the child a fright. I don't know what motive . . ."

Her face became positively interested—not angry at all; it was almost as though he had given her an idea for which she was grateful. "You mean you are taking the girl away?" He was touched by uneasiness; it hadn't been necessary to tell her that. Somebody seemed to be warning him—"Be careful." He looked round; of course there was nobody there; in the distance a door closed; it was like a premonition. He said unguardedly, "Be careful how you frighten that child again." He found it hard to tear himself away; he had the papers safe in his pocket, but he felt that he was leaving something else behind which needed his care. It was absurd; there could be no danger. He stared belligerently back at the square spotty veined face. He said, "I'll be back very soon. I shall ask her if you . . ."

He had noticed last night how big her thumbs were. She sat placidly there with them hidden in the large pasty fists—it was said to be a mark of neurosis. She wore no rings. She said firmly and rather loudly, "I still don't understand," and at the same time her face contorted—a lid dropped, she gave him an enormous crude wink full of an inexplicable amusement. He had an impression that she wasn't worried now any more, that she was mistress of the situation. He turned away, his heart still knocking in its cage, as if it were trying to transmit a message, a warning, in a code he didn't understand. It was the fault of the intellectual, he thought, always to talk too much. He could have told her all that when he returned. Suppose he didn't return? Well, the girl wasn't a slave, she couldn't be made to suffer. This was the best-policed city in the world.

As he came down into the hall a rather too humble voice said, "Would you do me the greatest favour?" It was an Indian with large brown impervious eyes, an expression of docility; he wore a shiny blue suit with rather orange shoes; it must be Mr. Muckerji. He said, "If you would answer me just one question? How do you save money?"

Was he mad? He said, "I never save money." Mr. Muckerji had a large open soft face which fell in deep folds around the mouth. He said anxiously, "Literally not? I mean that there are those who put aside all their copper coins—or Victorian pennies. There are the building societies and national savings."

"I never save."

"Thank you," Mr. Muckerji said, "that is exactly what I wished to know," and began to write something in a notebook. Behind Mr. Muckerji, Else appeared, watching him go. Again he felt irrationally glad, even for the presence of Mr. Muckerji. He wasn't leaving her alone with the manageress. He smiled at her across Mr. Muckerji's bent studious back and gave her a small wave of the hand. She smiled in return uncertainly. It might have been a railway station full of good-byes and curiosities, of curtailed intimacies, the embarrassments of lovers and parents, the chance for strangers, like Mr. Muckerji, to see, as it were, into the interiors of private houses. Mr. Muckerji looked up and said a little too warmly, "Perhaps we may meet again for another interesting talk." He put forward a hand and then too quickly withdrew it as if he were afraid of a rebuff; then he stood gently, humbly smiling, as D. walked out—into the fog.

Nobody ever knows how long a parting is for; otherwise we would pay more attention to the smile and the formal words. The fog came up all round him; the train had left the station; people would wait no longer on the platform; an arch will cut off the most patient waving hand.

He walked quickly, listening hard. A girl passed him, carrying an attaché case, and a postman zigzagged off the pavement into obscurity. He felt like an Atlantic flyer who is still over the traffic of the coast before the plunge. It couldn't take more than half an hour. Everything would have to be decided soon. It never occurred to him that he might not come to terms with Benditch; they were ready to go to almost any price for coal. The fog clouded everything; he listened for footsteps and heard only his own feet tapping on stone. The silence was not reassuring; he overtook people and became aware of them only when their figures broke the fog ahead. If he was followed, he would never be aware of it, but could they follow him in this blanketed city? Somehow, somewhere, they would have to strike.

A taxi drew slowly alongside him. The driver said, "Taxi, sir?" keeping pace with him along the pavement. He forgot his decision to take a taxi only from the rank. He said, "Gwyn Cottage, Chatham Terrace," and got in. They slid away into impenetrable mist, backed, turned. He thought with sudden uneasiness, This isn't the way. What a fool I've been! He said, "Stop," but the taxi went on; he couldn't see where they were—only the big back of the driver and the fog all round. He hammered on the glass. "Let me out," and the taxi stopped. He thrust a shilling into the man's hand and dived onto the pavement. He heard an astonished voice say, "What the bloody hell?"—the man had probably been quite honest. His nerve was horribly shaken. He ran into a policeman. "Russell Square Station?"

"You are going the wrong way," the policeman said. "Turn round, take the first to the left along the railings."

He came after what seemed a long while to the station. He waited for the lift and suddenly realized that this needed more nerve than he had thought—this going underground. He had never been below the surface of a street since the house had caved in on him—now he watched air raids from a roof. He would rather die quickly than slowly suffocate with a dead cat beside him. Before the lift doors closed he stood tensely; he wanted to bolt for the entrance. It was a strain his nerves could hardly stand; he sat down on the only bench, and the walls sailed up all round him. He put his head between his hands and tried not to see or feel the descent. It stopped. He was underground.

A voice said, "Like a hand? Give the gentleman your hand, Conway." He found himself urged to his feet by a small, horribly sticky fist. A woman with a bit of fur round a scrawny neck said, "Conway used to be taken that way in the lifts, didn't you, duck?" A pasty child of about seven held his hand glumly. He said, "Oh, I think I shall be all right now," still tense at the white below-ground passage, the dry stale wind, and the rumble of a distant train.

The woman said, "You going west? We'll put you off at the right station. You're a foreigner, aren't you?"

"Yes."

"Oh, I've nothing against foreigners."

He found himself led down the long passage; the child was clothed hideously in corduroy shorts, a lemon-yellow jumper, and a school cap, all chocolate and mauve stripes. The woman said, "I got quite worried about Conway. The doctor said it was just his age, but his father had duodenal ulcers." There was no escape; they herded him onto the train between them. She said, "All that's wrong with him now's he snuffles. Shut your mouth, Conway. The gentleman doesn't want to see your tonsils."

There were not many people in the carriage. He certainly hadn't been followed into the train. Would something happen at Hyde Park Corner? Or was he exaggerating the whole thing? This was England. But he remembered the chauffeur coming at him with a look of greedy pleasure on the Dover road, the bullet in the mews. The woman said, "The trouble with Conway is he won't touch greens."

An idea struck him. He said, "Are you going far west?"

"High Street, Kensington. We got to go to Barker's. That boy wears out clothes so quick—"

"Perhaps you would let me give you a lift in a taxi from Hyde Park Corner."

"Oh, we wouldn't bother you. It's quicker by underground."

They pulled in and out of Piccadilly, and he sat tense as they roared again into a tunnel. It was the same sound that reached you blowing back from where a high explosive bomb had fallen, a wind full of death and the noise of pain.

He said, "I thought perhaps the boy—Conway—"

"It's a funny name, isn't it, but we were at the pictures seeing Conway Tearle just before he came. My husband fancied the name. More than I did. He said, 'That's the one if it's a boy.' And when it happened that night it seemed—well, an omen."

"Wouldn't he perhaps—like the ride?"

"Oh, a taxi makes him sick. He's funny that way. A bus is all right—and a tube. Though there *were* times when I'd be ashamed to be with him in a lift. It wasn't nice for the others. He'd look at you and then—before you could say Jack Robinson—it was like a conjuring trick."

It was hopeless. Anyway, what could happen? They had shot

their bolt. You couldn't go further than attempted murder. Except, of course, a murder which succeeded. He couldn't imagine L.'s being concerned in that, but then, he would have a marvellous facility for disengaging himself from the unpleasant fact. "Here you are," she said. "This is your station. It's been pleasant having a chat. Give the gentleman your hand, Conway." He shook perfunctorily the sticky fingers and went up into the yellow morning.

There were cheers in the air; everyone was cheering; it might have been a great victory. The Knightsbridge pavement was crowded; over the road the tops of the Hyde Park gates appeared above the low fog; in another direction a chariot spurred behind four tossing horses above the dingy clouds. All round St. George's Hospital the buses were held up, vanishing gradually like alligators into the marshy air. Somebody was blowing on a whistle; a bath chair slowly emerged trundled by its invalid, while with the other hand he played a pipe, a painful progress along the gutter. The tune never got properly going; it whistled out, like the air from a rubber pig, and then started again with an effort. On a blackboard the man had written, "Gassed in 1917. One lung gone." The yellow air fumed round him and people were cheering.

A Daimler drew out of the traffic block, women squealed, several men took off their hats. D. was at a loss; he had seen religious processions in the old days, but nobody here seemed to be kneeling. The car moved slowly in front of him; two very small girls, stiffly dressed in tailored coats and wearing gloves, peered through the pane with pasty indifference. A woman screamed, "Oh, the darlings. They're going to shop at Harrod's." It was an extraordinary sight; the passage of a totem in a Daimler. A voice D. knew said sharply, "Take off your hat, sir." It was Currie.

For a moment he thought, He's followed me. But the embarrassment when Currie recognized him was too genuine. He grunted and sidled and swung his monocle. "Oh, sorry. Foreigner." D. might have been a woman with whom he had had shameful relations. You couldn't cut her, but you tried to pass on.

"I wonder," D. said, "if you'd mind telling me the way to Chatham Terrace?"

Currie flushed. "You going there—to Lord Benditch's?"

"Yes." The piping began again in the gutter brokenly. The buses moved ponderously on, and everybody scattered.

"Look here," Currie said. "I seem to have made a fool of myself the other night. Apologize."

"That's all right."

"Thought you were one of these confidence men. Stupid of me. But I've been caught that way myself, and Miss Cullen's a fine girl."

"Yes."

"I bought a sunken Spanish galleon once. One of the Armada fleet, you know. Paid a hundred pounds in cash. Of course there wasn't a galleon."

"No."

"Look here. I'd like to show there's no ill feeling. I'll walk you along to Chatham Terrace. Always glad to be of use to foreigners. Expect you'd do the same if I came to your country. Of course that's not likely."

"It's very good of you," D. said. He meant it; it was a great relief. This was the end of the battle; if they had planned a last desperate throw in the fog, they had been outfortuned. He could hardly call it outwitted. He put his hand up to his breast and felt through the overcoat the comforting bulge of his credentials.

"Of course," Captain Currie went on, explaining too much, "an experience like that—well, it makes you chary."

"Experience?"

"The Spanish galleon. The fellow was so plausible—gave me fifty pounds to hold while he cashed my cheque. I wouldn't hear of it, but he insisted. Said *he* had to insist on cash, so it was only fair."

"So you were only fifty pounds down?"

"Oh, they were dud notes. I suppose he saw I was a romantic. Of course it gave me an idea. You learn by your mistakes."

"Yes?" It was an immense pleasure to have this man prattling at his elbow down Knightsbridge.

"You've heard of the Spanish Galleon?"

"No—I don't think so."

"It was my first roadhouse. Near Maidenhead. But I had to sell out in the end. You know—the west, it's losing caste a bit. Kent's better—or Essex even. On the west you get a rather—popular element, on the way to the Cotswolds, you know." Violence seemed more than ever out of place in this country of complicated distinctions and odd taboos. Violence was too simple. It was a breach of taste. They turned to the left out of the main road; fantastic red towers and castellations emerged from the fog. Captain Currie said, "Seen any good shows?"

"I have been rather busy."

"Mustn't overdo it."

"And I've been learning Entrenationo."

"Good God, what for?"

"An international language."

"When you get down to it," Captain Currie said, "most people talk a bit of English." He said, "Well, I'll be damned. Do you know who we just passed?"

"I didn't see anyone."

"That chauffeur—what's-his-name's? The one you had the bout with."

"I never saw him."

"He was in a doorway. The car was there too. What do you say we go back and have a word with him?" He laid his unmaimed hand on D.'s sleeve. "There's heaps of time. Chatham Terrace is just ahead."

"No. No time." He felt panic. Was this a trap after all? The hand was urging him gently, remorselessly.

"I have an appointment with Lord Benditch."

"Won't take a moment. After all, it was fair fight and no favour. Ought to shake hands and show there's no ill feeling. Customary. It was *my* mistake, you know." He babbled breezily into D.'s ear, tugging at his sleeve; there was a slight smell of whisky.

"Afterwards," D. said. "After I've seen Lord Benditch."

"I wouldn't like to think there was any bad blood. My fault."

"No," D. said, "no."

"When's your appointment?"

"Noon."

"It's not five to. Shake hands all round and have a drink."

"No." He shook off the strong persistent hand; somebody whistled just behind him; he turned, desperately at bay, with his fists up. It was only a postman. He said, "Could you show me Gwyn Cottage?"

"You're almost on the doorstep," the postman said. "This way." He had a glimpse of Captain Currie's astonished and rather angry face. Afterwards he thought that he had probably been wrong—Captain Currie was merely anxious that everything should be smoothed away.

It was like an all-clear signal, seeing the big Edwardian door swing open upon the fantastic hall. He was able to smile again at a mine-owner's fondness for the mistresses of kings. There was a huge expanse of fake panelling, and all round the walls reproductions of famous paintings—Nell Gwyn sported in the place of honour above the staircase, among a number of cherubs who had all been granted peerages. What a lot of noble blood was based on the sale of oranges! He detected the Pompadour and Mme. de Maintenon; there was also—startlingly prewar in black silk stockings and black gloves—Mlle. Gaby Deslys. It was an odd taste.

"Coat, sir?"

He let the manservant take his overcoat. There was an appalling mixture of chinoiserie, Louis Seize, and Stuart in the furniture; he was fascinated. An odd haven of safety for a confidential agent. He said, "I'm afraid I'm a little early."

"His Lordship gave orders that you were to go straight in."

Most curious of all was the thought that somehow Rose had been produced among these surroundings, this vicarious sensuality. Did they represent the daydreams of an ambitious workingman's son? Money meant women. The manservant too was unbelievably exaggerated—very tall, with a crease that seemed to begin at the waist and to be maintained unimpaired only by an odd stance, by leaning back like the Tower of Pisa. He had always felt a faint distaste for menservants—they were so conservative, so established, such parasites; but this man made him want to laugh. He was a caricature. He was reminded of an actor-manager's house he had once dined in; there had been liveried footmen there.

The man swept open a door. "Mr. D." He found himself in an enormous parqueted room. It seemed to be hung with portraits—they could hardly be family ones. Some armchairs were grouped round a big log fire. They had high backs. It was difficult to see whether they were occupied. He advanced tentatively. The room would have been more effective, he thought, with someone else. It was meant to make you aware of the frayed sleeve, the shabbiness, the insecurity of your life, but as it happened he had been born without the sense of snobbery. He simply didn't mind his shabbiness. He hummed gently to himself, proceeding at a leisurely pace across the parquet. He was really too happy to be here at all to care about anything.

Somebody rose up from the central chair—a big man with a bullet head and a big mass of grey-black hair and the jaw of an equestrian statue. He said, "Mr. D.?"

"Lord Benditch?"

He waved his hand at three other chairs. "Mr. Forbes, Lord

Fetting, Mr. Brigstock." He said, "Mr. Goldstein could not come."

D. said, "I think you know the object of my visit."

"We had a letter," Lord Benditch said, "a fortnight ago, warning us." He flapped his hand towards a big desk of inlaid wood—it was a mannerism to use his hand like a signpost. "You will forgive me if we get to business straight away. I'm a busy man."

"I should like it."

Another man emerged from an armchair; he was small and dark and sharp featured, with a quick doggish air. He began to arrange chairs behind the desk with an air of importance. "Mr. Forbes," he said, "Mr. Forbes." Mr. Forbes came into view; he wore tweeds and carried very successfully the air of a man just up from the country; only the shape of the skull disclosed the Furtstein past. He said, "Coming, Brigstock," with a faint air of mockery.

"Lord Fetting."

"I should let Fetting sleep," Mr. Forbes said. "Unless, of course, he snores." They ranged themselves on one side of the desk, Lord Benditch in the middle. It was like the final viva voce examination for a degree. Mr. Brigstock, D. thought, would be the one who gave you the bad time; he would hang onto a question like a terrier.

"Sit down, won't you?" Lord Benditch said heavily.

"I would," D. said, "if there was a chair on this side the frontier." Forbes laughed. Lord Benditch said sharply, "Brigstock."

Brigstock swarmed round the desk and pushed up a chair. D. sat down. There was a horrible air of unreality about everything. This was the moment, but he could hardly believe it—in the fake house, among the fake ancestors and the dead mistresses; he couldn't even see Lord Fetting. This wasn't the sort of place where you expected a war to be decided. He said, "You know the amount of coal we require between now and April?"

"Yes."

"Can it be supplied?"

Lord Benditch said, "Granted I am satisfied, and Forbes and Fetting." He added, "And Brigstock," as an afterthought.

"A question of price?"

"Of course. And confidence."

"We will pay the highest market price—and a bonus of twenty-five per cent when delivery is completed."

Brigstock said, "In gold."

"A proportion in gold."

"You can't expect us to take notes," Brigstock said, "which may be valueless by the spring—or goods which you may not be able to get out of the country."

Lord Benditch leaned back in his chair and left it all to Brigstock; Brigstock had been trained to bring back the game. Mr. Forbes was drawing little pictures on the paper in front of him: girls with big circular googoo eyes, wearing bathing shorts.

"If we get this coal there is no question of the exchange falling. We've maintained an even level now for two years of war. This coal may mean the complete collapse of the rebels."

"We have other information," Brigstock said.

"I don't think it can be reliable."

Somebody suddenly snored—out of sight behind a chairback.

"We must insist on gold," Brigstock said. "Shall I wake Fetting?"

"Let him sleep," Mr. Forbes said.

"We will meet you halfway on that point," D. said. "We are prepared to pay the market price in gold, if you will accept the bonus in notes—or goods."

"Then it must be thirty-five per cent."

"That's very high."

Brigstock said, "We take a lot of risk. The ships have to be insured. A lot of risk." Behind his back was a picture by—was it Etty? Flesh and flowers in a pastoral landscape.

"When would you start delivery?"

"We have certain stocks—we could begin next month, but for the quantity you need we shall have to reopen several mines. That takes time—and money. There will have been depreciation of machinery. And the men will not be first-class workers any longer. They depreciate quicker than tools."

D. said, "Of course you hold a pistol to our heads. We must have the coal."

"Another point," Brigstock said. "We are businessmen; we are not politicians—or crusaders." Lord Fetting's voice came sharply from the fire. "My shoes. Where are my shoes?" Mr. Forbes smiled again, drawing googoo eyes, putting in the long lashes; was he thinking of the girl in Shepherd's Market? He had a look of healthy sensuality: sex in tweeds with a pipe.

Lord Benditch said heavily and contemptuously, "Brigstock means that we may get a better offer elsewhere."

"You may, but there's the future to think of. If they win they will cease to be your customers. They have other allies—"

"That is looking very far ahead. What concerns us is the immediate profit."

"You may find their gold is less certain than our paper. After all, it's stolen. We should bring an action. And there's your own government. To send coal to the rebels might prove illegal."

Brigstock said sharply, "If we come to terms—we should be prepared to take thirty per cent in notes at the rate prevailing on the last day of shipment—you must understand that any commission must come from your side. We have gone as far as we can towards meeting you."

"Commission? I don't quite understand."

"Your commission, of course, on the sale. Your people must look after that."

"I was not proposing," D. said, "to ask for a commission. Is it the usual thing? I didn't know, but in any case I wouldn't ask for it."

Benditch said, "You are an unusual agent," and loured at him as if he had expressed a heresy, had been found guilty of some sharp practice. Brigstock said, "Before we draw up the contract we had better see your credentials."

D. put his hand to his breast pocket. They were gone; it was incredible.

He began in panic-stricken haste to search all his pockets; there was nothing there. He looked up and saw the three men watching him. Mr. Forbes had stopped drawing and was gazing at him with interest. D. said, "It's extraordinary. I had them here in my breast pocket—"

Mr. Forbes said gently, "Perhaps they are in your overcoat."

"Brigstock," Lord Benditch said, "ring the bell." He said to the manservant, "Fetch this gentleman's coat." It was just a ceremony; he knew they wouldn't be there, but how had they gone? Could Currie possibly—? No, it wasn't possible. Nobody had had a chance except— The manservant came back with the coat over his arm. D. looked up at the trusty paid impassive eyes as if he might read there some hint—but they would take a bribe as they would take a tip without registering any feeling at all. "Well?" Brigstock asked sharply.

"They are not there."

A very old man appeared suddenly on his feet in front of the fire. He said, "When's this man going to turn up, Benditch? I've been waiting a very long time."

"He's here now."

"Somebody should have told me."

"You were asleep."

"Nonsense." One after the other, D. searched the pockets; he searched the lining; of course there was nothing. It was no more than a rather theatrical gesture—to convince them that he had once had the credentials. He felt himself that his acting was poor, that he wasn't really giving the impression that he expected to find them.

"Was I asleep, Brigstock?"

"Yes, Lord Fetting."

"Well, what if I was? I feel all the fresher for it. I hope nothing is settled."

"No, nothing, Lord Fetting." Brigstock looked smug and satisfied; he seemed to be saying, I suspected all the time.

"Do you really mean," Lord Benditch said, "that you've come out without your papers? It's very odd."

"I had them with me. They were stolen."

"Stolen! When?"

"I don't know. On the way to this room."

"Well," Brigstock said, "that's that."

"What's what?" Lord Fetting asked sharply. He said, "I shall not give my signature to anything any of you have decided."

"We've decided nothing."

"Quite right," Lord Fetting said. "It needs thinking over."

"I know," D. said, "you have only my word for this—but what possibly have I to gain?"

Brigstock leaned across the desk and said sharply, venomously, "There was the commission, wasn't there?"

"Oh, come, Brigstock," Forbes said, "he refused the commission."

"Yes, when he saw that it was useless to expect it."

Lord Benditch said, "There's no point in arguing, Brigstock. This gentleman is either genuine or not genuine. If he is genuine—and can prove it—I am quite prepared to sign a contract."

"Certainly," Forbes said. "So am I."

"But you, sir, will understand—as a businessman—that no contract can be signed with an unaccredited agent."

"And you will also understand," Brigstock said, "that there's a law in this country against trying to obtain money on false pretences."

"We'd better sleep on it," Lord Fetting said. "We'd better all sleep on it."

What am I to do now, he thought, what am I to do now? He sat in his chair, beaten. He had evaded every trap but one—that was no comfort. There remained only the long pilgrimage back—the Channel boat, the Paris train. Of course at home they would never believe his story. It would be odd if he had escaped—with no effort on his part—the enemy's bullets, to fall against a cemetery wall on his own side of the line. They carried out their executions at the cemetery to avoid the trouble of transporting bodies.

"Well," Lord Benditch said, "I don't think there's any more to be said. If when you get to your hotel you find your credentials, you had better telephone at once. We have another client; we can't hold matters up indefinitely."

Forbes said, "Is there nobody in London who would answer for you?"

"Nobody."

Brigstock said, "I don't think we need keep him any longer."

D. said, "I suppose it's useless telling you that I expected this. I've been here less than three days; my rooms have been searched; I have been beaten up." He put his hand to his face. "You can see the bruises. I have been shot at." He remembered, while he watched their faces, what Rose had warned him—no melodrama. It was like the putting up of shutters at night to guard—well, the royal mistresses and the Etty. Benditch, Fetting, Brigstock—they all became expressionless as if he had told a dirty story in unsuitable company. Lord Benditch said, "I'm prepared to believe you may have *lost* the papers—"

"This is a waste of time," Brigstock said. "This *shows*."

Lord Fetting said, "It's nonsense. There's the police."

D. got up. He said, "One thing more, Lord Benditch. Your daughter knows I was shot at. She has seen the place. She found the bullet."

Lord Fetting began to laugh. "Oh, that young woman," he said, "that young woman. The scamp." Brigstock looked nervously sideways at Lord Benditch; he looked as if he wanted to speak and dared not. Lord Benditch said, "What my daughter may say is not evidence—in this house." He frowned, staring down at his big hands, hairy on the knuckles.

D. said, "I must say good-bye then. But I haven't finished. I do implore you not to be rash."

"We are never rash," Lord Fetting said.

D. went the long way back across the cold room; it was like the beginning of a retreat—nobody could say whether a stand was possible before the cemetery wall. In the hall L. was waiting; it was a small satisfaction to feel that he had been kept a few minutes like someone of no account. He stood there, rather too deliberately aloof, examining Nell Gwyn among the cherubs. He didn't turn his head; he was the former patron forced by cruel circumstances to administer the cut direct; he leaned closely to the canvas and inspected the backside of the Duke of St. Albans.

D. said, "I should go carefully. Of course you have a lot of agents, but two can play at your game."

L. turned sadly away from the cherub to face a man with no social sense. He said, "I suppose you'll be catching the first boat back—but I shouldn't go farther than France."

"I'm not leaving England."

"What good can you do here?"

D. was silent; he had no ideas at all. His silence seemed to disconcert L. He said earnestly, "I do advise you—" Then there must be some angle from which he was still dangerous. Was it the simplest of all? He said, "You've made mistakes. That beating-up— Miss Cullen will never support you that I had stolen the car. And then the shooting—I didn't find the bullet. Miss Cullen did. I am going to bring a charge—"

A bell rang; the manservant appeared too quickly and too silently. "Lord Benditch will see you now, sir."

L. took no notice of him at all (that in itself was significant enough). He said, "If only you would give your word, there would be no more unpleasantness."

"I give you my word that my address for the next few days will be London." His confidence began to come back; the defeat had not been final. L. was shaken—about something. He seemed prepared to plead; he had some knowledge which D. did not possess. Then a bell rang; the servant opened the front door, and Rose came into her home like a stranger. She said, "I wanted to catch—" and then saw L. She said, "What a gathering!"

D. said, "I have been persuading him that I didn't steal your car."

"Of course you didn't."

L. bowed. He said, "I mustn't keep Lord Benditch waiting." The servant opened the door, and he was engulfed in the big room.

"Well," she said, "you remember what you said—about celebrating." She faced him with bogus bravado; it couldn't be easy—your first meeting again after telling a man you loved him; he wondered whether she would introduce some reason— "I've got such a head. Was I very drunk?" But she had an appalling honesty. She said, "You haven't forgotten about last night?"

He said, "I remember everything if you do. But there's nothing to celebrate. They got my papers."

She said quickly, "They didn't hurt you?"

"Oh, they did it painlessly. Is the man who opened the door new. here?"

"I don't know."

"Surely—"

She said, "You don't think, do you, that I live in this place?" But she swept that subject aside. "What did you tell them?"

"The truth."

"All the melodrama?"

"Yes."

"I warned you. How did Furt take it?"

"Furt?"

"Forbes. I always call him Furt."

"I don't know. Brigstock did most of the talking."

"Furt's honest," she said, "in his way." Her mouth was hard, as if she were considering his way. He felt again an immense pity for her, standing harshly in her father's house with a background of homelessness, private detectives, and distrust. She was so young— she had been a small child when he married. It takes such a short time to make appalling changes; they had both travelled too far for happiness in the same period. She said, "Isn't there anybody who'll answer for you at your embassy?"

"I don't think so. We don't trust them—except perhaps the Second Secretary."

She said, "It's worth trying. I'll get Furt. He's not a fool." She rang the bell and said to the servant, "I want to see Mr. Forbes."

"I'm afraid, madam, he's in conference."

"Never mind. Tell him I want to speak to him urgently."

"Lord Benditch gave orders—"

"You don't know who I am, do you? You must be new. It's not my business to know your face, but you'd better know mine. I'm Lord Benditch's daughter."

"I'm very sorry, miss. I didn't know—"

"Go in and take that message." She said, "So he's new."

When the door opened they could hear Fetting's voice. "No hurry. Better sleep." She said, "If he stole your papers—"

"I'm sure of it."

She said furiously, "I'll see he starves. There won't be a registry office in England—" Mr. Forbes came out. She said, "Furt, I want you to do something for me." He closed the door behind him and said, "Anything." He was like an oriental potentate in plus fours, ready to promise the most fantastic riches. She said, "Those fools don't believe him." His eyes were moist when he looked at her— whatever the detectives reported, he was a man hopelessly in love. He said to D., "Excuse me—but it *is* a tall story."

"I found the bullet," Rose said.

Away from the others, standing up, he looked more Jewish. He said, "I said a tall story, not an impossible one." Very far back in the past were the desert, the dead salt sea, the desolate mountains, and the violence on the road from Jericho. He had a basis of belief.

"What are they doing in there?" Rose said.

"Not much. Old Fetting is a wonderful brake—and so is Brigstock." He said to D., "Don't think you are the only man Brigstock distrusts."

Rose said, "If we can prove to you that we are not lying—"

"We?"

"Yes, we."

"If I'm satisfied," Forbes said, "I'll sign a contract for as much as I can supply. It won't be all you need, but the others will follow." He watched them anxiously, as if he was afraid of something; perhaps the man lived in perpetual fear of the announcement to the press—"A marriage has been arranged"—or of the ugly rumour— "Have you heard about Benditch's daughter?"

"Will you come to the Embassy now?" she asked.

"I thought you told us—"

"This isn't my idea," D. said. "I don't think it will be any use. You see, at home they don't trust the Ambassador—but there's always a chance."

They drove in silence, slowly, through the fog. Once Forbes said, "I'd like to get the pits started. It's a rotten life for the men there."

"Why should it bother you, Furt?"

He grinned painfully across the car at her. "I don't like being disliked." Then his dark raisin eyes stared out again into the yellow day with some of the patience of Jacob who served seven years. After all, D. thought, it was possible that even Jacob kept some consolation in a tent. Could you blame him? He felt almost envious of Forbes; it was something to be in love with a living woman, even if you got nothing from it but fear, jealousy, pain. It wasn't an ignoble emotion.

At the door of the Embassy he said, "Ask for the Second Secretary. There's a chance."

They were shown into a waiting-room. The walls were hung with prewar pictures. D. said, "That's the place where I was born." A tiny village died out against the mountains. He said, *"They* hold it now." He walked slowly round the room, leaving Forbes alone, as it were, with Rose. They were very bad pictures, very picturesque, full of thick cloud effects and heavy flowers. There was the university where he used to lecture—empty and cloistered and untrue. The door opened. A man like a mute in a black morning coat and a high white collar said, "Mr. Forbes?"

D. said, "Pay no attention to me. Ask what questions you like." There was a bookshelf; the books all looked unused in heavy uniform bindings—the national dramatist, the national poet . . . He turned his back on the others and pretended to study them.

Mr. Forbes said, "I've come to make some inquiries. On behalf of myself and Lord Benditch."

"Anything we can help you in—we shall be so pleased."

"We have been seeing a gentleman who claims to be an agent of your government. In connection with the sale of coal."

The stiff embassy voice said, "I don't think we have any information. I will ask the Ambassador, but I am quite certain—" His voice took on more and more assurance as he spoke.

"But I suppose it's possible that you would not be informed," Mr. Forbes said. "A confidential agent."

"It is most improbable."

Rose said sharply, "Are you the Second Secretary?"

"No, madam, I'm afraid he is on leave. I am the First Secretary."

"When will he be returning?"

"He will not be returning here."

So that, probably, was the end of things. Mr. Forbes said, "He claims that his credentials were stolen."

"Well—I'm afraid—we know nothing. It seems, as I say, very improbable."

Rose said, "This gentleman is not completely unknown. He is a scholar—attached to a university."

"In that case we could easily tell you."

What a fighter she was! he thought with admiration; she picked the right point every time.

"He is an authority on the romance languages. He edited the Berne MS. of the *Song of Roland*. His name is D."

There was a pause. Then the voice said, "I'm afraid—the name's completely unfamiliar to me."

"Well, it might be, mightn't it? Perhaps you aren't interested in the romance languages."

"Of course," he said with a small self-assured laugh, "but if you will wait two minutes, I will look the name up in a reference book."

D. turned away from the bookshelf. He said to Mr. Forbes, "I'm afraid we are wasting your time."

"Oh," Mr. Forbes said, "I don't value my time as much as all that." He couldn't keep his eyes off the girl; he followed every move she made with a tired sad sensuality. She was standing by the bookcase now, looking at the works of the national poet and the national dramatist. She said, "I wish you didn't have so many consonants in your language. So gritty." She picked a book out of a lower shelf and began to turn the pages. The door opened again. It was the secretary.

He said, "I have looked up the name, Mr. Forbes. There is no such person. I'm afraid you have been misled."

Rose turned on him furiously. She said, "You are lying, aren't you?"

"Why should I be, Miss—Miss—?"

"Cullen."

"My dear Miss Cullen, a civil war flings up these plausible people."

"Then why is his name printed here?" She had a book open. She said, "I can't read what it says, but here it is. I can't mistake the name. Here's the word Berne too. It seems to be a reference book."

"That's very odd. Can I see? Perhaps if you don't know the language—"

D. said, "But as I do, may I read it out? It gives the dates of my appointment as lecturer at the University of Zed. It refers to my book on the Berne MS. Yes, it's all here."

"You are the man?"

"Yes."

"May I see that book?" D. gave it him. He thought, By God, she's won! Forbes watched her with admiration. The secretary said,

"Ah, I am sorry. It was your pronunciation of the name, Miss Cullen, which set me wrong. Of course we know D. One of our most respected scholars." He let the words hang in the air: it was like a complete surrender, but all the time he kept his eyes on the girl, not on the man concerned. Somewhere there was a snag; there must be a snag. "There," the girl said to Forbes, "you see."

"But," the secretary went gently on, "he is no longer alive. He was shot by the rebels in prison."

"No," D. said, "that's untrue. I was exchanged. Here—I have my passport." He was thankful that he hadn't kept it in the same pocket as his papers. The secretary took it. D. said, "What will you say now? That it's forged?"

"Oh, no," the secretary said, "I think this is a genuine passport. But it isn't yours. You have only to look at the photograph." He held it out to them. D. remembered the laughing stranger's face he had seen in the passport office at Dover. Of course, nobody would believe— He said hopelessly, "War and prison change a man."

Mr. Forbes said gently, "There's a strong resemblance, of course."

"Of course," the secretary said. "He would hardly choose—"

The girl said furiously, "It's his face. I know it's his face. You've only to look—" but he could read the doubt somewhere behind, which whipped up anger only to convince herself.

"How he got it," the secretary said, "one doesn't know." He turned on D. and said, "I shall see you are properly punished. Oh, yes, I shall see to it." He lowered his voice respectfully. "I am sorry, Miss Cullen, but he was one of our finest scholars." He was extraordinarily convincing. It was like hearing yourself praised behind your back. D. felt an odd pleasure; it was, in a way, flattering.

Mr. Forbes said, "Better let the police get to the bottom of this. It's beyond me."

"If you will excuse me I will ring them up at once." The secretary sat down at a table and took the phone. D. said, "For a man who's dead I seem to be accumulating a lot of charges."

The secretary said, "Is that Scotland Yard?" He began to give the name of the Embassy.

"First there was stealing your car."

The secretary said, "The passport is stamped Dover; two days ago. Yes, that's the name."

"Then Mr. Brigstock wanted to have me up for trying to obtain money on false pretences—I don't know why."

"I see," the secretary said; "it certainly seems to fit in. Yes, we'll keep him here."

"And now I'm to be charged with using a false passport." He said, "For a university lecturer it's a dark record."

"Don't joke," the girl said. "This is crazy. You are D. I know you are D. If you aren't honest, then the whole putrid world—"

The secretary said, "The police were already looking for this fellow. Don't try to move. I have a gun in my pocket. They want to ask you a few questions."

"Not so few," D. said. "A car—false pretences—passport."

"And about the death of a girl," the secretary said.

Four

The nightmare was back; he was an infected man. Violence went with him everywhere. Like a typhoid carrier, he was responsible for the deaths of strangers. He sat down on a chair and said, "What girl?"

"You'll know very soon," the secretary said.

"I think," Mr. Forbes said, "we'd better go." He looked puzzled, out of his depth.

"I would much rather you stayed," the secretary said. "They will probably want an account of his movements."

Rose said, "I shan't go. It's fantastic, mad." She said, "You can tell them where you've been all day?"

"Oh, yes," he said, "I've got witnesses for every minute of the day." Despair began to lose its hold; this was a mistake, and his enemies couldn't afford many mistakes. But then he remembered that somebody somewhere must be dead; that couldn't be a mistake. He felt more pity than horror; one grew so accustomed to the deaths of strangers.

Rose said, "Furt, you don't believe all this!" He could read doubt again in her exclamation.

"Well," Forbes said, "I don't know. It's very odd."

But she was on again to the right fact, at the right moment. "If he's a fraud, why should anyone take the trouble to shoot at him?"

"If they did."

The secretary sat by the door with a polite air of not listening.

"But I found the bullet myself, Furt."

"A bullet, I suppose, can be planted."

"I won't believe it." She no longer said, D. noticed, that she didn't believe it. She turned back to him. "What else are they going to try now?"

Mr. Forbes said, "You'd better go."

"Where?" she said.

"Home."

She laughed—hysterically. Nobody else said a thing; they all just waited. Mr. Forbes began to look at the pictures carefully, one after another, as if they were important. Then the front doorbell rang. D. got to his feet. The secretary said, "Stay where you are. The officers will be coming through." Two men entered; they looked like a shopkeeper and his assistant. The middle-aged one said, "Mr. D.?"

"Yes."

"Would you mind coming along to the station to answer a few questions?"

"I can answer any you like here," D. said.

"As you please, sir." He stood and waited silently for the others to go. D. said, "I have no objection to these people being present. If it's a case of wanting to know my movements, they'll be of use to you."

Rose said, "How can he have done a thing? He can bring witnesses any moment of the day—"

The detective said with embarrassment, "This is a serious matter, sir. It would be better for all of us if you came to the station."

"Arrest me, then."

"I can't arrest you here, sir. Besides—we haven't got that far."

"Go on, then. Ask your questions."

"I believe, sir, you are acquainted with a Miss Crole?"

"I have never even heard of her."

"Oh, yes, you have. You are staying at the hotel where she worked."

"You don't mean Else?" He got up and advanced towards the officer with his hands out, imploring him. "They haven't done anything to her, have they?"

"I don't know who 'they' are, sir, but the girl's dead."

He said, "Oh, God, it's my fault."

The officer went gently on, like a doctor with a patient. "I ought to warn you, sir, that anything you say—"

"It was murder."

"Technically perhaps, sir."

"What do you mean? Technically?"

"Never mind that now, sir. All that concerns us at the moment is —the girl seems to have jumped out of a top-floor window." He remembered the look of the pavement far away below, between the shreds of fog. He heard Rose saying, "You can't implicate him. He's been at my father's since noon." He remembered how the news of his wife's death had come to him; he thought that news of that kind would never hurt him again. A man who has been burned by fire doesn't heed a scald. But this was like the death of an only child. How scared she must have been before she dropped. Why, why, why?

"Were you intimate with the girl, sir?"

"No. Of course not. Why, she was a child." They were all watching him closely; the police officer's mouth seemed to stiffen under the respectable shopkeeper's moustache. He said to Rose, "You had better go, ma'am. This isn't a case for lady's ears."

She said, "You're all wrong. I know you're all wrong." Mr. Forbes took her arm and led her out. The detective said to the secretary, "If you would stay, sir. The gentleman may want to be represented by his embassy."

D. said, "This isn't my embassy. Obviously. Never mind that now. Go ahead."

"There is an Indian gentleman, a Mr. Muckerji, staying in your hotel. He has made a statement that he saw the girl in your room this morning, undressing."

"It's absurd. How could he?"

"He makes no bones about that, sir. He was peeping. He said he was getting evidence—I don't know what for. He said the girl was on your bed, taking down her stocking."

"Of course. I see now."

"Do you still deny intimacy?"

"Yes."

"What was she doing then?"

"I had given her some valuable papers the night before to hide for me. She carried them in her instep under her stocking. You see I had reason to suppose that my room might be searched—or I might be attacked."

"What sort of papers, sir?"

"Papers from my government, establishing my position as their agent, giving me power to conclude certain business."

The detective said, "But this gentleman denies that you are—in fact—Mr. D. He suggests that you are travelling with the passport of a dead man."

D. said, "Oh, yes, he has his reasons." The toils were round him now all right; he was inextricably tied.

The detective said, "Could I see those papers?"

"They were stolen from me."

"Where?"

"In Lord Benditch's house." It was of course an incredible story. He said with a kind of horrified amusement at the whole wild tale, "By Lord Benditch's manservant." There was a pause; nobody said anything; the detective didn't even trouble to make a note. His companion pursed his lips and stared mildly round as if he was no longer interested in the tales criminals told. The detective said, "Well, to come back to the girl." He paused as if to give D. time to reconsider his story. He said, "Can you throw any light on this —suicide?"

"It wasn't suicide."

"Was she unhappy?"

"Not today."

"Had you threatened to leave her?"

"I wasn't her lover, man. I don't pursue children."

"Had you, by any chance, suggested that you should both kill yourselves?" The cat was out of the bag now; a suicide pact—that was what the detective had meant by technically murder. They imagined he had brought her to that pitch and then climbed down himself, the worst kind of coward. What in heaven's name had put them on that track? He said wearily, "No."

"By the way," the detective said, looking away at the bad pictures on the walls, "why were you staying at this hotel?"

"I had my room booked before I came."

"So you knew the girl before?"

"No, no, I haven't been in England for nearly eighteen years."

"You chose a curious hotel."

"My employers chose it."

"Yet you gave the Strand Palace as your address to the passport office at Dover."

He felt like giving up; everything he had done since he landed seemed to add a knot to the cord. He said stubbornly, "I thought that was a formality."

"Why?"

"The officer winked at me."

The detective sighed uncontrollably and seemed inclined to shut his notebook. He said, "Then you can throw no light on this—suicide?"

"She was murdered—by the manageress and a man called K."

"What motive?"

"I'm not sure yet."

"Then it would surprise you, I suppose, to hear that she left a statement."

"I do not believe it."

The detective said, "It would make things easier for all of us if you would make a proper statement yourself." He said with contempt, "These suicide pacts are not hanging matters. I only wish they were."

"Can I see the girl's statement?"

"I don't mind reading you a few extracts—if it'll help you to make up your own mind." He leaned back in his chair and cleared his throat as if he were going to read a poem or an essay of his own composition. D. sat with his hands hanging down and his eyes on the secretary's face; treachery darkened the whole world. He thought, This is the end. They can't kill a young child like that. He remembered the long drop to the cold pavement; how long did two seconds seem when you were helplessly falling? A dull rage stirred him. He had been pushed about like a lay figure long enough; it was time he began to act. If they wanted violence, let them have violence. The secretary stirred uneasily under his gaze. He put his hand in his pocket where the revolver lay; presumably he had fetched it when he went out to speak to the Ambassador.

The detective read: " 'I can't stand this any longer. Tonight he said we would both go away forever.' " He explained, "She kept a diary, you see. Very well written, too." It wasn't; it was atrocious, like the magazines she read, but D. could hear her tone of voice, the awkward phrases stumbling on the tongue. He swore hopelessly to himself. Somebody had got to die. That was what he had sworn when his wife was shot, but nothing had come of it. " 'Tonight,' " the detective read, " 'I thought he loved another, but he said no. I do not think he is one of those men who flit from flower to flower. I have written to Clara to tell her of our plan. She will be sad, I think.' " The detective said with emotion, "Wherever did she learn to write like that? It's as good as a novel."

"Clara," D. said, "is a young prostitute. You ought to be able to find her easily enough. Presumably the letter will explain what all this means."

"It sounds clear enough, what's written here."

"Our plan," D. went dully on, "was simply this: I was going to take her away today from the hotel."

"Below the age of consent," the detective said.

"I am not a beast. I asked Miss Cullen to find her a job."

The detective said, "Would it be right to say that you had got her to agree to go away with you, promising her employment?"

"Of course it wouldn't."

"It's what you said. And what about this woman called Clara? Where does she come in?"

"She had invited the child to come and be her maid. It didn't seem to me—suitable."

The detective began to write. "She had been offered employment by a young woman, but it did not seem to me suitable, so I persuaded her to come away with me—"

D. said, "You don't write—do you?—as well as she did."

"This isn't a joking matter."

Rage grew in him slowly like a cancer. He began to remember phrases—"Most of the boarders like kippers"—turns of the head, her fear at being left alone, the appalling immaturity of her devotion. "I'm not joking. I'm telling you there was no question of suicide. I charge the manageress and Mr. K. with deliberate murder. She must have been pushed—"

The detective said, "It's up to us to do the charging. The manageress has been questioned—naturally. She was very upset. She admits she's been cross with the child, for slatternly ways. As for Mr. K., I've never heard of him. There's no one of that name in the hotel."

He said, "I'm warning you. If you don't do the job I will."

"That's enough now," the detective said. "You won't be doing anything more in *this* country. It's time we moved."

"There's not enough evidence to arrest me."

"Not on this charge there isn't—yet. But the gentleman here says you are carrying a false passport."

D. said slowly, "All right. I'll come with you."

"We've got a car outside."

D. stood up. He said, "Do you put on handcuffs?" The detective mellowed a little. He said, "Oh, I don't think that will be necessary."

"Will you need me?" the secretary asked.

"I'm afraid you'll be wanted down at the station, sir. You see, we haven't any right here—it's your country. In case there's questions asked by some of these politicians we'll need a statement that you called us in. I suppose there may be more charges to come. Peters," he said, "go and see the car's outside. We don't want to stand about in this fog."

It was apparently the absolute end—not only the end of Else but of thousands at home—because there would be no coal now. Her death was only the first, and perhaps the most horrible because she was alone; the others would die in company in underground shelters. Rage slowly ate its way—he had been pushed around. He watched Peters out of the room. He said to the detective, "That's my birthplace over there, that village under the mountains." The detective turned and looked at it. He said, "It's very picturesque," and D. struck—right on the secretary's Adam's apple just where the high white collar ended. He went down with a whistle of pain, scrabbling for his gun. That helped. D. had it in his hand before the detective moved. He said quickly, "Don't make the mistake of thinking I won't shoot. I'm on active service."

"Now," the detective said, holding up his hand as coolly as if he were on traffic duty, "don't act wild. What we've got on you won't put you away for more than three months."

D. said to the secretary, "Get over to that wall. I've had a gang of traitors after me ever since I came across. Now I'm going to do the shooting."

"Put away that gun," the detective said in a gentle reasonable voice. "You've got overwrought. We'll look into your story when we get to the station."

D. started to move backwards towards the door. "Peters," the detective called sharply. D. had his hand on the handle; he began to turn it but met resistance. Somebody outside wanted to get in. He dropped his hand and stood back against the wall, with the gun covering the detective. The door swung open, hiding him. Peters said, "What is it, Sarge?"

"Look out." But Peters had advanced into the room. D. turned the gun on him. "Back against the wall with the others," he said.

The elderly detective said, "You are acting very silly. If you do get out of here, you'll be picked up in a few hours. Drop that gun and we'll say no more about it."

D. said, "I need the gun."

The door was open. He went backwards slowly and slammed

the door to. He couldn't lock it. He called, "I'll fire at the first one who opens the door." He was in the hall, among tall old portraits and marble consoles. He heard Rose say, "What are you doing?" and swung round, the gun in his hand. Forbes was beside her. He said, "No time to talk. That child was murdered. Somebody's going to die."

Forbes said, "Drop that gun, you fool. This is London."

He took no notice of him at all. He said, "My name *is* D." He felt that much of an avowal was due to Rose. He wasn't likely to see her again; he didn't want her to believe that she was always double-crossed by everyone. He said, "There must be some way of checking up." She was watching the gun with horror; she was probably not listening. He said, "I once gave a copy of my book to the Museum—inscribed to the reading-room attendants—in thanks." The handle began to turn. He called out sharply, "Let go or I'll fire." A man in black, carrying a portfolio, came running lightly down the wide marble steps. He exclaimed, "I say!" seeing the gun, and stood stock still. They made quite a crowd in the hall now, waiting for something to happen. D. hesitated; he had a belief that she would say something, something important like "Good luck" or "Be careful," but she was silent, staring at the gun. It was Forbes who spoke. He said in a puzzled voice, "You know there's a police car just outside." The man on the stairs said, "I say," again, incredulously. A bell tinkled and was silent. Forbes said, "Don't forget they've got the telephone in there."

He had forgotten it. He backed quickly, then by the glass doors of the hall thrust the gun in his pocket and walked quickly out. The police car was there, against the curb. If Forbes called to the others, he hadn't ten yards' start. He walked as fast as he dared; the driver gave him a sharp look—he had forgotten that he had no hat. In the fog it was possible to see for about twenty yards; he dared not run.

Perhaps Forbes hadn't called. He looked back; the car was obscured; he could see the tail light, that was all. He began to run on his toes; behind there was suddenly a clash of voices, the starting of an engine. They were after him. He ran—but there was no exit. He hadn't noticed that the Embassy was in a square to which there was only one entrance; he had turned the wrong way and had three sides to cover. There wasn't time. He could hear the car whine into top. They were not wasting time by turning, they were driving straight round the square.

Was this the end again? He nearly lost his head, running down the railings in what was now the direction of the car. Then his hand missed railing; there was a gap—the head of basement stairs. He ran to the bottom and crouched close under the wall and heard the car go by above. He was saved for the moment by fog; they couldn't be sure that he wasn't all the time just ahead. They couldn't be certain he hadn't turned when they started and outrun them to the street.

But they weren't taking chances. He could hear a whistle blowing and presently footsteps coming slowly round the square—they were looking in the areas. One must be going round one way, one the other; the car probably blocked the street and they were getting more men. Had they lost their fear of his gun, or had they had arms of their own in the police car? He didn't know how these things went in England. They were coming close.

There wasn't a light on. That alone was dangerous; they wouldn't expect to find him in an occupied basement. He peered through the window; he couldn't see much—the corner of what looked like a divan. It was probably a basement flat. There was a notice on the door—"No milk till Monday"—he tore it down. A little brass plate beside the bell—"Glover." He tried the door—hopeless; bolted and double-locked. The footsteps came nearer, very slowly. They must be searching thoroughly. There was only one chance; people were careless. He took out a knife and slipped it under the catch of the window, levered it; the pane slid up. He scrambled through and fell—silently—on the divan. He could hear somebody working up the square the other way; he felt weak and out of breath, but he daren't rest yet. He closed the window and turned on the light.

The place was stuffy with the smell of pot-pourri from a decorated pot on the mantelpiece; a divan covered with an art needlework counterpane, blue and orange cushions, a gas fire. He took it quickly in, to the homemade water colours on the walls and the radio set by the dressing table. It spoke to him of an unmarried ageing woman with few interests. He heard steps coming down into the area; on no account must the place seem empty. He looked for the switch, plugged in the radio. A bright feminine voice said, "But what is the young housewife to do if her table only seats four? To borrow from a neighbour at such short notice may be difficult." He opened a door at random and found himself in the bathroom. "Why not put two tables of the same height on end? The join will not be visible under the cloth. But where is the cloth to come from?" Somebody—it could only be a policeman—rang the area bell. "Even this need not be borrowed if you have a plain counterpane upon your bed."

Rage dictated his movements—they were pushing him around still; his turn had to come. He opened a cupboard door, found what he wanted—one of the tiny razors women use for their armpits, a stick of shaving soap, a towel. He tucked the towel into his collar, lathered over his moustache and the scar on his chin. The bell rang again; a voice said, "That was Lady Mersham in the second talk of a series, Hints to the Young Housewife."

D. moved slowly to the door, opened it. A policeman stood outside. He had a crumpled piece of paper in his hand. He said, "Seeing as this said 'No milk till Monday,' I thought the flat might be empty and the light left on." He peered at D. closely. D. said, pronouncing his words carefully as if he had to pass an examination in English, "That was last week."

"You haven't seen any stranger about?"

"No."

"Good day," the man said and moved reluctantly away. Suddenly he came back and said sharply, "Funny sort of razor you use."

D. realized that he was holding the woman's razor in his hand. He said, "Oh, it's my sister's. I lost my own. Why?"

It was a young man. He lost his poise and said, "Oh, well, sir. We got to keep our eyes open."

D. said, "You'll excuse me. I am in rather a hurry."

"That's all right, sir." He watched the man climb up into the fog. Then he closed the door and went back into the bathroom. The trapdoor had opened and let him out. He cleared the soap away from his mouth—no moustache. It made a difference, an enormous difference. It took ten years off his age. Rage was like vitality in his veins. Now they were going to have some of their own medicine; he had stood up to the watcher, the beating, the bullet; now it was their turn. Let them stand up to it equally well if they could. He thought of Mr. K. and the manageress and the dead child, and, moving back into the stuffy female room which smelled of dead roses, he swore that from now on he would be the hunter, the watcher, the marksman in the mews.

PART II

The Hunter

One

A hollow B.B.C. voice said, "Before we turn you over to the Northern Regional for a cinema organ recital from the Super-Palace, Newcastle, here is an S.O.S. from Scotland Yard. Wanted by the police: an alien passing under the name of D. who was arrested this morning at the request of the —— Embassy and made his escape after assaulting the Ambassador's secretary. Age about forty-five, five feet nine inches in height, hair dark inclined to grey, a heavy moustache, a scar on the right side of his chin. He is believed to carry a revolver."

The waitress said, "That's funny. You got a scar too. Don't you go and get into trouble."

"No," D. said, "no. I must be careful, mustn't I?"

"The things that happen," the waitress said. "It's awful, isn't it? I was just going down the street, an' there was a crowd. Somebody committed suicide, they said, out of a window. Of course I stopped an' watched, but there wasn't anything to see. So at lunchtime I go round to the hotel—to see Else an' ask what it was all about. When they said it was Else—you could've knocked me down with a feather."

"You and she were friends?"

"Oh, she hadn't got a better."

"And of course you're upset?"

"I can't hardly believe it yet."

"It doesn't seem likely, does it, a girl of that age? You don't think it was—perhaps—an accident."

"Oh, it couldn't 'a' been. If you ask me, it's a case of still waters —I know more than most people, an' I think she was crossed in love."

"You do?"

"Yes—with a married man living in Highbury."

"Have you told the police that?"

"I'm to be called at the inquest."

"Did *she* tell you that?"

"Oh, no. She was a quiet one. But you pick up things." He watched her with horror; this was friendship. He watched the small brown heartless eyes while she invented things even as she talked. There wasn't a man at Highbury—only in that romantic and squalid brain. Was it she who had lent Else those novelettes that had conditioned her speech? She said, "I think it was the children was the difficulty." There was a kind of gusto of creation in the voice. Else was safely dead; she could be reconstructed now to suit anybody at all. "Else was mad about him. It was a proper spell."

He laid the money down beside his plate. He said, "Well, it was interesting to hear about your—adventure."

"It'll be a long while before I forget it. I tell you—you could've knocked me down . . ."

He went out into the icy evening. It had been just chance which had led him to that café—or the fact that it was only two blocks from the hotel, and he wanted to make up his mind on the spot. The story was in all the papers now—"Gunman in Embassy" stared at him from a poster. They had his description—the charge, entering the country with a false passport; and one of the papers had routed out from somebody the fact that he had been staying in a hotel where a maid had committed suicide that morning. The fact was printed with a hint at a mystery, at developments to follow. Well, there were going to be developments.

He moved boldly down the road towards the hotel. The fog had nearly lifted now. He felt like a man exposed by the drawing back of a curtain. He wondered if they would have posted a policeman at the hotel; he came cautiously along the railings, holding an evening paper in front of his face, reading. There was nobody about. The door stood open as usual. He went quickly in, through the glass inner door, closing it behind him. The keys hung on their hooks; he took down his own. A voice—it was the manageress's—called down from the first floor. "Is that Mr. Muckerji?"

He said, "Yes," hoping that Mr. Muckerji had no pet phrase. Two foreign intonations were much alike. She seemed satisfied. He heard no more. The whole place was oddly quiet, as if death had touched it. No clatter of forks from the dining room—no sound from the kitchen. He trod softly up the carpeted stairs. The door of the manageress's room was half shut; he went by and up the wooden stairs. What window had she dropped from? He put the key into his door and softly opened it. Somewhere out of sight somebody was coughing—cough, cough, cough. He left the door ajar behind him; he wanted to listen. Sooner or later he would hear Mr. K. He had marked down Mr. K. as the simplest to deal with; he would break quicker than the manageress when the screw was turned.

He turned into the dim room; the curtains were drawn for a death. He reached the bed and realized with a shock that *she* was there, laid out ready for burial. Did they have to wait for the inquest? Presumably it was the only vacant room; her own would already have been filled—life goes on. She lay there, stiff, clean, and unnatural. People talked as if death were like sleep; it was like nothing but itself. He was reminded of a bird discovered at the bottom of a cage, on its back, with the claws rigid as grape stalks; nothing could look more dead. He had seen people dead in the street after an air raid, but they fell in curious humped positions—a lot of embryos in the womb. This was different—a unique position reserved for one occasion. Nobody in pain or asleep lay like this.

Some people prayed. That was a passive part; he was eager to express himself in action. Lying there, the body seemed to erase the fear of pain; he could have faced the chauffeur now on any lonely road. He felt fear like an irrelevancy. He didn't speak to it; it couldn't hear; it was no longer she. He heard steps on the stairs, voices. He went behind the curtain, sat back on the sill to keep his feet off the floor. Light came into the room. The manageress's voice said, "I could have sworn I locked that door. There. That's her."

A girl's voice said with avid emotion, "She looks lovely."

"She often talked of you, Clara," the manageress said heavily.

"The dear. Of course she did. Whatever made her, do you think?"

"We never know, do we, another person's heart?" He could see one of them now through a crack between the curtains—a girl with a coarse amiable pretty face a little smudged with facile tears. She said, "Was it here?" in a tone of awe.

"Yes. Through that window."

This window. But why hadn't she struggled? he wondered. Why were there no marks for the police to see?

"That very window?"

"Yes."

They began to move across the room; were they going to examine the scene a little more closely and discover him? Feet came towards him, paused as Clara spoke.

"If she'd come to me, it wouldn't have happened."

"She was all right here," the manageress said, "before *he* came."

"He's got something on his conscience, all right. Though when she wrote to me she was going away with him, I never thought she meant *this* way." He thought, Then even that letter doesn't help. She had been, poor child, incurably vague to the last with her novelette phrases.

The manageress said, "If you don't mind, I'll bring up Mr. Muckerji. He was most anxious to see her—for the last time."

"It's only right," Clara said. He heard the manageress go. Through the crack he could see Clara making up—the dab of powder, the lipstick; a man was on his way. But she didn't touch the tears—they too were only proper.

The manageress returned. She was alone. She said, "It's very odd. He's not in his room."

"Perhaps he's not come in."

"I heard him, though. He was in the hall, taking his key. I called out to him and he answered."

"Perhaps he's in—you know—the place."

"Oh, no. I tried the door." She was ill at ease. She said, "I can't understand. Somebody came in."

Clara said, "It sort of makes you think of ghosts, doesn't it, this sort of thing?"

"I think I'll go upstairs," she said, "and see how things are going. We have to get the room ready, you know, for the new maid."

"Else wasn't much, was she, for cleanness? Poor dear. I don't suppose she'd 'ave suited me. You want things just so when you have gentlemen friends." She was framed for a moment in the crack of the curtain, looking complacently down at the invisible dead. "Well, I must be going now. A gentleman has an appointment for eight sharp. And he doesn't like to be kept." She moved out of sight. The manageress's voice said, "You don't mind if I don't come down with you, dear, do you? There's things . . ."

He put his hand upon his gun, waiting. The light went out. The door shut. He heard the lock turn; the manageress must have her master key with her. He gave her a small start and then came out from behind the curtain. He didn't look at the body again; it had no interest now that it had no voice, no brain. If you believed in God, you could also believe that it had been saved from much misery and had a finer future. You could leave punishment then to God—just because there was no need of punishments when all a murderer did was to deliver. But he hadn't that particular faith. Unless people received their deserts, the world to him was chaos; he was faced with despair. He unlocked the door.

The manageress was on the floor above, talking. He closed the door behind him very softly; he didn't lock it. Let them be haunted by the inexplicable. Suddenly he heard K.'s voice. "You just forgot, I suppose. What else could it be?"

"I don't forget things," the manageress said. "And, anyway, who answered me if it wasn't Mr. Muckerji?"

"He may have gone out again."

"It isn't like him to pop in and out."

There was a strong smell of paint. D. slowly mounted. He could see into the room now; the light was on, while he bowed in obscurity on the dark stairs. Mr. K. was standing by the window with a paint-brush—of course, D. saw it now, it was from her own window she had fallen; there *had* been scratches, but there were no scratches any more. The room was redecorated for the next maid, the whole place whitened and freshened and free from crime. But Mr. K. had been awkward with the brush—they had been afraid to use a handyman—he had green paint on his jacket; it had even got onto his steel-rimmed spectacles. He said, "Who could it have been, anyway?"

"I thought of D."

"He'd never dare." He asked sharply, for reassurance, "Surely he'd never dare?"

"You can't tell what a man will dare when he hasn't anything to lose."

"But he doesn't *know*. You don't really believe he's here—now —somewhere in the house? Perhaps—with *her*." His voice broke a little. "What could he want here?"

"He might be wanting us."

It was a pleasure to D. to watch Mr. K.'s face, puckered behind the steel rims. Unquestionably he'd break under pressure. He said, "Oh, God, the radio says he has a gun."

"Better not talk so loud. He may be listening. We can't tell where he is. I'm sure I locked that door."

Mr. K. screamed at her. "You can tell, can't you, if he has the key!"

"Sh-sh!" She wasn't easy herself; the big spotty face was pastier than ever. "To think he may have been there with me and Clara."

D. began to move back down the stairs. He heard Mr. K. call sharply, "Don't leave me alone," and her contemptuous reply— "We've got to be sure. I'll just go down and see if the key's there on the rack for his room. If it's not, we can always dial the police," she added doubtfully.

D. went quickly down, risking a creaking stair, risking the Indian on the second floor—perhaps he'd packed and gone; people don't like a suicide in the house. Everything was very quiet. He hung up his key—no need for the police to interfere in this vendetta—then stood inside the dining-room door and listened. He heard the manageress come cautiously down into the hall, heavily breathing, and then call out, "The key's here." Mr. K. could be heard on the stairs. He was moving very quickly; the paint slopped up and down in its pot. She called out encouragingly, "It must have been a mistake. Just feel the door as you go by."

"I don't like to."

"Go on, you fool. I locked it only a minute ago."

He panted down to her. "It's not locked now."

D. could see her face in a mirror over the aspidistra; it showed more than fear—calculation, listening. It occurred to him that she mightn't want to call the police while the paint was still wet upstairs and the smell of it about the house; the less they had to explain the better. Mr. K. was in the hall now. He said anxiously, "You must have thought you turned the key. He wouldn't dare."

"And the voice?"

"Of course it was Mr. Muckerji."

"Well," she said, "here he is, isn't he? You can ask him now— for yourself." The hall door opened. In the mirror he could see her eyes—absorbed, planning. She said, "You're late, Mr. Muckerji. I thought I heard you ten minutes ago."

"Not me, madam. I have been busy, very busy—among the neighbours."

"Oh. God," Mr. K. said, "then it was—"

"What have you been busy about, Mr. Muckerji?"

"Well—you will not be offended—you have a phrase, 'the show goes on'—haven't you?—and when that poor child committed suicide, it seemed an occasion—of anthropological importance. You know how it is, Mrs. Mendrill, we mass observers are always on duty."

What was that? D. wondered. He could make no sense of it.

"So I have been collecting data. All the many reasons for her death—a married man in Highbury, a boy in Lambeth—all untrue, of course, but it shows the working of *their* minds. *We* know, of course, that the foreign gentleman—"

"Listen," Mr. K. said, "listen. I won't stay here. Get the police."

Mr. Muckerji said reprovingly, "There has been a lot of hysteria, too. And this will interest you, Mrs. Mendrill. There was somebody who said she saw the child fall. But she didn't."

"No?"

"No. Because she told me the wrong window. Everything else was right—but she had read the papers, you see, so she filled in— about your being there, trying to hold her back, the scream, all of it. But she got the window wrong. That is very interesting, I think."

"What do you do," the manageress said, "with all this information?"

"I type it out on my little Corona and send it to the organizers."

"Do they print it?"

"They file it—for reference. Perhaps one day in a big book— without my name. We work," he said regretfully, "for science."

Mr. K. said, "You've got to send for the police."

"Don't be a fool," the manageress said sharply. She explained, "He sees that man—you know the one who drove her to it—he sees him everywhere."

Mr. Muckerji said automatically, "That is interesting." He sniffed. "Ah, repainting. That is very interesting too. Are you being practical—to eliminate traces—or superstitious?"

"What do you mean—traces?" Mr. K. said excitedly.

"Oh, I mean untidiness, stains—things you do not want in an elegant hotel, which you were planning to redo in any case. Or is it superstition? Because there has been a death. You see there are tribes in West Africa who behave like that. They will even destroy the hut, the clothes, everything of the dead person. They want quite to forget that there has been a death. I am anxious to discover if your desire to put a new coat of paint over your hotel belongs to that category."

Mr. K. said, "I'm going. I can't stand this. If you want any help—"

Suddenly D. realized that he too was visible to the manageress in the same mirror. Their eyes had met. The manageress said slowly, "I shall be all right. With Mr. Muckerji. It's you who had better be careful." She said, "Didn't you want to see the body, Mr. Muckerji?"

"Yes. If it is convenient. I have brought a few flowers. That is superstition, but it is also practical. Because of the scent."

"I don't like flowers in a bedroom as a rule, but in this case I don't suppose it matters, does it?"

D. watched her narrowly, and she returned his look—at second hand. There were people, he thought, who could shoot like that. At shows. With the help of a mirror.

Mr. K. said, "I'm going, Marie," as if he expected something more than this heartless warning. It was as though in the mirror she were encouraging D. to do his worst. She was strong, all right; she would be the last to break; square and spotty and determined, she surrendered him, as it were—one victim.

Mr. Muckerji said, "A moment. I left my glasses, I think, in the dining room at breakfast time." D. drew the gun from his pocket and waited.

"Oh, no, Mr. Muckerji," the manageress said, "you'll find them in your room. We always clear away." She led him up the stairs with a hand on his arm. He was carrying a few untidy flowers wrapped in newspaper. It was extraordinary how the whole world could alter after a single violent act. They had thought they would put him safely away, but it was he now who was safe, because he had nothing to think about now but punishment—no duties. And it was they who welcomed the presence of Mr. Muckerji, as he had done only that morning.

The hall door shut; he followed Mr. K. into the street. Mr. K. walked fast, without looking behind him, carrying an umbrella. They went rapidly down towards the Gray's Inn Road—D. twenty paces behind. He made no effort to disguise his purpose; it seemed improbable that Mr. K. would really have the nerve to call a policeman. Suddenly, desperately, Mr. K. came to bay—on the pavement, by a bus stop. He must have heard the footsteps behind him, crossing the road when he crossed, pausing when he paused. He turned and watched D. approach. He had a cigarette in his hand; it wobbled. He said, "Excuse me. Might I have a light?"

"Certainly." D. struck the match and held it so that it lit the scared short-sighted eyes. They peered at him with haunted relief —no recognition. It was astonishing what difference a moustache made. He had to steady the cigarette with his own fingers. K. said, "I see you've got an evening paper in your pocket. Might I see?"

He was the kind of man who always borrowed if he could; he saved a match and saved a paper.

"You can have it," D. said. They had had only two interviews together, he and K., but something about the voice worried the man. He looked up sharply and then down at the paper again. He wasn't sure. A bus drew up. He said, "Thank you," climbing on board. D. followed—up to the top deck. They swayed forward one behind the other. Mr. K. took the front seat; D. was just behind. Mr. K. looked sharply up and saw D.'s face reflected in the glass. He sat there, not reading the paper, thinking, hunched in his seat; his old and seedy overcoat registered sickness like a cat's fur.

The bus turned into Holborn; the queue was going into the Empire; big windows full of office furniture lined the street; a milk bar, and then more furniture. The bus moved west. D. watched Mr. K.'s face in the window. Where did he live? Had he the courage to go home? They crossed St. Giles's Circus into Oxford Street. Mr. K. looked out and down with a kind of nostalgia at the policeman on traffic duty, the Jews outside the Astoria. He took off his spectacles and rubbed the glass; he wanted to see clearly. The paper was open on his knee at the story of the gunman in the Embassy. He began to read the description—as if he could trust that more than his own memory. Once again he took a quick snaky look at D.'s face; his eyes were on the scar this time. He said sharply, "Oh," before he could stop himself.

"Did you speak to me?" D. said, leaning forward.

"Me? Oh, no," Mr. K. said. He coughed with a dry throat—hack, hack, hack. He got on his feet, swaying with the bus.

"Do you get out here?"

"Me? Yes. Yes."

"So do I," said D. "You look ill. Do you want a hand?"

"No, no. I'm quite all right."

He made for the stairs, and D. followed at his heels.

They were side by side on the pavement, waiting for the traffic lights to change. D. said, "Things have changed for the better, haven't they?" He felt himself shaken by a reckless and malicious mirth.

"What do you mean?" Mr. K. said.

"I mean the weather. This morning there was so much fog."

The traffic lights turned green, and they crossed the entrance of Bond Street, side by side. D. could see Mr. K. taking quick looks

in the plate-glass windows at his companion, but he couldn't see
—his eyes were spoiled by poverty and too much reading; and he
daren't speak directly. It was as if, so long as D. did not declare
himself, he wasn't D.

Mr. K. suddenly turned into a doorway, into a dark passage, and
almost ran towards the electric globe at the far end. The passage
was somehow familiar; D. had been too absorbed to notice where
they had come. He followed after Mr. K.; an old lift was wheezing
down towards his victim. Mr. K. suddenly said in a voice pitched
high to go up the lift shaft to the rooms above, "You are following
me. Why are you following me?"

D. said gently, "Surely you ought to be speaking Entrenationo—
to a pupil." He laid his hand confidingly on Mr. K.'s sleeve. "I
should never have believed a moustache made all that difference."

Mr. K. pulled the lift door open. He said, "I don't want any more
to do with you."

"But we're on the same side, surely."

"You were superseded."

D. pushed him gently backwards and shut the lift gates. He said,
"I forgot. This is the night of the soirée, isn't it?"

"You ought to be on your way home by now."

"But I've been prevented. You must know that." He touched
the emergency button, and they stopped between two floors.

Mr. K. said, "Why did you do that?" He leaned against the lift
wall, blinking, blinking behind the steel rims. Somebody was playing a piano upstairs, rather badly.

D. said, "Did you ever read Goldthorb's detective stories?"

"Let me out of here," Mr. K. said.

"Schoolteachers generally read detective stories."

"I shall scream," Mr. K. said. "I shall scream."

"It wouldn't be good manners at a soirée. By the way, you've still
got some of that paint on your coat. That's not clever of you."

"What do you want?"

"It was so lucky that Mr. Muckerji found the woman who *saw*
it happen—from the other window."

"I wasn't there," Mr. K. said. "I know nothing."

"That's interesting."

"Let me out."

"But I was telling you about Goldthorb's detective story. One
man killed another in a lift. Rang the lift down. Walked up the

stairs. Rang the lift up and—before witnesses—discovered the body. Of course luck was on his side. You have to have a fortunate hand for murder."

"You wouldn't dare."

"I was just telling you Goldthorb's story."

Mr. K. said weakly, "There's no such man. The name's absurd."

"He wrote in Entrenationo, you see."

Mr. K. said, "The police are looking for you. You'd better clear out—quickly."

"They have no picture, and the description's wrong." He said mildly, "If there was a way of dropping you down the lift shaft—to make the punishment, you know, fit the crime—"

Suddenly the lift began to move upwards. Mr. K. said triumphantly, "There. You see. You'd better run for it." It wheezed and shook very slowly beyond the second floor—the offices of *Mental Health*.

D. said, "I shouldn't speak if I were you. You read about the revolver."

"It's not me you need be afraid of," Mr. K. said. "I bear you no malice—but Miss Carpenter or Dr. Bellows—"

There wasn't time to finish; the lift stopped, and Dr. Bellows came out of the big waiting-room to greet them; a faded woman in brown silk got into the lift, waving a hand thick with art jewellery like barnacles, squeaking a mysterious phrase which sounded like "Nougat." Dr. Bellows said, *"Bona nuche. Bona nuche,"* and smiled at them happily.

Mr. K. glared at him and waited. D. had his hand upon his pocket—but Dr. Bellows seemed unaware of anything wrong. He took a hand of each and shook them warmly. He said, "To a new pupil I may perhaps be allowed to speak a few words in English." He added in a slightly puzzled way: "You are a new pupil, surely. I *thought* I knew you."

D. said, "You are looking for my moustache."

"Of course. That's it."

"I told myself, for a new language a new face. Have you by any chance seen the evening paper?"

"No," Dr. Bellows said, "and please, please don't tell me. I never read the daily press. I find that in a good weekly paper fact has been sifted from rumour. All the *important* news is there. And so much less distress."

"It's an admirable idea."

"I recommend it. Miss Carpenter, my secretary, you know her, adopted it and has been so much happier ever since."

"It must make for everyone's happiness," D. said. Mr. K., he noticed, had slipped away. "I must speak to Miss Carpenter about it."

"You'll find her presiding over the coffee. For these soirées rules are a little relaxed. We hope people will speak Entrenationo if possible—but the great thing is to get together." He led D. into the waiting-room. There was a big urn on the counter and plates of rock buns. Miss Carpenter waved to him from behind the steam; she was still wearing her blue wool jumper with the bobbles. *"Bona nuche,"* she called to him. *"Bona nuche."* A dozen faces turned to look at him; it was like one of those illustrations in a children's encyclopedia, which show the races of the world. There were a good many Orientals, wearing glasses. Mr. K. stood with a rock bun in his hand, not eating.

"I must introduce you," Dr. Bellows said, "to our Siamese."

He pressed D. gently onwards towards the far wall. *"Hi es* Mr. D.—Doctor Li."

Dr. Li looked at him inscrutably through very thick lenses. *"Bona nuche."*

"Bona nuche," D. said.

Conversation went on among the leather armchairs spasmodically; little bursts of conversation rose up in corners and then withered away for want of nourishment. Miss Carpenter poured out coffee, and Mr. K. stared at his rock bun. Dr. Bellows moved here and there erratically, like love—the smooth white hair, the weak and noble face.

D. said, "An idealist."

"Qua?"

"I'm afraid," D. said, "I am a new pupil. I cannot yet speak much Entrenationo."

"Qua?" Dr. Li said sternly. He watched D. narrowly through the thick glasses like portholes, as if he suspected him of rudeness. Mr. K. began edging towards the door, still carrying his rock bun.

Dr. Li said sharply, *"Parla Entrenationo."*

"Parla Anglis."

"No," Dr. Li said firmly and angrily. *"No parla."*

"I am sorry," D. said. *"Un momento."* He crossed the room rapidly and took Mr. K.'s arm. He said, "We mustn't leave yet. It would look strange."

Mr. K. said, "Let me go. I implore you. I know nothing. I am feeling ill."

Dr. Bellows appeared again. He said, "How did you get on with Dr. Li? He is a very influential man. A professor at Chulalankarana University. It gives me great hopes of Siam."

"I found it a little difficult," D. said. "He seems to speak no English." He kept his hand through Mr. K.'s arm.

"Oh," Dr. Bellows said, "he speaks it perfectly. But he feels— quite rightly, of course—that the only object of learning Entrenationo is to speak it. Like so many Orientals he is a little—intransigent." They all three looked at Dr. Li, who stood in an island of silence with his eyes half closed. Dr. Bellows went across to him and began to talk earnestly in Entrenationo. Silence spread around the room; it was a privilege to hear the inventor speak his own language; he gave the impression of gliding rapidly among the cases like a skater.

Mr. K. said rapidly, "I can't stand this. What are you trying to get out of me?"

"A little justice," D. said gently. He felt no pity at all; the odd occasion—the surroundings of office coffee and homemade cakes, of withered women in old-fashioned evening dresses which had had too little wear, and of Orientals, shrewd and commercial behind their glasses—only lifted Mr. K. further out of the category of human beings who suffer pain and exact sympathy. Dr. Bellows was back again. He said, "Dr. Li asked me to say that he would be pleased to meet you another time—when you have learned rather more Entrenationo." He smiled feebly. "Such a firm character," he said. "I have not met such faith—no, not in all Israel."

"Mr. K. and I," D. said, "were just regretting that it was nearly time for us to leave."

"So soon? And I did so much want to introduce you to a Rumanian lady—oh, I see that she is talking to Dr. Li." He smiled across the room at them as if they were a young couple whose timid courtship he was encouraging and superintending. He said, "There. That is what I mean. Communication instead of misunderstanding, strife . . ." It seemed unlikely, D. thought, that Rumania and Siam were ever likely to come into serious conflict, but Dr. Bellows was already off again, forging his links between the most unlikely countries, and Miss Carpenter stood behind the coffee urn and smiled and smiled.

D. said, "It's time for us to move."

"I won't move. I am going to see Miss Carpenter home."

D. said, "I can wait."

He went over to the window and looked down; the buses moved slowly along Oxford Street like gigantic beetles. Across the top of the opposite building a sky sign spelled out slowly the rudimentary news, "2 goals to one." Far away, foreshortened on the pavement, a squad of police moved in single file towards Marlborough Street. What next? The news petered out and began again. "Another advance reported . . . 5000 refugees . . . four air raids . . ." It was like a series of signals from his own country. What are you doing here? Why are you wasting time? When are you coming back? He felt homesick for the dust after the explosion, the noise of engines in the sky. You have to love your home for something—if only for its pain and violence. Had L. come to terms, he wondered, with Benditch? The deal was closed to him; no credentials would avail him now in this respectable country—a man wanted on suspicion of murder. He thought of the child screaming at the window, scratching with her nails at the paint, breaking through the fog, smashed on the pavement; she was one of thousands. It was as if by the act of death she had become naturalized to his own land—a countrywoman. His territory was death; he could love the dead and the dying better than the living. Dr. Bellows, Miss Carpenter—they were robbed of reality by their complacent safety. They must die before he could take them seriously. He moved away from the window and said to Miss Carpenter, "Is there a telephone I could use?"

"Oh, certainly. In Dr. Bellows' office."

He said, "I hear Mr. K. is seeing you home?"

"Oh, but that's sweet of you, Mr. K. You really oughtn't to bother. It's such a long way to Morden."

"No trouble," Mr. K. muttered; he still held the rock bun—like an identification disc; they would be able to recognize his body by it.

D. opened the door of the office and quickly apologized. A middle-aged man with a shaven Teutonic skull was sitting out with an angular girl on Dr. Bellows' desk. There was a slight smell of onions —one of them must have been eating steak. "I am so sorry. I came to telephone." The angular girl giggled; she was singularly unattractive, with a large wrist watch and a lapel pin in the shape of an Aberdeen dog.

"Not at all. Not at all," the German said. "Come, Winifred."

He bowed stiffly to D. from the doorway. *"Korda,"* he said. *"Korda."*

"*Korda?*"

"Entrenationo—for the heart."

"Ah, yes, yes."

"I have a great passion," the German frankly explained, "for the English girls."

"Yes?" The German kept Winifred's bony hand in a tight grip; she had bad teeth and mouse-coloured hair; she carried with her a background of blackboards and chalk and children asking permission to leave the room—and Sunday walks in ruined fields with dogs.

"They have so much innocence," the German said and bowed again and closed the door.

D. rang up Lord Benditch's house. He said, "Is Miss Cullen there?"

"Miss Cullen doesn't live here." Luck favoured him; it was a woman—not the manservant, who might have remembered his voice. He said, "I can't find her in the telephone book. Would you give me her number?"

"Oh, I don't know that I can do that."

"I am a very old friend. Only over in England for a day or two."

"Well—"

"She will be very disappointed."

"Well—"

"She particularly asked—"

"It's Mayfair 301."

He dialled again and waited. He had to trust Miss Carpenter to keep a grip on Mr. K.; he knew very well how convention can be stronger than fear—especially when the fear is still a little vague and unbelievable; you have to learn to fear successfully. He said, "Is Miss Cullen there?"

"I don't think so. Hold on." Even if he couldn't get the coal himself, there must be some way of stopping L. If only he could prove that the murder—was a murder.

Rose's voice suddenly said, "Who's that?"

He said, "The name is Glover."

"What do you want? I don't know a Glover."

"I live," he said, "at three Chester Gardens—nearly next door to the Embassy."

There was silence at the other end. He said, "Of course, if you believe that story—of the suicide pact—you can send the police round tonight. Or if you believe that I am not D. at all."

She made no reply; had she rung off? He said, "Of course the girl was murdered. It was ingenious, wasn't it?"

She replied suddenly in a tone of fury, "Is that all you care?"

He said, "I shall kill whoever did it. I am not sure yet—I want the right person. One can't afford to kill more than one."

"You're crazy. Can't you get out of the country, go home?"

"They would probably shoot me. Not that that matters. But I shouldn't like L.—"

She said, "You're too late. They've signed."

"I was afraid—" He said, "Do you know what the contract is? I don't see how they can hope to get the coal out of the ports. There's the neutrality agreement."

She said, "I'll ask Furt."

"Has he signed too?"

"Yes, he's signed." Somebody was playing the piano again and singing; it seemed to be an Entrenationo song; the word *korda, korda* came in a lot. Presently she said, "He couldn't do anything else." She excused him. "When all the others signed—the shareholders—"

"Of course." He felt an odd prick of jealousy because she had taken the trouble to defend Forbes. It was like feeling painfully returning to a frozen hand. He didn't love, he was incapable of loving anyone alive, but nevertheless the prick was there.

She said, "Where are you? I keep on hearing the oddest sounds."

"At a soirée," he said. "That's what they call it. Of the Entrenationo School."

"You're such a fool," she said despairingly. "Don't you realize there's a warrant out for you? Resisting arrest. Forged passport. God knows what else."

He said, "It seems safe here. We are eating rock buns."

"Why be such a fool?" she said. "You're old enough, aren't you, to look after yourself?"

He said, "Will you find out for me—from Forbes?"

"You didn't mean that, did you, about killing—?"

"Yes, I meant that."

The voice came fiercely and vividly out of the vulcanite; she might have been standing at his elbow, accusing him. "So you did love the little bitch?"

"No," he said. "Not more than all the others. There have been four raids today. I daresay they've killed fifty children besides her. One has to get one's own back a little." He suddenly realized how absurd it all was. He was a confidential agent employed in an important coal deal on which the fate of a country might depend; she was a young woman, the daughter of a peer whose coal he wanted, and the beloved, apparently, of a Mr. Forbes, who also controlled several mines and kept a mistress in Shepherd's Market (that was irrelevant); a child had been murdered by the manageress or Mr. K.—acting presumably on behalf of the rebels, although they were employed by his own people. That was the situation: a strategical and political—and criminal—one. Yet here they were, talking to each other down the telephone like human beings, jealous of each other, as if they were in love, as if they had a world at peace to move about in, and the whole of time.

She said, "I don't believe it. You must have loved her."

"She was only fourteen, I should think."

"Oh, I daresay you've reached the age when you like them young."

"No."

"But you can't do anything of that kind here—killing, I mean —don't you understand? They'll hang you. Only the Irish try that on here—and they are always hanged."

"Oh, well," he said vaguely.

"Oh, God," she said. "The door's been open all the time." There was silence; then she said, "I've probably given you away. They'll have guessed—after the newspapers. Probably Scotland Yard's listening in now. They could have dialled 999 on the downstairs phone."

"Who are they?"

"Oh, the maid or my friend. You can't trust anyone. Get away from there—wherever you are."

"Yes," he said. "It's time to move on. *Bona nuche.*"

"What on earth's that?"

"Entrenatïono," he said, and rang off.

He opened the door into the waiting-room; there were fewer people about, less buns; the coffee was cooling in the urn. Mr. K. stood against the counter, grasped firmly in the conversational hold of Miss Carpenter. D. made for them, and Mr. K. wilted. It occurred to D. that he didn't look like the kind of man you killed. On the other hand, he was a traitor, and somebody had to die. It was unsporting perhaps, but Mr. K. might be the easiest—he would be a warning to other traitors. He said to Miss Carpenter, "I'm afraid I've got to tear away your escort," drawing on a pair of gloves he must be careful not to take off again.

"I won't go," Mr. K. said, and Miss Carpenter pouted delightedly and set a wool bobble swinging.

"It's really important," D. said, "or of course I would never take him."

"I don't see," Miss Carpenter said playfully, "that it could be so important."

"I have been onto my embassy," D. said; his imagination was unbridled, he feared nobody; it was his turn to be feared, and he felt exhilaration like laughter in his brain. "We have been discussing the possibility of setting up an Entrenationo centre at home."

"What's that?" Dr. Bellows said. He appeared at the buffet with a dark middle-aged woman in pink cretonne. The mild eyes gleamed excitedly. "But how—in the middle of a war?"

"It's no good fighting," D. said, "for a particular civilization if we don't—at the same time—keep it alive behind the lines." He felt a very slight horror at his own appalling fluency, a very little regret at the extravagant hopes he had aroused beside the coffee urn, in the dingy office. The old liberal eyes were full of tears. Dr. Bellows said, "Then some good may come of all the anguish."

"So you'll understand if I and my countryman here—we must rush away." It was the wildest story, but no story is too wild for a man who hopes. Everyone in this room lived in an atmosphere of unreality—high up above Oxford Street in an ivory tower, waiting for miracles. Dr. Bellows said, "I never thought when I got up this morning—so many years. 'This is the birthday of my life.' That was what one of our poetesses wrote." He held D.'s hand; everybody was watching; Miss Carpenter wiped the corner of her eye. He said, "God bless you, all of you."

Mr. K. said, "I will not go. I will not go," but nobody paid him any attention. He was hustled out beside D., towards the lift, by the lady in cretonne, hailed on his road. In his fear he lost his English altogether; he began to beseech them all to wait and listen in a language only D. could understand. He looked ill, beaten; he sought to express something, anything, in Entrenationo. He said, *"Mi korda, mi korda,"* white about the lips, but nobody else was talking Entrenationo now, and then they were together in the lift, going down. Dr. Bellows' face disappeared, his waistcoat buttons, his boots— he wore boots. Mr. K. said, "There's nothing you can do. Nothing."

D. said, "You've got nothing to fear if you weren't concerned in her death. Keep close beside me. Don't forget I have that revolver." They walked side by side into Oxford Street; suddenly Mr. K. sidestepped; somebody came in between; they were separated by shopwindow gazers. Mr. K. began to dart down the pavement, zigzagging. He was a small man and agile, but shortsighted; he bumped into people and went on without apology. D. let him go; it was no good pursuing him through the crowd. He called a taxi and said to the driver, "Go as slow as you can. There's a drunk friend of mine just in front—I've lost him in the crowd. He needs a lift before he gets in any trouble." Through the window he could watch Mr. K.; he was wearing himself down; it all helped.

Mr. K. bounded from right to left and back again; people turned round and stared at him. A woman said, "Ought to be ashamed," and a man said, "Guinness ain't so good for *him.*" His steel spectacles had slipped halfway down his nose, and every now and then he looked backwards; his umbrella got between people's legs, and a child howled at the sight of his little scared red eyes. He was creating a sensation. At the corner of South Audley Street he ran full tilt into a policeman. The policeman said kindly, "Hi. You can't behave like that here." Mr. K. stared up at him, his eyes blind above his glasses.

"Now go home quietly," the policeman said.

"No," Mr. K. said suddenly, "no."

"Put your head under the tap and go to bed."

"No." Mr. K. suddenly put his head down and rammed it at the policeman's stomach—ineffectually; a big gentle hand diverted him. "Do you want to come to the station?" the policeman asked mildly. A small crowd collected. A man with a high hollow voice in a black hat said, "You've no reason to interfere; he was doing no harm."

"I only said—" the policeman began.

"I heard what you said," the stranger retorted quickly. "On what charge, may I ask, do you intend—?"

"Drunk and disorderly," the policeman said.

Mr. K. watched with an appearance of wild hope; he forgot to be disorderly.

"Nonsense," the stranger said. "He's done nothing. I'm quite prepared to stand in the witness box."

"Now, now, now," the policeman said indignantly. "What's all the fuss about? I only told him to go home to bed."

"You suggested he was drunk."

"He is drunk."

"Prove it."

"What's it to do with you, anyway?"

"This is supposed to be a free country."

The policeman said plaintively, "What I want to know is, what have I *done?*"

The man in the black hat produced a card and said to Mr. K., "If you want to charge this constable with slander, I am quite prepared to give evidence." Mr. K. held the card as if he didn't understand. The policeman suddenly flung his arms above his head and shouted at the crowd, "Get on there. Move on."

"Do nothing of the kind," the stranger said sharply. "You are all witnesses."

"You'll make me lose my patience," the policeman said with a breaking voice. "I warn you."

"What of? Speak up now. What of?"

"Interfering with an officer in the performance of his duty."

"Duty," the stranger said sarcastically.

"But I am drunk," Mr. K. said suddenly, imploringly, "I am disorderly." The crowd began to laugh. The policeman turned on Mr. K., "Now you've started again," he said. "We aren't concerned with you."

"Oh, yes, we are," the stranger said.

A look of agony crossed the policeman's face. He said to Mr. K., "Now why don't you get quietly into a taxi and go home?"

"Yes. Yes. I'll do that," Mr. K. said.

"Taxi."

The taxi drew up beside Mr. K., and he grabbed thankfully at the handle, opened the door. D. smiled at him and said, "Step in."

"An' now," the policeman said, "for you—whatever your name is."

"My name is Hogpit."

"No more back answers," the policeman said.

Mr. K. backed onto the pavement. He said, "Not that taxi. I won't take that taxi."

"But my name *is* Hogpit." Several people laughed. The man said angrily, "It's no funnier than Swinburne."

Mr. K. struggled to get by.

"Moses!" the policeman said. "You again."

"There's a man in that taxi." Mr. K. said.

D. got out and said, "That's all right, officer. He's a friend of

mine. He *is* drunk—I lost him up the road at the Carpenter's Arms."
He took Mr. K.'s arm and led him firmly back. Mr. K. said, "He'll
kill me," and tried to flop onto the pavement. "Would you mind
giving me a hand, officer?" D. said. "I'll see he's no more trouble."
"That's all right, sir. I'm glad to be rid of him." He bent and
lifted Mr. K. as if he were a baby and piled him onto the floor of
the taxi. Mr. K. cried weakly, "I tell you he's been following me."
The man whose name was Hogpit said, "What right have you to
do that, constable? You heard what he said? How do you know
he's not telling the truth?"

The constable slammed the door and turned. He said, "Because
I use my judgment. An' now are *you* going to go quietly?" The taxi
drove on. The group slipped backwards, gesticulating. D. said,
"You only made yourself look a fool."

"I'll break the window. I'll scream," Mr. K. said.

"If the worst came to the worst," D. said in a low voice, as if he
meant to confide a secret, "I'd shoot."

"You couldn't get away. You wouldn't dare."

"That's the kind of argument they use in stories. It doesn't apply
any more in these days. There's a war on. It's not likely that any
of us will 'get away,' as you call it, for long."

"What are you going to do?"

"I'm taking you home for a talk."

"What do you mean, home?" But D. had no more to say as
they bumped slowly on across the park. The soapbox orators talked
in the bitter cold at Marble Arch with their mackintoshes turned up
around the Adam's apples, and all down the road the cad cars
waited for the right easy girls, and the cheap prostitutes sat hopelessly in the shadows, and the blackmailers kept an eye open on the
grass, where the deeds of darkness were quietly and unsatisfactorily
accomplished. This was technically known as a city at peace. A
poster said, "Bloomsbury Tragedy Sensation."

Two

The fight was out of Mr. K. He left the taxi without a word and
went on down the basement steps. D. turned up the light in the
little bed-sitting room and lit the gas; bent over the fire with the
match between his fingers, he wondered whether he was really going

to commit a murder. It seemed hard luck on Glover—whoever she might be; a person's home had a kind of innocency. When a house-front gave way before an explosion and showed the iron bed, the chairs, the hideous picture, and the chamber pot, you had a sense of rape; intrusion into a stranger's home was an act of lust. But you were driven always to copy what your enemy did. You dropped the same bombs, you broke up the same private lives. He turned with sudden fury on Mr. K. and said, "You've asked for this."

Mr. K. backed against the divan, sat down. Above his head was a small bookshelf with a few meagre books in limp morocco bind-ings—the inconsiderable library of a pious woman. He said, "I swear to you, I wasn't there."

"You don't deny, do you, that you and she planned to get my papers?"

"You were superseded."

"I know all that." He came close up to him; this was the moment for the blow in the face, the worked-up rage; they had shown him the other day how a man was beaten up. But he couldn't do it. To touch K. at all was to start a relationship. His mouth quivered in distaste. He said, "Your only chance of getting out alive is to be frank. They bought you both, didn't they?"

Mr. K.'s glasses dropped onto the divan; he felt for them over the art-needlework cover. He said, "How were we to know you had not sold out?"

"There was no way, was there?" D. said.

"They didn't trust you—or why should we have been employed?"

He listened, with his fingers on the gun. If you were the jury as well as the judge—the attorney too—you had to give every chance; you had to be fair even if the whole world was biased. "Go on."

Mr. K. was encouraged. His pink-rimmed eyes peered up, trying to focus; he moved the muscles of his mouth into a testing smile. He said, "And then, of course, you did behave oddly—didn't you? How could we tell that you wouldn't sell at a price?"

"True."

"Everyone has to look after himself. If you had sold—we should have got nothing."

It was a rather dreadful revelation of human depravity; Mr. K. had been more bearable when he was frightened, cringing. Now his courage was coming back. He said, "It's no good being left behind. After all, there's no hope."

"No hope?"

"You've only to read the paper tonight. We are beaten. Why, you know yourself how many ministers have ratted. You don't think they are getting nothing, do you?"

"I wonder what you got."

Mr. K. found his glasses and shifted on the divan. Fear had almost entirely left him; he had a look of old and agile cunning. He said, "I thought sooner or later we'd come to that."

"It would be best to tell me everything."

"If you want a cut," Mr. K. said, "you won't get it. Not even if I wanted—"

"Surely you haven't been foolish enough to sell for credit?"

"They knew better than to offer—to a man like me—money."

D. was at a loss. He said incredulously, "You mean—you've got nothing out of it?"

"What I've got's in writing. Signed by L."

"I never thought you were quite such a fool. If it was only promises you wanted, you could have had as many from us."

"This isn't a promise. It's an appointment. Signed by the Chancellor. You know L.'s the Chancellor now. That would be since your time." He sounded positively at ease again.

"Chancellor of what?"

"The university, of course. I have been made a professor. I am on the faculty. I can go home again."

D. laughed, he couldn't help it; but there was disgust behind the laughter. This was to be the civilization of the future, the scholarship of the future. He said, "It's a comfort to think if I kill you I'm killing Professor K." He had a hideous vision of a whole world of poets, musicians, scholars, artists—in steel-rimmed spectacles with pink eyes and old treacherous brains—the survivals of an antique worn-out world, teaching the young the useful lessons of treachery and dependence. He took out the secretary's gun. He said, "I wonder whom they'll appoint in your place." But he knew they had hundreds to choose from.

"Don't play about with a gun like that. It's dangerous."

D. said, "If you were at home now, you would be put on trial by a military court and sentenced. Why do you think you ought to escape here?"

"You're joking," Mr. K. said, trying to laugh.

D. opened the revolver; there were two shots in it.

Mr. K. said frantically, "You said if I hadn't killed the girl, I'd be safe."

"Well?" He closed the breech again.

"I didn't kill her. I only telephoned to Marie—"

"Marie? Oh, yes, the manageress. Go on."

"L. told me to. He rang me up from the Embassy. He said, 'Just tell her—do what you can.' "

"And you didn't know what that meant?"

"Not exactly. How could I? I only knew she had a plan—to get you deported. She never meant it to look like murder. It was when the police read the diary—it all fitted in. There was what you said —about taking her away."

"You know a lot."

"Marie told me—afterwards. It all came to her like a revelation. She had meant to frame a robbery. And then the girl, you see, was —insolent. She just thought she'd give her a scare—and then she lost her temper. You know she has an awful temper, and no control. No control at all." He tried again that testing smile. "It's only one girl," he said, "out of thousands. They die every day at home. It's war." Something in D.'s face made him add too quickly, "That was how Marie argued it."

"And what did you say?"

"Oh, I was against it."

"Before it happened—you were against it?"

"Yes. No, no, I mean—afterwards. When I saw her afterwards."

D. said, "It won't hold water. You knew, all right, all along."

"I swear I wasn't there—"

"Oh, I believe you. You wouldn't have the nerve. That was left to her."

"It's *her* you want."

"I've got a prejudice," D. said, "against killing women. But she'll suffer all right, when you are found dead. She'll be left wondering, I daresay—listening to sounds. Besides, I've only two bullets. And I don't know how to get more." He put up the safety catch.

"This is England!" the little grey man shrieked, as if he wanted to convince himself. He started to his feet and knocked a book off the shelf; it fell open upon the divan—a little book of devotional verse with God in capital letters. Certainly it was England—England was the divan, the wastepaper basket made out of old flower prints, the framed Speed map, and the cushions; the alien atmosphere plucked at D.'s sleeve, urged him to desist. He said furiously, "Get off that divan."

Mr. K. got tremulously up. He said, "You'll let me go."

Years of academic life might make you a good judge; it didn't make you a good executioner.

"Why not L.?" Mr. K. implored him.

"Oh, I'll deal with L. one day. But he isn't one of us." The distinction was real; you couldn't feel the same rage towards a museum piece.

Mr. K. thrust out his ink-stained hands with an air of pleading. He said, "You couldn't blame me if you knew. The life I've had. Oh, they write books about slavery." He began to cry. "You pity *her,* but it's me," he said, "it's me . . ." Words failed him.

"Get back through that door," D. said. The bathroom couldn't be seen from outside. It had ventilation but no window. The hand which held the gun shook with the impending horror. They had pushed him around—it was his turn now, but fear was returning, the fear of other people's pain, their lives, their individual despairs. He was damned like a creative writer to sympathy. He said, "Go on. Hurry," and Mr. K. began to stumble back. D. raked his mind for any heartless joke—"We haven't got a cemetery wall . . ."—but it petered out. You could joke only about your own death. Other people's deaths were important.

Mr. K. said, "She hadn't lived through what I had—fifty-five years of it. And then to have only six months more, and no hope at all."

D. tried not to listen, didn't in any case understand. He followed Mr. K., with the gun held before him with revulsion.

"If you had only six months, wouldn't you choose a little comfort?" The glasses slipped off his nose and smashed. He said, "Respect," with a sob. He said, "I always dreamed one day—the university." He was in the bathroom now, staring blindly where he supposed D. to be, backing towards the basin. "And then the doctor said six months." He gave a yelp of mournful anguish like a dog. "Die in harness—with that fool in Oxford Street—'*bona matina,*' '*bona matina*'—cold—the radiator's never on." He was raving now —the first words that came into his head, as if he had a sense that as long as he talked he was safe; and any words which emerged from that tormented and embittered brain couldn't help but carry the awful impress of the little office, the cubicle, the cold radiator, the roller picture on the wall—"*un famil gentilbono.*" He said, "The old man creeping round on rubber soles—I'd get the pain—had to apologize in Entrenationo—or else the fine—no cigarettes for a week." With every word he came alive—and the condemned must not come alive; he must be dead long before the judge passes sentence. "Stop," D. said. Mr. K.'s head switched round like a tortoise's. The blind eyes had got the direction wrong. "Can you blame me?" he said. "Six months at home—a professor—" D. shut his eyes and pressed the trigger; the noise took him by surprise, and the enormous kick of the gun; glass smashed, and somewhere a bell rang.

He opened his eyes; he had missed; he must have missed. The mirror over the basin was smashed a foot away from Mr. K.'s old head. Mr. K. was on his feet, blinking, with a look of perplexity. Somebody was knocking on the door. One bullet gone.

D. said, "Don't move. Don't make a sound. I won't miss twice," and shut the door. He was alone by the divan again, listening to the knock, knock on the area door. If it was the police, what was he to do with his only bullet? There was silence again everywhere else. The little book lay open on the divan.

> God is in the sunlight,
> Where the butterflies roam,
> God is in the candlelight,
> Waiting in your home.

The absurd poem was like a wax impress on his brain; he didn't believe in God, he had no home; it was like the incantation of a savage tribe which has an effect on even the most civilized beholder. Knock. Knock. Knock, and then a ring again. Was it one of the owner's friends, the owner herself? No, she would have a key. It must be the police.

He moved slowly across the room, gun in hand. He had forgotten the gun just as he had forgotten the razor. He opened the door like a doomed man.

It was Rose.

He said slowly, "Of course. I forgot. I gave you my address, didn't I?" He looked over her shoulder as if he expected to see the police—or Forbes.

She said, "I came to tell you what Furt said."

"Oh, yes, yes."

She said, "You haven't done anything, have you—wild?"

"No."

"Why the gun?"

"I thought you might be the police."

They came into the room and shut the area door. He had his eye on the bathroom; it was no good, he knew now he would never shoot. He might be a good judge, but he would never make an executioner. War toughened you but not to that extent; he carried around his neck like a dead albatross the lectures in romance languages, the *Song of Roland,* the Berne MS.

She said, "My dear—how strange you look! Younger."

"The moustache—"

"Of course. It suits you like that."

He said impatiently, "What did Furt say?"

"They've signed."

"But it's against your own law."

"They haven't signed a contract direct with L. You can always get round the law. The coal will go by Holland."

He had a sense of complete failure; he wasn't even capable of shooting a traitor. She said, "You'll have to go. Before the police find you." He sat on the divan with the gun hanging between his knees. He said, "And Forbes signed too?"

"You can't blame him." Again he felt the odd prick of jealousy. She said, "He doesn't like it."

"Why?"

She said, "You know, he's honest in a way. You can trust him when the wind's blowing east."

He said thoughtfully, "I've got another shot."

"What do you mean?" She sounded scared. She was looking at the gun.

"Oh," he said. "I didn't mean that. I mean the miners. The unions. If they knew what this really meant, mightn't they—?"

"What?"

"Do something?"

"What could they do?" she said. "You don't know how things are here. You've never seen a mining village when all the pits are closed. You've lived in a revolution—you've had too much cheering and shouting and waving of flags." She said, "I've been with my father to one of these places. He was making a tour—with royalty. There's no spirit left."

"Do you care then?"

She said, "Of course I care. Wasn't my grandfather—?"

"Do you know anybody there among the workers?"

She said, "My old nurse is there. She married a miner. But my father gives her a pension. She's not as badly off as some."

"Anybody would do for a start."

"You still don't understand. You can't go making speeches. You'd be in jail at once. You're wanted."

"I'm not going to give up yet."

"Listen. We can smuggle you out of here somehow. Money will do a lot. From one of the small ports. Swansea—"

He looked carefully up at her. "Would you like that?"

"Oh, I know what you mean, all right. But I like a man alive—not dead or in prison. I couldn't love you for a month if you were dead. I'm not that sort. I can't be faithful to people I don't see. Like you are." He was playing absent-mindedly with the revolver. She said, "Give me that thing. I can't bear . . ."

He handed it across to her without a word. It was his first action of trust.

She said, "Oh, God, that's the smell. I thought there was something wrong. You've used it. You *have* killed—"

"Oh, no. I tried to, but it wouldn't work. I'm a coward, I suppose. All I hit was the mirror. That's bad luck, isn't it?"

"Was it just before I rang?"

"Yes."

"I heard something. I thought it was a car backfiring."

He said, "Luckily nobody in this place knows the *real* sound."

"Where is he, then?"

"In there."

She pulled the door open. Mr. K. must have been listening hard; he came forward into the room on his knees. D. said gloomily, "That's Professor K." The man slumped over and lay with his knees drawn up on the floor. D. said, "He's fainted." She stood over Mr. K. and looked at him with disgust. She said, "You are sure you missed?"

"Oh, yes, I missed all right."

"Because," she said, "he's dead. Any fool can see that."

Three

Mr. K. was laid carefully out on the divan; the pious book lay by his ear. "God is in the candlelight, waiting in your home." He looked excessively unimportant, with a red rim across the bridge of his nose where the spectacles had rubbed it. D. said, "His doctor had given him six months. He was afraid he was going to end—suddenly—teaching Entrenationo. They paid him two shillings an hour."

"What are we going to do?"

"It was an accident."

"He died because you shot at him—they can call that murder."

"Technically murder?"

"Yes."

"It's the second time. I should like to be charged with an honest malice-aforethought murder for a change."

"You always joke when it's you who are concerned," she said. "Do I?"

She was in a rage again about something. When she was angry she was like a child, stamping and raging against authority and reason. Then he could feel an immense tenderness for her because she might have been his daughter. She made no demands on him for passionate love. She said, "Don't stand there as if nothing had happened. What are we going to do with him—it?"

He said gently, "I've been thinking about that. This is Saturday night. The woman who has this flat put out a notice—'No milk till Monday.' That means she won't be back before tomorrow night at the earliest. It gives me twenty-four hours. I can get to the mines by the morning, can't I, if I catch a train now?"

"They'll pick you up at the station. You're wanted already. Besides," she said furiously, "it's a waste of time. I tell you they haven't got any spirit left. They just live, that's all. I was born there. I know the place."

"It's worth a try."

She said, "I don't mind your being dead. But I can't bear your dying." She had no sense of shame at all—she acted and spoke without reserve. He remembered her coming down the foggy platform with the buns. It was impossible not to love her—in a way. After all, they had something in common. They had both been pushed around—and they were both revolting against the passive past with a violence which didn't really belong to them. She said, "It's no good saying—for my sake—like they do in stories. I know that."

"I'd do a lot," he said, "for your sake."

"Oh, God," she said, "don't pretend. Go on being honest. That's why I love you—that and my neuroses. Œdipus complexes, and the rest."

"I'm not pretending." He took her in his arms. This time it wasn't such a failure; everything was there except desire. He couldn't feel desire. It was as if he had made himself a eunuch for his people's sake. Every lover was in his way a philosopher; nature saw to that. A lover had to believe in the world, in the value of birth. Contraception didn't alter that. The act of desire remained an act of faith, and he had lost his faith.

She wasn't furious any more. She said sadly, "What happened to your wife?"

"They shot her accidentally."

"How?"

"They took her as a hostage for the wrong man. They had hundreds. I expect to the warders they all looked much alike." He wondered whether it would seem odd to quiet people, this making love with a dead wife on the tongue and a dead man on the divan. It wasn't very successful anyway. A kiss gives away too much—it is far more difficult to falsify than a voice. The lips when together expressed a limitless vacancy.

She said, "It seems odd to me, this loving someone who's dead."

"It happens to most people. Your mother—"

"Oh, I don't love her," she said. "I'm a bastard. Legitimized by marriage, of course. It oughtn't to matter—ought it?—but in a curious way one resents having been unwanted—even then."

It was impossible to tell what was pity and what was love, without a trial. They embraced again beside Mr. K. Over her left shoulder he could see Mr. K.'s open eyes, and he let her go. He said, "It's no use. I'm no good to you. I'm not a man any longer. Perhaps one day when all the killing has stopped . . ."

She said, "My dear, I don't mind waiting—as long as you're alive."

It was, in the circumstances, an enormous qualification.

He said, "You'd better go now. Make sure nobody sees you when you go out. Don't take a taxi within a mile of this place."

"What are you going to do?"

"Which station?"

She said, "There's a train from Euston somewhere near midnight. God knows when it gets there on a Sunday morning—you'd have to change. They'll recognize you, anyway."

"Shaving off the moustache made a difference."

"The scar's still there. That's what people look for." She said, "Wait a moment," and when he tried to speak she interrupted him. "I'll go. I'm going to be sensible, do anything that you say, let you go—anywhere. There's no point in not being sensible. But wait just a moment." She disappeared into the bathroom; her feet crunched on Mr. K.'s spectacles. She returned very quickly. "Thank God," she said, "she's a careful woman." She had some cotton wool in her hand and some plaster. She said, "Stand still. No one's going to see that scar." She laid the cotton-wool over his cheek and stuck it down with the plaster. "It looks convincing," she said, "like a boil."

"But it's not over the scar."

"That's the cunning. The plaster's over the scar. The cotton-wool's right up on your cheek. Nobody's going to notice that you are covering something on your chin." She held his head between her hands and said, "I'd make a good confidential agent, don't you think?"

"You're too good for that," he said. "Nobody trusts a confidential agent." He suddenly felt a tremendous gratitude that there was somebody in the warring crooked uncertain world he could trust besides himself. It was like finding in the awful solitude of a desert a companion. He said, "My dear, my love's not much good to anyone now, but it's all yours—what's left of it," but while he spoke he could feel the steady tug of a pain that united him to a grave.

She said gently, as if she were speaking in terms of love, "You've got a chance. Your English is good—but it's terribly literary. Your accent's sometimes queer, but it's the books you've read which really give you away. Try to forget you were ever a lecturer in the romance languages." She began to put her hand up to his face again when the bell rang.

They stood motionless in the middle of the little female room. It was like a legend where death interrupts love. The bell rang again.

He said, "Isn't there somewhere where you can hide?" But of course there wasn't. He said, "If it's the police, you must accuse me straight away. I won't have you mixed up in things."

"What's the use?"

"Go and open the door." He took Mr. K. by the shoulders and turned him over to face the wall. He pulled the counterpane up round him. He was in shadow; you couldn't very easily see the open eyes; it was just possible to believe that he was asleep. He heard the door open; a voice said, "Oh, excuse me. My name's Fortescue."

The stranger came timidly and penetratingly in—an old-young

man with receding hair and a double-breasted waistcoat. Rose tried
to bar his way. She said, "Well?" He repeated, "Fortescue," with
weak good humour.

"Who the hell are you?"

He blinked at them. He had no hat or coat. He said, "You know,
I live up above. Isn't Emily—that is, Miss Glover—here?"

D. said, "She's away for the week end."

"I knew she meant to go—but when I saw a light—" He said,
"Good God, what's that?"

"That," Rose said, "as you so winningly put it, is Jack—Jack
Owtram."

"Is he ill?"

"He will be—he's passed out. We've been having a party."

He said, "How very extraordinary! I mean, Emily—Miss
Glover—"

"Oh, call her Emily," Rose said. "We're all friends here."

"Emily never has parties."

"She lent us the flat."

"Yes. Yes. So I see."

"Do you want a drink?"

That's going too far, D. thought; this flat can't supply everything; we may be wrecked, but this isn't a schoolboy wreck which
supplies the right thing to Crusoe at the right time.

"No, no, thank you," Fortescue said. "As a matter of fact, I don't.
Drink, I mean."

"You must. Nobody can live without drinking."

"Oh, water. I drink water of course."

"You do?"

"Oh, yes, undoubtedly." He looked nervously again at the body
on the bed; then at D. like a sentry beside it. He said, "You've hurt
your face."

"Yes." Silence was present; it was the most prominent thing
there, like the favoured guest who outwaits all the others. Fortescue
said, "Well, I must be getting back."

"Must you?" Rose said.

"Well, not literally. I mean, I don't want to interrupt a party."
He was looking round—for the bottles and glasses; there were
things about this room he obviously couldn't understand. But the
awful fact was beyond his suspicion; his world didn't contain horror.
He said, "Emily didn't warn me . . ."

"You seem to see a lot of Emily."

He blushed. He said, "Oh, we're good friends. We're both Groupers, you see."

"Gropers?"

"No, no. Groupers. Oxford Groupers."

"Oh, yes," Rose said. "I know—house parties, Brown's Hotel, Crowborough . . ." She reeled off a string of associations which were incomprehensible to D. Was she going to be hysterical?

Fortescue brightened. His old-young face was like a wide white screen on which you could project only selected and well-censored films for the family circle. He said, "Have you ever been?"

"Oh, no. It wouldn't suit me."

He began to penetrate back into the room towards the divan. He had a liquid manner; you had to be very careful how you tilted the conversation or he would flow all over the place. He said, "You ought to try. We have all kinds of people—businessmen, Blues— we once had the Undersecretary for Overseas Trade. And of course there's always Frankie." He was almost up to the divan, explaining ardently. "It's religion—but it's practical. It helps you to get on—because you feel *right* towards people. We've had an enormous success in Norway."

"That's fine," Rose said, trying to tilt him the other way.

He said with his rather protuberant eyes upon the head of Mr. K., "And if you feel bad about things—you know what I mean— there's nothing clears the air like sharing—at a house party. The other fellows are always sympathetic. They've been through it too." He leaned a little forward and said, "He does look ill. Are you quite sure?"

It was a fantastic country, D. thought. Civil war provided nothing so fantastic as peace. In war life became simple—you didn't worry about sex or international languages or even getting on; you worried about the next meal and cover from high explosives. Fortescue said, "Wouldn't he feel better if—well—you know—if he brought it up?"

"Oh, no," Rose said, "he's better as he is—just lying quiet."

"Of course," he said meekly, "I don't know much about these things. Parties, I mean. I suppose he doesn't hold his drink very well. He oughtn't to do it, ought he?—it can't be good for him. And such an old man too. Forgive me—if he's a great friend—"

"You needn't mind," Rose said. D. wondered, Will he never go? Only the warmest heart could have failed to be frozen by Rose's manner.

"I know I must sound prejudiced. You see, in the Group we learn to be ascetic—in a reasonable way." He said, "I suppose you wouldn't care to step upstairs to my place—I've got a kettle boiling now for tea. I was going to ask Emily—" He leaned suddenly forward and said, "Good heavens, his eyes are open!" This is the end, D. thought.

Rose said slowly, "You didn't think—did you?—he was asleep."

You could almost see a terrible surmise come up behind the eyes, then fall again for the mere want of foothold. There was no room for murder in his gentle and spurious world. They waited for what he would say next; they had no plan at all. He said in a whisper, "How dreadful to think that he heard everything I said about him!"

Rose said harshly and nervously, "Your kettle will be all over the floor."

He looked from one to the other of them—something was wrong. "Yes, it will be, won't it? I hadn't meant to stay." Back and forth from one to the other as if he wanted reassurance—tonight he would have bad dreams. "Yes, I must be going. Good night."

They watched him climbing up the area steps into the safe familiar reassuring dark. At the top he turned and waved his hand to them, tentatively.

PART III

The Last Shot

One

It was still dark over the whole quiet Midland countryside. The small unimportant junction lay lit up like a centrepiece in a darkened shop window; oil lamps burned beside the general waiting-room, an iron footbridge straddled across towards another smoky flame, and the cold wind took the steam of the engine and flapped it back along the platform. It was Sunday morning.

Then the tail light of the train moved on like a firefly and was suddenly extinguished in some invisible tunnel. D. was alone except for one old porter hobbling back from where the luggage van had stood; the platform sloped down past a lamp into the indecipherable wilderness of lines. Somewhere not far away a cock crew, and a light which hung in midair changed from red to green.

"Is this right for the Benditch train?" D. called out.

"It'll be right," the porter said.

"Is it a long wait?"

"Oh, it'll be an hour—if it's on time."

D. shivered and beat his arms against his body for warmth. "That's a long time," he said.

"You can't expect different," the porter said. "Not on a Sunday."

"Don't they have any through trains?"

"Ah, they used to when the pits was working—but no one goes to Benditch now."

"Is there a restaurant here?" D. said.

"A restaurant!" the porter exclaimed, peering closely up at him. "What call would there be for a restaurant at Willing?"

"Somewhere to sit?"

"I'll open the waiting-room for you—if you like," the porter said. "It's cold in there, though. Better to keep moving."

"Isn't there a fire?"

"Well, it might've kept in." He took a monstrous key out of his pocket and opened a chocolate-coloured door. "Ah, well," he said, "it's not so bad," switching on the light. There were old faded photographs all round the walls, of hotels and resorts, fixed benches round the walls, two or three hard movable chairs, and an enormous table. A faint warmth—the memory of a fire—came out of the grate. The porter picked up a black ornamental cast-iron scuttle and shook a lot of coal dust onto the dying embers. He said, "That'll keep it in."

D. said, "And the table. What's the table for?"

The porter looked at him with sharp suspicion. He said, "To sit at. What d'you think?"

"But the benches won't move."

"That's true. They won't." He said, "Darn it, I've been here twenty years an' I never thought of that. You're a foreigner, ain't you?"

"Yes."

"They're sharp, foreigners." He stared moodily at the table. "Most times," he said, "they sit on it." Outside there was a cry, a roar, a cloud of white steam, wheels pounding past and fading out, a whistle again, and silence. He said, "That'll be the four fifty-five."

"An express?"

"Fast goods."

"But not for the mines?"

"Oh, no—for Woolhampton. Munitions."

D. bent his arms for warmth and walked slowly round the room. A tiny pillar of smoke fumed upwards in the grate. There was a photograph of a pier: a gentleman in a grey bowler and a Norfolk jacket was leaning over a handrail, talking to a lady in a picture hat and white muslin; there was a perspective of parasols. D. felt himself touched by an odd happiness, as if he were out of time altogether and already belonged to history with the gentleman in the bowler; all the struggle and violence over, wars decided one way or another, out of pain. A great Gothic pile marked "Midland Hotel" stared out across some tram lines, the statue of a man in a leaden frock coat, and a public lavatory. "Ah," the porter said, giving the coal dust a stir with a broken poker. "What you're looking at's Woolhampton itself. I was there in nineteen two."

"It looks a busy place."

"It is busy. An' that hotel—you won't find a better in the Midlands. We 'ad a lodge dinner there—in nineteen two. Balloons," he said; "a lady sang. An' there's Turkish baths."

"You miss it, I daresay."

"Oh, I don't know. There's something to be said for any place— that's how I look at it. Of course at Christmas time I miss the panto. The Woolhampton Empire's famous for its panto. But on the other 'and—it's 'ealthy here. You can see too much of life," he said, poking at the coal dust.

"I suppose this was quite an important station once."

"Ah, when the mines was working. I've had Lord Benditch waiting in this very room. *And* his daughter—the Honourable Miss Rose Cullen."

D. realized that he was listening—avidly, as if he were a young man in love. He said, "You've seen Miss Cullen?" and an engine whistled somewhere over the waste of rails and was answered, like a dog calling to other dogs in the suburb of a city.

"Ah, that I have. The last time I saw her here, it was only a week before she was presented—at the Court—to the King an' Queen." It filled D. with sadness—the vast social life going on all round her in which he had no part at all. He felt like a divorced man whose child is in another's custody—somebody richer and abler than himself; he has to watch a stranger's progress through the magazines. He found he wanted to claim her. He remembered her on the platform at Euston. She said, "We are unlucky. We don't believe in God. So it's no use praying. If we did I could tell beads, burn candles—oh, a hundred things. As it is, I can only keep my fingers crossed." In the taxi at his request she had given him back his gun. She had said, "For God's sake be careful. You are such a fool. Remember the Berne MS. You aren't Roland. Don't walk under ladders—or spill salt."

The porter said, "Her mother came from these parts. There's stories . . ."

Here he was, shut out for a little while from the monstrous world. He could see—from the security and isolation of this cold waiting-room—just how monstrous it was. And yet there were people who talked of a superintending design. It was a crazy mixture—the presentation at Court, his own wife shot in the prison yard, pictures in the *Tatler,* and the bombs falling—it was all hopelessly jumbled together by their mutual relationship as they had stood side by side near Mr. K.'s body and talked to Fortescue. The accomplice-to-be of a murderer had received an invitation to a royal garden party. It was as if he had the chemical property of reconciling irreconcilables. After all, even in his own case it might have seemed a long way from his lectures on romance to the blind shot at K. in the bathroom of a strange woman's basement flat. How was it possible for anyone to plan his life or regard the future with anything but apprehension?

But he had to regard the future. He came to a stop in front of a beach scene—bathing huts and sand castles and all the dreary squalor of a front reproduced with a remarkable veracity—the sense of blown newspapers and half-eaten bananas. The railway companies had been well advised to leave photography and take to art. He thought, If they catch me, of course, there *is* no future—that was simple. But if somehow he evaded them and returned home, *there* was the problem. She had said, "It's no good shaking me off now."

The porter said, "When she was a little thing she used to give away the prizes—for the best station garden in the country. That was before her ma died. Lord Benditch, he always overmarked for roses."

She couldn't come back with him to his sort of life—the life of an untrusted man in a country at war. And what could he give her anyway? The grave held him.

He went outside; it was still pitch-dark beyond the little platform, but you were aware that somewhere there was light. Beyond the rim of the turning world a bell, as it were, had rung in warning —perhaps there was a greyness. He walked up and down, up and down. There was no solution except failure. He paused by a slot machine—a dry choice of raisins, chocolate creams, matches, and chewing gum. He inserted a penny under the raisins, but the drawer remained stuck: The porter appeared suddenly behind him and said accusingly, "Did you try a crooked penny?"

"No. But it doesn't matter."

"Some of them are so artful," the man said, "you can't trust them not to get two packets with one penny." He rattled the machine. "I'll just go an' get the key," he said.

"It doesn't matter. It really doesn't matter."

"Oh, we can't have that," the porter said, limping away.

A lamp lit each end of the platform; he walked from one to the other and back again. The dawn came with a kind of careful and prepared slowness. It was like a ritual—the dimming of the lamps, the cocks crowing again, and then the silvering of the sky. The siding loomed slowly up with a row of trucks marked "Benditch Collieries," the rails stretched out towards a fence, a dark shape which became a barn, and then an ugly blackened winter field. Other platforms came into sight, shuttered and dead. The porter was back, opening the slot machine. "Ah," he said, "it's the wet. They don't care for raisins here. The drawer's rusty." He pulled out a greyish paper carton. "There," he said, "there you are." It felt old and damp to the fingers.

"Didn't you say it was healthy here?"

"That's right. The 'ealthy Midlands."

"But the damp—"

"Ah," he said, "but the station's in the holler, see." And sure enough the dark was shredding off like vapour from a long hillside. The light came drably up behind the barn and the field, over the station and the siding, crept up the hill. Brick cottages detached themselves; the stumps of trees reminded him of a battlefield; an odd metallic object rose over the crest. He said, "What's that?"

"Oh, that," the porter said, "that's nothing. That was just a notion they got."

"An ugly-looking notion."

"Ugly? You'd say that, would you? I don't know. You get used to things. I'd miss it if it weren't there."

"It looks like something to do with oil."

"That's what it is. They had a fool notion they'd find oil here. We could've told 'em—but they were Londoners. They thought they knew."

"There was no oil?"

"Oh, they got enough to light these lamps with, I daresay." He said, "You won't have so long to wait now. There's Jarvis coming down the hill." You could see the road now as far as the cottages; there was a little colour in the east, and all the world except the sky had the blackness of frostbitten vegetation.

"Who is Jarvis?"

"Oh, he goes into Benditch every Sunday. Weekdays too, sometimes."

"Works at the mines?"

"No, he's too old for that. Says he likes the change of air. Some says his old woman's there—but Jarvis, he says he's not married." He came plodding up the little gravelled drive to the station—an elderly man in corduroys with bushy eyebrows and dark evasive eyes and a white stubble on the chin. "How's things, George?" the porter said.

"Aw—might be worse."

"Going in to see the old woman?"

Jarvis gave a sidelong and suspicious glance and looked away.

"This gentleman's going to Benditch. He's a foreigner."

"Ah!"

D. felt as a typhoid carrier must feel when he finds himself among the safe and inoculated—these he couldn't infect. They were secured from the violence and horror he carried with him. He felt an enormous inanition as if at last, among the frostbitten fields, in the quiet of the deserted junction, he had reached a place where he could sit down, rest, let time pass. The voice of the porter droned on beside him—"bloody frost killed every one of the bloody . . ."; every now and then Jarvis said, "Ah," staring down the track. Presently a bell rang twice in a signal box; one noticed suddenly that unobtrusively the night had quite gone. He could see a man in the signal box holding a teapot; he put it down out of sight and tugged a lever. A signal—somewhere—creaked down, and Jarvis said, "Ah."

"Here's your train," the porter said. At the far end of a track a small blob of steam like a rose advanced, became an engine, a string of vibrating carriages. "Is it far to Benditch?" D. asked.

"Oh, it wouldn't be more than fifteen miles, would it, George?"

"Fourteen miles from the church to the Red Lion."

"It's not the distance," the porter said, "it's the stops."

A row of frosty windows split up the pale early morning sun like crystals. A few stubby faces peered out into the early day. D. climbed into an empty carriage after Jarvis and saw the porter, the general waiting-room, the ugly iron footbridge, the signalman holding a cup of tea, go backwards like peace. The low frosty hills closed round the track; a farm building, a ragged wood like an old fur toque, ice on a little ditch beside the line—it wasn't grand, it wasn't even pretty, but it had a quality of quiet and desertion. Jarvis stared out at it without a word.

D. said, "You know Benditch well?"

"Ah."

"You might know Mrs. Bennett?"

"George Bennett's wife or Arthur's?"

"The one who was nurse to Lord Benditch's girl."

"Ah."

"You know her?"

"Ah."

"Where does she live?"

Jarvis gave him a long suspicious look from his blue pebbly eyes. He said, "What do you want *her* for?"

"I've got a message for her."

"She's one door up from the Red Lion."

The woods and meagre grass gave out as they pottered on from stop to stop. The hills became rocky; a quarry lay behind a halt, and a rusting single line led out to it; a small truck lay overturned in the thorny grass. Then even the hills gave out and a long plain opened up, dotted with strange erratic heaps of slag—the height of the hills behind. Short unsatisfactory grass crept up them like gas flames; miniature railways petered out, going to nowhere at all, and right beneath the artificial hills the cottages began—lines of grey stone like scars. The train no longer stopped; it rattled deeper into the shapeless plain, passing halts under every slag heap dignified by names like Castle Crag and Mount Zion. It was like a gigantic rubbish heap into which everything had been thrown of a whole way of life—great rusting lift shafts and black chimneys and Nonconformist chapels with slate roofs and hopeless washing darkening on the line and children carrying pails of water from common taps. It was odd to think the country lay only just behind—ten miles away the cocks were crowing outside the junction. The cottages were continuous now, built up against the slag and branching out in narrow streets towards the railway; the only division the branch tracks to each black hill. D. said, "Is this Benditch?"

"Naw. This is Paradise."

They ground over a crossing under the shadow of another heap. "Is *this* Benditch?"

"Naw. This is Cowcumberill."

"How do you tell the difference?"

"Ah."

He stared moodily out—had he got an old woman here or was it for the change of air he came? He said at last very grudgingly, as if he had a grievance, "Anyone can tell Cowcumberill ain't Benditch." He said, "There's Benditch," as another slag heap loomed blackly up and the long grey scar of houses just went on. "Why," he said, working himself up into a kind of gloomy and patriotic rage, "you might as well say it was like Castle Crag—or Mount Zion, come to that. You've only got to look."

He did look; he was used to ruin, but it occurred to him that bombardment was a waste of time. You could attain your ruined world as easily by just letting go.

Benditch had the honour of a station, not a halt. There was even a first-class waiting-room, bolted, with broken glass. He waited for the other to get down, but Jarvis outwaited him, as if he suspected he was being spied on. He gave an effect of innocent and natural secrecy; he distrusted, as an animal distrusts, the strange footstep or the voice near the burrow.

When D. left the station the geography of his last stand stood plainly before him—one street ran down towards the slag heap and another street crossed it like a T, pressed up under the black hill. Every house was the same; the uniformity was broken only by an inn sign, the front of a chapel, an occasional impoverished shop. There was an air of rather horrifying simplicity about the place, as if it had been built by children with bricks. The two streets were curiously empty for a working-class town; but then there was no work to go to; it was probably warmer to stay in bed. D. passed a Labour Exchange and then more grey houses with the blinds down in the windows. Once he got a glimpse of horrifying squalor in a back yard where a privy stood open. It was like war, but without the spirit of defiance war usually raised.

The Red Lion had once been a hotel; this must have been where

Lord Benditch stayed; it had a courtyard and a garage and an old yellow A.A. sign. A smell of gas and privies hung about the street. People watched him—a stranger—through glass, without much interest; it was too cold to come out and exchange greetings. Mrs. Bennett's house was just the same grey stone as all the rest, but the curtains looked cleaner; there was almost a moneyed air when you looked in through the window to the little unused and crowded parlour. D. beat the knocker; it was of polished brass, in the shape of a shield and a coat of arms—the Benditch arms?—a mysterious feathered animal seemed to be holding a leaf in its mouth. It looked curiously complicated in the simple town—like an algebraic equation, it represented an abstract set of values out of place in the stony concrete street.

An elderly woman in an apron opened the door. Her face was withered and puckered and white, like old clean bone. "Are you Mrs. Bennett?" D. said.

"I am." She barred the way into the house with her foot like a doorstop on the threshold.

"I have a letter for you," D. said, "from Miss Cullen."

"Do you know Miss Cullen?" she asked him with disapproval and incredulity.

"You will read it all there." But she wouldn't let him in until she had read it, very slowly, without spectacles, holding the paper up close to the pale obstinate eyes. "She writes here," she said, "that you're her dear friend. You'd better come in. She says I'm to help you—but she doesn't say how."

"I'm sorry it's so early."

"It's the only train on a Sunday. You can't be expected to walk. Was George Jarvis on the train?"

"Yes."

"Ah."

The little parlour was crammed with china ornaments and photographs in tortuous silver frames. A round mahogany table, a velvet-covered sofa, hard chairs with twisted backs and velvet seats, newspaper spread on the floor to save the carpet—it was like a scene set for something which had never happened, which would never happen now. Mrs. Bennett said sternly with a gesture towards a silver frame, "You'll recognize that, I suppose?" A white plump female child held a doll unconvincingly. He said, "I'm afraid—"

"Ah," Mrs. Bennett said with a kind of bitter triumph. "She hasn't shown you everything, I daresay. See that pincushion?"

"Yes."

"That was made out of her presentation dress—what she wore to meet Their Majesties. Turn it over and you'll see the date." It was there—picked out in white silk. That was the year he had been in prison waiting to be shot. It was one of the years in her life too. "And there," Mrs. Bennett said, "she is—in the dress. You'll know *that* picture." Very formal and absurdly young and recognizably Rose, she watched him from a velvet frame. The little room seemed full of her.

"No," he said, "I have never seen that either."

She glared at him with satisfaction. She said, "Oh, well, old friends are best, I daresay."

"You must be a very old friend."

"The oldest," she rapped out at him. "I knew her when she was a week old. Even His Lordship didn't see her then—not till she'd passed her first month."

"She spoke of you," D. lied, "very warmly."

"She had cause," Mrs. Bennett said, tossing her white bony head. "I did everything for her—after her mother died." It's always odd, learning at second hand the biography of someone you love—like finding a secret drawer in a familiar desk full of revealing documents.

"Was she a good child?" he inquired with amusement.

"She had spirit. I don't ask for more," Mrs. Bennett said. She went agitatedly around, patting the pincushion, pushing the photographs a little this way and that. She said, "Nobody expects to be remembered. Though I don't complain of His Lordship. He's been generous. As was only proper. I don't know how we'd manage otherwise, with the pits closed."

"Rose told me she writes to you—regularly. So *she* remembers you."

"At Christmas," Mrs. Bennett said. "Yes. She doesn't say much —but of course she hasn't time in London with parties and so on. I thought she might have told me what His Majesty said to her— but then—"

"Perhaps he said nothing."

"Of course he said something. She's a lovely girl."

"Yes. Lovely."

"I only hope," Mrs. Bennett said, looking daggers across the china ornaments, "she knows her friends."

"I don't think she'd be easy to deceive," he said, thinking of Mr. Forbes and the private detectives and the whole dreary background of distrust.

"You don't know her like I do. I remember once—at Gwyn Cottage—she cried her eyes out. She was only four and that boy Peter Triffen—deceitful little monkey—he'd got a clockwork mouse." The old face flushed with ancient battle. "I'll be sworn that boy never came to any good." It was strange to think that—in a way—this woman had made her. Her influence had probably been as great as that of the mother who had died; perhaps the old bony face sometimes bore expressions he could detect in Rose—if he knew her better. The old woman said suddenly, "You're a foreigner, aren't you?"

"Yes."

"Ah."

He said, "Miss Cullen will have told you that I'm here on business."

"She didn't write *what* business."

"She thought you could tell me a few things about Benditch."

"Well?"

"I wondered who was the local union leader."

"You don't want to see *him*, do you?"

"Yes."

"I can't help you," Mrs. Bennett said. "We don't mix with *their* kind. An' you can't tell me Miss Cullen wants anything to do with that lot. Socialists."

"After all, her mother—"

"We know what her mother was," Mrs. Bennett said sharply, "but she's dead now, an' what's dead's forgotten."

"Then you can't help me at all?"

"Won't's the word."

'Not even his name?"

"Oh, you'll find that out soon enough. For yourself. It's Bates." A car went by outside; they could hear the brakes go on. "Now who," Mrs. Bennett said, "would be stopping at the Red Lion?"

"Where does he live?"

"Down Pit Street. We had royalty once," Mrs. Bennett said, with her face against the window, trying to see the car. "Such a pleasant-spoken young man. He came into this house and had a cup of tea

—just to show him there was miners' folk who kept their homes clean. He wanted to go into Mrs. Terry's, but they told him she was sick. Oh, she was furious when she heard. She'd cleaned up special —on the chance. Not that she'd got anything to clean. Everything's popped. It's as bare as a bone at Terry's. That's why of course. It wouldn't have been nice for him."

"I must be going."

"You can tell her from me," Mrs. Bennett said, "that she's got no business with Bates." She spoke with bitter and wavering authority, the manner of one who could at one time have commanded anything—"Change your stockings. No more sweets. Drink up that medicine"—but is now afraid that things have changed.

Luggage was being carried into the Red Lion, and the street had come alive. People stood in knots, defensively, as if ready to retreat, watching the car. He heard a child say, "Is it a dook?" He wondered whether Lord Benditch was already acting; it was quick work—the contract signed yesterday. Suddenly a rumour began; you couldn't tell where it started; somebody called out, "The pit's opening." The knots converged, became a small crowd; they stared at the car as if on its polished and luxurious body they could read definite news. A woman raised a feeble cheer which died out doubtfully. D. said to a man, "Who is it?"

"Lord Benditch's agent."

"Can you tell me where Pit Street is?"

"Turn left at the end of the road."

People were coming out of their houses now all the way along; he walked against a growing tide of hope. A woman called up to a bedroom window, "The agent's at the Red Lion, Nell." He was reminded of an occasion when in the hungry capital a rumour spread that food had arrived; he had watched them swarming down onto the quay, just like this. It hadn't been food but tanks, and they had watched the tanks unloaded with angry indifference. Yet they had needed tanks. He stopped a man and said, "Where's Bates?"

"Number seventeen—if he's there."

It was just beyond the Baptist Chapel, a grey stony symbol of religion with a slate roof. A Wayside Thought said enigmatically, "The Beauty of Life Is Only Invisible to Tired Eyes."

He knocked on the door of Number 17 again and again; nobody answered, and all the time the people went by—the old mackintoshes which wouldn't keep out the cold, the shirt too often washed for any warmth to be left in the thinned flannel. They were the people he was fighting for—and he had a frightening sense now that they were his enemies; he was here to stand between them and hope. He knocked and knocked and knocked, without reply.

Then he tried Number 19, and the door came open at once before he expected it. He was off his guard. He looked up, and there was Else.

She said, "Well, who do you want?" standing there like a ghost in the stone doorway, harried and undernourished and too young. He was shaken; he had to look closely before he saw the differences —the gland scar on the neck, a missing tooth. Of course it wasn't Else. It was only somebody out of the same mould of injustice and bad food.

"I was looking for Mr. Bates."

"He's next door."

"I can't make anyone hear."

"He'll have gone up to the Red Lion then—most like."

"There seems to be a lot of excitement."

"They say the pit's starting."

"Aren't you going up?"

"Somebody," she said, "has got to light the fire, I suppose." She looked at him with faint curiosity. "You the foreigner that came in the train with George Jarvis?"

"Yes."

"He said you wasn't up to any good." He thought with a touch of fear that he hadn't been much good to her double. Why carry this burden of violence into another country? Better be beaten at home, perhaps, than involve others—that was undoubtedly heresy. His party was quite right, of course, not to trust him. She said kindly, "Not that anyone pays attention to George. What do you want Bates for?"

Well, he wanted everyone to know; this after all was a democracy; he had to begin sometime—why not here? He said, "I wanted to tell him where the coal's going—to the rebels in my country."

"Oh," she said wearily, "you're one of that lot, are you?"

"Yes."

"What's it to do with Bates?"

"I want the men to refuse to work the pits."

She looked at him with amazement. "Refuse? Us?"

"Yes."

"You're off your nut," she said. "What's it got to do with us where the coal goes?"

He turned away. It was hopeless—he felt it now as a conviction. Out of the mouths of children . . . She called after him, "You're crazy. Why should we care?" He went stubbornly back up the street; he had to go on trying until they shut him up, hanged him, shot him, stopped his mouth somehow and relieved him of loyalty and let him rest.

They were singing now outside the Red Lion; events must be moving fast. There must have been some definite announcement. Two songs were fighting for supremacy—both old ones. He had heard them both when he was working in London years ago. The poor were extraordinarily faithful to old tunes. "Pack up Your Troubles" and "Now Thank We All Our God"—the crowd swayed between the two, and the secular song won. More people knew it. He could see papers being handed from hand to hand—Sunday papers. There seemed to be loads of them on the back seat of the car. D. caught a man's arm and said urgently, "Where's Bates?"

"He's upstairs with the agent."

He struggled through the crowd. Somebody stuck a paper into his hand. He couldn't help seeing the headlines—"Foreign Coal Deal. Pits to Reopen." It was a staid Sunday paper of limited imagination which carried conviction. He ran into the lounge of the hotel; he felt an urgent need to do something now—before the hope was too strong. The place was empty; big stuffed fish hung on the walls in glass cases—there must have been a time when people came to the district for sport. He went upstairs—nobody about. They were cheering now outside; something was happening. He threw open a big door marked "Drawing Room" and immediately faced his own image in a tall gilt mirror—unshaven, with cotton wool hanging out of the plaster dressing. A big french window was open; a man was speaking. There were two men at a table with their backs to him. The place smelled of musty velvet.

"All the stokers, lift men, mechanics are wanted at once—first thing in the morning. But don't be afraid. There'll be work for every man jack of you in less than a week. This is the end of *your* depression." He said, "You can ask your Mr. Bates in here. This isn't a four-day week for you—it's a three-hundred-and-sixty-five-day year." He lifted himself up and down on his toes in the window, a little dark astute man in gaiters who looked like an estate agent.

D. came across the room behind him. He said, "Excuse me—may I have a word with you?"

"Not now. Not now," the little man said, without turning round.

He said, "Now go home and have a good time. There'll be work for everyone before Christmas. And in return we hope—"

D. said to the two backs, "Is one of you Mr. Bates?"

Both men turned. One of them was L.

"—that you'll put your backs into it. You can trust the Benditch Colliery Company to help *you*."

"I'm Bates," the other said.

He could tell that L. hadn't quite recognized him. He was looking puzzled. D. said, "Well, I see you've met the general's agent, then. It's time I had a word." Then L.'s face cleared. He gave a tiny smile of recognition; an eyelid twitched.

The orator turned from the window and said, "What's all this?"

D. said, "This coal contract—it's said to be for Holland. It's nothing of the kind." He had his eye on Bates, a youngish man with a melodramatic shock of hair and a weak mouth. He said, "What's this got to do with me?"

"The men trust you, I suppose. Tell them to keep away from the pit."

"Look here. Look here," Benditch's agent said.

D. said, "Your unions declared they'd never work for them."

"This is for Holland," Bates said.

"That's cover. I came over to buy coal for the government. That man there had my credentials stolen."

"He's cuckoo," the agent said with conviction, lifting himself up and down on his toes. "That gentleman's a friend of Lord Benditch."

Bates shifted uneasily. "What can I do?" he said. "It's a government matter."

L. said gently, "I do know this man. He's a fanatic—and he's wanted by the police."

"Send for a constable," the agent said.

"I've got a gun in my pocket," D. said. He kept his eye on Bates. He said, "I know this means a year's work to your people. But it's death to ours. Why, it's been death to yours too if you only knew."

Bates suddenly broke out furiously. He said, "Why the hell should I believe a story like that? This is coal for Holland."

He had an uncertain night-school accent; he had risen—you could see that—and the marks of his rising he had tucked away with shame. He said, "I've never heard such a story." But D. knew that he half believed. His weak mouth carried his shock of hair like a disguise, suggesting a violence, a radicalism which wasn't his at all.

D. said, "If you won't speak to them, I will." The agent started for the door. D. said, "Sit down. You can call the police when I've done. I'm not trying to escape, am I? You can ask that man there— how many charges. I begin to forget—false passport, stealing a car, carrying firearms without a licence. Now I'm going to add incitement to violence."

He went to the window and called out, "Comrades!" At the back of the crowd he could see old Jarvis watching him sceptically. There were about a hundred and fifty people outside; a good many had already gone to spread the news. He said, "I've got to speak to you." Somebody called out, "Why?" He said, "You don't know where this coal's going."

They were hilarious and triumphant. A voice said, "The North Pole." He said, "It's not going to Holland—" They began to drift away; he had been a lecturer once, but he had never been a public speaker; he didn't know how to hold them. He said, "By God, you've got to listen!" He picked up an ash tray from the table and smashed the window with it.

"Here," Bates said in a shocked voice, "that's hotel property."

The sound of breaking glass brought the crowd round. D. said, "Do you want to dig coal to kill children with?"

"Aw, shut up," a voice said.

He said, "I know this means a lot to you. But it means everything to us." Glancing sideways, he saw in the mirror L.'s face— complacent, unmoved, waiting for him to finish. Nothing would make any difference. He shouted, "Why do they want *your* coal? Because the miners at home won't work for them. They shoot them, but they won't work." Over the heads of the crowd he could see old George Jarvis, keeping a little apart, secretive, not believing a word about anything. Somebody called out, "Let's hear Joe Bates," and the cry was taken up here and there. "Joe Bates. Joe."

D. said, "Here's your chance," turning back into the room towards the union secretary.

The little man like an estate agent said, "I'll see you get six months for this."

"Go on," D. said.

Bates went unwillingly to the window. He had a mannerism, learned from his leaders, of tossing back his unruly hair—it was the only unruly thing, D. thought, about him. He said, "Comrades.

You've heard a very serious charge." Was it possible, after all, that he was going to act?

A woman's voice shouted, "Charity begins at 'ome."

"I think the best thing we can do," Bates said, "is to ask a definite assurance from Lord Benditch's agent that this coal is going to Holland—and only Holland."

"What's the good of an assurance?" D. said.

"If he gives us that, why, we can go to work tomorrow with a clear conscience."

The little man in gaiters bustled forward. He said, "That's right. Mr. Bates is right. And I give you the assurance in Lord Benditch's name. . . ." What he said was drowned in cheers. D. found himself alone with L. as the cheers went on and the two men moved from the window. L. said, "You should've taken my offer, you know. You're in a very awkward situation. Mr. K. has been found."

"Mr. K.?"

"A woman called Glover came home late last night. She told the police she had psychic feelings. It's in the papers this morning."

The agent was saying, "As for this man, he's wanted by the police for fraud—and theft—"

L. said, "They want to interview a man who was seen in the flat with a young woman—by a man called Fortescue. He had a bandaged cheek, but the police seem to think that may have hidden a scar."

Bates said, "Let the constable pass, men."

"You'd better go, hadn't you?" L. said.

"I've a bullet left."

"You mean me—or yourself?"

"Oh," D. said, "I wish I knew just how far you'd go." He wanted to be driven to shoot—to know that L. had given the orders for the child's death; to hate him, despise him, and shoot. But L. and the child hadn't belonged to the same world—it was unbelievable that he could have given any order; you had something in common with people you killed, unless death was dealt out impersonally from a long-range gun or a plane.

"Come up here, constable," Lord Benditch's agent called out of the window to somebody below. He had the simple faith of his class that one constable could deal with an armed man.

L. said, "Almost any distance—to get back." It was unnecessary to say what or where; a whole way of life lay behind the quiet unfrightened voice—long corridors and formal gardens and expensive books, a picture gallery, a buhl desk and old servants who admired him. But would it be getting back to have a ghost tagged forever at your side as a reminder? D. hesitated—with the gun pointed through his pocket. L. said, "I know what you're thinking, but that woman was mad—literally mad."

D. said, "Thank you. In that case—" He felt a sudden lightening of the heart as if madness had brought a kind of normality into his world. It even eased his own responsibility a little. He made for the door.

Lord Benditch's agent turned from the window and said, "Stop him."

"Let him go," L. said. "The police—"

He ran down the stairs; the police constable, an elderly man, was coming into the hall. He looked sharply at D. and said, "Hi, sir, h've you seen—?"

"Up the stairs, officer."

He turned towards the yard at the back; Lord Benditch's agent squealed over the banisters, "That's him, officer. That's him."

D. ran; he had a few yards' start; the yard looked empty. He heard a shout and a crash behind him—the constable had slipped. A voice said, "This way, mate," and he swerved automatically into an outside lavatory. Things were going too fast. Somebody said, "Give him a leg up," and he found himself being propelled over a wall. He fell heavily on his knees beside a rubbish can, and a voice whispered, "Quiet." He was in a tiny back garden—a few square feet of thin grass, a cinder track, a ragged piece of coconut hanging on a broken brick to attract birds. He said, "What are you doing? What's the good?" This must be Mrs. Bennett's, he wanted to explain; what was the good? She'd only call the police—but everybody had gone. He was alone, like something you throw over a wall and forget. There was a lot of shouting in the street. He knelt, exhausted, like a garden image, while thoughts raced this way and that—he might have been holding a bird bath. He felt sick and angry; he was being pushed around again. What was the good? He was finished. A prison cell attracted him like quiet. Surely he'd tried enough. He put his head between his knees to cure his dizziness. He remembered he had had nothing to eat since a rock bun at the soirée.

A voice whispered to him urgently, "Get up."

He looked up and focused on three young faces. He said, "Who are you?"

They watched him with glee—the oldest couldn't have been more than twenty. They had soft, unformed, anarchic faces. The oldest said, "Never mind who *we* are. Come into the shed."

He obeyed them dreamily. In the little dark box there was just room for the four of them; they squatted on the coke and coal dust and the bits of old boxes torn up for firewood. A little light came in through the knots in the planks which someone had poked out with a finger. He said, "What's the good of this? Mrs. Bennett—"

"The old woman won't carry coal on a Sunday. She's strict."

"What about Bennett?"

"He's properly boozed."

"Somebody must have seen?"

"Naw. We've scouted."

"They'll search the houses."

"How can they without a warrant? Magistrate's in Woolhampton."

He gave it up and said wearily, "Well, I suppose I ought to thank you."

"Stow the thanks," the oldest boy said. "You got a gun, ain't you?"

"Yes."

The boy said, "The Gang want that gun."

"They do, do they? Who are the Gang? You?"

"We're the exekutive."

They squatted round him, watching greedily. He said evasively, "What happened to the constable?"

"The Gang saw to 'im."

The youngest boy rubbed his ankle thoughtfully.

"It was smart work."

"We're organized, you see," the oldest boy said.

"An' we've got—scores."

"Joey 'ere," the oldest boy said, "got the birch once."

"I see."

"Six strokes."

"That was before we organized."

The oldest boy said, "An' now we want your gun. You don't need it any more. The Gang's looking after you."

"It is, is it?"

"We got arranged. You stay here, an' when it's dark—when you hear seven strike—you go along up Pit Street. They'll all be at tea then. Those that aren't in Chapel. There's an alley up by Chapel. You wait there for the bus. Crikey'll be on the watch for you."

"Who's Crikey?"

"He's one of the Gang. He punches tickets. He'll see you get over to Woolhampton safe."

"You've got it all planned. But what do you want the gun for?" The oldest boy leaned close. He had a pale thick skin; his eyes had the blankness of a pit pony's. There was no enthusiasm anywhere—no wildness; anarchy was just an absence of certain restraints. He said, "We was listening to you. You don't want that pit worked. We'll stop them for you. It's all the same to us."

"Don't your fathers work there?"

"That don't worry us."

"But how?"

"We know where they keep the dynamite. All we got to do is bust the shed open an' pitch the sticks down. They won't be able to work that pit for months."

The boy's breath smelled sour. D. felt revulsion. He said, "Is nobody working there?"

"There's nobody up there at all."

It was his duty, of course, to take the chance, but he was reluctant. He said, "Why the gun?"

"We'll shoot out the lock."

"Do you know how to use one?"

"Of course we do."

He said, "There's only one bullet." They were all cramped together in the little shed; hands were against his hands; sour breath whistled in his face. He felt as if he were surrounded by animals— who belonged in the dark and had senses adjusted to the dark, while he could see only in the light. He said, "Why?" and an uninterested boy's voice came back. "Fun." A goose went winging by somewhere above his grave—where? He shivered. He said, "Suppose there *is* someone up there."

"Oh, we'll be careful. We don't want to swing." But they wouldn't swing. That was the trouble—they had no responsibility; they were under age. But all the same, he told himself, it was his duty—even if there should be an accident. You couldn't count strangers' lives in the balance against your own people's. When war began, the absolute moral code was abolished; you were allowed to do evil that good might come.

He took the gun out of his pocket and immediately the scaly

hand of the oldest boy dropped on it. D. said, "Throw the gun down the pit first. You don't want fingermarks."

"That's all right. You can trust us."

He kept his fingers on it, reluctant to let it go; it was his last shot. The boy said, "We shan't squeal. The Gang never squeals."

"What are they doing in the town now? The police, I mean."

"There's only two of 'em. One of them's got a bike. He's fetching a warrant from Woolhampton. They think you're in Charlie Stowe's—an' Charlie won't let them in to look. Charlie's got a score too."

"You won't have long—after you've shot the lock—to throw the sticks and get away."

"We'll wait to dark." The hand disengaged the gun; immediately it disappeared in someone's pocket. "Don't forget," the leader said. "Seven—at Chapel. Crikey'll be watchin' out."

When they had gone he remembered that he might at least have asked them for a little food.

Without it the hours went all the more slowly; he opened the door of the shed a crack, but all he could see was a dry shrub, a few feet of cinder path, the piece of coconut on its dirty string. He tried to plan ahead, but what was the good when life took you like a high sea and flung you . . . ? If he got to Woolhampton, would it be any use trying the station, or would it be watched? He remembered the bandage on his cheek; that was no longer any good; he tore it off. It had been bad luck that the woman should have found Mr. K.'s body so soon. But he had been pursued by bad luck ever since he landed; he saw Rose again, coming down the platform with the bun. If he had not taken a lift from her, would everything have been different? He would not have been beaten up, delayed. Mr. K. perhaps would not have suspected him of selling out and become determined to sell out himself first. The manageress—but she was mad, L. said. What exactly had he meant by that? Whichever track he took seemed to begin with Rose on the platform and end with Else lying dead on the third floor.

A small bird—he didn't know the names of English birds—was sitting on the coconut. It pecked very quickly and pecked again; it was having a good meal. Suppose he got to Woolhampton, should he aim at getting back to London—or where? That had been the idea when he said good-bye to Rose, but things had changed now— if he was wanted for Mr. K.'s murder too. The hunt would be far more serious than before. He didn't want to mix her up more than he had already done. It would be so much simpler, he thought wearily, if a policeman now just walked in. The bird suddenly took off from the coconut; there was a sound on the cinder path of somebody walking on tiptoe. He waited patiently for capture.

But it was only a cat. It looked in at him, black and tailored, from the bright winter daylight—regarded him, as it were, on an equality, as one animal another, and moved again out of sight, leaving behind a faint smell of fish. He thought suddenly, The coconut. When it's dark enough I can get the coconut. But the hours went by with appalling slowness; at one time there was a smell of cooking, at another high words came down to him from an upper window—the phrase "bringing disgrace" and "drunken brute." Mrs. Bennett was probably trying to get her husband out of bed. He thought he heard her say, "His Lordship," and then a window slammed, and what went on after that went on without the neighbours' knowing, in the dreadful secrecy of a home—man's castle. The bird returned to the coconut, and he watched it jealously; it used its beak as a labourer does a pick; he was tempted to scare it away. The afternoon light flattened over the garden.

What troubled him now more than all was the fate of the gun. Those boys were not to be trusted. Probably the whole story of the explosives shed was false, and they wanted the weapon merely to play with. Anything might happen at any moment. They might let it off in mere devilry—not that you could think of high spirits in relation to those pasty and unwanted faces. Once he was startled by what might have been a shot—until it was repeated. It was probably the agent's car. At last the dark did fall. He waited until he couldn't see the coconut before he ventured out. He found his mouth was actually watering at the prospect of that dry bird's-leaving. His foot crunched over-loudly on the cinder track, and a curtain in the house was drawn aside. Mrs. Bennett glared out at him. He could see her plainly, dressed up to go out, flattening her nose against the kitchen window, beside the cooker, the jealous heartless bony face. He waited, motionless; it seemed impossible that she shouldn't see him, but the garden was dark and she let the curtain fall.

He waited awhile and then went on—to the coconut.

It wasn't after all much of a feast; he found it tough and dry in the throat. He crouched in the shed and ate it in small shreds; he hadn't a knife and he wore down his fingernails scraping off the hard white food. At last even the longest wait is over; he had thought of everything—of Rose, the future, the past, the boys with the gun—until there was no more to think about at all. He had tried to remember the poem he had copied out into the notebook which L.'s chauffeur had stolen— "The beat . . . something of thy heart and feet, how passionately and irretrievably . . ." He gave it up. It had seemed at the time to mean a great deal. He thought of his wife; it represented all the ignobility of life that he felt the tie weakening between him and the grave. People should die together, not apart. A clock struck seven.

Two

He came carefully out of the shed with what was left of the coconut in his pocket. He realized suddenly that the boys had never told him how he was to get out of this back garden. That was like a child—the immense organized plan, and the small practical detail forgotten. It was madness to trust them with a gun. He supposed they had gone themselves over the wall—the way they had come. But he wasn't young; he was a weak hungry middle-aged man. He put his hands up. He could reach the top of the wall, but he hadn't the strength in the arms to raise himself. He tried again and again, each time more weakly. A very young voice from the lavatory whispered, "That you, mate?"

So they hadn't forgotten the detail.

He whispered, "Yes."

"There's a loose brick."

He felt along the wall until he found it. "Yes."

"Come over quick."

He landed on his feet where his escape had begun. A small dirty urchin watched him critically. "I'm the lookout," he said.

"Where are the others?"

He jerked his head up towards the dark background of slag which hung like a storm cloud above the village. "They'll be at the pit." He felt the sense of apprehension grow; it was like the five minutes between the warning and the first bombs. He had a feeling of merciless anarchy let loose like thunder on the hill.

"You go an' wait for Crikey," the minute and grubby creature commanded him harshly.

He obeyed; there wasn't anything else to do. The long grey street was badly lighted, and the Gang seemed to have chosen the time correctly—there was nobody about at all. He might have been going through a deserted town, a relic shown to tourists of the coal age, if it had not been for the light in the Chapel windows. He felt very tired and very sick, and with every step he took his apprehensions gathered. He felt a physical shrinking from the sudden noise which at any moment now would tear across this quiet. In the northwest sky there was a glow of light cast by Woolhampton, like a city on fire.

A narrow passage ran up between the Baptist Chapel and the next house; it gave it a spurious detached dignity in the crammed village. He waited there with his eyes on the street for Crikey and the Woolhampton bus. The only policeman left was presumably keeping an eye on Charlie Stowe's while he waited for the search warrant. Straight up at the back rose the mountains of slag, and somewhere in the dark the boys were gathering round the explosives shed. Inside the Chapel the tuneless voices of women were singing, "Praise to the Holiest in the height . . ."

A thin rain began to fall, blowing from the north across the hills of slag. It was impregnated with dust; it streaked the face like diluted paint. A man's voice, rough and tender and assured, said distinctly close to his elbow, "Let us all pray," and the impromptu prayer began to roll magnificently on its way—"Fountain of all goodness and truth . . . we bless Thee for all Thy gifts so freely bestowed . . ." The cold seeped through his mackintosh and lay like a wet compress on his breast. Was that the sound of a car? It was. He heard it backfiring furiously down the street, and he came cautiously to the entrance of his burrow, hoping for Crikey.

But he started quickly back into the dark. It wasn't the bus; it was a motor-bicycle ridden by a policeman. He must have got back from Woolhampton with the warrant; they would soon discover that he wasn't at Charlie Stowe's. How long would the bus be? They'd search it, surely—unless the Gang had thought of that too, and got a plan. He flattened himself against the Chapel wall, presenting as little surface as he could to the penetrating rain, and heard the prayer going on and imagined the big bare lighted interior with the pitch-pine panels and the table instead of an altar and the hot radiator and all the women in their Sunday best—Mrs. Bennett—"We pray Thee for our torn and tortured world . . . we would remember before Thee the victims of war, the homeless and destitute . . ." He smiled grimly, thinking, They are praying for me if they only knew it; how would they like that? They began to sing a hymn; the words came erratically and obscurely out from their prison of stone and flesh—"In heavenly love abiding, no change my heart shall fear . . ."

He was flung right across the passage and fell with the back of his head against a stone; glass flew like shrapnel. He had a sense that the whole wall above him was caving in to fall upon his face, and he screamed and screamed. He was aware of violence and not of noise—the noise was too great to be heard. You became conscious of it only when it was over, and there were only barking dogs and people shouting and the soft sifting of dust from a broken brick. He put his hands over his face to protect his eyes and screamed again; people ran along the street, nor far away a harmonium began defiantly to play, but he didn't hear it—he was back in the foundations of a house with a dead cat's fur touching his lips.

A voice said, "That's him." They were digging him out, but he couldn't move to avoid the edge of a spade or the point of a pick; he sweated with fear and called out in his own language. Somebody's hand was passing over him—and his mind went flick, flick, and he was back on the Dover road and the chauffeur's large and brutal hands were touching him. He said fiercely, "Take your hands off."

"Has he got a gun?"

"No."

"What's that in his right pocket?"

"Well, now isn't that a funny thing? It's a piece of coconut."

"Hurt?"

"I don't think so," the voice said. "Just scared, I reckon."

"Better put on the cuffs."

He came back down the long track which led from the dead cat to Benditch village by way of the Dover road. He felt his hands gripped and his eyes were uncovered. The wall still stood above him and the thin rain came steadily down; there was no change. Violence had passed, leaving only a little broken glass. Two policemen stood over him, and a small dismal crowd had collected at the entrance of the alley and watched avidly. A voice said, "The Scripture lesson is taken from . . ."

"It's all right," D. said. "I'm coming." He got up painfully; the fall had strained his back. He said, "I'd be glad to sit down if you don't mind."

A policeman said, "You'll have plenty of time for that."

One of them took his arm and led him out into the dingy street. A little way off stood a bus marked Woolhampton; a youth with a satchel slung across his shoulder watched him with poker face from the step.

He said, "What are the charges?"

"There'll be plenty," the policeman said, "don't you worry."

"I think," D. said, "I have the right—" looking at his cuffed hands.

"Using words likely to lead to a breach of the peace—an' being on enclosed premises with the purpose of committing a felony. That'll be enough to get on with."

D. laughed. He couldn't help it. He said, "Those are two fresh ones. They mount up, don't they?"

At the station they gave him a cup of cocoa and some bread and butter and locked him in a cell. He had not experienced such peace for a long time. He could hear them telephoning to Woolhampton about him, but he couldn't hear what was said beyond a few words. Presently the younger policeman brought him a bowl of soup. He said, "You're quite a catch, aren't you?"

"Am I?"

"They want you up in London—and in a hurry too." He said with respect, "They want to question you."

"What about?"

"I couldn't tell you, but you've seen the paper, I suppose. You've got to go up by the midnight train. With me. I won't mind taking a look at London, I can tell you."

D. said, "Would you mind telling me—that explosion—was anybody hurt?"

The policeman said, "Some kids set the explosives shed off up at the mine. But nobody was hurt—for a wonder. Except old George Jarvis; what he was doing up there no one knows. He complains of shock, but it would need an earthquake to shock old George."

"Then the damage wasn't great?"

"There wasn't any damage—if you don't count the shed and some windows broken."

"I see."

So even the last shot had failed.

PART IV

The End

One

The magistrate had thin white hair and pince-nez and deep lines around the mouth—an expression of soured kindliness. He kept on tapping his blotter impatiently with his fountain pen. It was as if the endless circumlocutions of police witnesses were at last getting his nerves frayed beyond endurance. "We proceeded to so-and-so . . ." "On information received . . ." He said with irritation, "What you mean to say is, I suppose . . ."

They had allowed D. to sit down in the dock. Where he sat he could see nobody but a few solicitors and policemen, the clerk at a table under the magistrate's dais, all strangers. But as he had stood at the entrance of the court waiting for his name to be called, all sorts of familiar faces had been visible—Mr. Muckerji, old Dr. Bellows, even Miss Carpenter was there. He had smiled painfully towards them as he climbed into the dock before he turned his back. How puzzled they must be—except, of course, Mr. Muckerji, who was certain to have his theories. He felt inexpressibly tired.

It had been a long thirty-six hours. First the journey up to London with an excited police officer who kept him awake all night talking about a boxing match he might or might not get to at the Albert Hall. And then the questioning at Scotland Yard. At first he had been amused—it contrasted oddly with the sort of questioning he had had in prison at home, with a club. Three men sat or strolled about the room; they were meticulously fair, and sometimes one of them would bring in tea and biscuits on a tray for him—very strong cheap tea and rather sweet biscuits. They also offered him cigarettes, and he had returned the compliment. They hadn't liked his black strong kind, but he noticed with secret amusement that they unobtrusively made a note of the name on the packet—in case it should come in useful later.

They were obviously trying to pin Mr. K.'s death on him; he

wondered what had happened to the other charges, the false passport and Else's so-called suicide—not to speak of the explosion at
Benditch. "What did you do with the gun?" they said. That was the
nearest they came to the odd scene at the Embassy.

"I dropped it in the Thames," he said with amusement.

They pursued the point very seriously; they seemed quite prepared to employ divers, dredgers.

He said, "Oh, one of your bridges—I don't know all their
names."

They had found out all about his visit to the Entrenationo soirée
with Mr. K., and a man had come forward who said that Mr. K.
had made a scene because he was being followed. A man called
Hogpit. "He wasn't being followed by me," D. said. "I left him outside the Entrenationo office."

"A witness called Fortescue saw you and a woman . . ."

"I don't know anyone called Fortescue."

The questioning had gone on for hours. Once there was a telephone call. A detective turned to D. with the receiver in his hand
and said, "You do know, don't you, that this is all voluntary? You
can refuse to answer any questions without your solicitor being
present."

"I don't want a solicitor."

"He doesn't want a solicitor," the detective said down the phone
and rang off.

"Who was that?" D. asked.

"Search me," the detective said. He poured D. out his fourth
cup of tea and said, "Two lumps? I always forget."

"No sugar."

"Sorry."

Later in the day there had been an identification parade. It was
rather disillusioning to a former lecturer in the romance languages
to see the choice of faces. This—it seemed to indicate—is what
you're like to us. He looked with distress down a line of unshaven
Soho types—they looked, most of them, like pimps, or waiters in
undesirable cafés. He was amused to find, however, that the police
had been only too fair. Fortescue suddenly came through a door
into the yard, carrying an umbrella in one hand and a bowler hat
in the other. He walked down the seedy parade like a shy young
politician inspecting a guard of honour and hesitated a long while
before a blackguard on D.'s right—a man who looked as if he
would kill you for a packet of cigarettes. "I think—" Fortescue said.

"No—perhaps." He turned pale earnest eyes towards the detective with him and said, "I'm very sorry, but you know I'm shortsighted, and everything here looks so different."

"Different?"

"Different, I mean, to Emily's—I mean Miss Glover's flat."

"You aren't identifying furniture," the officer said.

"No. But then the man I saw was wearing a plaster dressing. None of these——"

"Can't you just imagine the dressing?"

"Of course," Fortescue said, with his eye on D.'s cheek, "this one's got a scar. He might have been . . ."

But they were very fair. They wouldn't allow that. They had led him out and brought in a man in a big black hat whom D. vaguely remembered having seen—somewhere. "Now, sir," the detective said, "can you see here the man you say was in the taxi?"

He said, "If your man had paid proper attention at the time instead of trying to arrest him for drunkenness——"

"Yes, yes. It was a mistake."

"And a mistake, I suppose, hauling me into court for obstruction?"

The detective said, "After all, sir, we've apologized."

"All right, then. Bring out these men."

"They are here."

"Oh, these, yes." He said sharply, "Are they here willingly?"

"Of course. They get paid—all except the prisoner."

"And which is he?"

"Why, that's for you to say, sir."

The man in the hat said, "Yes, yes, of course," and strode rapidly down the line. He stopped in front of the same scoundrelly looking fellow that Fortescue had noticed and said firmly, "That's your man."

"Are you quite sure, sir?"

"Of course."

"Thank you very much." They hadn't brought anybody else in after that. Perhaps they felt they had so many charges against him that they had plenty of time ahead to pin onto him the most serious charge of all. He felt complete apathy; he had failed and he contented himself with denying everything. Let them prove what they wanted. At last they left him alone again in a cell, and he slept fitfully. The old dreams were returning with a difference. He was arguing with a girl up and down a riverbank—she was saying the

Berne manuscript was of much later date than the Bodleian one. They were fiercely happy, walking up and down by the quiet stream. He said, "Rose . . ." There was a smell of spring, and over the river very far away the skyscrapers stood—like tombs. A policeman was shaking him by the shoulders. "There's a solicitor to see you, sir."

He hadn't really wanted to see the solicitor. It was too tiring. He said, "I don't think you understand. I haven't got any money. That is to say—to be accurate, I have a couple of pounds and a return ticket."

The solicitor was a smart agile young man with a society manner. He said, "That's all right; that's being seen to. We're briefing Sir Terence Hillman. We feel that it's necessary, as it were, to show that you are not friendless, that you are a man of substance."

"If you call two pounds—"

"Don't let's discuss the money now," the solicitor said. "I assure you *we* are satisfied."

"But I must know, if I'm to consent—"

"Mr. Forbes is taking care of everything."

"Mr. Forbes!"

"And now," the solicitor said, "to go into details. They certainly seem to have chalked up a good few charges against you. Anyway, we've disposed of one. The police are satisfied now that your passport is quite correct. It was lucky you remembered that presentation copy at the Museum."

D. thought, with a slight awakening of interest, Good girl, trust her to remember the right thing and to go for it. He said, "And that child's death?"

"Oh, they never had any evidence there. And as it happens the woman's confessed. She's mad, of course. She went off into hysterics. You see, an Indian living there had been going round among the neighbours asking questions. No, we've got more serious things to guard against than that."

"When did all this happen?"

"Saturday evening. It was in the last edition of the Sunday papers." D. remembered how, driving across the park, he had seen a poster—something about a sensation, a Bloomsbury sensation—a Bloomsbury tragedy sensation; the whole absurd phrase came back. If only he had bought a copy he might have let Mr. K. alone and all this trouble would have been saved. An eye for an eye—but one didn't necessarily demand two eyes.

The solicitor said, "Of course in a way our chance lies in the number of charges."

"Doesn't murder take precedence?"

"I doubt if they can charge you with that yet."

It all seemed to D. abysmally complicated and not very interesting. They had got him, and they could hardly fail to get their evidence. He hoped that Rose would be kept safely out of it. It was a good thing she hadn't visited him; he wondered whether it was safe to send a message by the solicitor, and then decided that she had a lot of sense—enough sense to stay away. He remembered her candid statement, "I couldn't love you if you were dead," and he felt a slight unreasoning pain that you could depend on her now to do nothing rash.

She wasn't in court either. He was sure of that—one glance would have been enough to pick her out. Perhaps if she had been there he would have paid more attention to the proceedings. One tried to show off with quickness or bravado if one was in love—if he was in love.

Every now and then an elderly man with a nose like a parrot's got up to cross-examine a policeman. D. supposed he was Sir Terence Hillman. The affair dragged on. Then quite suddenly it all seemed to be over; Sir Terence was asking for a remand. His client had had no time to get his evidence together; there were issues which were not clear lying behind this case. They were not even clear to D. Why ask for a remand? Apparently he hadn't yet been charged with murder. Surely the less time the police were given the better.

Counsel for the police said they had no objection. He smirked sardonically—an inferior little birdlike man—towards the distinguished K.C. as if he had gained an unexpected point through the other's stupidity.

Sir Terence was on his feet again, asking that bail should be allowed.

A prolonged squabble began in court; it seemed to D. quite meaningless. He would really rather stay in a cell than a hotel room —and anyway, who would stand bail for so shady and undesirable an alien?

Sir Terence said, "I do object, Your Worship, to the attitude of the police. They drop hints about a more serious charge. Let them bring it, so that we can see what it is. At present they've mustered a long array of very minor charges. Being in possession of firearms, resisting arrest—and arrest for what? Arrest on a false charge which the police hadn't taken the trouble to investigate properly."

"Incitement to violence," the birdlike man said.

"Political!" Sir Terence exclaimed. He raised his voice and said, "Your Worship, a habit seems to be growing on the police which I hope you will be the means of checking. They will put a man in prison over some trivial offence while they try to get their evidence together on another charge—and if they fail, well, the man comes out again and we hear no more about those weighty reasons. *He* has had no chance of getting his witnesses together. . . ."

The wrangle went on. The magistrate said suddenly, impatiently, stabbing at his blotting paper, "I can't help feeling, Mr. Fennick, that there's something in what Sir Terence says. Really there's nothing in these charges at present which would prevent me granting bail. Wouldn't it meet your objections if the bail were made a very substantial one? After all, you have his passport." Then the arguments began all over again.

It was all very fictitious; he had only two pounds in his pocket —not literally in his pocket because, of course, they had been taken away from him when he was arrested. The magistrate said, "In that case I'll remand him for a week on bail in two recognizances of one thousand pounds each." He couldn't help laughing—two thousand pounds. A policeman opened the door of the dock and plucked his arm. "This way." He found himself back in the tiled passage outside the court. The solicitor was there, smiling. He said, "Well, Sir Terence was a bit of a surprise for them, wasn't he?"

"I don't understand what all the fuss was about," D. said. "I haven't the money—and anyway I'm quite comfortable in a cell."

"It's all arranged," the solicitor said.

"But who by?"

"Mr. Forbes. He's waiting for you now outside."

"Am I free?"

"Free as the air. For a week. Or until they've got enough evidence to re-arrest."

"I don't see why we should give them all that trouble."

"Ah," the solicitor said, "you've got a good friend in Mr. Forbes."

He came out of the court and down the steps; Mr. Forbes in loud plus fours wandered restlessly round the radiator of a Packard. They looked at each other with some embarrassment, not shaking hands. D. said, "I understand I've got you to thank—for somebody they call Sir Terence and for my bail. It really wasn't necessary."

"That's all right," Mr. Forbes said. He gave D. a long unhappy look as if he wanted to read in his face some explanation—of something. He said, "Will you get in beside me? I've left the chauffeur at home."

"I shall have to find somewhere to sleep. And I must get my money back from the police."

"Never mind about that now."

They climbed in, and Mr. Forbes started up. He said, "Can you see the petrol gauge?"

"Full."

"That's all right then."

"Where are we off to?"

"I want to call in—if you don't mind—at Shepherd's Market." They drove in silence all the way—into the Strand, round Trafalgar Square, Piccadilly. . . . They came into the little square in the middle of the market, and Mr. Forbes sounded his horn twice, looking up at a window over a fishmonger's. He said apologetically, "I won't be a minute." A face came to the window, a little plump pretty face over a mauve wrap. A hand waved; an unwilling smile. "Excuse me," Mr. Forbes said and disappeared through a door next the fishmonger's. A large tomcat came along the gutter and found a fish head; he spurred it once or twice with his claws and then moved on; he wasn't all that hungry.

Mr. Forbes came out again and climbed in; they backed and turned. He gave a cautious look sideways at D. and said, "She's not a bad girl."

"No?"

"I think she's really fond of me."

"I shouldn't wonder."

Mr. Forbes cleared his throat, driving on down Knightsbridge. He said, "You're a foreigner. You won't think it odd of me, keeping on Sally when—well, when I'm in love with Rose."

"It's nothing to do with me."

"A man must live—and I never thought I had a chance until this week."

"Ah," D. said. He thought, I'm beginning to talk like George Jarvis.

"And it's useful too," Mr. Forbes said.

"I'm sure it is."

"I mean—today, for instance. She is quite ready to swear that I spent the day with her if necessary."

"I don't see why it should be." They were silent through Hammersmith.

It wasn't until they were upon Western Avenue that Mr. Forbes said, "I expect you're a bit puzzled."

"A little."

"Well," Mr. Forbes said, "you realize, of course, that you've got to leave the country at once—before the police get any more evidence to connect you with that unfortunate affair. The gun would be enough—"

"I don't think they'll find the gun."

"You can't take any risks. You know, whether you hit him or not, it's technically murder. They wouldn't hang you, I imagine. But you'd get fifteen years—at the least."

"I daresay. But you forget the bail."

"I'm responsible for the bail. You've got to leave tonight. It won't be comfortable, but there's a tramp steamer with a cargo of food leaving for your place tonight. You'll probably be bombed on the way—that's your own affair." There was an odd break in his voice. D. glanced quickly at the domed Semitic forehead, the dark eyes over the rather gaudy tie; the man was crying. He sat at the wheel, a middle-aged Jew crying down Western Avenue. He said, "Everything's been arranged. You'll be smuggled on board in the Channel after they've cleared the customs."

"It's very good of you to take so much trouble."

"I'm not doing it for you." He said, "Rose asked me to do my best."

So he was crying for love. They turned south. Mr. Forbes said sharply, as if he had been accused, "Of course I made my conditions."

"Yes?"

"That she wasn't to see you. I wouldn't let her go to the court."

"And she said she'd marry you—in spite of Sally?"

"Yes." He said, "How did you know she knew?"

"She told me." He said to himself, Everything's for the best; I'm not in a condition for love; in the end she'll find that—Furt is good for her. In the old days nobody ever married for love. People made marriage treaties. This was a treaty. There's no point in feeling pain. I must be glad—glad to be able to turn to the grave again without infidelity. Mr. Forbes said, "I am going to drop you at a hotel near Southcrawl. They'll see you are picked up there by motorboat. You won't be conspicuous—it's quite a resort, even at this time of year."

He added irrelevantly, "Climate's as good as Torquay." Then they sat in gloomy silence, driving southwest, the bridegroom and the lover—if he were a lover.

It was well on into the afternoon, among the high bare downs of Dorset, that Mr. Forbes said, "You know, you haven't done so badly. You don't think there'll be—trouble when you get home?"

"It seems likely."

"But that explosion at Benditch—you know it blew L.'s contract sky high. That and K.'s death."

"I don't understand."

"You haven't got the coal yourself, but L. hasn't got it either. We had a meeting early this morning. We've cancelled the contract. The risk is too great."

"The risk?"

"To reopen the pits and then find the government stepping in. You couldn't have advertised the affair better if you'd bought the front page of the *Mail*. Already there's been a leading article—about political gangsters and the civil war being fought out on English soil. We had to decide whether to sue the paper for libel or cancel the contract and announce that we had signed in good faith under the idea the coal was going to Holland. So we cancelled."

It was certainly half a victory. He thought grimly that it would probably postpone his death—he would be left to an enemy bomb instead of reaching a solution of his problems quickly in front of the cemetery wall. On the crown of the hill they came in sight of the sea. He hadn't seen it since that foggy night at Dover with the gulls crying—the limit of his mission. Far away to the right a rash of villas began; lights were coming out, and a pier crept out to sea like a centipede with an illuminated spine. "That's Southcrawl," Mr. Forbes said. There were no ship's lights visible anywhere on the wide grey vanishing Channel. "It's late," Mr. Forbes said with a touch of nervousness.

"Where do I go?"

"See that hotel over on the left about two miles out of Southcrawl?" They cruised slowly down the hill; it was more like a village than a hotel as they came down towards it—or, nearer comparison still, an airport; circle after circle of chromium bungalows round a central illuminated tower—fields and more bungalows. "It's called the Lido," Mr. Forbes said. "A new idea in popular hotels. A thousand rooms, playing fields, swimming pools."

"What about the sea?"

"That's not heated," Mr. Forbes said. He looked slyly sideways. "As a matter of fact I've bought the place." He said, "We're advertising it as a cruise on land. Organized games with a secretary. Concerts. A gymnasium. Young people encouraged—no reception clerk looking down his nose at the new Woolworth ring. Best of all, of course, no seasickness. And cheap." He sounded enthusiastic; he said, "Sally's very keen. She's great, you see, on physical fitness."

"You take a personal interest?"

"I wish sometimes I could do more. A man must have a hobby. But I've got a fellow down now taking a look round the place; he's had a lot of experience with roadhouses and things. If he likes the idea I'm putting him in complete charge at fifteen hundred a year and all found. We want to make it an all-the-year-round resort. You'll see—the Christmas season's beginning."

A little way up the road Mr. Forbes stopped the car. He said, "Your room's been booked for a night. You won't be the first in this place to slip away without paying the bill. We shall report it, of course, to the police—but I daresay you don't mind one more minor charge. Your number's one hundred and five C."

"It sounds like a convict's."

Mr. Forbes said, "You'll be fetched from your room. I don't see that anything can go wrong. I won't come any further. You ask at the office for your key."

D. said, "I know there's no point in thanking you, but all the same——" He stood beside the car; he felt at a loss for the right words. He said, "You'll give my love to Rose, won't you? And my congratulations. I do congratulate her——" He broke off; he had surprised a look on Mr. Forbes's face which was almost one of hate. It must be a bitter thing to be accepted on such humiliating conditions—a dowry is less personal. He said, "She couldn't have a better friend." Mr. Forbes leaned passionately forward and jabbed at the self-starter. He began to back; D. had a glimpse of the red-rimmed eyes. If it wasn't hate, it was grief. He left Mr. Forbes and walked down the road to the two neon-lighted pillars which marked the entrance of the Lido. Two enormous plum puddings in electric light bulbs had been set up on the pillars, but the wiring wasn't completed; they looked black, steely, unappetizing.

The reception clerk occupied a little lodge just inside the grounds. He said, "Oh, yes, your room was booked by telephone last night,

Mr."—he took a look at the register—"Davis. Your luggage, I suppose, is coming up?"

"I walked from Southcrawl. It should be here."

"Shall I telephone to the station?"

"Oh, we'll give them an hour or two. One doesn't have to dress for dinner, I imagine."

"Oh, no. Nothing of that sort, Mr. Davis. Perfect liberty. May I send the sports secretary along to your room for a chat?"

"I think I'll just breathe the air for twenty-four hours first."

He strolled round and round the big chromium circles—every room with a sunbathing roof. Men in shorts, their knees a little blue with cold, were chasing each other hilariously in the dusk; a girl in pajamas called out, "Have they picked up for basketball, Spot?" to a man with a bald head. Number 105C was like a cabin —there was even a sham porthole instead of a window, and the washing basin folded back against the wall to make more room; you could almost imagine a slight smell of oil and the churning of the engines. He sighed; England, it appeared, was to maintain a certain strangeness to the very end, the eccentricities of a country which had known civil peace for two hundred and fifty years. There was a good deal of noise—the laughter which is known technically as happy, and several radios were playing, plugged in to different stations; the walls were very thin, so that you could hear everything that went on in the neighbouring rooms—a man seemed to be flinging his shoes against the wall. Like a cabin, the room was overheated; he opened a porthole, and almost at once a young man put his head through. "Hullo," he said. "Hullo in there."

"Yes?" D. inquired wearily, sitting on the bed; it didn't seem likely that this was the summons he was waiting for. "Do you want me?"

"Oh, sorry. I thought this was Chubby's room."

"What is it, Pig?" a girl's voice said.

The young man's head disappeared. He whispered penetratingly on the gravel, "It's a foreign bloke."

"Let me take a look."

"Don't be silly. You can't."

"Oh, can't I?" A beaky girl with fluffy fair hair thrust her head through the window, giggled, and disappeared again. A voice said, *"There's* Chubby. What've you been doing with yourself, you old rotter?"

D. lay on his back, thinking of Mr. Forbes driving back through

the dusk to London; was he going to see Rose—or Sally? Somewhere a clock struck. This at last was the end; the sooner he was
back now, the better; he could begin to forget the absurd comic
image which remained fixed in his mind of a girl tossing a bun into
the fog. He fell asleep and woke again; half an hour had passed,
by his watch. How much longer? He went to the window and
looked out; beyond the bar of lights from his own outer circle of
steel bungalows there was nothing—just night and the sound of the
sea washing up on shingle and withdrawing, the long sigh of a
defeated element. In the whole arc of darkness not a light to show
that any ship was standing in to shore.

He opened his door. There were no passages; every room opened
immediately, as it were, onto the unsheltered deck; the clock tower
like the bridge of a ship heaved among the clouds; a moon raced
backwards through the marbled sky—a wind had risen, and the sea
seemed very near. It seemed odd not to be pursued; for the first
time since he landed nobody "wanted" him; he had the safe legal
existence of a man on bail.

He walked briskly in the cold evening air past the little lighted
overheated rooms. Music came up from Luxemburg, Stuttgart, and
Hilversum; radio was installed everywhere. Warsaw suffered from
atmospherics, and National gave a talk on the problem of Indo-
China. Below the clock tower wide rubber steps led up to the big
glass doors of the recreation centre. He walked in; evening papers
were laid out for sale on a central table; a saucer full of pennies
showed that the trust system was in operation. There was a lot of
boisterous laughter in one corner where a group of men were drinking whisky; otherwise the big draughty steel and glass room was
empty—if you could talk of emptiness among all the small tables
and club armchairs, the slot machines and boards for Corinthian
bagatelle. There was even a milk bar, up beside the service door.
D. realized that he hadn't a single penny in his pockets; Mr. Forbes
had not given him time to get his money back from the police. It
would be awkward if the ship didn't turn up. He looked down at
the evening papers; he thought, With so many crimes on my head,
I may as well add petty larceny. Nobody was looking. He sneaked
a paper.

A voice he knew said, "It's a damned fine show."

God, he thought, could only really be pictured as a joker. It
was absurd to have come all this way only to encounter Captain
Currie at the end of it. He remembered that Mr. Forbes had

spoken of a man with experience of roadhouses. Well, it hardly seemed a moment for amicable greetings. He spread the paper open and sheltered himself behind it. A rather servile voice said, "Excuse me, sir, but I think you've forgotten your penny." A waiter must have come in under cover of that boisterous laughter; the trust system might be in operation, but they kept a careful watch on the number of pennies in the saucer. It didn't say much, he thought, for Chubby and Spot and the rest of Mr. Forbes's clientele.

He said, "Sorry. I haven't got any change."

"Oh, I can give you change, sir."

D. had his back to the drinkers now, but he had a sense that the laughter had stopped and that they were listening. He said with his hand in his pocket, "I seem to have left my money in my other suit. I'll pay you later."

"What room, sir?" If counting pennies made you rich, they deserved a fortune.

He said, "105C."

Captain Currie's voice said, "Well, I'm damned."

It was no good trying to avoid the encounter. After all he was on bail; there was nothing Currie could do. He turned and felt his poise a little shaken by Captain Currie's shorts—he had obviously been entering into the life of the place. D. said, "I hadn't expected to meet you here."

"I bet you hadn't," Captain Currie said.

"Well, I'll be seeing you, I expect, at dinner." Paper in hand, he moved towards the door.

Captain Currie said, "No, you don't. You stay where you are."

"I don't understand."

"This is the fellow I was telling you about, boys." Two moony middle-aged faces stared at him with awe, a little flushed with scotch.

"No!"

"Yes."

"I'm damned if he wasn't pinching a paper," one of them said.

"He's capable of anything," Captain Currie said.

"Would you mind," D. said, "getting out of my way? I want to go to my room."

"I daresay," Captain Currie said.

One of his companions said timidly, "Be careful, old man. He might carry a gun."

D. said, "I don't quite know what you gentlemen think you are doing. I'm not a fugitive from justice—isn't that the phrase? I happen to have been bailed, and there's no law which says I can't spend my time where I like."

"He's a regular sea-lawyer," one of the men said.

"You'd better take things quietly," Captain Currie said. "You've shot your bolt, man. You thought you'd get out of the country, I suppose—but you can't fool Scotland Yard. Best police force in the world."

"I don't understand."

"Why, man, you must know there's a warrant out. Look in the stop press. You're wanted for murder."

D. looked; it was there. Sir Terence Hillman had not fooled the police for long; they must have decided to take out a warrant as soon as he'd left the court. They were looking for him—and Captain Currie had, triumphantly, found him, and now watched him firmly, but with a kind of respect. Murder wasn't like stealing a car. It was the English tradition to treat a condemned man kindly —the breakfast before the execution. Captain Currie said, "Now, we are three to one. Take things quietly. It's no good making a scene."

Two

D. said, "Can I have a cigarette?"

"Yes, yes, of course," Captain Currie said. "Keep the whole packet." He told the waiter, "Ring up Southcrawl police station and tell them that we've got him."

"Well," one of his companions said, "we may as well sit down."

They had an air of embarrassment, standing between him and the door; they were obviously doubtful whether they ought not to pinion his arms or tie him up or something, but at the same time they had a horror of being conspicuous; the place was too public. They were obviously relieved when D. sat down himself; they pulled their chairs up around him. "I say, Currie," one of them said, "there'd be no harm in giving the fellow a drink." He added, rather unnecessarily it seemed to D., "He's not likely to get another."

"What will you have?" Currie said.

"I think a whisky and soda."

"Scotch?"

"Please."

When the waiter came back, Currie said, "A scotch. Get that message off?"

"Yes, sir. They said they would be over in five minutes and you was to keep him."

"Of course we'll keep him. We aren't fools. What do they think?"

D. said, "I thought in England people are supposed to be innocent until they are proved guilty."

"Oh, yes," Currie said, "that's right. But of course the police don't arrest a man unless they've got the right dope."

"I see."

"Of course," Captain Currie said, siphoning his whisky, "it's a mistake you foreigners make. In your own country you kill each other and nobody asks questions, but if you do that sort of thing in England, well, you're for it."

"Do you remember Blue?" one of the other men asked Currie.

"Tony Blue?"

"That's right. The one who played so badly in the Lancing-Brighton match in twenty-one. Muffed five catches."

"What about Blue?"

"He went to Rumania once. Saw a man fire at a bobby in the street. So he said."

"Of course Blue was a stinking liar."

D. said, "Would you mind if I went to my room for my things? One of you could come with me." It occurred to him that once in his room it might be possible—when the messenger arrived—They'd never find him here.

"Better wait for the police," Blue's friend said. "Mustn't take any risks."

"Might hit and run."

"I couldn't run far, could I?" D. said. "You're an island."

"I'm not taking any chances," Currie said.

D. wondered whether whoever was fetching him had already gone to room 105C and found it empty.

Currie said, "Would you two fellows mind keeping an eye on the door for a moment while I have a word with him alone?"

"Of course not, old man."

Currie leaned over his chair arm and said in a low voice, "Look here, you're a gentleman, aren't you?"

"I'm not sure—it's an English word."

"What I mean is—you won't say more than you need? One doesn't want a decent girl mixed up in this sort of thing."

"I don't quite follow—"

"Well, there was that story of a woman with you in the flat when that fellow Forester—"

"I read Fortescue in the papers."

"Yes, that was it."

"Oh, I imagine the woman—of course I don't know anything about it—was some prostitute or other."

"That's the idea," Currie said. "Stout fellow."

He called out to the others: "All right, you chaps. What about another scotch all round?"

Blue's friend said, "This one's on me."

"No, you did the last. This is my turn."

"As a matter of fact," the third said, "it's my turn."

"No, you did the one before last."

"Let's toss for it."

While they argued D. stared out between the hopeless barrier of their shoulders to the big glass doors. The floodlights were on, so that beyond a few feet of grass outside nothing could be seen at all. The hotel was there for the world to look at, but the world itself was invisible. Somewhere in that invisibility the cargo ship was passing—to his own country. He almost wished that he hadn't surrendered his gun to the gang of children in Benditch, even though they had, in a way, proved successful. The one shot would have put an end to a very boring and long-drawn-out process.

A party of girls pushed in, bringing a little cold air into the overheated room. They were noisy and heavily made up and rather unconvincing; they were trying to imitate the manner of a class more privileged than their own. They called loudly out, "Hullo, there's Captain Curly."

Currie blushed all down the back of his neck. He said, "Look here, girls. Get yourselves drinks somewhere else. This is a private party."

"Why, Curly?"

"We are talking important business."

"I expect it's just dirty stories. Tell."

"No, really, girls—I mean it."

"Why do they call you Curly?" D. said.

Currie blushed again.

"Introduce us to the fascinating stranger," a fat girl said.

"No, no. It's impossible. Absolutely no go."

Two men in mackintoshes pushed open the door and looked into the recreation room. One of them said, "Is there anybody here called—?"

Captain Currie said, "Thank God, are you the police?"

They watched him from the door. One of them said, "That's right."

"Here's your man."

"Are you D.?" one of them said.

"Yes." D. stood up.

"We have a warrant for your arrest on the charge of—"

"Never mind," D. said. "I know what it's all about."

"Anything you say—"

"Yes. Yes. Let's go." He said to the girls who stood gaping by the table, "You can have Curly now."

"This way," the detective said. "We've a car at the gate."

"No handcuffs?"

"I don't think they'll be needed," the man said with a heavy smile. "Come on. Get moving."

One of them took him by the arm, unobtrusively. They might have been friends leaving after a few drinks. The English law, he thought, was remarkably tactful; everybody in this country hated a scene. The night embraced them. Floodlights drowned the stars in favour of Mr. Forbes's fantastic hobby. Far out at sea a light burned. Perhaps that was the ship in which he was supposed to leave—leave this country free from his infection and his friends free from embarrassment, from the dangerous disclosure and the untimely reticence. He wondered what Mr. Forbes would say when he read the morning papers and found he hadn't gone.

"Come on," the detective said. "We've not got all night."

They led him out past the neon lights, saluting the clerk with a flick of the hand as they went. After all, the charge of leaving without paying his bill would not be added to the other misdemeanours. The car was up on the grass verge with the lights discreetly out. It would not have been good for the hotel, he supposed, if a police car had been too prominently on view. The taxpayer in this country was always protected. A third man sat at the wheel. He started up as soon as they appeared and switched on the lights.

D. got into the back between the two others. They swerved out onto the road and drove down towards Southcrawl.

One of the men in the back began to wipe his forehead. "Goddam!" he said.

They swerved left down a byroad away from Southcrawl. He said, "When they told me you were being taken care of, you could've knocked me down with a feather."

"You're not detectives?" He felt no elation; everything was starting all over again.

"Of course we're not detectives. You gave me a turn in there. I thought you were going to ask for my warrant. Haven't you any sense?"

"You see, detectives are on the way."

"Step on it, Joe."

They ricocheted down the rough path towards the sound of the sea. It came more boisterously up at them now every minute, the noise of surf beating on the rocks. "You a good sailor?" one of the men said.

"Yes. I think so."

"You need to be. It's a fierce night—and it'll be worse in the bay."

The car drew up. The headlights illuminated for a few feet a rough red chalk track and then ploughed on into nothing. They were at the edge of a low cliff. "Come on," the man said, "we've got to hurry. It won't take them long to tumble to things."

"Surely they can stop the ship—somehow."

"Oh, they'll send us a wire or two. We radio back that we haven't seen you. You don't think they'll turn out the Navy, do you? You aren't all that important."

They led the way down the steps cut in the cliff. In the little cove below a motorboat bobbed at the end of a chain. "What about the car?" D. said.

"Never mind the car."

"Won't it be traced?"

"I daresay—back to the shop it was bought at this morning, for twenty pounds. Anyone who likes is welcome to it. I wouldn't drive a car like that again—not for a fortune." But it seemed likely that a small fortune had been spent already—by Mr. Forbes. They puttered out of the cove and immediately met the force of the sea. It smashed at them deliberately, like an enemy. It was not like an impersonal force at all, riding in long regular breakers; it was like a madman with a pickaxe, smashing at them now on this side, now on the other. They would be lured, as it were, into a calm trough, and then the blows would come one after another in rapid succession; then calm again. There wasn't much time or chance to look back; only once, as they bobbed up on what seemed the top of the world, D. caught a glimpse of the floodlit hotel foundering in the far distance, as the moon swept up the sky.

It took them more than an hour to reach the ship, a dingy black coaster of about three thousand tons, flying a Dutch flag. D. came up the side like a piece of cargo and was immediately shipped below. An officer in an old jumper and dirty grey flannel trousers said, "You keep below for an hour or two. It is better so."

The cabin was tiny and close to the engine room. Somebody had had the forethought to lay out an old pair of trousers and a waterproof; he was wet through. The porthole was battened down, and a cockroach moved rapidly up the steel wall by the bunk. Well, he thought, I am nearly home. I am safe—if it is possible to think in terms of safety at all. He was safe from one danger and going back to another.

He sat on the edge of his bunk; he felt dizzy. After all, he thought, I am old—for this kind of life. He felt a sensation of pity for Mr. K., who had dreamed in vain of a quiet life in a university far behind the lines—well, at least he hadn't died in an Entrenationo cubicle in the presence of some sharp Oriental like Mr. Li who would resent the interruption of a lesson he had paid for in advance. And there was Else—the terror was over, she was secure from all the worse things which might have happened to her. The dead were to be envied. It was the living who had to suffer from loneliness and distrust. He got up; he needed air.

The deck was uncovered, and the wind whipped the sharp spray against his mouth. He leaned over the side and saw the great creamy tops rise up against the galley lights and surge away down into some invisible abyss. Somewhere far off a light went on and off—Land's End? No, they couldn't be as far as that yet from London, and Mr. Forbes driving through the dark, and Rose waiting—or Sally.

A voice he knew said, "That'll be Plymouth."

He didn't turn; he didn't know what to say. His heart had missed a beat like a young man's; he was afraid. He said, "Mr. Forbes—"

"Oh, Furt," she said, "Furt turned me down." He remembered the tears on Western Avenue, the look of hate on the hill above

Southcrawl. "He's sentimental," she said, "he preferred a gesture. Poor old Furt." In a phrase she dismissed him; he moved back into the salt and noisy dark at ten knots.

He said, "I'm an old man."

"If I don't care," she said, "what does it matter what you are? Oh, I know you're faithful—but I've told you I shan't go on loving a dead man." He took a quick look at her. Her hair was lank with spray. She looked older than he had ever seen her yet—plain. It was as if she were assuring him that glamour didn't enter into *this* business. She said, "When you are dead she can have you. I can't compete then—and we'll all be dead a long, long time."

The light went by astern; ahead there was only the splash, the long withdrawal, and the dark. She said, "You'll be dead very soon; you needn't tell me that, but *now* . . ."

The Ministry of Fear

BOOK I

The Unhappy Man

One: The Free Mothers

1

There was something about a fête which drew Arthur Rowe irresistibly, bound him a helpless victim to the distant blare of a band and the knock-knock of wooden balls against coconuts. Of course this year there were no coconuts because there was a war on: you could tell that too from the untidy gaps between the houses—a flat fireplace halfway up a wall like a painted fireplace in a cheap doll's house and lots of mirrors and green wallpaper, and from round a corner of the sunny afternoon the sound of glass being swept up, like the lazy noise of the sea on a shingled beach. Otherwise the Bloomsbury square was doing its very best with the flags of the Free Nations and a mass of bunting which had obviously been preserved by somebody ever since the Jubilee.

Arthur Rowe looked wistfully over the railings—there were still railings. The fête called him like innocence: it was entangled in childhood, with vicarage gardens, and girls in white summer frocks, and the smell of herbaceous borders, and security. He had no inclination to mock at these elaborately naïve ways of making money for a cause. There was the inevitable clergyman presiding over a rather timid game of chance; an old lady in a print dress that came down to her ankles and a floppy garden hat hovered officially, but with excitement, over a treasure hunt (a little plot of ground like a child's garden was staked out with claims), and as the evening darkened—they would have to close early because of the blackout—there would be some energetic work with trowels. There in a corner under a plane tree was the fortune-teller's booth—unless it was an impromptu outside lavatory. It all seemed perfect in the late summer Sunday afternoon. "My peace I give unto you not as the world knoweth peace. . . ." Arthur Rowe's eyes filled with tears as the small military band they had somehow managed to borrow struck up again a faded song of the last war: "Whate'er befall I'll still recall that sunlit mountainside."

Pacing round the railings he came towards his doom: pennies were rattling down a curved slope onto a chequerboard—but not very many pennies. The fête was ill attended: there were only three stalls and people avoided those. If they had to spend money they would rather try for a dividend, of pennies from the chequerboard or savings stamps from the treasure hunt. Arthur Rowe came along the railings, hesitantly, like an intruder, or an exile who has returned home after many years and is uncertain of his welcome.

He was a tall stooping lean man with black hair going grey and a sharp narrow face with a nose a little twisted out of the straight and a too sensitive mouth. His clothes were good but gave the impression of being uncared for; you would have said a bachelor if it had not been for an indefinable married look.

"The charge," said the middle-aged lady at the gate, "is a shilling, but that doesn't seem quite fair. If you wait another five minutes you can come in at a reduced rate. I always feel it's only right to warn people when it gets as late as this."

"It's very thoughtful of you."

"We don't want people to feel cheated—even in a good cause, do we?"

"I don't think I'll wait all the same. I'll come straight in. What exactly is the cause?"

"Comforts for free mothers—I mean mothers of the Free Nations."

Arthur Rowe stepped joyfully back into adolescence, into childhood. There had always been a fête about this time of year in the vicarage garden, a little way off the Trumpington road, with the flat Cambridgeshire fields beyond the extemporized bandstand and at the end of the fields the pollarded willows by the stickleback stream and the chalk pit on the slopes of what in Cambridgeshire they called a hill. He came to these fêtes every year with an odd feeling of excitement—as if anything might happen, as if the familiar pattern of life that afternoon might be altered forever. The band beat in the warm late sunlight, the brass quivered like haze, and the strange faces of young women would get mixed up with Mrs. Troup, who kept the general store and post office, Miss Savage the Sunday School teacher, the publican's and the vicar's wives. When he was a child he would follow his mother round the stalls— the baby clothes, the pink woollies, the art pottery, and always last and best the white elephants. It was as if there might always be discovered on the white-elephant stall some magic ring which would give three wishes or the heart's desire, but the odd thing was that when he went home that night with only a second-hand copy of *The Little Duke* by Charlotte Yonge or an out-of-date atlas advertising Mazawattee tea, he felt no disappointment; he carried with him the sound of brass, the sense of glory, of a future that would be braver than today. In adolescence the excitement had a different source; he might find at the vicarage some girl whom he had never seen before, and courage would touch his tongue, and in the late evening there would be dancing on the lawn and the smell of stocks. But because these dreams had never come true there remained the sense of innocence. . . .

And the sense of excitement. He couldn't believe that when he had passed the gate and reached the grass under the plane trees nothing would happen, though now it wasn't a girl he wanted or a magic ring, but something far less likely—to mislay the events of twenty years. His heart beat and the band played and inside the lean experienced skull was childhood.

"Come and try your luck, sir?" said the clergyman in a voice which was obviously baritone at socials.

"If I could have some coppers."

"Thirteen for a shilling, sir."

Arthur Rowe slid the pennies one after the other down the little inclined groove and watched them stagger on the board.

"Not your lucky day, sir, I'm afraid. What about another shilling's worth, another little flutter in a good cause?"

"I think perhaps I'll flutter farther on." His mother, he remembered, had always fluttered farther on, carefully dividing her patronage in equal parts, though she left the coconuts and the gambling to the children. At some stalls it was difficult to find anything at all even to give away to the servants.

Under a little awning there was a cake on a stand surrounded by a small group of enthusiastic sightseers. A lady was explaining. "We clubbed our butter rations—and Mr. Tatham was able to get hold of the currants."

She turned to Arthur Rowe and said, "Won't you take a ticket and guess its weight?"

He lifted it and said at random, "Three pounds five ounces."

"A very good guess, I should say. Your wife must have been teaching you."

He winced away from the group. "Oh, no, I'm not married."

War had made the stallholder's task extraordinarily difficult: second-hand Penguins for the Forces filled most of one stall, while another was sprinkled rather than filled with the strangest second-hand clothes—the cast-offs of old age—long petticoats with pockets, high lacy collars with bone supports, routed out of Edwardian drawers and discarded at last for the sake of the free mothers, and corsets that clanked. Baby clothes played only a very small part now that wool was rationed and the second-hand was in demand among friends. The third stall was the traditional one—the white elephant—though black elephant might have described it better since so many Anglo-Indian families had surrendered their collections of ebony elephants. There were also brass ash trays, embroidered match cases which had not held matches now for a very long time, books too shabby for the bookstall, two postcard albums, a complete set of Dickens cigarette cards, an electroplated egg-boiler, a long pink cigarette holder, several embossed boxes for pins from Benares, a signed postcard of Mrs. Winston Churchill, and a plateful of mixed foreign copper coins.

Arthur Rowe turned over the books and found with an ache of the heart a dingy copy of *The Little Duke*. He paid sixpence for it and walked on. There was something threatening, it seemed to him, in the very perfection of the day: between the plane trees which shaded the treasure ground he could see the ruined section of the square. It was as if Providence had led him to exactly this point to indicate the difference between then and now. These people might have been playing a part in an expensive morality for his sole benefit.

He couldn't, of course, not take part in the treasure hunt, though it was a sad declension to know the nature of the prize, and afterwards there remained nothing of consequence but the fortune-teller: it *was* a fortune-teller's booth and not a lavatory. A curtain made of a cloth brought home by somebody from Algiers dangled at the entrance. A lady caught his arm and said, "You must. You really must. Mrs. Bellairs is quite wonderful. She told my son . . ." and clutching another middle-aged lady as she went by, she went breathlessly on, "I was just telling this gentleman about wonderful Mrs Bellairs and my son."

"Your younger son?"

"Yes. Jack."

The interruption enabled Rowe to escape. The sun was going down; the square garden was emptying; it was nearly time to dig up the treasure and make tracks, before darkness and blackout and siren time. So many fortunes one had listened to, behind a country hedge, over the cards in a liner's saloon, but the fascination remained even when the fortune was cast by an amateur at a garden fête. Always, for a little while, one could half believe in the journey overseas, in the strange dark woman, and the letter with good news. Once somebody had refused to tell his fortune at all—it was just an act, of course, put on to impress him—and yet that silence had really come closer to the truth than anything else.

He lifted the curtain and felt his way in.

It was very dark inside the tent, and he could hardly distinguish Mrs. Bellairs, a bulky figure shrouded in what looked like cast-off widow's weeds—or perhaps it was some kind of peasant's costume. He was unprepared for Mrs. Bellairs' deep powerful voice: a convincing voice. He had expected the wavering tones of a lady whose other hobby was water-colours.

"Sit down, please, and cross my hand with silver."

"It's so dark."

But now he could just manage to make her out: it was a peasant's costume with a big headdress and a veil of some kind tucked back over the shoulder. He found a half-crown and sketched a cross upon her palm.

"Your hand."

He held it out and felt it gripped firmly as though she intended to convey: expect no mercy. A tiny electric night light was reflected down on the girdle of Venus, the little crosses which should have meant children, the long long line of life. . . .

He said, "You're up-to-date. The electric light, I mean."

She paid no attention to his flippancy. She said, "First the character, then the past; by law I am not allowed to tell the future. You're a man of determination and imagination and you are very sensitive—to pain, but you sometimes feel you have not been allowed a proper scope for your gifts. You want to do great deeds not dream them all day long. Never mind. After all, you have made one woman happy."

He tried to take his hand away, but she held it too firmly: it would have been a tug of war. She said, "You have found the true contentment in a happy marriage. Try to be more patient though. Now I will tell you your past."

He said quickly, "Don't tell me the past. Tell me the future."

It was as if he had pressed a button and stopped a machine. The silence was odd and unexpected. He hadn't hoped to silence her, though he dreaded what she might say, for even inaccuracies about things which are dead can be as painful as the truth. He pulled his hand again and it came away. He felt awkward sitting there with his hand his own again.

Mrs. Bellairs said, "My instructions are these. What you want is the cake. You must give the weight as four pounds eight and a half ounces."

"Is that the right weight?"

"That's immaterial."

He was thinking hard and staring at Mrs. Bellairs' left hand, which the light caught: a square ugly palm with short blunt fingers prickly with big art-and-crafty rings of silver and lumps of stone. Who had given her instructions? Did she refer to her familiar spirits? And if so why had she chosen him to win the cake? Or was it really just a guess of her own? Perhaps she was backing a great number of weights, he thought, smiling in the dark, and expected at least a slice from the winner. Cake, good cake, was scarce nowadays.

"You can go now," Mrs. Bellairs said.

"Thank you very much."

At any rate, Arthur Rowe thought, there was no harm in trying the tip: she might have stable-information, and he returned to the cake stall. Although the garden was nearly empty now except for the helpers, a little knot of people always surrounded the cake, and indeed it was a magnificent cake. He had always liked cake, especially rich Dundees and dark brown homemade fruit cakes tasting elusively of Guinness. He said to the lady at the stall, "You won't think me greedy if I have another sixpennyworth?"

"No. Please."

"I should say then four pounds eight and a half ounces."

He was conscious of an odd silence, as if all the afternoon they had been waiting for just this but hadn't somehow expected it from him. Then a stout woman who hovered on the outskirts gave a warm and hearty laugh. "Lawks," she said, "anybody can tell you're a bachelor."

"As a matter of fact," the lady behind the stall rebuked her sharply, "this gentleman has won. He is not more than a fraction of an ounce out. That counts," she said with nervous whimsicality, "as a direct hit."

"Four pounds eight ounces," the stout woman said. "Well, you be careful, that's all. It'll be as heavy as lead."

"On the contrary, it's made with real eggs."

The stout woman went away, laughing ironically, in the direction of the clothing stall.

Again he was aware of an odd silence as the cake was handed over: they all came round and watched—three middle-aged ladies, the clergyman who had deserted the chequerboard, and, looking up, Rowe saw the gipsy's curtain lifted and Mrs. Bellairs peering out at him. He would have welcomed the laughter of the stout outsider as something normal and relaxed: there was such an intensity about these people, as though they were attending the main ceremony of the afternoon. It was as if the experience of childhood renewed had taken a strange turn, away from innocence. There had never been anything quite like this in Cambridgeshire. It was dusk and the stallholders were ready to pack up. The stout woman sailed towards the gates carrying a corset (no paper wrappings allowed). Arthur Rowe said, "Thank you. Thank you very much." He felt so conscious of being surrounded that he wondered whether anyone would step aside and let him out. Of course the clergyman did, laying a hand upon his upper arm and squeezing gently. "Good fellow," he said, "good fellow."

The treasure hunt was being hastily concluded, but this time there was nothing for Arthur Rowe. He stood with his cake and *The Little Duke* and watched. "We've left it very late, very late," the lady wailed beneath her floppy hat.

But late as it was somebody had thought it worth his while to pay his entrance at the gate. A taxi had driven up, and a man made hastily for the gipsy tent rather as a mortal sinner in fear of immediate death might dive towards a confessional box. Was this another who had great faith in wonderful Mrs. Bellairs, or was it perhaps Mrs. Bellairs' husband come prosaically to fetch her home from her unholy rites?

The speculation interested Arthur Rowe, and he scarcely took in the fact that the last of the treasure hunters was making for the garden gate and he was alone under the great planes with the stall-keepers. When he realized it he felt the embarrassment of the last guest in a restaurant who notices suddenly the focused look of the waiters lining the wall.

But before he could reach the gate the clergyman had intercepted him jocosely. "Not carrying that prize of yours away so soon?"

"It seems quite time to go."

"Wouldn't you feel inciined—it's usually the custom at a fête like this—to put the cake up again—for the Good Cause?"

Something in his manner—an elusive patronage as though he were a kindly prefect teaching to a new boy the sacred customs of the school—offended Rowe. "Well, you haven't any visitors left surely?"

"I meant to auction—among the rest of us." He squeezed Rowe's arm again gently. "Let me introduce myself. My name's Sinclair. I'm supposed, you know, to have a touch—for touching." He gave a small giggle. "You see that lady over there—that's Mrs. Fraser—*the* Mrs. Fraser. A little friendly auction like this gives her the opportunity of presenting a note to the cause, unobtrusively."

"It sounds quite obtrusive to me."

"They're an awfully nice set of people. I'd like you to know them, Mr.—"

Rowe said obstinately, "It's not the way to run a fête—to prevent people taking their prizes."

"Well, you don't exactly come to these affairs to make a profit, do you?" There were possibilities of nastiness in Mr. Sinclair that had not shown on the surface.

"I don't want to make a profit. Here's a pound note, but I fancy the cake."

Mr. Sinclair made a gesture of despair towards the others, openly and rudely.

Rowe said, "Would you like *The Little Duke* back? The Mrs. Fraser might give a note for that just as unobtrusively."

"There's really no need to take that tone."

The afternoon had certainly been spoiled: brass bands lost their old associations in the ugly little fracas. "Good afternoon," Rowe said.

But he wasn't to be allowed to go yet: a kind of deputation advanced to Mr. Sinclair's support—the treasure-hunt lady flapped along in the van. She said, smiling coyly, "I'm afraid I am the bearer of ill tidings."

"You want the cake too," Rowe said.

She smiled with a sort of elderly impetuosity. "I must *have* the cake. You see—there's been a mistake. About the weight. It wasn't —what you said." She consulted a slip of paper. "That rude woman was right. The real weight was three pounds seven ounces. And that gentleman," she pointed towards the stall, "won it."

It was the man who had arrived late in the taxi and made for Mrs. Bellairs' booth. He kept in the dusky background by the cake stall and let the ladies fight for him. Had Mrs. Bellairs given him a better tip?

Rowe said, "That's very odd. He got the exact weight?"

There was a little hesitation in her reply, as if she had been cornered in a witness box undrilled for that question. "Well, not exact. But he was within three ounces." She seemed to gain confidence. "He guessed three pounds ten ounces."

"In that case," Rowe said, "I keep the cake because, you see, I guessed three pounds five the first time. Here is a pound for the cause. Good evening."

He'd really taken them by surprise this time: they were wordless, they didn't even thank him for the note. He looked back from the pavement and saw the group from the cake stall surge forward to join the rest, and he waved his hand. A poster on the railings said: "The Comforts for Mothers of the Free Nations Fund. A fête will be held . . . under the patronage of royalty. . . ."

2

Arthur Rowe lived in Guilford Street. A bomb early in the blitz had fallen in the middle of the street and blasted both sides, but Rowe stayed on. Houses went overnight, but he stayed. There were boards instead of glass in every room, and the doors no longer quite fitted and had to be propped at night. He had a sitting room and a bedroom on the first floor, and he was done for by Mrs. Purvis who also stayed—because it was her house. He had taken the rooms furnished and simply hadn't bothered to make any alterations. He was like a man camping in a desert. Any books there were came from the twopenny or the public library except for *The Old Curiosity Shop* and *David Copperfield,* which he read, as people used to read the Bible, over and over again till he could have quoted chapter and verse, not so much because he liked them as because he had read them as a child and they carried no adult memories.

The pictures were Mrs. Purvis's—a wild water-colour of the Bay of Naples at sunset and several steel engravings and a photograph of the former Mr. Purvis in the odd, dated uniform of 1914. The ugly armchair, the table covered with a thick woollen cloth, the fern in the window—all were Mrs. Purvis's, and the radio was hired. Only the packet of cigarettes on the mantelpiece belonged to Rowe, and the toothbrush and shaving tackle in the bedroom (the soap was Mrs. Purvis's), and inside a cardboard box his bromides. In the sitting room there was not even a bottle of ink or a packet of stationery: Rowe didn't write letters, and he paid his income tax at the post office.

You might say that a cake and a book added appreciably to his possessions.

When he reached home he rang for Mrs. Purvis. "Mrs. Purvis," he said, "I won this magnificent cake at the fête in the square. Have you by any chance a tin large enough?"

"It's a good-size cake for these days," Mrs. Purvis said hungrily. It wasn't the war that had made her hungry; she had always, she would sometimes confide to him, been like it from a girl. Small and thin and bedraggled, she had let herself go after her husband died; she could be seen eating sweets at all hours of the day; the stairs smelled like a confectioner's shop; little sticky paper bags would be found mislaid in corners, and if she couldn't be discovered in the house, you might be sure she was standing in a queue for fruit gums. "It weighs two and a half pounds if it weighs an ounce," Mrs. Purvis said.

"It weighs nearly three and a half."

"Oh, it couldn't do that."

"You weigh it."

When she was gone he sat down in the armchair and closed his eyes. The fête was over: the immeasurable emptiness of the week ahead stretched before him. His proper work had been journalism, but that had ceased two years ago. He had three hundred pounds a year of his own, and, as the saying goes, he didn't have to worry. The army wouldn't have him, and his short experience of civil defence had left him more alone than ever—they wouldn't have him either. There were munition factories, but he was tied to London. Perhaps if every street with which he had associations was destroyed, he would be free to go—he might find a factory near Trumpington. After a raid he used to sally out and note with a kind of hope that this restaurant or that shop existed no longer—it was like loosening the bars of a prison cell one by one.

Mrs. Purvis brought the cake in a large biscuit tin. "Three and a half," she exclaimed scornfully. "Never trust these charities. It's just under three."

He opened his eyes. "That's strange," he said, "that's very strange." He thought for a while. "Let me have a slice," he said. Mrs. Purvis hungrily obeyed. It tasted good. He said, "Put it away in the tin now. It's the kind of cake that improves with keeping."

"It'll get stale," Mrs. Purvis said.

"Oh, no, it's made with real eggs." But he couldn't bear the yearning way in which she handled it. "You can give yourself a slice, Mrs. Purvis," he said. People could always get things out of him by wanting them enough: it broke his precarious calm to feel that people suffered. Then he would do anything for them. Anything.

3

It was the very next day that the stranger moved into Mrs. Purvis's back room on the third floor. Rowe met him the evening of the second day in the dusk of the stairs: the man was talking to Mrs. Purvis in a kind of vibrant undertone, and Mrs. Purvis stood back against the wall with an out-of-depth scared expression. "One day," the man was saying, "you'll see." He was dark and dwarfish and twisted in his enormous shoulders with infantile paralysis.

"Oh, sir," Mrs. Purvis said to Rowe with relief, "this gentleman wants to hear the news. I said I thought perhaps you'd let him listen . . ."

"Come in," Rowe said and opened his door and ushered the stranger in: his first caller. The room at this time of the evening was very dim: beaverboard in the windows kept out the last remains of daylight, and the single globe was draped for fear of cracks. The Bay of Naples faded into the wallpaper: the little light that went on behind the radio dial had a homely effect like a night light in a child's nursery—a child who is afraid of the dark. A voice said with hollow cheeriness, "Good night, children, good night."

The stranger hunched down in one of the two easy chairs and began to comb his scalp with his fingers for scurf. You felt that sitting was his natural position: he became powerful then with his big out-of-drawing shoulders in evidence and his height disguised.

He said, "Just in time," and without offering his case he lit a cigarette: a black bitter tang of Caporal spread over the room.

"Will you have a biscuit?" Rowe asked, opening his cupboard door. Like most men who live alone, he believed his own habits to be the world's: it never occurred to him that other men might not eat biscuits at six.

"Wouldn't you like the cake?" Mrs. Purvis asked, lingering in the doorway.

"I think we had better finish the biscuits first."

"Cakes," said the stranger, "are hardly worth eating these days."

"But this one," Mrs. Purvis said with vicarious pride, "was made with real eggs. Mr. Rowe won it in a raffle." And just at that moment the news began—"and this is Joseph Macleod reading it." The stranger crouched back in his chair and listened; there was something supercilious in his manner, as though he were listening to stories of which only he was in a position to know the real truth.

"It's a little more cheerful tonight," Rowe said.

"They feed us," the stranger said.

"You won't want the cake?" Mrs. Purvis asked.

"Well, perhaps this gentleman would rather have a biscuit?"

"I'm very fond of cake," the stranger said sharply, "when it's good cake," as though his taste was the only thing that mattered, and he stamped out his Caporal on the floor.

"Then fetch it, Mrs. Purvis, and a pot of tea."

The stranger hoisted his deformed figure round in the chair to watch the cake brought in; certainly he was fond of cake: it was as though he couldn't keep his eyes off it. He seemed to hold his breath until it had reached the table safely; then he sat impatiently forward in his chair.

"A knife, Mrs. Purvis?"

"Oh, dear, oh, dear. This time of night," Mrs. Purvis explained, "I always get forgetful. It's the sirens."

"Never mind," Rowe said, "I'll use my own." He brought tenderly out of his pocket his last remaining treasure—a big schoolboy's knife. He couldn't resist displaying its beauties to a stranger—the corkscrew, the tweezers, the blade that shot open and locked when you pressed a catch. "There's only one shop you can get these in now," he said, "a little place off the Haymarket." But the stranger paid him no attention, waiting impatiently to see the knife slide in. Far away on the outskirts of London the sirens began their nightly wail.

The stranger's voice said, "Now you and I are intelligent men. We can talk freely . . . about things." Rowe had no idea what he meant. Somewhere two miles above their heads an enemy bomber came up from the estuary. "Where are you? Where are you?" its uneven engines pronounced over and over again. Mrs. Purvis had left them; there was a scrambling on the stairs as she brought her bedding down, a slam of the front door; she was making for her favourite shelter down the street. "There's no need for people like you and me to get angry," the stranger said, "about things."

He pushed his great deformed shoulder into the light, getting nearer to Rowe, sidling his body to the chair's edge. "The stupidity of this war," he said. "Why should you and I—intelligent men . . . ?" He said, "They talk about democracy, don't they? But you and I don't swallow stuff like that. If you want democracy—I don't say you do, but if you want it—you must go to Germany for it. What do you want?" he suddenly inquired.

"Peace," Rowe said.

"Exactly. So do we."

"I don't suppose I mean your kind of peace."

But the stranger listened to nobody but himself. He said, "We can give you peace. We are working for peace."

"Who are we?"

"My friends and I."

"Conscientious objectors?"

The deformed shoulder moved impatiently. He said, "One can worry too much about one's conscience."

"What else could we have done? Let them take Poland too without a protest?"

"You and I are men who know the world." When the stranger leaned forward, his chair slid an inch with him, so that he bore steadily down on Rowe like something mechanized. "We know that Poland was one of the most corrupt countries in Europe."

"Who are we to judge?"

The chair groaned nearer. "Exactly. A government like the one we had—and have . . ."

Rowe said slowly, "It's like any other crime. It involves the innocent. It isn't any excuse that your chief victim was—dishonest, or that the judge drinks . . ."

The stranger took him up. Whatever he said had an intolerable confidence. "How wrong you are. Why, even murder can sometimes be excused. We've all known cases, haven't we?"

"Murder . . ." Rowe considered slowly and painfully. He had never felt this man's confidence about anything at all. He said, "They say, don't they, that you shouldn't do evil that good may come?"

"Oh, cock," sneered the little man. "The Christian ethic. You're intelligent. Now I challenge you. Have you ever really followed that rule?"

"No," Rowe said. "No."

"Of course not," the stranger said. "Haven't we checked up on you? But even without that I could have told—you're intelligent." It was as if intelligence was the password to some small exclusive society. "The moment I saw you, I knew you weren't—one of the sheep." He started violently as a gun in a square nearby went suddenly off, shaking the house, and again faintly up from the coast came the noise of another plane. Nearer and nearer the guns opened up, but the plane pursued its steady deadly tenor until again one heard, "Where are you? Where are you?" overhead and the house shook to the explosion of the neighbouring gun. Then a whine began, came down towards them like something aimed deliberately at this one insignificant building; but the bomb burst half a mile away: you could feel the ground dent. "I was saying," the stranger said, but he'd lost touch: he had mislaid his confidence; now he was just a cripple trying not to be frightened of death. He said, "We're going to have it properly tonight. I hoped they were just passing."

Again the drone began.

"Have another piece of cake?" Rowe asked. He couldn't help feeling sorry for the man; it wasn't courage that freed him from fear so much as loneliness. "It may not be"—he waited till the scream stopped and the bomb exploded, very near this time, probably the end of the next street: *The Little Duke* had fallen on its side— "much." They waited for a stick to drop, pounding a path towards them, but there were no more.

"No, thank you—that's to say, please, yes." The man had a curious way of crumbling the cake when he took a slice: it might have been nerves. To be a cripple in wartime, Rowe thought, is a terrible thing; he felt his dangerous pity stirring in the bowels. "You say you checked upon me, but who are *you?*" He cut himself a piece of cake and felt the stranger's eyes on him all the time, like a starving man watching through the heavy plate-glass window the gourmet in the restaurant. Outside a fire engine went by, and again a plane came up. The night's noise and fires and deaths were now in train: they would go on like a routine till three or four in the morning—a bombing pilot's eight-hour day. He said, "I was telling you about this knife." During the intense preoccupation of a raid it was hard to stick to any one line of thought.

The stranger interrupted, laying a hand on his wrist—a nervous bony hand attached to an enormous arm. "You know there's been a mistake. That cake was never meant for you."

"I won it. What do you mean?"

"You weren't meant to win it. There was a mistake in the figures."

"It's a bit late now to worry, isn't it?" Rowe said. "We've eaten nearly half."

But the cripple took no notice of that. He said, "They've sent me here to get it back. We'll pay in reason."

"Who are 'they'?"

But he knew who *they* were: it was comic; he could see the whole ineffective rabble coming across the grass at him: the elderly woman in the floppy hat who almost certainly painted water-colours, the rather intense whimsical lady who had managed the raffle, and wonderful Mrs. Bellairs. He smiled and drew his hand away. "What are you all playing at?" he asked. Never had a raffle, surely, ever been treated quite so seriously before. "What good is the cake to you now?"

The other watched him with gloom. Rowe tried to raise the cloud. "I suppose," he said, "it's the principle of the thing. Forget it and have another cup of tea. I'll fetch the kettle."

"You needn't bother. I want to discuss—"

"There's hardly anything left to discuss, and it isn't any bother."

The stranger picked at the scurf which had lodged below his fingernail. He said, "There's no more to say then?"

"Nothing at all."

"In that case," the stranger said—he began to listen as the next plane came remorselessly up. He shifted uneasily as the first guns fired, far away in East London. "Perhaps I will have another cup."

When Rowe returned the stranger was pouring out the milk, and he had cut himself another piece of cake. He was conspicuously at home with his chair drawn nearer to the gas fire. He waved his hand towards Rowe's chair as if *he* were the host, and he seemed quite to have forgotten the squabble of a moment ago. "I was thinking," he said, "while you were out of the room, that it's intellectuals like ourselves who are the only free men. Not bound by conventions, patriotic emotions, sentimentality—we haven't what they call a stake in the country. We aren't shareholders and it doesn't matter to us if the company goes on the rocks. That's quite a good image, don't you think?"

"Why do you say 'we'?"

"Well," the cripple said, "I see no sign that you are taking any active part. And of course we know why, don't we?" And suddenly, grossly, he winked.

Rowe took a sip of tea: it was too hot to swallow—an odd flavour haunted him like something remembered, something unhappy. He took a piece of cake to drown the taste and, looking up, caught the anxious eyes of the cripple, fixed on him, waiting. He took another slow sip and then he remembered. Life struck back at him like a scorpion, over the shoulder. His chief feeling was astonishment and anger that anybody should do this to *him*. He dropped the cup on the floor and stood up: the cripple trundled away from him like something on wheels; the huge back and the long strong arms prepared themselves—and then the bomb went off.

They hadn't heard the plane this time; destruction had come drifting quietly down on green silk cords; the walls suddenly caved in. They were not even aware of noise.

Blast is an odd thing; it is just as likely to have the appearance of an embarrassing dream as of man's serious vengeance on man, landing you naked in the street or exposing you in your bed or on your lavatory seat to the neighbours' gaze. Rowe's head was singing; he felt as though he had been walking in his sleep: he was lying in a strange position, in a strange place. He got up and saw an enormous quantity of saucepans all over the floor; something like the twisted engine of an old car turned out to be a refrigerator. He looked up and saw Charles's Wain heeling over an armchair which was poised thirty feet above his head; he looked down and saw the Bay of Naples intact at his feet. He felt as though he were in a strange country without any maps to help him, trying to get his position by the stars.

Three flares came sailing slowly, beautifully, down, clusters of spangles like something off a Christmas tree; his shadow shot out in front of him and he felt exposed, like a jailbreaker caught in a searchlight beam. The awful thing about a raid is that it goes on: your own private disaster may happen early, but the raid doesn't stop. They were machine-gunning the flares: two broke with a sound like cracking plates and the third came to earth in Russell

Square; the darkness came coldly and comfortingly back again.

But in the light of the flares Rowe had seen several things: he had discovered where he was—in the basement kitchen; the chair above his head was in his own room on the first floor; the front wall had gone and all the roof, and the cripple lay beside the chair, one arm swinging loosely down at him. He had dropped neatly and precisely at Rowe's feet a piece of uncrumbled cake. A warden called from the street, "Is there anyone hurt in there?" and Rowe said aloud in a sudden return of his rage, "It's beyond a joke; it's beyond a joke."

"You're telling me," the warden called down to him from the shattered street as yet another raider came up from the southeast, muttering to them both like a witch in a child's dream, "Where are you? Where are you? Where are you?"

Two: Private Inquiries

1

Orthotex: the Longest Established Private Inquiry Bureau in the Metropolis still managed to survive at the unravaged end of Chancery Lane, close to a book auctioneer's, between a public house which in peacetime had been famous for its buffet and a legal bookshop. It was on the fourth floor, but there was no lift. On the first floor was a notary public, on the second floor the office of a monthly called *Fitness and Freedom,* and the third was a flat which nobody occupied now.

Arthur Rowe pushed open a door marked Inquiries, but there was no one there. A half-eaten sausage roll lay in a saucer beside an open telephone directory: it might, for all one knew, have lain there for weeks. It gave the office an air of sudden abandonment, like the palaces of kings in exile where the tourist is shown the magazines yet open at the page which royalty turned before fleeing years ago. Arthur Rowe waited a minute and then explored farther, trying another door.

A bald-headed man hurriedly began to put a bottle away in a filing cabinet.

Rowe said, "Excuse me. There seemed to be nobody about. I was looking for Mr. Rennit."

"I'm Mr. Rennit."

"Somebody recommended me to come here."

The bald-headed man watched Rowe suspiciously with one hand on the filing cabinet. "Who, if I may ask?"

"It was years ago. A man called Keyser."

"I don't remember him."

"I hardly do myself. He wasn't a friend of mine. I met him in a train. He told me he had been in trouble about some letters—"

"You should have made an appointment."

"I'm sorry," Rowe said. "Apparently you don't want clients. I'll say good morning."

"Now, now," Mr. Rennit said, "you don't want to lose your temper. I'm a busy man, and there's ways of doing things. If you'll be brief . . ." Like a man who deals in something disreputable—pornographic books or illegal operations—he treated his customer with a kind of superior contempt, as if it were not he who wanted to sell but only the other who was anxious to buy. He sat down at his desk and said as an afterthought, "Take a chair." He fumbled in a drawer and hastily tucked back again what he found there; at last he discovered a pad and a pencil. "Now," he said, "when did you first notice anything wrong?" He leaned back and picked at a tooth with his pencil point, his breath whistling slightly between the uneven dentures. He looked abandoned like the other room; his collar was a little frayed and his shirt was not quite clean. But beggars, Rowe told himself, could not be choosers.

"Name?" Mr. Rennit went on as an afterthought. "Present address?" He stubbed the paper fiercely, writing down the answers. At the name of a hotel he raised his head and said sombrely, "In your position you can't be too careful."

"I think perhaps," Rowe said, "I'd better begin at the beginning."

"My good sir," Mr. Rennit said, "you can take it from me that I know all the beginnings. I've been in this line of business for thirty years. Thirty years. Every client thinks he's a unique case. He's nothing of the kind. He's just a repetition. All I need from you is the answer to certain questions. The rest we can manage without you. Now then—when did you notice anything wrong, wife's coldness?"

"I'm not married," Rowe said.

Mr. Rennit shot him a look of disgust; he felt guilty of a quibble. "Breach of promise, eh?" Mr. Rennit said. "Have you written any letters?"

"It's not breach of promise either."

"Blackmail?"

"No."

"Then why," Mr. Rennit asked angrily, "do you come to me?" He added his tag, "I'm a busy man," but never had anyone been so palpably unemployed. There were two trays on his desk marked In and Out, but the Out tray was empty and all the In tray held was a copy of *Men Only*. Rowe would have left if he had known any other address and if he had not felt the sense of pity which is so much more promiscuous than lust. Mr. Rennit was so obviously angry because he had not been given time to set his stage, and he could so obviously not afford his anger.

"Doesn't a detective deal with anything but divorces and breaches of promise?"

Mr. Rennit said, "This is a respectable business with a tradition. I'm not Sherlock Holmes. You don't expect to find a man in my position, do you, crawling about floors with a microscope, looking for bloodstains?" He added stiffly, "If you are in any trouble of that kind, I advise you to go to the police."

"Listen," Rowe said, "be reasonable. You know you can do with a client just as much as I can do with you. I can pay, pay well. Be sensible and unlock that cupboard and let's have a drink on it together. These raids are bad for the nerves. One has to have a little something . . ."

The stiffness drained slowly out of Mr. Rennit's attitude as he looked cautiously back at Rowe. He stroked his bald head and said, "Perhaps you're right. One gets rattled. I've never objected to stimulants *as* stimulants."

"Everybody needs them nowadays."

"It was bad last night at Purley. Not many bombs but the waiting. Not that we haven't had our share, and land mines—"

"The place where I live went last night."

"You don't say," Mr. Rennit said without interest, opening the filing cabinet and reaching for the bottle. "Now last week, at Purley . . ." He was like a man discussing his operations. "Not a hundred yards away . . ."

"We both deserve a drink," Rowe said.

Mr. Rennit—the ice broken—became suddenly confiding. "I suppose I was a bit sharp. One does get rattled. War plays hell with a business like this." He explained. "The reconciliations—you wouldn't believe human nature could be so contrary. And then of course the registrations have made it very difficult. People daren't go to hotels as they used to. And you can't *prove* anything from motorcars."

"It must be difficult for you."

"It's a case of holding out," Mr. Rennit said, "keeping our backs to the wall until the peace comes. Then there'll be such a crop of divorces, breaches of promise . . ." He contemplated the situation with uncertain optimism over the bottle. "You'll excuse a teacup?" He said, "When peace comes an old-established business like this —with connections—will be a gold mine." He added gloomily, "Or so I tell myself."

Listening, Rowe thought as he so often did, You couldn't take such an odd world seriously, though all the time he did in fact take it with a mortal seriousness. The grand names stood permanently like statues in his mind: names like Justice and Retribution, though what they both boiled down to was simply Mr. Rennit, hundreds and hundreds of Mr. Rennits. But of course if you believed in God —and the Devil—the thing wasn't quite so comic. Because the Devil—and God too—had always used comic people, futile people, little suburban natures and the maimed and warped to serve His purposes. When God used them you talked emptily of Nobility, and when the Devil used them Wickedness; but the material was only dull shabby human mediocrity in either case.

". . . new orders. But it will always be the same world I hope," Mr. Rennit was saying.

"Queer things do happen in it all the same," Rowe said. "That's why I'm here."

"Ah, yes," Mr. Rennit said. "We'll just fill our cups and then to business. I'm sorry I have no soda water. Now just tell me what's troubling you—as if I was your best friend."

"Somebody has tried to kill me. It doesn't sound important when so many of us are being killed every night—but it made me angry at the time."

Mr. Rennit looked at him imperturbably over the rim of his cup. "Did you say you were *not* married?"

"There's no woman in it. It all began," Rowe said, "with a cake." He described the fête to Mr. Rennit, the anxiety of all the helpers to get the cake back, the stranger's visit—and then the bomb. "I wouldn't have thought twice about it," Rowe said, "if it hadn't been for the taste the tea had."

"Just imagination probably."

"But I knew the taste. It was—hyoscine," he admitted reluctantly.

"Was the man killed?"

"They took him to hospital, but when I called today he'd been fetched away. It was only concussion and his friends wanted him back."

"The hospital would have the name and address."

"They had a name and address, but the address—I tried the London directory—simply didn't exist." He looked up across the desk at Mr. Rennit, expecting some sign of surprise—even in an odd world it was an odd story—but Mr. Rennit said calmly, "Of course there are a dozen explanations." He stuck his fingers into his waistcoat and considered. "For instance," he said, "it might have been a kind of confidence trick. They are always up to new dodges, those people. He might have offered to take the cake off you—for a large sum. He'd have told you something valuable was hidden in it."

"Something hidden in it?"

"Plans of a Spanish treasure off the coast of Ireland. Something romantic. He'd have wanted you to give him a mark of confidence in return. Something substantial like twenty pounds while he went to the bank. Leaving you the cake of course."

"It makes one wonder . . ."

"Oh, it would have worked out," Mr. Rennit said. It was extraordinary, his ability to reduce everything to a commonplace level. Even air raids were only things that occurred at Purley.

"Or take another possibility," Mr. Rennit said. "If you are right about the tea—I don't believe it, mind—he might have introduced himself to you with robbery in mind. Perhaps he followed you from the fête. Did you flourish your money about?"

"I did give them a pound when they wanted the cake."

"A man," Mr. Rennit said with a note of relief, "who gives a pound for a cake is a man with money. Thieves don't carry drugs as a rule, but he sounds a neurotic type."

"But the cake?"

"Pure patter. He hadn't really come for the cake."

"And your next explanation? You said there were a dozen."

"I always prefer the straightforward," Mr. Rennit said, running his fingers up and down the whisky bottle. "Perhaps there was a genuine mistake about the cake and he had come for it. Perhaps it contained some kind of a prize—"

"And the drug was imagination again?"

"It's the straightforward explanation."

Mr. Rennit's calm incredulity shook Rowe. He said with resentment, "In all your long career as a detective have you never come across such a thing as murder—or a murderer?"

Mr. Rennit's nose twitched over the cup. "Frankly," he said, "no. I haven't. Life isn't like a detective story. Murderers are rare people to meet. They belong to a class of their own."

"That's interesting to me."

"They are very, very seldom," Mr. Rennit said, "what we call gentlemen. Outside of story books. You might say that they belong to the lower orders."

"Perhaps," Rowe said, "I ought to tell you that I am a murderer myself."

2

"Ha, ha," said Mr. Rennit miserably.

"That's what makes me so furious," Rowe said. "That they should pick on me—me. They are such amateurs."

"You are—a professional?" Mr. Rennit asked with a watery and unhappy smile.

Rowe said, "Yes, I am, if thinking of the thing for two years before you do it, dreaming about it nearly every night until at last you take the drug out from the unlocked drawer, makes you one . . . and then sitting in the dock trying to make out what the judge is really thinking, watching each one of the jury, wondering what *he* thinks . . . there was a woman in pince-nez who wouldn't be separated from her umbrella . . . and then you go below and wait hour after hour till the jury come back ̍and the warder tries to be encouraging, but you know if there's any justice left on earth there can be only one verdict."

"Would you excuse me one moment?" Mr. Rennit said. "I think I heard my man come back." He emerged from behind his desk and then whisked through the door behind Rowe's chair with surprising agility. Rowe sat with his hands held between his knees, trying to get a grip again on his brain and his tongue. "Set a watch, O Lord, before my mouth and a door round about my lips. . . ." He heard a bell tinkle in the other room and followed the sound. Mr. Rennit was at the phone. He looked piteously at Rowe and then at the sausage roll as if that were the only weapon within reach.

"Are you ringing up the police?" Rowe asked. "Or a doctor?"

"A theatre," Mr. Rennit said despairingly. "I just remembered I promised my wife—"

"You are married, are you, in spite of all your experience?"

"Yes." An awful disinclination to talk convulsed Mr. Rennit's features as a thin faint voice came up the wires. He said, "Two seats —in the front row," and clapped the receiver down again.

"The theatre?"

"The theatre."

"And they didn't even want your name? Why not be reasonable," Rowe said. "After all, I had to tell you. You have to have all the facts. It wouldn't be fair otherwise. It might have to be taken into consideration; mightn't it, if you work for me?"

"Into consideration?"

"I mean—it might have a bearing. That's something I discovered when they tried me—that everything may have a bearing. The fact that I had lunch on a certain day alone at the Holborn Restaurant. Why was I alone? they asked me. I said I liked being alone sometimes, and you should have seen the way they nodded at the jury. It had a bearing." His hands began to shake again. "As if I really wanted to be alone for life. . . ."

Mr. Rennit cleared a dry throat.

"Even the fact that my wife kept love birds—"

"You *are* married?"

"It was my wife I murdered." He found it hard to put things in the right order: people oughtn't to ask unnecessary questions; he really hadn't meant to startle Mr. Rennit again. He said, "You needn't worry. The police know all about it."

"You were acquitted?"

"I was detained during His Majesty's pleasure. It was quite a short pleasure; I wasn't mad, you see. They just had to find an excuse." He said with loathing, "They pitied me, so that's why I'm alive. The papers all called it a mercy killing." He moved his hand in front of his face as though he were troubled by a thread of cobweb. "Mercy to her or mercy to me. They didn't say. And I don't know even now."

"I really don't think," Mr. Rennit said, swallowing for breath in the middle of a sentence and keeping a chair between them, "I can undertake— It's out of my line."

"I'll pay more," Rowe said. "It always comes down to that, doesn't it?" and as soon as he felt cupidity stirring in the little dusty room, over the half-eaten sausage roll and the saucer and the tattered telephone directory, he knew he had gained his point. Mr. Rennit after all could not afford to be nice. Rowe said, "A murderer is rather like a peer: he pays more because of his title. One tries to travel incognito, but it usually comes out."

Three: Frontal Assault

1

Rowe went straight from Orthotex to the Free Mothers. He had signed a contract with Mr. Rennit to pay him fifty pounds a week for a period of four weeks to carry out investigations: Mr. Rennit had explained that the expenses would be heavy—Orthotex employed only the most experienced agents—and the one agent he had been permitted to see before he left the office was certainly experienced. (Mr. Rennit introduced him as A2, but before long he was absent-mindedly addressing him as Jones.) Jones was small and at first sight insignificant, with his thin pointed nose, his soft brown hat with a stained ribbon, his grey suit which might have been quite a different colour years ago, and the pencil and pen on fasteners in the breast pocket. But when you looked a second time you saw experience: you saw it in the small, cunning, rather frightened eyes, the weak defensive mouth, the wrinkles of anxiety on the forehead —experience of innumerable hotel corridors, of bribed chambermaids and angry managers, experience of the insult which could not be resented, the threat which had to be ignored, the promise which was never kept. Murder had a kind of dignity compared with this muted second-hand experience of scared and secretive passions.

An argument developed almost at once in which Jones played no part, standing close to the wall, holding his old brown hat, looking and listening as though he were outside a hotel door. Mr. Rennit who obviously considered the whole investigation the fantastic fad of an unbalanced man argued that Rowe himself should take no part. "Just leave it to me and A2," he said. "If it's a confidence trick . . ."

He would not believe that Rowe's life had been threatened. "Of course," he said, "we'll look into the poison books—not that there'll be anything to find."

"It made me angry," Rowe repeated. "He said he'd checked up

—and yet he had the nerve." An idea came to him and he went excitedly on, "It was the same drug. People would have said it was suicide, that I'd managed to keep some of it hidden."

"If there's anything in your idea," Mr. Rennit said, "the cake was given to the wrong man. We've only got to find the right one. It's a simple matter of tracing. Jones and I know all about tracing. We start from Mrs. Bellairs: she told you the weight, but why did she tell you the weight? Because she mistook you in the dark for the other man. There must be some resemblance." Mr. Rennit exchanged a look with Jones. "It all boils down to finding Mrs. Bellairs. That's not very difficult. Jones will do that."

"It would be easiest of all for me to ask for her—at the Free Mothers."

"I'd advise you to let Jones see to it."

"They'd think he was a tout."

"It wouldn't do at all for a client to make his own investigations, not at all."

"If there's nothing in my story," Rowe said, "they'll give me Mrs. Bellairs' address. If I'm right they'll try to kill me, because, though the cake's gone, I know there was a cake, and that there are people who want the cake. There's work for Jones, to keep his eye on me."

Jones shifted his hat uneasily and tried to catch his employer's eye. He cleared his throat and Mr. Rennit said, "What is it, A2?"

"Won't do, sir," Jones said.

"No?"

"Unprofessional, sir."

"I agree with Jones," Mr. Rennit said.

All the same, in spite of Jones, Rowe had his way. He came out into the shattered street and made his sombre way between the ruins of Holborn. In his lonely state to have confessed his identity to someone was almost like making a friend. Always before it had been discovered—even at the warden's post; it came out sooner or later like cowardice. It was extraordinary the tricks and turns of fate, the way conversations came round, the long memories some people had for names. Now in the strange torn landscape where London shops were reduced to a stone ground plan like those of Pompeii, he moved with a kind of familiarity: he was part of this as he was no longer part of the past—the long week ends in the country, the laughter up lanes in the evening, the swallows gathering on telegraph wires, peace. It was as if the ruins were part of his own mind.

Peace had come to an end quite suddenly on an August 31—the world waited another year. He moved like a bit of stone among the other stones: he was protectively coloured, and he felt at times, breaking the surface of his remorse, a kind of evil pride, like that a leopard might feel moving in harmony with all the other spots on the world's surface, only with greater power. He had not been a criminal when he murdered; it was afterwards that he began to grow into criminality like a habit of thought. That these men should have tried to kill him who had succeeded at one blow in destroying beauty, goodness, peace: it was a form of impertinence. There were times when he felt the whole world's criminality was his; and then suddenly at some trivial sight—a woman's bag, a face on an elevator going up as he went down, a picture in a paper—all the pride seeped out of him. He was aware only of the stupidity of his act; he wanted to creep out of sight and weep; he wanted to forget that he had ever been happy. A voice would whisper, "You say you killed for pity; why don't you have pity on yourself?" Why not indeed? Except that it is easier to kill someone you love than to kill yourself.

2

The Free Mothers had taken over an empty office in a huge white modern block off the Strand. It was like going into a mechanized mortuary with a separate lift for every slab. Rowe moved steadily upwards in silence for five floors: a long passage, frosted glass, somebody in pince-nez stepped into the lift carrying a file marked Most Immediate, and they moved on smoothly upwards. A door on the seventh floor was marked "Comforts for the Mothers of the Free Nations. Inquiries."

He began to believe that after all Mr. Rennit was right. The stark efficient middle-class woman who sat at a typewriter was so obviously incorruptible—and unpaid. She wore a little button to show she was honorary. "Yes?" she asked sharply, and all his anger and pride seeped away. He tried to remember what the stranger had said—about the cake not being intended for him. There was really nothing sinister in the phrase as far as he could now remember it, and as for the taste, hadn't he often woken at night with it upon his tongue?

"Yes?" the woman repeated briskly.

"I came," Rowe said, "to try and find out the address of a Mrs. Bellairs."

"No lady of that name works here."

"It was in connection with the fête."

"Oh, they were all voluntary helpers. We can't possibly disclose addresses of voluntary helpers."

"Apparently," Rowe said, "a mistake was made. I was given a cake which didn't belong to me."

"I'll inquire," the stark lady said and went into an inner room. He had just long enough to wonder whether after all he had been wise. He should have brought A2 up with him. But then the normality of everything came back: he was the only abnormal thing there. The honorary helper stood in the doorway and said, "Will you come through please?" He took a quick glance at her typewriter as he went by: he could read, "The Dowager Lady Cradbrooke thanks Mrs. J. A. Smythe-Philipps for her kind gift of tea and flour. . . ." Then he went in.

He had never become accustomed to chance stabs: only when the loved person is out of reach does love become complete. The colour of the hair and the size of the body—something very small and neat and incapable, you would say, of inflicting pain—this was enough to make him hesitate just inside the room—there were no other resemblances, but when the girl spoke, in the slightest of foreign accents, he felt the kind of astonishment one feels at a party, hearing the woman one loves talking in a stranger's tone to a stranger. It was not an uncommon occurrence: he would follow people into shops, he would wait at street corners because of a small resemblance, just as though the woman he loved was only lost and might be discovered any day in a crowd.

She said, "You came about a cake?"

He watched her closely; they had so little in common compared with the great difference, that one was alive and the other dead. He said, "A man came to see me last night—I suppose from this office."

He fumbled for words because it was just as absurd to think that this girl might be mixed up in a crime as to think of Jean—except as a victim. "I had won a cake in a raffle at your fête, but there seemed to be some mistake."

"I don't understand."

"A bomb fell before I could make out what it was he wanted to tell me."

"But no one could have come from here," she said. "What did he look like?"

"Very small and dark with twisted shoulders—practically a cripple."

"There is no one like that here."

"I thought perhaps that if I found Mrs. Bellairs." The name seemed to convey nothing. "One of the helpers at the fête."

"They were all volunteers," the girl explained. "I daresay we could find the address for you through the organizers, but is it so—important?"

A screen divided the room in two; he had imagined they were alone, but as the girl spoke a young man came round the screen. He had the same fine features as the girl: she introduced him, "This is my brother, Mr.—"

"Rowe."

"Somebody called on Mr. Rowe to ask about a cake. I don't quite understand. It seems he won it at our fête."

"Now let me see, who could that possibly be?" The young man spoke excellent English; only a certain caution and precision marked him as a foreigner. It was as if he had come from an old-fashioned family among whom it was important to speak clearly and use the correct words; his caution had an effect of charm, not of pedantry. He stood with his hand laid lightly and affectionately on his sister's shoulder, as though they formed together a Victorian family group. "Was he one of your countrymen, Mr. Rowe? In this office we are most of us foreigners, you know." He smilingly took Rowe into his confidence. "If health or nationality prevents us fighting for you, we have to do something. My sister and I are, technically, Austrian."

"This man was English."

"He must have been one of the voluntary helpers. We have so many. I don't know half of them by name. You want to return a prize, is that it? A cake?"

Rowe said cautiously, "I wanted to inquire about it."

"Well, Mr. Rowe, if I were you, I should be unscrupulous. I should just 'hang on' to the cake." When he used a colloquialism you could hear the inverted commas drop gently and apologetically round it.

"The trouble is," Rowe said, "the cake's no longer there. My house was bombed last night."

"I'm sorry. About your house, I mean. The cake can't seem very important now surely?"

They were charming, they were obviously honest, but they had caught him neatly and effectively in an inconsistency.

"I shouldn't bother," the girl said, "if I were you."

Rowe watched them, hesitating. But it is impossible to go through life without trust; that is to be imprisoned in the worst cell of all, oneself. For more than a year now Rowe had been so imprisoned—there had been no change of cell, no exercise yard, no unfamiliar warder to break the monotony of solitary confinement. A moment comes to a man when a break must be made whatever the risk. Now cautiously he tried for freedom. These two had lived through terror themselves, but they had emerged without any ugly psychological scar. He said, "As a matter of fact it wasn't simply the cake which was worrying me."

They watched him with a frank and friendly interest; you felt that in spite of the last years there was still the bloom of youth on them—they still expected life to offer them other things than pain and boredom and distrust and hate. The young man said, "Won't you sit down and tell us?" They reminded him of children who liked stories. They couldn't have accumulated more than fifty years' experience between them. He felt immeasurably older.

Rowe said, "I got the impression that whoever wanted that cake was ready to be—well, violent." He told them of the visit and the stranger's vehemence and the odd taste in his tea. The young man's very pale blue eyes sparkled with his interest and excitement. He said, "It's a fascinating story. Have you any idea who's behind it —or what? How does Mrs. Bellairs come into it?"

He wished now that he hadn't been to Mr. Rennit—these were the allies he needed, not the dingy Jones and his sceptical employer.

"Mrs. Bellairs told my fortune at the fête, and told me the weight of the cake—which wasn't the right weight."

"It's extraordinary," the young man said enthusiastically.

The girl said, "It doesn't make sense." She added almost in Mr. Rennit's words, "It was probably all a misunderstanding."

"Misunderstanding," her brother said and then dropped his inverted commas round the antiquated slang, "my eye." He turned to Rowe with an expression of glee. "Count this society, Mr. Rowe, as far as the secretary's concerned, at your service. This is really interesting." He held out his hand. "My name—our name is Hilfe. Where do we begin?"

The girl sat silent. Rowe said, "Your sister doesn't agree."

"Oh," the young man said, "she'll come round. She always does in the end. She thinks I'm a romantic. She's had to get me out of too many scrapes." He became momentarily serious. "She got me out of Austria." But nothing could damp his enthusiasm for long. "That's another story. Do we begin with Mrs. Bellairs? Have you any idea what it's all about? I'll get our grim volunteer in the next room' on the hunt," and, opening the door, he called through, "Dear Mrs. Dermody, do you think you could find the address of one of our voluntary helpers called Mrs. Bellairs?" He explained to Rowe, "The difficulty is she's probably just the friend of a friend—not a regular helper. Try Canon Topling," he suggested to Mrs. Dermody.

The greater the young man's enthusiasm, the more fantastic the whole incident became. Rowe began to see it through Mr. Rennit's eyes—Mrs. Dermody, Canon Topling . . . He said, "Perhaps after all your sister's right."

But young Hilfe swept on. "She may be, of course she may be. But how dull if she is. I'd much rather think, until we *know,* that there's some enormous conspiracy—"

Mrs. Dermody put her head in at the door and said, "Canon Topling gave me the address. It's number five Park Crescent."

"If she's a friend of Canon Topling," Rowe began and caught Miss Hilfe's eye. She gave him a secret nod as much as to say: now you're on the right track.

"Oh, but let's 'hang on' to the stranger," Hilfe said.

"There may be a thousand reasons," Miss Hilfe said.

"Surely not a thousand, Anna," her brother mocked. He asked Rowe, "Isn't there anything else you can remember which will convince her?" His keenness was more damping than her scepticism. The whole affair became a game one couldn't take seriously.

"Nothing," Rowe said.

Hilfe was at the window, looking out. He said, "Come here a moment, Mr. Rowe. Do you see that little man down there—in the shabby brown hat? He arrived just after you, and he seems to be staying. There he goes now, up and down. Pretends to light a cigarette. He does that too often. And that's the second evening paper he's bought. He never comes quite opposite, you see. It almost looks as if you are being trailed."

"I know him," Rowe said. "He's a private detective. He's being paid to keep an eye on me."

"By Jove," young Hilfe said—even his exclamations were a little Victorian—"you do take this seriously. We're allies now you know—you aren't 'holding out' on us, are you?"

"There is something I haven't mentioned." Rowe hesitated.

"Yes?" Hilfe came quickly back and with his hand again on his sister's shoulder waited with an appearance of anxiety. "Something which will wipe out Canon Topling . . . ?"

"I think there was something in the cake."

"What?"

"I don't know. But he crumbled every slice he took."

"It may have been habit," Miss Hilfe said.

"Habit," her brother teased her.

She said with sudden anger, "One of these old English characteristics you study so carefully."

Rowe tried to explain to Miss Hilfe, "It's nothing to do with me. I don't want their cake, but they tried, I'm sure they tried, to kill me. I know it sounds unlikely, now, in daylight, but if you had seen that wretched little cripple pouring in the milk, and then waiting, watching, crumbling the cake—"

"And you really believe," Miss Hilfe said, "that Canon Topling's friend—?"

"Don't listen to her," Hilfe said. "Why not Canon Topling's friend? There's no longer a thing called a criminal class. *We* can tell you that. There were lots of people in Austria you'd have said couldn't—well, do the things we saw them do. Cultured people, pleasant people, people you had sat next to at dinner."

"Mr. Rennit," Rowe said, "the head of the Orthotex Detective Agency, told me today that he'd never met a murderer. He said they were rare and not the best people."

"Why, they are dirt cheap," Hilfe said, "nowadays. I know myself at least six murderers. One was a cabinet minister, another was a heart specialist, the third a bank manager, an insurance agent—"

"Stop," Miss Hilfe said, "please stop."

"The difference," Hilfe said, "is that in these days it really pays to murder, and when a thing pays it becomes respectable. The rich abortionist becomes a gynecologist and the rich thief a bank director. Your friend is out of date." He went on explaining gently, his very pale blue eyes unshocked and unshockable. "Your old-fashioned murderer killed from fear, from hate—or even from love, Mr. Rowe—very seldom for substantial profit. None of these reasons is quite—respectable. But to murder for position—that's different, because when you've gained the position nobody has a right to criticize the means. Nobody will refuse to meet you if the position's high enough. Think of how many of your statesmen have shaken hands with Hitler. But of course to murder for fear or from love, Canon Topling wouldn't do that. If he killed his wife he'd lose his preferment," and he smiled at Rowe with a blithe innocence of what he was saying.

When he came out of what wasn't called a prison, when His Majesty's pleasure had formally and quickly run its course, it had seemed to Rowe that he had emerged into quite a different world —a secret world of assumed names, of knowing nobody, of avoiding faces, of men who leave a bar unobtrusively when other people enter; one lived where least questions were asked, in furnished rooms. It was the kind of world that people who attended garden fêtes, who went to Matins, who spent week ends in the country and played bridge for low stakes and had an account at a good grocer's, knew nothing about. It wasn't exactly a criminal world, though eddying along its dim and muted corridors you might possibly rub shoulders with genteel forgers who had never actually been charged or the corrupter of a child. One attended cinemas at ten in the morning with other men in mackintoshes who had somehow to pass the time away. One sat at home and read *The Old Curiosity Shop* all the evening. When he had first believed that someone intended to murder him, he had felt a sort of shocked indignation: the act of murder belonged to him like a personal characteristic, and not to the inhabitants of the old peaceful places from which he was an exile, and of which Mrs. Bellairs, the lady in the floppy hat, and the clergyman called Sinclair were so obviously inhabitants. The one thing a murderer should be able to count himself safe from was murder—by one of these.

But he was more shocked now at being told by a young man of great experience that there was no division between the worlds. The insect underneath the stone has a right to feel safe from the trampling superior boot.

Miss Hilfe told him, "You mustn't listen." She was watching him with what looked like sympathy. He could almost have imagined pity, as though she were able to understand. But that was impossible.

"Of course," Hilfe said easily, "I exaggerate. But all the same you have to be prepared in these days for criminals—everywhere. They call it having ideals. They'll even talk about murder being the most merciful thing."

Rowe looked quickly up, but there was no personal meaning in the pale blue theoretical eyes. "You mean the Prussians?" Rowe asked.

"Yes, if you like, the Prussians. Or the Nazis. The Fascists. The Reds. The Whites."

A telephone rang on Miss Hilfe's desk. She said, "It's Lady Dunwoody."

Hilfe, leaning quickly sideways, said, "We are so grateful for your offer, Lady Dunwoody. We can never have too many woollies. Yes, if you wouldn't mind sending them to this office, or shall we collect? You'll send your chauffeur. Thank you. Good-bye." He said to Rowe with a rather wry smile, "It's an odd way for someone of my age to fight a war, isn't it?—collecting woollies from charitable old dowagers, but it's useful, I'm allowed to do it, and it's something not to be interned. Only—you do understand, don't you?—a story like yours excites me. It seems to give one an opportunity—well, to take a more violent line." He smiled at his sister and said with affection, "Of course she calls me a romantic."

But the odd thing was she called him nothing at all. It was almost as if she not only disapproved of him, but had disowned him, wouldn't cooperate in anything—outside the woollies. She seemed to Rowe to lack her brother's charm and ease: the experience which had given him an amusing nihilistic abandon had left her brooding on some deeper more unhappy level. He felt no longer sure that they were without scars. Her brother had the ideas, but she felt them. When he looked at her it was as if his own unhappiness recognized a friend and signalled, signalled, but got no reply.

"And now," Hilfe said, "what next?"

"Leave it alone." Miss Hilfe addressed herself directly to Rowe —the signal when it did at last come was simply to say that communication was at an end.

"No, no," Hilfe said, "we can't do that. This is war."

"How do you know," Miss Hilfe said, still speaking only to Rowe, "that even if there is something behind it, it isn't just—theft, drugs, things like that?"

"I don't know," Rowe said, "and I don't care. I'm angry, that's all."

"What is your theory though?" Hilfe asked. "About the cake?"

"It might have contained a message, mightn't it?"

Both the Hilfes were silent for a moment as though that were an idea that had to be absorbed. Then Hilfe said, "I'll go with you to Mrs. Bellairs'."

"You can't leave the office, Willi," Miss Hilfe said. "I'll go with Mr. Rowe. You have an appointment."

"Oh, only with Trench. You can handle Trench for me, Anna."
He said with glee, "This is important. There may be trouble."

"We could take Mr. Rowe's detective."

"And warn the lady? He sticks out a yard. No," Hilfe said, "we
must very gently drop him. I'm used to dropping spies. It's a thing
one has learned since thirty-three."

"But I don't know what you want to say to Mr. Trench."

"Just stave him off. Say we'll settle at the beginning of the month.
You'll forgive us talking business, Mr. Rowe?"

"Why not let Mr. Rowe go alone?"

Perhaps, Rowe thought, she does after all believe there's something in it: perhaps she fears for her brother. She was saying, "You
don't both of you want to make fools of yourselves, Willi."

Hilfe ignored his sister completely. He said to Rowe, "Just a
moment while I write a note for Trench," and disappeared behind
the screen.

When they left the office together it was by another door: dropping Jones was as simple as that, for he had no reason to suppose
that his employer would try to evade him. Hilfe called a taxi, and
as they drove down the street Rowe was able to see how the shabby
figure kept his vigil, lighting yet another cigarette with his eyes
obliquely on the great ornate entrance, like a faithful hound who
will stay interminably outside his master's door. Rowe said, "I wish
we had let him know."

"Better not," Hilfe said. "We can pick him up afterwards. After
all we shan't be long," and the figure slanted out of sight as the taxi
wheeled away; he was lost among the buses and bicycles, absorbed
among all the other loitering seedy London figures, never to be
seen again by anyone who knew him.

Four: An Evening with Mrs. Bellairs

1

Mrs. Bellairs' house was a house of character: that is to say, it was
old and unrenovated, standing behind its little patch of dry and
weedy garden among the "To Let" boards on the slope of Campden Hill. A piece of statuary lay back in a thin thorny hedge, like
a large block of pumice stone, chipped and grey with neglect, and

when you rang the bell under the little early Victorian portico you seemed to héar the sound pursuing the human inhabitants into back rooms, as though what was left of life had ebbed up the passages.

The snowy-white cuffs and the snowy-white apron of the maid who opened the door came as a surprise. She was keeping up appearances as the house wasn't, though she looked nearly as old. Her face was talcumed and wrinkled and austere like a nun's.

Hilfe said, "Is Mrs. Bellairs at home?"

The old maid watched them with the kind of shrewdness people learn in convents. She said, "Have you an appointment?"

"Why, no," Hilfe said, "we were just calling. I'm a friend of Canon Topling."

"You see," the maid explained, "this is one of her evenings."

"Yes?"

"If you are not one of the group . . ."

An elderly man with a face of extraordinary nobility and thick white hair came up the path. "Good evening, sir," the maid said. "Will you come right in?" He was obviously one of the group, for she asked him into a room on the right and they heard her announce, "Dr. Forester." Then she came back to guard the door.

Hilfe said, "Perhaps if you would take my name to Mrs. Bellairs, we might join the group. Hilfe—a friend of Canon Topling."

"I'll *ask* her," the maid said dubiously.

But the result was after all favourable. Mrs. Bellairs herself swam out into the little jumbled hall. She wore a Liberty dress of shot silk and a toque and she held out both hands as though to welcome them simultaneously. "Any friend of Canon Topling," she said.

"My name is Hilfe. Of the Free Mothers Fund. And this is Mr. Rowe."

Rowe watched for a sign of recognition, but there was none. Her broad white face seemed to live in worlds beyond them.

"If you'd join our group," she said, "we welcome newcomers. So long as there's no settled hostility."

"Oh, none, none," Hilfe said.

She swayed in front of them, like a figurehead, into a drawing room all orange curtain and blue cushion as though it had been furnished once and for all in the twenties. Blackout globes made the room dim like an oriental café. There were indications among the trays and occasional tables that it was Mrs. Bellairs who had supplied the fête with some of its Benares work.

Half a dozen people were in the room, and one of them immediately attracted Rowe's attention—a tall broad black-haired man; he couldn't think why until he realized that it was his normality which stood out. "Mr. Cost," Mrs. Bellairs was saying, "this is—"

"Mr. Rowe." Hilfe supplied the name, and the introductions went round with a prim formality. One wondered why he was here, in the company of Dr. Forester with his weak mouth and his nobility; Miss Pantil, a dark young-middle-aged woman with black beads and a hungry eye; Mr. Newey—"Mr. Frederick Newey"— Mrs. Bellairs made a proud point of the name—who wore sandals and no socks and had a grey shock of hair; Mr. Maude, a short-sighted young man who kept as close as he could to Mr. Newey and fed him devotedly with thin bread and butter; and Collier who obviously belonged to a different class and had worked himself in with some skill. He was patronized, but at the same time he was admired. He was a breath of the larger life and they were interested. He had been a hotel waiter and a tramp and a stoker, and he had published a book—so Mrs. Bellairs whispered to Rowe—of the most fascinating poetry, rough but spiritual. "He uses words," Mrs. Bellairs said, "that have never been used in poetry before." There seemed to be some antagonism between him and Mr. Newey.

All this scene became clear to Rowe over the cups of very weak China tea which were brought round by the austere parlour maid.

"And what," Mrs. Bellairs asked, "do you do, Mr. Rowe?" She had been explaining Collier in an undertone—calling him plain Collier because he was a Player and not a Gentleman.

"Oh," Rowe said, watching her over his teacup, trying to make out the meaning of her group, trying in vain to see her in a dangerous role, "I sit and think."

It seemed to be the right as well as the truthful answer. He was encircled by Mrs. Bellairs' enthusiasm as though by a warm arm. "I shall call you our philosopher," she said. "We have our poet, our critic—"

"What is Mr. Cost?"

"He is Big Business," Mrs. Bellairs said. "He works in the City. I call him our mystery man. I sometimes feel he is a hostile influence."

"And Miss Pantil?"

"She has quite extraordinary powers of painting the inner world. She sees it as colours and circles, and sometimes oblongs, rhythmical arrangements . . ."

It was fantastic to believe that Mrs. Bellairs could have anything to do with crime—or any of her group. He would have made some excuse and gone if it had not been for Hilfe. These people, whatever Hilfe might say, did not belong under the stone with him.

He asked vaguely, "You meet here every week?"

"Always on Wednesdays. Of course we have very little time because of the raids. Mr. Newey's wife likes him to be back at Welwyn before the raids start. And perhaps that's why the results are bad. They can't be driven, you know." She smiled. "We can't promise a stranger anything."

He couldn't make out what it was all about. Hilfe seemed to have left the room with Cost. Mrs. Bellairs said, "Ah, the conspirators. Mr. Cost is always thinking up a test."

Rowe tried out a question tentatively. "And the results are sometimes bad?"

"So bad I could cry—if I knew at the time. But there are other times—oh, you'd be surprised how good they are."

A telephone was ringing in another room. Mrs. Bellairs said, "Who can that naughty person be? All my friends know they mustn't ring me on Wednesdays."

The old parlour maid had entered. She said with distaste, "Somebody is calling Mr. Rowe."

Rowe said, "But I can't understand it. Nobody knows—"

"Would you mind," Mrs. Bellairs said, "being very quick?"

Rowe left a track of disapproving silence behind him: they watched him following the maid. He felt as though he had made a scene in church and was now being conducted away. He could hear behind him nothing but the tinkle of teacups being laid away.

Hilfe was in the hall, talking earnestly to Cost. He asked, "For you?" He too was discomposed.

Rowe thought, Perhaps it's Mr. Rennit, but how can he have found me? Or Jones? He leaned across Mrs. Bellairs' desk in a small packed dining room. He said, "Hullo," and wondered again how he could have been traced. "Hullo."

But it wasn't Mr. Rennit. At first he didn't recognize the voice— a woman's. "Mr. Rowe?"

"Yes."

"Are you alone?"

"Yes."

The voice was blurred: it was as if a handkerchief had been stretched across the mouthpiece. She couldn't know, he thought, that there were no other women's voices to confuse with hers.

"Please will you leave the house as soon as you can."

"It's Miss Hilfe, isn't it?"

The voice said impatiently, "Yes. Yes. All right. It is."

"Do you want to speak to your brother?"

"Please do not tell him. And leave. Leave quickly."

He was amused for a moment. The idea of any danger in Mrs. Bellairs' company was absurd. He realized how nearly he had been converted to Mr. Rennit's way of thinking. Then he remembered that Miss Hilfe had shared those views. Something had converted her—the opposite way. He said, "What about your brother?"

"If you go away, he'll go too."

The dimmed urgent voice fretted at his nerves. He found himself edging round the desk so that he could face the door, and then he moved again because his back was to a window. "Why don't you tell this to your brother?"

"He would want to stay all the more." That was true. He wondered how thin the walls were. The room was uncomfortably crowded with trashy furniture: one wanted space to move about—the voice was disturbingly convincing—to manœuvre in. He said, "Is Jones still outside—the detective?"

There was a long pause: presumably she had gone to the window. Then the voice sprang at him unexpectedly loud—she had taken away the handkerchief. "There's nobody there."

"Are you sure?"

"Nobody."

He felt deserted and indignant. What business had Jones to leave his watch? Somebody was approaching down the passage. He said, "I must ring off."

"They'll try to get you in the dark," the voice said, and then the door opened. It was Hilfe.

He said, "Come along. They are all waiting. Who was it?"

Rowe said, "When you were writing your note I left a message with Mrs. Dermody, in case anyone wanted me urgently."

"And somebody did?"

"It was Jones—the detective."

"Jones?" Hilfe said.

"Yes."

"And Jones had important news?"

"Not exactly. He was worried at losing me. But Mr. Rennit wants me at his office."

"The faithful Rennit. We'll go straight there—afterwards."

"After what?"

Hilfe's eyes expressed pleasure, excitement, and malice. "Something we can't miss—at any price." He added in a lower voice, "I begin to believe we were wrong. It's lots of fun, but it's not—dangerous."

He laid a confiding hand on Rowe's arm and gently urged him, "Keep a straight face, Mr. Rowe, if you can. You mustn't laugh. She *is* a friend of Canon Topling."

The room when they came back was obviously arranged for something. A rough circle had been formed with the chairs, and everyone had an air of impatience politely subdued. "Just sit down, Mr. Rowe, next to Mr. Cost," said Mrs. Bellairs, "and then we'll turn out the lights."

In nightmares one knows the cupboard door will open; one knows that what will emerge is horrible; one doesn't know what it is. . . .

Mrs. Bellairs said again, "If you'll just sit down, so that we can turn out the light."

He said, "I'm sorry. I've got to go."

"Oh, you can't go now," Mrs. Bellairs cried. "Can he, Mr. Hilfe?"

Rowe looked at Hilfe, but the pale blue eyes sparkled back at him without understanding. "Of course he needn't go," Hilfe said. "We'll both wait. What did we come for?" An eyelid momentarily flickered as Mrs. Bellairs with a gesture of appalling coyness locked the door and dropped the key down her blouse and shook her fingers at them. "We always lock the door," she said, "to satisfy Mr. Cost."

In a dream you cannot escape: the feet are leaden-weighted; you cannot stir from before the ominous door which almost imperceptibly moves. It is the same in life: sometimes it is more difficult to make a scene than to die. A memory came back to him of someone else who wasn't certain, wouldn't make a scene, gave herself sadly up and took the milk. . . . He moved through the circle and sat down on Cost's left like a criminal taking his place in an identity parade. On his own left side was Miss Pantil. Dr. Forester was on one side of Mrs. Bellairs and Hilfe on the other. He hadn't time to see how the others were distributed before the light went out. "Now," Mrs. Bellairs said, "we'll all hold hands."

The blackout curtains had been drawn and the darkness was almost complete. Cost's hand in his felt hot and clammy, and Miss Pantil's hot and dry. This was the first séance he had ever attended, but it wasn't the spirits he feared. He wished Hilfe was beside him, and he was aware all the time of the dark empty space of the room behind his back in which anything might happen. He tried to loosen his hands, but they were firmly gripped. There was complete silence in the room: a drop of sweat formed above his right eye and trickled down; he couldn't brush it away, it hung on his eyelid and tickled him. Somewhere in another room a gramophone began to play.

It played and played—something sweet and onomatopœic by Mendelssohn, full of waves breaking in echoing caverns. There was a pause and the needle was switched back and the melody began again. The same waves broke interminably into the same hollow. Over and over again. Underneath the music he became aware of breathing on all sides of him—all kinds of anxieties, suspenses, excitements controlling the various lungs. Miss Pantil's had an odd dry whistle in it, Cost's was heavy and regular, but not so heavy as another breath which laboured in the dark, he couldn't tell whose. All the time he listened and waited. Would he hear a step behind him and have time to snatch away his hands? He no longer doubted at all the urgency of that warning— "They'll try to get you in the dark." This was danger: this suspense was what somebody else had experienced, watching from day to day his pity grow to the monstrous proportions necessary to action.

"Yes," a voice called suddenly, "yes, I can't hear," and Miss Pantil's breath whistled and Mendelssohn's waves moaned and withdrew. Very far away a taxi horn cried through an empty world.

"Speak louder," the voice said; it was Mrs. Bellairs' with a difference: a Mrs. Bellairs drugged with an idea, with an imagined contact beyond the little dark constricted world in which they sat. He wasn't interested in any of that: it was a human movement he waited for. Mrs. Bellairs said in a husky voice, "One of you is an enemy. He won't let it come through." Something—a chair, a table—creaked, and Rowe's fingers instinctively strained against Miss Pantil's. That wasn't a spirit. That was the human agency which shook tambourines or scattered flowers or imitated a child's touch upon the cheek—it was the dangerous element, but his hands were held.

"There is an enemy here," the voice said. "Somebody who doesn't believe, whose motives are evil." Rowe could feel Cost's fingers tighten round his. He wondered whether Hilfe was still completely oblivious to what was happening; he wanted to shout a plea for help, but convention held him as firmly as Cost's hand. Again a

board creaked. Why all this mummery, he thought, if they are all
in it? But perhaps they were not all in it. For anything he knew he
was surrounded by friends—but he didn't know which they were.

"Arthur."

He pulled at the hands holding him: that wasn't Mrs. Bellairs'
voice.

"Arthur."

The flat hopeless voice might really have come from beneath the
heavy graveyard slab.

"Arthur, why did you kill . . . ?" The voice moaned away into
silence, and he struggled against the hands. It wasn't that he recognized the voice; it was no more his wife's than any woman's dying
out in infinite hopelessness, pain, and reproach; it was that the voice
had recognized him. A light moved near the ceiling, feeling its way
along the walls, and he cried, "Don't. Don't."

"Arthur," the voice whispered; he forgot everything, he no
longer listened for secretive movements, the creak of boards. He
simply implored, "Stop it, please stop it," and felt Cost rise from
the seat beside him and pull at his hand and then release it, throw
the hand violently away as though it was something he didn't like
to hold. Even Miss Pantil let him go, and he heard Hilfe say, "This
isn't funny. Put on the light."

It dazzled him, going suddenly on. They all sat there with joined
hands watching him: he had broken the circle—only Mrs. Bellairs
seemed to see nothing, with her head down and her eyes closed
and her breathing heavy. "Well," Hilfe said, trying to raise a laugh,
"that was certainly quite an act," but Mr. Newey said, "Cost. Look
at Cost," and Rowe looked with all the others at his neighbour. He
was taking no more interest in anything, leaning forward across the
table with his face sunk on the French polish.

"Get a doctor," Hilfe said.

"I'm a doctor," Dr. Forester said. He released the hands on either
side of him, and everyone became conscious of sitting there like
children playing a game and surreptitiously let each other go. He
said gently, "A doctor's no good, I'm afraid. The only thing to do is
call the police."

Mrs. Bellairs had half woken up and sat with leery eyes and her
tongue a little protruding.

"It must be his heart," Mr. Newey said. "Couldn't stand the excitement."

"I'm afraid not," Dr. Forester said, "he has been murdered." His old noble face was bent above the body; one long sensitive delicate hand dabbled and came up stained, like a beautiful insect that feeds incongruously on carrion.

"Impossible," Mr. Newey said, "the door was locked."

"It's a pity," Dr. Forester said, "but there's a very simple explanation of that. One of us did it."

"But we were all," Hilfe said, "holding—" Then they all looked at Rowe.

"He snatched away his hand," Miss Pantil said.

Dr. Forester said softly, "I'm not going to touch the body again before the police come. Cost was stabbed with a kind of schoolboy's knife."

Rowe put his hand quickly to an empty pocket and saw a roomful of eyes noting the movement.

"We must get Mrs. Bellairs out of this," Dr. Forester said. "Any séance is a strain, but this one—" He and Hilfe between them raised the turbaned bulk; the hand which had so delicately dabbled in Cost's blood retrieved the key of the room with equal delicacy. "The rest of you," Dr. Forester said, "had better stay here, I think. I'll telephone to Notting Hill police station, and then we'll both be back."

For a long while there was silence after they had gone; nobody looked at Rowe, but Miss Pantil had slid her chair well away from him, so that he now sat alone beside the corpse as though they were two friends who had got together at a party. Presently Mr. Newey said, "I'll never catch my train unless they hurry." Anxiety fought with horror—any moment the sirens might go—he caressed his sandalled foot across his knee, and young Maude said hotly, "I don't know why *you* should stay," glaring at Rowe.

It occurred to Rowe that he had not said one word to defend himself: the sense of guilt for a different crime stopped his mouth. Besides, what could he, a stranger, say to Miss Pantil, Mr. Newey, and Maude to convince them that in fact it was one of their friends who had murdered. He took a quick look at Cost, half expecting him to come alive again and laugh at them—"one of my tests"— but nobody could have been deader than Cost was now. He thought: somebody here *has* killed him—it was fantastic, more fantastic really than that he should have done it himself. After all he belonged to the region of murder—he was a native of that country. As the police will know, he thought, as the police will know.

The door opened and Hilfe returned. He said, "Dr. Forester is looking after Mrs. Bellairs. I have telephoned to the police." His eyes were saying something to Rowe which Rowe couldn't understand. Rowe thought, I must see him alone, surely he can't believe . . .

He said, "Would anybody object if I went to the lavatory and was sick?"

Miss Pantil said, "I don't think anybody ought to leave this room till the police come."

"I think," Hilfe said, "somebody should go with you. As a formality of course."

"Why beat about the bush?" Miss Pantil said. "Whose knife is it?"

"Perhaps Mr. Newey," Hilfe said, "wouldn't mind going with Mr. Rowe."

"I won't be drawn in," Newey said. "This has nothing to do with me. I only want to catch my train."

"Perhaps I had better go then," Hilfe said, "if you will trust me." No one objected.

The lavatory was on the first floor. They could hear from the landing the steady soothing rhythm of Dr. Forester's voice in Mrs. Bellairs' bedroom. "I'm all right," Rowe whispered. "But, Hilfe, I didn't do it."

There was something shocking in the sense of exhilaration Hilfe conveyed at a time like this. "Of course you didn't," he said. "This is the real thing."

"But why? Who did it?"

"I don't know, but I'm going to find out." He put his hand on Rowe's arm with a friendliness that was very comforting, urging him into the lavatory and locking the door behind them. "Only, old fellow, you must be off out of this. They'll hang you if they can. Anyway they'll shut you up for weeks. It's so convenient for *them.*"

"What can I do? It's my knife."

"They are devils, aren't they?" Hilfe said with the same lighthearted relish he might have used for a children's clever prank. "We've just got to keep you out of the way till Mr. Rennit and I— By the way, better tell me who rang you up."

"It was your sister."

"My sister?" Hilfe grinned at him. "Good for her. She must have got hold of something. I wonder just where. She warned you, did she?"

"Yes, but I was not to tell you."

"Never mind that. I shan't eat her, shall I?" The pale blue eyes became suddenly lost in speculation.

Rowe tried to recall them. "Where can I go?"

"Oh, just underground," Hilfe said casually. He seemed in no hurry at all. "It's the fashion of our decade. Communists are always doing it. Don't you know how?"

"This isn't a joke."

"Listen," Hilfe said. "The end we are working for isn't a joke, but if we are going to keep our nerve we've got to keep our sense of humour. You see *they* have none. Give me only a week. Keep out of the way as long as that."

"The police will be here soon."

Hilfe said, "It's only a small drop from this window to the flower-bed. It's nearly dark outside and in ten minutes the sirens will be going. Thank God, one can set one's clock by them."

"And you?"

"Pull the plug as you open the window. No one will hear you then. Wait till the cistern refills, then pull the plug again and knock me out 'good and hard.' It's the best alibi you can give me. After all, I'm an enemy alien."

Five: Between Sleeping and Waking

1

There are dreams which belong only partly to the unconscious: these are the dreams we remember so vividly on waking that we deliberately continue them, and so fall asleep again and wake and sleep and the dream goes on without interruption, with a thread of logic the pure dream doesn't possess.

Rowe was exhausted and frightened: he had made his way half across London while the nightly raid got under way. It was an empty London with only occasional bursts of noise and activity; an umbrella shop was burning at the corner of Oxford Street; in Wardour Street he walked through a cloud of grit; a man with a grey dusty face leaned against a wall and laughed and a warden said sharply, "That's enough now. It's nothing to laugh about." None of these things mattered. They were like something written about:

they didn't belong to his own life and he paid them no attention. But he had to find a bed, and so somewhere south of the river he obeyed Hilfe's advice and at last went underground.

He lay on the upper tier of a canvas bunk and dreamed that he was walking up a long hot road near Trumpington, scuffing the white chalk dust with his shoe caps. Then he was having tea on the lawn at home behind the red brick wall, and his mother was lying back in a garden chair, eating a cucumber sandwich. A bright blue croquet ball lay at her feet, and she was smiling and paying him the half-attention a parent pays a child. The summer lay all round them, and evening was coming on. He was saying, "Mother, I murdered her . . ." and his mother said, "Don't be silly, dear. Have one of these nice sandwiches."

"But, Mother," he said, "I did. I did." It seemed terribly important to him to convince her: if she were convinced, she could do something about it, she could tell him it didn't matter and it would matter no longer, but he had to convince her first. But she turned her head away and called out in a little vexed voice to someone who wasn't there, "You *must* remember to dust the piano."

"Mother, please listen to me," but he suddenly realized that he was a child; so how could he make her believe? He was not eight years old, he could see the nursery window on the second floor with the bars across, and presently the old nurse would put her face to the glass and signal to him to come in. "Mother," he said, "I've killed my wife, and the police want me." His mother smiled and shook her head and said, "My little boy couldn't kill anyone."

Time was short: from the other end of the long peaceful lawn, beyond the croquet hoops and out of the shadow of the great somnolent pine, came the vicar's wife, carrying a basket of apples. Before she reached them he must convince his mother, but he had only childish words. "I have. I have."

His mother leaned back, smiling in the deck chair, and said, "My little boy wouldn't hurt a—beetle." (It was a way she had, always to get the conventional phrase just wrong.)

"But that's why," he said. "That's why," and his mother waved to the vicar's wife and said, "It's a dream, dear, a nasty dream."

He woke up to the dim lurid underground place—somebody had tied a red silk scarf over the bare globe to shield it. All along the walls the bodies lay two deep, while outside the raid rumbled and receded. This was a quiet night: any raid which happened a mile away wasn't a raid at all. An old man across the aisle snored, and at the end of the shelter two lovers lay on a mattress with their hands and knees touching.

Rowe thought, This would be a dream too to her; she wouldn't believe it. She had died before the first Great War, when airplanes —strange crates of wood—just staggered across the Channel. She could no more have imagined this than that her small son in his brown corduroy knickers and his blue jersey with his pale serious face—he could see himself like a stranger in the yellowing snapshots of her album—should grow up to be a murderer..Lying on his back, he caught the dream and held it—pushed the vicar's wife back into the shadow of the pine—and argued with his mother.

"This isn't real life any more," he said. "Tea on the lawn, evensong, croquet, the old ladies calling, the gentle unmalicious gossip, the gardener trundling the wheelbarrow full of leaves and grass. People write about it as if it still went on; lady novelists describe it over and over again in books of the month, but it's not there any more."

His mother smiled at him in a scared way but let him talk: he was the master of the dream now. He said, "I'm wanted for a murder I didn't do. People want to kill me because I know too much. I'm hiding underground, and up above the Germans are methodically smashing London to bits all round me. You remember St. Clement's—the bells of St. Clement's? They've smashed that—St. James's, Piccadilly, the Burlington Arcade, Garland's Hotel where we stayed for the pantomime, Maples, and John Lewis. It sounds like a thriller, doesn't it?—but the thrillers are like life—more like life than you are, this lawn, your sandwiches, that pine. You used to laugh at the books Miss Savage read—about spies, and murders, and violence, and wild motorcar chases, but, dear, that's real life: it's what we've all made of the world since you died. I'm your little Arthur who wouldn't hurt a beetle and I'm a murderer too. The world has been remade by William Le Queux." He couldn't bear the frightened eyes which he had printed himself on the cement wall: he put his mouth to the steel frame of his bunk and kissed the white cold cheek. "My dear, my dear, my dear. I'm glad you are dead. Only do you know about it? Do you know?" He was filled with horror at the thought of what a child becomes, and what the dead must feel watching the change from innocence to guilt and powerless to stop it.

"Why, it's a madhouse," his mother cried.

"Oh, it's much quieter there," he said. "I know. They put me in one for a time. Everybody was very kind there. They made me librarian." He tried to express clearly the difference between the madhouse and this. "Everybody in the place was very—reasonable." He said fiercely, as though he hated her instead of loving her, "Let me lend you the *History of Contemporary Society*. It's in hundreds of volumes, but most of them are sold in cheap editions: *Death in Piccadilly, The Ambassador's Diamonds, The Theft of the Naval Papers, Diplomacy, Seven Days' Leave, The Four Just Men . . .*"

He had worked the dream to suit himself, but now the dream began to regain control. He was no longer on the lawn; he was in the field behind the house where the donkey grazed which used to take their laundry to the other end of the village on Mondays. He was playing in a haystack with the vicar's son and a strange boy with a foreign accent and a dog called Spot. The dog caught a rat and tossed it, and the rat tried to crawl away with a broken back, and the dog made little playful excited rushes. Suddenly he couldn't bear the sight of the rat's pain any more: he picked up a cricket bat and struck the rat on the head over and over again; he wouldn't stop for fear it was still alive, though he heard his nurse call out, "Stop it, Arthur! How can you? Stop it!" and all the time Hilfe watched him with exhilaration. When he stopped he wouldn't look at the rat: he ran away across the field and hid. But you always had to come out of hiding some time, and presently his nurse was saying, "I won't tell your mother, but don't you ever do it again. Why, she thinks you wouldn't hurt a fly. What came over you, I don't know." Not one of them guessed that what had come over him was the horrible and horrifying emotion of pity.

That was partly dream and partly memory, but the next was altogether dream. He lay on his side, breathing heavily, while the big guns opened up in North London, and his mind wandered again freely in that strange world where the past and future leave equal traces, and the geography may belong to twenty years ago or to next year. He was waiting for someone at a gate in a lane: over a high hedge came the sound of laughter and the dull thud of tennis balls, and between the leaves he could see mothlike movements of white dresses. It was evening; and soon it would be too dark to play and someone would come out, and he waited dumb with love. His heart beat with a boy's excitement, but it was the despair of a grown man that he felt when a stranger touched his shoulder and said, "Take him away." He didn't wake. This time he was in the main street of a small country town where he had sometimes when a boy stayed with an elder sister of his mother's. He was standing outside the innyard of the King's Arms, and up the yard he could see the lit windows of the barn in which dances were held on Saturday nights. He had a pair of pumps under his arm and he was waiting for a girl much older than himself who would presently come out of her cloakroom and take his arm and go up the yard with him. All the next few hours were with him in the street: the small crowded hall full of the familiar peaceful faces—the chemist and his wife, the daughters of the headmaster, the bank manager, and the dentist with his blue chin and his look of experience; the paper streamers of blue and green and scarlet, the small local orchestra, the sense of a life good and quiet and enduring, with only the gentle tug of impatience and young passion to disturb it for the while and make is doubly dear forever after. And then without warning the dream twisted towards nightmare: somebody was crying in the dark with terror—not the young woman he was waiting there to meet, whom he hadn't yet dared to kiss and probably never would, but someone whom he knew better even than his parents, who belonged to a different world altogether, to the sad world of shared love. A policeman stood at his elbow and said in a woman's voice, "You had better join our little group," and urged him remorselessly towards a urinal where a rat bled to death in the slate trough. The music had stopped, the lights had gone, and he couldn't remember why he had come to this dark vile corner where even the ground whined when he pressed it as if it had learned the trick of suffering. He said, "Please let me go away from here," and the policeman said, "Where do you want to go to, dear?" He said, "Home," and the policeman said, "This is home. There isn't anywhere else at all," and whenever he tried to move his feet the earth whined back at him: he couldn't move an inch without causing pain.

He woke and the sirens were sounding the All Clear. One or two people in the shelter sat up for a moment to listen, but then they lay down again. Nobody moved to go home: this was their home now. They were quite accustomed to sleeping underground; it had become as much part of life as the Saturday night film or the Sunday service had ever been. This was the world *they* knew.

Six: Out of Touch

1

Rowe had breakfast in an A.B.C. in Clapham High Street. Boards had taken the place of windows and the top floor had gone; it was like a shack put up in an earthquake town for relief work. For the enemy had done a lot of damage in Clapham. London was no longer one great city; it was a collection of small towns. People went to Hampstead or St. John's Wood for a quiet week end, and if you lived in Holborn you hadn't time between the sirens to visit friends as far away as Kensington. So special characteristics developed, and in Clapham, where day raids were frequent, there was a hunted look which was absent from Westminster, where the night raids were heavier but the shelters were better. The waitress who brought Rowe's toast and coffee looked jumpy and pallid, as if she had lived too much on the run: she had an air of listening whenever gears shrieked. Grey's Inn and Russell Square were noted for a more reckless spirit, but only because they had the day to recover in.

The night raid, the papers said, had been on a small scale. A number of bombs had been dropped, and there had been a number of casualties, some of them fatal. The morning communiqué was like the closing ritual of a midnight Mass. The sacrifice was complete and the papers pronounced in calm invariable words the *Ite Missa Est*. Not even in the smallest type under a single headline was there any reference to an "Alleged Murder at a Séance." Nobody troubled about single deaths. Rowe felt a kind of indignation. He had made the headlines once, but his own disaster if it had happened now would have been given no space at all. He had almost a sense of desertion; nobody was troubling to pursue so insignificant a case in the middle of a daily massacre. Perhaps a few elderly men in the C.I.D. who were too old to realize how the world had passed them by were still allowed by patient and kindly superiors to busy themselves in little rooms with the trivialities of a murder. They probably wrote minutes to each other; they might even be allowed to visit the scene of the "crime," but he could hardly believe that the results of their inquiries were read with more interest than the

scribblings of those eccentric clergymen who were still arguing
about evolution in country vicarages. "Old So-and-so," he could
imagine a senior officer saying, "poor old thing, we let him have a
few murder cases now and then. In his day, you know, we used
to pay quite a lot of attention to murder, and it makes him feel that
he's still of use. The results— Oh, well, of course, he never dreams
that we haven't time to read his reports."

Rowe, sipping his coffee, seeking over and over again for the
least paragraph, felt a kinship with the detective inspectors, the Big
Five, *My Famous Cases:* he was a murderer and old-fashioned; he
belonged to their world, and whoever had murdered Cost belonged
there too. He felt a slight resentment against Willi Hilfe, who
treated murder as a joke with a tang to it. But Hilfe's sister hadn't
treated it as a joke: she had warned him, she had talked as if death
were still a thing that mattered. Like a lonely animal, he scented the
companionship of his own kind.

The pale waitress kept an eye on him: he had had no chance of
shaving, so that he looked like one of those who leave without
paying. It was astonishing what a single night in a public shelter
could do to you; he could smell disinfectant on his clothes as
though he had spent the night in a workhouse infirmary.

He paid his bill and asked the waitress, "Have you a telephone?"
She indicated one near the cash desk, and he dialled Rennit. It was
risky but something had to be done. Of course the hour was too
early. He could hear the bell ringing uselessly in the empty room,
and he wondered whether the sausage roll still lay on the saucer
beside the telephone. It was always questionable in these days
whether a telephone bell would ring at all, because overnight an
office might have ceased to exist. He knew now that part of the
world was the same: Orthotex still stood.

He went back to his table and ordered another coffee and some
notepaper. The waitress regarded him with increasing suspicion.
Even in a crumbling world the conventions held: to order again
after payment was unorthodox, but to ask for notepaper was continental. She could give him a leaf from her order pad, that was
all. Conventions were far more rooted than morality: he had himself found that it was easier to allow oneself to be murdered than
to break up a social gathering. He began to write carefully in a
spidery hand an account of everything that had happened. Something had got to be done; he wasn't going to remain permanently
in hiding for a crime he hadn't committed, while the real criminals

got away with—whatever it was they were trying to get away with. In his account he left out Hilfe's name—you never knew what false ideas the police might get and he didn't want his only ally put behind bars. He was already deciding to post his narrative straight to Scotland Yard.

When he had finished it he read it over while the waitress watched: the story was a terribly thin one—a cake, a visitor, a taste he thought he remembered, until you got to Cost's body and all the evidence pointing to him. Perhaps after all he would do better not to post it to the police, but rather to some friend. But he had no friend, unless he counted Hilfe—or Rennit. He made for the door and the waitress stopped him. "You haven't paid for your coffee."

"I'm sorry. I forgot."

She took the money with an air of triumph: she had been right all the time. She watched him, through the window from between the empty cake stands, making his uncertain way up Clapham High Street.

Promptly at nine o'clock he rang again, from close by Stockwell Station, and again the empty room drummed on his ear. By nine-fifteen when he rang a third time Mr. Rennit had come in. He heard his sharp anxious voice saying, "Yes. Who's there?"

"This is Rowe."

"What have you done with Jones?" Mr. Rennit accused him.

"I left him yesterday," Rowe said, "outside—"

"He hasn't come back," Mr. Rennit said.

"Maybe he's shadowing—"

"I owe him a week's wages. He said he'd be back last night. It's not natural." Mr. Rennit wailed up the phone, "Jones wouldn't stay away with me owing him money."

"Worse things have happened than that."

"Jones is my right arm," Mr. Rennit said. "What have you done with him?"

"I went and saw Mrs. Bellairs—"

"That's neither here nor there. I want Jones."

"And a man was killed."

"What?"

"And the police think I murdered him."

There was another wail up the line. The small shifty man was being carried out of his depth: all through his life he had swum safely about among his prickly little adulteries, his compromising letters, but the tide was washing him out to where the bigger fishes hunted. He moaned, "I never wanted to take up your case—"

"You've got to advise me, Rennit. I'll come and see you."

"No." He could hear the breath catch down the line. The voice imperceptibly altered. "When?"

"At ten o'clock. Rennit, are you still there?" He had to explain to somebody. "I didn't do it, Rennit. You must believe that. I don't make a habit of murder." He always bit on the word murder as you bite a sore spot on the tongue: he never used the word without self-accusation. The law had taken a merciful view; himself he took the merciless one. Perhaps if they had hanged him he would have found excuses for himself between the trapdoor and the bottom of the drop, but they had given him a lifetime to analyze his motives in.

He analyzed now—an unshaven man in dusty clothes sitting in the Tube between Stockwell and Tottenham Court Road. (He had to go a roundabout route because the Tube had been closed at many stations.) The dreams of the previous night had set his mind in reverse. He remembered himself twenty years ago, daydreaming and in love: he remembered without self-pity, as one might watch the development of a biological specimen. He had in those days imagined himself capable of extraordinary heroisms and endurances which would make the girl he loved forget the awkward hands and the spotty chin of adolescence. Everything had seemed possible. One could laugh at daydreams, but so long as you had the capacity to daydream there was a chance that you might develop some of the qualities of which you dreamed. It was like the religious discipline: words however emptily repeated can in time form a habit, a kind of unnoticed sediment at the bottom of the mind, until one day to your own surprise you find yourself acting on the belief you thought you didn't believe in. Since the death of his wife Rowe had never daydreamed; all through the trial he had never even dreamed of an acquittal. It was as if that side of the brain had been dried up; he was no longer capable of sacrifice, courage, virtue, because he no longer dreamed of them. He was aware of the loss: the world had dropped a dimension and become paper thin. He wanted to dream, but all he could practice now was despair, and the kind of cunning which warned him to approach Mr. Rennit with circumspection.

2

Nearly opposite Mr. Rennit's was an auction room which specialized in books. It was possible from before the shelves nearest the door to keep an eye on the entrance to Mr. Rennit's block. The weekly auction was to take place next day, and visitors flowed in with catalogues; an unshaven chin and a wrinkled suit were not out of place here. A man with a ragged moustache and an out-at-elbows jacket, the pockets bulging with sandwiches, followed him in and looked carefully through a folio volume of landscape gardening; a bishop—or he might have been a dean—was examining a set of the Waverley Novels; a big white beard brushed the libidinous pages of an illustrated Brantôme. Nobody here was standardized; in teashops and theatres people are cut to the pattern of their environment, but in this auction room the goods were too various to appeal to any one type. Here was pornography—eighteenth-century French with beautiful little steel engravings celebrating the copulations of elegant overclothed people on Pompadour couches; here were all the Victorian novelists, the memoirs of obscure pig-stickers, the eccentric philosophies and theologies of the seventeenth century—Newton on the geographical position of Hell, and Jeremiah Whiteley on the Path of Perfection. There was a smell of neglected books, of the straw from packing cases, and of clothes which had been too often rained upon. Standing by the shelves containing lots one to thirty-five, Rowe was able to see anyone who came in or out by the door Mr. Rennit used.

Just on the level of his eyes was a Roman missal of no particular value, included in lot twenty with religious books various. A big round clock which itself had once formed part of an auction, as you could tell from the torn label below the dial, pointed 9:45 above the auctioneer's desk. Rowe opened the missal at random, keeping three-quarters of his attention for the house across the street. The missal was ornamented with ugly, coloured capitals: oddly enough it was the only thing that spoke of war in the old quiet room. Open it where you would, you came on prayers for deliverance, the angry nations, the unjust, the wicked, the adversary like a roaring lion—the words stuck out between the decorated borders like cannon out of a flowerbed. "Let not man prevail," he read—and the truth of the appeal chimed like music. For in all the world outside that room man had indeed prevailed; he had himself prevailed. It wasn't only evil men who did these things. Courage smashes a cathedral, endurance lets a city starve, pity kills . . . we are trapped and betrayed by our virtues. It might be that whoever killed Cost had for that instant given his goodness rein, and Rennit, perhaps for the first time in his life, was behaving like a good citizen by betraying his client. You couldn't mistake the police officer who had taken his stand behind a newspaper just outside the auction room.

He was reading the *Daily Mirror*. Rowe could see the print over his shoulder with Zec's cartoon filling most of the page. Once, elusively, from an upper window Mr. Rennit peered anxiously out and withdrew. The clock in the auction room said five minutes to ten. The grey day full of last night's debris and the smell of damp plaster crept on. Even Mr. Rennit's desertion made Rowe feel a degree more abandoned.

There had been a time when he had friends: not many because he was not gregarious, but for that very reason in his few friendships he had plunged deeply. At school there had been three; they had shared hopes, biscuits, measureless ambitions, but now he couldn't remember their names or their faces. Once he had been addressed suddenly in Piccadilly Circus by an extraordinary grey-haired man with a flower in his buttonhole and a double-breasted waistcoat and an odd finicky manner, an air of uncertain and rather seedy prosperity. "Why, if it isn't Boojie!" the stranger said and led the way to the bar of the Piccadilly Hotel, while Rowe sought in vain for some figure in the lower fourth—in black Sunday trousers or football shorts, inky or mudstained—who might be connected with this overplausible man who now tried unsuccessfully to borrow a fiver, then slid away to the gents and was no more seen, leaving the bill for Boojie to pay.

More recent friends he had had, of course: perhaps half a dozen. Then he married and his friends became his wife's friends even more than his own—Tom Curtis, Crooks, Perry, and Vane. Naturally they had faded away after his arrest. Only poor silly Henry Wilcox continued to stand by, because, he said, "I know you are innocent. You wouldn't hurt a fly"—that ominous phrase which had been said about him too often. He remembered how Wilcox had looked when he said, "But I'm not innocent. I did kill her." After that there wasn't even Wilcox or his small domineering wife who played hockey. (Their mantelpiece was crowded with the silver trophies of her prowess.)

The plain-clothes man looked impatient. He had obviously read every word of his paper because it was still open at the same place. The clock said five past ten. Rowe closed his catalogue, after marking a few lots at random, and walked out into the street. The plain-clothes man said, "Excuse me," and Rowe's heart missed a beat.

"Yes?"

"I've come out without a match."

"You can keep the box," Rowe said.

"I couldn't do that, not in these days." He looked over Rowe's shoulder, up the street to the ruins of the Safe Deposit, where safes stood about like the aboveground tombs in Latin cemeteries, then followed with his eye a middle-aged clerk trailing his umbrella past Rennit's door.

"Waiting for someone?" Rowe asked.

"Oh, just a friend," the detective said clumsily. "He's late."

"Good morning."

"Good morning, sir." The "sir" was an error in tactics, like the soft hat at too official an angle and the unchanging page of the *Daily Mirror*. They don't trouble to send their best men for mere murder, Rowe thought, touching the little sore again with his tongue.

What next? He found himself, not for the first time, regretting Henry Wilcox. There were men who lived voluntarily in deserts, but they had their God to commune with. For nearly ten years he had felt no need for friends—one woman could include any number of friends. He wondered where Henry was in wartime. Perry would have joined up and so would Curtis. He imagined Henry as an air-raid warden, fussy and laughed at when all was quiet, a bit scared now during the long pavement vigils but carrying on in dungarees that didn't suit him and a helmet a size too large. Goddam it, he thought, coming out on the ruined corner of High Holborn, I've done my best to take part too. It's not my fault I'm not fit enough for the army, and as for the damned heroes of civil defence—the little clerks and prudes and what-have-you—they didn't want me: not when they found I had done time— even time in a loony bin wasn't respectable enough for Post Four or Post Two or Post any number. And now they've thrown me out of their war altogether: they want me for a murder I didn't do. What chance would they give me with my record?

He thought, Why should I bother about that cake any more? It's nothing to do with me: it's their war, not mine. Why shouldn't

I just go into hiding until everything's blown over? (Surely in war-time a murder does blow over?) It's not my war: I just seem to have stumbled into the firing line, that's all. I'll get out of London and let the fools scrap it out, and the fools die. . . . There may have been nothing important in the cake; it may have contained just a paper cap, a motto, a lucky sixpence. . . . Perhaps that hunchback hadn't meant a thing: perhaps the taste was imagination. Perhaps the whole scene never happened at all as I remember it: blast often did odd things, and it certainly wasn't beyond its power to shake a brain that had too much to brood about already. . . .

As if he were escaping from some bore who walked beside him explaining things he had no interest in, he dived suddenly into a telephone box and rang a number. A stern dowager voice admonished him down the phone as though he had no right on the line at all. "This is the Free Mothers. Who is that please?"

"I want to speak to Miss Hilfe."

"Who is that?"

"A friend of hers." A disapproving grunt twanged the wires. He said sharply, "Put me through please," and almost at once he heard the voice which if he had shut his eyes and washed out the telephone booth and smashed Holborn he could have believed was his wife's. There was really no resemblance, but it was so long since he had spoken to a woman except his landlady or a girl behind a counter that any feminine voice took him back.

"Please. Who is that?"

"Is that Miss Hilfe?"

"Yes. Who are you?"

He said as though his name were a household word, "I'm Rowe."

There was such a long pause that he thought she had put the receiver back and said, "Hullo, are you there?"

"Yes."

"I wanted to talk to you."

"You shouldn't ring me."

"I've nobody else to ring—except your brother. Is he there?"

"No."

"You heard what happened?"

"He told me."

"You had expected something, hadn't you?"

"Not that. Something worse." She explained, "I didn't know *him*."

"I brought you some worries, didn't I, when I came in yesterday?"

"Nothing worries my brother."

"I rang up Rennit."

"Oh, no, no. You shouldn't have done that."

"I haven't learned the technique yet. You can guess what happened."

"Yes. The police."

"You know what your brother wants me to do?"

"Yes."

Their conversation was like a letter which has to pass a censorship. He had an overpowering desire to talk to someone frankly. He said, "Would you meet me somewhere—for five minutes?"

"No," she said. "I can't. I can't get away."

"Just for two minutes."

"It's not possible."

It suddenly became of great importance to him. "Please," he said.

"It wouldn't be safe. My brother would be angry."

He said, "I'm so alone. I don't know what's happening. I've got nobody to advise me. There are so many questions . . ."

"I'm sorry."

"Can I write to you—or him?"

She said, "Just send your address here—to me. No need to sign the note—or sign it with any name you like."

Refugees had such stratagems on the tip of the tongue: it was a familiar way of life. He wondered whether if he were to ask her about money she would have an answer equally ready. He felt like a child who is lost and finds an adult hand to hold, a hand that guides understandingly homewards. He became reckless of the imaginary censor. He said, "There's nothing in the papers."

"Nothing."

"I've written a letter to the police."

"Oh," she said, "you shouldn't have done that. Have you posted it?"

"No."

"Wait and see," she said. "Perhaps there won't be any need. Just wait and see."

"Do you think it would be safe to go to my bank?"

"You are so helpless," she said, "so helpless. Of course you mustn't. They will watch for you there."

"Then how can I live?"

"Haven't you a friend who would cash you a cheque?"

Suddenly he didn't want to admit to her that there was no one at all. "Yes," he said, "yes. I suppose so."

"Well then. Just keep away," she said so gently that he had to strain his ears.

"I'll keep away."

She had rung off. He put the receiver down and moved back into Holborn, keeping away. Just ahead of him, with bulging pockets, went one of the bookworms from the auction room.

Haven't you a friend? she had said. Refugees always had friends: people smuggled letters, arranged passports, bribed officials; in that enormous underground land as wide as a continent there was companionship. In England one hadn't yet learned the technique. Whom could he ask to take one of his cheques? Not a tradesman. Since he began to live alone he had dealt with shops only through his landlady. He thought for the second time that day of his former friends. It hadn't occurred to Anna Hilfe that a refugee might be friendless. A refugee always had a party—or a race.

He thought of Perry and Vane: not a chance even if he had known how to find them. Crooks, Boyle, Curtis—Curtis was quite capable of knocking him down. He had simple standards, primitive ways, and immense complacency. Simplicity in friends had always attracted Rowe; it was a complement to his own qualities. There remained Henry Wilcox. There was just a chance there—if the hockey-playing wife didn't interfere. Their two wives had had nothing in common. Rude health and violent pain were too opposed, but a kind of self-protective instinct would have made Mrs. Wilcox hate him. Once a man started killing his wife, she would have ungrammatically thought, you couldn't tell where it would stop.

But what excuse could he give Henry? He was aware of the bulge in his breast pocket where his statement lay, but he couldn't tell Henry the truth: no more than the police would Henry believe that he had been present at a murder as an onlooker. . . . He must wait till after the banks closed—that was early enough in wartime, and then invent some urgent reason.

What? He thought about it all through lunch in an Oxford Street Lyons and got no clue. Perhaps it was better to leave it to what people called the inspiration of the moment, or better still give it up, give himself up. . . . It only occurred to him as he was paying his bill that probably he wouldn't be able to find Henry anyway. Henry had lived in Battersea, and Battersea was not a good district to live in now. He might not even be alive—twenty thousand people were dead already. He looked him up in a telephone book. He was there.

That meant nothing, he told himself: the blitz was newer than the edition. All the same he dialled the number just to see—it was as if all his contacts now had to be down a telephone line. He was almost afraid to hear the ringing tone, and when it came he put the receiver down quickly and with pain. He had rung Henry up so often—before things happened. Well, he had to make up his mind now; the flat was still there, though Henry mightn't be in it. He couldn't brandish a cheque down a telephone line; this time the contact had got to be physical. And he hadn't seen Henry since the day before the trial.

He would almost have preferred to throw his hand in altogether.

He caught a number 19 bus from Piccadilly. After the ruins of St. James's Church one passed at that early date into peaceful country. Knightsbridge and Sloane Street were not at war, but Chelsea was, and Battersea was in the front line. It was an odd front line that twisted like the track of a hurricane and left patches of peace. Battersea, Holborn, the East End, the front line curled in and out of them . . . and yet there were pieces of Battersea where the public house stood at the corner with the dairy and the baker beside it and as far as you could see there were no ruins anywhere.

It was like that in Wilcox's street: the big middle-class flats stood rectangular and gaunt like railway hotels, completely undamaged, looking out over the park. There were "To Let" boards up all the way down, and Rowe half hoped he would find one outside number 63. But there was none. In the hall was a frame in which occupants could show whether they were in or out, but the fact that the Wilcoxes' was marked "In" meant nothing at all, even if they still lived there, for Henry had a theory that to mark the board "Out" was to invite burglary. Henry's caution had always imposed on his friends a long tramp upstairs to the top floor (there were no lifts).

The stairs were at the back of the flats looking towards Chelsea, and as you climbed above the second floor and your view lifted, the war came back into sight. Most of the church spires seemed to have been snapped off two-thirds up, like sugar sticks, and there was an appearance of slum clearance where there hadn't really been any slums.

It was painful to come in sight, up a turn of the stairs, of the familiar 63. He used to pity Henry because of his masterful wife, his conventional career, the fact that his work—chartered account-ancy—seemed to offer no escape: three hundred a year of Rowe's own had seemed like wealth, and he had for Henry some of the feeling a rich man might have for a poor relation. He used to give Henry things. Perhaps that was why Mrs. Wilcox hadn't liked him. He smiled with affection when he saw a little plaque on the door marked A.R.P. Warden: it was exactly as he had pictured. But his fingers hesitated on the bell.

3

He hadn't had time to ring when the door opened and there was Henry. An oddly altered Henry. He had always been a neat little man—his wife had seen to that. Now he was in dirty blue dun-garees, and he was unshaven. He walked past Rowe as though he didn't see him and leaned over the well of the staircase. "They aren't here," he said.

A middle-aged woman with red eyes who looked like a cook followed him out and said, "It's not time, Henry. It's really not time." For a moment—so altered was Henry—Rowe wondered whether the war had done this to Henry's wife too.

Henry suddenly became aware of him—or half aware of him. He said, "Oh, Arthur—good of you to come," as though they'd met yesterday. Then he dived back into his little dark hall and became a shadowy abstracted figure beside a grandfather clock.

"If you'd come in," the woman said, "I don't think they'll be long now."

He followed her in and noticed that she left the door open as though others were expected: he was getting used now to life taking him up and planting him down without volition of his own in sur-roundings where only he was not at home. . . . On a chest—made he remembered to Mrs. Wilcox's order by the Tudor Manufactur-ing Company—a pair of dungarees was neatly folded with a steel hat on top. He was reminded of prison, where you left your own clothes behind. In the dimness Henry repeated, "Good of you, Arthur," and fled again.

The middle-aged woman said, "Any friend of Henry's is welcome. I am Mrs. Wilcox." She seemed to read his astonishment even in the dark and explained, "Henry's mother." She said, "Come and wait inside. I don't suppose they'll be long. It's so dark here. The black-out, you know. Most of the glass is gone." She led the way into what Rowe remembered was the dining room. There were glasses laid out as though there was going to be a party. It seemed an odd time of day—too late or too early. Henry was there: he gave the effect of having been driven into a corner, of having fled here. On the mantelpiece behind him were four silver cups with the names of teams engraved in double entry under a date: to have drunk out of one of them would have been like drinking out of an account book.

Rowe, looking at the glasses, said, "I didn't mean to intrude," and Henry remarked for the third time as though it were a phrase he didn't have to use his brain in forming, "Good of you." It was as if he had no memory left of that prison scene on which their friend-ship had foundered. Mrs. Wilcox said, "It's so good the way Henry's old friends are all rallying to him." Then Rowe, who had been on the point of inquiring after Henry's wife, suddenly under-stood. Death was responsible for the glasses, the unshaven chin, the waiting—even for what had puzzled him most of all, the look of youth on Henry's face. People say that sorrow ages, but just as often sorrow makes a man younger—ridding him of responsibility, giving in its place the lost unanchored look of adolescence.

He said, "I didn't know. I wouldn't have come if I'd known."

Mrs. Wilcox said with gloomy pride, "It was in all the papers."

Henry stood in his corner; his teeth chattered while Mrs. Wilcox went remorselessly on—she had had a good cry, her son was hers again. "We are proud of Doris. The whole post is doing her honour. We are going to lay her uniform—her clean uniform—on the coffin, and the clergyman is going to read about 'Greater love hath no man . . .' "

"I'm sorry, Henry."

"She was crazy," Henry said angrily. "She had no right. I told her the wall would collapse."

"But we are proud of her, Henry," his mother said, "we are proud of her."

"I should have stopped her," Henry said. "I suppose," his voice went high with rage and grief, "she thought she'd win another of those blasted pots."

"She was playing for England, Henry," Mrs. Wilcox said. She

turned to Rowe and said, "I think we ought to lay a hockey stick beside the uniform, but Henry won't have it."

"I'll be off," Rowe said. "I'd never have come if—"

"No," Henry said, "*you* stay. *You* know how it is." He stopped and looked at Rowe as though he realized him fully for the first time. He said, "I killed my wife too. I could have held her, knocked her down . . ."

"You don't know what you are saying, Henry," his mother said. "What will this gentleman think?"

"This is Arthur Rowe, Mother."

"Oh," Mrs. Wilcox said. "Oh," and at that moment up the street came the slow sad sound of wheels and feet.

"How dare he!" Mrs. Wilcox said.

"He's my oldest friend, Mother," Henry said. Somebody was coming up the stairs. "Why *did* you come, Arthur?" Henry said.

"To get you to cash me a cheque."

"The impudence," Mrs. Wilcox said.

"I didn't know about this—"

"How much, old man?"

"Twenty?"

"I've only got fifteen. You can have that."

"Don't trust him," Mrs. Wilcox said.

"Oh, my cheques are good enough. Henry knows that."

"There are banks to go to."

"Not at this time of day, Mrs. Wilcox. I'm sorry. It's urgent."

There was a little trumpery Queen Anne desk in the room; it had obviously belonged to Henry's wife. All the furniture had an air of flimsiness: walking between it was like walking, in the old parlour game, blindfold between bottles. Perhaps in her home the hockey player had reacted from the toughness of the field. Now moving to get at the desk, Henry's shoulder caught a silver cup and set it rolling across the carpet. In the open door appeared a very fat man in dungarees, carrying a white steel helmet. He picked up the cup and said solemnly, "The procession's here, Mrs. Wilcox."

Henry dithered by the desk.

"I have the uniform ready," Mrs. Wilcox said, "in the hall."

"I couldn't get a Union Jack," the post warden said, "not a big one. And those little ones they stick on ruins didn't somehow look respectful." He was painfully trying to exhibit the bright side of death. "The whole post's turned out, Mr. Wilcox," he said, "except those that have to stay on duty. And the A.F.S.—they've sent a contingent. And there's a rescue party and four salvage men—and the police band."

"I think that's wonderful," Mrs. Wilcox said. "If only Doris could see it all."

"But she *can* see it, ma'am," the post warden said. "I'm sure of that."

"And afterwards," Mrs. Wilcox said, gesturing towards the glasses, "if you'll all come up here . . ."

"There's a good many of us, ma'am. Perhaps we'd better make it just the post. The salvage men don't really expect . . ."

"Come along, Henry," Mrs. Wilcox said. "We can't keep all these brave kind souls waiting. You must carry the uniform down in your arms. Oh dear, I wish you looked more tidy. Everybody will be watching you."

"I don't see," Henry said, "why we shouldn't have buried her quietly."

"But she's a heroine," Mrs. Wilcox exclaimed.

"I wouldn't be surprised," the post warden said, "if they give her the George Medal—posthumously. It's the first in the borough —it would be a grand thing for the post."

"Why, Henry," Mrs. Wilcox said, "she's not just your wife any more. She belongs to England."

Henry moved towards the door; the post warden still held the silver cup awkwardly—he didn't know where to put it. "Just anywhere," Henry said to him, "anywhere." They all moved into the hall, leaving Rowe. "You've forgotten your helmet, Henry," Mrs. Wilcox said. He had been a very precise man, and he'd lost his precision: all the things which had made Henry Henry were gone; it was as if his character had consisted of a double-breasted waistcoat, columns of figures, a wife who played hockey; without these things he was unaccountable, he didn't add up. "You go," he said to his mother, "you go."

"But, Henry . . ."

"It's understandable, ma'am," the post warden said. "It's feeling that does it. We've always thought Mr. Wilcox a very sensitive gentleman at the post. They'll understand," he added kindly, meaning, one supposed, the post, the police band, the A.F.S., even the four salvage men. He urged Mrs. Wilcox towards the door with a friendly broad hand, then picked up the uniform himself. Hints of the past penetrated the anonymity of the dungarees—the peaceful past of a manservant, or perhaps of a commissionaire who runs out into the rain carrying an umbrella. War was very like a bad dream in which familiar people appear in strange and terrible and unlikely disguises. Even Henry.

Rowe made an indeterminate motion to follow; he couldn't help hoping it would remind Henry of the cheque. It was his only chance of getting any money; there was nobody else. Henry said, "We'll just see them go off and then we'll come back here. You do understand, don't you? I couldn't bear to watch." They came out together into the road by the park; the procession had already started: it moved like a little dark trickle towards the river. The steel hat on the coffin lay blackened and unreflecting under the winter sun, and the Rescue Party didn't keep step with the post. It was like a parody of a State funeral—but this *was* a State funeral. The brown leaves from the park were blowing across the road, and the drinkers coming out at closing time from the Duke of Rockingham took off their hats. Henry said, "I told her not to do it . . ." and the wind blew the sound of footsteps back to them. It was as if they had surrendered her to the people—to whom she had never belonged before.

Henry said suddenly, "Excuse me, old man," and started after her. He hadn't got his helmet: his hair was beginning to go grey; he broke into a trot for fear after all of being left behind. He was rejoining his wife and his post. Arthur Rowe was left alone. He turned his money over in his pocket and found there wasn't much of it.

Seven: A Load of Books

1

Even if a man has been contemplating the advantages of suicide for two years, he takes time to make his final decision—to move from theory to practice. Rowe couldn't simply go then and there and drop into the river . . . besides he would have been pulled out again. And yet watching the procession recede he could see no other solution. He was wanted by the police for murder and he had thirty-five shillings in his pocket. He couldn't go to the bank and he had no friend but Henry: of course he could wait till Henry came back, but the cold-blooded egotism of that act repelled him. It would be simpler and less disgusting to die. A brown leaf settled on his coat—that, according to the old story, meant money, but the old story didn't say how soon.

He walked along the embankment towards Chelsea Bridge: the tide was low and the seagulls walked delicately on the mud. One noticed the absence of perambulators and dogs: the only dog in sight looked stray and uncared for and evasive; a barrage balloon staggered up from behind the park trees; its huge nose bent over the thin winter foliage and then it turned its dirty old backside and climbed.

It wasn't only that he had no money: he had no longer what he called a home—somewhere to shelter from people who might know him. He missed Mrs. Purvis coming in with the tea: he used to count the days by her; punctuated by her knock they would slide smoothly towards the end—annihilation, forgiveness, punishment or peace. He missed *David Copperfield* and *The Old Curiosity Shop:* he could no longer direct his sense of pity towards the fictitious sufferings of little Nell—it roamed around and saw too many objects —too many rats that needed to be killed. And he was one of them.

Leaning over the embankment in the time-honoured attitude of would-be suicides, he began to go into the details. He wanted as far as possible to be unobtrusive: now that his anger had died it seemed to him a pity that he hadn't drunk that cup of tea—he didn't want to shock any innocent person with the sight of an ugly death. And there were very few suicides which were not ugly. Murder was infinitely more graceful because it was the murderer's object not to shock—a murderer went to infinite pains to make death look quiet, peaceful, happy. Everything, he thought, would be so much easier if he only had a little money.

Of course he could go to the bank and let the police get him. It seemed probable that then he would be hanged. But the idea of hanging for a crime he hadn't committed still had power to anger him: if he killed himself it would be for a crime of which he was guilty. He was haunted by a primitive idea of Justice. He wanted to conform; he had always wanted to conform.

A murderer is regarded by the conventional world as something rather monstrous, but to himself a murderer is only an ordinary man—a man who takes either tea or coffee for breakfast and afterwards excretes, a man who likes a good book and perhaps prefers biography or travel to fiction, a man who at a regular hour goes to bed, who tries to develop good physical habits but possibly suffers from constipation, who prefers dogs or cats and has certain views about politics.

It is only if the murderer is a good man that he can be regarded as monstrous.

Arthur Rowe was monstrous. His early childhood had been passed before the first World War, and the impressions of childhood are ineffaceable. He was brought up to believe that it was wrong to inflict pain, but he was often ill, his teeth were bad and he suffered agonies from an inefficient dentist he knew as Mr. Griggs. He learned before he was seven what pain was like—he wouldn't willingly allow even a rat to suffer it. In childhood we live under the brightness of immortality—heaven is as near and actual as the seaside. Behind the complicated details of the world stand the simplicities: God is good, the grown-up man or woman knows the answer to every question, there is such a thing as truth, and justice is as measured and faultless as a clock. Our heroes are simple: they are brave, they tell the truth, they are good swordsmen, and they are never in the long run really defeated. That is why no later books satisfy us like those which were read to us in childhood, for those promised a world of great simplicity of which we knew the rules, but the later books are complicated and contradictory with experience: they are formed out of our own disappointing memories—of the V.C. in the police-court dock, of the faked income-tax return, the sins in corners, and the hollow voice of the man we despise talking to us of courage and purity. The little duke is dead and betrayed and forgotten: we cannot recognize the villain and we suspect the hero and the world is a small cramped place. That is what people are saying all the time everywhere; the two great popular statements of faith are: "What a small place the world is" and "I'm a stranger here myself."

But Rowe was a murderer—as other men are poets. The statues still stood. He was prepared to do anything to save the innocent or to punish the guilty. He believed against all the experience of life that somewhere there was justice, and justice condemned him. He analyzed his motives minutely and always summed up against himself. He told himself, leaning over the wall, as he had told himself a hundred times, that it was he who had not been able to bear his wife's pain—and not she. Once, it was true, in the early days of the disease, she had broken down, said she wanted to die, not to wait: that was hysteria. Later it was her endurance and her patience which he had found most unbearable. He was trying to escape his own pain, not hers, and at the end she had guessed or half guessed what it was he was offering her. She was scared and afraid to ask. How could you go on living with a man if you had once asked him whether he had put poison into your evening drink? Far easier when you love him and are tired of pain just to take the hot milk and sleep. But he could never know whether the fear had been worse than the pain, and he could never tell whether she might not have preferred any sort of life to death. He had taken the stick and killed the rat, and saved himself the agony of watching. . . . He had gone over the same questions and the same answers daily, ever since the moment when she took the milk from him and said, "How queer it tastes," and lay back and tried to smile. He would have liked to stay beside her till she slept, but that would have been unusual, and he must avoid anything unusual: so he had to leave her to die alone. And she would have liked to ask him to stay—he was sure of that—but that would have been unusual too. After all, in an hour he would be coming up to bed. Convention held them at the moment of death. He had in mind the police questions, "Why did you stay?" and it was quite possible that she too was deliberately playing his game against the police. There were so many things he would never know. But when the police did ask questions he hadn't the heart or the energy to tell them lies. Perhaps if he had lied to them a little they would have hanged him.

It was about time now to bring the trial to an end.

2

"They can't spoil Whistler's Thames," a voice said.

"I'm sorry," Rowe said, "I didn't catch . . ."

"It's safe underground. Bomb-proof vaults."

Somewhere, Rowe thought, he had seen that face before: the thin depressed grey moustache, the bulging pockets, out of which the man now took a piece of bread and threw it towards the mud; before it had reached the river the gulls had risen; one outdistanced the others, caught it and sailed on, down past the stranded barges and the paper mill, a white scrap blown towards the blackened chimneys of Lots Road.

"Come, my pretties," the man said, and his hand suddenly became a landing ground for sparrows. "They know uncle," he said, "they know uncle." He put a bit of bread between his lips and they hovered round his mouth, giving little pecks at it as though they were kissing him.

"It must be difficult in wartime," Rowe said, "to provide for all your nephews."

"Yes, indeed," the man said—and when he opened his mouth you saw his teeth were in a shocking condition, black stumps like the remains of something destroyed by fire. He sprinkled some crumbs over his old brown hat and a new flock of sparrows landed there. "Strictly illegal," he said, "I daresay. If Lord Woolton knew." He put a foot up on a heavy suitcase, and a sparrow perched on his knee. He was overgrown with birds.

"I've seen you before," Rowe said.

"I daresay."

"Twice today, now I come to think of it."

"Come, my pretties," the elderly man said.

"In the auction room in Chancery Lane."

A pair of mild eyes turned to him. "It's a small world."

"Do you buy books?" Rowe asked, thinking of the shabby clothes.

"Buy and sell," the man said. He was acute enough to read Rowe's thoughts. "Working clothes," he said. "Books carry a deal of dust."

"You go in for old books?"

"Landscape gardening's my specialty. Eighteenth century. Fullove, Fulham Road, Battersea."

"Do you find enough customers?"

"There are more than you'd think." He suddenly opened his arms wide and shooed the birds away as though they were children with whom he'd played long enough. "But everything's depressed," he said, "these days. What they want to fight for I don't understand." He touched the suitcase tenderly with his foot. "I've got a load of books here," he said, "I got from a lord's house. Salvage. The state of some of them would make you weep, but others— I don't say it wasn't a good bargain. I'd show them to you, only I'm afraid of bird droppings. First bargain I've had for months. In the old days I'd have treasured them, treasured them. Waited till the Americans came in the summer. Now I'm glad of any chance of a turnover. If I don't deliver these to a customer at Regal Court before five, I lose a sale. He wants to take them down to the country before the raid starts. I haven't a watch, sir. Could you tell me the time?"

"It's only four o'clock."

"I ought to go on," Mr. Fullove said. "Books are heavy though and I feel just tired out. It's been a long day. You'll excuse me, sir, if I sit down a moment." He sat himself down on the suitcase and drew out a ragged packet of Tenners. "Will you smoke, sir? You look a bit done, if I may say so, yourself."

"Oh, I'm all right." The mild exhausted ageing eyes appealed to him. He said, "Why don't you take a taxi?"

"Well, sir, I work on a very narrow margin these days. If I take a taxi that's four bob gone. And then when he gets the books into the country, perhaps he won't want one of them."

"They are landscape gardening?"

"That's right. It's a lost art, sir. There's a lot more to it, you know, than flowers. That's what gardening means today," he said with contempt, "flowers."

"You don't care for flowers?"

"Oh, flowers," the bookseller said, "are all right. You've got to have flowers."

"I'm afraid," Rowe said, "I don't know much about gardening—except flowers."

"It's the tricks they played." The mild eyes looked up with cunning enthusiasm. "The machinery."

"Machinery?"

"They had statues that spurted water at you when you passed, and the grottoes—the things they thought up for grottoes. Why, in a good garden you weren't safe anywhere."

"I should have thought you were meant to feel safe in a garden."

"They didn't think so, sir," the bookseller said, blowing the stale smell of carious teeth enthusiastically in Rowe's direction. Rowe wished he could get away; but automatically with that wish the sense of pity worked and he stayed.

"And then," the bookseller said, "there were the tombs."

"Did they spurt water too?"

"Oh, no. They gave the touch of solemnity, sir, the *memento mori.*"

"Black thoughts," Rowe said, "in a black shade?"

"It's how you look at it, isn't it, sir?" But there was no doubt that the bookseller looked at it with a kind of gloating. He brushed a little bird lime off his jacket and said, "You don't have a taste, sir, for the Sublime—or the Ridiculous?"

"Perhaps," Rowe said, "I prefer human nature plain."

The little man giggled. "I get your meaning, sir. Oh, they had room for human nature, believe me, in the grottoes. Not one without a comfortable couch. They never forgot the comfortable couch," and again with sly enthusiasm he blew his carious breath towards his companion.

"Don't you think," Rowe said, "you should be getting on? You mustn't let me rob you of a sale," and immediately he reacted from his own harshness, seeing only the mild tired eyes, thinking, Poor devil, he's had a weary day, each one to his taste . . . after all he liked me. That was a claim he could never fail to honour because it astonished him.

"I suppose I ought, sir." He rose and brushed away some crumbs the birds had left. "I enjoy a good talk," he said. "It's not often you can get a good talk these days. It's a rush between the shelters."

"You sleep in a shelter?"

"To tell you the truth, sir," he said as if he were confessing to an idiosyncrasy, "I can't bear the bombs. But you don't sleep as you ought in a shelter." The weight of the suitcase cramped him: he looked very old under its weight. "Some people are not considerate. The snores and squabbles . . ."

"Why did you come into the park? It's not your shortest way."

"I wanted a rest, sir—and the trees invited, and the birds."

"Here," Rowe said, "you'd better let me take that. There's no bus this side of the river."

"Oh, I couldn't bother you, sir. I really couldn't." But there was no genuine resistance in him: the suitcase was certainly very heavy; folios of landscape gardening weighed a lot. He excused himself, "There's nothing so heavy as books, sir—unless it's bricks."

They came out of the park and Rowe changed the weight from one arm to the other. He said, "You know, it's getting late for your appointment."

"It's my tongue that did it," the old bookseller said with distress. "I think—I really think I shall have to risk the fare."

"I think you will."

"If I could give you a lift, sir, it would make it more worth while. Are you going in my direction?"

"Oh, in any," Rowe said.

They got a taxi at the next corner, and the bookseller leaned back with an air of blissful relaxation. He said, "If you make up your mind to pay for a thing, enjoy it, that's my idea."

But in the taxi with the windows shut it wasn't easy for another to enjoy it: the smell of dental decay was very strong. Rowe talked for fear of showing his distaste. "And have you gone in yourself for landscape gardening?"

"Well, not what you would call the garden part." The man kept peering through the window—it occurred to Rowe that his simple enjoyment rang a little false. He said, "I wonder, sir, if you'd do me one last favour. The stairs at Regal Court—well, they are a caution to a man of my age. And no one offers somebody like me a hand. I deal in books, but to them, sir, I'm just a tradesman. If you wouldn't mind just taking up the bag for me. You needn't stay a moment. Just ask for Mr. Travers in number six. He's expecting the bag—there's nothing you have to do but leave it with him." He took a quick sideways look to catch a refusal on the wind. "And afterwards, sir, you've been very kind, I'd give you a lift anywhere you wanted to go."

"You don't know where I want to go," Rowe said.

"I'll risk that, sir. In for a penny, in for a pound."

"I might take you at your word and go a very long way."

"Try me. Just try me, sir," the other said with a kind of forced glee. "I'd sell you a book and make it even." Perhaps it was the man's servility—or it may have been only the man's smell—but Rowe felt unwilling to oblige him. "Why not get the commissionaire to take it up for you?" he asked.

"I'd never trust him to deliver—straight away."

"You could see it taken up yourself."

"It's the stairs, sir, at the end of a long day." He lay back in his seat and said, "If you must know, sir, I oughtn't to have been carrying it," and he made a movement towards his heart, a gesture for which there was no answer.

Well, Rowe thought, I may as well do one good deed before I go away altogether—but all the same he didn't like it. Certainly the man looked sick and tired enough to excuse any artifice, but he had been too successful. Why, Rowe thought, should I be sitting here in a taxi with a stranger, promising to drag a case of eighteenth-century folios to the room of another stranger? He felt directed, controlled, moulded, moulded by some agency with a surrealist imagination.

They drew up outside Regal Court—an odd pair, both dusty, both unshaven. Rowe had agreed to nothing, but he knew there was no choice: he hadn't the hard strength of mind to walk away and leave the little man to drag his own burden. He got out under the suspicious eye of the commissionaire and lugged the heavy case after him. "Have you got a room booked," the commissionaire asked and added dubiously, "sir?"

"I'm not staying here. I'm leaving this case for Mr. Travers."

"Ask at the desk, please," the commissionaire said and leaped to serve a more savoury carload.

The bookseller had been right: it was a hard pull up the long wide stairs of the hotel. You felt they had been built for women in evening dress to walk slowly down: the architect had been too romantic; he hadn't seen a man with two days' beard dragging a load of books. He counted fifty steps.

The clerk at the counter eyed him carefully. Before Rowe had time to speak he said, "We are quite full up, I'm afraid."

"I've brought some books for a Mr. Travers in room six."

"Oh, yes," the clerk said. "He was expecting you. He's out, but he gave orders"—you could see that he didn't like the orders—"that you were to be allowed in."

"I don't want to wait. I just want to leave the books."

"Mr. Travers gave orders that you were to wait."

"I don't care a damn what orders Mr. Travers gave."

"Page," the clerk called sharply, "show this man to number six, Mr. Travers. Mr. Travers has given orders that he's to be allowed in." He had very few phrases and never varied them. Rowe wondered on how few he could get through life, marry and have children. . . . He followed at the page's heels down interminable corridors lit by concealed lighting; once a woman in pink mules and a dressing gown squealed as they went by. It was like the corridor of a monstrous Cunarder—one expected to see stewards and stewardesses, but instead a small stout Jew wearing a bowler hat padded to meet them from what seemed a hundred yards away, then suddenly veered aside into the intricacies of the building. "Do you unreel a thread of cotton?" Rowe asked, swaying under the weight of the case which the page never offered to take, and feeling the strange lightheadedness which comes, we are told, to dying men. But the back—the tight little blue trousers and the bumfreezer jacket—just went on ahead. It seemed to Rowe that one could be lost here for a lifetime: only the clerk at the desk would have a clue to one's whereabouts, and it was doubtful whether he ever penetrated very far in person into the enormous wilderness. Water would come regularly out of taps, and at dusk one would emerge and collect tinned foods. He was touched by a forgotten sense of adventure, watching the numbers go backwards, 49, 48, 47: once they took a short cut which led them through the 60's to emerge suddenly among the 30's.

A door in the passage was ajar and odd sounds came through it, as though someone were alternately whistling and sighing, but nothing to the page seemed strange. He just went on: he was a child of this building. People of every kind came in for a night with or without luggage and then went away again: a few died here and the bodies were removed unobtrusively by the service lift. Divorce suits bloomed at certain seasons: corespondents gave tips and detectives out-trumped them with larger tips—because their tips went on the expense account. The page took everything for granted.

Rowe said, "You'll lead me back?" At each corner arrows pointed above the legend "Air Raid Shelter." Coming on them every few minutes, one got the impression that one was walking in circles.

"Mr. Travers left orders you was to stay."

"But I don't take orders from Mr. Travers," Rowe said.

This was a modern building; the silence was admirable and disquieting. Instead of bells ringing lights went on and off. One got the impression that all the time people were signalling news of great importance that couldn't wait. The silence, now that they were out of earshot of the whistle and the sigh, was like that of a stranded liner: the engines had stopped, and in the sinister silence you listened for the faint depressing sound of lapping water.

"Here's six," the boy said.

"It must take a long time to get to a hundred."

"Third floor," the boy said, "but Mr. Travers gave orders—"

"Never mind," Rowe said. "Forget I said it."

Without the chromium number you could hardly have told the difference between the door and the wall: it was as if the inhabitants had been walled up. The page put in a master key and pushed the wall in. Rowe said, "I'll just put the case down," but the door had shut behind him. Mr Travers, who seemed to be a much-respected man, had given his orders, and if he didn't obey them he would have to find his way back alone. There was an exhilaration in the absurd episode: he had made up his mind now about everything—justice as well as the circumstances of the case demanded that he should kill himself (he had only to decide the method), and now he could enjoy the oddness of existence; regret, anger, hatred, too many emotions had obscured for too long the silly shape of life. He opened the sitting-room door.

"Well," he said, "this beats all."

It was Anna Hilfe.

He asked, "Have you come to see Mr. Travers too? Are you interested in landscape gardening?"

She said, "I came to see you."

It was really his first opportunity to take her in. Very small and thin, she looked too young for all the things she must have seen, and now taken out of the office frame she no longer looked efficient —as though efficiency were an imitative game she could only play with adult properties, a desk, a telephone, a black suit. Without them she looked just decorative and breakable, but he knew that life hadn't been able to break her. All it had done was to put a few wrinkles round eyes as straightforward as a child's.

"Do you like the mechanical parts of gardening too?" he asked. "Statues that spurt water . . ."

His heart beat at the sight of her, as though he were a young man and this his first assignation outside a cinema, in a Lyons Corner House . . . or in an innyard in a country town where dances were held. She was wearing a pair of shabby blue trousers, ready for the night's raid, and a wine-coloured jersey. He thought with melancholy that her thighs were the prettiest he had ever seen.

"I don't understand," she said.

"How did you know I was going to cart a load of books here for Mr. Travers—whoever Mr. Travers is. I didn't know myself until ten minutes ago."

"I don't know what excuse they thought up for you," she said. "Just go. Please."

She looked the kind of child you want to torment—in a kindly way: in the office she had been ten years older. He said, "They do people well here, don't they? You get a whole flat for a night. You can sit down and read a book and cook a dinner . . ."

A pale brown curtain divided the living room in half; he drew it aside, and there was the double bed, a telephone on a little table, a bookcase. He asked, "What's through here?" and opened a door. "You see," he said, "they throw in a kitchen, stove and all." He came back into the sitting room and said, "One could live here and forget it wasn't one's home." He no longer felt carefree: it had been a mood which had lasted minutes only.

She said, "Have you noticed anything?"

"How do you mean?"

"You don't notice much for a journalist."

"You know I was a journalist?"

"My brother checked up on everything."

"On everything?"

"Yes." She said again, "You didn't notice anything?"

"No."

"Mr. Travers doesn't seem to have left behind him so much as a used piece of soap. Look in the bathroom. The soap's wrapped up in its paper."

Rowe went to the front door and bolted it. He said, "Whoever he is, he can't get in now till we've finished talking. Miss Hilfe, will you please tell me slowly—I'm a bit stupid, I think—first how you knew I was here and secondly why you came?"

She said obstinately, "I won't tell you how. As to why—I've asked you to go away quickly. I was right last time, wasn't I, when I telephoned?"

"Yes, you were right. But why worry? You said you knew all about me, didn't you?"

"There's no harm in you," she said simply.

"Knowing everything," he said, "you wouldn't worry—"

"I like justice," she said, as if she were confessing an eccentricity.

"Yes," he said, "it's a good thing if you can get it."

"But *they* don't."

"Do you mean Mrs. Bellairs," he asked, "and Canon Topling?" It was too complicated: he hadn't any fight left. He sat down in the armchair—they allowed in the ersatz home one armchair and a couch.

"Canon Topling is quite a good man," she said and suddenly smiled. "It's too silly," she said, "the things we are saying."

"You must tell your brother," Rowe said, "that he's not to bother about me any more. I'm giving up. Let them murder whom they like—I'm out of it. I'm going away."

"Where?"

"It's all right," he said. "They'll never find me. I know a place so safe— But they won't want to. I think all they were really afraid of was that I should find *them*. I'll never know now, I suppose, what it was all about. The cake—and Mrs. Bellairs. Wonderful Mrs. Bellairs."

"They are bad," she said, as if that simple phrase disposed of them altogether. "I'm glad you are going away. It's not your business." To his amazement she added, "I don't want you to be hurt any more."

"Why," he said, "you know everything about me. You've checked up." He used her own childish word, "I'm bad too."

"Mr. Rowe," she said, "I have seen so many bad people where I come from, and you don't fit: you haven't the right marks. You worry too much about what's over and done. People say English justice is good. Well, they didn't hang you. It was a mercy killing, that was what the papers called it."

"You've read all the papers?"

"All of them. I've even seen the pictures they took. You put your newspaper up to hide your face."

He listened to her with dumb astonishment. No one had ever talked to him openly about it. It was painful, but it was the sort of pain you feel when iodine is splashed on a wound—the sort of pain you can bear. She said, "Where I come from I have seen a lot of killings, but they were none of them mercy killings. Don't think so much. Give yourself a chance."

"I think," he said, "we'd better decide what to do about Mr. Travers."

"Just go. That's all."

"And what will you do?"

"Go too. I don't want any trouble either."

Rowe said, "If they are your enemies, if they've made you suffer, I'll stay and talk to Mr. Travers."

"Oh, no," she said. "They are not mine. This isn't my country."

He said, "Who are they? I'm in a fog. Are they your people or my people?"

"They are the same everywhere," she said. She put out a hand and touched his arm tentatively—as if she wanted to know what he felt like. "You think you are so bad," she said, "but it was only because you couldn't bear the pain. But *they* can bear pain—other people's pain—endlessly. They are the people who don't care."

He could have gone on listening to her for hours: it seemed a pity that he had to kill himself, but he had no choice in the matter. Unless he left it to the hangman. He said, "I suppose if I stay till Mr. Travers comes, he'll hand me over to the police."

"I don't know what they'll do."

"And that little smooth man with the books was in it too. What a lot of them there are."

"An awful lot. More every day."

"But why should they think I'd stay—when once I'd left the books?" He took her wrist—a small bony wrist—and said sadly, "You aren't in it too, are you?"

"No," she said, not pulling away from him, just stating a fact. He had the impression that she didn't tell lies. She might have a hundred vices, but not the commonest one of all.

"I didn't think you were," he said, "but that means—it means they meant us both to be here."

She said, "Oh," as if he'd hit her.

"They knew we'd waste time talking, explaining. They want us both, but the police don't want you." He exclaimed, "You're coming away with me now."

"Yes."

"If we are not too late. They seem to time things well." He went into the hall and very carefully and softly slid the bolt, opened the door a crack, and then very gently shut it again. He said, "Just now I was thinking how easy it would be to get lost in this hotel, in all these long passages."

"Yes?"

"We shan't get lost. There's someone at the end of the passage waiting for us. His back's turned. I can't see his face."

"They do think of everything," she said.

He found his exhilaration returning. He had thought he was going to die today—but he wasn't: he was going to live, because he could be of use to someone again. He no longer felt that he was dragging round a valueless and ageing body. He said, "I don't see how they can starve us out. And they can't get in. Except through the window."

"No," Miss Hilfe said. "I've looked. They can't get in there. There's twelve feet of smooth wall."

"Then all we have to do is sit and wait. We might ring up the restaurant and order dinner. Lots of courses, and a good wine. Travers can pay. We'll begin with a very dry sherry—"

"Yes," Miss Hilfe said, "if we were sure the right waiter would bring it."

He smiled. "You think of everything. It's the continental training. What's your advice?"

"Ring up the clerk—we know him by sight. Make trouble about something. Insist that he must come along, and then we'll walk out with him."

"You're right," he said. "Of course that's the way."

He lifted the curtain and she followed him. "What are you going to say?"

"I don't know. Leave it to the moment. I'll think of something." He took up the receiver and listened—and listened. He said, "I think the line's dead." He waited for nearly two minutes, but there was only silence.

"We *are* besieged," she said. "I wonder what they mean to do." They neither of them noticed that they were holding hands: it was as though they had been overtaken by the dark and had to feel their way.

He said, "We haven't got much in the way of weapons. You don't wear hatpins nowadays, and I suppose the police have got the only knife I've ever had." They came back hand in hand into the small living room. "Let's be warm anyway," he said, "and turn on the fire. It's cold enough for a blizzard, and we've got the wolves outside."

She had let go his hand and was kneeling by the fire. She said, "It doesn't go on."

"You haven't put in the sixpence."

"I've put in a shilling."

It was cold and the room was darkening. The same thought struck both of them. "Try the light," she said, but his hand had already felt the switch. The light didn't go on.

"It's going to be very dark and very cold," he said. "Mr. Travers is not making us comfortable."

"Oh," Miss Hilfe said, putting her hand to her mouth like a child. "I'm scared. I'm sorry, but I am scared. I don't like the dark."

"They can't do anything," Rowe said. "The door's bolted. They can't batter it down, you know. This is a civilized hotel."

"Are you sure," Miss Hilfe said, "that there's no connecting door? In the kitchen . . . ?"

A memory struck him. He opened the kitchen door. "Yes," he said. "You're right again. The tradesmen's entrance. These are good flats."

"But you can bolt that too. Please," Miss Hilfe said.

Rowe came back. He said gently, "There's only one flaw in this well-furnished flat. The kitchen bolt is broken." He took her hand again quickly. "Never mind," he said. "We're imagining things. This isn't Vienna, you know. This is London. We are in the majority. This hotel is full of people—on *our* side." He repeated, "On our side. They are all round us. We've only to shout." The world was sliding rapidly towards night: like a torpedoed liner heeling too far, she would soon take her last dive into darkness. Already they were talking louder because they couldn't clearly see each other's faces.

"In half an hour," Miss Hilfe said, "the sirens will go. And then they'll all go down into the basement, and the only ones left will be us—and *them*." Her hand felt very cold.

"Then that's our chance," he said. "When the sirens go, we go too with the crowd."

"We are at the end of the passage. Perhaps there won't be a crowd. How do you know there *is* anyone left in this passage? They've thought of so much. Don't you think they'll have thought of that? They've probably booked every room."

"We'll try," he said. "If we had any weapon at all—a stick, a stone." He stopped and let her hand go. "If those aren't books," he said, "perhaps they are bricks. Bricks." He felt one of the catches. "It isn't locked," he said. "Now we'll see." But they both looked at the suitcase doubtfully. Efficiency is paralyzing. *They* had thought of everything, so wouldn't they have thought of this too?

"I wouldn't touch it," she said.

They felt the inertia a bird is supposed to feel before a snake: a snake too knows all the answers.

"They must make a mistake some time," he said.

The dark was dividing them. Very far away the guns grumbled.

"They'll wait till the sirens," she said, "till everybody's down there, out of hearing."

"What's that?" he said. He was getting jumpy himself.

"What?"

"I think someone tried the handle."

"How near they are getting," she said.

"By God," he said, "we aren't powerless. Give me a hand with the couch." They stuck the end of it against the door to the kitchen. They could hardly see a thing now: they were really in the dark. "It's lucky," Miss Hilfe said, "that the stove's electric."

"But I don't think it is. Why?"

"We've shut them out of here. But they can turn on the gas . . ."

He said, "You ought to be in the game yourself. The things you think of. Here. Give me a hand again. We'll push this couch through into the kitchen . . ." But they stopped almost before they started. He said, "It's too late. Somebody's in there." The tiniest click of a closing door was all they had heard.

"What happens next?" he asked. Memories of *The Little Duke* came incongruously back. He said, "In the old days they always called on the castle to surrender."

"Don't," she whispered. "Please. They are listening."

"I'm getting tired of this cat and mouse act," he said. "We don't even know he's in there. They are frightening us with squeaking doors and the dark." He was moved by a slight hysteria. He called out, "Come in, come in. Don't bother to knock," but no one replied.

He said angrily, "They've chosen the wrong man. They think they can get everything by fear. But you've checked up on me. I'm a murderer, aren't I? You know that. I'm not afraid to kill. Give me any weapon. Just give me a brick." He looked at the suitcase.

Miss Hilfe said, "You're right. We've got to do something, even if it's the wrong thing. Not just let them do everything. Open it."

He gave her hand a quick nervous pressure and released it. Then he opened the lid of the suitcase. . . .

BOOK II

The Happy Man

One: Conversations in Arcady

1

The sun came into the room like pale green underwater light. That was because the tree outside was just budding. The light washed over the white clean walls of the room, over the bed with its primrose yellow cover, over the big armchair and the couch and the bookcase which was full of advanced reading. There were some early daffodils in a vase which had been bought in Sweden, and the only sounds were a fountain dripping somewhere in the cool out-of-doors and the gentle voice of the earnest young man with rimless glasses.

"The great thing, you see, is not to worry. You've had your share of the war for the time being, Mr. Digby, and you can lie back with an easy conscience."

The young man was always strong on the subject of conscience. His own, he had explained weeks ago, was quite clear. Even if his views had not inclined to pacifism, his bad eyes would have prevented him from being of any active value—the poor things peered weakly and trustfully through the huge convex lenses like bottle glass: they pleaded all the time for serious conversation.

"Don't think I'm not enjoying myself here. I am. You know it's a great rest. Only sometimes I try to think . . . who am I?"

"Well, we know that, Mr. Digby. Your identity card—"

"Yes, I know my name's Richard Digby, but who is Richard Digby? What sort of life do you think I led? Do you think I shall ever have the means to repay you all—for this?"

"Now that needn't worry you, Mr. Digby. The doctor is repayed all he wants simply by the interest of your case. You're a very valuable specimen under his microscope."

"But he makes life on the slide so very luxurious, doesn't he?"

"He's wonderful," the young man said. "This place—he planned it all, you know. He's a very great man. There's not a finer shell-shock clinic in the country. Whatever people may say," he added darkly.

"I suppose you have worse cases than mine—violent cases."

"We've had a few. That's why the doctor arranged the sick bay for them. A separate wing and a separate staff. He doesn't want even the attendants in this wing to be mentally disturbed. You see, it's essential that we should be calm too."

"You're certainly all very calm."

"When the time's ripe I expect the doctor will give you a course of psychoanalysis, but it's really much better, you know, that the memory should return of itself—gently and naturally. It's like a film in a hypo bath," he went on, obviously drawing on another man's patter. "The development will come out in patches."

"Not if it's a good hypo bath, Johns," Digby said. He lay back in the armchair, smiling lazily, lean and bearded and middle aged. The angry scar on his forehead looked out of place—like duelling cuts on a professor.

"Hold on to that," Johns said—it was one of his favourite expressions. "You went in for photography then?"

"Do you think that perhaps I was a fashionable portrait photographer?" Digby asked. "It doesn't exactly ring a bell, though of course it goes—doesn't it?—with the beard. No, I was thinking of a dark room on the nursery floor at home. It was a linen cupboard too, and if you forgot to lock the door, a maid would come in with clean pillow slips and bang went the negative. You see, I remember things quite clearly until say eighteen."

"You can talk about that time," Johns said, "as much as you like. You may get a clue and there's obviously no resistance—from the Freudian censor."

"I was just wondering in bed this morning which of the people I wanted to become I did in fact choose. I remember I was very fond of books on African exploration—Stanley, Baker, Livingstone, Burton, but there doesn't seem much opportunity for explorers nowadays."

He brooded without impatience. It was as if his happiness were drawn from an infinite fund of tiredness. He didn't want to exert himself. He was comfortable exactly as he was. Perhaps that was why his memory was slow in returning. He said dutifully, because of course one had to make some effort, "One might look up some old Colonial Office lists. Perhaps I went in for that. It's odd, isn't it, that knowing my name, you shouldn't have found any acquaintance. You'd think there would have been inquiries. If I had been married, for instance. That does trouble me. Suppose my wife is trying to find me." If only that could be cleared up, he thought, I should be perfectly happy.

"As a matter of fact," Johns said and stopped.

"Don't tell me you've unearthed a wife?"

"Not exactly, but I think the doctor has something to tell you."

"Well," Digby said, "it *is* the hour of audience, isn't it?"

Each patient saw the doctor in his study for a quarter of an hour a day, except those who were being treated by psychoanalysis—they were given an hour of his time. It was like visiting a benign headmaster out of school hours to have a chat about personal problems. One passed through the common room where the patients could read the papers, play chess or draughts, or indulge in the rather unpredictable social intercourse of shell-shocked men. Digby as a rule avoided the place; it was disconcerting, in what might have been the lounge of an exclusive hotel, to see a man quietly weeping in a corner. He felt himself to be so completely normal—except for the gap of he didn't know how many years and an inexplicable happiness as if he had been relieved suddenly of some terrible responsibility—that he was ill at ease in the company of men who all exhibited some obvious sign of an ordeal—the twitch of an eyelid, a shrillness of voice, or a melancholy that fitted as completely and inescapably as the skin.

Johns led the way. He filled with perfect tact a part which combined assistant, secretary, and male nurse. He was not qualified, though the doctor occasionally let him loose on the simpler psyches. He had an enormous fund of hero worship for the doctor, and Digby gathered that some incident in the doctor's past—it might have been the suicide of a patient but Johns was studiously vague—enabled him to pose before himself as the champion of the great misunderstood. He said, "The jealousies of medical people—you wouldn't believe it. The malice. The lies." He would get quite pink on the subject of what he called the doctor's martyrdom. There had been an inquiry: the doctor's methods were far in advance of his time; there had been talk—so Digby gathered—of taking away the doctor's license to practise. "They crucified him," he said once with an illustrative gesture and knocked over the vase of daffodils. But eventually good had come out of evil (one felt the good included Johns): the doctor in disgust at the West End world had retired to the country, had opened his private clinic where he refused to accept any patient without a signed personal request—even the more violent cases had been sane enough to put themselves voluntarily under the doctor's care.

"But what about me?" Digby had asked.

"Ah, you are the doctor's special case," Johns said mysteriously. "One day he'll tell you. You stumbled on salvation all right that night. And anyway you did sign."

It never lost its strangeness—to remember nothing of how he had come here. He had simply woken to the restful room, the sound of the fountain, and a taste of drugs. It had been winter then. The trees were black, and sudden squalls of rain broke the peace. Once very far across the fields came a faint wail like a ship signalling departure. He would lie for hours, dreaming confusedly. . . . It was as if then he might have remembered, but he hadn't got the strength to catch the hints, to fix the sudden pictures, he hadn't the vitality to connect. . . . He would drink his medicines without complaint and go off into deep sleep which was only occasionally broken by strange nightmares in which a woman played a part. . . . It was a long time before they told him about the war, and that involved an enormous amount of historical explanation. What seemed odd to him, he found, was not what seemed odd to other people. For example, the fact that Paris was in German hands appeared to him quite natural—he remembered how nearly it had been so before in the period of his life that he could recall, but the fact that we were at war with Italy shook him like an inexplicable catastrophe of nature.

"Italy," he exclaimed. Why, Italy was where two of his maiden aunts went every year to paint. He remembered too the Primitives in the National Gallery and Caporetto and Garibaldi, who had given a name to a biscuit, and Thomas Cook's. Then Johns patiently explained about Mussolini.

2

The doctor sat behind a bowl of flowers at his very simple unpainted desk and he waved Digby in as if this were a favourite pupil. His elderly face under the snow-white hair was hawklike and noble and a little histrionic, like the portrait of a Victorian. Johns sidled out: he gave the impression of stepping backwards the few paces to the door and he stumbled on the edge of the carpet.

"Well, and how are you feeling?" the doctor said. "You look more yourself every day."

"Do I?" Digby asked. "But who knows really if I do? I don't, and you don't, Dr. Forester. Perhaps I look less myself."

"That brings me to a piece of important news," Dr. Forester said. "I have found somebody who *will* know. Somebody who knew you in the old days."

Digby's heart beat violently. He said, "Who?"

"I'm not going to tell you that. I want you to discover everything for yourself."

"It's silly of me," Digby said, "but I feel a bit faint."

"That's only natural," Dr. Forester said. "You aren't very strong yet." He unlocked a cupboard and took out a glass and a bottle of sherry. "This'll put you to rights," he said.

"Tio Pepe," Digby said, draining it.

"You see," the doctor said, "things are coming back. Have another glass?"

"No, it's blasphemy to drink this as medicine."

The news had been a shock. He wasn't sure that he was glad. He couldn't tell what responsibilities might descend on him when his memory returned. Life is broken as a rule to every man gently:

duties accumulate so slowly that we hardly know they are there. Even a happy marriage is a thing of slow growth: love helps to make imperceptible the imprisonment of a man, but in a moment, by order, it would be impossible to love a stranger who entered bearing twenty years of emotional claims. Now, with no memories nearer than his boyhood, he was entirely free. It wasn't that he feared to face himself; he knew what he was and he believed he knew the kind of man the boy he, remembered would have become; it wasn't failure he feared nearly so much as the enormous tasks that success might confront him with.

Dr. Forester said, "I have waited till now, till I felt you were strong enough."

"Yes," Digby said.

"You won't disappoint us, I'm sure," the doctor said. He was more than ever the headmaster, and Digby a pupil who had been entered for a University scholarship: he carried the prestige of the school as well as his own future with him to the examination. Johns would be waiting with anxiety for his return—the form master. Of course they would be very kind if he failed. They would even blame the examiners.

"I'll leave the two of you alone," the doctor said.

"He's here now?"

"*She* is here," the doctor said.

3

It was an immense relief to see a stranger come in. He had been afraid that a whole generation of his life would walk through the door, but it was only a thin pretty girl with reddish hair, a very small girl—perhaps she was too small to be remembered. She wasn't, he felt certain, anybody he needed to fear.

He rose: politeness seemed the wrong thing; he didn't know whether he should shake hands—or kiss her. He did neither. They looked at each other from a distance, and his heart beat heavily.

"How you've changed," she said.

"They are always telling me," he said, "that I'm looking quite myself."

"Your hair is much greyer. And that scar. And yet you look so much younger—happier."

"I lead a very pleasant easy life here."

"They've been good to you?" she asked with anxiety.

"Very good."

He felt as though he had daringly taken a stranger out to dinner and now couldn't hit on the right conversational move. He said, "Excuse me. It sounds so abrupt. But I don't know your name."

"You don't remember me at all?"

"No."

He had occasionally had dreams about a woman, but it wasn't this woman. He couldn't remember any details of the dream except the woman's face, and that had been filled with pain. He was glad that this was not the one. He looked at her again. "No," he said. "I'm sorry. I wish I could."

"Don't be sorry," she said with strange ferocity. "Never be sorry again."

"I just meant—this silly brain of mine."

She said, "My name's Anna." She watched him carefully. "Hilfe."

"That sounds foreign."

"I am Austrian."

He said, "All this is so new to me. We are at war with Germany. Isn't Austria—?"

"I'm a refugee."

"Oh, yes," he said. "I've read about them."

"You had even forgotten the war?" she asked.

"I have a terrible lot to learn," he said.

"Yes, terrible. But need they teach it you?" She repeated, "You look so much happier."

"One wouldn't be happy, not knowing anything." He hesitated and again said, "You must excuse me. There are so many questions. Were we simply friends?"

"Just friends. Why?"

"You are very pretty. I couldn't tell . . ."

"You saved my life."

"How did I do that?"

"When the bomb went off—just before it went off—you knocked me down and fell on me. I wasn't hurt."

"I'm very glad. I mean," he laughed nervously, "there might be all sorts of discreditable things to learn. I'm glad there's one good one."

"It seems so strange," she said. "All these terrible years since nineteen thirty-three—you've just read about them, that's all. They are history to you. You're fresh. You aren't tired like all the rest of us everywhere."

"Nineteen thirty-three," he said. "Nineteen thirty-three. Now ten sixty-six, I can give you that easily. And all the kings of England—at least—I'm not sure—perhaps not all."

"Nineteen thirty-three was when Hitler came to power."

"Of course. I remember now. I've read it all over and over again, but the dates don't stick."

"And I suppose the hate doesn't either."

"I haven't any right to talk about these things," he said. "I haven't lived them. They taught me at school that William Rufus was a wicked king with red hair, but you couldn't expect us to hate him. People like yourself have a right to hate. I haven't. You see I'm untouched."

"Your poor face," she said.

"Oh, the scar. That might have been anything—a motorcar accident. And after all they were not meaning to kill *me.*"

"No?"

"I'm not important." He had been talking foolishly, at random. He had assumed something, and after all there was nothing he could safely assume. He said anxiously, "I'm not important, am I? I can't be, or it would have been in the papers."

"They let you see the papers?"

"Oh, yes, this isn't a prison, you know." He repeated, "I'm not important?"

She said evasively, "You are not famous."

"I suppose the doctor won't let you tell me anything. He says he wants it all to come through my memory, slowly and gently. But I wish you'd break the rule about just one thing. It's the only thing that worries me. I'm not married, am I?"

She said slowly as if she wanted to be very accurate and not to tell more than was necessary, "No, you are not married."

"It was an awful idea that I might suddenly have to take up an old relationship which would mean a lot to someone else and nothing to me. Just something I had been told about like Hitler. Of course a new one's different." He added with a shyness that looked awkward with grey hair, "You are a new one."

"And now there's nothing left to worry you?" she asked.

"Nothing," he said. "Or only one thing—that you might go out of that door and not come back." He was always making advances and then hurriedly retreating, like a boy who hasn't learned the technique. He said, "You see, I've suddenly lost all my friends except you."

She said rather sadly, "Did you have a great many?"

"I suppose—by my age—one would have collected a good many." He said cheerfully, "Or was I such a monster?"

She wouldn't be cheered up. She said, "Oh, I'll come back. They want me to come back. They want to know, you see, as soon as you begin to remember."

"Of course they do. And you are the only clue they can give me. But have I got to stay here till I remember?"

"You wouldn't be much good, would you, without a memory—outside?"

"I don't see why not. There's plenty of work for me. If the army won't have me, there's munitions."

"Do you want to be in it all again?"

He said, "This is lovely and peaceful. But it's only a holiday after all. One's got to be of use." He went on, "Of course it would be much easier if I knew what I'd been, what I could do best. I can't have been a man of leisure. There wasn't enough money in my family." He watched her face carefully while he guessed. "There aren't so many professions. Army, Navy, Church—I wasn't wearing the right clothes, if these are my clothes." There was so much room for doubt. "Law? Was it law, Anna? I don't believe it. I can't see myself in a wig getting some poor devil hanged."

Anna said, "No."

"It doesn't connect. After all the child does make the man. I never wanted to be a lawyer. I did want to be an explorer—but that's unlikely. Even with this beard. They tell me the beard really does belong. I wouldn't know. Oh," he went on, "I had enormous dreams of discovering unknown tribes in Central Africa. Medicine? No, I never liked doctoring. Too much pain. I hated pain." He was troubled by a slight dizziness. He said, "It made me feel ill, sick, hearing of pain. I remember—something about a rat."

"Don't strain," she said. "It's not good to try too hard. There's no hurry."

"Oh, that was neither here nor there. I was a child then. Where did I get to? Medicine—trade. I wouldn't like to remember suddenly that I was the general manager of a chain store. That wouldn't connect either. I never particularly wanted to be rich. I suppose in a way I wanted to lead—a good life."

Any prolonged effort made his head ache. But there were things he had to remember. He could let old friendships and enmities remain in oblivion, but if he were to make something of what was left of life he had to know of what he was capable. He looked at his hand and flexed the fingers: they didn't feel useful.

"People don't always become what they want to be," Anna said.

"Of course not, a boy always wants to be a hero. A great explorer. A great writer. But there's usually a thin disappointing connection. The boy who wants to be rich goes into a bank. The explorer becomes—oh, well, some underpaid colonial officer marking minutes in the heat. The writer joins the staff of a penny paper." He said, "I'm sorry. I'm not as strong as I thought. I've gone a bit giddy. I'll have to stop—work—for the day."

Again she asked with odd anxiety, "They are good to you here?"

"I'm a prize patient," he said. "An interesting case."

"And Dr. Forester—you like Dr. Forester?"

"He fills one with awe," he said.

"You've changed so much." She made a remark he couldn't understand. "This is how you should have been." They shook hands like strangers. He said, "And you'll come back often?"

"It's my job," she said, "Arthur." It was only after she had gone that he wondered at the name.

4

In the mornings a servant brought him breakfast in bed: coffee, toast, a boiled egg. The Home was nearly self-supporting; it had its own hens and pigs and a good many acres of rough shooting. The doctor did not shoot, himself; he did not approve, Johns said, of taking animal life, but he was not a doctrinaire. His patients needed meat, and therefore shoots were held, though the doctor took no personal part. "It's really the idea of making it a sport," Johns explained, "which is against the grain. I think he'd really rather trap."

On the tray lay always the morning paper. Digby had not been allowed this privilege for some weeks until the war had been gently broken to him. Now he could lie late in bed, propped comfortably on three pillows, and take a look at the news: "Air raid casualties this week are down to 255," sip his coffee and tap the shell of his boiled egg; then back to the paper: "The Battle of the Atlantic. . . ." The eggs were always done exactly right: the white set and the yolk liquid and thick. Back to the paper: "The Admiralty regret to announce . . . lost with all hands." There was always enough butter to put a little in the egg, for the doctor kept his own cows.

This morning as he was reading Johns came in for a chat, and Digby, looking up from the paper, asked, "What's a Fifth Column?"

There was nothing Johns liked better than giving information. He talked for quite a while, bringing in Napoleon.

"In other words, people in enemy pay?" Digby said. "That's nothing new."

"There's this difference," Johns said. "In the last war—except for Irishmen like Casement—the pay was always cash. Only a certain class was attracted. In this war there are all sorts of ideologies. The man who thinks gold is evil—he's naturally attracted to the German economic system. And the men who for years have talked against nationalism—well, they are seeing all the old national boundaries obliterated. Pan-Europe. Perhaps not quite in the way they meant. Napoleon too appealed to idealists." His glasses twinkled in the morning sun with the joys of instruction. "When you come to think of it, Napoleon was beaten by the little men, the materialists. Shopkeepers and peasants. People who couldn't see beyond their counter or their field. They'd eaten their lunch under that hedge all their life and they meant to go on doing it. So Napoleon went to St. Helena."

"You don't sound a convinced patriot yourself," Digby said.

"Oh, but I am," Johns said earnestly. "I'm a little man too. My father's a chemist, and how he hates all these German medicines that were flooding the market. I'm like him. I'd rather stick to Burroughs and Wellcome than all the Beyers." He went on, "All the same the other does represent a mood. It's we who are the materialists. The scrapping of all the old boundaries, the new economic ideas—the hugeness of the dream. It *is* attractive to men who are not tied—to a particular village or town they don't want to see scrapped. People with unhappy childhoods, progressive people who learn Esperanto, vegetarians who don't like shedding blood."

"But Hitler seems to be shedding plenty."

"Yes, but the idealists don't see blood like you and I do. They aren't materialists. It's all statistics to them."

"What about Dr. Forester?" Digby asked. "He seems to fit the picture."

"Oh," Johns said enthusiastically, "he's sound as a bell. He's written a pamphlet for the Ministry of Information. 'The Psychoanalysis of Nazidom.' But there was a time," he added, "when there was—talk. You can't avoid witch-hunting in wartime, and of course there were rivals to hallo on the pack. You see, Dr. Forester —well, he's so alive to everything. He likes to know. For instance, spiritualism—he's very interested in spiritualism, as an investigator."

"I was just reading the questions in Parliament," Digby said. "They suggest there's another kind of Fifth Column. People who are blackmailed."

"The Germans are wonderfully thorough," Johns said. "They did that in their own country. Card indexed all the so-called leaders, socialites, diplomats, politicians, labour leaders, priests—and then presented the ultimatum. Everything forgiven and forgotten, or the public prosecutor. It wouldn't surprise me if they'd done the same thing over here. They formed, you know, a kind of Ministry of Fear—with the most efficient undersecretaries. It isn't only that they get a hold on certain people. It's the general atmosphere they spread, so that you feel you can't depend on a soul."

"Apparently," Digby said, "this M.P. has got the idea that important plans have been stolen from the Ministry of Home Security. They had been brought over from a Service Ministry for a consultation and lodged overnight. He claims that next morning they were found to be missing."

"There must be an explanation," Johns said.

"There is. The Minister says that the honourable member was misinformed. The plans were not required for the morning conference, and at the afternoon conference they were produced, fully discussed, and returned to the Service Ministry."

"These M.P.'s get hold of odd stories," Johns said.

"Do you think," Digby asked, "that by any chance I was a detective before this happened? That might fit the ambition to be an explorer, mightn't it? Because there seem to me to be so many holes in the statement."

"It seems quite clear to me."

"The M.P. who asked the question must have been briefed by someone who knew about those plans. Somebody at the conference —or somebody who was concerned in sending or receiving the plans. Nobody else could have known about them. Their existence is admitted by the Minister."

"Yes, yes. That's true."

"It's strange that anyone in that position should spread a canard. And do you notice that in that smooth elusive way politicians have the Minister doesn't in fact deny that the plans were missing? He says that they weren't wanted, and that when they were wanted they were there."

"You mean there was time to photograph them?" Johns said excitedly. "Would you mind if I smoked a cigarette? Here, let me take your tray." He spilled some coffee on the bedsheet. "Do you know," he said, "there was a suggestion of that kind made nearly three months ago. It was just after your arrival. I'll look it up for you. Dr. Forester keeps a file of the *Times*. Some papers were missing then for several hours. They tried to hush that up—said it was just a case of carelessness and that the papers had never been out of the Ministry. An M.P. made a fuss—talked about photographs, and they came down on him like a sledgehammer. Trying to undermine public confidence. The papers had never left the possession— I can't remember whose possession. Somebody whose word you had to take or else one of you would go to Brixton and you could feel sure that it wouldn't be he. The papers shut down on it right away."

"It would be strange, wouldn't it, if the same thing had happened again?"

Johns said excitedly, "Nobody outside would know. And the others wouldn't say."

"Perhaps the first time was a failure. Perhaps the photos didn't come out properly. Someone bungled. And of course they couldn't use the same man twice. They had to wait until they got their hands on a second man. Until they had him carded and filed in the Ministry of Fear." He thought aloud, "I suppose almost the only men they couldn't blackmail for something shabby would be saints—or outcasts with nothing to lose."

"You weren't a detective," Johns exclaimed, "you were a detective writer."

Digby said, "You know I feel quite tired. The brain begins to tick and then suddenly I feel so tired I could lie down and sleep. Perhaps I will." He closed his eyes and then opened them again. "The thing to do," he said, "would be to follow up the first case—the bungled one, to find the point of failure." Then he slept.

5

It was a fine afternoon, and Digby went for a solitary walk in the garden. Several days had passed since Anna Hilfe's visit, and he felt restless and moody, like a boy in love. He wanted an opportunity to show that he was no invalid, that his mind could work as

well as another man's. There was no satisfaction in shining before
Johns. . . . He dreamed wildly between the box hedges.

The garden was of a rambling kind which should have belonged
to childhood and only belonged to childish men. The apple trees
were old apple trees and gave the effect of growing wild: they
sprang unexpectedly up in the middle of a rosebed, trespassed on
a tennis court, shaded the window of a little outside lavatory like a
potting shed which was used by the gardener—an old man who
could always be located from far away by the sound of a scythe or
the trundle of a wheelbarrow. A high red brick wall divided the
flower garden from the kitchen garden and the orchard, but flowers
and fruit could not be imprisoned by a wall. Flowers broke among
the artichokes and sprang up like flames under the trees. Beyond
the orchard the garden faded gradually out into paddocks and a
stream and a big untidy pond with an island the size of a billiard
table.

It was by the pond that Digby found Major Stone. He heard him
first: a succession of angry grunts like a dog dreaming. Digby
scrambled down a bank to the black edge of the water and Major
Stone turned his very clear blue military eyes on him and said, "The
job's got to be done." There was mud all over his tweed suit and
mud on his hands: he had been throwing large stones into the
water and now he was dragging a plank he must have found in
the potting shed along the edge of the water.

"It's sheer treachery," Major Stone said, "to leave a place like
that unoccupied. You could command the whole house." He slid
the plank forward so that one end rested on a large stone. "Steady
does it," he said. He advanced the plank inch by inch towards the
next stone. "Here," he said, "you ease it along. I'll take the other
end."

"Surely you aren't going in?"

"No depth at this side," Major Stone said and walked straight
into the pond. The black mud closed over his shoes and the turn-
ups of his trousers. "Now," he said, "push. Steady does it." Digby
pushed but pushed too hard: the plank toppled sideways into the
mud. "Damnation," said Major Stone. He bent and heaved and
brought the plank up; scattering mud up to his waist, he lugged it
ashore.

"Apologize," he said. "My temper's damned short. You aren't a
trained man. Good of you to help."

"I'm afraid I wasn't much good."

"Just give me half a dozen sappers," Major Stone said, "and you'd see." He stared wistfully across at the little bushy island. "But it's no good asking for the impossible. We've just got to make do. We'd manage all right if it weren't for all this treachery." He looked Digby in the eyes as though he were sizing him up. "I've seen you about here a lot," he said. "Never spoke to you before. Liked the look of you, if you don't mind my saying so. I suppose you've been sick like the rest of us. Thank God, I'll be leaving here soon. Able to be of use again. What's been your trouble?"

"Loss of memory," Digby said.

"Been out there?" the major asked, jerking his head in the direction of the island.

"No, it was a bomb. In London."

"A bad war this," the major said. "Civilians with shell-shock." It was uncertain whether he disapproved of the civilians or the shell-shock. His stiff fair hair was grizzled over the ears, and his very blue eyes peered out from under a yellow thatch. The whites were beautifully clear: he was a man who had always kept himself fit—and ready to be of use. Now that he wasn't fit and wasn't of use, an awful confusion ruled the poor brain. He said, "There was treachery somewhere or it would never have happened," and, turning his back abruptly on the island and the muddy remnants of his causeway, he scrambled up the bank and walked briskly towards the house.

Digby strolled on. At the tennis court a furious game was in progress—a really furious game. The two men leaped and sweated and scowled: their immense concentration was the only thing that looked abnormal about Still and Fishguard, but when the set was over they would grow shrill and quarrelsome and a little hysterical. The same climax would be reached at chess.

The rose garden was sheltered by two walls: one the wall of the vegetable garden, the other the high wall that cut communication—except for one small door—with what Dr. Forester and Johns called euphemistically "the sick bay." Nobody cared to talk about the sick bay; grim things were assumed, a padded room, strait jackets: you could see only the top windows from the garden and they were barred. Not one man in the sanatorium was ignorant of how close he lived to that quiet wing. Hysteria over a game, a sense of treachery, in the case of Davis tears that came too easily—they knew those things meant sickness just as much as violence did. They had signed away their freedom to Dr. Forester in the hope of escaping worse, but if worse happened the building was there on the spot—"the sick bay"—there would be no need to travel to a strange asylum. Only Digby felt quite free from its shadow: the sick bay was not there for a happy man. Behind him the voices rose shrilly from the tennis court: Fishguard's "I tell you it was inside." "Out." "Are you accusing me of cheating?" "You ought to have your eyes seen to"—that was Still. The voices sounded so irreconcilable that you would have said such a quarrel could have no other end than blows —but no blow was ever struck. Fear of the sick bay perhaps. The voices went suddenly off the air like an unpopular turn. When the dusk fell, Still and Fishguard would be in the lounge playing chess together.

How far was the sick bay, Digby sometimes wondered, a fantasy of disordered minds? It was there of course, the brick wing and the barred windows and the high wall: there was even a segregated staff whom other patients had certainly met at the monthly social evening which he had not yet attended. (The doctor believed that these occasions on which strangers were present—the local clergyman, a sprinkling of elderly ladies, a retired architect—helped the shell-shocked brains to adapt themselves to society and the conventions of good behaviour.) But was anybody certain that the sick bay was occupied? Sometimes it occurred to Digby that the wing had no more reality than the conception of Hell presented by sympathetic theologians—a place without inhabitants which existed simply as a warning.

Suddenly Major Stone appeared again, walking rapidly. He saw Digby and veered towards him down one of the paths. Little beads of sweat stood on his forehead. He said to Digby, "You haven't seen me, do you hear? You haven't seen me," and brushed by. He seemed to be making for the paddock and the pond. In another moment he was out of sight among the shrubberies, and Digby walked on. It seemed to him that the time had come for him to leave. He wasn't in place here: he was normal. A faint uneasiness touched him when he remembered that Major Stone too had considered himself cured.

As he came in front of the house Johns emerged. He looked ruffled and anxious. He said, "Have you seen Major Stone?" Digby hesitated for a second only. Then he said, "No."

Johns said, "The doctor wants him. He's had a relapse."

The camaraderie of a fellow-patient weakened. Digby said, "I did see him earlier."

"The doctor's very anxious. He may do himself an injury—or someone else." The rimless glasses seemed to be heliographing a warning, Do *you* wish to be responsible?

Digby said uneasily, "You might have a look round the pond."

"Thanks," Johns said and called out, "Poole. Poole."

"I'm coming," a voice said.

A sense of apprehension moved like a heavy dark curtain in Digby's brain: it was as though someone had whispered faintly to him so that he couldn't be sure of the words, "Take care." A man stood at the gate from the sick bay, wearing the same kind of white coat that Johns wore on duty but not so clean. He was a dwarfish man with huge twisted shoulders and an arrogant face. "The pond," Johns said.

The man blinked and made no movement, staring at Digby with impertinent curiosity. He had obviously come from the sick bay: he didn't belong in the garden. His coat and fingers were stained with what looked like iodine.

"We've got to hurry," Johns said. "The doctor's anxious—"

"Haven't I met you," Poole said, "somewhere before?" He watched Digby with a kind of enjoyment. "Oh, yes, I'm sure I have."

"No," Digby said. "No."

"Well, we know each other now," Poole said. He grinned at Digby and said with relish, "I'm the keeper," swinging a long simian arm towards the sick bay.

Digby said loudly, "I don't know you from Adam. I don't want to know you," and had time to see Johns' look of amazement before he turned his back and listened to their footsteps hurrying towards the pond.

It was true: he didn't know the man, but the whole obscurity of his past had seemed to shake—something at any moment might emerge from behind the curtain. He had been frightened and so he had been vehement, but he felt sure that a black mark would be made on his chart of progress and he was apprehensive. Why should he fear to remember anything? He whispered to himself, "After all, I'm not a criminal."

6

At the front door a servant met him. "Mr. Digby," she told him, "there's a visitor for you," and his heart beat with hope.

"Where?"

"In the lounge."

She was there, looking at a *Tatler,* and he had no idea what to say to her. She stood there as he seemed to remember her from very far back, small, tense, on guard, and yet she was part of a whole world of experience of which he was innocent.

"It's good of you," he began and stopped. He was afraid if he once began making the small talk of a stranger, they would be condemned for life to that shadowy relationship. The weather would lie heavily on their tongues, and they would meet occasionally and talk about the theatre. When they passed in the street he would raise his hat, and something which was only just alive would be safely and hopelessly dead.

He said slowly, "I have been longing for this ever since you came before. The days have been very long with nothing to do in them but think and wonder. This is such a strange life."

"Strange and horrible," she said.

"Not so horrible," he said, but then he remembered Poole. He said, "How did we talk before my memory went? We didn't stand stiffly, did we, like this—you holding a paper and I—we were good friends, weren't we?"

"Yes."

He said, "We've got to get back. This isn't right. Sit down here and we'll both shut our eyes. Pretend it's the old days before the bomb went off. What were you saying to me just then?" She sat in miserable silence, and he said with astonishment, "You shouldn't cry."

"You said shut your eyes."

"They are shut now."

The bright artificial lounge where he felt a stranger, the glossy magazines and the glass ash trays were no longer visible: there was just darkness. He put out his hand and touched her. He said, "Is this strange?"

After a long time a small dried-up voice said, "No."

He said, "Of course I loved you, didn't I?" When she didn't answer he said, "I must have loved you. Because directly you came in the other day—there was such a sense of relief, of peace, as if I'd been expecting someone different. How could I have helped loving you?"

"It doesn't seem likely," she said.

"Why not?"

"We'd only known each other a few days."

"Too short of course for you to care about me."

Again there was a long silence. Then she said, "Yes, I did."

"Why? I'm so much older. I'm not much to look at. What sort of a person was I?"

She replied at once as though this was easy; this was part of the lesson she had really learned: she had turned this over in her mind again and again. "You had a great sense of pity. You didn't like people to suffer."

"Is that unusual?" he asked, genuinely seeking information: he knew nothing of how people lived and thought outside.

"It was unusual," she said, "where I came from. My brother—" She caught her breath sharply.

"Of course," he said, quickly snatching at a memory before it went again, "you had a brother, hadn't you? He was a friend of mine too?"

"Let's stop playing this game," she said. "Please." They opened their eyes simultaneously on the suave room.

He said, "I want to leave here."

"No," she said, "stay. Please."

"Why?"

"You are safe here."

He smiled. "From more bombs?"

"From a lot of things. You are happy here, aren't you?"

"In a way."

"There"—she seemed to indicate the whole external world beyond the garden wall—"you weren't happy." She added slowly, "I would do anything to keep you happy. This is how you should be. This is how I like you."

"You didn't like me out there?" He tried to catch her humorously in a contradiction, but she wouldn't play. She said, "You can't go on seeing someone unhappy all day, every day, without breaking."

"I wish I could remember."

"Why bother to remember?"

He said simply—it was one of the few things of which he was certain: "Oh, of course one's got to remember."

She watched him with intensity as though she were making up her mind to some course of action. He went on, "If only to remember you, how I talked to you—"

"Oh, don't," she said, "don't," and added harshly like a declaration of war, "dear heart."

He said triumphantly, "That was how we talked."

She nodded, keeping her eyes on him. He said, "My dear . . ."

Her voice was dry like an old portrait: the social varnish was cracking. She said, "You always used to say that you'd do impossible things for me."

"Yes?"

"Do some possible ones. Just be quiet. Stay here a few more weeks till your memory comes back."

"If you'll come often."

"I'll come."

He put his mouth against hers: the action had all the uncertainty of an adolescent kiss. "My dear, my dear," he said, "why did you say we were only friends?"

"I wasn't going to bind you."

"You've bound me now."

She said slowly as though she were astonished, "And I'm glad."

All the way upstairs to his room he could smell her. He could have gone into any chemist's shop and picked her powder, and he could have told in the dark the texture of her skin. The experience was as new to him as adolescent love: he had the blind passionate innocence of a boy. Like a boy, he was driven relentlessly towards inevitable suffering, loss, and despair and called it happiness.

7

Next morning there was no paper on his tray. He asked the woman who brought his breakfast where it was, but all she could tell him was that she supposed it hadn't been delivered. He was touched again by the faint fear he had felt the previous afternoon when Poole came out of the sick bay, and he waited impatiently for Johns to arrive for his morning chat and smoke. But Johns didn't come. He lay in bed and brooded for half an hour and then rang his bell. It was time for his clothes to be laid out, but when the maid came she said she had no orders.

"But you don't need orders," he said. "You do it every day."

"I has to have my orders," she said.

"Tell Mr. Johns I'd like to see him."

"Yes, sir"—but Johns didn't come. It was as if a cordon sanitaire had been drawn around his room.

For another half-hour he waited, doing nothing. Then he got out of bed and went to the bookcase, but there was little that promised him distraction—only the iron rations of learned old men. Tolstoy's *What I Believe,* Freud's *The Psychoanalysis of Everyday Life,* a biography of Rudolf Steiner. He took the Tolstoy back with him and, opening it, found faint indentations in the margin where pencil marks had been rubbed out.

It is always of interest to know what strikes another human being as remarkable, and he read: "Remembering all the evil I have done, suffered and seen, resulting from the enmity of nations, it is clear to me that the cause of it all lay in the gross fraud called patriotism and love of one's country. . . ."

There was a kind of nobility in the blind shattering dogma, just as there was something ignoble in the attempt to rub out the pencil mark. This was an opinion to be held openly, if at all. He looked farther up the page: "Christ showed me that the fifth snare depriving me of welfare is the separation we make of our own from other nations. I cannot but believe this, and therefore if in a moment of forgetfulness feelings of enmity towards a man of another nation may arise within me . . ."

But that wasn't the point, he thought: he felt no enmity towards any individual across the frontier; if he wanted to take part again, it was love which drove him and not hate. He thought, Like Johns, I am one of the little men, not interested in ideologies, tied to a flat Cambridgeshire landscape, a chalk quarry, a line of willows across the featureless fields, a market town—his thoughts scrabbled at the curtain—where he used to dance at the Saturday hops. He fell back on one face with a sense of immeasurable relief: he could rest there. Ah, he thought, Tolstoy should have lived in a small country —not in Russia which was a continent rather than a country. And why does he write as if the worst thing we can do to our fellow-man is to kill him? Everybody has to die and everybody fears death, but when we kill a man we save him from his fear which would otherwise grow year by year. . . . One doesn't necessarily kill because one hates; one may kill because one loves. . . . And again the old dizziness came back as though he had been struck over the heart.

He lay back on his pillow, and the brave old man with the long beard seemed to buzz at him: "I cannot acknowledge any States or nations. . . . I cannot take part . . . I cannot take part." A kind of waking dream came to him of a man—perhaps a friend, he couldn't see his face—who hadn't been able to take part: some private grief had isolated him and hidden him like a beard. What was it? He couldn't remember. The war and all that happened round him had seemed to belong to other people. The old man in the beard he felt convinced was wrong. He was too busy saving his own soul. Wasn't it better to take part even in the crimes of people you loved, if it was necessary hate as they did, and if that were the end of everything suffer damnation with them rather than be saved alone?

But that reasoning, it could be argued, excused your enemy. And why not? he thought. It excused anyone who loved enough to kill or be killed. Why shouldn't you excuse your enemy? That didn't mean you must stand in lonely superiority, refuse to kill, and turn the intolerable cheek. "If a man offend *thee* . . ." There was the point—not to kill for one's own sake. But for the sake of people you loved, and in the company of people you loved, it was right to risk damnation.

His mind returned to Anna Hilfe. When he thought of her it was with an absurd breathlessness. It was as if he were waiting again years ago outside—wasn't it the King's Arms?—and the girl he loved was coming down the street, and the night was full of pain and beauty and despair because one knew one was too young for anything to come of this. . . .

He couldn't be bothered with Tolstoy any longer. It was unbearable to be treated as an invalid. What woman outside a Victorian novel could care for an invalid? It was all very well for Tolstoy to preach non-resistance: he had had his heroic violent hour at Sevastopol. Digby got out of bed and saw in the long narrow mirror his thin body and his grey hair and his beard.

The door opened: it was Dr. Forester. Behind him, eyes lowered, subdued like someone found out, came Johns. Dr. Forester shook his head and, "It won't do, Digby," he said, "it won't do. I'm disappointed."

Digby was still watching the sad grotesque figure in the mirror. He said, "I want my clothes. And a razor."

"Why a razor?"

"To shave. I'm certain this beard doesn't belong."

"That only shows your memory isn't returning yet."

"And I had no paper this morning," he went weakly on.

Dr. Forester said, "I gave orders that the paper was to be stopped. Mr. Johns has been acting unwisely. These long conversations about the war—you've excited yourself. Poole has told me how excited you were yesterday."

Digby with his eyes on his own ageing figure in the striped pajamas said, "I won't be treated like an invalid or a child."

"You seem to have got it into your head," Dr. Forester said, "that you have a talent for detection, that you were a detective perhaps in your previous life."

"That was a joke," Digby said.

"I can assure you you were something quite different. Quite different," Dr. Forester repeated.

"What was I?"

"It may be necessary one day to tell you," Dr. Forester said, as though he were uttering a threat. "If it will prevent foolish mistakes." Johns stood behind the doctor, looking at the floor.

"I'm leaving here," Digby said.

The calm noble old face of Dr. Forester suddenly crumpled into lines of dislike. He said sharply, "And pay your bill, I hope?"

"I hope so too."

The features re-formed, but they were less convincing now. "My dear Digby," Dr. Forester said, "you must be reasonable. You are a very sick man, a very sick man indeed. Twenty years of your life have been wiped out. That's not health. And yesterday and just now you showed an excitement which I've feared and hoped to avoid." He put his hand gently on the pajama sleeve and said, "I don't want to have to restrain you, to have you certified—"

Digby said, "But I'm as sane as you are. You must know that."

"Major Stone thought so too. But I've had to transfer him to the sick bay. He had an obsession which might at any time have led to violence."

"But I—"

"Your symptoms are very much the same. This excitement." The doctor raised his hand from the sleeve to the shoulder, a warm soft moist hand. He said, "Don't worry. We won't let it come to that, but for a little we must be very quiet—plenty of food, plenty of sleep, some very gentle bromides, no visitors for a while, not even our friend Johns, no more of these exciting intellectual conversations."

"Miss Hilfe," Digby said.

"I made a mistake there," Dr. Forester said. "We were not strong enough. I have told Miss Hilfe not to come again."

Two: The Sick Bay

1

When a man rubs out a pencil mark he should be careful to see that the line is quite obliterated. For if a secret is to be kept no precautions are too great. If Dr. Forester had not so inefficiently rubbed out the pencil marks in the margins of Tolstoy's *What I Believe,* Mr. Rennit might never have learned what had happened to Jones, Johns would have remained a hero worshipper, and it is possible that Major Stone would have slowly wilted into further depths of insanity between the padded hygienic walls of his room in the sick bay. And Digby—might have remained Digby.

For it was the rubbed-out pencil marks which kept Digby awake and brooding at the end of a day of loneliness and boredom. You couldn't respect a man who dared not hold his opinions openly, and when respect for Dr. Forester was gone, a great deal went with it. The noble old face became less convincing: his qualifications even became questionable. What right had he to forbid the newspapers? Above all, what right had he to forbid the visits of Anna Hilfe?

Digby still felt like a schoolboy, but he now knew that his headmaster had secrets of which he was ashamed: he was no longer austere and self-sufficient. And so the schoolboy planned rebellion. At about half-past nine in the evening he heard the sound of a car and, watching between the curtains, he saw the doctor drive away. Or rather Poole drove and the doctor sat beside him.

Until Digby saw Poole he had planned only a petty rebellion— a secret visit to Johns' room; he felt sure he could persuade that young man to talk. Now he became bolder: he would visit the sick bay itself and speak to Stone. The patients must combine against tyranny, and an old memory slipped back of a deputation he had once led to his real headmaster because his form against all precedent—for it was a classical form—had been expected by a new master to learn trigonometry. The strange thing about a memory like that was that it seemed young as well as old: so little had happened since that he could remember. He had lost all his mature experience.

A bubble of excited merriment impeded his breath as he opened the door of his room and took a quick look down the corridor. He was afraid of undefined punishments, and for that reason he felt his action was heroic and worthy of someone in love. There was an innocent sensuality in his thought: he was like a boy who boasts to a girl of a beating he has risked, sitting in the sunshine by the cricket ground, drinking ginger beer, hearing the pad, pad of wood and leather, under the spell, daydreaming and in love. . . .

There was a graduated curfew for patients according to their health, but by half-past nine all were supposed to be in bed and asleep. But you couldn't enforce sleep. Passing Davis's door, he could hear the strange uncontrollable whine of a man weeping. Farther down the passage Johns' door was open and the light was on. Taking off his bedroom slippers, he passed quickly across the doorway, but Johns wasn't there. Incurably sociable, he was probably chatting with the housekeeper. On his desk was a pile of newspapers: he had obviously picked them out for Digby before the doctor had laid his ban. It was a temptation to stay and read them, but the small temptation didn't suit the mood of high adventure. Tonight he would do something no patient had ever voluntarily done before—enter the sick bay. He moved carefully and silently—the words of the Pathfinder and Indian came to his mind—downstairs.

In the lounge the lights were off, but the curtains were undrawn and the moonlight welled in with the sound of the plashing fountain and the shadow of silver leaves. The *Tatlers* had been tidied on the tables, the ash trays taken away, and the cushions shaken on the chairs—it looked now like a room in an exhibition where nobody crossed the ropes. The next door brought him into the passage by Dr. Forester's study. As he quietly closed each door behind him he felt as though he were cutting off his own retreat. His ribs seemed to vibrate to the beat, beat of his heart. Ahead of him was the green baize door he had never seen opened, and beyond that door lay the sick bay. He was back in his own childhood, breaking out of dormitory, daring more than he really wanted to dare, proving himself. He hoped the door would be bolted on the other side; then there would be nothing he could do but creep back to bed, honour satisfied.

The door pulled easily open. It was only the cover for another door, to deaden sound and leave the doctor in his study undisturbed. But that door too had been left unlocked, unbolted. As he passed into the passage beyond, the green baize swung to behind him with a long sigh.

2

He stood stone still and listened. Somewhere a clock ticked with a cheap tinny sound, and a tap had been left dripping. This must once have been the servants' quarters; the floor was stone, and his bedroom slippers pushed up a little smoke of dust. Everything spoke of neglect; the woodwork when he reached the stairs had not been polished for a very long time and the thin drugget had been worn threadbare. It was an odd contrast to the spruce nursing home beyond the door; everything round him shrugged its shoulders and said, "We are not important. Nobody sees us here. Our only duty is to be quiet and not disturb the doctor." And what could be quieter than dust? If it had not been for the clock ticking he would have doubted whether anyone really lived in this part of the house —the clock and the faintest tang of stale cigarette smoke, of Caporal, that set his heart beating again with apprehension.

Where the clock ticked Poole must live. Whenever he thought of Poole he was aware of something unhappy, something imprisoned at the bottom of the brain trying to climb out. It frightened him in the same way as birds frightened him when they beat up and down in closed rooms. There was only one way to escape that fear—the fear of another creature's pain. That was to lash out until the bird was stunned and quiet or dead. For the moment he forgot Major Stone and smelled his way towards Poole's room.

It was at the end of the passage where the tap dripped, a large square comfortless room with a stone floor, divided in half by a curtain—it had probably once been a kitchen. Its new owner had lent it an aggressive and squalid masculinity, as if he had something to prove: there were ends of cigarettes upon the floor, and nothing was used for its right purpose. A clock and a cheap brown teapot served as bookends on a wardrobe to prop up a shabby collection —Carlyle's *Heroes and Hero Worship,* lives of Napoleon and Cromwell, and numbers of little paper-covered books about what to do with Youth, Labour, Europe, God. The windows were all shut, and when Digby lifted the drab curtain he could see the bed had not been properly made—or else Poole had flung himself down for a rest and hadn't bothered to tidy it afterwards. The tap dripped into a fixed basin and a razor strop dangled from a bedpost. An old tin which had once held lobster paste now held old razor blades. The place was as comfortless as a transit camp; the owner might have been someone who was just passing on and couldn't be bothered to change so much as a stain on the wall. An open suitcase full of soiled underclothes gave the impression that he hadn't even troubled to unpack.

It was like the underside of a stone: you turned up the bright polished nursing home and found beneath it this.

Everywhere there was the smell of Caporal, and on the bed there were crumbs, as though Poole took food to bed with him. Digby stared at the crumbs a long while; a feeling of sadness and disquiet and dangers he couldn't place haunted him—as though something were disappointing his expectations, as though the cricket match were a frost, nobody had come to the half-term holiday, and he waited and waited outside the King's Arms for a girl who would never turn up. He had nothing to compare this place with. The nursing home was something artificial, hidden in a garden. Was it possible that ordinary life was like this? He remembered a lawn and afternoon tea and a drawing room with water-colours and little tables and a piano no one played on and the smell of eau de cologne: was this the real adult life to which we all came in time? Had he too belonged to this world? He was saddened by a sense of familiarity. And yet this was not what he had dreamed a few years back at school. But then he remembered that the years since then were not few but many.

At last the sense of danger reminded him of poor imprisoned Stone. He might not have long before the doctor and Poole returned, and though he could not believe they had any power over him, he was yet afraid of sanctions he couldn't picture. His slippers padded again up the passage and up the dingy stairs to the first floor. There was no sound here at all: the tick of the clock didn't reach so far; large bells on rusty wires hung outside what might have been the butler's pantry. They were marked Study, Drawing Room, 1st Spare Bedroom, 2nd Spare Bedroom, Day Nursery. . . . The wires sagged with disuse and a spider had laid its scaffolding across the bell marked Dining Room.

The barred windows he had seen over the garden wall had been on the second floor and he mounted unwillingly higher. He was endangering his own retreat with every step, but he had dared himself to speak to Stone, and if it were only one syllable he must speak it. He went down a passage, calling softly, "Stone. Stone."

There was no reply and the old cracked linoleum creaked under his feet and sometimes caught his toes. Again he felt a familiarity—

as if this cautious walking, this solitary passage, belonged more to his world than the sleek bedroom in the other wing. "Stone," he called, "Stone," and heard a voice answer, "Barnes. Is that you, Barnes?" coming startlingly from the door beside him.

"Hush," he said and, putting his lips close to the keyhole, "it's not Barnes. It's Digby."

He heard Stone sigh. "Of course," the voice said, "Barnes is dead. I was dreaming."

"Are you all right, Stone?"

"I've had an awful time," Stone said, so low that Digby could hardly hear him, "an awful time. I didn't really mean I wouldn't eat . . ."

"Come to the door so that I can hear you better."

Stone said, "They've got me in one of these strait jackets. They said I was violent. I don't think I was violent. It's just the treachery." He must have got nearer the door because his voice was much clearer. He said, "Old man, I know I've been a bit touched. We all are in this place, aren't we? But I'm not *mad*. It just isn't right."

"What did you do?"

"I wanted to find a room to enfilade that island from. They'd begun to dig, you see, months ago. I saw them one evening after dark. One couldn't leave it at that. The Hun doesn't let the grass grow. So I came through into this wing and went to Poole's room . . ."

"Yes?"

"I didn't mean to make them jump. I just wanted to explain what I was after."

"Jump?"

"The doctor was there with Poole. They were doing something in the dark—" The voice broke; it was horrible hearing a middle-aged man sobbing invisibly behind a locked door.

"But the digging?" Digby asked. "You must have dreamed . . ."

"That tube—it was awful, old man. I hadn't really meant I wouldn't eat. I was just afraid of poison."

"Poison?"

"Treachery," the voice said. "Listen, Barnes—"

"I'm not Barnes."

Again there was a long sigh. "Of course. I'm sorry. It's getting me down. I *am* touched you know. Perhaps they are right."

"Who's Barnes?"

"He was a good man. They got him on the beach. It's no good,

Digby. I'm mad. Every day in every way I get worse and worse."

Somewhere from far away, through an open window on the floor below, came the sound of a car. Digby put his lips to the door and said, "I can't stay, Stone. Listen. You are not mad. You've got ideas into your head, that's all. It's not right putting you here. Somehow I'll get you out. Just stick it."

"You're a good chap, Digby."

"They've threatened me with this too."

"You," Stone whispered back. "But you're sane enough. By God, perhaps I'm not so touched after all. If they want to put you here, it must be treachery."

"Stick it."

"I'll stick it, old man. It was the uncertainty. I thought perhaps they were right."

The sound of the car faded.

"Haven't you any relations?"

"Not a soul," the voice said. "I had a wife, but she went away. She was quite right, old chap, quite right. There was a lot of treachery."

"I'll get you out. I don't know how, but I'll get you out."

"That island, Digby—you've got to watch it, old man. I can't do anything here, and I don't matter anyway. But if I could just have fifty of the old bunch . . ."

Digby reassured him gently, "I'll watch the island."

"I thought the Hun had got hold of it. They don't let the grass grow. But I'm sometimes a bit confused, old man."

"I must go now. Just stick it."

"I'll stick it, old man. Been in worse places. But I wish you didn't have to go."

"I'll come back for you."

But he hadn't the faintest idea of how. A terrible sense of pity moved him: he felt capable of murder for the release of that gentle tormented creature. He could see him now, walking into the muddy pond—the very clear blue eyes and the bristly military moustache and the lines of care and responsibility. That was a thing you learned in this place: that a man kept his character even when he was insane. No madness would ever dim that military sense of duty to others.

His reconnaissance had proved easier than he had any right to expect: the doctor must be taking a long ride. He reached the green baize door safely, and when it sighed behind him it was like Stone's weary patience asking him to come back. He passed quickly through the lounge and then more carefully up the stairs until he came again within sight of Johns' open door. Johns wasn't there: the clock on his desk had only moved on twelve minutes; the papers lay in the lamplight. He felt as though he had explored a strange country and returned home to find it all a dream—the calendar not turned a single page during all his wanderings.

3

He wasn't afraid of Johns. He went in and picked up one of the offending papers. Johns had arranged them in order and marked the passages. He must have been bitten by the passion for detection. The Minister of Home Security, Digby read, had replied months ago to a question about a missing document in much the same terms as in the later case. It had never been missing. There had been at most a slight indiscretion, but the document had never left the personal possession of—and there was the great staid respected name which Johns had forgotten. In the face of such a statement how could anyone continue to suggest that the document had been photographed? That was to accuse the great staid name not of an indiscretion but of treason. It was perhaps a mistake not to have left the document in the office safe overnight, but the great name had given his personal assurance to the Minister that not for one second had the document been out of his possession. He had slept with it literally under his pillow. . . . The *Times* hinted that it would be interesting to investigate how the calumny had started. Was the enemy trying to sap our confidence in our hereditary leaders by a whisper campaign? After two or three issues there was silence.

A rather frightening fascination lay in these months-old newspapers. Digby had slowly had to relearn most of the household names, but he could hardly turn the page of any newspaper without encountering some great man of whom he had never heard, and occasionally there would crop up a name he did recognize—someone who had been a figure twenty years ago. He felt like a Rip van Winkle returning after a quarter of a century's sleep; the people of whom he had heard hardly connected better than he did with his youth. Men of brilliant promise had lapsed into the Board of Trade, and of course in one great case a man who had been considered too brilliant and too reckless ever to be trusted with major office was the leader of his country. One of Digby's last memories was of hearing him hissed by ex-servicemen from the public gallery of a law court because he had told an abrupt unpalatable truth about an old campaign. Now he had taught the country to love his unpalatable truths.

He turned a page and read casually under a photograph: "Arthur Rowe whom the police are anxious to interview in connection . . ." He wasn't interested in crime. The photograph showed a lean shabby clean-shaven man—all photographs of criminals looked much alike. Perhaps it was the spots—the pointillist technique of the newspaper photograph. There was so much of the past he had to learn that he couldn't be bothered to learn the criminals—at any rate of the domestic kind.

A board creaked and he turned. Johns hovered and blinked in the doorway. "Good evening, Johns," Digby said.

"What are you doing here?"

"Reading the papers," Digby said.

"But you heard the doctor say—"

"This isn't a prison, Johns," Digby said, "except for poor Stone. It's a very charming nursing home and I'm a private patient with nothing wrong except loss of memory, due to a bomb." He realized that Johns was listening to him with intensity. "Isn't that about it?" he asked.

"It must be, mustn't it?" Johns said.

"So we must keep a sense of proportion, and there's no earthly reason why, if I don't feel like sleep, I shouldn't stroll down the passage to your room for a chat and a read."

"When you put it like that," Johns said, "it sounds so simple."

"The doctor makes you see it differently, doesn't he?"

"All the same a patient ought to follow the treatment—"

"Or change his doctor. You know I've decided to change my doctor."

"To leave?" Johns asked. There was fear in his voice.

"To leave."

"Please don't do anything rash," Johns said. "The doctor's a great man. He's suffered a lot—and that may have made him a bit —eccentric. But you can't do better than stay here, really you can't."

"I'm going, Johns."

"Just another month," Johns entreated. "You've been doing so well. Until that girl came. Just a month. I'll speak to the doctor. He'll let you have the papers again. Perhaps he'll even let *her* come.

Only let me put it to him. I know the way. He's so sensitive: he takes offence."

"Johns," Digby asked gently, "why should you be afraid of my going?"

The unrimmed glasses caught the light and set it flickering along the wall. Johns said uncontrollably, "I'm not afraid of your going. I'm afraid—I'm afraid of his not letting you go." Very far away they both heard the purr, purr of a car.

"What's wrong with the doctor?" Johns shook his head and the reflection danced again upon the wall. "There's something wrong," Digby pressed him. "Poor Stone saw something odd and so he's put away."

"For his own good," Johns said imploringly. "Dr. Forester knows. He's such a great man, Digby."

"For his own good be damned. I've been to the sick bay and talked to him."

"You've been *there?*" Johns said.

"Haven't you—ever?"

"It's forbidden," Johns said.

"Do you always do exactly what Dr. Forester tells you?"

"He's a great doctor, Digby. You don't understand: brains are the most delicate mechanisms. The least thing to upset the equilibrium and everything goes wrong. You have to trust the doctor."

"I don't trust him."

"You mustn't say that. If you only knew how skilful he is, the endless care he takes. He's trying to shelter you until you are really strong enough—"

"Stone saw something odd and Stone's put away."

"No, no." Johns put out a weak hand and laid it on the newspapers, like a badgered politician gaining confidence from the dispatch box. "If you only knew, Digby. They've made him suffer so with their jealousies and misunderstandings, but he's so great and good and kind—"

"Ask Stone about that."

"If you only knew—"

A soft savage voice said, "I think he'll have to know." It was Dr. Forester, and again that sense of possible and yet inconceivable sanctions set Digby's heart beating.

Johns said, "Dr. Forester, I didn't give him leave—"

"That's all right, Johns," Dr. Forester said, "you are very loyal, I know. I like loyalty." He began to take off the gloves he had been wearing in the car: he drew them slowly off the long beautiful fingers. "I remember after Conway's suicide how you stood by me. I don't forget a friend. Have you ever told Digby about Conway's suicide?"

"Never," Johns protested.

"But he should know, Johns. It's a case in point. Conway also suffered from loss of memory. Life, you see, had become too much for him—and loss of memory was his escape. I tried to make him strong, to stiffen his resistance so that when his memory came back he would be able to meet his very difficult situation. The time I spent, wasted on Conway. Johns will tell you I was very patient—he was unbearably impertinent. But I'm human, Digby, and one day I lost my temper. I do lose my temper—very seldom, but sometimes. I told Conway everything, and he killed himself that night. You see his mind hadn't been given time to heal. There was a lot of trouble, but Johns stood by me. He realizes that to be a good psychologist you sometimes have to share the mental weakness of the patient: one cannot be quite sane all the time. That's what gives one sympathy—and the other thing."

He spoke gently and calmly, as though he were lecturing on an abstract subject, but the long surgical fingers had taken up one of the newspapers and was tearing it in long strips.

Digby said, "But my case is different, Dr. Forester. It was only a bomb that destroyed my memory. Not trouble."

"Do you really believe that?" Dr. Forester said. "And I suppose you think it was just gunfire, concussion, which drove Stone out of his mind? That isn't how the mind works. We make our own insanity. Stone failed—shamefully—so now he explains everything by treachery. But it wasn't other people's treachery that left his friend Barnes—"

"And you have a revelation up your sleeve for me too, Dr. Forester?" He remembered the pencil marks in the Tolstoy rubbed out by a man without the courage of his opinions and that heartened him. He asked, "What were you doing with Poole in the dark when Stone found you?" He had meant it only as a piece of impertinent defiance he had believed that the scene existed only in Stone's persecuted imagination—like the enemy digging on the island. He hadn't expected to halt Dr. Forester in the middle of his soft tirade. The silence was disagreeable. He tailed weakly off, "And digging . . ."

The noble old face watched him, the mouth a little open: a tiny dribble ran down the chin.

Johns said, "Please go to bed, Digby. Let's talk in the morning."

"I'm quite ready to go to bed," Digby said. He felt suddenly ridiculous in his trailing dressing gown and his heel-less slippers; he was apprehensive too—it was like turning his back on a man with a gun.

"Wait," Dr. Forester said. "I haven't told you yet. When you know you can choose between Conway's method and Stone's method. There's room in the sick bay."

"You ought to be there yourself, Dr. Forester."

"You're a fool," Dr. Forester said. "A fool in love. I watch my patients. I know. What's the good of you being in love? You don't even know your real name." He tore a piece out of one of the papers and held it out to Digby. "There you are. That's you. A murderer. Go and think about that."

It was the photograph he hadn't bothered to examine. The thing was absurd. He said, "That's not me."

"Go and look in the glass," Dr. Forester said. "And then begin to remember. You've got a lot to remember."

Johns protested weakly, "Doctor, that's not the way—"

"He asked for it," Dr. Forester said, "just like Conway did."

But Digby heard no more of what Johns had to say: he was running down the passage towards his room: halfway he tripped on his dressing-gown cord and fell. He hardly felt the shock. He got to his feet a little giddy—that was all. He wanted a looking glass.

The lean bearded face looked out at him in the familiar room. There was a smell of cut flowers. This was where he had been happy. How could he believe what the doctor had said? There must be a mistake. It didn't connect. At first he could hardly see the photograph: his heart beat and his head was confused. This isn't me, he thought, as that lean shaven other face with the unhappy eyes and the shabby suit came into focus. It didn't connect: the memories he had of twenty years ago and Arthur Rowe whom the police had wanted to interview in connection with—but Dr. Forester had torn the paper too carelessly. In those twenty years he couldn't have gone astray as far as this. He thought, Whatever they say, this man standing here is me. I'm not changed because I lose my memory. This photograph and Anna Hilfe, he protested—and suddenly he remembered what had momentarily puzzled him and he had quite forgotten: Anna's voice saying, "It's my job, Arthur." He put his hand up to his chin and hid the beard: the long twisted nose told its tale, and the eyes which were unhappy enough now.

He steadied himself with his hands on the dressing table and thought, Yes, I'm Arthur Rowe. He began to talk to himself under his breath, But I'm not Conway. I shan't kill myself.

He was Arthur Rowe with a difference. He was next door to his own youth: he had started again from there. He said, In a moment it's going to come back, but I'm not Conway—and I won't be Stone. I've escaped for long enough; my brain will stand it. It wasn't all fear that he felt; he felt also the untired courage and the chivalry of adolescence. He was no longer too old and too habit-ridden to start again. He shut his eyes and thought of Poole, and an odd medley of impressions fought at the gateway of his unconsciousness to be let out: a book called *The Little Duke* and the word Naples— see Naples and die—and Poole again, Poole sitting crouched in a chair in a little dark dingy room, eating cake, and Dr. Forester, Dr. Forester stooping over something dark and bleeding. . . . The memories thickened—a woman's face came up for a moment with immense sadness and then sank again like someone drowned, out of sight: his head was racked with pain as other memories struggled to get out, like a child out of the mother's body. He put his hands on the dressing table and held to it. He said to himself over and over again, I must stand up. I must stand up, as though there were some healing virtue in simply remaining on his feet while his brain reeled with the horror of returning life.

BOOK III

Bits and Pieces

One: The Roman Death

1

Rowe followed the man in the blue uniform up the stone stairs and along a corridor lined with doors: some of them were open, and he could see that they led into little rooms all the same shape and size like confessionals. A table and three chairs: there was never anything else, and the chairs were hard and upright. The man opened one door—but there seemed no reason why he should not have opened any of the others—and said, "Wait here, sir."

It was early in the morning: the steel rim of the window enclosed a grey cold sky. The last stars had only just gone out. He sat with his hands between his knees in a dull tired patience; he wasn't important, he hadn't become an explorer, he was just a criminal. The effort of reaching this place had exhausted him; he couldn't even remember with any clearness what he had done—only the long walk through the dark countryside to the station, trembling when the cows coughed behind the hedgerows and an owl shrieked; pacing up and down upon the platform till the train came, the smell of grass and steam. The collector had wanted his ticket and he had none; nor had he any money to pay with. He knew his name or thought he knew his name, but he had no address to give. The man had been very kind and gentle: perhaps he looked sick. He had asked him if he had no friends to whom he was going, and he replied that he had no friends. "I want to see the police," he said, and the collector rebuked him mildly, "You don't have to go all the way to London for that, sir."

There was a moment of dreadful suspense when he thought he would be returned like a truant child. The collector said, "You are one of Dr. Forester's patients, aren't you, sir? Now if you get out at the next station, they'll telephone for a car. It won't take more than thirty minutes."

"No."

"You lost your way, sir, I expect, but you don't need to worry with a gentleman like Dr. Forester."

He gathered all the energy of which he was capable and said, "I am going to Scotland Yard. I'm wanted there. If you stop me, it's your responsibility."

At the next stop—which was only a halt, a few feet of platform and a wooden shed among dark level fields—he saw Johns: they must have gone to his room and found it empty and Johns had driven over. Johns saw him at once and came with strained naturalness to the door of the compartment; the guard hovered in the background. "Hullo, old man," Johns said uneasily, "just hop out. I've got the car here—it won't take a moment to get home."

"I'm not coming."

"The doctor's very distressed. He'd had a long day and he lost his temper. He didn't mean half of what he said."

"I'm not coming."

The guard came nearer to show that he was willing to lend a hand if force were necessary. Rowe said furiously, "You haven't certified me yet. You can't drag me out of the train," and the guard edged up. He said softly to Johns, "The gentleman hasn't got a ticket."

"It's all right," Johns said surprisingly, "there's nothing wrong." He leaned forward and said in a whisper, "Good luck, old man." The train drew away, laying its steam like a screen across the car, the shed, the figure which didn't dare to wave.

Now all the trouble was over; all that was left was a trial for murder.

Rowe sat on; the steely sky paled and a few taxis hooted. A small fat distrait man in a double-breasted waistcoat opened the door once, took a look at him, and said, "Where's Beavis?" but didn't wait for an answer. The long wounded cry of a boat came up from the Pool. Somebody went whistling down the corridor outside, once there was the chink-chink of teacups, and a faint smell of kipper blew in from a distance.

The little stout man came briskly in again: he had a round over-sized face and a small fair moustache. He carried the slip Rowe had filled in down below. "So you are Mr. Rowe," he said sternly. "We are glad you've come to see us at last." He rang a bell and a uniformed constable answered it. He said, "Is Beavis on duty? Tell him to come along."

He sat down and crossed his neat plump thighs and looked at his nails. They were very well kept. He looked at them from every angle and seemed worried about the cuticle of his left thumb. He said nothing. It was obvious that he wouldn't talk without a witness. Then a big man in a ready-to-wear suit came with a pad and a pencil and took the third chair. His ears were enormous and stuck out straight from his skull and he had an odd air of muted shame, like a bull who has begun to realize that he is out of place in a china shop. When he held the pencil to the pad you expected one or the other to suffer in his awkward grasp, and you felt too that he knew and feared the event.

"Well," the dapper man said, sighed, and tucked his nails away for preservation under his thighs. He said, "You've come here, Mr. Rowe, of your own accord and volunteer a statement?"

Rowe said, "I saw a photograph in the paper . . ."

"We've been asking you to come forward for months."

"I knew it for the first time last night."

"You seem to have lived a bit out of the world."

"I've been in a nursing home. You see . . ."

Every time he spoke the pencil squeaked on the paper, making a stiff consecutive narrative out of his haphazard sentences.

"What nursing home?"

"It was kept by a Dr. Forester." He gave the name of the railway station. He knew no other name. He explained, "Apparently there was a raid." He touched the scar on his forehead. "I lost my memory. I found myself at this place knowing nothing—except bits of my childhood. They told me my name was Richard Digby. I didn't even recognize the photograph at first. You see, this beard . . ."

"And your memory has come back now, I hope?" the little man asked sharply, with a touch—a very faint touch—of sarcasm.

"I can remember something, but not much."

"A very convenient sort of memory."

"I am trying," Rowe said with a flash of anger, "to tell you all I know. In English law isn't a man supposed to be innocent until you prove him guilty? I'm ready to tell you everything I can remember about the murder, but I'm not a murderer."

The plump man began to smile. He drew out his hands and looked at his nails and tucked them back again. "That's interesting, Mr. Rowe," he said. "You mentioned murder, but I have said nothing about murder to you, and no paper has mentioned the word murder—yet."

"I don't understand."

"We play strictly fair. Read out his statement so far, Beavis."

Beavis obeyed, blushing nervously, as though he were an overgrown schoolboy at a lectern, reading Deuteronomy. "I, Arthur Rowe, have made this statement voluntarily. Last night, when I saw a photograph of myself in a newspaper, I knew for the first time that the police wanted to interview me. I have been in a nursing home kept by a Dr. Forester for the last four months, suffering from loss of memory due to an air raid. My memory is not fully restored, but I wish to tell everything I know in connection with the murder of—"

The detective stopped Beavis. He said, "That's quite fair, isn't it?"

"I suppose it is."

"You'll be asked to sign it presently. Now tell us the name of the murdered man."

"I don't remember it."

"I see. Who told you we wanted to talk to you about a murder?"

"Dr. Forester."

The promptness of the reply seemed to take the detective by surprise. Even Beavis hesitated before the pencil bore down again upon the pad. "Dr. Forester told you?"

"Yes."

"How did he know?"

"I suppose he read it in the papers."

"We have never mentioned murder in the papers."

Rowe leaned his head wearily on his hand. Again his brain felt the pressure of associations. He said, "Perhaps . . ." The horrible memory stirred, crystallized, dissolved. "I don't know."

It seemed to him that the detective's manner was a little more sympathetic. He said, "Just tell us—in any order—in your own words—what you do remember."

"It will have to be in any order. First there's Poole. He's an attendant in Dr. Forester's sick bay—where the violent cases go, only I don't think they are always violent. I know that I met him in the old days—before my memory went. I can remember a little shabby room with a picture of the Bay of Naples. I seemed to be living there—I don't know why. It's not the sort of place I'd choose. So much of what's come back is just feelings, emotion—not fact."

"Never mind," the detective said.

"It's the way you remember a dream when most of it has gone. I remember great sadness—and fear, and, yes, a sense of danger, and an odd taste."

"Of what?"

"We were drinking tea. He wanted me to give him something."

"What?"

"I can't remember. What I do remember is absurd. A cake."

"A cake?"

"It was made with real eggs. Then something happened. . . ." He felt terribly tired. The sun was coming out. People all over the city were going to work. He felt like a man in mortal sin who watches other people go up to receive the sacrament . . . abandoned. If only he knew what *his* work was.

"Would you like a cup of tea?"

"Yes. I'm a bit tired."

"Go and find some tea, Beavis, and some biscuits—or cake."

He asked no more questions until Beavis had returned, but suddenly as Rowe put out his hand to take a piece of cake, he said, "There are no real eggs in that, I'm afraid. Yours must have been homemade. You couldn't have bought it."

Without considering his reply, Rowe said, "Oh, no, I didn't buy it, I won it—" and stopped. "That's absurd. I wasn't thinking." The tea made him feel stronger. He said, "You don't treat your murderers too badly."

The detective said, "Just go on remembering."

"I remember a lot of people sitting round a room and the lights going out. And I was afraid that someone was going to come up behind me and stab me or strangle me. And a voice speaking. That's worse than anything—a hopeless pain, but I can't remember a word. And then all the lights are on, and a man's dead, and I suppose that's what you say I've done. But I don't think it's true."

"Would you remember the man's face?"

"I think I would."

"File Q seven, Beavis."

It was growing hot in the small room. The detective's forehead was beaded and the little fair moustache looked damp. He said, "You can take off your coat if you like," and took his own off, and sat in a pearl-grey shirt with silvered armlets to keep the cuffs exactly right. He looked doll-like, as though only the coat were made to come off.

Beavis brought a paper-covered file and laid it on the table. The detective said, "Just look through these—you'll find a few loose photographs too—and see if you can find the murdered man."

A police photograph is like a passport photograph: the intelligence which casts a veil over the crude common shape is never recorded by the cheap lens. No one can deny the contours of the flesh, the shape of nose and mouth, and yet we protest, This isn't me.

The turning of the pages became mechanical. Rowe couldn't believe that it was among people like these that his life had been cast. Only once he hesitated for a moment: something in his memory stirred at sight of a loose photograph of a man with a lick of hair plastered back, a pencil on a clip in the lower left-hand corner, and wrinkled evasive eyes that seemed to be trying to escape too bright a photographer's lamp.

"Know him?" the detective asked.

"No. How could I? Or is he a shopkeeper? I thought for a moment, but no, I don't know him." He turned on. Looking up once, he saw that the detective had got his hand out from under his thigh:

he seemed to have lost interest. There were not many more pages to turn—and then unexpectedly there the face was: the broad anonymous brow, the dark city suit, and with him came a whole throng of faces bursting through the gate of the unconscious, rioting horribly into the memory. He said, "There," and lay back in his chair, giddy, feeling the world turn around him.

"Nonsense," the detective said. The harsh voice hardly penetrated. "You had me guessing for a moment—a good actor—waste any more time. . . ."

"They did it with my knife."

"Stop play-acting," the detective said. "That man hasn't been murdered. He's just as alive as you are."

2

"Alive?"

"Of course he's alive. I don't know why you picked on him."

"But in that case"—all his tiredness went; he began to notice the fine day outside— "I'm not a murderer. Was he badly hurt?"

"Do you really mean—?" the detective began incredulously. Beavis had given up the attempt at writing. He said, "I don't know what you are talking about. Where did this happen? When? What was it you think you saw?"

As Rowe looked at the photograph it came back in vivid patches. He said, "Wonderful Mrs.—Mrs. Bellairs. It was her house. A séance." Suddenly he saw a thin beautiful hand bloodstained. He said, "Why, Dr. Forester was there. He told us the man was dead. They sent for the police."

"The same Dr. Forester?"

"The same one."

"And they let you go?"

"No, I escaped."

"Somebody helped you?"

"Yes."

"Who?"

The past was swimming back to him, as though now that there was nothing to fear the guard had been removed from the gate. Anna's brother had helped him: he saw the exhilarated young face and felt the blow on his knuckles. He wasn't going to betray him. He said, "I don't remember that."

The little plump man sighed. "This isn't for us, Beavis," he said.

"We'd better take him across to fifty-nine." He put a call through to someone called Prentice. "We turn 'em in to you," he complained, "but how often do you turn 'em in to us?" Then they accompanied Rowe across the big collegiate courtyard under the high grey block; the trams twanged on the embankment, and pigeons' droppings gave a farmyard air to the sandbags stacked around. He didn't care a damn that they walked on either side of him, an obvious escort: he was a free man still and he hadn't committed murder, and his memory was coming back at every step. He said suddenly, "It was the cake he wanted," and laughed.

"Keep your cake for Prentice," the little man said sourly. "He's the surrealist round here."

They came to an almost identical room in another block where a man in a tweed suit with a drooping grey Edwardian moustache sat on the edge of a chair as though it were a shooting stick. "This is Mr. Arthur Rowe we've been advertising for," the detective said and laid the file on the table. "At least he says he is. No identity card. Says he's been in a nursing home with loss of memory. We are the lucky fellows who've set his memory going again. Such a memory. We ought to set up a clinic. You'll be interested to hear he saw Cost murdered."

"Now that *is* interesting," Mr. Prentice said with middle-aged courtesy. "Not *my* Mr. Cost?"

"Yes. And a Dr. Forester attended the death."

"*My* Dr. Forester?"

"It seems likely. This gentleman has been a patient of his."

"Take a chair, Mr. Rowe, and you, Graves."

"Not me. You like the fantastic. I don't. I'll leave you Beavis in case you want any notes taken." He turned at the door and said, "Pleasant nightmares to you."

"Nice chap, Graves," Mr. Prentice said. He leaned forward as though he were going to offer a hip flask. The smell of good tweeds came across the table. "Now would you say it was a *good* nursing home?"

"So long as you didn't quarrel with the doctor."

"Ha, ha, exactly. And then?"

"You might find yourself in the sick bay for violent cases."

"Wonderful," Mr. Prentice said, stroking his long moustache. "One can't help admiring— You wouldn't have any complaint to make?"

"They treated me very well."

"Yes. I was afraid so. You see if only someone would complain —they are all voluntary patients—one might be able to have a look at the place. I've been wanting to for a long time."

"When you get in the sick bay it's too late. If you aren't mad, they can soon make you mad." In his blind flight he had temporarily forgotten Stone. He felt a sense of guilt, remembering the tired voice behind the door. He said, "They've got a man in there now. He's not violent."

"A difference of opinion with our Dr. Forester?"

"He said he saw the doctor and Poole—he's the attendant— doing something in the dark in Poole's room. He told them he was looking for a window from which he could enfilade—" Rowe broke off. "He *is* a little mad, but quite gentle, not violent."

"Go on, go on," Mr. Prentice said.

"He thought the Germans were in occupation of a little island in a pond. He said he'd seen them digging in."

"And he told the doctor that?"

"Yes." Rowe implored him, "Can't you get him out? They've put him in a strait jacket, but he wouldn't hurt a soul."

"Well," Mr. Prentice said, "we must think carefully." He stroked his moustache with a milking movement. "We must look all round the subject, mustn't we?"

"He'll go really mad."

"Poor fellow," Mr. Prentice said unconvincingly. There was a merciless quality in his gentleness. He switched, "And Poole?"

"He came to me once—I don't know how long ago—and wanted a cake I'd won. There was an air raid on. I have an idea that he tried to kill me because I wouldn't give him the cake. It was made with real eggs. Do you think I'm mad too?" he asked with anxiety.

Mr. Prentice said thoughtfully, "I wouldn't say so. Life can be very odd. Oh, very odd. You should read more history. Silkworms, you know, were smuggled out of China in a hollow walking stick. One can't really mention the places diamond smugglers use. And at this very moment I'm looking—oh, most anxiously—for something which may not be much bigger than a diamond. A cake— very good, why not? But he didn't kill you."

"There are so many blanks," Rowe said.

"Where was it he came to see you?"

"I don't remember. There are years and years of my life I still can't remember."

"We forget very easily," Mr. Prentice said, "what gives us pain."

"I almost wish I *were* a criminal so that there could be a record of me here."

Mr. Prentice said gently, "We are doing very well, very well. Now let's go back to the murder of—Cost. Of .course that might have been staged to send you into hiding, to stop you coming to us. But what came next? Apparently you didn't go into hiding and you didn't come to us. And what was it you knew—or we knew?" He put his hands flat on the table and said, "It's a beautiful problem. One could almost put it into algebraic terms. Just tell me all you told Graves."

He described again what he could remember: the crowded room and the light going out and a voice talking and fear.

"Graves didn't appreciate all that, I daresay," Mr. Prentice said, clasping his bony knees and rocking slightly. "Poor Graves—the passionate crimes of railway porters are his spiritual province. In this branch our interests have to be rather more bizarre. And so he distrusts us—really distrusts us."

He began turning the pages of the file rather as he might have turned over a family album, quizzically. "Are you a student of human nature, Mr. Rowe?"

"I don't know what I am."

"This face, for instance."

It was the photograph over which Rowe had hesitated; he hesitated again.

"What profession do you think *he* followed?" Mr. Prentice asked.

The pencil clipped in the breast pocket, the depressed suit, the air of a man always expecting a rebuff, the little lines of knowledge round the eyes—when he examined it closely he felt no doubt at all. "A private detective," he said.

"Right the first time. And this little anonymous man had his little anonymous name—"

Rowe smiled. "Jones I should imagine."

"You wouldn't think it, Mr. Rowe, but you and he—let's call him Jones—had something in common. You both disappeared. But you've come back again. What was the name of the agency that employed him, Beavis?"

"I don't remember, sir. I could go and look it up."

"It doesn't matter. The only one I can remember is the Clifford. It wasn't that."

"Not the Orthotex?" Rowe asked. "I once had a friend—" and stopped.

"It comes back, doesn't it, Mr. Rowe? His name was Jones, you see. And he did belong to the Orthotex. What made you go there? We can tell you even if you don't remember. You thought that someone had tried to murder you—about a cake. You had won the cake unfairly at a fair (what a pun!) because a certain Mrs. Bellairs had told you the weight. You went to find out where Mrs. Bellairs lived—from the offices of the Fund for the Mothers of the Free Nations (if I've got the outlandish name correct) and Jones followed, just to keep an eye on them—and you. But you must have given him the slip somehow, Mr. Rowe, because Jones never came back, and when you telephoned next day to Mr. Rennit you said you were wanted for murder."

Rowe sat with his hand over his eyes—trying to remember? trying not to remember?—while the voice drove carefully and precisely on.

"And yet no murder had been committed in London during the previous twenty-four hours—so far as we knew—unless poor Jones had gone that way. You obviously knew something: perhaps you knew everything; we advertised for you and you didn't come forward. Until today when you arrive in a beard you certainly used not to wear, saying you had lost your memory, but remembering at least that you had been accused of murder—only you picked out a man we know is alive. How does it all strike you, Mr. Rowe?"

Rowe said, "I'm waiting for the handcuffs," and smiled unhappily.

"You can hardly blame our friend Graves," Mr. Prentice said.

"Is life really like this?" Rowe asked. Mr. Prentice leaned forward with an interested air as though he were always ready to abandon the particular in favour of the general argument. He said, "This is life, so I suppose one can say it's like life."

"It isn't how I had imagined it," Rowe said. He went on, "You see, I'm a learner. I'm right at the beginning, trying to find my way about. I thought life was much simpler and—grander. I suppose that's how it strikes a boy. I was brought up on stories of Captain Scott writing his last letters home, Oates walking into the blizzard, I've forgotten who it was losing his hands from his experiments with radium, Damien among the lepers. . . ." The memories which are overlaid by the life one lives came freshly back in the little stuffy office in the great grey yard. It was a relief to talk. "There was a book called the *Book of Golden Deeds* by a woman called Yonge . . . *The Little Duke.* . . ." He said, "If you were suddenly taken from that world into this job you are doing now you'd feel bewildered. Jones and the cake, the sick bay, poor Stone, all this talk of a man called Hitler, your files of wretched faces, the cruelty and meaninglessness—it's as if one had been sent on a journey with the wrong map. I'm ready to do anything you want, but remember I don't know my way about. Everybody else has changed gradually and learned. This whole business of war and hate—even that's strange. I haven't been worked up to it. I expect much the best thing would be to hang me."

"Yes," Mr. Prentice said eagerly, "yes, it's a most interesting case. I can see that to you"—he became startlingly colloquial—"this is rather a dingy hole. We've come to terms with it of course."

"What frightens me," Rowe said, "is not knowing how I came to terms with it before my memory went. When I came in to London today I hadn't realized there would be so many ruins. Nothing will seem as strange as that. God knows what kind of a ruin I am myself. Perhaps I *am* a murderer?"

Mr. Prentice reopened the file and said rapidly, "Oh, we no longer think you killed Jones." He was like a man who has looked over a wall, seen something disagreeable and now walks rapidly, purposefully away, talking as he goes. "The question is—what made you lose your memory? What do you know about that?"

"Only what I've been told."

"And what have you been told?"

"That it was a bomb. It gave me this scar.'

"Were you alone?"

Before he could brake his tongue he said, "No.'

"Who was with you?"

"A girl." It was too late now: he had to bring her in, and after all, if he were not a murderer, why should it matter that her brother had aided his escape? "Anna Hilfe." The plain words were sweet on the tongue.

"Why were you with her?"

"I think we were lovers."

"You think?"

"I don't remember."

"What does she say about it?"

"She says I saved her life."

"The Free Mothers," Mr. Prentice brooded. "Has she explained how you got to Dr. Forester's?"

"She was forbidden to." Mr. Prentice raised an eyebrow. "They wanted—so they told us—my memory to come back naturally and slowly of itself. No hypnotism, no psychoanalysis."

Mr. Prentice beamed at him and swayed a little on his shooting stick: you felt he was taking a well-earned rest in the middle of a successful shoot. "Yes, it wouldn't have done, would it, if it had come back too quickly? Although of course there was always the sick bay."

"If only you'd tell me what it's all about."

Mr. Prentice stroked his moustache: he had the fainéant air of Arthur Balfour, but you felt that he knew it. He had stylized himself —life was easier that way. He had chosen a physical mould just as a writer chooses a technical form. "Now were you ever a habitué of the Regal Court?"

"It's a hotel?"

"You remember that much."

"Well, it's an easy guess."

Mr. Prentice closed his eyes: it was perhaps an affectation, but who could live without affectations?

"Why do you ask about the Regal Court?"

"It's a shot in the dark," Mr. Prentice said. "We have so little time."

"Time for what?"

"To find a needle in a haystack."

3

One wouldn't have said that Mr. Prentice was capable of much exertion, rough shooting, you would have said, was beyond him. From the house to the brake and from the brake to the butts was about as far as you could expect him to walk in a day. And yet during the next few hours he showed himself capable of great exertion, and the shooting was indubitably rough

He had dropped his enigmatic statement into the air and was out of the room almost before the complete phrase had formed, his long legs moving stiffly like stilts. Rowe was left alone with Beavis, and the day wore slowly on The sun's early promise had been false: a cold unseasonable drizzle fell like dust outside the window. After a long time they brought him some cold pie and tea on a tray.

Beavis was not inclined to conversation. It was as though *his* words might be used in evidence, and Rowe only once attempted to break the silence. He said, "I wish I knew what it was all about," and watched Beavis's long-toothed mouth open and clap to like a rabbit snare. "Official secrets," Beavis said and stared with flat eyes at the blank wall.

Then suddenly Mr. Prentice was with them again, rushing the room in his stiff casual stride, followed by a man in black who held a bowler hat in front of him with both hands like a basin of water and panted a little in the trail of Mr. Prentice. He came to a stop inside the door and glared at Rowe. He said, "That's the scoundrel. I haven't a doubt of it. I can see through the beard. It's a disguise."

Mr. Prentice gave a giggle. "That's excellent," he said. "The pieces are really fitting."

The man with the bowler said, "He carried in the suitcase and he wanted just to leave it. But I had my instructions. I told him he must wait for Mr. Travers. He didn't want to wait. Of course he didn't want to, knowing what was inside. Something must have gone wrong. He didn't get Mr. Travers, but he nearly got the poor girl. And when the confusion was over, he'd gone."

"I don't remember ever seeing him before," Rowe said.

The man gesticulated passionately with his bowler. "I'll swear to him in any court of law."

Beavis watched with his mouth a little open and Mr. Prentice giggled again. "No time," he said. "No time for squabbles. You two can get to know each other later. I need you both now."

"If you'd tell me a little," Rowe pleaded. To have come all this way, he thought, to meet a charge of murder and to find only a deeper confusion.

"In the taxi," Mr. Prentice said. "I'll explain in the taxi." He made for the door.

"Aren't you going to charge him?" the man asked, panting in pursuit.

Mr. Prentice without looking round said, "Presently, presently, perhaps," and then darkly, "Who?"

They swept into the courtyard and out into broad bleak stony Northumberland Avenue, policemen saluting; into a taxi and off along the ruined front of the Strand; the empty eyes of an insurance building; boarded windows; sweet shops with one dish of mauve cachous in the window.

Mr. Prentice said in a low voice, "I just want you two gentlemen to behave naturally. We are going to a City tailor's where I'm being measured for a suit. I shall go in first, and after a few minutes you,

Rowe, and last you, Mr. Lloyd," and he touched the bowler hat with the tip of a finger where it balanced on the stranger's lap.

"But what's it all about, sir?" Lloyd asked. He had edged away from Rowe, and Mr. Prentice curled his long legs across the taxi, sitting opposite them in a tip-up.

"Never mind. Just keep your eyes open and see if there's anyone in the shop you recognize." The mischief faded from his eyes as the taxi looped round the gutted shell of St. Clement Danes. He said, "The place will be surrounded. You needn't be afraid."

Rowe said, "I'm not afraid. I only want to know . . ." staring out at odd devastated boarded-up London.

"It's really serious," Mr. Prentice said. "I don't know quite how serious. But you might say that we all depend on it." He shuddered away from what was almost an emotional statement, giggled, touched doubtfully the silky ends of his moustache, and said with sadness in his voice, "You know there are always weaknesses that have to be covered up. If the Germans had known after Dunkirk just how weak. . . . There are still weaknesses of which if they knew the exact facts   ⸴⸴ The ruins around St. Paul's unfolded, the obliterated acres of Paternoster Row, like a Pompeian landscape. He said, "This would be nothing to it. Nothing." He went slowly on, "Perhaps I was wrong to say there was no danger. If we are on the right track, of course, there must be danger, mustn't there? It's worth—oh, a thousand lives to them."

"If I can be of any use," Rowe said. "This is so strange to me. I didn't imagine war was like this," staring out at desolation. Jerusalem must have looked something like this in the mind's eye of Christ when he wept.

"I'm not scared," the man with the bowler said sharply, defensively

"We are looking," Mr. Prentice said, clasping his bony knees and vibrating with the taxi, "for a little roll of film—probably a good deal smaller than a cotton reel. Smaller than those little rolls you put in Leica cameras. You must have read the questions in Parliament about certain papers which were missing for an hour. It was hushed up publicly. It doesn't help anybody to ruin confidence in a big name—and it doesn't help us to have the public and the press muddying up the trail. I tell you two only because—well, we could have you put quietly away for the duration if there was any leakage. It happened twice—the first time the roll was hidden in a cake and the cake was to be fetched from a certain fête. But you won it"—Mr. Prentice nodded at Rowe. "The password, as it were, was given to the wrong man."

"Mrs. Bellairs," Rowe said.

"She's being looked after at this minute." He went on explaining with vague gestures of his thin useless-looking hands. "That attempt failed. A bomb that hit your house destroyed the cake and everything—and probably saved your life. But they didn't like the way you followed the case up. They tried to frighten you into hiding, but for some reason that was not enough. Of course they meant to blow you into pieces, but when they found you'd lost your memory, that was good enough. It was better than killing you because by disappearing you took the blame for the bomb—as well as for Jones."

"But why the girl?"

"We'll leave out the mysteries," Mr. Prentice said. "Perhaps because her brother helped you. They aren't above revenge. There isn't time for all that now." They were at the Mansion House. "What we know is this—they had to wait until the next chance came. Another big name and another fool. He had this in common with the first fool—he went to the same tailor."

The taxi drew up at the corner of a city street.

"We foot it from here," Mr. Prentice said. A man on the opposite curb began to walk up the street as they alighted.

"Do you carry a revolver?" the man in the bowler asked nervously.

"I wouldn't know how to use it," Mr. Prentice said. "If there's trouble of that kind just lie flat."

"You had no right to bring me into this."

Mr. Prentice turned sharply. "Oh, yes," he said, "every right. Nobody's got a right to his life these days. My dear chap, you are conscripted for your country." They stood grouped on the pavement; bank messengers with chained boxes went by in top hats; stenographers and clerks hurried past, returning late from their lunch. There were no ruins to be seen: it was like peace. Mr. Prentice said, "If those photographs leave the country, there'll be a lot of suicides—at least that's what happened in France."

"How do you know they haven't left?" Rowe asked.

"We don't. We just hope, that's all. We'll know the worst soon enough." He said, "Watch when I go in. Give me five minutes with our man in the fitting room, and then you, Rowe, come in and ask for me. I want to have him where I can watch him—in all the mirrors. Then, Lloyd, you count a hundred and follow. *You* are going to be too much of a coincidence. You are going to be the last straw."

They watched the lean, stiff, old-fashioned figure make his way up the street: he was just the kind of man to have a City tailor—somebody reliable and not expensive whom he would recommend to his son. Presently about fifty yards along he turned in. A man stood at the next corner and lit a cigarette. A motorcar drew up next door and a woman got out to do some shopping, leaving a man at the wheel.

Rowe said, "It's time for me to be moving." His pulse beat with excitement: it was as if he had come to this adventure unsaddened, with the freshness of a boy. He looked suspiciously at Lloyd, who stood there with a nerve twitching in his cheek. He said, "A hundred and you follow." Lloyd said nothing. "You understand. You count a hundred."

"Oh," he said furiously, "this play-acting. I'm a plain man."

"Those were his orders."

"Who's he to give me orders?"

Rowe couldn't stay to argue; time was up.

War had hit the tailoring business hard. A few rolls of grey inferior cloth lay on the counter; the shelves were nearly empty. A man in a frock coat with tired lined anxious face said, "What can we do for you, sir?"

"I came here," Rowe said, "to meet a friend." He looked down the narrow aisle between the little mirrored cubicles. "I expect he's being fitted now."

"Will you take a chair, sir?" and, "Mr. Ford," he called, "Mr. Ford." Out from one of the cubicles, a tape measure slung round his neck, a little bouquet of pins in his lapel, solid, City-like, came Cost whom he had last seen dead in his chair when the lights went on. Like a piece of a jigsaw puzzle which clicks into place and makes sense of a whole confusing block, that stolid figure took up its place in his memory with the man from Welwyn and the proletarian poet and Anna's brother. What had Mrs. Bellairs called him? He remembered the whole phrase, "Our mystery man."

Rowe stood up as though this were someone of great importance who must be greeted punctiliously, but there seemed to be no recognition in the stolid respectable eyes. "Yes, Mr. Bridges?" Those were the first words he had ever heard him speak; his whole function before had been one of death.

"This gentleman has come to meet the other gentleman."

The eyes swivelled slowly and rested; no sign of recognition broke their large grey calm—or did they rest a shade longer than was absolutely necessary? "I have nearly taken the gentleman's measurements. If you would not mind waiting two minutes . . ." Two minutes, Rowe thought, and then the other, the straw which will really break you down.

Mr. Ford—if that was now to be his name—walked slowly up to the counter; everything he did, you felt, was carefully pondered: his suits must always be well built; there was no room in that precision for the eccentricity, the wayward act, and yet what a wild oddity lay hidden under the skin. He saw Dr. Forester dabbling his fingers in what had looked like blood.

A telephone stood on the counter. Mr. Ford picked up the receiver and dialled. The dial faced Rowe. He watched with care each time where the finger fitted. B A T. He felt sure of the letters, but one number he missed, suddenly wavering and catching the serene ponderous gaze of Mr. Ford as he dialled. He was unsure of himself: he wished Mr. Prentice would appear.

"Hullo," Mr. Ford said, "hullo. This is Pauling and Crosthwaite."

Along the length of the window towards the door dragged the unwilling form of the man with the bowler hat. Rowe's hands tightened in his lap. Mr. Bridges was sadly straightening the meagre rolls of cloth, his back turned. His listless hands were like a poignant criticism in the *Tailor and Cutter*.

"The suit was dispatched this morning, sir," Mr. Ford was saying, "I trust in time for your journey." He clucked his satisfaction calmly and inhumanly down the telephone. "Thank you very much, sir. I felt very satisfied myself at the last fitting." His eyes shifted to the clanging door as Lloyd looked in with a kind of wretched swagger. "Oh, yes, sir, I think when you've worn it once, you'll find the shoulders will settle." Mr. Prentice's whole elaborate plot was a failure: that nerve had not broken.

"Mr. Travers," Lloyd exclaimed with astonishment.

Carefully putting his hand over the mouthpiece of the telephone, Mr. Ford said, "I beg your pardon, sir?"

"You are Mr. Travers." Then Lloyd, meeting those clear calm eyes, added weakly, "Aren't you?"

"No, sir."

"I thought . . ."

"Mr. Bridges, would you mind attending to this gentleman?"

"Certainly, Mr. Ford."

The hand left the receiver and Mr. Ford quietly, firmly, authoritatively continued to speak up the wire. "No, sir. I find at the last moment that we shall not be able to repeat the trousers. It's not a matter of coupons, no. We can obtain no more of that pattern from the manufacturers—no more at all." Again his eyes met Rowe's and wandered like a blind man's hand delicately along the contours of his face. "Personally, sir, I have no hope. No hope at all." He put the receiver down and moved a little way along the counter. "If you can spare these a moment, Mr. Bridges . . ." He picked up a pair of cutting shears.

"Certainly, Mr. Ford."

Without another word he passed Rowe, not looking at him again, and moved down the aisle, without hurry, serious, professional, as heavy as stone. Rowe quickly rose: something he felt must be done, be said, if the whole plan were not to end in fiasco. "Cost," he called after the figure, "Cost." It was only then that the extreme calm and deliberation of the figure with the shears struck him as strange, the gaze that had felt round his face. He called out "Prentice" sharply in warning as the fitter turned aside into a cubicle.

But it was not the cubicle from which Mr. Prentice emerged. He came bewilderedly out in his silk shirt sleeves from the other end of the aisle. "What is it?" he asked, but Rowe was already at the other door straining to get in. Over his shoulder he could see the shocked face of Mr. Bridges, Lloyd's goggling eyes. "Quick," he said, "your hat," and grabbed the bowler and crashed it through the glass of the door.

Under the icicles of splintered glass he could see Cost-Travers-Ford. He sat in the armchair for clients opposite the tall triple mirror: leaning forward, his throat transfixed with the cutting shears held firmly upright between his knees. It was like a Roman death.

Rowe thought, This time I *have* killed him, and heard that quiet, respectful, but authoritative voice speaking down the telephone. "Personally, I have no hope. No hope at all."

Two: Mopping Up

1

Mrs. Bellairs had less dignity.

They had driven straight to Campden Hill, leaving Lloyd with his wrecked bowler. Mr. Prentice was worried and depressed. "It does no good," he said. "We want them alive and talking."

Rowe said, "It shocked me for a moment. He must have had great courage. I don't know why that's so surprising. One doesn't associate it with tailors—except for that one in the story who killed a giant. I suppose you'd say this one was on the side of the giants. I wonder why."

Mr. Prentice burst suddenly out as they drove up through the park in the thin windy rain. "Pity is a terrible thing. People talk about the passion of love. Pity is the worst passion of all: we don't outlive it like sex."

"After all, it's war," Rowe said with a kind of exhilaration. The old fake truism, like a piece of common pyrites in the hands of a child, split open and showed its sparkling core to him. He was taking part.

Mr. Prentice looked at him oddly, with curiosity. "You don't feel it, do you? Adolescents don't feel pity. It's a mature passion."

"I expect," Rowe said, "that I led a dull, humdrum, sober life, and so all this excites me. Now that I know I'm not a murderer I can enjoy—" He broke off at sight of the house dimly remembered like the scene of a dream: that unweeded little garden with the grey fallen piece of statuary and the small iron gate that creaked. All the blinds were down as though somebody had died, and the door stood open; you expected to see auction tickets on the furniture.

"We pulled her in," Mr. Prentice said, "simultaneously."

There was silence about the place; a man in a dark suit who might have been an undertaker stood in the hall. He opened a door for Mr. Prentice and they went in. It wasn't the drawing room that Rowe vaguely remembered but a small dining room crammed full with ugly chairs and a too large table and a desk. Mrs. Bellairs sat in an armchair at the head of the table with a pasty grey, closed face, wearing a black turban. The man at the door said, "She won't say a thing."

"Well, ma'am," Mr. Prentice greeted her with a kind of gallant jauntiness.

Mrs. Bellairs said nothing.

"I've brought you a visitor, ma'am," Mr. Prentice said, and, stepping to one side, he allowed her to see Rowe.

It is a disquieting experience to find yourself an object of terror: no wonder the novelty of it intoxicates some men. To Rowe it was horrible—as though he had suddenly found himself capable of an atrocity. Mrs. Bellairs began to choke, sitting grotesquely at the table head: it was as if she had swallowed a fish bone at a select dinner party. She must have been holding herself in with a great effort, and the shock had upset the muscles of her throat.

Mr. Prentice was the only one equal to the occasion. He wormed round the table and slapped her jovially on the back. "Choke up, ma'am," he said, "choke up. You'll be all right."

"I've never seen the man," she moaned, "never."

"Why, you told his fortune," Mr. Prentice said. "Don't you remember that?"

A glint of desperate hope slid across the old congested eyes. She said, "If all this fuss is about a little fortune-telling. I only do it for charity."

"Of course we understand that," Mr. Prentice said.

"And I never tell the future."

"Oh, if we could see into the future . . ."

"Only character."

"And the weight of cakes," Mr. Prentice said, and all the hope went suddenly out. It was too late now for silence.

"And your little séances," Mr. Prentice went cheerily on as though they shared a joke between them.

"In the interests of science," Mrs. Bellairs said.

"Does your little group still meet?"

"On Wednesdays."

"Many absentees?"

"They are all personal friends," Mrs. Bellairs said vaguely; now that the questions seemed again on safer ground she put up one plump powdered hand and adjusted the turban.

"Mr. Cost now—he can hardly attend any longer."

Mrs. Bellairs said carefully, "Of course I recognize this gentleman now. The beard confused me. That was a silly joke of Mr. Cost's. I knew nothing about it. I was far, far away."

"Far away?"

"Where the Blessed are."

"Oh, yes, yes. Mr. Cost won't play such jokes again."

"It was meant quite innocently, I'm sure. Perhaps he resented two strangers—we are a very compact little group. And Mr. Cost was never a real believer."

"Let's hope he is now." Mr. Prentice did not seem worried at the moment by what he had called the terrible passion of pity.

He said, "You must try to get into touch with him, Mrs. Bellairs, and ask him why he cut his throat this morning."

Into the goggle-eyed awful silence broke the ringing of the telephone. It rang and rang on the desk, and there were too many people in the little crowded room to get to it quickly. A memory shifted like an uneasy sleeper—this had happened before.

"Wait a moment," Mr. Prentice said. "You answer it, ma'am."

She repeated, "Cut his throat . . ."

"It was all he had left to do. Except live and hang."

The telephone cried on. It was as though someone far away had his mind fixed on that room, working out the reason for the silence.

"Answer it, ma'am," Mr. Prentice said again.

Mrs. Bellairs was not made of the same stuff as the tailor. She heaved herself obediently up, jangling a little as she moved. She got momentarily stuck between the table and the wall, and the turban slipped over one eye. She said, "Hullo. Who's there?"

The three men in the room stayed motionless, holding their breaths. Suddenly Mrs. Bellairs seemed to recover: it was as if she felt her power—the only one there who could speak. She said, "It's Dr. Forester. What shall I say to him?" speaking over her shoulder with her mouth close to the receiver. She glinted at them, maliciously, intelligently, with her stupidity strung up like a piece of camouflage she couldn't be bothered to perfect. Mr. Prentice took the receiver from her hand and rang off. He said, "This isn't going to help you."

She bridled, "I was only asking—"

Mr. Prentice said, "Get a fast car from the Yard. God knows what those local police are doing. They should have been at the house by this time." He told a second man, "See that this lady doesn't cut her throat. We've got other uses for it."

He proceeded to go through the house from room to room as destructively as a tornado; he was white and angry. He said to Rowe, "I'm worried about your friend—what's his name?—Stone." He said, "The old bitch," and the word sounded odd on the Edwardian lips. In Mrs. Bellairs' bedroom he didn't leave a pot of cream unchurned—and there were a great many. He tore open her pillows himself with vicious pleasure. There was a little lubricious book called *Love in the Orient* on a bed table by a pink-shaded lamp; he tore off the binding and broke the china base of the lamp. Only the sound of a car's horn stopped the destruction. He said, "I'll want you with me—for identifications," and took the stairs in three strides and a jump. Mrs. Bellairs was weeping now in the drawing room, and one of the detectives had made her a cup of tea.

"Stop that nonsense," Mr. Prentice said. It was as if he were determined to give an example of thoroughness to weak assistants. "There's nothing wrong with her. If she won't talk, skin this house alive." He seemed consumed by a passion of hatred and perhaps despair. He took up the cup from which Mrs. Bellairs had been about to drink and emptied the contents on the carpet. Mrs. Bellairs wailed at him, "You've got no right—"

He said sharply, "Is this your best tea service, ma'am?" wincing ever so slightly at the gaudy Prussian blue.

"Put it down," Mrs. Bellairs implored, but he had already smashed the cup against the wall. He explained to his man, "The handles are hollow. We don't know how small these films are. You've got to skin the place."

"You'll suffer for this," Mrs. Bellairs said tritely.

"Oh, no, ma'am, it's you who'll suffer. Giving information to the enemy is a hanging offence."

"They don't hang women. Not in this war."

"We may hang more people, ma'am," Mr. Prentice said, speaking back at her from the passage, "than the papers tell you about."

2

It was a long and gloomy ride. A sense of failure and apprehension must have oppressed Mr. Prentice: he sat curled in the corner of the car, humming lugubriously. It became evening before they had unwound themselves from the dirty edge of London, and night before they reached the first hedge. Looking back, one could see only an illuminated sky—bright lanes and blobs of light like city squares, as though the inhabited world were up above and down below only the dark unlighted heavens.

It was a long and gloomy ride, but all the time Rowe repressed, for the sake of his companion, a sense of exhilaration: he was happily drunk with danger and action. This was more like the life he had imagined years ago. He was helping in a great struggle, and when he saw Anna again he could claim to have played a part against her enemies. He didn't worry very much about Stone; none of the books of adventure one read as a boy had an unhappy ending. And none of them was disturbed by a sense of pity for the beaten side. The ruins from which they emerged were only a heroic backdrop to his personal adventure: they had no more reality than the photographs in a propaganda album: the remains of an iron bedstead on the third floor of a smashed tenement only said, "They shall not pass," not, "We shall never sleep in this room, in this home again." He didn't understand suffering because he had forgotten that he had ever suffered.

Rowe said, "After all nothing can have happened there. The local police—"

Mr. Prentice observed bitterly, "England is a very beautiful country. The Norman churches, the old graves, the village green and the public house, the policeman's home with his patch of garden. He wins a prize every year for his cabbages—"

"But the county police—"

"The chief constable served twenty years ago in the Indian Army. A fine fellow. Has a good palate for port. Talks too much about his regiment, but you can depend on him for a subscription to any good cause. The superintendent—he was a good man once, but they'd have retired him from the metropolitan police after a few years' service without a pension, so the first chance he got he transferred to the county. You see, being an honest man he didn't want to lay by in bribes from bookmakers for his old age. Only of course in a small county there's not much to keep a man sharp. Running in drunks. Petty pilfering. The judge at the assizes compliments the county on its clean record."

"You know the men?"

"I don't know *these* men, but if you know England you can guess it all. And then suddenly into this peace—even in wartime it's still peace—comes the clever, the warped, the completely unscrupulous, ambitious, educated criminal. Not a criminal at all as the county knows crime. He doesn't steal and he doesn't get drunk —and if he murders, they haven't had a murder for fifty years and can't recognize it."

"What do you expect to find?" Rowe asked.

"Almost anything except what we are looking for. A small roll of film."

"They may have got innumerable copies by this time."

"They may have, but they haven't innumerable ways of getting them out of the country. Find the man who's going to do the smuggling—and the organizer. It doesn't matter about the rest."

"Do you think Dr. Forester—?"

"Dr. Forester," Mr. Prentice said, "is a victim—oh, a dangerous victim, no doubt, but he's not the victimizer. He's one of the used, the blackmailed. That doesn't mean, of course, that he isn't the courier. If he is we are in luck. He couldn't get away—unless these country police . . ." Again the gloom of defeat descended on him.

"He might pass it on."

"It isn't so easy," Mr. Prentice said. "There are not many of these people at large. Remember, to get out of the country now you must have a very good excuse. If only the country police . . ."

"Is it so desperately important?"

Mr. Prentice said gloomily, "We've made so many mistakes since this war began and they've made so few. Perhaps this one will be the last we'll make. To trust a man like Dunwoody with anything secret—"

"Dunwoody?"

"I shouldn't have let it out, but one gets impatient. Have you heard the name? They hushed it up because he's the son of the grand old man."

"No, I've never heard of him—I think I've never heard of him."

A screech owl cried over the dark flat fields; their dimmed headlights just touched the near hedge and penetrated no farther into the wide region of night; it was like the coloured fringe along the unexplored spaces of a map. Over there among the unknown tribes a woman was giving birth, rats were nosing among sacks of meal, an old man was dying, two people were seeing each other for the first time by the light of a lamp: everything in that darkness was of such deep importance that their errand could not equal it— this violent superficial chase, this cardboard adventure hurtling at forty-five miles an hour along the edge of the profound natural common experiences of men. Rowe felt a longing to get back into that world: into the world of homes and children and quiet love and the ordinary unspecified fears and anxieties the neighbour shared; he carried the thought of Anna like a concealed letter promising just that; the longing was like the first stirring of maturity when the rare experience suddenly ceases to be desirable.

"We shall know the worst soon," Mr. Prentice said. "If we don't find here . . ." His hunched hopeless figure expressed the weariness of giving up.

Somebody a long way ahead was waving a torch up and down, up and down. "What the hell are they playing at?" Mr. Prentice said. "Advertising—they can't trust a stranger to find his way through their county without a compass."

They drew slowly along a high wall and halted outside big heraldic gates. It was unfamiliar to Rowe: he was looking from the outside at something he had only seen from within. The top of a cedar against the sky was not the same cedar that cast a shadow round the bole. A policeman stood at the car door and said, "What name, sir?"

Mr. Prentice showed a card. "Everything all right?"

"Not exactly, sir. You'll find the superintendent inside."

They left the car and trailed, a little secretive dubious group, between the great gates. They had no air of authority; they were stiff with the long ride and subdued in spirit: they looked like a party of awed sightseers taken by the butler round the family seat. The policeman kept on saying, "This way, sir," and flashing his torch, but there was only one way.

It seemed odd to Rowe, returning like this. The big house was silent—and the fountain was silent too. Somebody must have turned off the switch which regulated the flow. There were lights on in only two of the rooms. This was the place where for months he had lain happily in an extraordinary peace: this scene had been grafted by the odd operation of a bomb onto his childhood. Half his remembered life lay here. Now that he came back like an enemy, he felt a sense of shame. He said, "If you don't mind, I'd rather not see Dr. Forester."

The policeman with the torch said, "You needn't be afraid, sir, he's quite tidy."

Mr. Prentice had not been listening. "That car," he said, "who does it belong to?"

A Ford V8 stood in the drive—that wasn't the one he meant, but an old tattered car with cracked and stained wind-screen, one of those cars that stand with a hundred others in lonely spoiled fields along the highway—yours for five pounds if you can get it to move away.

"That, sir—that's the Reverend's."

Mr. Prentice asked sharply, "Are you holding a party?"

"Oh, no, sir. But as one of them was still alive we thought it only right to let the vicar know."

"Things seemed to have happened," Mr. Prentice said gloomily. It had been raining and the constable tried to guide them with his torch between the puddles in the churned-up gravel and up the stone steps to the hall door.

In the lounge where the illustrated papers had lain in glossy stacks, where Davis had been accustomed to weep in a corner and the two nervous men had fumed over the chess pieces, Johns sat in an armchair with his head in his hands. Rowe went to him. He said "Johns," and Johns looked up. He said, "He was such a great man . . . such a great man."

"Was?"

"I killed him."

3

It had been a massacre on an Elizabethan scale. Rowe was the only untroubled man there—until he saw Stone. The bodies lay where they had been discovered: Stone bound in his strait jacket with the sponge of anesthetic on the floor beside him and the body twisted in a hopeless attempt to use his hands. "He hadn't a chance," Rowe said. This was the passage he had crept up, excited, like a boy breaking a school rule: in the same passage, looking in through the open door, he grew up—learned that adventure didn't follow the literary pattern, that there weren't always happy endings, felt the awful stirring of pity that told him something had got to be done, that you couldn't let things stay as they were, with the innocent struggling in fear for breath and dying pointlessly. He said slowly, "I'd like . . . how I'd like . . ." and felt cruelty waking beside pity, its old and tried companion.

"We must be thankful," an unfamiliar voice said, "that he felt no pain." The stupid complacent and inaccurate phrase stroked at their raw nerves.

Mr. Prentice said, "Who the hell are you?" He apologized reluctantly, "I'm sorry. I suppose you are the vicar."

"Yes. My name's Sinclair."

"You've got no business here."

"I *had* business," Mr. Sinclair corrected him. "Dr. Forester was still alive when they called me. He was one of my parishioners." He added in a tone of gentle remonstrance, "You know, we are allowed on a battlefield."

"Yes, yes, I daresay. But there are no inquests on those bodies. Is that your car at the door?"

"Yes."

"Well, if you wouldn't mind going back to the vicarage and staying there till we are through with this."

"Certainly. I wouldn't want to be in the way."

Rowe watched him: the cylindrical black figure, the round collar glinting under the electric light, the false, hearty intellectual face. Mr. Sinclair said to him slowly, "Haven't we met   . ?" confronting him with an odd bold stare.

"No," Rowe said.

"Perhaps you are one of the patients here?"

"I was."

Mr. Sinclair said with nervous enthusiasm, "There. That must be it. I felt sure that somewhere—on one of the doctor's social evenings, I daresay. Good night."

Rowe turned away and considered again the man who had felt no pain. He remembered him stepping into the mud, desperately anxious, then fleeing like a scared child towards the vegetable garden. He had always believed in treachery. He hadn't been so mad after all.

They had had to step over Dr. Forester's body: it lay at the bottom of the stairs. A sixth snare had entangled the doctor: not love of country but love of one's fellow-man, a love which had astonishingly flamed into action in the heart of respectable hero-worshipping Johns. The doctor had been too sure of Johns; he had not realized that respect is really less reliable than fear: a man may be more ready to kill one he respects than to betray him to the police. When Johns shut his eyes and pulled the trigger of the revolver which had once been confiscated from Davis and had lain locked away for months in a drawer, he was not ruining the man he respected—he was saving him from the interminable proceedings of the law courts, from the crudities of prosecuting counsel, the unfathomable ignorances of the judge, and the indignity of depending on the shallow opinion of twelve men picked at random. If love of his fellow-man refused to allow him to be a sleeping partner in the elimination of Stone, love also dictated the form of his refusal.

Dr. Forester had shown himself disturbed from the moment of Rowe's escape. He had been inexplicably reluctant to call in the police, and he seemed worried about the fate of Stone There were consultations with Poole from which Johns was excluded, and during the afternoon there was a trunk call to London. .   Johns took a letter to the post and couldn't help noticing the watcher outside the gate. In the village he saw a police car from the county town. He began to wonder.

He met Poole on his way back. Poole too must have seen. All the fancies and resentments of the last few days came back to

Johns. Sitting in a passion of remorse in the lounge, he couldn't explain how all these indications had crystallized into the belief that the doctor was planning Stone's death. He remembered theoretical conversations he had often had with the doctor on the subject of euthanasia: arguments with the doctor who was quite unmoved by the story of the Nazi elimination of old people and incurables. The doctor had once said, "It's what any State medical service has sooner or later got to face. If you are going to be kept alive in institutions run by and paid for by the State, you must accept the State's right to economize when necessary." He intruded on a colloquy between Poole and Forester which was abruptly broken off; he became more and more restless and uneasy; it was as if the house were infected by the future; fear was already present in the passages. At tea Dr. Forester made some remark about "poor Stone."

"Why poor Stone?" Johns asked sharply and accusingly.

"He's in great pain," Dr. Forester said. "A tumour. Death is the greatest mercy we can ask for him."

He went restlessly out into the garden in the dusk; in the moonlight the sundial was like a small sheeted figure of someone already dead at the entrance to the rose garden. Suddenly he heard Stone crying out. . . . His account became more confused than ever. Apparently he ran straight to his room and got out the gun. It was just like Johns that he had mislaid the key and found it at last in his pocket. He heard Stone cry out again. He ran through the lounge, into the other wing, made for the stairs—the sickly confected smell of chloroform was in the passage, and Dr. Forester stood on guard at the foot of the stairs. He said crossly and nervously, "What do you want, Johns?" and Johns, who still believed in the misguided purity of the doctor's fanaticism, saw only one solution: he shot the doctor. Poole with his twisted shoulder and his malign conceited face backed away from the top of the stairs—and he shot him too in a rage because he guessed he was too late.

Then, of course, the police were at the door. He went to meet them, for apparently the servants had all been given the evening off, and it was that small banal fact of which he had read in so many murder stories that brought the squalid truth home to him. Dr. Forester was still alive, and the local police thought it only right to send for the parson. That was all. It was extraordinary the devastation that could be worked in one evening in what had once seemed a kind of earthly paradise. A flight of bombers could not have eliminated peace more thoroughly than had three men.

The search was then begun. The house was ransacked. More police were sent for. Lights were switched on and off restlessly through the early morning hours in upstairs rooms. Mr. Prentice said, "If we could find even a single print," but there was nothing. At one point of the long night watch Rowe found himself back in the room where Digby had slept. He thought of Digby now as a stranger—a rather gross, complacent, parasitic stranger whose happiness had lain in too great an ignorance. Happiness should always be qualified by a knowledge of misery. There on the bookshelf stood the Tolstoy with the pencil marks rubbed out. Knowledge was the great thing—not abstract knowledge in which Dr. Forester had been so rich, the theories which lead one enticingly on with their appearance of nobility, of transcendent virtue, but detailed, passionate, trivial human knowledge. He opened the Tolstoy again: "What seemed to me good and lofty—love of fatherland, of one's own people—became to me repulsive and pitiable. What seemed to me bad and shameful—rejection of fatherland and cosmopolitanism—now appeared to me on the contrary good and noble." Idealism had ended up with a bullet in the stomach at the foot of the stairs: the idealist had been caught out in treachery and murder. Rowe didn't believe they had had to blackmail him much. They had only to appeal to his virtues, his intellectual pride, his abstract love of humanity. One can't love humanity. One can only love people.

"Nothing," Mr. Prentice said. He drooped disconsolately across the room on his stiff lean legs and drew the curtain a little aside. Only one star was visible now; the others had faded into the lightening sky. "So much time wasted," Mr. Prentice said

"Three dead and one in prison."

"They can find a dozen to take their place. I want the films: the top man." He said, "They've been using photographic chemicals in the basin in Poole's room. That's where they developed the film probably. I don't suppose they'd print more than one at a time. They'd want to trust as few people as possible, and so long as they have the negative . . ." He added sadly, "Poole was a first-class photographer. He specialized in the life history of the bee. Wonderful studies. I've seen some of them. I want you to come over now to the island. I'm afraid we may find something unpleasant there for you to identify."

They stood where Stone had stood: three little red lights ahead

across the pond gave it in the three-quarter dark an illimitable air
as of a harbour just before dawn with the riding lamps of steamers
gathering for a convoy. Mr. Prentice waded out and Rowe followed
him; there was a thin skin of water over nine inches of mud. The
red lights were lanterns—the kind of lanterns which are strung at
night where roads are broken. Three policemen were digging in the
centre of the tiny island. There was hardly foothold for two more
men. "This was what Stone saw," Rowe said. "Men digging."

"Yes."

"What do you expect—?" He stopped: there was something
strained in the attitude of the diggers. They put in their spades carefully as though they might break something fragile and they seemed
to turn up the earth with reluctance. The dark scene reminded him
of something: something distant and sombre. Then he remembered
an old dark Victorian engraving in a book his mother had taken
away from him: men in cloaks digging at night in a graveyard with
the moonlight glinting on a spade.

Mr. Prentice said, "There's somebody you've forgotten—unac-
counted for."

Now as each spade cut down he waited himself with apprehension: he was held by the fear of disgust.

"How do you know where to dig?"

"They left marks. They were amateurs at this. I suppose that was
why they were scared of what Stone saw."

One spade made an ugly scrunching sound in the soft earth.

"Careful," Mr. Prentice said. The man wielding it stopped and
wiped sweat off his face; but the night was cold. Then he drew the
tool slowly out of the earth and looked at the blade. "Start again
on this side," Mr. Prentice said. "Take it gently. Don't go deep."
The other men stopped digging and watched, but you could tell
they didn't want to watch.

The man digging said, "Here it is." He left the spade standing
in the ground and began to move the earth with his fingers, gently
as though he were planting seedlings. He said with relief, "It's
only a box."

He took his spade again and with one strong effort lifted the box
out of its bed. It was the kind of wooden box which holds groceries
and the lid was loosely nailed down. He pried it open with the edge
of the blade and another man brought a lamp nearer. Then one by
one an odd sad assortment of objects was lifted out: they were like
the relics a company commander sends home when one of his men

has been killed. But there was this difference: there were no letters or photographs.

"Nothing they could burn," Mr. Prentice said.

These were what an ordinary fire would reject: a fountain-pen clip, another clip which had probably held a pencil.

"It's not easy to burn things," Mr. Prentice said, "in an all-electric house."

A pocket watch. He nicked open the heavy back and read aloud, "F.G.J. from N.L.J. on our silver wedding, 3.8.15." Below was added, "To my dear son in memory of his father. 1919."

"A good regular timepiece," Mr. Prentice said.

Two plaited metal armbands came next. Then the metal buckles off a pair of sock suspenders. And then a whole collection of buttons—little pearl buttons off a vest, large ugly brown buttons off a suit, brace buttons, pants buttons, trouser buttons—one could never have believed that one man's single change of clothes required so much holding together. Waistcoat buttons. Shirt buttons. Cuff buttons. Then the metal parts of a pair of braces. So is a poor human creature joined respectably together like a doll: take him apart and you are left with a grocery box full of assorted catches and buckles and buttons.

At the bottom there was a pair of heavy old-fashioned boots with big nails worn with so much pavement tramping, so much standing at street corners.

"I wonder," Mr. Prentice said, "what they did with the rest of him."

"Who was he?"

"He was Jones."

Three: Wrong Numbers

1

Rowe was growing up: every hour was bringing him nearer to hailing distance of his real age. Little patches of memory returned: he could hear Mr. Rennit's voice saying, "I agree with Jones," and he saw again a saucer with a sausage roll upon it beside a telephone. Pity stirred, but immaturity fought hard; the sense of adventure struggled with common sense as though it were on the side of happiness and common sense were allied to possible miseries, dis-appointments, disclosures.

It was immaturity which made him keep back the secret of the telephone number: the number he had so nearly made out in Cost's shop. He knew the exchange was B A T, and he knew the first three numbers were 271: only the last had escaped him. The infor-mation might be valueless—or invaluable. Whichever it was he hugged it to himself. Mr. Prentice had had his chance and failed; now it was his turn. He wanted to boast like a boy to Anna, "I did it."

About four-thirty in the morning they had been joined by a young man called Brothers. With his umbrella and his moustache and his black hat he had obviously modelled himself upon Mr. Prentice; perhaps in twenty years the portrait would have been adequately copied; it lacked at present the patina of age—the cracks of sadness, disappointment, and resignation. Mr. Prentice wearily surrendered the picked bones of investigation to Brothers and offered Rowe a seat in the car going back to London. He pulled his hat over his eyes, sank deep into the seat, and said, "We are beaten," as they splashed down a country lane with the moon-light flat on the puddles.

"What are you going to do about it?"

"Go to sleep." Perhaps to his fine palate the sentence sounded overconscious, for without opening his eyes he added, "One must avoid self-importance, you see. In five hundred years' time, to the historian writing the Decline and Fall of the British Empire, this little episode would not exist. There will be plenty of other causes You and me and poor Jones will not even figure in a footnote. It will be all economics, politics, battles."

"What do you think they did to Jones?"

"I don't suppose we shall ever know. In time of war so many bodies are unidentifiable. So many bodies," he said sleepily, "wait-ing for a convenient blitz." Suddenly, surprisingly, and rather shock-ingly, he began to snore.

They came into London with the early workers: along the indus-trial roads men and women were emerging from underground; neat elderly men carrying attaché cases and rolled umbrellas appeared from public shelters. In Gower Street they were sweeping up glass, and a building smoked into the new day like a candle which some late reveller has forgotten to snuff. It was odd to think that the usual battle had been going on while they stood on the island in the

pond and heard only the scrape of the spade. A notice turned them
from their course, and on a rope strung across the road already
flapped a few handwritten labels. "Barclay's Bank. Please inquire
at . . ." "The Cornwallis Dairy. New address . . ." "Marquis's
Fish Saloon . . ." On a long quiet empty expanse of pavement a
policeman and a warden strolled in lazy proprietory conversation,
like gamekeepers on their estate—a notice read "Unexploded
Bomb." This was the same route they had taken last night, but it
had been elaborately and trivially changed. What a lot of activity,
Rowe thought, there had been in a few hours—the sticking up of
notices, the altering of traffic, the getting to know a slightly different
London. He noticed the briskness, the cheerfulness on the faces:
you got the impression that this was an early hour of a national
holiday. It was simply, he supposed, the effect of finding oneself
alive.

Mr. Prentice muttered and woke. He told the driver the address
of a small hotel near Hyde Park Corner—"if it's still there"—and
insisted punctiliously on arranging for Rowe's room with the manager. It was only after he had waved his hand from the car—"I'll
ring you later, dear fellow"—that Rowe realized that his courtesy
of course had an object. He had been lodged where they could
reach him; he had been thrust securely into the right pigeonhole,
and would presently, when they required him, be pulled out again.
If he tried to leave it would be reported at once. Mr. Prentice had
even lent him five pounds—you couldn't go far on five pounds.

Rowe had a small early breakfast. The gas main apparently had
been hit, and the gas wouldn't light properly. It wasn't hardly more
than a smell, the waitress told him, not enough to boil a kettle or
make toast. But there was milk and Post Toasties and bread and
marmalade—quite an Arcadian meal, and afterwards he walked
across the park in the cool early sun and noticed, looking back over
the long empty plain, that he was not followed. He began to whistle
the only tune he knew: he felt a kind of serene excitement and
well being, for he was not a murderer. The forgotten years hardly
troubled him more than they had done in the first weeks at Dr.
Forester's home. How good it was, he thought, to play an adult part
in life again, and veered with his boy's secret into Bayswater towards a telephone box.

He had collected at the hotel a store of pennies. He was filled
with exhilaration, pressing in the first pair and dialling. A voice
said briskly, "The Hygienic Baking Company at your service," and

he rang off. It was only then he began to realize the difficulties ahead: he couldn't expect to know Cost's customer by a sixth sense. He dialled again and an old voice said "Hullo." He said, "Excuse me. Who is that please?"

"Who do you want?" the voice said obstinately—it was so old that it had lost sexual character and you couldn't tell whether it was a man's or a woman's.

"This is Exchange," Rowe said: the idea came to him at the moment of perplexity as though his brain had kept it in readiness all the while. "We are checking up on all subscribers since last night's raid."

"Why?"

"The automatic system has been disarranged. A bomb on the district exchange. Is that Mr. Isaacs of Prince of Wales Road?"

"No, it isn't. This is Wilson."

"Ah, you see, according to our dialling you should be Mr. Isaacs."

He rang off again; he wasn't any the wiser: after all even a Hygienic Bakery might conceal Mr. Cost's customer—it was even possible that his conversation had been a genuine one. But no, that he did not believe, hearing again the sad stoical voice of the tailor, "Personally, sir, I have no hope. No hope at all." Personally—the emphasis had lain there. He had conveyed as clearly as he dared that it was for him alone the battle was over.

He went on pressing in his pennies: reason told him that it was useless, that the only course was to let Mr. Prentice into his secret —and yet he couldn't but believe that somehow over the wire some sense would be conveyed to him, the vocal impression of a will and a violence sufficient to cause so many deaths—poor Stone asphyxiated in the sick bay, Forester and Poole shot down upon the stairs, Cost with the shears through his neck, Jones. . . . The cause was surely too vast to come up the wire only as a commonplace voice saying, "Westminster Bank speaking."

Suddenly he remembered that Mr. Cost had not asked for any individual. He had simply dialled a number and begun to speak as soon as he heard a voice reply. That meant he could not be speaking to a business address, where some employee would have to be brought to the phone.

"Hullo."

A voice took any possible question out of his mouth. "Oh, Ernest," a torrential voice said, "I knew you'd ring. You dear sympathetic thing. I suppose David's told you Minny's gone. Last night in the raid, it was awful. We heard her voice calling to us from outside, but of course there was nothing we could do. We couldn't leave our shelter. And then a land mine dropped—it must have been a land mine. Three houses went, a huge hole. And this morning not a sign of Minny. David still hopes of course, but I knew at the time, Ernest, there was something elegiac in her mew . . ."

It was fascinating, but he had work to do. He rang off.

The telephone box was getting stiflingly hot. He had already used up a shilling's worth of coppers; surely among these last four numbers a voice would speak and he would know. "Police Station, Mafeking Road." Back onto the rest with the receiver. Three numbers left. Against all reason he was convinced that one of these three. . . . His face was damp with sweat. He wiped it dry and immediately the beads formed again. He felt suddenly an apprehension: the dryness of his throat, his heavily beating heart, warned him that this voice might present too terrible an issue. There had been five deaths already. . . . His head swam with relief when a voice said, "Gas Light and Coke Company." He could still walk out and leave it to Mr. Prentice. After all, how did he know that the voice he was seeking was not that of the operator at the Hygienic Baking Company—or even Ernest's friend?

But if he went to Mr. Prentice he would find it hard to explain his silence all these invaluable hours. He was not after all a boy; he was a middle-aged man. He had started something and he must go on. And yet he still hesitated while the sweat got into his eyes. Two numbers left: a fifty per cent chance. He would try one, and if that number conveyed nothing at all, he would walk out of the box and wash his hands of the whole business. Perhaps his eyes and his wits had deceived him in Mr. Cost's shop. His finger went reluctantly through the familiar arcs: B A T 271; which number now? He put his sleeve against his face and wiped, then dialled.

BOOK IV

The Whole Man

One: Journey's End

1

The telephone rang and rang: he could imagine the empty rooms spreading round the small vexed instrument. Perhaps the rooms of a girl who went to business in the City, or a tradesman who was now at his shop; of a man who left early to read at the British Museum: innocent rooms. He held the welcome sound of an unanswered bell to his ear. He had done his best. Let it ring.

Or were the rooms perhaps guilty rooms? The rooms of a man who had disposed in a few hours of so many human existences. What would a guilty room be like? A room, like a dog, takes on some of the characteristics of its master. A room is trained for certain ends—comfort, beauty, convenience. This room would surely be trained to anonymity. It would be a room which would reveal no secrets if the police should ever call: there would be no Tolstoys with pencilled lines imperfectly erased; no personal touches; the common mean of taste would furnish it—a wireless set, a few detective novels, a reproduction of Van Gogh's sunflower. He imagined it all quite happily while the bell rang and rang. There would be nothing significant in the cupboards: no love letters concealed below the handkerchiefs, no cheque book in a drawer; would the linen be marked? There would be no presents from anyone at all—a lonely room: everything in it had been bought at a standard store.

Suddenly a voice he knew said a little breathlessly, "Hullo. Who's that?" If only, he thought, putting the receiver down, she had been quite out of hearing when the bell rang, at the bottom of the stairs, or in the street. If only he hadn't let his fancy play so long, he need never have known that this was Anna Hilfe's number.

He came blindly out into Bayswater: he had three choices—the sensible and the honest choice was to tell the police. The second was to say nothing. The third was to see for himself. He had no doubt at all that this was the number Cost had dialled; he remembered how she had known his real name all along, how she had said—it was a curious phrase—that it was her "job" to visit him at the home. And yet he didn't doubt that there was an answer, an answer he couldn't trust the police to find. He went back to his hotel and up to his room, carrying the telephone directory with him from the lounge—he had a long job to do. In fact it was several hours before he reached the number. His eyes were swimming and he nearly missed it: 16 Prince Consort Mansions Battersea—a name which meant nothing at all. He thought wryly: of course a guilty room would be taken furnished. He lay down on his bed and closed his eyes.

It was past five o'clock in the afternoon before he could bring himself to act, and then he acted mechanically. He wouldn't think any more: what was the good of thinking before he heard her speak? A 19 bus took him to the top of Oakley Street, and a 49 to Albert Bridge. He walked across the bridge, not thinking. It was low tide and the mud lay up under the warehouses. Somebody on the embankment was feeding the gulls: the sight obscurely distressed him and he hurried on, not thinking. The waning sunlight lay in a wash of rose over the ugly bricks, and a solitary dog went nosing and brooding into the park. A voice said, "Why, Arthur," and he stopped. A man wearing a beret on untidy grey hair and warden's dungarees stood at the entrance to a block of flats. He said doubtfully, "It is Arthur, isn't it?"

Since Rowe's return to London many memories had slipped into place—this church and that shop, the way Piccadilly ran into Knightsbridge. He hardly noticed when they took up their places as part of the knowledge of a lifetime. But there were other memories which had to fight painfully for admission: somewhere in his mind they had an enemy who wished to keep them out—and often succeeded. Cafés and street corners and shops would turn on him a suddenly familiar face, and he would look away and hurry on as though they were the scenes of a road accident. The man who spoke to him belonged to these, but you can't hurry away from a human being as you can hurry away from a shop.

"The last time you hadn't got the beard. You are Arthur, aren't you?"

"Yes, Arthur Rowe."

The man looked puzzled and hurt. He said, "It was good of you to call that time."

"I don't remember."

The look of pain darkened like a bruise. "The day of the funeral."

Rowe said, "I'm sorry. I had an accident: my memory went. It's only beginning to come back in parts. Who are you?"

"I'm Henry—Henry Wilcox."

"And I came here—to a funeral?"

"My wife got killed. I expect you read about it in the papers. They gave her a medal. I was a bit worried afterwards because you'd wanted me to cash a cheque for you and I forgot. You know how it is at a funeral: so many things to think about. I expect I was upset too."

"Why did I bother you then?"

"Oh, it must have been important. It went right out of my head —and then I thought, I'll see him afterwards. But I never saw you."

Rowe looked up at the flats above them. "Was it here?"

"Yes."

He looked across the road to the gate of the park: a man feeding gulls; an office worker went by carrying a suitcase; the road reeled a little under his feet. He said, "Was there a procession?"

"The post turned out. And the police and the rescue party."

Rowe said, "Yes. I couldn't go to the bank to cash the cheque. I thought the police thought I was a murderer. But I had to find money if I was going to get away. So I came here. I didn't know about the funeral. I thought all the time about this murder."

"You brood too much," Henry said. "A thing that's done is done," and he looked quite brightly up the road the procession had taken.

"But this was never done, you see. I know that now. I'm not a murderer," he explained.

"Of course you aren't, Arthur. No friend of yours—no proper friend—ever believed you were."

"Was there so much talk?"

"Well, naturally."

"I didn't know." He turned his mind into another track: along the embankment wall—the sense of misery and then the little man feeding birds, the suitcase—he lost the thread until he remembered the face of the hotel clerk, and then he was walking down interminable corridors, a door opened and Anna was there. They shared the danger—he clung to that idea. There was always an explanation. He remembered how she had told him he had saved her life. He said stiffly, "Well, good-bye. I must be getting on."

"It's no use mourning someone all your life," Henry said. "That's morbid."

"Yes. Good-bye."

"Good-bye."

2

The flat was on the third floor. He wished the stairs would never end, and when he rang the bell he hoped the flat would be deserted. An empty milk bottle stood outside the door on the small dark landing; there was a note stuck in it: he picked it out and read it— "Only half a pint tomorrow please." The door opened while he still held it in his hand, and Anna said hopelessly, "It's you."

"Yes, me."

"Every time the bell rang I've been afraid it would be you."

"How did you think I'd find you?"

She said, "There's always the police. They are watching the office now." He followed her in.

It wasn't the way he had at one time—under the sway of the strange adventure—imagined that he would meet her again. There was a heavy constraint between them. When the door closed they didn't feel alone. It was as if all sorts of people they both knew were with them. They spoke in low voices so as not to intrude. He said, "I got your address by watching Cost's fingers on the dial— when he telephoned you just before he killed himself."

"It's so horrible," she said. "I didn't know you were there."

" 'I've no hope at all.' That's what he said. 'Personally, I've no hope.' "

They stood in a little ugly crowded hall as though it wasn't worth the bother of going any farther. It was more like a parting than a reunion—a parting too sorrowful to have any grace. She wore the same blue trousers she had worn at the hotel: he had forgotten how small she was. With the scarf knotted at her neck she looked heartbreakingly impromptu. All around them were brass trays, warming pans, knickknacks, an old oak chest, a Swiss cuckoo clock carved with heavy trailing creepers. He said, "Last night was not good either. I was there too. Did you know that Dr. Forester was dead— and Poole?"

"No."

He said, "Aren't you sorry—such a massacre of your friends?"

"No," she said, "I'm glad." It was then that he began to hope. She said gently, "My dear, you have everything mixed up in your head, your poor head. You don't know who are your friends and who are your enemies. That's the way they always work, isn't it?"

"They used you to watch me, didn't they, down there at Dr. Forester's, to see when my memory would begin to return? Then they'd have put me in the sick bay like poor Stone."

"You're so right and so wrong," she said wearily. "I don't suppose we'll ever get it straight now. It's true I watched you for them. I didn't want your memory to return any more than they did. I didn't want you hurt." She said with sharp anxiety, "Do you remember everything now?"

"I remember a lot and I've learned a lot. Enough to know I'm not a murderer."

She said, "Thank God."

"But you knew I wasn't?"

"Yes," she said, "of course. I knew it. I just meant—oh, that I'm glad *you* know." She said slowly, "I like you happy. It's how you ought to be."

He said as gently as he could, "I love you. You know that. I want to believe you are my friend. Where are the photographs?"

A painted bird burst raspingly out of the hideous carved clock case and cuckooed the half-hour. He had time to think between the cuckoos that another night would soon be on them. Would that contain horror too? The door clicked shut and she said simply, "He has them."

"He?"

"My brother." He still held the note to the milkman in his hand. She said, "You are so fond of investigation, aren't you? The first time I saw you you came to the office about a cake. You were so determined to get to the bottom of things. You've got to the bottom now."

"I remember. He seemed so helpful. He took me to that house—"

She took the words out of his mouth. "He staged a murder for you and helped you to escape. But afterwards he thought it safer to have you murdered. That was my fault. You told me you'd written a letter to the police, and I told him."

"Why?"

"I didn't want to get him into trouble for just frightening you. I never guessed he could be so thorough."

."But you were in that room when I came with the suitcase," he said: he couldn't work it out. "You were nearly killed too."

"Yes. He hadn't forgotten, you see, that I telephoned to you at Mrs. Bellairs'. *You* told him that. I wasn't on his side any longer—not against you. He told me to go and meet you—and persuade you not to send the letter. And then he just sat back in another flat and waited."

He accused her, "But you are alive."

"Yes," she said, "I'm alive, thanks to you. I'm even on probation again—he won't kill his sister if he doesn't feel it's necessary. He calls that family feeling. I was only a danger because of you. This isn't *my* country. Why should I have wanted your memory to return? You were happy without it. I don't care a damn about England. I want you to be happy, that's all. The trouble is he understands such a lot."

He said obstinately, "It doesn't make sense. Why am I alive?"

"He's economical." She added, "They are all economical. You'll never understand them if you don't understand that." She repeated wryly like a formula, "The maximum of terror for the minimum time directed against the fewest objects."

He was bewildered: he didn't know what to do. He was learning the lesson most people learn very young, that things never work out in the expected way. This wasn't an exciting adventure, and he wasn't a hero, and it was even possible that this was not a tragedy. He became aware of the note to the milkman. "He's going away?"

"Yes."

"With the photographs of course?"

"Yes."

"We've got to stop him," he said. The "we" like the French *tu* spoken for the first time conveyed everything.

"Yes."

"Where is he now?"

She said, "He's here."

It was like exerting a great pressure against a door and finding it ajar all the time. "Here?"

She jerked her head. "He's asleep. He had a long day with Lady Dunwoody about woollies."

"But he'll have heard us?"

"Oh, no," she said. "He's out of hearing, and he sleeps so sound. That's economy too. As deep a sleep and as little of it—"

"How you hate him," he said with surprise.

"He's made such a mess," she said, "of everything. He's so fine, so intelligent—and yet there's only this fear. That's all he makes."

"Where is he?"

She said, "Through there is the living room and beyond that is his bedroom."

"Can I use the telephone?"

"It's not safe. It's in the living room and the bedroom door's ajar."

"Where's he going?"

"He has permission to go to Ireland—for the Free Mothers. It wasn't easy to get, but your friends have made such a sweep. Lady Dunwoody worked it. You see he's been so grateful for her woollies. He gets the train tonight." She said, "What are you going to do?"

"I don't know."

He looked helplessly round. A heavy brass candlestick stood on the oak chest: it glittered with polish; no wax had ever sullied it. He picked it up. "He tried to kill me," he explained weakly.

"He's asleep. That's murder."

"I won't hit first."

She said, "He used to be sweet to me when I cut my knees. Children always cut their knees. . . . Life is horrible, wicked."

He put the candlestick down again.

"No," she said. "Take it. You mustn't be hurt. He's only my brother, isn't he?" she asked with obscure bitterness. "Take it. Please." When he made no move to take it, she picked it up herself: her face was stiff and schooled and childish and histrionic. It was like watching a small girl play Lady Macbeth. You wanted to shield her from the knowledge that these things were really true.

She led the way, holding the candlestick upright as though it were a rehearsal: only on the night itself would the candle be lit. Everything in the flat was hideous except herself: it gave him more than ever the sense that they were both strangers here. The heavy furniture must have been put in by a company, bought by an official buyer at cut rates, or perhaps ordered by telephone—suite 56a of the autumn catalogue. Only a bunch of flowers and a few books and a newspaper and a man's sock in holes showed that people lived here. It was the sock which made him pause: it seemed to speak of long mutual evenings, of two people knowing each other over many years. He thought for the first time, It's her brother who's going to die. Spies like murderers were hanged, and in this case there was no distinction. He lay asleep in there and the gallows was being built outside.

They moved stealthily across the anonymous room towards a door ajar. She pushed it gently with her hand and stood back so that he might see. It was the immemorial gesture of a woman who shows to a guest after dinner her child asleep.

Hilfe lay on the bed on his back without his jacket, his shirt open at the neck. He was deeply and completely at peace, and so defenceless that he seemed to be innocent. His very pale gold hair lay in a hot streak across his face, as though he had lain down after a game. He looked very young; he didn't, lying there, belong to the same world as Cost bleeding by the mirror, and Stone in the strait jacket. One was half impelled to believe, It's propaganda, just propaganda; he isn't capable. . . . The face seemed to Rowe very beautiful, more beautiful than his sister's which could be marred by grief or pity. Watching the sleeping man, he could realize a little of the force and the grace and the attraction of nihilism—of not caring for anything, of having no rules and feeling no love. Life became simple. . . . He had been reading when he fell asleep; a book lay on the bed and one hand still held the pages open; it was like the tomb of a young student: bending down, you could read on the marble page the epitaph chosen for him, a verse:

> Denn Orpheus ists. Seine Metamorphose
> in dem und dem. Wir sollen uns nicht mühn
> um andre Namen. Ein für alle Male
> ists Orpheus, wenn es singt. . . .

The knuckles hid the rest.

It was as if he were the only violence in the world and when he slept there was peace everywhere.

They watched him and he woke. People betray themselves when they wake: sometimes they wake with a cry from an ugly dream; sometimes they turn from one side to the other and shake the head and burrow as if they are afraid to leave sleep. Hilfe just woke: his lids puckered for a moment, like a child's when the nurse draws the curtain and the light comes in; then they were wide open and he was looking at them with complete self-possession. The pale blue eyes held full knowledge of the situation: there was nothing to explain. He smiled and Rowe caught himself in the act of smiling back. It was the kind of trick a boy plays suddenly, capitulating, admitting everything, so that the whole offence seems small and the fuss absurd. There are moments of surrender when it is so much easier to love one's enemy than to remember.

Rowe said weakly, "The photographs . . ."

"The photographs." He smiled frankly up. "Yes, I've got them." He must have known that everything was up—including life, but he still retained the air of badinage, the dated colloquialisms which made his speech a kind of light dance of inverted commas. "Admit," he said, "I've led you 'up the garden.' And now I'm 'in the cart.' " He looked at the candlestick which his sister stiffly held and said, "I surrender," with amusement, lying on his back on the bed, as though they had all three been playing a game.

"Where are they?"

He said, "Let's strike a bargain. Let's swap," as though he were suggesting the exchange of foreign stamps for toffee.

Rowe said, "There's no need for me to exchange anything. You're through."

"My sister loves you a lot, doesn't she?" He refused to take the situation seriously. "Surely you wouldn't want to eliminate your brother-in-law?"

"You didn't mind trying to eliminate your sister."

He said blandly and unconvincingly, "Oh, that was a tragic necessity," and gave a sudden grin which made the whole affair of the suitcase and the bomb about as important as a booby trap on the stairs. He seemed to accuse them of a lack of humour: it was not the kind of thing they ought to have taken to heart.

"Let's be sensible civilized people," he said, "and come to an agreement. Do put down the candlestick, Anna. I can't hurt you here even if I wanted to." He made no attempt to get up, lying on the bed, displaying his powerlessness like evidence.

"There's no basis for an agreement," Rowe said. "I want the photographs, and then the police want you. You didn't talk about terms to Stone—or Jones."

"I know nothing about all that," Hilfe said. "I can't be responsible—can I?—for all my people do. That isn't reasonable, Rowe." He asked, "Do you read poetry? There's a poem here which just seems to meet the case." He sat up, lifted the book, and dropped it again. With a gun in his hand he said, "Just stay still. You see there's still something to talk about."

Rowe said, "I've been wondering where you kept it."

"Now we can bargain sensibly. We're both in a hole."

"I still don't see," Rowe said, "what you've got to offer. You don't really imagine, do you, that you can shoot us both and then get to Ireland? These walls are as thin as paper. You are known as the tenant. The police would be waiting for you at the port."

"But if I'm going to die anyway, I might just as well—mightn't I?—have a massacre."

"It wouldn't be economical."

He considered the objection half seriously and then said with a grin, "No, but don't you think it would be rather grand?"

"It doesn't much matter to me how I stop you. Being killed would be quite useful."

Hilfe exclaimed, "Do you mean your memory's come back?"

"I don't know what that's got to do with it."

"Such a lot. Your past history is really sensational. I went into it all carefully and so did Anna. It explained so much I didn't understand at first when I heard from Poole what you were like. The kind of room you were living in, the kind of man you were. You were the sort of man I thought I could deal with quite easily until you lost your memory. That didn't work out right. You got so many illusions of grandeur, heroism, self-sacrifice, patriotism. . . ." Hilfe grinned at him. "Here's a bargain for you. My safety against your past. I'll tell you who you were. No trickery. I'll give you all the references. But that won't be necessary. Your own brain will tell you I'm not inventing."

"He's just lying," Anna said. "Don't listen to him."

"She doesn't want you to hear, does she? Doesn't that make you curious? She wants you as you are, you see, and not as you were."

Rowe said, "I only want the photographs."

"You can read about yourself in the newspaper. You were really quite famous. She's afraid you'll feel too grand for her when you know."

Rowe said, "If you give me the photographs . . . ?"

"And tell you your story . . . ?"

He seemed to feel some of Rowe's excitement. He shifted a little on his elbow and his gaze moved for a moment. The wristbone cracked as Anna swung the candlestick down, and the gun lay on the bed. She took it up and said, "There's no need to bargain with him."

He was moaning and doubled with pain, and his face was white with it. Both their faces were white. For a moment Rowe thought she would go on her knees to him, take his head on her shoulder, surrender the gun to his other hand.

"Anna," Hilfe whispered, "Anna."

She said, "Willi," and rocked a little on her feet.

"Give me the gun," Rowe said.

She looked at him as if he were a stranger who shouldn't have been in the room at all: her ears seemed filled with the whimper from the bed. Rowe put out his hand and she backed away, so that she stood beside her brother. "Go outside," she said, "and wait. Go outside." In their pain they were like twins. She pointed the gun at him and moaned, "Go outside."

He said, "Don't let him talk you round. He tried to kill you," but, seeing the family face in front of him, his words sounded flat. It was as if they were so akin that either had the right to kill the other: it was only a form of suicide.

"Please don't go on talking," she said. "It doesn't do any good." Sweat stood on both their faces; he felt helpless.

"Only promise," he said, "you won't let him go."

She moved her shoulders and said, "I promise." When he went she closed and locked the door behind him.

For a long time afterwards he could hear nothing—except once the closing of a cupboard door and the chink of china. He imagined she was bandaging Hilfe's wrist; he was probably safe enough, incapable of further flight. Rowe realized that now if he wished he could telephone to Mr. Prentice and have the police surround the flat—he was no longer anxious for glory: the sense of adventure had leaked away and left only the sense of human pain. But he felt that he was bound by her promise: he had to trust her, if life was to go on.

A quarter of an hour dragged by and the room was full of dusk. There had been low voices in the bedroom: he felt uneasy. Was Hilfe talking her round? He was aware of a painful jealousy: they had been so alike and he had been shut out like a stranger. He went to the window and, drawing the blackout curtain a little aside, looked out over the darkening park. There was so much he had still to remember: the thought came to him like a threat in Hilfe's dubious tones

The door opened, and when he let the curtain fall he realized how dark it had become. Anna walked stiffly towards him and said, "There you are. You've got what you wanted." Her face looked ugly in the attempt to avoid tears; it was an ugliness which bound him to

her more than any beauty could have done. It isn't being happy together, he thought as though it were a fresh discovery, that makes
one love—it's being unhappy together. "Don't you want them," she
asked, "now I've got them for you?"

He took the little roll in his hand: he had no sense of triumph at
all. He asked, "Where is he?"

She said, "You don't want him now. He's finished."

"Why did you let him go?" he asked. "You promised."

"Yes," she said, "I promised." She made a small movement with
her fingers, crossing two of them—he thought for a moment that she
was going to claim that child's excuse for broken treaties.

"Why?" he asked again.

"Oh," she said vaguely, "I had to bargain."

He began to unwrap the roll carefully: he didn't want to expose
more than a scrap of it. "But he had nothing to bargain with," he
said. He held the roll out to her on the palm of his hand. "I don't
know what he promised to give you, but this isn't it."

"He swore that's what you wanted. How do you know?"

"I don't know how many prints they made. This may be the only
one or there may be a dozen. But I do know there's only one negative."

She asked sadly, "And that's not it?"

"No."

3

Rowe said, "I don't know what he had to bargain with, but he
didn't keep his part."

"I give up," she said. "Whatever I touch goes wrong, doesn't it?
Do what you want to do."

"You'll have to tell me where he is."

"I always thought," she said, "I could save both of you. I didn't
care what happened to the world. It couldn't be worse than it's always been, and yet the globe, the beastly globe, survives. But people, you, him . . ." She sat down on the nearest chair—a stiff, polished, ugly upright chair: her feet didn't reach the floor. She said,
"Paddington, the seven-twenty. He said he'd never come back. I
thought you'd be safe then."

"Oh," he said, "I can look after myself," but, meeting her eyes, he
had the impression that he hadn't really understood. He said,
"Where will he have it? They'll search him at the port anyway."

"I don't know. He took nothing."

"A stick?"

"No," she said, "nothing. He just put on his jacket—he didn't even take a hat. I suppose it's in his pocket."

He said, "I'll have to go to the station."

"Why can't you leave it to the police now?"

"By the time I get the right man and explain to him, the train will have gone. If I miss him at the station, then I'll ring the police." A doubt occurred. "If he told you that, of course he won't be there."

"He didn't tell me. I didn't believe what he told me. That was the original plan. It's his only hope of getting out of here."

When he hesitated she said, "Why not just let them meet the train at the other end? Why do it all yourself?"

"He might get out on the way."

"You mustn't go like this. He's armed. I let him have his gun."

He suddenly laughed. "By God," he said, "you have made a mess of things, haven't you?"

"I wanted him to have a chance."

"You can't do much with a gun in the middle of England except kill a few poor devils." She looked so small and beaten that he couldn't preserve any anger. She said, "There's only one bullet in it. He wouldn't waste that."

"Just stay here," Rowe said.

She nodded. "Good-bye."

"I'll be back quite soon." She didn't answer, and he tried another phrase. "Life will begin all over again then." She smiled unconvincingly, as though it was he who needed comforting and reassurance, not she.

"He won't kill me."

"I'm not afraid of that."

"What are you afraid of then?"

She looked up at him with a kind of middle-aged tenderness, as though they'd grown through love into its later stage. She said, "I'm afraid he'll talk."

He mocked at her from the door. "Oh, he won't talk *me* round," but all the way downstairs he was thinking again, I didn't understand her.

The searchlights were poking up over the park: patches of light floated like clouds along the surface of the sky. It made the sky seem very small; you could probe its limit with light. There was a

smell of cooking all along the pavement from houses where people
were having an early supper to be in time for the raid. A warden
was lighting a hurricane lamp outside a shelter. He said to Rowe,
"Yellow's up." The match kept going out—he wasn't used to lighting lamps; he looked a bit on edge: too many lonely vigils on deserted pavements; he wanted to talk. But Rowe was in a hurry; he
couldn't wait.

On the other side of the bridge there was a taxi rank with one
cab left. "Where do you want to go?" the driver asked and considered, looking up at the sky, the pillows of light between the few
stars, one pale just visible balloon. "Oh, well," he said, "I'll take a
chance. It won't be worse there than here."

"Perhaps there won't be a raid."

"Yellow's up," the driver said, and the old engine creaked into
life.

They went up across Sloane Square and Knightsbridge and into
the park and on along the Bayswater Road. A few people were
hurrying home; buses slid quickly past the Request stops; Yellow
was up; the saloon bars were crowded. People called to the taxi
from the pavement, and when a red light held it up an elderly gentleman in a bowler hat opened the door quicky and began to get in.
"Oh," he said, "I beg your pardon. Thought it was empty. Are you
going towards Paddington?"

"Get in," Rowe said.

"Catching the seven-twenty," the stranger said breathlessly. "Bit
of luck for me this. We'll make it."

"I'm catching it too," Rowe said.

"Yellow's up."

"So I've heard."

They creaked forward through the thickening darkness. "Any
land mines your way last night?" the old gentleman asked.

"No, no. I don't think so."

"Three near us. About time for the Red I should think."

"I suppose so."

"Yellow's been up for quarter of an hour," the elderly gentleman
said, looking at his watch as though he were timing an express train
between stations. "Ah, that sounded like a gun. Over the estuary I
should say."

"I didn't hear it."

"I should give them another ten minutes at most," the old gentleman said, holding his watch in his hand as the taxi turned up into

Praed Street. They swung down the covered way and came to rest. Through the blacked-out station the season-ticket holders were making a quick getaway from the nightly death: they dived in earnest silence towards the suburban trains, carrying little attaché cases, and the porters stood and watched them go with an air of sceptical superiority. They felt the pride of being a legitimate objective: the pride of people who stayed.

The long train stood darkly along number one platform: the bookstalls closed, the blinds drawn in most of the compartments. It was a novel sight to Rowe and yet an old sight. He had only to see it once, like the sight of a bombed street, for it to take up its place imperceptibly among his memories. This was already life as he'd known it.

It was impossible to see who was in the train from the platform: every compartment held its secrets close. Even if the blinds had not been lowered, the blued globes cast too little light to show who sat below them. He felt sure that Hilfe would travel first class; as a refugee he lived on borrowed money, and as the friend and confidant of Lady Dunwoody he was certain to travel in style.

He made his way down the first-class compartments along the corridor: they were not very full; only the more daring season-ticket holders remained in London as late as this. He put his head in at every door and met at once the disquieting return stare of the blue ghosts.

It was a long train, and the porters were already shutting doors higher up before he reached the last first-class coach. He was so accustomed to failure that it took him by surprise, sliding back the door, to come on Hilfe.

He wasn't alone. An old lady sat opposite him, and she had made Hilfe's hands into a cat's cradle for winding wool. He was handcuffed in the heavy oiled raw material for seamen's boots. His right hand stuck stiffly out, the wrist bandaged and roughly splinted, and round and round and ever so gently the old lady industriously wound her wool. It was ludicrous and it was sad. Rowe could see the weighted pocket where the revolver lay, and the look that Hilfe turned on him was not reckless or amused or dangerous: it was humiliated. He had always had a way with old ladies.

Rowe said, "You won't want to talk here."

"She's deaf," Hilfe said, "stone deaf."

"Good evening," the old lady said, "I hear there's a Yellow up."

"Yes," Rowe said.

"Shocking," the old lady said and wound her wool.

"I want the negative," Rowe said.

"Anna should have kept you longer. I told her to give me enough start. After all," he added with gloomy disappointment, "it would have been better for both."

"You cheated her too often," Rowe said. He sat down by his side and watched the winding—up and over and round.

"What are you going to do?"

"Wait till the train starts and then pull the cord."

Suddenly from very close the guns cracked—once, twice, three times. The old lady looked vaguely up as though she had heard something very faint intruding on her silence. Rowe put his hand into Hilfe's pocket and slipped the gun into his own. "If you'd like to smoke," the old lady said, "don't mind me."

Hilfe said, "I think we ought to talk things over."

"There's nothing to talk about."

"It wouldn't do, you know, to get me and not to get the photographs."

Rowe began, "The photographs don't matter by themselves. It's you." But then he thought, They do matter. How do I know he hasn't passed them on already? If they are hidden, the place may be agreed on with another agent; even if they are found by a stranger, they are not safe. He said, "We'll talk," and the siren sent up its tremulous howl over Paddington. Very far away this time there was a pad, pad, pad like the noise a fivesball makes against the glove, and the old lady wound and wound. He remembered Anna saying, "I'm afraid he'll talk," and he saw Hilfe suddenly smile at the wool as if life had still the power to tickle him into savage and internal mirth.

Hilfe said, "I'm still ready to swap."

"You haven't anything to swap."

"You haven't much, you know, either," Hilfe said. "You don't know where the photos are."

"I wonder when the sirens will go," the old lady said.

Hilfe moved his wrists in the wool. He said, "If you give me back the gun, I'll let you have the photographs."

"If you can give me the photographs, they must be with you There's no reason why I should bargain."

"Well," Hilfe said, "if it's your idea of revenge, I can't stop you. I thought perhaps you wouldn't want Anna dragged in. She let me escape, you remember."

"There," the old lady said, "we've nearly done now."

Hilfe said, "They probably wouldn't hang her. Of course that would depend on what I say. Perhaps it would be just an internment camp till the war's over—and then deportation if you win. From my point of view," he explained dryly, "she's a traitor, you know."

Rowe said, "Give me the photographs and then we'll talk." The word "talk" was like a capitulation. Already he was beginning painfully to think out the long chain of deceit he would have to practise on Mr. Prentice if he were to save Anna.

The train rocked with an explosion. The old lady said, "At last we are going to start," and, leaning forward, she released Hilfe's hands. Hilfe said with a curious wistfulness, "What fun they are having up there." He was like a mortally sick man saying farewell to the sports of his contemporaries: no fear, only regret. He had failed to bring off the record himself in destruction. Five people only were dead: it hadn't been much of an innings compared with what they were having up there. Sitting under the darkened globe, he was a long way away: wherever men killed, his spirit moved in obscure companionship.

"Give them to me," Rowe said.

He was surprised by a sudden joviality. It was as if Hilfe after all had not lost all hope—of what? Escape? Further destruction? He laid his left hand on Rowe's knee with a gesture of intimacy. He said, "I'll be better than my word. How would you like to have your memory back?"

"I only want the photographs."

"Not here," Hilfe said. "I can't very well strip in front of a lady, can I?" He stood up. "We'd better leave the train."

"Are you going?" the old lady asked.

"We've decided, my friend and I," Hilfe said, "to spend the night in town and see the fun."

"Fancy," the old lady vaguely said, "the porters always tell you wrong."

"You've been very kind," Hilfe said, bowing. "Your kindness disarmed me."

"Oh, I can manage nicely now, thank you."

It was as if Hilfe had taken charge of his own defeat. He moved purposefully up the platform and Rowe followed like a valet. The rush was over: he had no chance to escape; through the glassless roof they could see the little trivial scarlet stars of the barrage flashing and going out like matches. A whistle blew and the train began to move very slowly out of the dark station: it seemed to move surreptitiously; there was nobody but themselves and a few porters to see it go. The refreshment rooms were closed, and a drunk soldier sat alone on a waste of platform, vomiting between his knees.

Hilfe led the way down the steps to the lavatories: there was nobody there at all—even the attendant had taken shelter. The guns cracked; they were alone with the smell of disinfectant, the greyish basins, the little notices about venereal disease. The adventure he had pictured once in such heroic terms had reached its conclusion in the Gentleman's. Hilfe looked in an L.C.C. mirror and smoothed his hair.

"What are you doing?" Rowe asked.

"Oh, saying good-bye," Hilfe said. He took off his jacket as though he were going to wash, then threw it over to Rowe. Rowe saw the tailor's tag marked in silk, Pauling and Crosthwaite. "You'll find the photographs," Hilfe said, "in the shoulder."

The shoulder was padded.

"Want a knife?" Hilfe asked. "You can have your own," and he held out a boy's compendium.

Rowe slit the shoulder up and took out from the padding a roll of film: he broke the paper which bound it and exposed a corner of negative. "Yes," he said. "This is it."

"And now the gun?"

Rowe said slowly, "I promised nothing."

Hilfe said with sharp anxiety, "But you'll let me have the gun?"

"No."

Hilfe suddenly was scared and amazed. He exclaimed in his odd dated vocabulary, "It's a caddish trick.".

"You've cheated too often," Rowe said.

"Be sensible," Hilfe said. "You think I want to escape. But the train's gone. Do you think I could get away by killing you in Paddington station? I wouldn't get a hundred yards."

"Why do you want it then?" Rowe asked.

"I want to get farther away than that." He said in a low voice, "I don't want to be beaten up." He leaned earnestly forward and the L.C.C. mirror behind him showed a tuft of fine hair he hadn't smoothed.

"We don't beat up our prisoners here."

"Oh, no?" Hilfe said. "Do you really believe that? Do you think you are so different from us?"

"Yes."

"I wouldn't trust the difference," Hilfe said. "I know what we do to spies. They'll think they can make me talk—they will make me talk." He brought up desperately the old childish phrase, "I'll swap." It was difficult to believe that he was guilty of so many deaths. He went urgently on, "Rowe, I'll give you your memory back. There's no one else will."

"Anna," Rowe said.

"She'll never tell you. Why, Rowe, she let me go to stop me. Because I said I'd tell you. She wants to keep you as you are."

"Is it as bad as that?" Rowe said. He felt fear and an unbearable curiosity. Digby whispered in his ear that now he could be a whole man again: Anna's voice warned him. He knew that this was the great moment of a lifetime: he was being offered so many forgotten years, the fruit of twenty years' experience. His breast had to press the ribs apart to make room for so much more: he stared ahead of him and read, "Private Treatment Between the Hours of . . ." On the far edge of consciousness the barrage thundered.

Hilfe grimaced at him. "Bad?" he said. "Why—it's tremendously important."

Rowe shook his head sadly. "You can't have the gun."

Suddenly Hilfe began to laugh: the laughter was edged with hysteria and hate. "I was giving you a chance," he said. "If you'd given me the gun, I might have been sorry for you. I'd have been grateful. I might have just shot myself. But now"—his head bobbed up and down in front of the cheap mirror—"now I'll tell you gratis."

Rowe said, "I don't want to hear," and turned away. A very small man in an ancient brown homburg came rocking down the steps from above and made for the urinal. His hat came down over his ears: it might have been put on with a spirit level. "Bad night," he said, "bad night." He was pale and wore an expression of startled displeasure. As Rowe reached the steps a bomb came heavily down, pushing the air ahead of it like an engine. The little man hastily did up his flies; he crouched as though he wanted to get farther away. Hilfe sat on the edge of the wash basin and listened with a sour nostalgic smile as though he were hearing the voice of a friend going away forever down the road. Rowe stood on the bottom step and waited and the express roared down on them and the little man stooped lower and lower in front of the urinal. The sound began to diminish, and then the ground shifted very slightly under their feet at the explosion. There was silence again except for the tiny sifting of dust down the steps. Almost immediately a second bomb was under way. They waited in fixed photographic attitudes, sitting, squatting, standing: this bomb could not burst closer without destroying them. Then it too passed, diminished, burst a little farther away.

"I wish they'd stop," the man in the homburg said, and all the urinals began to flush. The dust hung above the steps like smoke, and a hot metallic smell drowned the smell of ammonia. Rowe climbed the steps.

"Where are you going?" Hilfe said. He cried out sharply, "The police?" and when Rowe did not reply, he came away from the wash basin. "You can't go yet—not without hearing about your wife."

"My wife?" He came back down the steps; he couldn't escape now: the lost years waited for him among the wash basins. He asked hopelessly, "Am I married?"

"You *were* married," Hilfe said. "Don't you remember now? You poisoned her." He began to laugh again. "Your Jean."

"An awful night," the man in the homburg said; he had ears for nothing but the heavy uneven stroke of the bomber overhead.

"You were tried for murder," Hilfe said, "and they sent you to an asylum. You'll find it in all the papers. I can give you the dates."

The little man turned suddenly to them and, spreading out his hands in a gesture of entreaty, he said in a voice filled with tears, "Shall I ever get to Wimbledon?" A bright white light shone through the dust outside, and through the glassless roof of the station the glow of the flares came dripping beautifully down.

It wasn't Rowe's first raid: he heard Mrs. Purvis coming down the stairs with her bedding; the Bay of Naples was on the wall and *The Old Curiosity Shop* upon the shelf. Guilford Street held out its dingy arms to welcome him, and he was home again. He thought, What will that bomb destroy? Perhaps with a little luck the flower shop will be gone near Marble Arch, the sherry bar in Adelaide Crescent, or the corner of Quebec Street where I used to wait so many hours, so many years . . . there was such a lot which had to be destroyed before peace came.

"Go along," a voice said, "to Anna now," and he looked across a dimmed blue interior to a man who stood by the wash basins and laughed at him.

"She hoped you'd never remember." He thought of a dead rat and a policeman, and then he looked everywhere and saw reflected in the crowded court the awful expression of pity: the judge's face was bent, but he could read pity in the old fingers which fidgeted with an Eversharp. He wanted to warn them, Don't pity me. Pity is cruel. Pity destroys. Love isn't safe when pity's prowling round.

"Anna," the voice began again, and another voice said with a kind of distant infinite regret at the edge of consciousness, "And I might have caught the six-fifteen." The horrible process of connection went on: his Church had once taught him the value of penance, but penance was a value only to oneself. There was no sacrifice, it seemed to him, that would help him to atone to the dead. The dead were out of reach of the guilty. He wasn't interested in saving his own soul.

"What are you going to do?" a voice said. His brain rocked with its long journey: it was as if he were advancing down an interminable passage towards a man called Digby—who was so like him and yet had such different memories. He could hear Digby's voice saying, "Shut your eyes. . . ." There were rooms full of flowers, the sound of water falling, and Anna sat beside him, strung up, on guard, in defence of his ignorance. He was saying, "Of course you have a brother. I remember . . ."

Another voice said, "It's getting quieter. Don't you think it is?"

"What are you going to do?"

It was like one of those trick pictures in a children's magazine: you stare at it hard and you see one thing—a vase of flowers—and then your focus suddenly changes and you see only the outlined faces of people. In and out the two pictures flicker. Suddenly, quite clearly, he saw Hilfe as he had seen him lying asleep—the graceful shell of a man, all violence quieted. He *was* Anna's brother. Rowe crossed the floor to the wash basins and said in a low voice that the man in the homburg couldn't hear, "All right. You can have it. Take it."

He slipped the gun quickly into Hilfe's hand.

"I think," a voice behind him said, "I'll make a dash for it. I really think I will. What do you think, sir?"

"Be off," Hilfe said sharply, "be off."

"You think so too. Yes. Perhaps." There was a scuttle on the steps and silence again.

"Of course," Hilfe said, "I could kill you now. But why should I? It would be doing you a service. And it would leave me to your thugs. How I hate you though."

"Yes?" He wasn't thinking of Hilfe: his thoughts swung to and

fro between two people he loved and pitied. It seemed to him that
he had destroyed both of them.

"Everything was going so well," Hilfe said, "until you came blun-
dering in. What made you go and have your fortune told? You had
no future."

"No." He remembered the fête clearly now: he remembered
walking round the railings and hearing the music; he had been
dreaming of innocence . . . Mrs. Bellairs sat in a booth behind a
curtain. . . .

"And just to have hit on that one phrase," Hilfe said. " 'Don't
tell me the past. Tell me the future.' "

And there was Sinclair too. He remembered with a sense of
responsibility the old car standing on the wet gravel. He had better
go away and telephone to Prentice. Sinclair probably had a
copy. . . .

"And then on top of everything, Anna. Why the hell should any
woman love you?" He cried out sharply, "Where are you going?"

"I've got to telephone to the police."

"Can't you give me just five minutes?"

"Oh, no," Rowe said. "No. It's not possible." The process was
completed: he was what Digby had wanted to be—a whole man.
His brain held now everything it had ever held. Willi Hilfe gave an
odd little sound like a retch. He began to walk rapidly towards the
lavatory cubicles, with his bandaged hand stuck out. The stone floor
was wet and he slipped but recovered. He began to pull at a lavatory door, but of course it was locked. He didn't seem to know what
to do: it was as if he needed to get behind a door, out of sight, into
some burrow. He turned and said imploringly, "Give me a penny,"
and everywhere the sirens began to wail the All Clear. The sound
came from everywhere; it was as if the floor of the urinal whined
under his feet. The smell of ammonia came to him like something
remembered from a dream. Hilfe's strained white face begged for
his pity. Pity again. He held out a penny to him and then tossed it
and walked up the steps. Before he reached the top he heard the
shot. He didn't go back: he left him for others to find.

4

One can go back to one's own home after a year's absence and
immediately the door closes it is as if one had never been away. Or

one can go back after a few hours and everything is so changed that one is a stranger.

This of course, he knew now, was not his home. Guilford Street was his home. He had hoped that wherever Anna was there would be peace: coming up the stairs a second time, he knew that there would never be peace again while they lived.

To walk from Paddington to Battersea gives time for thought. He knew what he had to do long before he began to climb the stairs. A phrase of Johns came back to mind about a Ministry of Fear. He felt now that he had joined its permanent staff. But it wasn't the small bureau to which Johns had referred, with limited aims like winning a war or changing a constitution. It was a ministry as large as life to which all who loved belonged. If one loved one feared. That was something Digby had forgotten, full of hope among the flowers and *Tatlers*.

The door was open as he had left it, and it occurred to him almost as a hope that perhaps she had run out into the raid and been lost forever. If one loved a woman one couldn't hope that she would be tied to a murderer for the rest of her days.

But she was there—not where he had left her but in the bedroom where they had watched Hilfe sleeping. She lay on the bed face downwards with her fists clenched. He said, "Anna."

She turned her head on the pillow: she had been crying, and her face looked as despairing as a child's. He felt an enormous love for her, enormous tenderness, the need to protect her at any cost. She had wanted him innocent and happy, she had loved Digby. He had got to give her what she wanted. Life had no other task for him. He said gently, "Your brother's dead. He shot himself," but her face didn't alter. It was as if none of that meant anything at all—all that violence and gracelessness and youth had gone without her thinking it worth attention. She asked with terrible anxiety, "What did he say to you?"

Rowe said, "He was dead before I could reach him. Directly he saw me he knew it was all up."

The anxiety left her face: all that remained was that tense air he had observed before—the air of someone perpetually on guard to shield him. He sat down on the bed and put his hand on her shoulder. "My dear," he said, "my dear. How much I love you." He was pledging both of them to a lifetime of lies, but only he knew that.

"Me too," she said. "Me too."

They sat for a long while without moving and without speaking:

they were on the edge of their ordeal like two explorers who see at last from the summit of the range the enormous dangerous plain. They had to tread carefully for a lifetime, never speak without thinking twice: they must watch each other like enemies because they loved each other so much. They would never know what it was not to be afraid of being found out. It occurred to him that perhaps after all one could atone even to the dead if one suffered for the living enough.

He tried tentatively a phrase. "My dear, my dear, I am so happy," and heard with infinite tenderness her prompt and guarded reply, "Me too." It seemed to him that after all one could exaggerate the value of happiness. . . .